The Dark World Saga: In Need of Protection

Steve Shoemake

Table of Contents

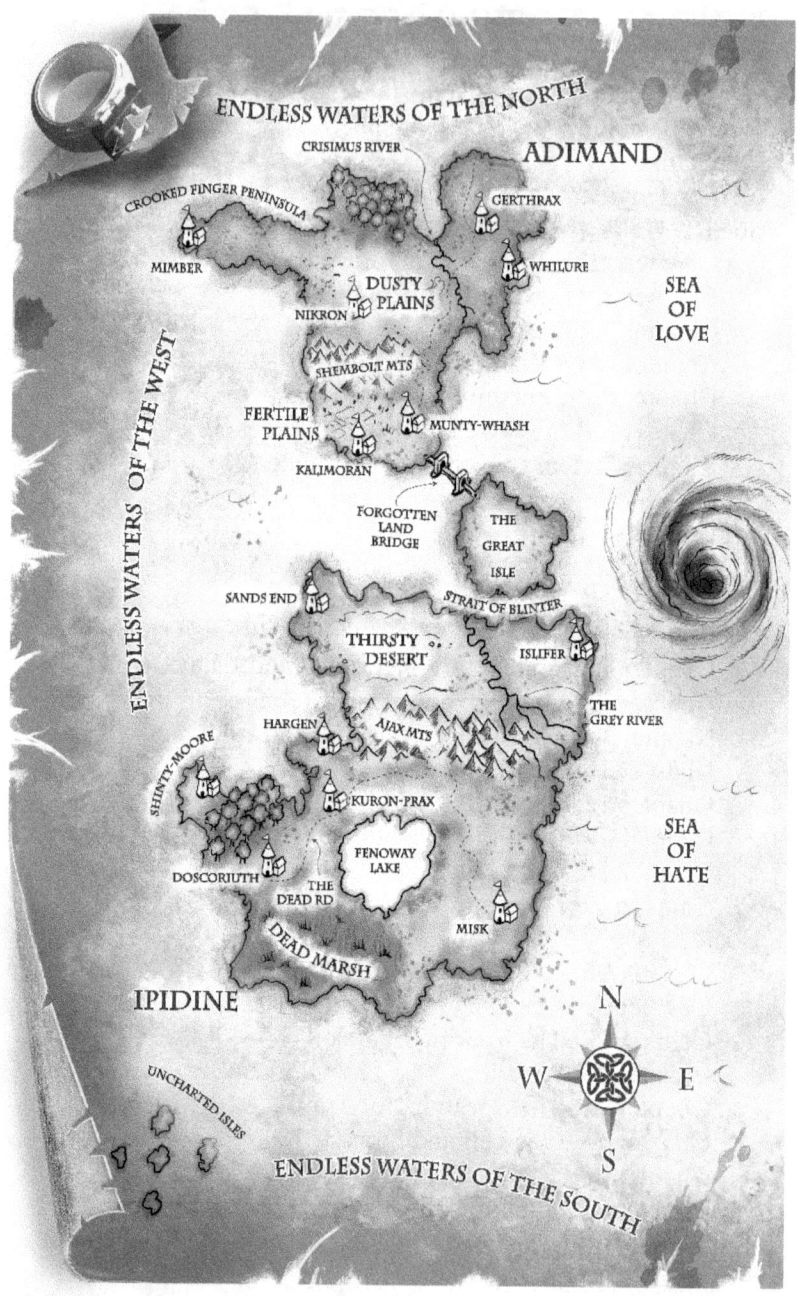

ENDLESS WATERS OF THE NORTH

ADIMAND

CRISIMUS RIVER

CROOKED FINGER PENINSULA

GERTHRAX

MIMBER

WHILURE

SEA
OF
LOVE

DUSTY
PLAINS

NIKRON

SHEMBOLT MTS

FERTILE
PLAINS

MUNTY-WHASH

KALIMORAN

FORGOTTEN
LAND
BRIDGE

THE
GREAT
ISLE

ENDLESS WATERS OF THE WEST

SANDS END

STRAIT OF BLINTER

THIRSTY
DESERT

ISLIFER

THE
GREY RIVER

HARGEN

AJAX MTS

SHINTY-MOORE

KURON-PRAX

SEA
OF
HATE

DOSCORIUTH

FENOWAY
LAKE

THE
DEAD RD

MISK

DEAD MARSH

IPIDINE

N

W   E

S

UNCHARTED ISLES

ENDLESS WATERS OF THE SOUTH

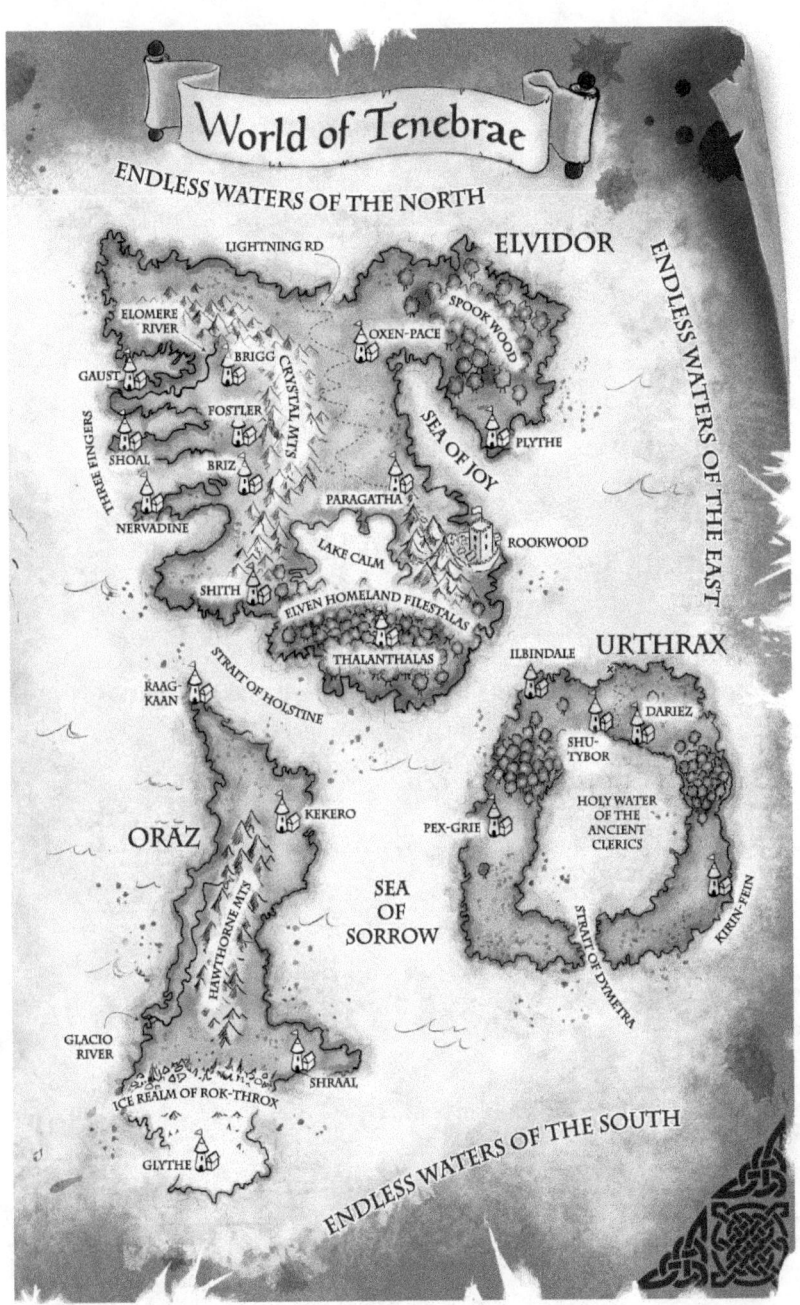

World of Tenebrae

ENDLESS WATERS OF THE NORTH

ENDLESS WATERS OF THE EAST

ELVIDOR

LIGHTNING RD

SPOOK WOOD

ELOMERE RIVER

OXEN-PACE

BRIGG

CRYSTAL MTS

GAUST

FOSTLER

SEA OF JOY

PLYTHE

THREE FINGERS

SHOAL

BRIZ

NERVADINE

PARAGATHA

ROOKWOOD

LAKE CALM

SHITH

ELVEN HOMELAND FILESTALAS

THALANTHALAS

URTHRAX

ILBINDALE

RAAG-KAAN

STRAIT OF HOLSTINE

DARIEZ

SHU-TYBOR

KEKERO

HOLY WATER OF THE ANCIENT CLERICS

ORĀZ

PEX-GRIE

SEA OF SORROW

HAWTHORNE MTS

STRAIT OF DYMETRA

KIRIN-FEIN

GLACIO RIVER

SHRAAL

ICE REALM OF ROK-THROX

GLYTHE

ENDLESS WATERS OF THE SOUTH

DEDICATION

For my Mother, who always loved to read. Without your encouragement as a child, this never comes to light…

Rest in His Peace, Lucy.

ACKNOWLEDGEMENTS

First and foremost, I would like to thank the *real* One True God for the blessing that is this book.

To my wife Thea, I could not possibly keep up the enthusiasm of the nightly grind without your encouragement. Thank you for joining me on this journey through Tenebrae.

To my Aunt Midge and my Aunt Leah, thank you for the deep interest you've built in these characters, and for your nosey questions about what happens next.

Mark…thank you for lending an ear and helping to keep me focused on the finish line.

Thank you again Joanne Burns, for the encouragement along the way.

Thank you John Helfers, my story editor, for invaluable feedback. Your collaboration on specific plot elements has made me a better novelist. You're a pro at your craft.

Thank you Donna Harriman Murillo, my cover artist, for capturing the essence of the underground cavern of Shields. Your attention to detail makes that scene real.

Thank you, Tim Greenan, my map illustrator, for bringing the world of Tenebrae to life.

And lastly, to my readers of Volume I, *In Pursuit of Wisdom*, thank you for taking a chance on a new author. The reviews and interaction has been more gratifying than I could ever have imagined.

Book 1: Gold

CHAPTER ONE: TRUTH, FAITH, AND FURY

~Veronica~

"I'm not keen to take a woman aboard," said the greasy captain of the *Fury*. "Winter thaw, not much food. Rough seas and a rougher crew. What be yer business in Rookwood?" he asked, tugging at his ear. His face was covered with a week's worth of stubble, or dirt—it was hard to distinguish. The smell of sweat, leather, and rotting fish, however, was hard to miss.

Seated across from this repugnant man, Veronica sipped her drink. It was common cider. The captain was three tankards in, and no worse the wear.

She was growing tired of these conversations. This was the fourth captain this week that was reluctant to take her. She sighed. Having spent a week now in Shoal, she was anxious to get back to Rookwood to pursue her contract on Strongiron, whom she had agreed to kill. Xaro had hired her to assassinate the Queen's General, making his assault for the throne more like a victory parade than a pitched battle. Completing that contract, however, had thus far proven much more difficult than Veronica imagined. She found herself, once again, west of the peaks that all but cut Elvidor in two.

But the thought of travelling overland this winter through her secret passage in the Crystal Mountains was daunting. She'd done it twice now, but it was hard, and food would be extremely scarce this time of year. It would take two or three months, at least. She really needed to find a ship.

"Captain Kilroy, my business with the Queen is my own business. I only ask to book passage on your ship. I have the gold and will bring my own food. You'll not even know I'm aboard." *Seems like the same conversation every time.*

"Hah! Three weeks, likely four on a ship alone with a crew of twenty hard men. A lady doesn't travel alone. There'll be questions." Since she was buying, he motioned for a fourth, banging his hand on the table.

"I'm no lady," said Veronica, stabbing the table with the dagger as she leaned forward, the blade point landing between two of his fingers. "I can take care of myself."

Captain Kilroy regarded the knife with a low, throaty chuckle. In a flash, he drew his own dagger and buried it in the battered oak tabletop as well, parting her thin, pale fingers in a similar fashion. Veronica blinked in surprise.

"Ye think yer the first woman I've met who knows her way around a blade? You're more common than a bent copper. Like I said—I've a rough crew."

He pulled his dagger free and made it disappear. "I'll take yer gold, but I can't guarantee yer safety aboard my ship. It's a Dark World, lass. But aye, I'll take ye to see our Queen. Ye just keep yer knives to yerself."

~Krishnan~

A slight hiss emanated from the bubbling pot suspended over the magical flame. The special iron cauldron was capable of handling extreme heat. Krishnan grinned wickedly as he finished his chanting. The small flame he'd conjured up was beyond white-hot. Waves of heat permeated his small workshop, and his sweat tasted salty as it slid down his tan, angular face, over his tight black goatee, and onto his thin lips.

He picked up a short iron rod, about six inches long, and uttered one final spell over it, his voice rising to a crescendo. The rod levitated, floating out of his hand, and his eyes grew large as he guided it above the brew, allowing it to fall into the cauldron. The hissing and smoke continued, stinging his eyes. But he kept the spell going, repeating a new chant, his voice steady and loud.

Finally the smoke began dissipating, and he drew his spell to a close. The flame began to wane, and the small cauldron started to cool. Though he was a little tired, Krishnan could not contain his excitement. *This time I've got it.*

Slowly he approached the cauldron, peering inside. At the bottom, instead of a short iron rod, was a tiny pebble, still glowing in the clear liquid.

Krishnan peered closer. He levitated the pebble out of the potion; it was the size of a pea. Watching it cool, the color faded from bluish to white hot, to fiery red, to orange…to copper.

Not gold!

Disgusted, he hurled the pebble through a wall with no more than a thought. Seventy-seven similar pea-sized holes already existed where he'd lost his temper and "flung" his creation as far away as he could.

It was one of his life's ambitions to turn iron into gold. Gold was the only thing in this Dark World that other men understood and respected. He would not waste his talents entertaining children at the fair. He would not beg for food, and he had no interest serving some King or Queen who had inherited their station in life. Krishnan could crush most men with little more effort than your average daydream took. All he lacked was *gold*.

"That pebble of copper won't even pay for my spell components," he muttered out loud. Frustrated, he kicked over his cauldron, spilling the clear liquid that immediately began hissing and eating away at his stone floor. "There *must* be a way—" He stopped suddenly, peering at his holey wall.

He had failed to turn even one of the previous seventy-seven failures into silver, let alone gold. Most were still iron, some stone, occasionally he made copper, like today, but he had never really looked at his wall of failure—until now.

Peering closely at the pattern of holes for the first time, he could make out two words: *Sands End*.

~Queen Najalas~

"That is quite a story," said the Queen to the young mage standing before her. She wore no crown and no make up. Her mousy hair hung straight and flat to her shoulders, and her thin lips barely stood out from the rest of her pale complexion. Yet, when she spoke, there was no doubt who was in charge.

She was seated in her council chambers, along with her Steward, Jonathon; her Admiral, Peter; and Captain of the Guard, Simon. Together with her General, Strongiron, and her Head Mage, Niku, the five of them made up her council. Strongiron and Niku were away on a mission on Urthrax, and in Niku's place the Queen had invited Belara Kassar to sit in on their meeting. Belara was Niku's Number Two mage—a gifted Illusionist with remarkable abilities. The scent of her hair filled the chamber with the smell of roses, vanilla, and other exotic spices.

Queen Najalas glanced at Belara, who was wearing a rich green dress, with a matching cloak and hooded cowl worn fashionably close to her head. The sorceress's face was completely hidden. *I wonder if she believes a word of this*, she thought.

Strongiron and Niku were on a quest commissioned by the Queen herself. They were escorting a young lady, Kari Quinlan, who was determined to become a True Cleric. All of them were looking for signs of an ancient God. When the young mage first reappeared, she'd gathered her council to hear the story of the most wanted mage in her realm: Magi Blacksmooth—a man that she, along with at least fifty other witnesses, had seen kill one of her guests right in the Great Hall. She stared at the True Mage, wishing she could see the thoughts behind his pure white eyes.

"You'll understand if I'm skeptical," she continued. A quick look at her advisors saw them all nodding, save Belara. Simon, in particular, seemed to be straining to contain himself.

Magi was as relaxed as a lion amidst a pack of sheep. "I would be shocked if you didn't require proof of my tale."

"And what proof do you offer, murderer?" said Simon.

"This." Magi took the Staff of Insight and placed it on the table. "As I have said, I see things as they truly are with this Staff. It is blessed beyond measure by Dymetra herself. Through me, all that would be hidden can be exposed."

Magi continued, a smile beginning to sprout from the corner of his mouth. "Let me propose this. Ask me to reveal a truth or expose a lie that I could never know—something only you would know. If I am successful, then you can trust my story. If I am unsuccessful, I will turn myself in, and you may judge me here and now. I will not *Teleport* away, nor will I fight. Will you accept this test?"

"How do we know you won't just read or try and control our minds?" asked Jonathon.

"You are not zombies—I know of no way to do that through my Art. But if you doubt my word, I will disrobe and leave all my spell components in front of you. Ask your colleague." He nodded at Belara.

They all turned to her. "It is true—no such spell exists to read minds that I am aware of." She leaned forward, tilting her head. The Queen picked up a whiff of the subtle scent of roses, vanilla, and exotic spices that seemed to follow the ambitious Illusionist everywhere. "However, new spells *are* created every day. Perhaps he has figured out how to read minds, but I doubt it. Better to be safe though, my Queen. We *should* remove his spell components." Though Belara had no discernable eyes, the Queen could almost feel her gaze boring into Magi's robes, coveting whatever spell components he might have.

"That won't be necessary," said the Queen, nodding to a few mage-guards that had slipped silently into the back of the room. Wordlessly, they wove a spell around Magi, binding his hands and freezing his body. "I noticed you are not wearing the ring you spoke about at your trial in Gaust. The one that protects its wearer from magical attacks…" The Queen smiled as Magi stiffened. "We accept your proposal. Release his tongue, and let him hold this Staff."

Magi tried to smile. He tried to nod, but could not move anything but his tongue, eyelids, and fingers.

"Thank you, my Queen." Holding his staff, he asked softly, "Which of you would like to go first?"

~Kari~

Kari carefully rolled up a prayer scroll; this was her time to meditate, but she couldn't clear her mind. The prayer was an appeal to Dymetra for wisdom, but the recited words rang hollow for her at the moment. Had she tried to cast a spell with such a distracted mind, she was liable to fail miserably. She found it hard to believe prayers would be any different. Frustrated, she began to run her fingers absently through her thick, dark hair.

It should be me. The Ol' Shakoor sent me *to speak to the Queen about becoming a True Cleric.* That had been the gist of her prophesy. *Strongiron had accompanied me,* so she told herself, *because I prayed for a protector.* She couldn't shake the feeling that he was only accompanying her because *she* had brought it to pass. This was not the plan. Strongiron, a True Cleric? The man was the Queen's General—a True Warrior, for god's sake. His purpose in life was basically to kill the Queen's enemies and break things.

Yet the True Clerics knew him. Expected him. Took him in. And for several weeks now, he'd been training long hours. Reading, praying, learning. The acolytes had separated him from the others, who now saw him rarely, a couple evenings a week. "Amazing" was all he would say when Niku and Rebecca grilled him on his studies.

The weeks rolled on. Niku was anxious to return, but hesitant to leave Strongiron behind in the Ancient Tower of Dariez. After six weeks their mission, however, was beyond complete. Not only had they uncovered proof, remnants, and relics of the True Clerics of old—they were creating a new one as well.

"It's time, Kari." Niku had an annoying habit of sneaking up on people in his soft boots. "We need to provide an update to our Queen. If you are coming, now is the time."

Kari looked at the small pile of travelling clothes that lay washed and folded in the corner of her spartan room. She pushed herself away from the table of scrolls and looked down at the plush white robe she now wore, with a deep hood folded in back that sometime caught her hair if she spun around too quickly. It was simple garb, and comfortable. The scent of wildflowers filled her room—and much of Dariez—from the Cleric's preferred oil lamps.

She had changed her mind a dozen times. On one hand, she definitely felt like leaving. Getting far away from this place. Let Strongiron go through the "special" training; she was fed up whiling away her days pouring over old scrolls in a language she was only beginning to grasp. Go back and become a Master Illusionist. Climb the Staircase and be done with this new training. Perhaps she might still catch up with Tarsh...

Still...she felt compelled to stay. *Surely it wasn't just to stay close to the General. Surely not.* There was something about him...something that stirred her in a manner that Tarsh or even Magi couldn't. But it was more than *him*; it just seemed like she was in the right place, even though she was bored and didn't feel like she was moving forward in any discernable way. Still—something in the way Strongiron looked and sounded when she saw him made her not want to leave. It wasn't a sense of peace, or calm. Far from it. He exuded power in a way that surpassed his bulging arms. There was just something different about this place. The prayer scrolls she studied were beautiful. It felt right...but she was still restless. *Bored.*

"Young lady, I plan on sailing home. I will take you with me, but the time is now." The Queen's Head Mage smiled, trying not to sound impatient. His grey hair was now clean, but the deep creases in his face hinted of a man far older. Niku stood in her doorway, dressed for sea travel with a thick cloak and high boots, clutching a plain staff tightly.

"Is it wise for us to leave Strongiron here? Without you, he won't be able to *Teleport*, and if we take the ship—he will be trapped here."

"As I've said, at the pace he's progressing, Strongiron will soon be able to *Teleport* himself. I've seen firsthand True Clerics *Teleport*—Malenec called on his dark God to save him before we could execute him. What's more, apparently water is not a teleportation boundary for them. The Elfs assure me that as a True Cleric, Strongiron will be able to return to Rookwood with Dymetra's blessing. His work continues here. Mine is back at Rookwood, beside our Queen. And now the time has come for you to choose."

"And Rebecca?" *I'm stalling.*

"She will follow you for now, I'm sure."

"And Quentin?" *More stalling.*

"He will come with me, of course." Niku fixed his white, unblinking gaze on her.

One of the three elfs, the True Cleric Faralon, had also approached quietly. It was just as unnerving as having Niku approach. "I could not help but overhear, Miss Kari. If I may—I would encourage you to stay. Your studies have progressed well these last few weeks. The world will need more True Clerics than just Strongiron."

"But all I do is read these ancient prayers all day! You three elfs spend all your time with Strongiron—your *champion*. I am not learning anything!"

Faralon seemed to glide over to her. "Kari, dear child. Those ancient prayers are no small thing. A simple prayer for courage can change the course of a losing battle. A prayer for healing can restore a body ravaged by injury or disease. A prayer for wisdom can reveal hidden truth. A prayer for justice can kill a man despite the strongest of armor. Your memorization of these and other "ancient" prayers are more powerful than the greatest spell your Art can conceive."

"Then why don't they work?" She asked pointedly. "Where is my wisdom, my justice?"

"Just as the strength of a spell within your Art depends on the depth of your own potential well, so to does the strength of a prayer depend on the depth of your Faith. Dymetra rewards the Faithful. And you are building that Faith. *Trust in it now.* Stay, Kari."

She nodded slowly. She looked down at her soft, white robe, then at the pile of clothes in the corner, and finally back up at Faralon. She sighed. Turning to Niku, she said, "Let's go. I'm ready to leave."

She turned back to the old elf, who looked crestfallen. "You're in good hands here with Strongiron, Faralon. But I have other studies I also need to pursue."

~Captain Kilroy~

"What good is gold if there be no taverns at the bottom of the sea?" roared the *Fury's* first mate. "Cap'n Kilroy, this be madness. Throw the vixen into the sea and let us turn about. All the gold in her pack won't buy us summer seas."

Kilroy wiped the freezing spray from his beard and harrumphed. The Whirlpool had nearly toppled the boat, and the Straight of Holstine had nearly run them into the cliffs. One mast was down, and every third oar was splintered. A steady rotation of crewmen bailing out the bottom deck kept the *Fury* afloat, aided by some tar and pitch work. But there would be no return journey. Once they reached Rookwood, the ship would need extensive repairs over the winter and likely on into spring.

And the Captain intended to bleed his rich patron for every last piece of gold she had in the process.

Down a mast, and with the delays and horrendous weather, it would take at least eight weeks. They were already six weeks in, and the latest storms pounded the *Fury* anew, as if drawn to the irony.

Veronica did not dare show herself outside her quarters. Only a handful of the men even knew she existed. "Safer for you, safer for me," was all he'd said while smuggling her aboard one evening. She had agreed.

As the storm coated the ship with yet another layer of ice, Captain Kilroy headed down to his guest's cabin for a little chat. He knocked sharply on her door, checking the lock (which, naturally, was locked). He heard the bolt slide out of the way as Veronica said, "enter" pleasantly enough.

Captain Kilroy came in, dripping and shivering. He didn't bother sitting down, but reached into his long coat and pulled the cork from an oversized flask. He fixed his eyes on Veronica, who sat calmly in a corner, brandishing her knife. The captain took a long pull and tucked it back away, never offering her any "for the chill." She seemed as if she could care less.

"Woman, you'll have more gold in repairs for me ship than it would have cost you to buy it a month ago. This trip is madness, as I said it would be. The winter seas don't like our wood. The *Fury* is holding together, but barely."

Veronica stood up and stretched. "We are closer to Rookwood than we are to any other port, no? The last port was Raag-Kaan, off the coast of Oraz, at the entrance to the Straights, and we sailed through them two weeks ago. What options do we have, Captain?"

Kilroy narrowed his eyes. "The crew thinks I ought to throw you into the sea. Hell, half of 'em say you don't even exist." He chuckled. "I've a mind to parade you on deck and let 'em throw yer bony arse over. Better fer morale."

Veronica laughed. "Perhaps. But I have found that men bleeding to death in front of their shipmates tends to have the opposite effect on morale."

Kilroy's eyes glinted at the shiny dagger Veronica twirled casually in her hands, the way a potter might fidget with wet clay. "Aye. I'm not keen to see me crew carved up. But you would die, lady, sure as winter. And yer gold would stay with me—know that I could care less fer yer hide. Frankly, if you took a few of me crew with you, I'd hardly shed a tear for some of these curs, with all their whinin'. I care for two things and two things only: yer gold, and my arse. And right now, this trip's puttin' both at risk!"

Veronica grinned. "So, are *you* done whining, Captain? I see no other options for you to pursue besides our present course, given your, ah, priorities." She flawlessly balanced her perfectly weighted dagger on the tip of her finger, point down. Years of training had put a callous on this finger, allowing for the dramatic effect.

Captain Kilroy sneered, and with a deftness that belied his size, he flicked his wrist and threw a tiny blade at the ornate dagger, knocking it off her finger with a modest prick. She shook her hand, surprised by the drop of her own blood. "Yer parlor tricks don't impress me. I've forgotten more knife work than a two-bit Assassin like you could ever know. Aye—I know yer part of the Black Guild. I'm no fool. Like I said, you may know yer way around a blade, but don't think yer alone in that regard. Why, I've—"

The first mate barged in, crowding the small cabin uncomfortably. He was drenched. "She's sinking, Cap'n! The *Fury* has had her fill!"

~Strongiron~

"It is time."

Faralon was dressed in his usual white robes, seated in a comfortable, oversized chair in one of his reading rooms. A scroll of parchment was half-curled on a side table, and subtle incense filled the room with a faint smell of cloves and cinnamon.

Strongiron paced back and forth. He wore a new coat of armor, custom-made in a gleaming shade of ivory. The three clerics at Dariez had made it for him. Of Elfish design, it was light but surprisingly strong, with intricate details woven into the shoulder plates. The breastplate bore no crest or sigil, just a beautiful woven pattern of ivory-looking steel, highlighted in gold. It fit perfectly, and Strongiron wore it at Faralon's request, but it wouldn't be his first choice. "Perfect for impressing the nobles over dinner; useless in the forest," he quietly said to himself when it was presented to him. He had graciously accepted the gift, but it was uncomfortably ornate for Strongiron's taste.

Yet, out of respect, he wore it to his meeting with Faralon, Jasper, and Nowahiram—the three Elfen True Clerics that maintained the Tower of Dariez. He fixed Faralon with a resigned stare from his bright blue eyes. "So soon?"

The ancient elf smiled. His dark, formerly smooth skin, framed by a simple white hood, showed the lines of age. "You are ready. Your prayers are memorized, and your increasing Faith has shown itself to be strong. Dymetra favors you, Strongiron. Another month or another year will not grow you as a Cleric. Besides, the time is fast approaching where the events of the world will compel your newfound Faith to be put into practice. As we have discussed, it is a Dark World, Strongiron, and it is growing darker."

Faralon grabbed a small vial of red liquid sealed with a cork and wax. He tore open the vial and repeated, "It is time."

"Surely there are some other means? This is barbaric!" Strongiron rolled his eyes and spread his arms in frustration before sighing loudly. He bowed his head when his words were greeted in silence. "I don't even know what I am to do."

Faralon stood up. He looked at the two other elfs and nodded before he approached Strongiron, placing one hand on his shoulder, holding the open vial in the other. "It is not an act of barbarism, my friend. It is an act of obedience. A True Cleric has Faith enough to heal any man of his most grievous wounds, even unto his death. That has always been the standard by which a True Cleric is known: the power to bring life from death. That is a power reserved for God, and only the One True God has such power, and only Her True Clerics shall be blessed to wield it. Consider this the ultimate test—no Mage, no Clerical charlatan can bring the dead back to life. Even the most Unholy One, the demon Kuth-Cergor, who was once secretly worshipped here in our midst, cannot raise the dead. His power can only animate their corpses." For some reason, Faralon looked over at Nowahiram and smiled at him sadly. The other elf simply lowered his eyes.

"No, true resurrection—that is a gift from Dymetra and Her alone," Faralon said, focusing on the large man once again. "And it is your final test. I have faith in your faith, Strongiron."

"And if I fail?"

"Then you will study further and your faith will grow stronger. My colleagues will pray that I may rejoin you." Faralon winked. "I hope."

"And what if they fail?" Strongiron gestured toward the other two with a half-smile, trying to lighten the mood, calm his nerves, or both.

"Then I suppose it is my time to serve Dymetra in her real Kingdom, and frankly, that's not a bad proposition, given the events that are unfolding here in Tenebrae." Faralon grew serious again and took a step back. He slowly began swirling the red liquid in the vial.

"These events—you have mentioned before that you have seen certain things. What is happening in the broader world? I feel so disconnected from the realm, from my Queen, in the months I've been here. Since the rest of my campaign left, I've felt increasingly isolated." Strongiron looked over at Jasper and Nowahiram, both of whom were like ghosts, speechless.

Faralon looked up from his vial. "As we have discussed, Kuth-Cergor has re-entered this world, and we have unfortunately aided his efforts by training two clerics of his. It was a mistake in our judgment and a corruption of our Faith that has since been fixed," he hastily added. "And it is a story for another day. But a warrior such as you had been foretold as one who would bring the truth of Dymetra back to Tenebrae. Your True Warrior status will make you credible among the people; your signs of healing will make your testimony believable. It is your destiny, Strongiron."

"Part of it. Tell him of the rest, Faralon." Jasper said quietly from the corner.

"Tell me what?" Strongiron tilted his head from Faralon to Jasper.

Faralon frowned slightly at Jasper. "I was hoping Dymetra would share that with Her cleric Herself, when the time is right. A destiny is never really set in stone, my friend—events can and do shape and change it."

"Perhaps she *is* telling him; perhaps she's using *us* to do so." Jasper raised his eyebrows. "Tell him, Faralon."

"Very well. It is no big thing that you should hear it from us, Strongiron. Have you heard of the Shield of Life?" Faralon asked.

"No, I can't say that I have."

"No matter. It is one of three Artifacts of the Ancients. It is a wondrous shield, last worn by Windomere, one of the last True Clerics from a bygone age—the last age when the True God was known and worshipped. Legend says it was buried with him, and we believe he was buried somewhere in the Dusty Plains in Adimand." He took his eyes off the vial of red liquid and looked directly at Strongiron. "Tenebrae will need that shield, Strongiron, for it protects from dark prayers, my friend."

He, too, began to pace, placing his thumb over top of the vial while he walked. "You see, when Kuth-Cergor and his clerics lay claim to our cities, we may be able to match them sword for sword. We may even be able to match them spell for spell. But a True Cleric is a terrible thing to behold, Strongiron, and one who channels the full power of the Unholy One can usher in an era of misery beyond description in the most woeful lamentation. It—"

"But there are three—perhaps soon to be four—of us, two of them. Surely we can match them 'prayer for prayer' as well?" Strongiron looked at the three elfs hopefully.

Nobody said a word for an uncomfortable pause. Finally, Jasper broke the silence. "When you are fully trained as a True Cleric, our time will be at an end. Each of us has lived an unnaturally long life, Strongiron, even for Elfs. Assuming you are successful in your final test, you will be the last, and only, True Cleric in all of Tenebrae who is blessed by Dymetra. Others may come to the Tower in time, but it will fall on you to pass on what you have learned."

"And thus," Faralon said, "we believe it to be a good idea for you to pursue the Shield of Life."

"A good idea, or my destiny? Is this coming from you, or from Dymetra?" Strongiron pressed. "I pray and hear Her voice now, too. She has not mentioned this to me."

Faralon shifted a bit uncomfortably, and looked over at Nowahiram and Jasper. "Well…who's to say? It has the ring of wisdom to it, does it not?" He smiled, but it looked a bit forced for someone who was typically so wise. He straightened his face. "No matter. Continue praying about it, Strongiron. My colleagues and I simply believe that it is a prudent course for you to follow. The three artifacts are not trifling trinkets; they are objects of extraordinary power, and you will need them to defend Tenebrae. And we can all agree that your destiny—from *Her*—is to defend Tenebrae, yes?" His two friends nodded.

"By enlightening the world, yes," Jasper finished.

"What are the other two?" asked Strongiron, changing the subject slightly.

"The Staff of Wisdom is one. It allows the rightful owner to see the truth of all things; it tolerates no lies. It was last wielded by a contemporary of Windomere, the Archmage Quixatalor. The other is the Blade of Justice—a terrible dagger, ever sharp, that kills its intended victim in a single throw, always returning to the thrower. Neither armor nor spell can save the victim from its power, as long as a line-of-sight exists between victim and assailant. The famed True Warrior Ajax was last known to possess it. His exploits were such that an entire mountain range is named after him.

"These three Artifacts—the Staff of Wisdom, the Shield of Life, and the Blade of Justice can bring Wisdom, Protection, and Justice to a Dark World," Faralon continued, "if the right leaders find and wield them."

"We believe you are one such leader," Jasper finished.

Strongiron didn't say anything immediately. He simply nodded. "Very well. I understand, and will most certainly seek Her guidance on the matter. But now, I suppose the time has indeed come."

Faralon nodded.

"Then let us put my faith to the test. Dymetra knows the right timing. If now is the time, than now is the time." He walked over to Faralon, who was still standing, and put his hand firmly on his shoulder, looking intently at the soft brown eyes of his Elfish teacher. The elf took one last look at his two ancient friends, then looked up into the bright blue eyes of his new friend.

Faralon took his thumb off the top of the vial and drank the red liquid in one large swig, smiling momentarily before slowly falling into Strongiron's grasp.

The elf died in less than a minute.

~Magi~

It was an odd sensation, actually. Unable to move, completely paralyzed, yet fully conscious—frozen in the Queen's council chambers. Magi knew there were several mage guards behind him, holding him in check. *Be patient*, he thought. *These poor souls have not seen what I've seen.* Odd as it may have seemed, he was very relaxed, even while standing stiff as a board in front of his Queen, gripping the Staff of Insight.

Peter, the head of Queen Najalas's Navy, strode forward. He stroked his well-oiled beard, a small goatee that terminated in a sharp point at the bottom of his chin. Curly black hair rimmed the rest of his face, and only his well-worn boots seemed out of place for a man of his status. He was lean—almost too fit—and looked like he was as much at home hoisting sails as he was commanding the Queen's Navy.

"So, you claim to have met Dymetra, and that you came back to Tenebrae with that fabled Staff. How fascinating. What would you say about me?"

Magi closed his eyes. Not that he needed to, but it helped him sift through the Admiral's words, his intent. His secrets. "Admiral," Magi began, "Judge me on this. You wish that the Queen had sent you, not Strongiron, on the quest to secure evidence that Dymetra does, indeed, exist. You long for such proof. Eighteen years ago, you killed a sailor, and the guilt haunts you to this day. On a ship sailing toward the port cities along the Three Fingers, you drank too much while on watch, keeping a flask of spirits by your side the entire night. When a young sailor came to relieve you, he saw the state you were in, and was about to report it to your captain. Your promising career would be cut off for a night of lonely consumption. He didn't care why you were drinking. It didn't matter that your brother had caught the dying disease. Outcast, never to be seen again—your brother would go where all the afflicted gather, in the tribal communities North of Rookwood, near Oxen-Pace. 'Where the lepers die,' as they say. You were thinking of him, and drinking heavily that night. If men knew your brother had the dying disease, it would only be a matter of time before they shunned you as well, out of fear of contagion. The guilt was horrible."

Peter's eyes grew wider with each word Magi said. He would have reached out a hand to put on the other man's shoulder, but only his eyes and mouth were free to move. He tried to look sympathetic, but knowing how awkward this was, he hastened to finish his insight into Peter.

"In the end, the outcome was tragic: one young sailor looking to make his mark with the captain, turning in a fellow crew mate for dereliction of duty; and you, intent on preserving your well-earned reputation. It was a simple matter to put your dagger into his back, push him over the side of the boat, and sober yourself up. When they asked where he was, you simply lied and said he never came to relieve you, so you took his shift as well. When he never turned up, they figured he fell overboard or something. Nobody questioned you. Nobody even thought to look for blood on your dagger. But years later, the dual guilt of both your murder, your cover-up, and of having an abandoned brother, not knowing whether he's dead or alive, living in the harshness of a disease-ridden encampment, still gnaws at you. You live in a castle with your lovely wife, Felicity, and your two small children, Brandon and Chelsea, and serve the Queen of all the land. Yet, your brother suffers. This is why you wanted to find Dymetra. Why you seek her. Why you embrace a Faith that you don't fully understand."

The others looked at Peter, shocked. His friend Jonathon ran up to him. "Peter—is this true?"

Eyes glistening, Peter put his head down slightly before raising it again. "Aye," he said, nodding vigorously. "Yes—the mage speaks the truth. Can you see him—my brother Garin? Does your Staff allow you to see him? Is he alive?"

"No. I don't know, Peter. I wish I could offer you that. I'm not given to visions about what might be happening in other parts of the world. I only know the truth of a man or woman's heart that is in my presence."

Simon narrowed his eyes. "Take the Staff, my Queen! This man does not need to be around us, reading our minds!" He approached Magi with outstretched hands, but the Queen cut him off. She had heard enough. She nodded at the mage-guards, and they released Magi.

Rising from her throne, she approached him carefully, but confidently. "So, young Magi. Let us assume your story is true. What would you have me do with you? Give me one reason why I shouldn't just take your Staff and punish you for the murder *you* yourself committed in my very presence not long ago."

Magi smiled as he knelt before her. It felt good to move his legs again. "Queen Najalas, I would offer to serve you as the Archmage Quixatalor once served the Kings and Queens of old. A life of service does not make up for my killing Kyle, but there is nothing in your power that you could inflict upon me that could balance that scale anyhow. Besides, my debt is first with Kyle and also with Kari. Kyle—as I related...I've made my peace with him. Eventually, I will need to seek Kari's forgiveness, too, but you, my Queen...I have dishonored your Hall. Surely a fair punishment and a fair trade is my gift of service—to bring wisdom and insight beyond our human limitations to this realm? I don't seek to replace anyone on your council—just let me lend my voice...and my Staff, to your thought process."

"My Queen, no." Simon shook his head. "Do not bring this man into our Council."

"Peter? Jonathon?" the Queen asked.

Peter nodded. "There is no way any man, untouched by some God, would possibly know my burden of guilt that I have carried all these years. You already have one reformed murderer on your council. Perhaps you can see clear to add a second. The man speaks the truth."

Jonathon just sighed. "I'm not crazy about an even number of councilors, but I suppose you still can break any ties. I guess in the end, I just think it would be better to have more truth, not less, in this Dark World."

The elf's body was hardly heavy for Strongiron, who was a massive man by any measure. He gently bent his six-and-one-half foot frame over to lay the elf on a simple bed. A True Warrior, Knight of Thunder, Commander of the Realm, Bearer of the Ancient Crest of House Tuitio—Strongiron was about to add one more simple title that would dwarf them all: True Cleric.

He looked over at Jasper and Nowahiram, who would witness his prayers. "Faralon is dead," he said.

"Indeed he is. The question is, will Dymetra return him to us at your request?" Jasper smiled and opened his palm, gesturing toward his fallen friend encouragingly.

Strongiron nodded, and started to kneel, but he stopped. He looked over at Nowahiram. "Before I pray, tell me about Kuth-Cergor, Nowahiram. I would like to know more about whom I am fighting against, and Faralon, bless him, would never humor my questions. You knew him best." He did not say it bitingly; he was simply stating a fact. The elves made no secret of Nowahiram's fall; it was the how and why that nobody discussed.

The elf shifted uncomfortably. "Would you fill your head with thoughts of Kuth-Cergor before asking our precious God for the miracle of miracles? That isn't the way I would clear my head, Strongiron."

"On a battlefield, I won't ever have a clear head. If my faith depends on a distraction-free environment, than we shall all surely fail because I doubt I'll ever have it. I am a Warrior Cleric, brother. My head will never be clear—I'm not going to have the luxury of a deserted tower in which to put my faith into practice. So I ask again…tell me more about Kuth-Cergor." Strongiron had the uncanny ability to strike a tone that was both deferential and commanding at the same time.

Jasper smiled at his fellow Cleric. "He has a point, my friend. Tell him more. You have nothing to hide—let his questions be answered."

"Well, all right. I'm not sure what you wish to know. He is a demon at heart. A liar who can exploit your weaknesses a hundred different ways. He is a devourer, a slaver."

"That much I know. Why did you once worship him?" It was an obvious, blunt question.

Nowahiram stepped forward and sighed. "I was…curious…at first." He stopped and pointed at Strongiron. "Much like you are now. My curiosity opened a window, I suppose. I was a True Cleric, Strongiron. One of three left in all of Tenebrae. I am old and wise. Over the years I became quite proud of myself, of my holiness. Faith in Dymetra soon became faith in Nowahiram. I became self-righteous, impressed with my piety, by my prayer-life, by my knowledge. Oh, I kept it from my dear friends…they did not see the haughtiness grow. But the thoughts were there, and they grew. I began picturing myself in a different kingdom, in a different role. And then one day while meditating I heard a voice—and I knew whose it was. It was his. My lack of humility had pushed Dymetra into the furthest reaches of my mind, and it did not take long for my prayers to be addressed by Kuth-Cergor. It was as if he intercepted them before they reached Her, and answered them himself. Of course, she never left—I know that now. But it is amazingly simple to tune out Her voice, and he will gladly step into the silence left behind. That was the day he let me know that two acolytes would be coming, and that I should open their minds to his message, for they will be receptive. One of them you know—Xaro is his name. The other is Malenec. I am living proof that Malenec, at least, is also a True Cleric. A Dark Cleric, for sure, as he killed me before leaving. Only the mercy of Dymetra saved me from my fate as a soulless corpse, tethered forever to a rotting body."

He curled his lip and looked away before continuing. "Strongiron—I would have you understand one last thing. Kuth-Cergor will not rest until you and your message is extinguished. You said you wanted to know whom you are fighting. Let me be clear—you are *not* fighting him; you can't. He is not of this world, and has power neither of us understands nor could match." Nowahiram smiled and put two hands on Strongiron, one on each shoulder, to look him square in his bright blue eyes. "Your fight is against the lies of this world, the misconceptions perpetrated over generations. Your fight is against other men and their misguided beliefs. Do not try and fight Kuth-Cergor; you will only end up serving him, as I did. That is a fight for Dymetra, should She wish it."

"But are we not Her sword and shield?" Strongiron asked.

Here Jasper walked over. "Indeed. But even a True Warrior learns when to strike and when to sheath his weapon." He put a hand on top of both Strongiron and Nowahiram's head. "Now my friend, if you are satisfied with my brother's confession, I would greatly like to press on with the matter at hand."

Yes, I have procrastinated enough. But something else about what Nowahiram said bothered him. "What did you mean, 'the fight is Dymetra's, if She wishes it?'"

Nowahiram just raised his eyebrows slightly. "Tenebrae must be worth saving, Strongiron."

"Of course it's worth saving." *That's the point of this, isn't it?*

Jasper flashed a sad little smile while he shook his head slightly. "Perhaps, Strongiron, but that is not our call—it's Her's. And only a True God's love could save a world that hates the very God that created it. When you have walked the land as a True Cleric for as long as we have served as guardians of this tower, you may think differently." He sighed and turned his soft eyes on Strongiron. "But enough of that talk. Come now, it is time for your prayer."

With a nod, Strongiron distanced himself from the two Clerics and knelt next to Faralon's body. Taking a deep breath, he bowed his head and concentrated on the One True God, letting the words of his memorized prayer come forth. The exact wording of his prayer was not critical, but he also didn't want to stumble through his request, either.

"Dymetra, True God of all things, Your servant has fallen. If his life's work is not complete, I ask that You restore his spirit and heal his shattered body. Bring life to him, Dymetra, as only You can, that all who know him may be inspired by Your generosity. Grant Your humble servant this prayer request that all may know that You are with me."

Strongiron lifted his head and stared at Faralon's corpse. Nothing in the room moved. Strongiron looked down at the soft, white robes of his Elfen mentor; they matched his new white armor. He looked around and saw everything still—literally still. For the first time in months, Strongiron couldn't hear the sound of the silver waterfall outside. It seemed as if time itself had stopped. The Tower of Dariez was *completely* silent.

"Strongiron, why do you seek this man's life?" It was a voice that seemed painfully loud in contrast to the tomb-like silence. It was a familiar voice, one he had 'heard' many times before in the quiet of his mind. But this was different. This sounded like it came from the chair next to him. He spun his head around, but saw no one. He didn't have to. He knew who She was.

My God! Strongiron, already on his knees, could feel the presence of Dymetra. Trembling, he squeezed his eyes shut and buried his square jaw into his chest, lowered his head as far as he could go without breaking his neck. "My God!" was all he could say.

"Why do you seek this man's life?" the voice repeated.

Strongiron focused. This was not the same type of prayer that had routinely been answered during his previous studies. This was *very* different. He could feel the weight of Her presence, and it was getting harder to breathe. This was the most terrifying moment of his life—far more terrifying than when he faced the three Steele brothers in battle to earn the Mark of a True Warrior.

Gathering his thoughts, he finally decided what he would say and spoke up before his throat completely dried out. He started spilling his guts, speaking rapidly. "My God, I seek to be a True Cleric. My motivations are selfish, and I am probably the least worthy man in the realm for such a blessing. I've...I have killed men in battle. I don't know why I want Faralon back, other than the fact that I've been told I need to do this to earn Your blessing. I am lost, Dymetra. But he doesn't deserve to die just to prove my worth."

Dymetra did not pause. *"Indeed, he does deserve to die. He has earned the rest. You would have him suffer in his old body just to prove to the world that you are a True Cleric. Giving him his life back is not what makes you My Cleric, Strongiron. You are My Cleric because your faith is strong, like your name. I shall grant your prayer—and Faralon's—as well. He has prayed for rest, and I shall grant him, Nowahiram, and Jasper their due rest. Their work is coming to an end. Yours, Strongiron, is just beginning."*

Strongiron looked up—the room was white everywhere. He could not make out any objects. Just white light everywhere. "What would you have me do, My God? How do we win?"

Dymetra's voice was calm. *"My Clerics have told you to seek the Shield of Life. The world is in need of protection, yet the people do not know from whom they need it. You say you are lost...all are lost. You can win by spreading truth, and I shall accompany you for as long as you seek Me. When you no longer seek Me, then you will be alone. Do not delay unnecessarily, Strongiron."*

The white light slowly began to dim and the room, which had been completely whited-out, began to come back into focus.

"Dymetra!" Strongiron called out. "Don't leave yet!" Still on his knees, he swiveled his head around, looking for any sign of the God.

"She is always with us, brother." Faralon was sitting up, smiling at Strongiron. "Thank you for your prayers. We have a little more time." He looked over at the other two elfs and nodded.

Strongiron was more relieved than surprised by the elf's voice. "Faralon! You're alive!" He grabbed the elf and hugged him.

"Yes, brother, for a little while. Just long enough to say good-bye, really." He waved for the other two to join him. "For all of us to say good-bye."

He called me brother. The word finally hit Strongiron. "I'm a True Cleric." He stepped back slightly to look at his three mentors.

"Yes. The power of your prayers may reshape this world yet, Strongiron." Jasper came over to clasp his hand.

"I still am so unsure of what's next. Where do I find this tomb of Windomere? What does the shield look like? How—"

"Strongiron." Faralon interrupted. "There is a time for you to plan like a General, and there is time for you to trust like a Cleric. If you had all the answers, there would be no place for Faith, now would there?" He smiled again. "Take care, brother. It is your time now."

The three elfs took their leave and left the room, each heading to their private chambers. Strongiron looked around the empty reading room in the tower. "My time. My time for what?" he said, not meaning to think out loud. He chuckled at the sound of his own voice. *At the very least, the Queen is surely interested in an update.*

CHAPTER TWO: UNEXPECTED ENCOUNTERS

~Xaro~

Sweat poured off Xaro, soaking his tunic. "Again!" he yelled.

He was in a foul mood. Though winter never really came to his fortress, Sands End, the months rolled by with a daily dose of heat, dust, and issues. Weeks of recent prayer continued to go unanswered to his most pressing problem: he lacked the gold he needed to build the armada required to sail his army across the seas. There were no cities of real wealth close by that he could attack, even if he was so inclined, which he was not. Exhausting and depleting his army by sacking minor cities to fill his coffers would just create more problems than the gold solved anyhow, but there were no ready alliances, no natural resources to exploit. Nothing to sell even if there were buyers…just sand and heat. So he prayed and waited. And trained.

The fighter grunted, too proud to admit exhaustion, yet too tired to speak. He was the day's sparring partner—just a nameless, sunburned face for Xaro to focus his rage against. Tall, strong, and breathing—those seemed to be the basic requirements.

Hoisting himself up off the dirt of the pit that was one of the combat arenas at Sands End, the sparring partner carefully raised his sword, circling to his left. Deep gashes ran down his sword arm, and his small oaken shield had so many hack marks that shards of wood were starting to poke out. One of his eyes was swollen shut, and his calf had been slashed painfully. Yet he was lucky; had he been an inch or two shorter, that gash would be directly behind his knee. Every fighter worth his salt knew that was a deadly blow in battle.

"Fight, you coward!" Xaro bellowed. "It is an honor to battle me. Is this the best my troops have to offer?" With a forceful blow to his opponent's shield, he finally cracked it apart. The shield shattered, as did the bones in the fighter's forearm. Bits of wood and iron flew everywhere as the man crumpled to the ground, holding his sword up protectively across his head with his good arm.

"Bah! Better you die from our enemies. You're not even worth the distinction of dying by my hand." He sneered at the man before turning to his Cleric in exasperation. "Malenec! Heal this man, if you can. May Kuth-Cergor take mercy on you."

Malenec eyed the wounded man, and then turned to Xaro. "Every day, your butchery gets worse. It is your prerogative, of course, but if you keep this up, your army will consist of nothing but broken men and undead warriors. This one, to be sure, is likely beyond healing. He shall be my newest undead warrior."

The man blanched. "No, good sir! I can heal up just fine—I can fight! Please—do not turn me into…into them." He looked frightfully at a ring of zombies that circled the pit. They looked hungry, but said nothing, contenting themselves to stare lustfully at the pool of blood forming underneath the man's shattered arm and calf.

Xaro cocked his head. "Must everyone you surround yourself with be undead? Outside of that brother of yours you torture, you cloak yourself in death, and the stench follows you everywhere."

Malenec narrowed his eyes, a smile spreading across his lips. "My living brother and I shall meet again, if we ever launch our attack into Elvidor." He wrinkled his nose. "As for any 'stench,' *I* am not the one who reeks in this desert heat."

Xaro sneered. "Do whatever you see fit, Cleric." He pointed to the bleeding fighter. "See to it that you don't waste his body while he still lives." He then turned to his general, the massive half-ogre Tar-Tan. "Find me a better fighter tomorrow. My skills get duller by the day. Soon I will spar with *you* if there is no one else worthy to fight."

The half-ogre narrowed his eyes, but knew better than to speak hastily. He had only met one man that he feared to fight. And so he followed this one man, Xaro, but it was still difficult for him to hold his tongue. Fortunately, Malenec spoke up.

"Xaro, this training for you is pointless. Your skills are as sharp as ever. What does this prove—that you swing a fair sword? In battle, your skills will best be put to use from the back, anyhow. All you do is weaken your own army with this daily exhibit of superiority. Are you that insecure? Come, what has it been—sixty days? This is pointless. Spring will be here soon. Surely your time can better be spent planning our launch?" Malenec never minced words with Xaro. He feared no man.

But he should fear me, Xaro fumed.

"We will leave when all of the arrangements are made! Moving 75,000 men, both alive and undead, across the world is no small task. Do not presume to lecture me. Remember your place, Malenec."

The Dark Cleric smiled. "Why, my place is right here in support of Kuth-Cergor. Presumably we serve the same God still, no?" He turned his back on Xaro, and began walking away, hundreds of undead warriors protectively encircling the enigmatic cleric.

Scowling, Xaro turned and looked back at the fighter he had crushed, curled up on the ground, clutching his arm. He offered a quick prayer to Kuth-Cergor, and put his hand on the man's arm. "Get up, Captain." His wounds slowly began healing. "The True Cleric says your wounds were beyond his ability, yet Kuth-Cergor heals them for *me*. You are luckier than you deserve. My Cleric would have your soul in limbo. Let it never be said that I am not merciful."

He turned to Tar-Tan, his foul mood undeterred. "See that this lump is trained to fight like a man."

Nearby, Xaro saw a slender man with a tanned, angular, goateed face bending down, picking at the sand. "You there. What are you doing?"

Standing up, the man held out his hand. He was holding small pieces of iron from the wounded fighter's shield. "I'm looking for gold," Krishnan said with a dry smile. "And with your help, I believe I've found it."

~Tarsh~

After a time, the people of Gaust avoided eye contact with him completely. Nobody asked his name—he was simply called the 'Monster of Gaust,' though nobody would ever say that to his face. His brutally-scarred face. The simple healing spells common to his Art may have kept him alive, but could do nothing for his disfigured face.

Tarsh Minster was truly a monster.

In the weeks following his encounter with Magi, one of Lord Corovant's mage guards helped his body knit itself back together, but true healing was hard to find. His injuries from that one spell were extensive; he would forever limp, and was at least an inch shorter due to the compacting of his spine. Running and jumping were memories. A deep breath would bring about a coughing fit.

At seventeen, Tarsh should have been at the peak of health. Two events in the last several months forever changed that: his climbing of the Staircase, where he'd lost his hair and inherited a long scar from his right eye down, and his encounter with Magi, who had brought an air hammer down upon his head that reshaped his face and crushed him like a nail made of soft clay might flatten with a blow from a sledgehammer.

The scar he had earned climbing the Staircase had made him look tough; now it was white and wide and just made him look pitiful. His smiles looked awkward, with lips that didn't quite line up any longer, few teeth, and one eye that was essentially shut, though he could still see slightly through a slit. It was the only reason he didn't wear an eye patch. His other eye was forever tinted red and murky from the blood pooled behind it—the only real blessing of the entire event, for now it was impossible to tell from looking at him that he was a True Mage. Of the tell-tale white eyes, one was merely slit and the other bloodshot.

A True Mage he was, however…he still could cast all his spells. His fingers were still dexterous, and his mind was razor-sharp. When his strength returned, he began using his bitterness to fuel his goals, working from small tasks toward his ultimate objective: Revenge. But first he had to beg for money and food. In time he would regain his strength. Then he would find Magi Blacksmooth, and kill him. Make him *pay* for everything. All the pain and anguish in his life stemmed from his former roommate.

And so Tarsh dined on hate for breakfast, bitterness for lunch, and—his favorite meal of the day—wicked fantasies for dinner. One recurring supper "dish" he was most fond of involved a slow and painful disfigurement far surpassing his own.

Tarsh grinned his lopsided grin.

"Alms?" he continued to beg along the docks, moving frequently, as city officials kept trying to shoo him away. "A coin for the stricken?" Some would toss him a coin. Some hurried over to the other side of the street, but Tarsh usually found them and looted them—he had become quite talented at projecting fear. The few brave citizens or travelers in Gaust that withstood his fear spell were often inexplicably struck blind as they walked past. He would never be a master thief, but he was an effective thug.

A few weeks of this life—living on the streets, bathing in the cold sea water, dressing in rags, begging from some, stealing from others, sifting through garbage for food—had produced enough gold for him to sail from Gaust to Shoal, or maybe as far as Nervadine…but not clear across the sea.

Frustrated, he started venturing into the nicer parts of town, near the city center, hoping for more information. But it was nearly impossible for him to have a decent conversation with anyone. Sitting by the roadside with a battered cap, warming his hands by a makeshift fire, he occasionally threw out the name: "Magi Blacksmooth? Anyone heard of the man?" But a filthy, disfigured beggar calling out a name didn't invite extended conversation. Just the opposite; the more he spoke, the fewer coppers he collected.

I have to find him. Skillfully avoiding some of the Lord's guards, Tarsh parked himself just outside one of the fancier taverns in town, frequented by the wealthier, perhaps more well-travelled class. Snow had begun giving way to mud, but the night was still quite cold. Though spring may be coming, he could still see his breath on this cloudless night.

Tonight he would camp just off the road, not too close to *The Winking Lark*, but not too far from the door, either. Methodically, like every other night, he built a small campfire. He usually avoided magical flame, not wanting to waste any coins on spell components. He also knew he'd have a hard time claiming poverty as a magic-user, and most importantly, he preferred to keep his identity as a True Mage to himself—it was the one advantage his disfigurement provided.

A young soldier walked past, holding a modestly plump lady's hand as they strolled by the fire. "Pardon me sir, but have you ever heard of a man called Magi Blacksmooth?" The two ignored him completely.

Another gentleman, older and a bit wobbly, shuffled out, leaning on a rather nice staff. "Kind sir, excuse me. I'm looking for information about a young m—" Tarsh stopped when the man threw up mere feet from his campfire. He caught himself with his walking stick to keep from pitching headfirst into the mud and his own vomit, then staggered on, paying Tarsh nary a glance.

And so it went, and the hours rolled by as Tarsh fed his fire from odd pieces of wood he collected by the docks. Tired, thirsty, and sore, he called out one final time to a passerby who stumbled by. From the back of the man's head, all he could see was a shock of red hair blowing in the night wind. At his side was a too-thin woman hanging at his elbow, pawing at his hair from behind. The scent of heavy perfume trailed behind her.

Tarsh sighed. "Young man, ever hear of a fellow named Magi Blacksmooth?" he called out.

The man stopped, and he seemed to sober up instantly. He turned around and walked over to Tarsh. As he came closer, the True Mage immediately recognized him—he had the most unforgettable face Tarsh could remember. *Next to my own, of course,* he thought bitterly. Two mismatched eyes stared down at Tarsh as he came within full view, his features illuminated by the flickering fire.

"You're Marik's friend." He cocked his head and looked even closer. "I've been looking for you."

Tarsh rubbed the drowsiness out of his eyes, stretching his sore limbs to try and stand up. *He was drunk the first day I met him as well...no wonder he can't remember my name.* "Hello, Trevor. My name is Tarsh—we met at the *Lazy Pour*, remember? Do you know where I can find Marik? Or better yet, where I can find the mage that came upon us when we were set to leave—his name is Magi. Magi Bl—"

"I know who Magi is." He never took his eyes off Tarsh. "What in all of Tenebrae happened to your face?"

Tarsh narrowed his one red eye, his other being nearly shut as it was. "You were on the docks that night. Isn't it obvious?"

"Magi did that to you? Surely Lord Corovant's healers—"

"Bah! Healing. There is no healing in this Dark World. Spare me your concern, Thief." Tarsh sneered, making his hideous face all the more misshapen. "Can you tell me where Marik is, or Magi? I have much to discuss with my former roommate."

Trevor's lady friend began growing impatient, but he waved his hand dismissively at her, without ever taking his eyes off Tarsh. She balled her hands into fists, but must have thought better of it when she got a look at Tarsh's face. Head down, she slowly shuffled away down the street.

Trevor cracked the slightest of smiles. "I do, in fact, know where Marik and Magi are. Likely the same place, though that's hard to say."

"What do you mean? Where?"

Trevor rubbed his hands together next to the fire, and finally dropped his gaze and stared at the flames, slowly shaking his head. "If revenge is your aim, then I am sorry to disappoint you. A friend of mine already killed Magi, shortly after he killed Marik and nearly killed you. I was there—I saw the whole battle."

Tarsh's mouth sagged open. All he could think about was his wicked torture fantasy—his burning desire to pay Magi back. He *couldn't* be dead. "Dead? Both of them? Are you certain?" He stared into those mismatched eyes, one blue and one brown, looking for a hint of a lie.

Trevor returned Tarsh's stare down. "He is most assuredly dead. My friend slit his throat while I watched him bleed out. But I may be able to offer you something far greater than revenge, Tarsh. Far greater. Marik thought highly of your talent, and planned to introduce you to our Master. Do you still practice the Art, or have your wounds taken that from you, too?"

Tarsh closed his red eye and raised his hands above his head as he spoke the language of magic. A crack of lightning lit the cloudless night sky, hurling a bolt from nowhere straight into the diminishing figure of the woman that had walked arm-in-arm out of *The Winking Lark* with Trevor moments earlier. Her final cry was drowned out by the tremendous peal of thunder that accompanied the spell. In the fading light of the flash, the last they saw was her thin body pitching forward into a puddle by the side of the road. Trevor had covered his ears at the thunder, a stunned look on his face.

"My Art is the one thing that has not been taken from me, Trevor."

~Captain Kilroy~

Captain Kilroy was almost ready to open his eyes. Gentle warmth pulsated near him, and he made out the unmistakable sounds of a crackling fire. By God, it felt good against his stiff bones. He was still slowly trying to piece together his most recent memories, and frankly keeping his eyes closed helped him concentrate, though his head still hurt.

The *Fury*. She had sunk in a terrible gale off the coast of Elvidor. A few of his crew had crammed into some dinghies, but they quickly capsized. He lost his voice shouting orders. The last mast fell. He remembered his ship listing hard to port and vaguely saw his passenger racing to climb railings to try and stay atop the water as long as possible. The wind was deafening, and it felt like ice was falling from the sky instead of rain.

He seemed to hear some of his crew screaming from a rowboat as it crashed on its side, smashing the small craft to bits and crushing the sailors. A watery grave for all of them.

The battering waves finally split the capsized *Fury*, and Captain Kilroy found himself clutching a piece of wood, freezing to death in the seas, dead bodies all around, pelted by icy spray, buried in wave after wave. The last thing he remembered was surfacing after a brutal wave sent him and his piece of wood under for the third or fourth time. As he broke the surface, his head hit something, and he lost consciousness.

And now, warmth. He decided it was time to open his eyes and was glad he did. He was looking up at the most beautiful woman he'd ever seen.

"Are you well?" she asked. "That was a wicked storm."

"Aye. I'll live. Doing better now. Where is this place, and who might I be talking to?" *That came out a lot more direct than I meant it to. By God, she is spectacular.*

The woman smiled. She probably meant it to look sweet, but on her face it almost came across—coy? Her rich, dark skin was framed by long hair the color of midnight. But it was her light brown, almond-shaped eyes that captivated the captain—they sparkled in a manner that was both kind and playful. "I am sure you have many questions. We saved a few of your men, but alas, most were gone before we could help them. Our scouts saw the ship approach, so we attempted to help, but the seas were unforgiving. Your captain was either brave or foolish to sail in such a storm."

"Aye. He's both, and greedy, too. Name's Kilroy. Captain Kilroy—The Brave, The Foolish, and The Greedy. And now The Indebted." He extended his hand to the woman and refrained from winking, opting to go with a self-deprecating smile that he hoped hit just the right note. "And you are?"

She smiled back. Again. "I am Lady Elyn, and you are in Thalanthalas, capital city of the Elfs." She took his hand politely and quickly shook it. "My father had some of our Elfen mages levitate the few survivors out of the water as we found them. We healed as many as we could, as best as we were able, and transported you all here to recover. That was four days ago—you are the last of your crew to wake up."

"How many are left?"

Lady Elyn shook her head. "Three, including you. A young man and a young woman."

"Woman?" *She owes me gold!* "Miss, Elyn, I'd be grateful if I could see this woman."

The elven beauty smiled ruefully. "Alas, she has left our care, but she did ask that I leave you this pouch." She handed him a small pack. "And this note."

> *Captain Kilroy, here is three-fourths of our price, since you delivered me three-fourths of the way to Rookwood. A contract is a contract. The Gods were not kind to your ship. Hopefully this will help you get started on the rebuilding.*
>
> *Good luck, V.*

He crumpled up the note and dug his hands into the pouch, pulling a few handfuls of gold out. A mighty sum for a journey, for sure, but hardly enough to replace a ship. Disgusted, Captain Kilroy sneered.

Lady Elyn waited a moment to see if he had anything else to say. She finally asked if he'd like to see the other lone survivor from his crew.

He looked at his modest pouch of gold, now his entire fortune. "Nay—maybe on the morrow. I think I'll sleep a bit, if that be alright with you, m'lady." *Just a mouth to feed now, and no ship for him to earn his keep on. 'Gods were not kind'—ha! Now there's an understatement. There are no gods—just a Dark, Dark World.*

~Queen Najalas~

Winter trudged onward, and the lines were getting longer. They always did at the tail-end of the cold season, as food became scarcer and townsfolk became more desperate. But this was not an ordinary winter surge in petitioners. The Queen tried to listen sympathetically, but it was impossible to ignore the growing number of discontents. Swollen feet, scarred faces. More and more people began turning on neighbors, bringing complaints over a goat or a small bird. One group came calling to complain about the disputed ownership of a woodpile. Soon the numbers became so large that she had to begin delegating. Herodius, the leader of a slave rebellion who risked everything on a harrowing sea journey to bring news of the Queen's enemy to her court, emerged as a competent arbitrator of various disputes; he had the patience to listen intently without suffering frivolity. She was grateful he had shown up.

"I pay my taxes—where is our food? You promised us food!" The Queen was snapped out of her wandering thoughts by a young mother shrieking up at her. "Look at my son, *your Majesty*," she mocked.

The boy was pathetic-looking. His skin was ashen, and his eyes were far too large for his hollowed face.

Jonathon stepped up to the woman before she could get any closer. "Please come with me, Madam. You are not to speak to your Queen in such a manner." He grabbed the woman's arm and began to pull her away from the dais.

"You are supposed to feed us! To protect us! My son dies while you live in a castle off *our* gold. What more can you take from me? Tell me—what more will you take from *all of us*?!" she screamed around the Great Hall until the Queen's steward slapped her. Her boy didn't even cry as they were forcibly led away. The rest of the crowd became restless, but the guards quickly moved in to restore order before anything sparked into a bigger disturbance.

Queen Najalas sighed. When tensions became this high, she knew it was time to leave the Great Hall for awhile. Herodius led her to an antechamber, and went back to continue her work.

And on it went, day after day. Simon begged his Queen to quit seeing the masses, that there was no point. The Queen continued to collect taxes, of course, and Rookwood did offer protection. Didn't these people realize that war was brewing in the West? The guards, the knights, the roads—all required gold and silver. The winter was harsh, perhaps harder than typical, but nothing had prepared them for the complete lack of food. Did the people not save anything for the cold months? What did they honestly expect her to do?

"No, we shall hear them out. They need us, Simon. Our kingdom is hurting, and they need to know we understand."

"But my Queen—this is pointless. Reckless, even. Do you know how many knives I have found hidden in petitioners' boots as they approach with their complaint? Soon one will be clever enough to hide one where I don't look, and desperate enough to use it. If you wish to listen to them, then I must insist that you delegate this. Let your new pet listen to them. Perhaps he can use his fancy staff to ferret out those that are truly worthy of an audience with you."

The Queen smiled; she had heard this suggestion before. And she had to admit that it was not without merit. But she resisted. "Simon, my dear Simon. Magi can see truth, but can he offer protection? The people need protection, Simon. And as their Queen, it falls on me to provide them with it, even if they don't always see it the way we do inside Rookwood—the guards manning the city walls, the food subsidies, the wood subsidies, the ships patrolling the waters, the knights patrolling the roads. Spring will come soon, Captain. Until then, be patient with our people. Magi will see some, just as Herodius sees some. But only a Queen can truly give the people what they need in this Dark World: Protection. Protection…and maybe Hope."

She leaned back in her chair, already weary, but knowing the day was far from over. "Send in the next petitioner, but let's do it one at a time from now on, shall we?"

~Magi~

Magi sat and listened patiently, acutely aware of his surroundings. He was dressed in a hunter green tunic, dark brown pants, fine leather boots, and a travelling cloak around his shoulders, despite the large fire roaring nearby stocked with evergreen logs that gave the audience chamber a woodsy scent and a pleasing ambience.

In short, he was warm, well fed, and comfortable—everything that the people seeking his judgment were not. To top it off, he held a beautifully carved staff that drew the attention of everyone in the room whenever he so much as shifted his weight upon the Judgment Seat. *If only Lionel could see me now...I look to all the world a proper Ranger.* His eyes, of course, gave it away.

He considered the case before him. On one hand was a local miller—Ronbar was his name. He was dressed well enough, but Magi was not one to miss details. He did not need his Staff to see the small patches in the miller's shoes, or the seam where someone had stitched up a rip in his livery. The miller might have had gold at one time, but he was far from the merchant class now.

Standing across from him was the owner of *The Last Call*, a tavern on the very outskirts of Rookwood, well in the shadow of the great castle. She called herself Lady Velvet, and had to be one of the most disgusting women Magi had ever seen. Underneath a cloak that looked to be stitched together from the skins of a hundred different squirrels, she somehow had squeezed herself into a grease-stained, tight-fitting dress, with mountains of flesh bulging against the poor cloth whenever she took a breath. The way she held her head, however, you'd have thought she was Queen of all Tenebrae.

Ale. The dispute was over ale. Half the population is freezing, the other half starving, and he is required to make a ruling about ale. *Dymetra...increase my patience!*

"Hey—fancy pants! You payin' attention?" Lady Velvet croaked, sounding like an old campaigner who had spent all his gold on tobacco and mead. "As I been saying—I had a deal. One of the Queen's errand boys came calling and made a deal on behalf of the crown to get me decent ale from this wretch of a miller. We shook on it. All I got was three lousy barrels—hell, my regs went through that before the end of a good night! Don't suppose a real dandy like you knows anything about an honest mug of ale when times get hard though, do you? All warm up here in your shiny castle, stealin' our hard-earned gold and silver. Ain't right, you know, and this miller ain't been trading square for years! Always watering down the ale, thinkin' Lady Velvet won't know any better. But I do, and me regs do. It's a hard thing, keeping common folk warm and fed. This miller's no better than a thief!"

Ronbar shifted uncomfortably during her talk before straightening his back and shouting up at Magi. "I say! I am no such thing as a thief. This—*hag*—has been complaining about my ale for years. Go buy your ale from some other miller if mine is not, shall we say, up to your standards. But I will not sit here and be called a thief by an outsized prostitute who blackmailed her way into owning a tavern!"

The audience chamber, smaller than the Great Hall, was still filled with petitioners—all eager to warm themselves by one of the large fire pits brightening the room. When they heard Ronbar's accusation, the small group of peasantry erupted into raucous shouts and laughter, filling the room with a gossipy din. Magi rubbed his temples.

Holding his Staff, he sifted through their words. No one could hide the truth from Magi while he carried the Staff of Insight. No one. Half-truths and false intentions were all laid bare for the Staff's Master. Rolling the Staff from his left to right hand, he stood up. He didn't even need to say a word for a hush to fall over the room, punctuated only by some trapped tree sap cracking and popping in the blaze off to one side.

"Both of you have told the truth," he began wearily. "But neither of you told me all of it." He turned to Lady Velvet. "You did indeed make a deal with someone to speak on your behalf with the miller here. His name was Kyle, and he was a good friend of mine." Magi paused slightly. "The best of friends, actually, but no matter. Your deal was for him to barter on your behalf for better ale with the miller in exchange for room and board. Well—he never stayed one day at *The Last Call*, did he? And he did negotiate with Queen Najalas herself on your behalf to see that some stronger ale was shipped to your tavern, though he sought nothing in return from you. This is true." Magi again paused—making a statement of fact. "And therefore nothing more is owed you from the Crown."

Turning to the miller, he continued. "And you Ronbar, you know exactly that of which you accuse the Lady Velvet, seeing as she is the one who is blackmailing *you*, which is why you send her poor ale. She extorts your gold and then pays it back to you for ale, holding the secret of your affair. Well, your indiscretion is no longer secret, so there is nothing left for her to blackmail you with. This also is true."

He held up his hands to quiet the gasps in the crowd. Ronbar was mortified. Lady Velvet was irate. Magi pressed on. "Make your ale as it should be made, and trade fairly with everyone, including the Lady Velvet. If she is not getting a fair price for good ale, we'll sell the ale to her and take it directly from you in addition to our taxes. And she will be paying for it with her own gold, unless she finds some other fellow to blackmail." He paused here to give the crowd a few moments of laughter to shame them both a bit before continuing. "But there is a third factor that neither of you are considering."

Here Magi addressed seemingly everyone in the audience chamber. "Bread. A time is coming when we may be forced to choose between ale and bread. The baker may pay more for the miller's grain than he can charge for ale. We may all be drinking watered down ale, thin mead, and sour wine before this winter passes. Be prudent."

The effect of his message was not a calming one. Shouts of hoarding began to come up from the back of the room. Hungry eyes looked at the lavish tapestries on the castle walls with disdain. Angry mutterings could be heard as people moved closer to the warmth of the large fire. The guards were tense and many started moving forward, making it a point to bang the butt of their spears on the cold stone of the castle.

Holding his Staff high above his head, Magi uttered a calming spell—really a light, light, sleeping spell—and order was restored immediately.

Unexpectedly, Jonathon entered the audience chamber and trotted up to the Judgment Seat. Leaning over, he whispered to Magi, "The Queen wishes to see you immediately. Apparently, the person who you claimed killed you in Gaust was an acolyte of Dymetra—a seeker hoping to learn the ancient ways of becoming a True Cleric, back when such existed. She was known in this Court."

Magi gave Jonathon a puzzled look. "And? We've long since gone over my account of what happened. What is the urgency that I should leave this crowd—there must be at least 20 more grievances to air this afternoon."

Jonathon smiled. "They can wait. Queen Najalas, however, cannot. You see, Miss Sarah has returned, and will no doubt be disappointed to see that she won't be collecting the Queen's reward for your death." He turned to leave through an archway in the back of the room before glancing back at Magi. "And bring your Staff."

Bring the mage to me, if you think he is worthy.

His last conversation with Xaro had ended with this simple instruction. He stared at the man leaning over the deck, one hand on the rail, the other clutching his walking staff. It was a calm night—cold still—but calm. Spring may have been coming, but it still felt like winter on the sea, with the crisp air adding a salty tang to each breath. Yet a magical blue fire next to the brooding, hunched-over mage kept him warm and did nothing to consume the wood of the ship.

Trevor couldn't see his face, only the back of his ragged robe. *Not that I'm complaining.* This Tarsh was hideous. He almost didn't bother inviting him to meet with Xaro and frankly was hoping it might take a little longer to find the guy. He certainly hadn't been trying very hard—it took him a month of "searching" the city before the beggar had accosted him, and turned out to be the man he was supposed to be looking for. Ah, well...his leisure time in the city had just about run its course over the last month, anyhow.

If you think he is worthy... Technically, Xaro had left the judgment to him. He could have left Gaust at any time and told Xaro that he couldn't find him or that he was unfit to be of much use—both of which could have been true a few days ago. And even now, Trevor recognized that his estimation of Tarsh was based largely on a lightning bolt from the sky. It was impressive to him, but to another True Mage? Who knows? In the end, he figured it would be easier to let Xaro sort out whether this Tarsh—the "Monster of Gaust"—was of any value to his cause... but that wasn't the only reason he'd decided to bring him.

A modest wave caused *Sheila's Bane* to slowly rise and then suddenly drop, making Trevor spill half of his mug of ale down the front of his dark tunic. "Z! What are your sailors doing?" he shouted. Captain Zephyr, or Captain Z, could hardly hear Trevor's shouts.

Brushing off the front of his shirt, he quickly drank the rest of his mug (his fourth) before slowly pulling himself up. The bitter, hoppy brew was meant for long sea voyages. Trevor loved every last drop. He reached for the rail next to Tarsh to steady himself. "Drink?" he asked his companion.

"No. I'm fine." He kept staring out to sea over the rail, never even turning his head to face Trevor.

"Tarsh, do you know why I invited you?" Trevor was feeling a little chatty this evening. *Might as well find out.*

"You want me to meet Xaro—same reason Marik wanted to introduce me to him. To hear you and he talk about this guy, he sounds like the reincarnation of Quixatalor."

"Quixa-who?"

"Never mind. A famous True Mage." He turned and looked at Trevor, the expression on his ravaged face difficult to read. "Means nothing to a thief."

"Well, yes. Marik has told you all about Xaro and Kuth-Cergor, I suppose. Tell me—what do you think of that?"

"Of what? Of Kuth-Cergor? I don't know. I've seen no evidence of ancient gods, I've seen no evidence of new gods. The only reality I know is my face. The cruelest irony is that I won't have a chance to avenge myself or die trying. I came with you out of curiosity. That and…never mind."

"And what else?" Trevor pressed.

"Perhaps if Xaro is close to a god, perhaps this god can heal me. I don't know. I don't hold out much hope. It is a Dark World."

"Yes, indeed it is. As I told you several days ago, Xaro may offer you a seat at the table. Marik served him for years, and he coveted Magi. Both are dead. You could take their place. But…"

"But what?" Tarsh's head spun around, his one red eye narrowing.

Trevor smiled, and gently put his hand on Tarsh's shoulder. He leaned a little close, the blue flames casting a flickering light against his cheek. "I don't know about you, Tarsh, but I believe in *options*. Xaro means to take over the world, and usher in a new age with his God installed as Lord over us all. That sounds like a fun ride for as long as we stay in the inner circle. It doesn't sound quite as *enjoyable* if we ever find ourselves cross-wise with Xaro, if you catch my meaning." He curled his lip in a half-smile.

Tarsh stared at Trevor for an uncomfortable moment. "You seek to betray the very Master you would have me join? Tell me, are all thieves as treacherous as you?" Trevor, however, could see the beginning hint of a half-smile in return.

"Betray? No, no no no no," he replied, shaking his head. "*Options*," he whispered. "Before we met a few days ago, you were begging and stealing for food, an outcast from society. Xaro may elevate your station, for sure. Then again, he may not. Who can say for sure what he may do, or what our future might be in a world headed for war? I am simply providing you an audience with him. He may heal you, accept you, and together we may both serve long on his council, as would be proper."

"Or? What schemes fill your head, Thief?" Trevor could now see the tortured yet unmistakable smile of a scheming man reflected back at him in the dancing blue flame.

"Simply this—a True Thief and a True Mage ought to be able to disappear and live off the wealth of others much more easily than either alone could hope for in this Dark, Dark World. Wouldn't you agree?"

~Xaro~

"Gold," Krishnan continued, "is the key, Xaro. With our combined skill, we can surely complete the transfiguration of common iron. Every town will be ours to buy. Every warrior has his price. Your army will swell with every step. The best of every weapon, of every armor. But most important—we will drive up the price of food until only we can afford it. There is so little to be had as it is; only the hunters fill their bellies this cursed winter. You should hear the stories of suffering from Oraz and Elvidor. And yet we can turn this curse to a blessing! Not only will our soldiers be the best fed, but our enemies shall be the worst. What city, starving and bereft of gold, will not cry out to us for protection? We may conquer the world with little more than a shout from our well-fed army. *This* is what I can bring to you. *This* is the reality of a Dark World where gold controls everything...and *we* control the gold."

Krishnan smiled as he rolled a fat grape between his thumb and forefinger, staring at it before he tossed it into his mouth. The dark-skinned mage with the angular face had coal-black hair and a mouth wreathed by a tight goatee, all in contrast to his bright, white eyes. Krishnan lounged in Xaro's private chambers, with the soft scent of cinnamon smoking in a coal pit in the corner. Xaro often burned the incense after his training to mask the smell of a warrior's sweaty leather. He watched as Krishnan reached over to grab an enormous olive off a different platter.

Fool. You have no idea who controls everything. Still—the idea is not without merit. "For a newly-minted True Mage that has failed every attempt at this unusual alchemy, you sure seem content to claim an interest in *my* soldiers, *my* army, and most assuredly—*my* gold. You forget your place, metal-changer." He briefly allowed the *Illusion* of his faux eyes to fade away, revealing the pure white eyes that were the hallmark of every True Mage.

The affect this had on his face was not lost on Krishnan, who put the olive down and lowered his head instinctively. "Of course, Xaro. I only meant to describe my allegiance, not my station. Forgive me."

A little better. "Very well. So—we are to change iron to gold, you say. A virtual endless supply of gold would certainly help our campaign in the provinces that are suffering under this wretched winter. I see the logic in that. But let me cut to the quick with two questions: One, what will be different here since you've already failed seventy-seven times? And two, assuming *we* succeed, what is it that you expect in return for this skill?" Xaro made sure that this would not be a negotiation.

"What is missing, I believe, are the prayers of a faithful Cleric combined with my spells. All the ancient scrolls highlight the prayers of a faithful servant as the final step in the process. Until a few days ago, I had never met a Cleric. Now I've met two! Surely, it can be no coincidence that I came here. Surely, a man of god such as yourself can see the providence of our meeting? Come now—your god, the ancient one, this Kuth-Cergor, he must have ordained this! It is as if he *wants* us to build a mountain of gold before you launch your attack. You put your faith in this god, and he rewards you with gold! Xaro, it is *destiny*!" Krishnan whispered the last word for effect. A wicked smile crept across his face. "As for my expectations…I am sure if we are successful, that there will be enough gold for me to enjoy, shall we say, some modest privileges."

Xaro looked at this blasphemous young mage with mostly contempt. Slowly, however, he smiled, too. "Very well. We shall do this. Right now. But understand the stakes: if we succeed, you shall join my inner council, and commit yourself to worship Kuth-Cergor and him alone. You shall call me Master the rest of your life, and shall serve at my leisure. And we shall make much gold, and conquer all of Tenebrae, beginning with Elvidor."

"And if we fail?"

"I shall hand you over to my Cleric, Malenec, who will rip your soul from you and leave your body neither alive nor dead, but suspended forever until you burn, an undead shell of flesh answering to us and us alone."

Krishnan leaned forward slightly and extended his hand. "Either way, I am more protected than I am now in this Dark World. If your god is real, I have nothing to fear." He smiled back at Xaro. "Let's begin…Master."

~*Veronica*~

Veronica (whom everyone at court knew as Miss Sarah) sat calmly in one of the Queen's antechambers, modestly recounting the tale of her avengement of Kyle's murderer. The Queen listened patiently, joined by her guards, Simon of course, and a cloaked woman wearing a bright red, hooded dress that fit snugly around her head. Professing her loyalty to Dymetra, she explained how conflicted she was at the taking of this life, but ultimately felt at ease, knowing that she had Dymetra's blessing. She told a rather plain tale, devoid of many details, that culminated in a simple poisoning. A humane murder, if such a thing exists. Certainly a far more merciful punishment than the arcane missile this rogue mage had sent into Kari's brother.

"Magi, I believe his name is," the Queen helped as Veronica wrapped up her tale.

"Yes. Magi. That's it. I decided to come back in order to continue my pursuit of holiness and clerical studies. I still wish to join Strongiron and Kari in their quest of knowledge on Urthrax, and you may deduct whatever amount of gold is appropriate from the published reward in exchange for a ship to take me across the sea to join them." *A True Assassin never fails to collect on a contract, private or public.*

The Queen had the strangest look on her face—one that Veronica couldn't quite place. It was disconcerting. Inscrutable. *You should be calling for a feast in my honor, woman.* Yet Veronica just smiled pleasantly at her Queen.

Finally, the Queen broke the silence. "Well. Miss Sarah, that was quite...riveting. Tell me though—is there any evidence you have that would confirm that the rogue mage, Magi, is, in fact, dead? And where did this poisoning take place again?"

"My Queen, alas all I have is my word. I can only hope that the word of an acolyte of the one True God Dymetra is sufficient." Veronica bowed her head in humility for a brief pause before looking up when no one interrupted her. "As for the poisoning, I caught up with him in Gaust. However, I dumped the body into the sea once he was dead—there wouldn't be any trace of that man's wickedness left behind, I'm afraid."

The Queen fixed her with a steely stare for the briefest of moments, before softening. "I suppose we must take you at your word for now. But I am curious, where did you learn how to poison a man, and it must have been awfully heavy for you to drag his body into the sea…why would you do such a thing if you meant to collect the reward?"

Veronica, calm as ever, replied, "My Queen…things are different in the West. Even with a public warrant, one can never be sure how the local provinces will take such a sight. I thought a dead body would attract too much attention, and to be blunt—acting to collect a bounty from the Queen may not endear me to the restless population if they decided I was a murderer. Rolling a body over a dock is not too heavy, even for one as slight as me, your Majesty. And as for my knowledge of poisons, it is a woman's equalizer in this Dark World, is it not?" She smiled a bit coyly, hoping to appear sheepish and confident all at the same time.

The Queen tilted her head slightly. "A woman's equalizer. This may be true for some…" She glanced over at the woman in red and smiled. "But not for all. So—my grip on the West is light, is that what you are saying? Speak plainly, Miss Sarah."

"I would never say that your rule is diminished, my Queen, but west of the mountains can be a distant land, your Majesty. I destroyed the evidence of my killing perhaps out of shame, but also out of discretion. If proof is required to collect the crown's gold, than I respectfully withdraw my claim." She bowed her head to hide the clenching of her teeth before she finished her thought. She cleared her throat sharply and put a delicate smile on her face, looking up. "Vengeance for Kari shall be reward enough." *Not hardly enough, but Xaro would have tried to take it from me anyhow. Bother.* "Now, if I may continue my studies—is there any way you can help me rejoin Kari, Strongiron, and the others?" That *contract is still in force, at least.*

"I would gladly send you to join the expedition on Urthrax, but I don't believe that is necessary. You see, most of them have just now returned."

With a slight nod, Kari, another mage, Niku, and a female Ranger Veronica vaguely remembered as Rebecca entered. But no Strongiron. *Where's Strongiron? That's my contract!*

"Miss Kari—what happened to the General? Did you find what you were looking for?" Veronica steadied her breathing a bit to avoid sounding over-anxious.

Niku answered before Kari could say anything. "Miss Sarah, our General is fine. We did, indeed, find evidence of the True Clerics. More than evidence—we found remnants. I must admit that I was skeptical at first, and I doubted your calling and Miss Kari's. But I never would have dreamed that it was our own General who

Dymetra has called. He shall return as a True Warrior Cleric, and may we all be blessed when that occurs. The tales of Dymetra are true—we saw the fabled Tower of Dariez ourselves, and Quentin here can testify to the power that a True Cleric can wield. It is…virtually limitless."

The mage named Quentin stepped forward and described how the True Cleric Faralon had healed his tongue, giving him back his magic. Finally, Kari stepped forward and described her studies, and her choice to continue her pursuit of the Art while Strongiron continued his pursuit of God. At this, Veronica saw an eager smile spread across the woman in red's face.

Throughout this, Veronica listened attentively. Something was odd—the Queen never took her eyes off her, even when the others were speaking. Finally Veronica cleared her throat. "Miss Kari, Niku…that is an adventure worthy of a bard. Alas, I believe it puts my tale to shame. Although as I've related this already to our Queen, I do have what I hope is one piece of good news for you, Kari. The murderous mage who killed your brother is dead. I poisoned him myself to avenge your brother. May Dymetra have mercy on his soul."

"She has," Magi said casually, walking in behind Veronica silently with Jonathon, staff in hand.

CHAPTER THREE: POWER DISPLAYED

~Tarsh~

Dawn broke red over the horizon, with the rhythmic sound of *Sheila's Bane* cutting through the gentle seas as the only noise upon deck; no birds cawed as the majestic ship headed west into the gray light, leaving pink light to spread behind her. It was still too dark, but Tarsh knew that somewhere to the southwest lay the Great Whirlpool of Emotion—a giant maelstrom where the Sea of Love and the Sea of Hate comingled. Captain Z steered far north of it.

Tarsh rubbed his stubbled beard, absently fingering the smooth scar down his cheek where no hair would grow. He slept fitfully, often up early. Trevor would be asleep for hours still, nursing a headache from strong ale meant to last a long sea voyage. Tarsh just shook his head. *The Thief would sell his own Mother for a pint.*

He recounted their recent conversation—there was something Trevor had said that disturbed him. Or rather, *didn't* say.

Slowly, gray light spread over the westward sea. Tarsh leaned forward, letting the salty spray tickle his tortured face. He was going to meet Xaro—a man whom both Marik and Trevor spoke of as a real Cleric—a man to be respected, certainly feared. They were supposed to find Magi's ring and bring it him; Marik had recruited Tarsh for just such a purpose. Privately Tarsh hoped that the ring, and perhaps his faithful service—including even a religious conversion, if need be—would be enough incentive to encourage Xaro to heal him…and that was before his face and body were so misshapen. He was burned and scarred from the Staircase, to be sure, but what he had become since then…

He bunched his hand into a fist and slammed it down on the railing. Last he'd heard, Magi had the ring when he brought the Air Hammer down upon him. Soon after that, according to Trevor, Magi had killed Marik before some other "friend" of his found a way to slit Magi's throat, killing the mage and Tarsh's chance for revenge in one stroke.

But he never mentioned the ring. It just now occurred to Tarsh that he hadn't asked the Thief about it.

Where was it? He knew it was a ring of magical protection—Marik and Trevor could both attest to that. Without the ring, what would he and Trevor be bringing to Xaro? He was a True Mage, and would be welcome in any army, for sure, but he would need to prove himself if he was to have any hope of gaining Xaro's trust. Committing to alliances with a self-interested, turn-cloak Thief was not likely to engender that trust, for sure.

But what if Trevor is right? What if Xaro is unwilling to help me? What am I really signing up for? A small pairing, him and Trevor together, could live out their days in obscurity—literally just disappear. His thieving for gold, Tarsh's own magic for defense; they could easily live a merchant-class lifestyle without the danger of tyrants, of war—accountable to no one but themselves in a Dark World.

But would I really need the Thief? I am, after all, a True Mage— and few even know! I could easily disappear; who wants to come close to a man who looks as I do? Tarsh conveniently ignored his recent reality in Gaust, when he had last been 'on his own.'

Now…if I could just find this ring… Tarsh again stuck his face out over the rail as *Sheila's Bane* came down the backside of a modest wave, delighting in the crisp, salty spray in the morning air. He felt electric, alive. From his daydream or the cool sea smell, he didn't know, but he couldn't wait to ask the Thief what ever became of the ring. He wouldn't need a soul if he had a trinket such as *that*. Or perhaps he could barter with it—it would be a healthy bargaining chip for a healing prayer from this Xaro if indeed the man was blessed by an ancient god.

"Maelstrom!" yelled the lookout, breaking Tarsh from his reverie.

Tarsh limped across the deck to the other side of the ship. Unbelievably, the Giant Whirlpool yawned to port in the distance, and the ship was just beginning to tilt as the wind blew out of the north, pressing the ship south toward the massive swirling waters.

Captain Z scrambled up on deck as the call rang out. Soon more and more sailors spilled out from their bunks to take their spots. The wind had picked up, and was clearly pushing the sails as if to guide the vessel straight into the heart of the black, coiled water.

"To starboard!" the Captain yelled.

Booms were moved, sails bent, the wheel spun by the first mate. The ship straightened for a moment, but no longer seemed to be cutting through the water. All their efforts seemed to merely keep the boat in place. Instead of sailing past the enormous, black maw of the sea, it looked to Tarsh as if the giant whirlpool was slowly drifting *toward them*. He looked up at the sails and saw the seams straining. Men were pulling on ropes in every direction, trying to keep the ship from turning to port.

"Pull, men! Blast this cursed water! She's tryin' to feast on *Sheila*—she'll not have the *Bane!* Pull, I said! To starboard!" He paused for a second and then yelled, "To oars!"

That doesn't sound good, thought Tarsh. He was no sailor, but he doubted the oars would be helpful against such determined wind and seas. *They'll probably just get snapped off.* This seemed more like an act of desperation. He gazed out over the water, the wind whipping through his robes. Over the Giant Whirlpool was a dark cloud that followed it everywhere, with lightning forking out into an otherwise clear sky. Unmistakably, the massive Whirlpool was slowly inching closer.

"Heave! On my count! Heave!...Heave!...*Heave!*" Captain Z's voice carried up from the row deck just below Tarsh, over the sounds of wind and the crashing of water. Tarsh leaned over and saw the rhythmic hum of dozens of oars striking the water in near unison. He looked up...it seemed as if the dark cloud was no longer approaching.

Crack! Just as he was watching the cloud, he heard the unmistakable sound of wood splintering and looked down at the row of oars stabbing the sea. He saw one of the middle ones crack and poke awkwardly in the wrong direction, useless. *Crack!* Another broke, this one on the other side of the ship's hull. He looked up again and saw a test of wills almost in perfect balance: Mother Nature vs. Captain Z and *Sheila's Bane*—one fighting to hold its grip, the other fighting to break free. *Crack!*

Another oar gone. The current and the wind were conspiring to snap them like toothpicks. Tarsh closed his eyes, one of which was nearly always shut. *I've never tried this before.* If he was to die in a shipwreck, however, it would be with magic on his lips.

Tarsh called forth a simple levitation spell, only this time he wasn't trying to raise or lower himself; instead, he fixed his mind on *Sheila's Bane*.

The ship began to vibrate slightly, and Tarsh felt himself perspiring. He focused on the whole ship—careful to avoid ripping the mast from the hull or pulling planks up from the deck. Sailors began to cry out as the oars struggled to pierce the top of the water, rowing air instead. Slowly the ship rose up out of the sea. Raising his arms, Tarsh let go of the railing and moved to the center of the main deck, his robes flapping wildly in the fierce gale.

The crew could do nothing now but watch. The boat was out of the water, and every man held fast to whatever object they could.

Some cursed. Most shouted. Some simply gawked, rubbing the salty sea from their eyes, fixated on the True Mage in their midst.

Tarsh plumbed the depths of his potential well of energy and emptied himself into the moment, pushing the boat through the adversarial wind. Slowly they put more distance between the dark cloud, the black water, and *Sheila's Bane*. North and west the boat hovered, a mere thirty-five feet above the sea, but high enough that all but the meanest waves broke harmlessly beneath the floating ship. One league became two, two became three, and then as suddenly as the winds had picked up, they ceased. Far to the south and east the Giant Whirlpool lingered, no longer threatening.

Gently, Tarsh allowed the boat to descend back into the water. Exhausted, his strength failed him the last few feet, causing a rough re-entry onto the Sea of Love. He collapsed with most of the other sailors on splashdown.

"Not bad. Marik was right about one thing: you can never have too much magic on your side."

Tarsh slowly opened his bloodshot eye to see Trevor's ugly face, framed by the mid-morning sun, looking down at him.

~Magi~

Two thoughts raced through Magi's mind nearly simultaneously.

The first: *so this is the woman that I should thank.* He smiled at Veronica, leaning on the Staff of Wisdom out of habit more than weariness. She was a liar and cutthroat of the highest order. He should know; she had cut his own throat months ago.

And in so doing, she had unwittingly released his soul from the grip of the curse that his former master had put upon it. She also made it possible for him to make peace with his best friend, Kyle, whom he had brutally murdered while under the curse. Furthermore, if she hadn't killed Magi, he never would have come face to face with the one True God—never learned the truth about Dymetra. Never received the gift of Quixatalor's Staff of Wisdom.

All because this woman sliced his neck open as if she was bleeding a pig for a feast.

His second, parallel thought was much more painful: *Kari, I owe you more than my life.*

Before the shocked look could vanish from Veronica's face, Magi strode to Kari and fell on both knees, making sure he was looking up at her, neck raised. "Kari…" he began, his white eyes filling with tears. "Kari…you're back. I—"

Her brilliant green eyes were wide with—anger? Loathing? Fear? Magi couldn't tell for sure. He couldn't read her face, and there certainly wasn't any lie to see with his Staff. She never took her eyes off him, but she was clearly speaking to Veronica. "You just said that you killed him." She leaned forward, and now the rage in her face was undeniable. "What trick is this, Magi?"

He recoiled slightly, still on his knees. "No *Illusion*, Kari. My story is long, and I've told it to most of this court, save you and those that arrived with you recently..." He stood up and turned to look at Veronica. "And the Assassin."

How amusing. She stares at me like I'm a ghost...but there are more important matters at hand. He inclined his head slightly, and took a step toward Veronica. "You look familiar, but I don't believe we've formally met. My name is Magi—Magi Blacksmooth. The last time I saw you was when you were slipping an arm over my head from behind while drawing your blade across my throat."

Peter, who was standing next to Veronica, narrowed his eyes at her. "Like Miss Kari said, I thought you were just telling us you poisoned him." Peter nodded in Magi's direction.

Veronica appeared frozen, eyes darting furiously around the room. Magi saw her looking at Kari, at the Queen, at Herodius, the mage guards, Belara, Peter, Jonathon, Simon, Rebecca...but she quickly focused back on Magi. Her pause in addressing him was no more than a second or two, but the silence hung in the air for what felt like an hour. Magi could feel Kari's eyes boring into his back every second he stood facing Veronica, but right now she was the darker threat by far.

"You're alive, knave." Veronica turned to the Queen, raising her voice. "Your Majesty, the murderer walks freely in your Hall?"

"I imagine there are three, four, or even more murderers in this Hall as we speak, Miss Sarah. I'm afraid his story does not square with your own." The Queen stood tall, in front of a large chair, flanked by Simon on one side and Herodius on the other.

"Surely the man who killed *her* brother in cold blood right here in this very stronghold is the liar!" Veronica shouted, pointing at Kari.

Kari's hands stealthily moved toward some of her inner pouches. Illusionists rarely needed spell components to cast their typical spells. She might be thinking of something more real than *Illusion*.

Magi's head was spinning. *Confronting both of these women at the same time was not my plan.* It was time for the truth. He stepped forward, the smile on his face replaced with sadness. But his voice was stern. "Veronica Edgewild—and that is your given name, enough with this Miss Sarah nonsense—it is pointless for you to lie further about your plans and identity. Behold the Staff of Wisdom— it tolerates no lie in its presence. I have proven the validity of my story many times over to this group. But let me prove the same to you, so that you know my words are true." He turned to look at Kari. "Everything I am about to say is true, Kari. I have much to explain— and account for—with you, too. Especially with you."

Magi turned back to direct his comments to Veronica. "Born humble on a small farm, you watched your parents killed in front of you by a nameless murderer who wanted your land. You escaped, and spent several years in an orphanage in Fostler. I will spare all the retelling of the horrors you suffered there. But you were hardened, ripe for recruitment by the Assassin's Guild, and you rose quickly to the top of their ranks. Stealthy, your calling card is a throat slash— just like the one that ended your own mother's life. And like the one that ended mine.

"You were referred by your Guild leader to Xaro—a man who has made known his plan to usher in a new age of war and conquest and false worship. A man beholden to the anti-God. A man who takes aim on Rookwood as we speak. A man you call Master.

"Your kills are countless. Only one mark has thus far escaped you: Xaro has put a contract on the life of the Queen's General, Strongiron. You have failed to kill *him*, but were hoping to further ingratiate yourself to this court by presenting yourself as the one who killed *me*. It must be terribly inconvenient for you that I am still quite alive."

Veronica started to speak but Magi cut her off, jamming the butt of his Staff into the stone floor for emphasis. "Don't. Stop, Veronica. You and I know what I have just spoken aloud to be the absolute truth. The Staff of Wisdom tolerates no lie, not even from me. You cannot lie in my presence, Veronica. False words and half-guarded truths ring out like cymbals in my ears. The larger question is simply this: where is your Master now, and what do you know of his plans?" Magi leaned forward slightly, but did not take a threatening step.

All eyes were on her, and Magi could see the desperation grow in her eyes. Mage guards began slowly reaching into their pouches. Knights were moving to cover the doors.

It was Kari, however, who spoke first.

"Why did you kill my brother?" The question filled the room like a fast-gathering storm cloud, fueling the tension in the air with bitter energy. It was as if Kari hadn't heard a thing Magi had just said to Veronica, consumed with this singular thought.

Magi turned away from Veronica to focus on Kari. "Oh, Kari." He walked back toward her. "If I could take that back, I would. I was cursed, Kari. Marik cursed me. He played us all for fools. Like Veronica, he, too, served Xaro. He darkened my soul, and my heart was shrouded in jealousy, anger, bitterness. After I—" he paused, taking a deep breath. "After I hit you, your brother attacked me, and I snapped."

He wanted to reach out and hold her, but he didn't feel like he should get any closer. He stopped walking toward her. "Please forgive me, Kari. I have seen Kyle. He has forgiven me, and is with Her—with Dymetra. She sent me back. With *this*." He held the Staff, its white stone aglow. "It is as I described it—Quixatalor's Staff of Wisdom. Everything I have said is true, Kari." He shook his head gently. "I may not deserve your forgiveness, nor do I expect you to understand how deeply sorry I am. I loved your brother." He gripped the Staff so tight that the color drained from his knuckles. "If Kuth-Cergor's reach into Tenebrae leads to this kind of sorrow, then I will do everything I can to stop him. If I could bring Kyle back, I would. In fact, I tried." He looked straight into Kari's glistening eyes. "She wouldn't send him back. Not for me."

"What do you mean she wouldn't send him? What are you talking about?" Kari screamed at him.

For the first time since Magi entered the room he took his eyes off both Kari and Veronica and stared into the distance. He was picturing Kyle in his early 30s, like he was with Dymetra. Nobody could ever tell what a True Mage was *really* staring at, but still...

Magi addressed the entire room. "He was happy. Older, healthy, content. He would have come, but...Dymetra had a lesson for me to learn. I begged Her to send us both back. Kyle was happy in Her presence...but he would have come. I know it. For me, as my friend, he would have given his new life up to rejoin our fight here in Tenebrae. I know that this is hard for anyone of us to grasp, but Dymetra had a different lesson—especially for me. Sending Kyle back wouldn't absolve my guilt: only She could do that. How selfish would it have been for me to drag Kyle back from paradise, and for what? To fight the coming war? She has made it clear, at least to me, that having Kyle next to me is not what I needed most."

He looked into Kari's face again, hoping some of this would register. "He loves you, Kari. And he forgave me. He would have come back for love and friendship, but truly, he is to be envied now.

I'm no Cleric, but I have seen the one True God, and I can assure you that what She says, She does. I have been relieved of my guilt, and while I miss Kyle, and regret what I've done, I also understand that it was not really me who did it. My prayer is that, in time, you come to that understanding and can find a way to forgive me, too." Magi turned back around to look toward the Assassin.

At that moment, while the entire room was fixated on Magi and Kari, Veronica reached out cat-quick and grabbed Peter from behind, a hidden blade now painfully displayed against his throat. "If anyone moves to cast a spell, I will tear open your Admiral's throat. And ask your pet mage if I'm lying, Najalas. If my life is worth his, than by all means send in your knights and spell casters. Tell them to stand down if you value this man's life."

Magi held up a hand, palm outward, shouting to the room, yet staring at Veronica. "She is telling the truth, my Queen. Peter's life for hers. She has no great love for her own life, nor the life of others." He looked at Peter, who was shocked to find a knife digging into his throat so quickly. He thought of Peter's wife, Felicity, and of Brandon and Chelsea, who he had seen many times over the last few months while serving the Queen in Rookwood. He then looked around the room, then back at Queen Najalas.

"Sarah, or Veronica—put your knife away. No harm will come to you. This is madness. Let us continue our discussion." The Queen didn't smile, but tried to take a conciliatory tone. Peter tried to squirm out of Veronica's grip, but stopped as the blade bit into his neck, causing a red trickle to start sliding down his neck.

"Veronica!" The Queen yelled.

"Magi—you say your staff doesn't tolerate a lie. Than know this—if Peter moves another inch I will happily end this right now. I won't escape, but neither will he. Now tell *me* the truth: will Najalas harm me if I let him go? Will she let me go?" Veronica appeared to be digging a second blade into the man's back. Her back was to a wall; nobody could come up behind her. The mages in the room were at the ready. Swords were drawn from several knights and guards. Beads of sweat were perched on most people's brows in the room. Not Veronica's, however. Her skin was pale, smooth, and dry; her fingers were steady.

Magi turned and looked directly at the Queen, though he addressed Veronica. "Yes, Veronica. She is lying. You will be captured as soon as you release Peter." He sighed slightly. "I'm sorry, my Queen. The Staff has no guile. Veronica means to kill Peter, then herself, before you can extract any information."

Simon, who was near the back, shouted to Magi "You fool! Why say such things? Do you doubt the Queen's word? How dare you accuse the Queen of lying?!" Several groans and oaths were made, though Magi kept one eye on Veronica, one eye on the Queen. And if he had a third eye, he would have trained it on Kari, who suddenly seemed to be his third priority.

Herodius approached slowly, palms forward. "Let me exchange myself for this man. I have no family. Take me as your hostage. I will come willingly—Magi will attest to this."

Magi said nothing, he just slowly nodded, reading the situation.

"Why would I exchange a more valuable hostage for a less valuable one? I spent time in this court, though brief, and I know all about Peter's charming family. It would be a shame to have their father's death on your conscience, Najalas." Peter started to say something but winced, likely from the point in his back or the edge on his neck.

Veronica raised her voice to speak to the Queen. "Let me walk out of Rookwood with Peter as my hostage, and I will send him back unharmed when I am outside the city gates. Swear that you will not send anyone after me, and I will swear that he shall come back to you. Otherwise, we can spill blood here and now and be done with this—it's not like this would be the first time this room has tasted blood." She looked over at Kari, then over at Magi. "And you will verify the truth of this pact, or there will be blood here and now."

Magi turned to the Queen, and could see the wheels in her mind turning. All eyes were on her. "Very well. But you shall release Peter now. If I am to keep my word, than it does not matter whether you are outside the castle or not. I shall ensure that you leave the castle unharmed." Queen Najalas looked at Magi.

But Veronica shook her head. "You may intend for my safe passage, but your court may take matters into their own hands. No. Peter comes with me, and let his blood be on the hands of any who would break your order, and attack me until I am outside the city. If I break my oath, how long would it take for you to hunt me down with your cavalry and a division of Rangers at your disposal? No, Najalas. *My* word is not the least trustable one in this pact. I am an Assassin, and if you know anything about Assassins, you would know how highly we value our contracts."

Magi could see Simon bristle every time Veronica refused to acknowledge the Queen's title. Still, Magi turned to the Queen and said simply, "She is speaking the truth, your Majesty."

Queen Najalas sighed. "Very well. We have an understanding. You may leave the castle peaceably, and I order all to stand down and let this wretched Assassin pass our midst and trouble us no more. Send Peter back with nothing worse than a nick on his neck, or know that I will empty my castle hunting you down, and we will keep your bones alive to make you suffer all the greater if you go back on this pact."

She angrily turned to Magi. "I'm not lying this time, am I, mage?"

Magi's white eyes narrowed. "No. No you are not, my Queen."

~Xaro~

Rather than experiment in a dungeon or laboratory at Sands End, Xaro preferred an open-air setting. He stared at the young man who claimed to be the answer to his prayers for more gold: a true alchemist.

Standing atop the flat roof with a tower behind him, he then turned to look out across the desert. Everything was hazy from the waves of heat radiating from the sand surrounding them. Far off in the distance, he could make out the Endless Water of the West—his one port from which all his shipments came, and presumably where all his warships would launch. *Assuming we can finish building them.*

He and Krishnan were alone. He had dismissed everyone else, including Malenec. *Especially Malenec.* Whatever secrets were to be discovered would be learned before a limited audience. And if this would-be alchemist proved Xaro a fool for trying such a task as this, there would be a limited audience to his reaction as well.

He watched Krishnan work, asking questions, observing, memorizing everything he chanted as a small, black pot came to a slow boil. "It is time, Xaro. Now is when you must lend your prayers to the potion, if it is to work. I have researched and experimented more than seventy times to reach this point. It *must* take the faith of a True Cleric to transform the metal." He tried to sound determined, but Xaro could tell there was doubt in his voice. "Why else would I be directed here?" he said, seemingly to himself.

Why, indeed. He stared at Krishnan for a moment longer. A sheen of sweat covered every part of his exposed skin, making him looked as if he had been dipped into clear, shiny syrup. Xaro was convinced that he had been laboring—magically speaking—in preparing that potion. Beyond that, he wasn't quite sure what to make of the man yet.

Slowly approaching the small cauldron, suspended above a roaring blue fire, he looked in and saw a clear liquid boiling, giving off an intense smell of sulfur. He wrinkled his nose at the stench of rotten eggs. Krishnan pointed at the cauldron and nodded at Xaro in encouragement.

Very well. Xaro spread his arms wide and began praying loudly, never once closing his eyes. "Kuth-Cergor," he began. "You have guided my path to this point, through marshes and mountains, across the ocean and into the desert, and I ask you to guide it further still. I have prayed for gold, and you deliver me an alchemist, for which I offer my thanks. Now I beseech thee: your power is limitless. Your wealth is limitless. Your knowledge is limitless. Lend us this power, O Master, that we may use it to further your plans in this realm. I ask that you bless our efforts, specifically this kettle of potion, and turn it into the gold-transforming elixir of legend. With this gold, your servants will create an even mightier army, and more important, we shall finish building an armada worthy of your name, O God. Grant this power to us, and we will deliver you this realm, Kuth-Cergor. And the throne that we build for you will be made of the same pure gold that we ask you to show us now!" Xaro shouted at the end, his voice reaching a piercing crescendo.

And then there was silence. The echoes of his prayer had subsided, leaving Krishnan and Xaro alone atop the mountain. After an awkward minute, Krishnan sighed. "And now, we test it."

He took some of the iron bits scavenged from the fighting pits and slowly dropped them into the clear, foul-smelling liquid. It immediately began hissing, and smoke poured from the top and down the sides, obscuring everything.

"Is this what always happens?" Xaro asked, more loudly than needed over the hissing. "In all of your failed experiments, is this what happens?"

He stared at Krishnan, who was steadfastly sticking his face right into the stinking, smoking cauldron top, trying to see what was happening. "There is always smoke!" he shouted back. He looked up, smiling. "But not like this."

Xaro walked over, wrinkling his nose. Soon he, too, stared at the top of the black pot, suspended over a blue *Everflame*, waiting for the smoke to subside. Slowly, they began to make out an object at the bottom of the cauldron—and it wasn't iron fragments.

But it wasn't gold, either. It looked purplish. Krishnan narrowed his white eyes, frowning. Casting a levitation spell, he slowly raised the object from the bottom of the pot.

It looked like a purple jewel, shaped like a starburst. Xaro had seen it before and recognized it instantly. "That is the Purple Sun—the jewel of the Elfs." He looked at it as Krishnan rotated it magically. "My Thief possesses it, or once did, at least." Xaro was speaking his thoughts aloud, paying no attention to his companion.

"The answer to your prayer is this jewel. Add it to the potion, and your efforts will be successful. Do not delay. Our efforts are being countered as we speak. She has awoken, and Her Artifacts are being sought."

The booming voice came out of nowhere. Xaro knew it sounded like thunder to a non-Cleric, but to him it was as clear as if his Master was standing next to him. He spoke infrequently, but having studied and worshipped him for so long now, rarely was anything ambiguous to his messages.

He looked over at Krishnan, who had fallen to his knees, covering his ears when the thunderclap sounded. His levitation spell faltered, and the jewel fell to the ground. Xaro watched as the *Illusion* of the gemstone, perpetrated by his Master, faded, revealing nothing more than copper fragments on the stone roof of Sands End. Krishnan's eyes grew wide, and he screamed in frustration at the all-too-familiar remnants from his labors.

Xaro just smiled. He walked over to Krishnan, who was retreating backwards from his knees fearfully. "It's all right, Krishnan. I have no intention of handing you over to Malenec. Our God has spoken, and answered my prayer. In time, I will teach you to hear his voice as well."

He extended a hand to the terrified mage and helped him up. "Come. We have work to do. I believe I will include you in my next council meeting. It is time I get an update. From my Thief, in particular…"

~Strongiron~

The air felt like it was getting warmer. *Spring,* thought Strongiron.

The Warrior Cleric sat in one of his favorite spots outside the Tower of Dariez; a small clearing with marble benches placed in the lush grass, constantly watered from the silver mist that floated around the tower from the nearby waterfall. The clearing was surrounded by trees and was a favorite spot for prayer, meditation or exercise.

Or procrastination. Strongiron had gathered some things from the tower that he thought might come in handy—a few potions, some prayer scrolls. He found his new armor actually had places to hold such things. He packed up a chest with more extensive books and teachings.

After raising Faralon from the dead and saying his brief goodbyes, he couldn't find the elfs anywhere. All three of them had vanished, leaving Strongiron to his thoughts, alone in the Tower. He stared up at the waterfall—it literally looked as if Dymetra herself was pouring molten silver over the edge of the cliff. The delta that formed at the base of the waterfall and the opening of the massive lagoon was a pallet of lightening gray.

He found himself daydreaming, and his mind wandered back to the picture of a fiery, headstrong Illusionist with emerald eyes and rich, brown hair that felt like freshly spun silk. *Perhaps it is good that you left...it would be much harder to leave this place if the two of us were alone here.* He breathed in the mist that covered everything near the base of the waterfall and sighed.

Strongiron stood up and looked at the tower one last time. "Protect your Tower, Dymetra, from those who would seek to desecrate it, and reveal its location to those who truly seek You."

He took another deep breath, wondering what it would feel like to *Teleport* for the first time. "Return your Cleric to Rookwood, my God. Let me begin the task You have set before me there."

~Queen Najalas~

The last to arrive was Magi, who shut the door behind him. The Queen was seated on the Judgment Seat in the Great Hall. She towered over everyone else in the room, and that was by design for this discussion. She thought about limiting the meeting to her small council, but given what had just happened, she wanted all the witnesses she had selected, to at least provide different perspectives.

She looked over at Belara, who today had chosen a cherry-red dress that hugged her body like a second skin, right down to the hooded cowl framing her face. *Selfish ambition.* She looked at Herodius, his face hard and proud. *Vengeance.* She turned to Kari, who had literally walked off the ship with Niku moments ago to debrief everyone on their trip to Urthrax. *Conflicted.* She looked at Peter, who walked in right before Magi, holding a bandage to his neck. *Indignant.* Then Simon. *Outraged.* Niku. *Tired.* Jonathon. *Dutiful.* And so on, she took in each person, armed only with her wit, her two eyes, and whatever wisdom had been granted her. *I may not have a magical staff, but I seem to be able to rule quite capably without one.*

She finally looked at Magi, who walked over to take a seat directly in front of her. *Resolved. Magi has decided something.*

"So. I see we have our Admiral back. Good—" the Queen began.

"Your Majesty, please excuse my interruption, but surely we must send our best to recapture this killer!" Simon rose to his feet as he interrupted his Queen. "You cannot be held to your word on this. No oaths were made. Let—"

The Queen raised her hand. "Enough, Simon. Sit down."

He nodded and grudgingly sat back down.

The Queen addressed the room. "As I was saying. Peter—you are unharmed?"

"Yes, my Queen. A bit more than a shaving nick, but I've suffered far worse, your Majesty." Peter kept the cloth tightly pressed to his neck.

"Good. As I was saying, I won't order anyone to follow Miss…" she stopped, and looked at Magi. "Veronica. I have no intent on ordering her pursuit at this time. If, however, she turns up again, I would be *most* interested in continuing a discussion with her." She looked at Simon with a smile.

He smiled back. "I see, my Queen. Women travelling alone frequently need help from the crown."

Magi rolled his eyes, to no effect whatsoever. "My Queen, I don't care whether you officially order her tracked down or not. You are not accountable to me or my Staff. I have served you as an advisor, that is all."

The Queen looked at him. "You say 'served.' Am I to take it that you feel your debt to me has been repaid already?"

Magi shook his head. "No—my debts will be long in repayment. But the manner in which I serve may change. Send knights after her if you wish to break your word, but know that it is my intent to follow her myself. And I gave no assurances to her that I wouldn't."

Peter sucked in his breath a bit. "Why would you leave, Magi? Your Queen needs you."

Najalas looked down at Magi from her perch on the Judgment Throne, her eyes narrowing. "Why indeed."

"Is it not obvious? My ring. I will follow her back to Xaro, and do everything I can possibly do to keep him from obtaining my ring."

The Queen was unconvinced. "To keep him from obtaining it, or to re-obtain it yourself?"

"Well," Magi said, looking at the Staff he was holding and smiled. "To re-obtain it myself accomplishes both goals, does it not?" He looked up at the Queen. "Xaro commanding an army protected from magic with the ring's power—it would be almost too frightful to contemplate."

"And how will you track her, Mage?" Simon asked.

"I have some tracking skills, Simon. I spent a fair amount of time learning from one of the best." He looked over at Rebecca, who was standing next to Kari. "Do you remember Lionel? He taught me quite a few things, before he was…" Magi stopped, his white eyes widening as if he had just realized something.

The Queen was listening closely. "Before what, Magi?"

He turned and looked up at her. "Before he was killed, your Majesty. His throat was slit open as surely as my own." He sighed and shook his head, self-consciously rubbing the scar along his neck. "It would appear that my path and Veronica's have crossed well before this."

"And what will you do if you catch up to her? What is your plan?" asked the Queen.

Magi opened his arms a bit. "To be honest, I'm not quite sure, but following her shouldn't be too hard. I doubt one even needs to be a Ranger. It is a safe bet that she will head back to Xaro. She'll need to sail to do that, and it won't be from Rookwood. My guess is that she travels West; she came from that way. She'll know villages and the terrain. She may even know a way through the Crystal Mountains, or she'll head through the Elfsbane Pass."

He finally stood up. "It doesn't matter, Queen Najalas. Wherever she goes, I can follow her. She cannot *Teleport*. And when the time is right, I'll confront her. My hope is that she leads me to Xaro first. Whether she does so of her own volition, or does so unwittingly—I haven't planned that out yet. I just know we cannot let Xaro come to our shores with that ring on his hand." He clenched his fist, and then sighed. "The fact is, I'm of no use to you, my Queen, if he is wearing that ring. Neither is Belara, Niku, any of your Mage Guards. None of us! I just don't know who will face him if he is bearing my old ring."

"Oh, I don't know. Only caught the tail end of all this, but I think I'd give it a go. Sorry I'm late, your Majesty," said Strongiron, standing in the back, unannounced, gleaming in the most spectacular white armor the Queen had ever seen.

CHAPTER FOUR: OF PLANS AND SCHEMES

~Xaro~

Xaro was in such a fine mood, he decided to treat himself to some sweetwater, which he flavored with expensive lemons imported from Adimand. He was seated in a comfortable, airy room at Sands End that opened to the hot air outside. While spring may have been slowly spreading across most of the realm, it was always hot at Sands End—forever summer in the desert. But today there was a mild zephyr that stirred through the meeting room, high up in one of the turrets. The room had a door that led to a circular balcony, which Xaro decided to throw open today, given the breeze. The airflow merely added to his good humor.

Kuth-Cergor has spoken, shaping events, bending them to his will even as we speak. It was a comforting thought, knowing he could call upon such power, and that He would answer. *That* was why Xaro was in such a good mood. Only Malenec could truly relate, but he also despised how close the other man was to his God as well.

He looked over at his enormous General, the half-ogre Tar-Tan, his Dark Cleric, Malenec, along with the shadowy images of Veronica and Trevor, both of whom were attending his update meeting from afar. All of them were looking at the newest invitee, Krishnan, with his dark skin, white eyes, and a pointy chin covered in a meticulously-trimmed, well-oiled, black goatee. Krishnan just smiled, somewhat nervously, as he looked around from his seat next to Xaro.

"Ah, good. All assembled. It has been some time since our last update, and I am eager to know how your tasks have progressed." Xaro began with a smile as he sipped his lemon sweetwater. "Ah, excellent in this heat."

He turned to face the shimmering image of Trevor first. "Let us start with you, my Master Thief. Tell me, where are you in your journey back to Sands End?"

The shade of Trevor smiled. "All is well, Master. We sail aboard a vessel called *Sheila's Bane* northwest of the Whirlpool and will cross the Forgotten Land Bridge at high-tide within a fortnight, or so I'm told. Another fortnight and we should be anchored in Sands End."

A month. "Very well, and do you have the ring?"

"I do." Trevor did not take it out to show anyone.

"And that gemstone—the Purple Sun of the Elfs—the one you had to steal as part of your Final Test…you showed that to me long ago. Do you still have that with you as well?" Xaro asked.

Trevor hesitated, narrowing his eyes. He did not answer immediately. "You have never expressed any interest in that, Master. Why now?"

"Just tell me whether you still have it, Thief." Xaro was still smiling when he said this, but there was a keen edge in his voice.

"I suppose I do," Trevor replied, choosing his words carefully. "It is a gem of great worth and value to me."

Xaro never hesitated. "It is a gem of great worth and value, for sure. And you shall receive much gold in exchange for it."

Trevor's shade seemed to shift, whether in discomfort or from the rocking ship was hard to know. He finally said, "I would prefer to keep it, Master."

Xaro narrowed his eyes. *How much do I share with this group?* He then softened his face and smiled. *Kuth-Cergor has ordained this, what have I to fear from my own council?* "Trevor," he began. "I would like to introduce you and the rest of my council to our newest member. His name is Krishnan." Xaro smiled warmly and pointed to the Mage, who slowly nodded. "Krishnan is an alchemist. That pendant, whether you know it or not, can turn base metal into gold. Did you know this, Trevor?"

"I did not, Master." Trevor's image appeared to lean forward.

"I suspected as much. Neither did I. Even our alchemist didn't know. That is why alchemy is a failed discipline within our Art: without the Purple Sun, it does not work. Krishnan was led here by Kuth-Cergor, just as you are being led here. All these events are moving forward by the grace of his unseen hand." Xaro said with a flourish of his own hands. Malenec nodded while everyone else looked on eagerly. "His appearance is not by coincidence."

Xaro continued. "Soon we shall have our unlimited supply of gold, and I can assure you, my little Thief, that what you will be paid for that jewel will far exceed whatever you hoped to earn on the black market. Besides—it is a well-known artifact. Why would you risk trading it for gold anywhere else, knowing that the sale could trace the thievery back to your hand? Think before you do anything rash, Trevor. You do not want the Elfs hunting you on one side, and me on the other, do you?" He was smiling at Trevor, but the threat was plain.

Trevor just shook his head. "Of course not, Master. I am also eager to see how this might work."

"Good. Very wise decision. Now, any further updates?" Xaro asked.

"Only that I brought Tarsh, the Mage Marik was going to introduce you to. I did not invite him to our private meeting, but I can attest that his power is strong. He pulled our entire ship from the grip of the Maelstrom, Master. Your ring and this jewel would be at the bottom of the sea if he hadn't been aboard. We're all lucky."

"I can assure you that luck has nothing to do with it. As I just said, Kuth-Cergor moves events to pursue his will. I look forward to meeting this Tarsh. Magi would have been on that boat helping our cause, had events not led to his untimely death." Xaro looked at his assassin Veronica, who started to speak, but Xaro talked over her to address the rest of the group. "Yet Kuth-Cergor equips your boat with yet another Mage to help you deliver that ring and jewel to my hand. Never doubt that you are all caught up in larger events, supported by a *real* God of unlimited power and resolve."

"Yes, of course, Master. We are fortunate to have such a God on our side," Trevor said, somewhat woodenly.

I will deal with your patronizing tone later. He turned to Veronica. "And you, my dear? I think you wished to speak next, yes?" He took another sip of lemon sweetwater, rolling the cool liquid around his tongue to savor the taste.

"Magi is not dead," she said.

Xaro started coughing as his drink slid down the wrong pipe. After hacking a minute, he composed himself. "*What* did you just say?"

"Magi is not dead, Master. He lives. I saw him with my own eyes. And he carries an odd staff. He calls it the Staff of Wisdom— says it belonged to an ancient mage. Quix-something-or-other. I can't recall the exact name, as I had to focus on some other things at the time. But I can verify that it gives him some form of ability to see the truth in a person's words. It nearly got me killed."

"But—how? *How did he get it?!*" Xaro shouted, louder than he'd intended. "Veronica, tell me everything, right now."

She recounted the scene of her escape. "He claims to have died, and have been sent back to Tenebrae with this relic. I can only tell you what I saw and heard and did. I *know* he was dead when I slit his throat. I picked up his limp hand and removed the ring from his lifeless fingers, standing in a pool of his blood. Just yesterday in Rookwood, I saw the scar I gave him across his neck, as plain as lightning in the night sky. He died, and he now lives, and he carries an ancient staff." She paused. "And I would bet that he is following me even as we speak now."

"Of course he is. That's what I would do. He seeks revenge." Tar-Tan spoke up for the first time at the meeting. "The Mage wants to take your life." His little, yellow eyes were staring at the Master Assassin, his arms crossed, a hint of a smile on his lips.

"Perhaps," said Veronica. There was no smile on her lips. "I expect him to follow me because he wants his ring back. When I released my hostage, Magi asked me if I still had it. I told him I did."

"And?" asked Xaro.

"He knew I didn't. He gave me this message: 'Tell your Master that he cannot win. Tell him that faith in Dymetra has stirred, and that She hears. And tell your Master that I will have my ring.'" She shrugged. "He then watched me turn and head into the city. Looking back, I saw him lingering a minute or two after I had disappeared into a crowd. He will come, Xaro. I am sure that is his intent."

After a brief period of silence, Malenec started to laugh. A cold, mirthless laugh. "Let him come. Let *Her* come, for that matter. If She wishes to fight for this realm, so be it. None can stand the power and fury of Kuth-Cergor, neither man nor spirit."

Xaro kept his face expressionless. *This changes things.* He did not fear an attack on Sands End from a single Mage, but hadn't developed much of a defense plan, either. "Does he know where the ring is?"

"Only that I do not have it...but he knows I'm going to meet someone who does or will. He knows I'm headed to Sands End. There is simply no lying to him while he carries that staff."

An idea began forming in Xaro's head, but he wanted all the reports before he issued his orders. *More time to think.*

~Queen Najalas~

Peter, Jonathon, Niku, and Simon all came up to Strongiron, clapping him on the back, poking fun at his new armor (Simon thought it might save his life in a blizzard, but get him killed otherwise), and welcoming him back in general.

The Queen observed this for several minutes, in part because she wanted to see how he'd changed. To her eye, except for the white armor, he hadn't changed much at all. He always was holding court; he held court now. *The man just leads.*

As Strongiron recounted his time at the Tower of Dariez, she noticed other things. Magi seemed a bit impatient, though he let the old friends catch up without interrupting. Belara was staring at Strongiron, listening attentively. Kari, it seemed to the Queen, was trying hard *not* to stare. Strongiron caught her eye at one point, and Kari looked away quickly, almost as if she was embarrassed. The Queen sighed; *she's hardly the first maiden smitten with my General.*

It was the islander, however, that surprised her. At one point in his story, as Strongiron was relating how he had seen Dymetra, Herodius stepped forward and introduced himself with an unusual question:

"How do you know you were speaking to a God, and not some *Illusion*? Your sorceress could convince me that the dead lived if she set her mind to it. How can you be so certain, Strongiron?"

The conversation stopped. Everyone glanced toward Belara, who simply returned their gazes with a half smile and single raised eyebrow. Strongiron walked over to Herodius with a kind face and a gentle smile, extending his hand.

"I don't believe we have met. My name is Strongiron. You are?"

The islander clasped hands briefly, clearly out of politeness. "Herodius Cromwell. I come from the Uncharted Isles. Your Queen has shown us great kindness. Xaro and his army destroyed our homes, slaughtered our families, and enslaved our men. I will not sour your homecoming with the details, but I have pledged whatever strength I have to our common cause, and the men that escaped their fate serve in whatever manner they are able. Some farming, most fighting.

"This is now the second time I have heard a member of our Queen's court speak of a firsthand encounter with this ancient God." He nodded at Magi. "And I am certainly not unfamiliar with miracles—the fact that we are even here is one of the greatest miracles I've ever seen.

"But I find it hard to understand a God who sends this one back to the living—" he again gestured toward Magi, "—with an ancient staff, and then shows Herself to you to raise an ancient elf back to health *only* to allow the elf to die hours later, to hear your tale." Herodius looked into Strongiron's crystal-blue eyes and finished his thought. "Tell me, Cleric—where was Dymetra when my Maria's life needed to be returned to me?"

The Queen sucked in her breath a little. It was the first time she had heard Herodius mention his wife's name.

The warm smile on Strongiron's face quickly gave way to creases of concern as the awkward moment lingered. He finally said, "I can see that you have suffered greatly in this Dark World, Herodius. I am sorry for your loss. Dymetra gives us no assurances of an easy life. If Faith guaranteed safety, food, warmth, and long life—there would be none who did not follow Her."

He slowly approached the tall, dark islander, and put a hand on his shoulder. Herodius was one of the few men there as tall as Strongiron, and they were looking at eye-level with one another. Strongiron continued. "I would like to speak to you more about Dymetra, Herodius. I have learned much that I can share. But you had a specific question. You asked where She was. I can tell you that She is where She always is—" He gestured around the room with his other hand. "—all around us. She never left, Herodius. We left Her—"

Herodius stepped back from Strongiron, letting the Warrior-Cleric's arm fall as he interrupted. "*I* never left. My wife never left. My family never left. My village never left." His eyes smoldered with anger, but he composed himself. "I understand that my Queen has put her hope in this ancient God. And this Mage claims to have seen this same God, as do you. I mean no disrespect, but the war that is coming to Rookwood has already come to my home, my life. If this God aims to help us, then help us! If She aims to soothe us, then soothe us! I have seen neither, and I do not plan on dropping to my knees when the first sword is drawn. Our enemy surely plans for our death, while you stand here speaking of a silver waterfall and peaceful elfen clerics."

He turned to Queen Najalas. "My Queen, we are not yet prepared. Not nearly enough for the onslaught that is coming."

"Know your place, Herodius," said Simon. The Captain of the Queen's Guard apparently did not appreciate the islander's tone.

Before the Queen or Herodius could say a word to Simon, Strongiron spoke up. "Be at ease, Simon. Our friend has suffered greatly." He looked at Herodius. "No offense taken, Herodius. I understand you have questions. I don't pretend to have all the answers, but I do know this—good can still come from all this. It may not be clear, easy, or quick…but good can yet be made of your tragedy. We may not deserve to have our Dark World brightened, but She can shine brightly still within it. Do not lose hope."

"Hope." Herodius chuckled cynically. "You and the Mage both lecture about hope. Well, I have hope. You don't have to worry about that. I have the same hope that every clear-thinking man, woman, and child in Rookwood ought to have. I hope to find Xaro and his men, and kill them. Especially his ogre. That is hope enough to sustain me."

~*Xaro*~

Xaro turned his attention to his fellow Cleric. *Hopefully, we are perfecting how to orchestrate a battle with the dead and living fighting alongside one another.* "Malenec, your update?"

"The undead have gathered, and as you know, we have tried to simulate some battle scenarios that blend my army with yours. They—"

"All are *my* army, brother." Xaro interrupted, staring his Dark Cleric down.

"Hmmm. As you say. If we are going to be exact in our choice of words, let me rephrase. The undead and live fighters have fought together somewhat. My will keeps them from attacking 'friendly' troops, if you will, but as I have shared with Tar-Tan, they are meant to be a separate fighting force. The coordination of the mindless is, frankly, exhausting, and it is difficult to relay troop movements from your field general to me to them. I am, however, experimenting. With a different prayer, I am hoping to create a small subset of wights to complement our zombie horde. The wights kill by inflicting unbearable pain—they torture you to death, basically. But raising a wight from a corpse is far more complex, and requires far more energy for me to control, as they have a will of their own that I must constantly subvert. But they also can follow orders and react intelligently to changing battle scenarios, which makes them superior for grouping with our human troops. Of course, if you would just listen to reason and allow me to turn our entire army into undead warriors—"

"You will not lay a finger upon my men, Cleric," said Tar-Tan. "I allow the co-training, but only because Xaro requests it."

"These wights," Xaro began, ignoring his Cleric's request and his General's retort. "Who are you experimenting on, Malenec?"

Malenec's eyes glinted dangerously. "If you must know, there have been a few children in Misk that have gone missing recently. I started my experiments with children, as they are much easier to control in general. I wish to see how many I can control as wights before they begin to exert themselves as independent creatures. Six children seem to be doable when I am spending my resources on the thousands of zombies as well. Would you like to meet them?"

Malenec smiled fiendishly, standing up and gesturing to a side door leading off the upper room.

"I did not approve of this, Malenec!" Xaro screamed at his Dark Cleric. "We are to protect Misk, not abduct their children in the night and turn them into undead wights!"

"You are not the only one who speaks directly to our Lord and Master, Xaro. He answers my prayers, too. Perhaps I just pray for bigger things." The side door blew open, and six grotesque bodies walked out. Three boys, three girls, none of them could have been older than eight or nine, though their ages were impossible to discern because their little bodies were distorted: long necks and arms, thin, pale with crooked fingers that looked more like meat hooks.

The tallest one sneered, stepped forward and approached Krishnan, whose white eyes looked nearly circular. "I am Justin. I want to touch you…" Before the Mage could recoil, the boy snaked out his arm and gripped Krishnan's wrist like an iron shackle.

The True Mage let out a bloodcurdling scream, falling to his knees.

"Enough!" Xaro shouted. He instinctively cast a force spell and flung the wight away from his alchemist, thumping it against the far wall. Undeterred, the wight sprung back to its feet, gazing hungrily at Xaro.

"That was fun. You prefer me to touch you? I come to you now." Justin took three or four long, quick strides across the room, coming within arm's reach of Xaro before hissing and stopping as if he had run into an invisible barrier. He spun his head around to face Malenec. "I wish to touch this one. I wish to touch him *now*! I want to grab him—let me grab him!"

Malenec smiled despite Xaro's fury. "I do apologize, Xaro. Figuring some things out still, obviously. But the possibilities! Surely you can appreciate that. *Master*," he added with a grin.

I will need to deal with Malenec. And soon. He is too bold by far. Xaro looked at Krishnan, who was only now back on his knees, crawling into his chair, trying to breathe. "Here." He handed his alchemist the rest of his lemon sweetwater. The mage held the glass in a trembling hand as he gulped the drink down.

Xaro turned to Malenec. "You are not to create another wight, and you are to keep those monsters away from our men, our camps, and our fortress. Send them to the desert until I figure out how to use them, if at all. Do I make myself clear?"

"Xaro, I didn't imagine you to be squeamish. Just think for a min—"

Xaro hurled a jet of flame at Justin so hot that the shades of Trevor and Veronica shimmered in the heat, and even Malenec recoiled. The wight screamed before its body was consumed by fire, leaving angry, black burn marks on the stone wall behind it where the rock was scorched.

Malenec started to yell something when Xaro shouted over him, his voice amplified: *"Am I clear, Malenec?!"*

The silence after the roaring of Xaro's fire spell and his booming voice was unsettling to all, especially the wights. "We understand one another, Xaro. Yes." He nodded at the five remaining wights, and the two former boys and three former girls begrudgingly walked back out of the room, through the side door. They were whispering to one another in hushed, whiny tones. The only word Xaro could make out was "touch."

Xaro let the silence hang in the air a little longer, glaring at his Dark Cleric before finally exhaling. He turned to his half-ogre General. "Your update, Tar-Tan."

The half-ogre stood, his beady, yellow eyes shifting uncomfortably between Xaro and Malenec. He cleared his throat and slowly walked over to a small table, where he opened a large scroll case and unrolled a detailed map of Tenebrae, which he spread out. He motioned for the others to come closer. Soon even the shadowy images of Trevor and Veronica stood behind Tar-Tan, peering at the map. The half-ogre kept looking over his shoulders uncomfortably at their shades. *Can't say I blame him after that.*

"As you requested, Master, I have formulated a battle plan. Rookwood is mountain stronghold that is well defended. It will not be easy to defeat, but it is possible."

Xaro looked at his giant general. *Now we shall see how well you plan.* He waved, encouraging Tar-Tan to proceed.

"The key to victory is in siege. Who knows what escape routes they may have built within the mountains—we cannot let the Queen escape. She must fall if the east of Elvidor is to fall. The west...I'm not too worried west of the Crystal Mountains. They cannot provide swords or comfort to the Queen any easier than she can exert much in the way of law there. We will rule those villages through fear and occupation, but the Queen must fall, and for that to happen, we must cut off every avenue of escape.

"Therefore, here is what I propose: The Elfs must be taken down, as they protect her Southern border. They man the cliffs overlooking the Strait of Holstine. I would land two of our four divisions in Shith. One of our divisions will be led by me, and will travel north across Lake Calm and cut off the retreat for the Elfs. I would have—" He nodded at Malenec "—*him* lead his undead troops in the other division to head straight for Thalanthalas. It is unlikely that the Elfs would burn down their precious woods to fight off those things of yours."

"Doubtful they would," Malenec agreed.

"That will force all the Elfs back to Thalanthalas to defend their capital. Trevor can go with you—you've been there before, correct?"

"Yes, but—" Trevor began.

Tar-Tan kept talking. "It will be impossible to keep a pending assault on Rookwood secret once the Elfs are directly attacked. We must be swift. Our third division will be making its way down the lightning road to choke off any escape to the North. Xaro, I believe you are the best equipped to lead this group on land."

Xaro did not immediately say anything. Tar-Tan continued.

"Finally, that leaves the Sea of Joy to the East. Once the Elfs are pre-occupied, someone must take our fourth division and sail through the Strait of Holstine to bottle up their port. I would prefer a Mage to lead this. Marik would have been my first choice. Perhaps you?" He looked at Krishnan.

"I am a metal changer, not a warrior. My role is to finance this conquest." He looked at Xaro hopefully, still rubbing his pale wrist where the wight had grabbed him.

Xaro pursed his lips, and looked at Krishnan a bit disdainfully. "No, I don't think that is to be your role." He turned to Tar-Tan. "We don't need to name the leader yet. Perhaps this Tarsh might have the right mentality. You say he has served you well already on the seas?" He looked at Trevor.

Trevor shrugged. "He has, Master. He seems powerful enough to me."

The General narrowed his eyes. "That is the plan. Once we converge on Rookwood, we will have time to probe its defenses without worrying about their escape. We can lay siege, or we can attack. We have options, dominant land positions, resources, and time on our side."

Xaro looked at Tar-Tan. *A prudent, well thought out strategy. Not bad for a half-ogre. Not bad at all.* "I agree. When we have the gold, we'll start the building process for the ships we'll need. This is a good plan, Tar-Tan."

Veronica, who had been quietly listening, finally spoke up. "And where do I fit in, Master?"

Everyone turned to look at her shimmering shade. Xaro flashed an exultant smile. "You may be the key to the whole thing, Veronica. When you return to Sands End, I shall explain."

~Queen Najalas~

The Queen studied the two men standing in front of her. She would never doubt Herodius's passion. Ever. He stood facing Strongiron with an unwavering gaze. *Not trying to be his friend, not fawning over him, not hoping he's going to save the day. The man wants to act!*

"Herodius," she began. "Your point is well made. I sent Strongiron on an expedition to help Kari find God. Apparently God found him, so to speak, and hopefully we shall all be blessed for it." She held up her hand before Strongiron could interject. "Yes, yes, She never left, She doesn't need to be found—you know what I meant." The Queen smiled. "Good to have you back, my friend."

She stepped down from the raised dais she had been sitting on and hugged her General. "So. You are a True Cleric now. I look forward to hearing more of your time there, but Herodius is right—we must turn our attention to our defenses. You have reappeared at a moment where our focus is turned to planning. My initial thought is that our Northern boundary—"

"My Queen" Strongiron interrupted. "Najalas."

Everyone stopped to look at the General. The Queen cocked her head at the interruption.

"Queen Najalas," Strongiron started again. "I will gladly lend my thoughts to this planning, but you need to know that I have another mission to fulfill—one that I fear will take me away from Rookwood for some time. Dymetra Herself has asked me to seek out the Shield of Life. It is a blessed artifact—one of the three Artifacts of the Ancients—this one belonging to the True Cleric Windomere."

Magi stood and approached Strongiron as soon as he mentioned the Shield. He had never been introduced to Strongiron, and didn't bother to introduce himself now. "Do you know what it does?" he blurted.

Strongiron turned to the True Mage. "I know that it protects the bearer from dark prayers. Like your Staff, it is blessed by the One True God who will protect the Shield-bearer from all forms of spiritual harm that Kuth-Cergor might attempt, including undead spirits, as long as the Shield-bearer has faith." He winked at Magi. "I don't think even that ring you were talking about earlier can do that."

"Where is this shield, Strongiron?" asked the Queen.

He sighed. "I don't know, my Queen. But I know that my search begins in Adimand. Windomere is buried somewhere there. I will go and visit his grave for starters."

"Adimand?" said Peter. "That is on the other side of the world! We are preparing for war here, General!"

"This is absurd, Strongiron," weighed in Simon.

"The defense of this stronghold must be your priority, my Queen!" said Herodius.

Jonathon said nothing, but shook his head.

Kari, however, simply stared at the True Warrior in white.

Belara waved her hand, and a large map of Tenebrae appeared upon the very floor they stood on. "Even though you *Teleport* now, and apparently across water, look at the size of Adimand. You are looking for an object likely no bigger than this table over an entire continent. No one has found this shield in centuries. Have you considered this is a distraction from our enemy to pull you away from Rookwood when your Queen needs you here? We know they have tried to kill you already and failed…perhaps if they cannot kill you, they will simply make you disappear on a hopeless chase under the illusion of your God's will." She subtly moved her hands and the map image on the floor began to coalesce into the shape of a woman. The form of Dymetra. "As Herodius has rightly said—illusion can cause strange decisions." The Queen noticed that while she mentioned Herodius and was facing Strongiron, her head was turned toward Kari.

More shouts ensued, while Strongiron sighed. He finally held up his hands. "Friends, friends—I hear your concerns. I do. I would like nothing more to stay and fortify our defenses and prepare for battle. But I have been given this mission by our God—not some conjurer's fantasy." He waved his hand, and Belara's *Illusion* dissipated into smoke, to the amazed looks of everyone.

He has *changed,* thought the Queen.

"I will give you my thoughts, but Rookwood needs a General that will be here. It is for this reason that I will travel North to recall my Lieutenant General, Sir Victor, Knight of Thunder, to assume overall leadership of the forces here. Upon my return, I will provide any final input into the planning process that I can, and relinquish my command, by your grace, to search for Windomere's shield, and to bring it back for our protection against whatever terrors Xaro and his Dark Cleric may formulate. My Queen…it is not that I leave on the whims of a God. It is also the most prudent use of my skills. You are thinking and preparing for a physical battle. That is good, for there will be one, and we must be physically prepared. But what good are traps, walls, swords, spears, and provisions against undead spirits that walk through walls? Against curses that confound even our best Mage-guards?

"This war—I am trying to tell you—is to be won or lost by faith. If we trust only in wood and metal, bone and sweat, we will surely be abandoned to these devices. Our hope rests in Dymetra, or no one," he finished.

Herodius stepped toward him. "Very well, then by your logic we should just sit and wait here for you to bring us a shield—one that has been lost for a thousand years. Is this your council?"

Strongiron shook his head. "Herodius. You take everything past its point. The Queen needs you to help her prepare. Sir Victor needs men like you. The realm needs men like you. Dymetra needs men like you, too." He smiled at the hard-looking islander. "We will devise some defensive plans that give us options, rest assured. Dymetra calls us to have faith in Her. That does not mean we sit around and do nothing, my friend."

The Queen turned to Magi and Strongiron. "Then it would appear the two men who have been closest to our God have chosen to leave Rookwood when it would seem their presence is most needed here." She held up her hands, palms outward, immediately trying to pull her words back in. "That came out wrong—I am…frustrated. But I understand why each of you are doing this, and I won't order you to stay." *Could I? Would they listen? Am I the highest authority in their lives?*

She continued. "What is most pressing now is to understand when you are leaving." She turned to Magi. "You still intend to track down the Assassin to find your ring. When do you plan to depart?"

"As soon as this meeting adjourns. I have what I need." He tapped his staff on the ground. "I may visit the storeroom first, by your leave."

The Queen nodded and turned to Strongiron. "And you, my friend?"

"Soon. Within a week or two, I would hope, my Queen. Time is of the essence—I am anxious to get to Adimand, but Victor may respond better to this order in person. Besides, it would be good to see our Northern troops after this last winter."

"Very well, then. Let us meet again soon, before you depart, Strongiron." She turned to Magi. "Good luck, Magi Blacksmooth. Come back to us with that ring. And the head of that Assassin, too."

Everyone mumbled or chuckled darkly as they began filing out of the room, until only the women were left: Queen Najalas, Kari, and Belara. The Queen looked at the young Mage. "Yes, Kari? Is there something further you need?"

She turned to Belara. "I need her to show me how to climb the Staircase. I'm going to travel with Strongiron, and I'll need to be able to *Teleport*."

~Veronica~

The small room at *The Last Call* was filthy. It smelled like sour ale had been used to stain the wood floors. The beetles didn't seem to mind too much, however, as they were quite comfortable crawling all over the room.

Veronica could care less. She'd seen worse, slept in worse, and lived in worse than a night in this cheap, dank tavern. She was grateful the meeting with Xaro had finally ended; it seemed that might go on forever. Discussing troop movements and battle strategy bored her to tears. *Just give me my next contract.*

Only an hour had passed since she felt the familiar, tingly sensation of being summoned to a meeting, though in truth it felt like four by the time Tar-Tan finished his update. The air was still cold outside, especially at night, though spring was approaching, and the ground was wet and soggy from melting snow. It was good to be inside tonight.

Veronica stared at herself in a cracked, greasy mirror. She did not have long—she trusted the Queen's promise about as much as she trusted a thief to return a coin pouch. Knights, guards—even other Assassins in the employ of the Crown—they would surely send someone after her. Sparing Peter was the only thing that had kept Magi from his personal revenge, however.

Magi. She had no doubt he would follow her. He all but said so. Before she released Peter outside the castle walls, he had asked her: "Where is my ring?" In light of the given situation, with one knife at Peter's throat and another one pressed against the small of his back, the question struck her as odd. *A bit out of place, but telling.* She had said she had it, at which he called her out as a liar. Then she said she didn't know, to which he simply smiled. "When will you trust that you cannot lie to me, Veronica? I can read the half-truths and hidden truth behind your words. You know who has the ring and where it is headed. Tell your Master that he cannot win. Tell him that faith in

Dymetra has stirred, and that She hears. And tell your Master that I will have my ring."

How does he see that? She shared that part of their conversation with the others. It was what he said last that caught her completely off guard, however, and that she had kept to herself. "If Kyle can forgive me, then I can forgive you, Veronica. But your killing must stop, Assassin." And that was it. He pulled his hood up over his long, reddish-brown hair, until only his white eyes were visible in the light of the gleaming white stone atop his staff. Magi then walked backward, never taking his eyes off her, up the long path through the outer wall leading up into the mountain stronghold. She caught herself staring at his white eyes growing smaller in the distance as he ascended toward the inner walls leading up to Rookwood Castle.

Forgive me? Veronica curled her lip reflexively, though nobody was around to see it. *There is nothing for you to forgive, Mage. I pursue my own ends, as we all do. It's a Dark World, and if someone wishes to trade gold for death, what wrong is there in accelerating someone's peaceful sleep a bit?* She scoffed at the entire concept. *The only forgiveness I truly need is Xaro's, for failing to execute a contract for the first time.*

Shaking her head, she pushed that final conversation out of her mind. She had to move quickly. The whole reason she'd bought a room so close to the castle was two-fold. First, she needed to update Xaro (who conveniently reached out to her himself), second, and more importantly, she needed to transform herself into Vernon. In this terrain and season it would be impossible for her not to leave easy tracks wherever she headed, and men would take matters into their own hands even if the Queen had given an order to let her be. Her face would be splattered across posters, and a single woman travelling alone would be a dead give-away. She needed a quiet place to apply her disguise; thus the room at the luxurious *Last Call*...luxurious, at least, compared to the surrounding woods.

It took a couple hours to get it just about right—reshaping the nose, the eyebrows, the hair. The gray stubble was the hardest to create authentically, but it also did more to make her look like a middle-aged wayfarer than any other aspect of her disguise. She also changed clothes to complete the look. Vernon looked like a hungry farmer, desperate for work after a lean winter. *No different than most,* she thought with satisfaction. Only this farmer was deadly.

She then felt the all-too-familiar tingle. Xaro wanted to speak again.

"Yes, Master?" she asked. This time, it was only Xaro and her in the meeting.

"Veronica? Your transformation is—exceptional." His shimmering image from Sands End now stood between the edge of her straw mat and the broken mirror along the far wall.

"Thank you, Master. This should be a workable disguise during my travels back to Sands End." She grinned. Even her teeth had been worked on to show a gap or two, with more yellowing.

"That is what I wanted to discuss with you, my dear Assassin. I don't want you coming back to Sands End."

Veronica nodded. It had seemed strange that she should spend a month or longer sailing all the way to Sands End if they were all planning on coming to Elvidor. But she didn't question Xaro—he probably wanted her off the continent after her near capture by the Queen. And with Magi's ability to glean information...she did need to get away.

"You want me to continue my efforts against Strongiron, Master?" It bothered her immensely that she had barely missed his neck with that dart.

"Yes and no. What I am going to tell you is to remain between us, Veronica. At least until I deem it worth sharing. Everyone thinks you are coming back to Sands End to avoid pursuit by that insufferable Queen. Even Magi would assume you're coming back. But I have a different plan for you.

"In my recent prayers, Kuth-Cergor revealed to me that his enemy has been awakened to this world. I can only assume that my brother, the golden child of my father's eye, was successful in finding the last three True Clerics at the Tower of Dariez. You said that he stayed behind—he wasn't there at Rookwood when you returned. He must have stayed to study. If he has become a True Cleric, it will be difficult for you to kill him now; you've seen what *She* can do. I do not doubt that Dymetra raised Magi from his death and sent him back with the Staff She blessed. Two other Artifacts of the Ancients exist: A Shield a Blade. It is the Shield that I am most interested in at the moment."

"Why the Shield, Master?" asked Veronica.

Xaro did not immediately answer, as if he was choosing his words carefully. He slowly answered her question. "The so-called Shield of Life is reputed to protect the Shield-bearer from prayers whose power is derived from Kuth-Cergor, Veronica. It would render Malenec's prayers and my own...ineffective."

Veronica cocked her head to the side. "So, why would you need such protection?"

"It is not my protection I'm interested in; I wish to deny my enemies this protection!" he snapped.

Veronica's disguised face displayed no emotion. *If I had Magi's Staff, I bet it would tell me that you're lying.* She just nodded respectfully and followed up. "Of course. But what does this have to do with Strongiron's contract?"

Xaro's face softened a bit. "Kuth-Cergor has told me that the Artifacts are being sought. The Staff has obviously already been found. I suspect Strongiron, if he is truly a True Cleric, will seek the Shield. They have seen what Malenec can do, how he single-handedly turned a city into an army of the walking dead. I do not doubt that they will pursue the Shield; it is what I would do."

"Why would the Queen send forth her General, Xaro?" Veronica asked, taking a seat on the edge of the straw bedding. She looked at a small colony of beetles huddled in a nearby corner, scrambling over one another for stale food and crumbs on the floor. "She just sent him away—she wouldn't send him again, would she?"

"Perhaps. That is why I say 'yes and no.' I don't really know. If he does pursue it, then perhaps you will have another chance. Although I warn you, killing a True Cleric is much different than killing a True Mage. If indeed Strongiron is a True Cleric, he will wield a formidable power. Do not take needless chances, my dear. You are too valuable to me."

Veronica beamed and even slightly blushed at the compliment, but the effect was lost given her male disguise. "Thank you, Master. I only wish I had not failed you in the first place."

"So do I, Veronica. So do I." He held a brief smile before his shimmering image stood up. "Now then. I do need you to leave the continent of Elvidor, though. Even with your disguise, it is not safe for you, especially with Magi wielding Quixatalor's old staff. Which brings me to the ancillary benefit of this plan: you may end up delaying Magi from reaching Sands End. If he breaks off his quest to regain his ring to instead follow you, it would give us more time to build up our armada. Perhaps even deploy if your quest lasts a year. While I don't fear a lone True Mage…he could cause us an inconvenience if he showed up."

"But wasn't your plan for him to join you in Sands End at one point?" Veronica asked, somewhat confused.

"At one point, yes—he would have made a tremendous ally. Now I fear that ship has sailed, if you'll pardon my pun." Xaro said, somewhat wistfully. "No matter. If he comes, he shall be killed, and for good this time, as I will make sure Malenec puts his soul in limbo, forever out of *Her* reach. But if you can find and recover the Shield that once belonged to Windomere—the greatest True Cleric of Quixatalor's generation—and in the process distract Magi and perhaps even Strongiron, if the Queen is stupid enough to send him…well that would more than make up for your failure with Strongiron's contract."

"It shall be done, Master. Do you know where the Shield lies?" Veronica asked.

"Not precisely. Legend has it that it was buried with him. And Windomere is buried somewhere in Adimand, where he was from. Sail there, hopefully drawing Magi at least to follow you. I would tell you to let him think that you have his precious ring, but we both know that won't work."

"Or you could put a contract on his head. I've killed him once before, Master, I can kill him again. There is no need for me to lead him astray. Killing is what I do, and apart from Strongiron, I'm fairly good at it, if you recall." Veronica hands on her hips, indignant, caught the look of Vernon staring back at her in the dirty mirror. Coming from 'him,' the pose looked almost comical.

Xaro was serious, however. "Kill him again? So he can be sent back to us again, probably even stronger?"

"I can burn his body, Xaro. Surely She can't raise him from ashes."

"She can. And likely will. Do not waste your time. Kill him if you need to—and are able to—but unless you can bind his soul, I do not trust that he will stay dead. There is no contract on him. However, your contract will be ten times the normal rate for bringing me the Shield of Life. Kill as you see fit in search of this Artifact. Tell no one—not even your colleagues on my small council. This is your assignment. Do you accept?"

Ten times! Fifty thousand gold pieces! "Adimand it is, Master. This Shield shall be yours." She then uttered another thought. "And what is the contract for *both* the Shield and the Staff, if indeed I *can* separate it from Magi?"

Xaro smiled. "I would caution you from being too greedy, Veronica. I would have you try your luck at grave robbing before you seek the life of a True Mage who you are unlikely to catch unaware again. That said…if gold is what you most desire, it is gold you shall have. Bring me the Shield. If you can get your hands on the

Staff as well—then if it is in my power to grant, I will." He smiled, nodded, and faded out.

Veronica took a deep breath and sat down on the sticky straw bed. The exorbitant contract was exhilarating; clearly Xaro was counting on this Purple Sun to deliver him his gold, but that wasn't the final thought on her mind as she settled down for some quick sleep.

This was the first time she had ever seen Xaro afraid…of anything. *Why would Xaro be afraid?*

The last thing on her mind was the words of Silver, the head of the Black Guild. *"An Assassin never asks why."*

~Strongiron~

It felt good to remove his armor. It wasn't heavy—certainly not as heavy as plate armor should have been—but it felt good to be free of it nonetheless. *Such a long day.* He retired to his usual quarters in Rookwood, where he relaxed with a cup of particularly strong tea the Elfen clerics had taught him to brew. The bracing taste of spearmint always took his breath away at first sip.

"General Strongiron," hailed a guard from outside his private room. "You have a visitor."

Another one? He sighed. *Surely a moment of peace is not too much to ask?* "Thank you, Sir Henry. Perhaps we can schedule an audience tom—"

"It is Miss Quinlan, General," interrupted the guard.

Strongiron sat up. "I see. Send her in." He involuntarily tightened the cinch around his clerical robes.

Kari entered, and she had also changed clothes from their reunion with the Queen earlier. She walked in wearing an emerald green mage robe held tight around her slim waist with a simple brown cord—it had the effect of making her green eyes sparkle. The cowl was down, and her dark hair fell past her shoulders.

"I meant to tell you earlier—your hair has grown since you left the Tower." Strongiron stood as she entered. "May I fix you something to drink?"

Kari smiled. "My hair can be any length I wish, Strongiron." She inclined her head slightly. "But it is good of you to notice. Anything cool would be lovely, thank you."

Strongiron poured her a glass of lemon sweetwater and handed it to her before he sat back down, gesturing for her to do the same. "To what do I owe this visit, Kari?"

She took a drink, wrinkled her nose, but smiled. "A bit tart to be called 'sweet-water', don't you think?"

Strongiron shrugged. "Every palate is different, I suppose." He leaned forward. "What is on your mind, Kari?"

She put her drink down and stood. "I…I want to go with you."

"Where? To Adimand?" Strongiron stood as well. "Kari—"

She walked up to him and kissed him lightly, catching Strongiron off guard. He did not, however, pull away. "Kari—" he began again.

"Before you give me all the reasons why I shouldn't, let me give you the one that matters. I felt something for you when we travelled to Dariez together. Tell me that you felt nothing when we first boarded the Queen's ship to Urthrax—or all those weeks in the Tower—and I will leave you to your evening. I may have left to pursue my own destiny, but that doesn't mean it needs to be separate. Why can't I see the wide world of Adimand and give—whatever 'this' is—a chance to blossom?"

A dozen reasonable objections rose to his lips, but he voiced the over-arching one. "I must *Teleport*, Kari. How will you accompany me?"

"I'm working on that." She flashed him a smile. Strongiron let his hands slide from behind her neck to grip both shoulders. *By Dymetra, she is stunning when she smiles.*

Strongiron slowly shook his head. "Kari," he began. "I do not deny that you stir my emotions. But you must understand…this is not a camping trip. This is a mission given to me *directly from Dymetra*. The risk…"

"No greater a risk than when *Dymetra* sent me to learn about Her. Did I not prove my worth to you in Shu-Tybor?"

"But She gave *me* this task. You *left* Her. Why did you leave the Tower, Kari?"

Kari pulled away and began to walk around the room, turning her back to him. "Perhaps that was a mistake. Perhaps not. I felt like I was stagnating there, Strongiron! Scroll after scroll after scroll…I want to see the world—I want to see Tenebrae." She turned back to look at him. "I would like to see it with you, I think."

She folded her hands across her chest. "But I will see it regardless."

Strongiron approached her with his final objection. "We are on the precipice of war, Kari. Your skill could best be put to use in Rookwood, defending the crown." The irony of his argument was immediately apparent; he reflexively winced before Kari even opened her mouth.

"Now you make the same argument against me that was hurled at you this morning?! If you don't want my company, have the spine to tell me plainly. I just assume—"

Strongiron reached forward and pulled her close to him, kissing her passionately. "For good or ill, I don't know, but let me assure you of this: your company is desired, Kari Quinlan. God help me, but I do want you to join me. Learn how to *Teleport*—which I understand is no small thing for you mages—and we shall plan this journey together." He kissed her again, grabbing a fistful of her velvety green robe near the small of her back, just above the waist, pulling her close to him.

"And Kari," he whispered, more somber. "We don't have much time to delay."

CHAPTER FIVE: IN PURSUIT OF POWER

~Kari~

A tiny dribble of thick, dark cherry sauce clung to her fork as she sliced the succulent beef. A perfect medium, the meat was so tender she could cut through it with the side of her fork. But the taste—the sheer decadence of the perfectly seared steak with a warm glaze of deep red cherry sauce was exquisite. Kari closed her eyes to enjoy the rich meal. She couldn't believe the fare Belara had prepared for the two of them.

"Taste is one of the hardest illusions to create, my dear," said Belara. She smiled sweetly, and immediately the bite in Kari's mouth tasted like her morning oatmeal. The sudden change was so disconcerting that she started coughing.

Belara just laughed. "You would not be the first person to spew grain all over the place. But I would prefer that you avoid ruining my new yellow dress."

Kari smiled politely between her coughs. Belara's dress *was* yellow, and against her olive-skin, it looked quite bright, and frankly, garish. The dress culminated into a hood that fit snugly around her head, forming a point at the center of her forehead. The only give-away that she even had hair at all were the tufts of shoulder-length black poking out around her neck.

Kari stared down at her meal…a bowl of porridge. "That was an amazing *Illusion*, Belara. How did you do that?"

"It is hard to craft an *Illusion* that does not have some anchor of experience in your mind. If I had never tasted perfect steak, I will not likely create a good *Illusion* of what perfect steak tastes like. A True Illusionist must therefore have a rich catalogue of experiences from which to draw. If you have not seen a mountain, you cannot create a believable *Illusion* of one. If you've not heard a baby cry, you cannot create that sound. If you have not smelled death, you cannot create that smell.

"Personally, I have always enjoyed a thick, juicy steak, and this is one of my favorite sauces. I have created this *Illusion* so many times for myself as we ration our food during the hard winter months that it is second nature to me, right down to the level of saltiness you taste. Mastering the *Illusion* of taste is one of the last hurdles I want to see you perfect before you climb the Staircase, if that is still your goal."

Kari pushed the soupy gruel away from her and shrugged her shoulder. "I do. I want to *Teleport*. I *need* to *Teleport*. I just wish I could keep my eyes." Then it hit her. "Belara, why don't you create an *Illusion* to camouflage your eyes? Surely you don't like them being pure white, do you?"

She shook her head. "I have tried. I would imagine most True Mages have tried some type of spell. None work that I know of…the power it takes to counter the spell that transforms you…let me just say it would be exhausting. The last time I tried, it drained me for three days, and I didn't darken so much as a speck of my true eye color, which is now obviously white. Only a pact with one of the Gods—I'm sorry dear, with a True God—could yield such results. I forget that you are now a devotee of Dymetra."

Belara reached out and put a hand over Kari's. "But trust me—the power is worth it, Kari. And in time you may find you like the immediate respect your eyes garner for you in this Dark World. But you already know this…you would not have come back to finish your training had you not been convinced."

Kari nodded. "I am good at *Illusions*."

"You are. Now practice. Turn our winter grain into something edible for me, as I'm still hungry." Belara released Kari's hand with a wink and a smile, leaning back and crossing her arms.

Kari closed her eyes, and Belara immediately slapped the table. "Stop that. You do not need to telegraph your spell casting by closing your eyes. Concentrate without appearing to do so. Cast your spell while you finish your meal with me."

"Ok…" Kari pulled the bowl of gruel back toward her and reached her hand directly into the mush to pull out… a large, violet grape. "Here, Mistress. Try it."

Belara took the grape and bit into it, and juices started running down her fingers. She rubbed them together and said, "Not sticky enough." She then smiled at Kari and said, "You also forgot the seeds."

Kari tightened her lips. "Mistress, I suppose I can work on these details, but is it really necessary? How will mastering taste *Illusions* help me on the Staircase? Shouldn't I brush up on my *Magic Missiles* and other spells?"

Belara pressed both her hands onto the table and stood up, at which point the *Illusion* vanished, leaving wet oatmeal in the bowls. "Kari, you are an Illusionist; details are *all* that matter. Everyone's trip up the Staircase is tailored to their individual skills, their potential, their training. If you think you're just going to blast your way to the top, then you're more foolish than I thought. That isn't your gift, and certainly wouldn't be a measure of your talent. You must be convincing in *every* form of *Illusion* before I teach you how to open the doorway and climb." She sat back down and crossed her arms across her yellow chest once again, this time without the wink and smile. "Besides, I had not even commented on the taste of your grapes, which was too sour for my pallet. You messed up the *feel* of the juice running down my fingers and the *feel* of the seeds in my mouth—those you missed completely. We have a lot of work to do, Kari, and less than a week to do it if you truly hope to join Strongiron." She exhaled and leaned back. "But first, tell me one thing."

"Yes?"

"Why rush this? Why do you feel the need to join him on this ridiculous quest of his?"

"Ridiculous? He's doing this for *Dymetra!*" Kari crossed her arms.

"Dymetra can bring to light this ancient shield and plop it into his lap if it's so important to Her. I am sure Strongiron believes he is doing the right thing, but be practical, Kari. This makes no sense, and you know it…or you're not the intelligent young woman I thought you were. So let me ask you again—why are you so bound and determined to leave with him?"

Kari didn't answer immediately, and when she did, the words weren't crisp. "I—I want to—I just want to be close to him—to help him, I suppose, and —" Kari steeled herself and focused on the whites of Belara's eyes; the mark of a True Mage. "And I want the power, to be honest."

"Yes! I know you do, you should; you can do this, Kari. You *have* the gift. Just remember that Gods and Crowns come and go. You know what sustains them? Power. And you know what the source of True Power is? *Magic,* Kari. Magic.

"It is a Dark World, Kari, and it will be the True Mages that bring order and light to Tenebrae, regardless of the scrolls you read on Urthrax."

~Magi~

Magi groaned. Lady Velvet was one of the last people he wished to run into while tracking Veronica, but the trail unmistakably led to *The Last Call*. It took him less than four hours from leaving her outside the city to staring at the sign outside the run-down inn. The wooden sign hung lopsided from a single metal loop in one corner, and squeaked whenever the wind blew. The weathered carvings and faded paint were indistinguishable and too difficult to make out. Instead the words *Last Call* were garishly painted on both sides in blood red. *If it was just a little warmer outside…* Sighing, he tugged his heavy cloak around his shoulders and pushed open the door.

The common room inside was nearly empty, save for a handful of men huddled around a fireplace in the center. Four pairs of eyes turned toward him as the door hinges announced his presence with a shriek. He nodded before taking a seat away from them all in the corner. The looks on all their faces was predictable: True Mages always made people nervous. Just as quickly the four pairs of eyes turned their attention back to the bottom of their mugs, grumbling in hushed tones.

"Well, if it ain' Fancy Pants, come to play the common man, eh? Give me one good reason why I ought to serve you, after how you played me this morn'. You made Lady Velvet the subject of gossip and foolish talk. Ain' right, embarrassing a lady like that. Now you want my ale? I'll serve you the dishwater that good-fer-nuthin Miller keeps sendin' me. Lousy man, in every way. Can' trust no one in this Dark World. You come to apologize? What's yer game, Fancy Pants? We don' need no Mage in here." Lady Velvet was wearing the same outfit from this morning's session in court, with a few more grease spots and smudges added throughout the long day.

"Bitter tea. I came for bitter tea, and a room. I'm travelling and your inn is…convenient. Unless your rooms have sold out?" Magi asked.

Lady Velvet narrowed her eyes. "Nah, plenty of rooms, if I choose to let you stay. But yer 'convenience' will cost you two gold crowns, and not a copper less. And that don' include the tea!" She stalked off without even looking to see whether he'd accept and stay. All he heard was her muttering something about real men and drink.

Magi smiled. Tracking Veronica would have been easy enough without the Staff, just using the Ranger skills he'd picked up over his life. But her tracks soon led to heavily travelled paths, and became lost in a collage of footprints in the soft, wet roads. At virtually every turn, however, he could find someone in the shops, beggars in the street, or barkeeps in the taverns that had seen a tall, pale woman. And since no one could lie or even hide the truth from him, it took Magi a very short time to triangulate in on sightings and pick up her trail until it led him to *The Last Call* on the very outskirts of Rookwood.

"Here" said Lady Velvet, sloshing a third of his tea onto the table as she set it down. "Three gold pieces and I'll scare you up a room." She narrowed her eyes at the mage, puffing out her enormous chest. "A tip migh' help yer cause. Some rooms are nicer than others." She cackled as she strutted away.

Magi did his best to erase that image from his mind as he smelled the bitter, pungent tea. There was hardly any steam coming from it. *Lukewarm at best.* He sighed again and pulled his cowl up over his head to make up for the lack of warmth in his drink.

He knew Veronica was upstairs somewhere. He knew she didn't have the ring. He knew she was planning on meeting with Xaro, and he knew Xaro coveted the ring as much as Magi or any other mage would. He also knew that she knew who had the ring.

That was about it. If he was completely sure the ring was headed to Sands End, and that it would be there still when he arrived, he would have ditched Veronica completely and bought passage in the morning, sailing west, but he was hardly sure of that. His Staff allowed him to see through lies; he couldn't read minds. For all he knew, Xaro was already heading east with an undead horde.

No, his best chance of finding the ring was still Veronica, who clearly had a means of communicating with Xaro, probably through a distance-telepathy spell. A very difficult spell to put in place, but Magi thought it likely Xaro could handle it, from all he had heard of the man, from his prophesy to his father to Strongiron's parting words earlier in the day.

The more he thought about it, the more he leaned toward confronting Veronica directly. There was something…pure about her. Not in a holy way—goodness, no, but in his brief conversation with her, she seemed very pragmatic, very black and white. She had clearly been willing to trade her life for Peter's, and while his exposure to True Assassins was quite rare, he'd always heard that they were loyal to their contract. Perhaps if Magi could strike a contract with her…his mind raced ahead. *And I would know if she intended to honor it!*

That's what made up his mind in the end; when it got right down to it, in anything that involved dialogue and trust, Magi always had the upper hand. He could probably track her over all of Elvidor, but that would be tedious, and he might lose her on the sea anyhow. Why not approach her directly? As Magi thought about it, she really only had three options if he confronted her: *take me to the ring, fight me, or try and escape and evade me. Given those three choices, what is*

Veronica likely to do? He took a sip of the tea. *Weak…and gritty. Just dreadful.*

She's likely to take the pragmatic choice, and take me to Xaro and the ring. After all, wasn't that what Marik was planning to do all those years? Hand me over to Xaro, all trained up? And if I offer her a nice little contract to boot…

Magi pushed his mug of tea to one side and walked over to Lady Velvet. She was leaning into a man with no teeth at a table by the fire, now burning low. "Here, Miss Velvet," he said, handing her four gold pieces, which made the man by the fire snort in disgust at the outrageous sum. "I'd like the room next to the tall, pale woman who came in earlier this evening, if it's all the same to you."

~Trevor~

One shaft of moonlight shone through a porthole in the tiny cabin below deck that Trevor and Tarsh shared. The other light came from a small lantern on a simple table nailed to the wall between their bunks. Tarsh's side of the room was pristine; dirty clothes and ceramic flasks, bottles, and mugs littered the floor around Trevor's bed, clinking together as *Sheila's Bane* rocked gently in the early morning water.

"Could be a nice moonset if you want to head up on deck," said Trevor. "Half the crew worships you; the other half fears you. They all respect you, though. That was some trick you pulled." He reached for a pail in the corner and picked one of the clay mugs off the floor and sniffed it. Shrugging, he blew some dust out of it and dipped a ladle into the pail to pull out a drink of water.

"You go. Take some of your empty drinking vessels with you. The racket keeps me up, and I need my rest." Tarsh grumpily laid his head back down.

"Nah. I'll stay here." He pushed all the clanking mugs, flasks, and bottles into another corner and threw a pile of dirty clothing on top of them to keep them from rolling around with every sway of the ship. "That'll keep 'em quiet. Besides…there's something I want to discuss with you."

Tarsh sat up. The room they shared was so small that there was literally three feet between their bunks. Seated facing one another, they were uncomfortably close. "What?"

"I spoke to Xaro. He's agreed to meet you." Trevor reached into a carefully hidden pouch inside his vest that he wore all the time and put on the ring he'd been tasked to bring to Xaro. "However, I'm not so sure it makes sense for us to go there."

Tarsh narrowed his one, bloodshot eye. "More schemes? What now, Thief?"

Trevor didn't immediately answer, weighing his words. Finally, he asked, "How much do you know of alchemy?"

Tarsh blinked. "Alchemy? Spinning common metal into gold? Very little, Thief. Why?"

Trevor bit his lip. "Because you and I may have the secret to unlimited gold, and I'm not sure a Master Thief will be needed once Xaro has an unlimited supply of gold."

"Hmph," said Tarsh. "Are all Thieves this self-concerned? You seem awfully committed to disobeying your Master when all he asks is that you show up."

"And you are less self-concerned, worrying about your face?" Tarsh leaned forward with a snarl, and Trevor softened his expression, holding up his palm. "Relax. I simply believe there are options we should discuss."

"Then out with it," said Tarsh. "What are your options?"

Trevor opened up his vest showing the Purple Sun—the jewel he'd stolen from Lady Elyn—dangling from a strap around his neck. "Xaro said this is the key. Do you know what this is?"

"No, but it is beautiful. Key to what?"

"He has an alchemist with him, and he says *this jewel* is what's needed to change common metals to gold." Trevor said. He pulled it over his head and was holding it in his hand, turning it over, looking at it carefully. *Flawless.*

Tarsh fixed his one good eye on Trevor and cocked his head curiously. "Why are you telling me this, Trevor? What makes you think I'm more trustworthy than Xaro, a man who pays you?"

At this Trevor turned his attention back to Tarsh, leaned forward slightly, and smiled. "I don't. But I know you can't hurt me with your spells while I'm wearing this ring, and I like my chances in a knife fight with you if it comes to that." He chuckled slightly and leaned back. "If I can't trust you, then I think I can trust your self-interest. I can't figure out how to use this gem to create gold, but I bet you can. What I'm proposing is this: My gem, your magic—we split all the gold we create 50/50. We can stick together or go our separate ways, whatever. But you don't really want a part in Xaro's war council, do you? Cause I can tell you that the only role left for us after his last meeting is for me to lead an undead horde on an attack of Thalanthalas—where I am known for having stolen this very jewel—and for you to be a part of a blockade of the harbor in Rookwood. Neither seems real appetizing."

"So, you would throw your lot in with the Monster of Gaust, eh?" Tarsh stared out at the beautiful moonset, where it would soon fade from view in the pre-dawn sky. "Very well, then tell me why *I* should trust *you*? Say I do figure out the right spell or potion. Why wouldn't an accomplished Thief just take it all, if my magic is impervious to you?"

Here Trevor actually laughed out loud and stood up, daring to put his hand on Tarsh's shoulder. "Tarsh, you just levitated an entire ship out of the Great Maelstrom. If you don't trust my ethics, trust my pragmatism. When we're rich, we'll be targets, because I intend to enjoy my gold. You can protect me far better with your spellcraft than I could protect you with my thieving. The greater risk is *you* seeking to leave or harm *me*, I'm sure you'll agree. Not the other way around. Now, if you want to take your gold and leave, I won't stop you once our job is done, but I need this ring to protect me from you, lest you get any ideas of taking the gold for yourself. Admit it: I have far more to worry about with you than you have to worry about me. You're more valuable to me once the gold is made." He sat back down. "Simple as that."

Tarsh rubbed his chin, and Trevor could see he was seriously thinking about this. *Now close the deal.* "There's one more thing, Tarsh, you should know. I've also been told that your life-quest for revenge on Magi need not end. He's not dead. Some other God raised him, and he lives, carrying a Staff that once belonged to that ancient True Mage you referenced...Quixatalor. Help me turn this jewel into a fountain of gold, and I will help you kill Magi Blacksmooth."

Tarsh's red eye grew wide as he slowly sucked in his breath. "If you are lying to me, Thief—"

"I am not." Trevor extended his hand, the one holding the Purple Starburst. "Do we have a deal?"

Tarsh slowly smiled. He took the enormous amethyst, shaped like a starburst, from the thief's hand and held it up to the shaft of moonlight streaming into their room. Even the fading moonlight was thrown into a dozen colors scattered all over the room as the light bent its way through the jewel's intricate facets. "Deal."

Just then there was a heavy knock on the door. Tarsh quickly buried the jewel in his robes and turned to open it.

When the door opened, darkness immediately filled the room. It was as if night itself was unleashed, instantly filling the room with nothing but blackness. The lantern went out, the moonlight was gone—everything in their cabin was covered in an impenetrable, disorienting darkness.

Trevor grabbed a knife from his boot just as he heard Tarsh fall over with a groan and a *thump*.

~Kari~

Four eighteen-hour days of practice, and even Kari had to admit that her *Illusions* of all the senses were markedly better. *Nearly perfect*, if Mistress Belara was to be believed.

Her mind had been sharpened to the point where she saw details in everything: the subtle differences in scent between a white rose and red rose, the minute difference in shade between Palatinate Blue and Persian Blue, the texture differences between white sand and black, or the tonal differences between the voices of identical twins. Even her palate sensitivity had been heightened: she could easily distinguish between freshwater sourced from different springs, streams, and lakes now.

A week ago, Kari could wield *Illusions* that were impressive, but clumsy to the trained eye. By the fifth day of their intense training, Kari could wield *Illusions* that one could literally get lost in forever. She could form a different reality that was indistinguishable from your current reality.

Belara was draped in shimmering silver today, her trademark dress hugging her voluptuous curves, right to the top of her head, where the tight-fitting silver hood gave her an eerie, foreign look. She looked up from a scroll as Kari entered. "Come in, Kari. How did you rest?"

"Fine, Mistress. I feel sharp." And it's true. Kari did feel awake and alert, despite the long hours of fine-tuning her skills over the last few days.

"Good. Sit down." Belara stood and glided to a pot of tea hanging above a blue *Everflame* on a hearth in her study area. She poured Kari a mug full of deep red liquid, tinged with orange. "A nice calming potion to help you think more clearly than ever today."

"Thank you," said Kari, taking a sip. It was sweet at first, with an herbal finish. It did not take long for Kari to begin sensing things she normally couldn't pick up on, like a butterfly flapping its wings far down the mountain road toward the main walls of the city. "Oh my! This is extraordinary, Mistress." She took another sip. *I wonder if this is what Magi feels when he casts his spells.*

"Yes, it is extraordinary. I want you to finish a full mug, and then I will teach you how to open the Staircase. You are ready, Kari—assuming you still wish to go through with it." The blue light dancing off her silvery dress against her olive skin made her words come across almost ominously. She looked more exotic than ever. *Maybe it's the drink.*

Kari let the words hang there. *The power. Teleportation. Ability to see the world in an instant! The depth of her magical potential magnified. And then I can accompany Strongiron...as his equal.*

My eyes. I'll look like her. Kari stared at Belara's pure white eyes, imagining where the pupils and irises should have been. "Mistress, can you create an *Illusion* of what you looked like before you Climbed? I would like to see what you looked like before your transformation."

Belara smiled, only this was the first time Kari thought the smile was sad. That was another problem when your eyes were pure white; subtle facial expressions all looked sterile. She nodded and pointed to a nearby mirror.

Kari walked over and approached the mirror hanging on the True Mage's wall. Only instead of her own reflection, she saw Belara Kassar's. And her eyes were not white. They were light green. Like Kari's. Kari reached up to touch her face, and the reflection mirrored her movements. The young face of Belara Kassar looking back at her was simply stunning. Her hair, perpetually contained in those tight-fitting cowls that came up over her head, was now thick, long, and jet-black. *Much darker than mine.* She rivaled the Ol 'Shakoor for beauty.

Kari turned around. "I can't believe how beautiful you were. And you gave that up...to be a True Mage?" She turned to look at the image in the mirror again, but this time saw only her own reflection. "And...you are convinced it's worth it?" Kari didn't say it, perhaps didn't need to, but couldn't help but think *and now no man will grow close to you. But Strongiron would still find me attractive...surely he would?*

Belara approached her protégé reassuringly. "I have told you— yes, it is worth it. Knowing then what I know now, I would make the same decision. For me, the power is enough. But if you have any doubts, tell me now. You can continue to train, and you can still learn new spells, new branches of magic. But your power will always be at its current level. Good, but not great. Great power is reserved for those who make great sacrifices, Kari. But if you have reservations, it is not safe to Climb. People die in this ascent. You must be fully committed."

"One more question. The Ol 'Shakoor was a prophetess who revealed my prophesy last year. She was a True Mage, yet she kept her eyes. She implied that she 'negotiated' this with someone, but had a different price to pay. In catching up with Magi, I've since learned exactly what that price was; she's now blind. Will I have the same chance to negotiate?" Kari asked, looking at Belara hopefully.

Drawing her ruby-red lips into a thin, straight line, Belara shook her head. "No. This is not a negotiation, Kari, but rather a test to receive a gift if judged worthy. You won't be in a position to demand anything. Either the gift of this power is worth it to you, or not, and if not, then let's call it a week and I'll pursue other matters of state, and you can admire yourself in front of a mirror while the realm suffers from starvation and the general harshness of winter, preparing for a war we didn't invite, all while our Queen…" She shook her head and trailed off. Belara pointed at the mirror again, losing her patience. "Come—is this so hideous to you?"

Kari turned around, and saw her own reflection this time. Only her eyes were already white now. Gone were the brilliant green eyes that had garnered her so much attention the last several years, and in their place were the pure white eyes of a True Mage, set off against her tan skin, high cheekbones, thick brown hair. She didn't look hideous…

I look…terrifying. There was something about a female True Mage that seemed to look far more menacing than Magi or Niku ever did. She glanced at Belara. *Just like her.*

Kari took a deep breath. "I'm ready, Mistress. I was born to be a True Mage." She finished the last of her tea. "Show me how to open the door."

~Magi~

It was a simple awakening spell, really. The night before, Magi placed a charm outside Veronica's door that would create a mild "shock" to him when anybody opened the door.

It turned out to be unnecessary. The door screeched open on rusty hinges in the predawn hour, followed immediately by a shocking tingle up Magi's arm. Ready to leave immediately, he checked his travelling cloak for bugs, and then *Teleported* just outside the front of *The Last Call* and waited.

Looking to the east, the tavern was too far inland to see water, but the horizon was still low and unobstructed. The night was overcast, but a thin break in the clouds just above the horizon was starting to glow pinkish-orange, forming a short ribbon of color far off in the distance. *Dawn of a new day—chilly, but definitely warming up.*

A tall, thin man wearing a heavy, black cloak emerged from the tavern, heading north on a path toward Paragatha. He was alone. Magi fell in silently a few feet behind him, careful not to get too close.

"Hello, Veronica," he said.

The man spun around far too quickly for a middle-aged drifter, knife in hand. Magi knocked the blade out of his hand with his Staff. "I have no interest in harming you, Veronica. I wish to talk. Is it possible for you to talk without you trying to kill me—again, I might add—or do I need to restrain you first?"

The man cocked his head to one side slightly, narrowing his eyes. "How did you know it was me?" She then saw the Staff, with the white stone atop it. "Never mind."

"As I have told you, lies are pointless with me, and this disguise is nothing more than a lie." Magi walked around Veronica, never taking his eyes off her, staff poised to strike. He reached down and picked up her knife. "Can I trust you with this?" he asked, extending it.

"Yes" she said, reaching out for it.

Magi sighed and tucked it into his belt.

"Veronica, I want to talk to you, if you can bring yourself to tell the truth. Let me get right to the point. You know I want my ring back. And I know that you know where it is, or where it's headed. You have three options, as I see it. Number one, you can take me to meet Xaro. Number two, you can run and try and evade my pursuit. Or Number three, you can fight me right now. Or try and fight me later if you feel naked without your dagger. Regardless, I can assure you that option two is a waste of your time and option three is a waste of your life. And there are no hostages here for you to threaten."

Veronica spit at Magi's feet. "You like to be self-righteous with that staff of yours, but you lied to me as well. You said the Queen wouldn't have me followed."

"And she did not. I am not acting under the Queen's authority. Far from it; she would much rather I had stayed at Rookwood. But I will recover what was stolen from me. My interest, at least so far as you are concerned, is not to bring you to justice for your crimes. I'm not hunting you, Veronica. I only want my ring. Frankly, I'm a little stunned at your reluctance." Magi pulled his staff up into a vertical, non-threatening position, placing his free hand on his hip.

Veronica laughed, and the girlish sound coming from her disguised face would have made onlookers gawk had there been any. "Reluctant? To travel with a Mage who is motivated to kill me for revenge, back to disrupt my Master's plans, after I had already told him that you were dead? Why, that sounds like a fantastic option!"

Magi smiled. "You lie again. You can't help yourself. Your tone drips of sarcasm, yet you *want* me to come with you. At what point will it sink in to that thick head of yours that you might as well just tell me the truth?"

Veronica just stood there and said nothing.

Magi continued. "Assuming we are in agreement, let us begin our journey west, shall we? If I wanted to exact revenge, you'd already be dead. As for disrupting Xaro's plans—that part you got right. That is precisely what I intend to do, but I suspect he would just as soon have me away from Rookwood anyhow, so at this point both his and my interests are aligned. So let me try and align yours as well. Here." Magi tossed her a small scrollcase.

"What's this?" she said, wary of the True Mage's scroll.

"Open it."

She opened it. It was a contract for 10,000 gold pieces: 2,000 up front, and 8,000 when she brought him to whoever possessed his ring. The only caveat: no pre-meditated killing while on the journey.

She looked up and slowly approached Magi, who did not back away. "You are a fool, Mage. My Ma—"

"Call me Magi, Veronica," he interrupted. "If we're going to travel across the realm together, we ought to be on a first name basis."

"Very well. Magi, you are a fool. My Master will kill you if you try to take it, and what good will your magic be against him if he possesses it? This is the fool's errand that you wish to pay me for?"

She's not lying. She believes every word of that. "Yes. That is what the contract is for. As for my likely death, you of all people should know that I'm hard to kill." He smiled and unhooked a fairly large pouch from his belt. "I don't know if you wish to travel with this much gold on you or not, but I will send it wherever you want if we have a deal." He dropped the heavy pouch into her hand. "Count it if you like."

Veronica felt the significant weight of the small sack, opened it up and pulled out a handful of beautiful gold crowns. "No, I don't think that will be necessary." She cinched it up and stuck out her hand, a rueful smile on her manly face. "I trust you—or at least I trust your motivation. We have a deal. I think I'll keep this little bag on me, but I wouldn't mind if you could make it a bit lighter?"

Magi slowly nodded, said a word, and felt that familiar rush of his heightened senses that always thrilled him. A moment later, and the bag was light as a feather, and no longer jangled when she walked.

It quickly disappeared inside a pocket on her trousers. "Thanks…one more thing. Since I've agreed to this contract, may I have my knife back now? For self-defense? We do live in a Dark World."

Magi considered her words carefully, and slowly handed her the knife. *Even though she's still lying.*

~Trevor~

Slashing wildly through the blackness all around him with his short dagger, Trevor yelled, *"Here! Down Here!"*

He heard the bolt in his cabin door slide shut in response.

"Who's there? Who is it? Tarsh, are you conscious?" He repeatedly stabbed the darkness in all directions to keep a would-be assailant or rogue sailor at bay. It wasn't just that the room was dark; it was like everything in the room was black, as if light itself was the essence of blackness. Trevor was breathing rapidly and sweating. He was terrified. *"Show yourself!"* he screamed.

Suddenly a vice-like grip held his wrist, clenching down on him with tremendous strength. He cried out in agony, dropping his knife. Whoever was holding him controlled him easily. He couldn't make out their face—or even the fingers closed around his wrist—just blackness in all directions.

"Who…are…you?!" he gasped, struggling to wrench his wrist free.

"Trevor, I am disappointed that you don't recognize my work."

The voice. He had heard that voice before. It was hard to forget. "Malenec? Why are you here? How are you here? Let me go, you freak!" he pleaded. "We are on the same team!" Trevor swung a wild punch with his free hand, but he couldn't even split the darkness, let alone connect with the Dark Cleric.

"I'm glad you think so. Soon I can guarantee that." He gave Trevor's wrist a twist, forcing the Thief to his knees. He heard the whisperings of a nearly silent prayer, followed by the most excruciating pain he had ever experienced in his life. The flesh on his hand began to dissolve—slowly. Though he couldn't see a thing, he could hear the drops of flesh splattering onto his cabin floor. He could feel the intense pain as every nerve in his hand was exposed. All he could do is wail and scream as his hand essentially melted.

"Unfortunately for you, not a sound will leave this room. One of the more useful side effects from my darkness storm that Kuth-Cergor granted, praise be to him," Malenec said in an almost gleeful tone.

"My hand!" Trevor cried. "Please Malenec, my hand..." he begged as the last bit of flesh dissolved from his hand, leaving Trevor's exposed skeleton right up to the wrist where Malenec held him fast.

"Yes, you have something on your hand that I desire." He slowly bent Trevor's wrist downward until Magi's old ring easily slid off his finger bones. Trevor still couldn't see a thing, but he never heard the ring hit the floor. "It is a shame—for you, of course—that this magnificent ring protects you from a Mage's Art, yet it is powerless against my prayers."

"Take it! You can have it! Please, fix my hand, Malenec. Please—what good am I without a hand?" He pleaded with the Dark Cleric. "I won't tell a soul, I promise."

"No, you won't have a soul to tell," the Dark Cleric replied. Trevor felt a blade sink deep into his chest, and began choking on his own blood. "Your soul, in fact, will be mine. You will be a wonderful addition to my undead horde. Why, I may even put you in front when we attack the Elfs, since you're so familiar with Thalanthalas. *Then*—and only then—will we be on the same team, my little Thief."

"Malenec..." he gurgled, clawing at the blackness around him from his knees with his one free hand.

"Shhhh. Die, Trevor Blink." He gave the knife a twist.

Trevor tried to scream, but had no air in his lungs. Malenec released his grip on his wrist, pushing the dying Thief backward. He fell, and could feel the point of the blade protruding from his back catch on the wood floor beneath him.

The last thing he heard was Malenec laughing softly, muttering something about Xaro.

Chapter Six: Mage Dreams and Killer Quandries

~Kari~

Finishing the spell to open the door to the Staircase, she stepped back and watched the blue outline of the door begin to glow out of thin air in the middle of Belara's sitting room. Soon the edges connected and the door began filling in, heavy and wooden, attached to nothing.

"Remember—details, Kari! Trust in yourself, and you cannot fail," Belara encouraged as Kari placed her hand on the door ring leading to the Staircase. She looked back at her most recent teacher, a True Mage and Master Illusionist, and nodded reverently. Her heart beat at a maddening rate. *I haven't been this nervous since I was a child, with my brother and Magi and Tarsh, stealing Mikenese Melons before we were attacked by a wolf.*

She walked into the Staircase chamber, shutting the door behind her. The one torch that shed any light at all danced with a *whoosh* as the door closed behind her.

Kari looked around. In front of her were the first steps of a spiral staircase, hewn out of stone that curved to her right. The left side of the stairwell wall looked like rock and stone, rough and uneven. A copper-colored sconce held a torch, and looking around the bend in the staircase, she could see dancing shadows, likely indicating another flame on the wall up ahead. The right side of the stairwell was also made of a similar rock wall. The effect of having a winding staircase closed in on both sides was that you could not see the magnitude of how high it went…Kari could only see the half-dozen steps in front of her before they curved around. She imagined herself inside and at the bottom of a perfectly coiled snake, climbing from tail to forked tongue. *The belly of a snake would probably be less deadly.*

She cast a *Shield* spell, crushing a white marble, just to feel better prepared, despite the draw on her energy and started her climb. The steps were not symmetrical at all; some were large, others wide, still others narrow. Up she climbed.

And up. And up. Always turning to her right, bending around the center, interminable and mind numbing. After what must have been an hour by her reckoning, she finally cast a *Glowball*, tired of the spacing between the wall torches being as dark as they were. Barely enough light to dimly see, she worried she might be missing details on the steps—latches, trip wires—anything that might trigger an opening and a different path. Everything just looked so similar.

Finally, rounding a turn she came to a small landing, no more than four feet square, with a heavy door. *Thank God!* She paused on the landing to gather her breath. Though the cave-like atmosphere was cool, Kari was sweating from the exertion.

She walked up to the door and felt it. *Old, old wood. Smooth.* She listened. *Nothing—only the sound of the flickering flame of the nearest torch in the stairwell below me.* She took a deep breath through her nose. *Smells like a dank cave.* She did not try to taste the door.

Calling forth a dozen possible spells for anything that might await her on the other side, she took a final, deep breath and tested the door to see if it was locked. It wasn't. Heart pounding wildly, she pulled the door open...

...and saw more stairs. Suspicious, she walked through carefully, testing the placement of her feet before letting her full weight settle. *Wish I had Magi's staff now.* She took a few more steps and could not find a booby trap. She sighed and let the door close behind her. Once again, the closest torch that shed any light danced with a *whoosh* from its copper sconce as the door closed.

She continued her climb... and continued further. The steps were all different widths and heights, just as before. After what surely felt like another hour, she came again to a door, very similar to the first one. Kari looked closely, but couldn't see any major differences; *old smooth door in a nearly silent dank smelling cave.* She pulled the second door open...

...and groaned. More stone steps, curving upward in a spiral to the right. Kari was frustrated, tired, and almost dizzy from the constant turning. She wasn't feeling cautious at all, and strode right to the steps, letting the door slam behind her with a *whoosh* that nearly blew out the nearby torch again.

Kari stopped. She looked at the torch on the wall very closely. It looked like all the other torches she passed at regular intervals. She grabbed the torch and snuffed it out, leaving only her glowball to provide her with adequate light until she reached the next torch. She began to push herself, hopping two steps at a time when the heights of consecutive steps were low enough. Sweat ran freely down her face, neck, and back as she raced upwards.

It still took quite longer than she would have liked to reach the next door. She paused to catch her breath for a minute, trying to clear her head for some spells just in case, but finally pulled on the handle without even checking.

She saw more stairs…and a torch lying on the ground. These weren't more stairs. *They're the same stairs!* Kari pulled the door closed behind her, and felt the same *woosh* as always, without the flickering flame this time.

So this must all be one big Illusion? Kari rubbed her aching thigh muscles. *No Illusion there.* She began climbing again, but this time very slowly, more slowly than even the first time, looking for anything unusual in the steps or walls. She had no concept of time at this point, everything was just up and to the right, up and to the right. Nothing jumped out at her—just rock, stone, and the occasional torch. She couldn't spot so much as a beetle crawling around.

Finally, after hours (or so it seemed), she came again to a door. *The door. If I go through that door, I will be climbing for another day.* She was so frustrated she couldn't decide whether to cry or scream. *What am I missing?*

She walked up to the door, felt all over it, listening intently, searching for imperfections or hidden latches or knobs. She took deep breaths through her nose. *Still a dank breeze.* Shaking her head, she even put the tip of her tongue to the door. *Cold, dirty, wood. I can't believe I tasted a door.*

Frustrated, Kari hurled her *Glowball* at the door. It ricocheted and disappeared into the ceiling right above her. *Of course! How could I be so stupid?* This wasn't even the first time Kari had seen a false ceiling; she had spotted one in the Catacombs outside Shu-Tybor, leading to a secret entrance to the Tower of Dariez. She just hadn't been looking *up.* Casting a quick *Levitation* spell and a new *Glowball*, she could easily pick out the imperfections in the *Illusion*—the mismatching shades of rock, some textures that didn't line up. Of course this was an *Illusion.* She put her hands over her head to brace for the impact—just in case she was wrong—as she slowly lifted herself from the landing.

The impact never came, and she passed right through. She gathered up her first glowball, and now had one flanking each side of her as she propelled herself to a new landing, facing a new door.

This one was different. It was reinforced with heavy metal, with a large iron handle instead of a loop ring. No steps were present; just this landing, the door, and the false floor through which she had just levitated. Her *Glowballs* were the only light.

"No time to dawdle," she said to no one but herself. She grabbed the iron handle and pulled, behind which she found three more doors facing her in this large room. All of them looked the same. It was definitely a room, not a cave. The walls were smooth and white. She let the door shut behind her.

Immediately each door burst into flame. She turned around, and the door behind her was gone.

~Magi~

"Why would you wish to head North to Paragatha?" asked Magi as he walked alongside the fit Assassin, who was still disguised as a male peasant. "We could buy passage in the port of Rookwood to sail west."

The ground was still recovering from winter, with muddy, brown snow lining the main roads and paths. The sun lit up the morning; crisp, but not so cold that the walk was miserable. By midmorning, the air had warmed to the point where they could no longer see their breath, despite their purposeful strides. Veronica set a good pace, although on foot it was unlikely that they would make it to Paragatha in one day. It was a good three- or four-day hike to the nearby city.

She turned her head. "For the third time, I do not wish to sail out of Rookwood—even with a disguise. I am no good to you if I'm captured by the Queen's Guard, Magi. If this is too much a strain on your tired legs, why don't you just *Levitate* behind me?"

Magi made an indignant noise, striking a tone somewhere between laughter and anger. "I do not need to waste my energy floating behind you. I can walk farther and faster than you could ever dream." He thought of his long treks through the woods with his friend and mentor Lionel, a True Ranger from Brigg who had taught him how to track and hunt and survive. *Lionel...most likely another of your victims.*

"Suit yourself, but we will go overland, at least on this continent."

"I could protect us both if the Queen's Guard gives us trouble. Overland will put us at the Crystal Mountains by mid-spring at the earliest. We are losing time." Unsatisfied with her explanation, Magi thumped the butt end of his staff more forcibly into the ground as he walked.

"You are the one who is committed to following me. You wish me to lead you to this ring. Fine. Therefore I am the guide, and I say we are going by land—at least until we reach The Three Fingers."

Magi did not say anything immediately. He could not read her mind, but he knew something was amiss. "Why do you want our journey west to take weeks—if not months—longer than it needs to? It cannot be out of fear that you are discovered and arrested, given both your disguise and my standing with the Queen."

Veronica slowed, but did not stop. She kept her eyes forward and did not look at Magi. "If you must know, I was shipwrecked this winter in the Strait of Holstine, and I would prefer not to sail any more on this journey than I have to. Besides, the extra weeks will not hurt us. I don't know exactly where my colleague who has your ring is. After my next update with Xaro, I can provide you with more information, and we can change our plans if need be. But for now, it suits your best interest and my personal interest to travel overland. I would have us stay at a decent place one more night before the camping begins as we turn west toward the mountains. Is that truth enough for you and your staff?"

Her words carry the truth, at least as far as she knows. "It is. Now was it so hard to share the truth with me?" Magi asked, before softening his tone. "I am sorry for your shipwreck. What happened?"

"A storm. It was nothing. I survived." Veronica did not elaborate, and Magi detected no lies.

They walked in silence for some time, finding the well-worn path that would lead them to Paragatha over the next few days. Stopping by an outcropping of rock off the path, in the shadow of the small mountain range behind Rookwood, they shared a meal of dried pork. As he ate, Magi stared up at the jagged mountains still capped in snow. He was tempted to cast a simple spell, just to heighten his senses. He could imagine the eagles circling far above him, the bears stretching after a lean winter's nap, the first insects starting to buzz. He also imagined the sound of the snow melt forming icy-blue streams cascading down the mountain.

He stared at the Assassin, still disguised as a man. "There is something I've wanted to ask you for awhile now. Did you kill a Ranger and a Warrior in Gaust over a year ago, Veronica?" The question had bothered Magi since he first began connecting dots.

Veronica looked up from her morsel of dried pork into Magi's white eyes. "I've killed many. I may have. I may not. There are plenty of us who deal in death, Mage." She shrugged and turned her attention back to her meal.

She speaks in a manner that makes lying difficult to ascertain. No matter. Undeterred, Magi continued. "It was in a Library—the Great Library in Gaust is where my friend the Ranger was killed by an Assassin. Does that jog your memory at all?"

She said nothing, but shrugged again.

"Look at me!" Magi shouted.

Veronica looked up, and smiled charmingly. The effect would have been off-putting enough without the disguise; it was all the more so as a man, eyelashes fluttering. "So your friend was killed? Am I supposed to keep track of everyone I've slain?" she intimated in mock ignorance.

A lie. "You do keep track of everyone. Every baby, every mother, every old man, every enemy, every stranger. Everyone. And you know what I'm talking about. Tell me about that contract."

Veronica's expression sobered. "That is not part of our deal. I would never divulge the details of any of my contracts," she said, eyes flashing.

"I can make you talk, Veronica. Lionel was my friend. I would like you to tell me why you killed him." Magi finished his pork and stood.

Surprisingly—infuriatingly—she looked up at the towering mage and laughed. "Make me talk? It is bad enough you filter everything I say through that Staff of yours. Am I your guide or your captive? Will you now torture me for information? How will that go over with that precious God of yours that loved you *so much* that She sent you back to Tenebrae for more suffering?"

"She sent me back to do a job." Magi said, sitting back down. "And…that came out wrong. I don't want to torture you, Veronica. I just want the truth. Why did you kill Lionel and Sindar?"

"It is a Dark World, mage. I am an Assassin, and it was their time to die. That will have to be reason enough for now, unless you mean to harm me in an attempt to learn more. And I doubt highly there is anything you and your spells can do to me that is worse than what I've already endured.

"Let's get moving," she said as she stood, pulling her travelling cloak around her as she set out.

~Kari~

The room was tight, maybe fifteen square feet, and *hot*. The flames were not close enough to burn her directly, but the heat radiating from the three doorframes was enough to burn the sweat off her face before it could trickle down. The shimmering air itself seemed to be holding the heat in, as if Kari was in a tiny brick oven facing three mammoth, white-hot coals.

I must get out of here. She put her hands up to shield her eyes from the burning doors but could not step forward. Breathing was becoming more difficult as the fire seemed to consume the very air she was inhaling, with each breath beginning to sear her lungs. *I have to get out of here!*

Concentrating was almost impossible. She could feel her skin getting deep red, which would happen sometimes when she was younger and played outside in high summer too long on a sweltering afternoon. This was much worse, however; her skin would begin peeling in minutes—she knew she was baking alive.

Think! If this was an *Illusion*, it was the most realistic one she'd ever seen in her life. *Clearly, I must pick a door.* For Kari, the immediate decision was right or left—the center door was flanked by another flaming door on either side, so she figured that one would be hottest. Concentrating on a simple cooling spell, she cast it on the right-most door.

There was no change; if anything, the flames seemed to dance and gleam more after her spell, like the door had *drank in* the magic. Sighing, she tried to freeze the other two doors, and both times the flames grew higher and hotter.

Kari could feel the skin on her exposed arms beginning to blister. Frustrated, she summoned real water to try and quench the flames. The doors absorbed her magic again, this time sending a geyser of flames sprouting toward the low ceiling. She could almost feel the doors laughing, mocking her pitiful efforts.

What am I missing? She tore off a piece of her mage robes and covered half her face. Tiny blisters were beginning to burst and seep on the back of her hand and arm. The pain was worse than anything she had experienced in her eighteen years of life.

With a final scream, she picked the right-most door and ran for it, holding her arms ahead of her. *Dymetra, please let this fire be an Illusion. At the very least, I pray the door is unlocked!*

She grabbed the door ring and pushed. It wouldn't budge. She pulled—and the door slowly opened just as the frame of flame above her exploded in a blaze of orange across the side of her face. The stink of burning hair filled her nostrils.

The last thought Kari had before she stumbled through the door and passed out from the excruciating pain was: *That was not an Illusion.*

***

Time seemed to melt away like the skin on half her face. Kari finally opened her eyes and immediately knew something was wrong; the vision in her left eye was blurry. She was lying face down in a puddle of goo she hoped wasn't what was left of her face. If she had tears, they would have spilled forth, but all she could do was shudder.

Kari knew some rudimentary *Healing* spells, which she cast as soon as she could block out the pain all over her body. She watched as the extensive blistering and burns on her left arm and hand scabbed over. It wasn't a full healing, and the skin was still hard, cracked, and mismatched with the rich olive-toned skin covering the rest of her body. She had a small jar of jelly made from the sap of *sanitor* trees that worked as a burn salve, and she used the entire jar on her face and scalp. The pain was now dull instead of blinding, but it was still constant. She slowly stood up to take a look around.

More stairs. Kari looked behind her at the door she had just come through. *The Oven.* She couldn't bear the thought of re-entering that room. If there had been a door in front of her with a sign above that read *EXIT*, she would have left right then and there. Anything but more stairs…anything except The Oven, that is.

She didn't care about preserving her magical energy at this point; physically she was spent and gravely injured as well. She uttered a *Levitation* spell and began floating up, but not before she threw the first torch on the cave floor, just in case she was entering another *Illusion* loop.

Up and around to the right she floated. Same uneven steps, same torches, same walls, same colors, same stone feel, same scent in the air. Around and around she went upwards. She could cover much more ground than she could walking, so the height of wherever she was must have been dizzying. *Surely an hour has passed.*

Finally she reached another landing with another door just like the one that led to The Oven. Kari couldn't wait to get off the Staircase—she opened the door without hesitation…and stepped into the outskirts of a forest.

Reflexively Kari rubbed her eyes before her left one reacted painfully from her touch. She ended the levitation and let herself down gently, putting her feet on a small trail that looked oddly familiar. She took a few steps and glanced back at the blue outline of a door that hung on nothing in the middle of the woods along this trail. *Let me die on this Staircase than live my life as a failed mage, burned and untouchable.*

Rather than give in to depression or bitterness, she turned away from the door and continued down the trail. The woods ended abruptly, opening up to a small hamlet that caused what little hair she had left on her right arm to stand on end. Kari recognized the village immediately. She was back in Shu-Tybor. And that meant one thing: *Wraiths.*

"Hello, Kari. It's so good to see you again." Phillip, the former Elder of Brigg, flashed an icy smile toward Kari as he stepped out from behind some trees. "Although I must say you look dreadful."

When she last encountered Phillip, he had been possessed by the wraiths that inhabited Shu-Tybor. The wraiths were spirits that fed on hosts' fear and pain, and they could not be killed. She remembered watching vividly as Strongiron cleaved Phillip's head right off, only to watch him reattach it and continue fighting with that same, icy smile frozen on his face. They escaped only when she cast an *Illusion* of their retreat to get the wraiths to depart.

"What do you want?" she croaked. Her tongue felt thick, and her throat was dry and scratchy. It hurt to even speak.

"Your body, of course! Many here greatly desire warm flesh. Although I'll take it cold as well," Phillip said with a twinkle in his eye as he approached.

Kari began a soft chant, nearly under her breath, and a dozen Karis, all equally scarred and disheveled, appeared around her, encircling Phillip and causing him to pause. "Then take your pick."

The wraith spun its head around in a complete circle—literally. Returning to face the original Kari, he laughed, never losing that cold smile or the dead gleam in his eyes. "Silly girl. Your *Illusion* was better the first time we met. I can *feel* your fear." He took a step toward one of the Kari's to his right and grabbed her arm.

This time it was Kari's turn to flash a smile toward Phillip. "We all feel fear," said the twelve Karis in unison. The *Illusion* passed through the wraith's grip, and Kari spun the dozen doppelgangers around so that Phillip couldn't eliminate them one by one. "Guess again, creature."

This little game bought Kari some time—time to think while Phillip clawed at a different Kari each time, trying to figure out which one was real. In the end, she ruled out direct attacks and she ruled out running. She thought maybe if she levitated she might escape, but the wraiths were spirit; it would just leave Phillip and try and possess her as she rose above its host's reach.

So she prayed. *Dymetra, I know I am not worthy, but I pray that you turn this creature free. Let Phillip find rest, and let this wraith move on as well. Quench this tortured soul's thirst, so that it troubles your people no longer.*

It was a simple prayer, one that she remembered reading on a scroll from her few weeks of study at the Tower of Dariez. She amended it to call out the host by name.

This was the fifth time Phillip had tried to grab Kari's arms, and this time he was close, picking the *Illusion* of Kari two over from her left. He stopped and looked directly at the real her.

"What have you done for me?" it asked, its mouth open wide. The mouth began to soften—the plastic smile being replaced with a genuine one for the first time. "She is real…" Phillip mumbled, and Kari knew he wasn't talking about her. "Thank you, Kari…" he said as the body slowly collapsed to the ground. It began to fade away, revealing the trampled grass and dusty path beneath. And then it was gone, like a candle winking out.

A dozen heads all turned in unison to look around as Kari briefly maintained the *Illusion*. Perhaps it had always been there before, but she saw for the first time the blue outline of an unattached door just down the path a little further. She dispelled the multiple body *Illusion* and stolidly approached the door. Staring around one last time on the hamlet of Shu-Tybor, she opened the portal to re-enter the Staircase.

"It is so good to see you at last," said Strongiron with arms outstretched and a warm, concerned smile on his face.

~Magi~

The next few days passed unremarkably, with Magi making light conversation or none at all as they approached the city of Windomere, Paragatha. Having met the One True God, it felt strange seeing all those pillars lining the main entrance to the city, each adorned with a different God or Goddess. Moons, work, fertility, food, play, music, nature, love, war, fire, sea, gold—the list of things that were worshipped by people seemed endless, each embodied by a unique God situated on top. Figurines were sold in the marketplace, and beggars invoked all their names, hoping to attract niche worshippers, which Magi found ironic. You would think the beggars would concentrate on worshipping Venia, the Goddess of charity. *Then again, probably best to spread the love around when pleading for coppers.*

"Here's where I'm going," Veronica said as she turned toward a familiar tavern, *The Royal Steed.* As Magi recalled, it was a high-class inn, catering to knights and many servants of the crown.

"Why this inn? I've been here before—it will be crawling with the Queen's knights. Not that I care—your disguise is fine, but I am recognizable as well. Why attract the attention? There are dozens of places that are…less well travelled."

"You are correct. It is filled with Thunder, Thorns, and Blood. I'm not worried about the knights, but you should be. Not all of them may have heard that the Queen has decided to trust you. Your warrant picture that the Mage Guards sent out after you killed your friend may be the last image of you some of these men have seen. The bounty on your head may be more concerning than mine." She smiled sweetly, but disguised as a man, it looked toothy and awkward. "That is why I suggest you stay elsewhere."

"Forget it. You're not leaving my sight. We have a contract, remember?"

"We do. That is why you needn't worry about me 'escaping'—I think we can dispense with the illusion that I am anything other than your prisoner. But do use that stick of yours—am I lying when I say I have no intention of escaping tonight?"

Magi gripped the Staff of Insight reflexively, although he certainly didn't need to. He could see the truth in her statement, plain as the sun. "I do not believe you're lying, but that's not the point. I don't think it's a good idea for us to separate. Why don't we go somewhere else—I've been to several places in this city when I went in search of my father last year."

"That old man—" Veronica stopped as she looked at Magi's face.

Magi suddenly recalled the last image he had of his father. He was dead, his throat sliced open. *Like Lionel…* He immediately began connecting dots. "You—" was all he could say, his white eyes growing wide.

Veronica took a step back, her hand on the door to *The Royal Steed.* She stared at Magi, and even in disguise she could not hide her fear as recognition began to dawn on her travelling companion. She said nothing.

"You!" he said again, this time venomously. "You killed him! You killed my father! Do not lie to me!"

Veronica said nothing, and her face was impassive. She slowly nodded, her chin jutting out defiantly. But her eyes told another story. She was scared. Not remorseful, but intimidated.

Magi tried to keep his emotions in check as he stared at the woman who had murdered a father he barely knew. *And the time you did spend with him, you treated him worse yourself. At least in death he's now at peace, with your mother. You spit on him, for God's sake!* With the skill of an accomplished mage, he suppressed his emotional response. He closed his eyes for a couple seconds, and then stepped toward the Assassin. "Marik's contract?"

Veronica narrowed her eyes. "You know I'm not going to discuss my contracts with other clients. We've been over this." She paused. "He did not suffer, Magi, if that matters to you."

"Do not try and camouflage a profitable kill as a mercy killing. You took money from someone to kill my father. Forgiving you for killing me was easy compared to this," he said bitterly. Then he took a deep breath. "Perhaps it is best if we separate tonight. I should like to be alone this evening. I may pay my first visit to a temple—tonight would be a good time for prayer, and God knows this city is filled with temples. I will meet you in the common room here at first light, when we turn west to the Crystal Mountains."

"Agreed. We shall meet up in the morn." Veronica nodded, and without another word, pushed open the door to *The Royal Steed*, letting the sounds of laughter and the smells of spiced meat waft out toward them. She disappeared inside.

Less than a minute later, cloaked in a spell of *Invisibility*, Magi silently entered the tavern behind a small group of knights.

~Kari~

Kari would have run over to hug the True Warrior and Cleric if she had any strength left in her legs. Instead, she collapsed into Strongiron's arms as he approached.

"There, there—you made it. Here, sit down." He held her shuddering, scarred body, and finally just picked her up gently.

Her head cradled against his massive shoulder, Kari finally had a look around. They were in a comfortable room, almost identical to one of the studies Strongiron and she sometimes used in the Tower of Dariez, back when she thought her future might be as a High Priestess—a True Cleric. She could vaguely pick up the familiar smells of old parchment and the sweet smell of incense laced heavily with cloves. At her old copying table was a large, plush chair that would only be slightly less comfortable than her friend's warm, massive arms. And on the table was a glass pitcher of cool water with tiny mint leaves floating in it. Next to the large pitcher was a small vial of yellow liquid.

"Here, Kari. Let me look at you." Strongiron gently set her down onto the chair and kneeled to look at her more closely. She finally had a chance to see her reflection off a mirror hanging on the opposite wall, behind him. She gently pushed him aside to stare at the image facing her. Half of her visage was raw, blackened, and bloody where the doorframe had exploded into her face. Her one eye was milky and seeping.

"Is it as bad as it looks?" she asked through cracked lips as she unsteadily reached for the water. "Can you help me, Strongiron?" She turned to look into his bright blue eyes hopefully. "Please tell me that's why you're here."

He met her gaze, smiling warmly. "I may be able to. It is all up to Dymetra, of course. But I will pray that She shows you Her favor and heals your flesh. For now, drink this—it will help." Strongiron handed her that small vial of yellow liquid. "For the pain, for the nerves, and especially for the skin."

She uncorked it and smelled it, swirling it around. It smelled sweet, like peach nectar, and stuck to the sides of the vial. "What is it?"

"A form of ambrosia—a wonderful healing accelerant." Strongiron placed a hand gently on the right side of her head where she still had hair and stroked it softly. "It will help, Kari."

She gave a short nod and tipped it back into her mouth. The thick potion slowly slid down the long, glass vial and into her scorched mouth.

Ooh...so sweet! It felt like it was coating her entire stomach.

Strongiron suddenly stood. He backed away from the table with an expectant look to his face, which started to glow. Kari watched as his broad chest began to thin out, his arms began to lengthen, as did his chin. His eyes, once the most striking shade of blue, began to darken, first to grey, then to slate, then to black, encompassing his entire eyeball. She watched this thin creature make a tent with his long fingers, a wicked smile on his face. "It hurts, yes?"

That was when she convulsed onto the floor in agony. Even the *Illusion* of incense faded, and her nose was filled instead with the stench of decay that seemed to emanate from whatever was standing in front of her. He closed his eyes, hugging himself in ecstasy as Kari twisted on the floor. It felt like every nerve in her body was being set on fire all at once.

"W-w-what hav-ve you d-done to me-e?" Kari struggled to get out. She was on the very edge of passing out from the pain.

"My dearest Kari, I am sifting you. My name is Morsus, and I am Fate's Minister of Pain. The poison you ingested is, regrettably, lethal. Not everyone is meant to be a True Mage, I'm afraid. Death, while certain, is not quite immediate. That would be dreadfully unsatisfying, obviously. I'm afraid I'll just have to make do with only a few more scant, precious moments of your agony, however. That will have to suffice for awhile."

The gangly wight bent over Kari, pushing his face exceedingly close to the charred side of her body, sniffing loudly. "Exquisite. You won't mind if I touch you, will you?" Without waiting for her to even try and answer or recoil, he reached down and put his grotesquely large hand on her raw, burned shoulder.

"AHHH!" she screamed. Everything was going white in her mind.

Morsus immediately let go, a crestfallen look on his face. "No, no—can't have you dying while unconscious. But I had to feel it, just once. I'm sure you understand—the temptation and all."

Kari could only shake, her one good eye wild and wide. She could feel her throat constricting. Her heart was slowing down. The pain was actually subsiding now. Even though it was getting harder to breathe, the pain almost felt distant. She clawed at her throat for oxygen, but was too exhausted to panic.

"And so it ends, young Kari. The Staircase is unkind to the unworthy. Good bye, Mage." Morsus sighed, looking down on the twitching, raw, burned shell of a woman on the floor. She gasped once more, and then was still.

Morsus stepped over Kari's dead body, opened a door outlined in blue light that had just appeared, and left the room.

~Veronica~

"Silas," she called. "A glass of warm, spiced wine and a room."

The owner of *The Royal Steed* looked at the disheveled, dirty, pale man in front of him and furrowed his brow. "I'm sorry, have we met? It's a busy night, one of my bar wenches will bring you…wine." He said the last word almost disdainfully. "Show them your silver before you order, too." He started to walk away.

"I said I needed a room, Silas. Do your serving women also arrange rooms?" She handed him a gold crown. "One that is private and comfortable." Veronica normally would have flashed a charming smile, but instead just stared coldly at the innkeeper.

"Yes…well…I think I have just the room for you—what did you say your name was?" Silas asked, his large forehead starting to produce a few beads of sweat. He was a large man, with deep jowls, and sweating was apparently something that came quite easily to him.

"I haven't given you a name, Silas. Put it under Gold. Mr. Gold. That's all you need, right?" Veronica didn't want to step too closely to the innkeeper, in part because she didn't want any details of her actual features to shine through the disguise in the low light, but mostly because he smelled.

"Very shrewd. Mr. Gold—follow me to your room. I will send up some hot, eh, wine for you shortly." Silas smiled, slipping the gold coin into a greasy pocket inside his apron.

"No. Bring the wine to me first. I'll wait here, and we will go up together." Veronica took a seat at a nearby chair, and began drumming her fingers on the table. "Now, Silas."

"Yes, right away sir." Silas ran into the kitchen, barking orders.

Veronica looked around. As she suspected, the place was packed with the crests of the three Knightly Orders: Thunder—representing power, Thorns—representing loyalty, and Blood—representing sacrifice. That was all Veronica knew of the knights. She looked around further, and was so startled she nearly gave herself away.

Drinking alone in the corner was Silverfist, the head of her Guild. A Master Assassin. *What in the world is he doing in Paragatha?* If he recognized his star pupil, he didn't acknowledge it. His gaze continued to circulate the room, scanning and sipping.

Veronica desperately wanted to speak with him. Perhaps he might have some advice about her current set of contracts. She needed to talk to someone who would understand. She would update Xaro tonight—the whole point of a private room was for that purpose—but she wasn't sure he would understand.

She had just decided that she would try and talk to him when Silas burst through a swinging door back into the common room. "Your wine, sir. Now, if you'll follow me, I'll take you to your room." He handed her a rather ornate goblet filled nearly to the brim with a warm, deep red liquid. Silas nodded furtively and started heading toward a staircase in the back of the inn. Veronica put her hand on his shoulder and stopped him.

"That is too much for me. Please, take a sip yourself first, Silas." Again, no smiles—she just kept up her grim countenance.

"Ah—sir?" Silas said, stumbling a bit. "Beggin' your pardon, but that's your wine. Sip it yourself, finish what you can, leave the rest. You already paid for it."

"I insist. Please. A sip, Silas." Veronica squeezed his shoulder hard, digging in with her strong fingers while smiling so as to look nothing more than a familiar customer greeting an old innkeeper friend.

Silas did not reply or even groan immediately. Veronica felt the sweat rolling off the back of his head and pooling on her hand. "Yes. A taste. Just to prove the vintage and the temperature, of course."

He narrowed his eyes, but took the proffered goblet and drank. Afterward, he searched for the cleanest patch of his apron he could find and gently wiped the edge of the cup he had drunk from. "I do believe you will like it, Mr. Gold." He raised an eyebrow and offered it back.

"Thank you. Yes, I do believe I will as well. Before we go to my room, I have—" she looked over to where Silverfist had been seated. He was gone now. *Damn! Where did he go?*

"Yes?" asked Silas.

"Nothing. Take me to my room."

"Follow me." He led her up the stairs, with Veronica scanning the common room as they went, looking for signs. He was gone.

They walked all the way down a long hallway, poorly lit with guttering torches. The old wood floor creaked in protest with every step, and the smell of burned kitchen offerings from countless years dominated the senses.

At the very end, Silas pulled out a large single key attached to a ring meant to hold several. He unlocked a door, pushed it open, and handed Veronica a small candle he had carried up. "Enjoy your privacy this evening." With a curt nod, he turned and walked back toward the common room of his inn as fast as he could, rubbing his shoulder.

Veronica stood in the open doorway for a second, waving her candle around to shed some light on the room, which was pointless, as the light merely extended two or three feet at most. She sighed and gently shut the door.

"You are quite lucky that taking contracts against our own is frowned upon, Veronica. You've grown careless," said Silverfist, lighting a pipe in the corner of her room.

~Kari~

Given the way Kari felt right at this moment, it would have been harder to fake being alive than it was casting an *Illusion* of her death.

Physically drained and magically spent, she forced herself to stand. Up until this point, the hardest *Illusion* she had ever tried to create was the retreat of her and her friends in Shu-Tybor from Phillip and the other wraiths. But this was much different, much more difficult. *Much.*

It is one thing to create an *Illusion* of oneself while nobody is looking and send it off to do something while you disappear or blend into your environment. It is entirely different to seamlessly create an *Illusion* of oneself while someone else is looking directly at you—with no hint of transition or spell casting—while the "real" you backs away and hides in plain sight. But that is precisely what Kari had done once she'd realized the trap. *Strongiron would never offer me a drink in this place.*

The rest was just reading the verbal and non-verbal cues of what turned out to be a wight, hoping her *Illusion* wasn't moving too fast or too slow, or doing something unintended. When the wight gripped her shoulder, she knew it meant to cause pain, so she illustrated pain. When the wight gave her the drink, it telegraphed that it was lethal, so she died. But the *Illusion* had tapped even the fumes of her reserves; she could hardly concentrate on basic movement, let alone cast another spell.

After the wight left, Kari saw the door appear and gathered her strength. Her body was still scarred, half her head was burned down to the scalp, and her mind felt like warm jelly. She tried taking a deep breath, but it caused a coughing fit, rattling her lungs. Wheezing, she shuffled one foot in front of another until she reached the door. Closing her one good eye, she focused her attention on the simple iron ring near the edge of the magical door and pulled, watching it swing open soundlessly. She stood to one side in the doorframe.

Slowly, cautiously, she opened her eye and peered beyond the door into the scene beyond. It was a room—a very large room, filled with books, fine art, wall tapestries, and thick rugs with intricate patterns and colors. The room was so bright it hurt her eyes…at least the one good one that still functioned. There was some kind of fragrance to it. Not incense or anything heavy—but a fresh smell, like pinecones. In back of the room was a raised dais and an enormous chair that was obviously a throne, so ornate that it would have offended Kari, if she'd had the energy to care about such things.

Seated upon the chair was a strange-looking man wearing a bright green tunic, trousers, and a queer-looking hat with a small, yellow feather protruding from one side. He leaped down, from the throne and the dais, all the way to the floor with a vigor that was startling.

"Do come in, Kari! Come in! I am so *proud* of you!" He ran up to her and reached out to take the hand that wasn't blackened by fire. "I'd hug you child, but I know you're in no shape for hugging at present." His teeth were whiter than the snow-capped Crystal Mountains near her home.

"Who are you?" she asked, only slightly louder than a whisper. *I won't have another Illusion try and trick me.* She pulled her hand back.

"Relax, Kari Quinlan. There is no one who will harm you here. Your tests are concluded. You have reached the top of the Staircase, and I am Fatum, or Fate for short. You may know me by other names—some call me Fortune's Song, others have called me Destiny. But I prefer simply Fate. Come, I had good water and some fruit prepared for you." With a charming smile, he motioned to a table set before a comfortable-looking couch and long chair outfitted with at least a dozen matching pillows. "I will drink and eat first," he added, as if he'd guessed her suspicions.

Fate offered Kari the couch, then took a seat among the pillows in the facing chair. He poured himself some water from a pitcher and clipped some berries growing in bunches from a piece of vine he had brought and placed on the platter. He tore off a piece of hot bread that steamed when he broke it open and spread some soft cheese over it. "Please—you'll find none better on Tenebrae, I assure you."

Kari sat down and watched her strange host nibble on everything in front of her. She looked for any giveaway of an *Illusion*, but could not find any telltale shimmering or other tells. *If this isn't real, it's certainly as convincing as anything I've seen.*

After a few minutes, hunger and thirst gave out, and she helped herself. The soft butter melted into the piping hot bread, and she took as large a bite as she could without hurting her jaw, given the burns. But she was so hungry and thirsty that the pain of chewing and swallowing was a pittance to pay for the sheer joy of eating and drinking.

"A little better now?" asked Fate, again smiling brightly. He then let the smile fade and turned serious. "You have suffered."

"Yes." It was all she could say at first. After a moment, she added, "I hope it is worth it."

"Hmmm. You have regret."

"Look at me. How should I feel?" She put the cheese and thick bread down. "I am scarred forever."

"You are scarred, that is true. But would you choose a different path if you knew this was to be your fate, pardon the pun?"

Kari hesitated only a moment. "Probably. Most certainly. I don't feel like a True Mage—I don't know how this is supposed to work. But I don't feel any different magically. Physically, I'm dramatically different. I'm a monster. How can I answer that question if I don't know what I've gained?" As she ate and drank, she could feel her energy level beginning to rise. Her injuries, however, were unaffected.

Fate stood up and smiled. "Well, normally, I just give you a simple blessing, your eyes are whitened, and you walk out that door right there—" He pointed to an oaken door in the closest wall. "—which will lead you back to your entrance to the Staircase." He again let his smile fade, and turned serious in a way that was jarring. "However, that isn't going to be your transition."

"My transition?" Kari looked up at Fate as he suddenly stood.

"Your transition will be done by God Herself—Dymetra. When you are ready, She has told me to bring you to Her." He looked at Kari soberly. "So eat. Drink. They will give you your strength back. We need to leave soon." He gestured instead to a door behind his throne. "Through there."

Her throat suddenly dry, Kari nearly choked. "Dymetra? Meet Her?" *This must be some kind of dream.*

"This is no dream, Kari. Your thoughts play out in my mind long before you even have them. I assure you, She is quite real. But you already know that—you have sought her, worshipped Her, prayed to Her. Now, you will meet Her. Come, the way is not far—can you walk without difficulty now?" He sprung out of his chair with an energy that belied his somber tone.

"Yes—I'll manage." She looked at Fate and slowly stood up. *I do feel stronger...that was some kind of bread and berries!* "Why does She want to see me?"

"I don't know, Kari. She's never asked to meet anyone else who has successfully Climbed before. You, however, She wishes to meet, and so meet we shall." He turned around at the doorway and shrugged his shoulders. "Her world, Her rules."

Her world, Her rules. Very well, if this is all a trick, at least my head has cleared—I can probably cast something useful. "Lead the way."

Without so much as reaching for the handle, Fate waved his hand, and the door swung outward this time. He nodded at Kari, and again at the opening as if to say 'you first.'

Kari stepped lightly behind the throne and cautiously through the door…and onto a long, winding stone path. Smooth stones of all different shapes and sizes formed the road, with rolling hills dotted with pastel-colored wildflowers on either side. Far, far off into the distance were majestic, snow-capped mountains that must have been truly immense up close.

Immediately, an overwhelming sense of peace flooded her senses the moment her feet hit the path. She was so immersed in the flooding of her own senses that it took a few seconds to register a person approaching along the intricate stone walkway. Then he broke into a run toward her.

"Hello Kari!" shouted Kyle Quinlan, her brother, as he came up to her, threatening a bear hug.

~Veronica~

Large balls of blue smoke glowed eerily in the dim lighting of the small but comfortable room. Silverfist puffed away at his short-stem pipe while swirling a glass of wine in his other hand.

"Master," said Veronica. "You recognized me."

"The moment I saw you. It is a good disguise, but imperfect. It helps knowing what you look like as a young woman, of course. But even with a body as athletic as yours—there are signs, Veronica. Tell-tale signs." He smiled mischievously as he took a sip of wine. "You would do well to stick to female disguises."

"I see," Veronica acknowledged without even a hint of embarrassment. She changed the subject. "What are you doing here, Master? I must admit, I am glad to see you. I would like your advice on something."

The half-elf took a long pull on his pipe, causing the red embers in the bowl to flare briefly in the corner of her dark room. He still looked the same, nearly timeless, with his chiseled frame, dark skin and hair only mildly peppered with grey after a hundred years. He had the gift of long life that all Elfs enjoyed. He seemed to be thinking about something before answering. He finally said, "I am headed to Rookwood."

"Rookwood? What in all of Tenebrae does our Guild have to do there?" asked Veronica.

"Word has been sent that the Queen wanted to see me. I've been travelling for some time, using the opportunity to reconnect with some Guild members in the field, and old friends. I will be leaving Paragatha shortly to meet with the Queen before the week is done. Shall I give her your regards?" he asked with a chuckle.

"I don't see how this is funny. The woman would try and kill me on sight." Veronica finally sipped the wine Silas had brought her and hid her grimace. *Too sweet.*

"Yes, your exploits in the capital have travelled far and wide, my dear. Though if she has put a price on your head, it is not through the Guild. We frown on such contracts anyhow, as you know. But every Assassin has their price…" He trailed off wistfully, and narrowed his already almond-shaped eyes. "But you seek advice. It is by grand happenstance that we should run into one another in the whole land of Elvidor, so by all means—what troubles you?"

"In a minute. What does the Queen want with you?" snapped Veronica.

"I don't know. Could be anything. But I have my suspicions." He took long sip of wine. "Not as good as the western grapes, I daresay."

"What suspicions?"

Silverfist took the pipe out of his mouth. "Veronica, what does anyone want with the head of the Black Guild? Think for a minute, and draw your own conclusions. I'll not speculate here."

The Queen wants someone dead. Maybe me. Maybe Xaro. Maybe Silverfist himself for training me.

"Very well. Enjoy your chat with that ugly woman. My question is this: I have accepted a contract from Xaro to find an object for him, but I have also accepted a contract from…his enemy to find a different object that Xaro *also* covets. I am not sure I will be able to fulfill both contracts."

Silverfist put his wine glass down, stood up and walked slowly over to Veronica with a warm smile. After a few quick puffs to help him think, he took the pipe out of his mouth and sighed. Then he slapped Veronica clear across the face.

"Ow!" she exclaimed, falling over onto the bed. "Master!"

"You foolish twit. What are you doing taking contracts to find this or that in the first place? What Guild do you belong to?" he said in a hoarse—but loud—whisper before jamming the pipe back in his mouth.

Veronica rubbed her cheek. "The Black Guild."

"What are you?" he asked, leaning over her with the pipe firmly clenched in his teeth.

"An Assassin."

"A *True* Assassin. A *Master* Assassin," Silver corrected. "You were the top performer coming out of your apprenticeship. A gifted killer. Where is the woman who killed babies to save them from the misery of life? Where is the woman who crept into one of the largest libraries in Elvidor and slit a Ranger's throat *right in front of two adult mages* without even being seen? You remember your Selectivity Test—the final test that earned you the coveted contract with Xaro? And now look at you: Known throughout the land for a botched attempt on a General, forced to travel—quite literally—in a poor man's disguise, taking contracts to serve as little more than a common Thief or worse—as some poor excuse for a Ranger. Remember who you are, Veronica. You're better than that. You are a talented, remorseless killer. An ender of life."

Veronica blinked. *An ender of life. That is what I am.* "Yes, of course. You are right, Master. So I shouldn't have taken either contract?"

Silver puffed a few times with a "hmph" before he sat back down. "What's done is done. You have taken the contracts. I trust they are both good gold?"

"They are, Master. Fifty thousand for one, ten thousand for the other." She got up from the bed and sat back down in chair, still rubbing her stinging cheek.

"Oh ho. That is…lucrative." Silverfist finished his wine. "If you cannot honor them both, then you keep the larger one, of course."

"But that's the problem, Master. I can't break the second one, not easily. It is with…Magi. Magi Blacksmooth. Perhaps you've heard—"

"Good God, Veronica! You took a contract with the man you killed? Of course I've heard of Magi—the whole continent has. Your brethren in the Guild call him the Death Cheater. They say he cannot be killed. I hear the stories, Veronica, the Guild's reach is vast. For blood and bone, why would you take a contract with him, *especially* since your principal benefactor is a man bent upon war against him and his allies?"

"I should ask you the same question, Silver. Why do business with a Queen while I do business with an agent of her foe?" Veronica narrowed her own eyes this time.

Silver shook his head. "You naive, simple woman. The Guild is in the business of profiting from death. War is good for business. Unbelievably good. Think for a minute before you embarrass yourself again. We have agents working at cross-purposes all over the realm. Wherever there is greed, or lust, or hatred—you will find us. In other words: everywhere. It is a Dark World, Veronica. And we are in the business of profiting from such darkness.

"Your situation is different. It is one thing for the Guild to make money playing both sides; it is quite another for a single Assassin to do so. This is no lover's quarrel or a simple land feud between petulant nobles. Playing both sides in such affairs might make for a bit of sport, but not this. You are now engaged in political maneuvering and assassination attempts at the highest of levels, and have set yourself up to be an agent of both sides. You foolish, foolish woman. So young. Remember that the only rule—*the only one that truly matters*—is this: live to take another contract. The Black Guild are not mercenaries, we're not heroes, and we're not interested in suicide missions. We're contract killers, pure and simple." He stood up and walked toward the door, a plume of blue smoke trailing behind him.

"Where are you going? What would you do?" Veronica asked, standing and putting her hand on him as he walked past.

He stopped and turned to her. "I'm going for more wine and to clear my head of this entire mess. As for what I'd do, I see only one alternative that ends well for you. You must kill either Xaro or Magi."

He removed her hand from his shoulder. "At least you know you can. After all, you've done it once before. It's the only thing you've ever been good at."

~Kari~

"Kyle!" screamed Kari as she instinctively extended her arms. There wasn't any pain. She looked at her left shoulder and arm. They were still heavily scarred and blackened…but no longer in pain. She hugged her brother unabashedly, though he was far more tender with her. "You look—different."

Kyle gently pulled himself away from his sister to look directly at her face. He wore a sad smile. "I could say the same to you, Sis." He held her disfigured left hand in his right and placed his own left hand lightly on top of it. "Come with me."

"Ah—awkward reunions. They never get old." Fate mumbled behind Kari.

She had forgotten he was even standing there, she was so caught up in seeing her brother. She turned around. "Where are we?"

"Home. Paradise. Heaven. The Unblemished Realm. It has many names, but the best way to think about it is Home. You're Home."

"I don't have a home—not really, at least. Our parents live in Fostler, and Marik's school had been home for so many years...that seems like a lifetime ago." She turned to her brother. "So I died?"

Kyle didn't answer immediately. He looked up at Fate, who was shaking his head and rolling his eyes as he walked past them. "Kari, I told you. Dymetra asked to see you personally to transition you to True Mage status. It is an honor beyond words that She wishes to speak to you in person. You are not dead. You're a bit—wounded—but hopefully your increased power will help offset your physical presence."

He looked over to Kyle. "As for your brother—he is transformed into his ageless form, like me. When you saw him last, he was an 18-year-old boy. He looks different to you because he probably appears older, maybe 30 or so in your years. That is what you see as different in him. Now then," he said, somewhat impatiently, with his hands on his hips, "if there are no more immediate questions that need answering, may we continue on for a bit?"

Kari looked at the queer man standing there, his hat tilted to one side, with the little yellow feather poking out. For what seemed like the first time in an eon, she couldn't help but laugh. "By all means. Lead the way."

Kyle fell into step next to her, with Fate a few steps ahead. Kari was staring down at the way the stones all fit together beneath her feet. "It's like they're designed as a puzzle to fit together," she mused out loud, breaking a few moments of silence as they walked.

"It does. I could stare at the stones forever and not find two exactly the same, and yet they fit perfectly. You forget how mesmerizing they are until someone new discovers the path for the first time." Kyle looked over to Kari. "It is so good to see you, Sis. I'm proud of you."

"Proud of me? Look at me, Kyle. I'm a monster. Look at where my choices have brought me! I should have stayed in Rookwood, or in Dariez, or stayed anywhere. I wasn't—I wasn't ready for this." She could walk without pain, but she kept self-consciously reaching up to touch the left side of her head and face, where half her hair was burned away, leaving only charred, naked scalp.

"Proud of who you are, not what you look like." He changed the subject. "How's Magi doing?"

"Fine, I guess. He said he talked to you when he…died." *The only pain he has to show for his trials is a thin scar below his neck. And white eyes—he does have those.* Her mind was dominated by thoughts of her appearance.

"He did. I forgave him, Kari—he was not himself, as I'm sure he told you. He did come away from the whole ordeal with a different perspective, I'm sure. One might even say wisdom." Kyle smiled.

"And one heckuva Staff," said Fate, clearly eavesdropping.

Kari shrugged and looked ahead. "I see a house."

As the stone path meandered up a small hill, she indeed saw a home not far in the distance, near a fast flowing stream that probably cut its way down from the mountains. The path led to a short bridge that arched over the swift water, leading on the other side to the gates. Beyond the house stretched a thick forest that seemed endless. A canopy of dark green ran from behind this simple home to the base of the grey mountains. There were no other dwellings anywhere that she could see from the crest of the hilltop.

"Almost there!" said Fate, as he nearly skipped down the back of the hill toward the house. "Come on!"

A warm breeze carried the scent of hundreds of wildflowers and playfully blew back what was left of Kari's hair. It was the first time she registered the pleasant temperature; it seemed forever since she had left the grip of winter at the bottom of the Staircase.

As they hustled down the path toward the bridge and home behind it, Kari slowed her step slightly. "Kyle," she said. "What's She like? Dymetra?"

Kyle stopped. "You know Her better than I do, Kari. I don't know—She's…God. Knows all, sees all. Nothing is unclear to Her. Nothing is impossible for Her. She is fair, but…"

"But what?" she pressed.

"I would just say that Her definition of what is good or right or fair does not always square with those stuck in Tenebrae. Then again, I imagine I would think differently, too, if everything occurred to me in the present tense. Time has no effect on Her, or on us here, for that matter. Everything past and future is essentially the present for Her." He started walking again. "Fifty or sixty years may matter to you, I know. To Her, it's a moment…it's, er…now."

"We're here," announced Fate. He took in a deep breath, standing in front of the beautiful marble door, waiting for Kari and Kyle to catch up. When they did, he looked over at her and winked.

"Ready?" Without waiting for an answer, he pushed the door open, which silently swung inward.

I am now. With what little strength she'd regained, Kari created a simple *Illusion* of her former self, hiding her injuries, and followed him inside.

~Veronica~

"*Fennatulum,*" Veronica said, seated alone in her smoky room that smelled like fine tobacco with a hint of cloves. It was the one incantation she could use to initiate a discussion with Xaro, half a world away. The magic came from Xaro; the word was simply charmed to let him know that Veronica wanted to speak. Fortunately, he was available at this hour.

"Your timing is excellent, my dear. I was planning on calling a full meeting of my council soon, but it is well that you and I should speak first in private. We have much to discuss. Given that you saw fit to reach out in the wee hours of your night, I imagine I should let you proceed first." Xaro inclined his head slightly. "By the way—your disguise is terrible. What has happened since we last spoke?"

"Master, I apologize for my appearance and the hour of my contact—it has been a long week since I escaped Rookwood, and I do not have much time. I have been captured, essentially, by Magi. He asks that I lead him to the ring." Veronica went to sip her glass of wine, only to find it empty from her previous conversation. *Probably a short pour from that weasel. It was too sweet anyhow.*

"Captured? Is he there with you?" Xaro asked.

"No Master, he is praying. But he will be back at first light. I could leave now, but frankly I do not like my chances of escaping. It is mostly rolling hills, farms, and sparse woods from Paragatha to the mountains if I head west. East will take me to the sea. North, and I follow the main road. South puts me into Lake Calm and back into Elfen lands. He tracks like a Ranger, and can cover distance with ease. It will be difficult to throw him off my trail, and furthermore, it is unlikely I would win a direct confrontation, either." Veronica opened her hands. "I reached out because I—don't know what to do."

"I told you killing a True Mage would be much more difficult once he is on guard for it." Xaro stood up suddenly, rubbing his chin. "And what did you say he was doing? Praying?"

"He mentioned he was going to find a temple, yes."

"Hmm. Interesting." Xaro did not look pleased. *At all.*

"If I can't kill him and can't escape, then I fear I'm going to have to deliver him to you. It will delay your assignment for me—I can't make for the far west coast of Ipidine and also the shores of Adimand without losing many weeks at sea, Master."

Xaro narrowed his eyes. "Tell me, Assassin. You told me he knows that I am based here at Sands End. He thinks you can lead him to the person with his old ring. Well, I have an update for you: Trevor is dead. The same charm that allows you to request a meeting also binds me to your life force, as it does with all members of my small council. I knew immediately when Marik was dead. As I now know that Trevor is dead. I have asked Tar-Tan to sail out to where the ship was last located, to find what may have happened. Perhaps they were shipwrecked. Perhaps that fool of a Thief stumbled overboard in a drunken stupor. I do not know, but he was carrying very precious cargo to me."

"The ring and the jewel."

"Yes, the ring and the Purple Sun jewel," echoed Xaro. "My point in sharing this with you is simply this. If you tell Magi that you no longer know who has the ring, it will be true. And if you tell him that you have no idea how to find it, that will also be true. And if your value to him is thereby reduced, perhaps he will approach me without you. Or he may try and kill you—but I doubt it. That doesn't seem to fit with the new incarnation of Magi that you have described. In any event, we will be ready at Sands End. It is possible that he may just let you go, allowing you to proceed with haste on your real contract for the Shield of Life, somewhere in Adimand."

"It is worth a try, my Master," said Veronica, cocking her head to one side. She looked up with a crooked half-smile. "You are most wise when it comes to this kind of thing."

"Perhaps. Only logical. He will travel much faster without you. As I said, we shall make arrangements for our…guest." Xaro tented his hands. "Like our other conversation—this update stays between the two of us. Are we clear?"

"Yes, Master." Veronica knelt. "I will let you know as soon as I am able whether I have found a way to escape."

"See that you do, Veronica," finished Xaro. "And one last thing: fix your disguise—you look neither like a man nor a woman, just some sort of disheveled, thin figure. Whatever the opposite of blending in is, that is how you look." The shimmering image of Xaro wrinkled its nose and faded away.

Veronica yawned. Maybe, just maybe, in this case the truth would indeed set her free.

CHAPTER SEVEN: THE JUDGEMENTS WE MAKE

~Kari~

From the outside, Kari thought it would be about as large as Marik's school, or perhaps one of the floors in the Tower of Dariez. Stepping inside, however, changed her perspective.

The house was *immense*. Rooms upon rooms sprawled like shops on a busy city block. They all seemed to branch out, however, from a long, wide hallway framed with white-and-gray marble columns supporting a vaulted ceiling far higher than the roof appeared outside. Whether the exterior was an *Illusion* or the inside was, Kari couldn't fathom. Maybe they both were. But they sure didn't match.

She saw many people milling about, walking from one room to another, carrying scrolls and books and plates of food. *Something is odd.* She couldn't quite put her finger on it. There was much laughter and hugging, even some guffawing between two young couples.

Between two young couples... then she recognized what was strange. There were no old people. And there were no children. Everyone looked like her brother Kyle; young, healthy, and thirty-ish.

"Fate, everyone here is the same age." Kari stared at several people, not quite sure what to do when they saw her staring and waved. She feebly waved back.

"Yes. As I told you earlier, everyone here is fixed at that age, and time no longer works against you. Not such a bad gift, huh?" Fate took his hat off with a flourish, waving it around in all directions.

Kari kept walking, but Fate blocked her path with his arm. "Your *Illusion*—is pointless. No need for that here. Everyone can see through it; you might as well save your strength, Kari. Rather silly of you to think that your skills are such that you could hide your appearance from God. If you can't hide your thoughts and motives, how do you hope to hide your physical appearance?"

Hmm. And I thought this was one of my better Illusions. "Perhaps, but I would prefer not show myself in such a wretched state to Dymetra. I haven't—I just...I'm too vain, Fate. And embarrassed. That is the truth."

Fate sighed softly. "As you wish. Straight ahead to Her throne." He placed the hat back on his head and skipped forward.

The hallway stretched ahead of her for quite some time, always with what seemed to be endless rooms and sitting areas branching off. Soon a large, white throne on a raised dais was visible in the distance.

Kari felt Her long before she could see Her. The raw, unbounded *power* from the white throne left the Mage gasping for breath. She fell to her knees before they were even close, and threw her hands over her head. The *Illusion* surrounding her crumbled like a fistful of clenched, dry dirt. Her left side was horribly burned and scarred once again.

All Kari could think about was leaving. She did not belong here, did not want to be here. The overwhelming sense of *smallness* she felt was crushing. She had a better chance of counting every drop of water in all the seas than of looking this woman in the eye. It seemed like every bad thought she'd ever had—indeed, every memory of every wrong thing she'd said or done or considered was now flashing through her mind. All her motives, selfish or otherwise, were laid bare. Kari started to shake uncontrollably.

"Welcome, Kari Quinlan. Stand up, and be at ease." Her voice seemed to come from everywhere and right in front of her at once.

Kari forced herself to uncover her head and picked her head up only slightly, her eyes still firmly fixed on the carpet below. Dymetra had stepped down from the throne and was now right before her. Eyes still looking largely on the floor, Kari could make out the blinding light from her feet. "M—my G—god!" she rasped hoarsely.

"Arise, and rest." While a hint of softness lingered in Her voice, it was still too intimidating for Kari. She tried to speak, but only stuttered gibberish.

A strong hand on either arm gently lifted her to her feet. One belonged to her brother. The other was a kind-looking stranger. She turned her face away from Dymetra and mumbled "thank you" to both men. Her brother smiled gently and stayed close by, his arm around her for support.

"Would you like something to drink? Some lemon sweetwater, perhaps?" Dymetra asked.

She is speaking to me! "N-no. I'm okay. Thank you." She closed her eyes and shook her head. "I mean, yes. Please—that sounds wonderful."

A glass of a nearly clear liquid was brought to her, and the very smell of it seemed to clear her head even as it dazzled her senses. Crisp, bright, and tart—it was the most vivid tasting glass of lemon sweetwater Kari had ever indulged in. She blinked and felt more alert, less wobbly. "Thank you, my God." She bowed her head in silence. She still could not bear to look directly at Her.

Dymetra then spoke, her words filling the room. "Kari Quinlan, you have successfully Climbed. I wanted to see you. You sought Me after your prophesy. You searched for Me in the ancient Tower of Dariez, where My True Clerics were fond of gathering., then you left." Then after a slight pause: "I want you to tell Me truly why you left My Tower to pursue the life of an Illusionist."

Kari kept her head bowed, and cupped the glass of lemon sweetwater to keep it from shaking. *I can't possibly lie to God.* Instead of the glass trembling in her hands, she started shaking her head back and forth. Tears welled up in her eyes. *The shame...* "You already know," she mumbled, so softly that only Kari herself could hear it. Hearing no response, she let the tears spill over down her right cheek from her one good eye.

"Jealousy," she said, her voice a bit stronger now. "I was jealous of Strongiron. I thought I was the chosen one, yet all of the attention was being paid to him. I was restless and impatient, but mostly jealous. I wanted to be special more than I wanted to worship You…and my pride has cost me my face. Perhaps it is what I deserve. Forgive me, Dymetra. I should have stayed and learned and..." Her eyes were still downcast, as if not looking at Her could somehow hold the immensity of Her presence at bay.

"And?"

"And I could have grown closer to him, as well. He is a good man."

"To your standard, perhaps he is, but we are here to discuss you, and your motivations. You have spoken the truth of your heart, and I do forgive you, Kari. But that is not why I summoned Fate to bring you here. I summoned you here to offer you a gift. Ask Me for the singular desire of your heart, and I shall grant it to you, Kari. As one who put their faith in Me before I was shown to you, it is My pleasure to do this for you."

There were murmurs in the throne room. Kari looked around and saw all the thirty-year-old faces staring back at her expectantly. *Dymetra. Is. Granting. Me. A. Wish.*

She saw a young man that reminded her of Magi, and another that resembled Strongiron. She also could have sworn that one man who was looking at her was the former King Alomar, based on an old painting she once saw in Rookwood. She turned to her brother, who was smiling so wide he looked almost silly. He mouthed to her: *Go on! You know what you want! Be healed!*

She instinctively put her hand to her head and felt the flaky skin on her scalp. She held the back of her two hands up in front of her face next to one another. One blackened, raw, and scarred. The other soft, olive-skinned, flawless. Her mind was made up.

"My God," began Kari. "I don't deserve such a gift. Many on Tenebrae deserve your favor more than I."

"Do not presume to lecture Me about who is worthy and who is not, child," Dymetra interrupted. "My gifts are My own to give, for My own purposes."

Kari took a sip of her water and swallowed hard. "Yes, my God. I—" She paused and knelt low, bowing her head further. "Forgive me. I do not wish to turn my back on your gift." She took a very deep breath to steady herself. "If I may have the one desire of my heart, then I would ask for this: raise my brother from his untimely death, and let him rejoin the living on Tenebrae."

"Kari—" began Kyle.

"That is what I want most." Kari snapped before he could say another word, rising and turning toward him. "I miss my brother. I miss *you*." She turned back toward Dymetra, finally forcing herself to look up at her God's face directly. "I know You can do this, if it is Your will. I've seen You raise others."

She could not focus on Dymetra's face for very long. It was light and energy and timeless. She looked human, with long golden hair. No—an instant later it was short, and dark. Her tan complexion grew darker also—black like an islander—before turning paler once again.

After a few scant seconds, Kari dropped her face. It was too much. She could hear Her voice, could feel Her presence. But Kari could no more see Her appearance as she could hug Her. *She looks like everyone, but no one looks like Her.*

"Kari Quinlan." Dymetra spoke. "Your brother is well-loved. You are not the first to pray for his life."

Kari fell again to her knees again. She was truly terrified by the power standing over her. *Please, Dymetra. Heal him, not me. I left you.*

"Stand, Kari. For you, I will grant this request. He will return with you." Dymetra extended her arms wide. "Because you put your faith in Me when most choose to worship all manner of nonsense, I shall do one more thing. You speak of My will—here it is: that you shall return to Tenebrae not only a True Mage, but as My Priestess. You shall be a True Cleric, Kari, and I task you with helping bring hope, light, truth, and grace to your world. All True Clerics have shown the Faith necessary to bring someone back from My home in the land of the living to your home in the land of the dying. Kyle shall resume his life on Tenebrae with the rest of those who are dying."

She turned to Kyle. "My will is for you, Kyle, to seek out Elsa, whom you call the Ol' Shakoor. She prays for help and companionship, as she suffers alone with her blindness. May you be a comfort to her, Kyle. You will learn much from her."

Kyle looked stunned. He bowed low and said, "It would be my pleasure, my God. Thank You for Your gift."

"Your knowledge of My home will help many Mages who seek a glimpse of their future through prophesy. It is a gift for you, for your sister, and for Elsa. But mainly it is a gift to Tenebrae."

I am a True Cleric. Kari struggled to digest that. "My God, I thought my chance of being a True Cleric had passed. I chose magic back at the Tower. I don't know what to say."

At this, Dymetra laughed. It was not a sound that filled her heart with joy. Again, she felt small and terrified.

"My dear. Do you think it so easy to pluck yourself from My hand? I chose you long before you chose Me, long before you or your brother were even born. You *shall* be My Cleric, using all your skills to heal, to educate, and to spread the picture of hope to your realm."

"Thank you, Dymetra. It is more than I could have asked for." She was getting anxious, and looked over at her brother, who was scanning the room. Perhaps he was looking for someone, or a door. Kari was exhausted, feeling meek, small, and utterly overwhelmed by Her presence. "Is it time we leave, my God?"

"There is one more thing, Kari." Dymetra pointed a shimmering finger at Kari. "My Cleric must be approachable. The white eyes of a True Mage are meant to warn people to stay away, knowing the great power and advantage that they possess. My Clerics must do the opposite: draw people toward them—to Me. Therefore, be healed, Kari, and return to Tenebrae with the eyes that I first gave you. Let all you meet learn of My grace, for I am the only hope of your realm."

The room suddenly erupted with dozens and dozens of joyful shouts, surprised musings, and even a song. Tears of unbridled gratitude slid down her cheeks—both of them—as she watched her left arm transform once again into the picture of health. She reached back and felt her hair as it grew and thickened into the fullness it once had before she began her Climb.

She was then engulfed in a bear hug by her brother, but soon others joined in, surrounding her, hugging her, crying with her, laughing and praising Dymetra. They were all strangers, and yet it didn't feel strange at all. She shouted "Thank You!" over and over again, but she knew she could not possibly be heard.

As if in response, Her voice came into Kari's mind. *It is My pleasure to give you these gifts, Kari. Use them well, and remember that you are My True Cleric. As long as your faith runs true, you will find Me running alongside you. Go now…your work is only beginning.*

The ring of people around her began to part, and then she saw the blue outline of a door next to a window that she noticed for the first time. It was an enormous, circular window, and as she approached, she saw a silver river, similar to the metallic-looking water that cascaded over the mountain falls at the Tower of Dariez. The sun seemed to be hitting the water just right, for several rainbows almost seemed to bloom like flowers in the air over the river. All she could do was suck in her breath.

"Come on, sis," said Kyle. "I don't think this door leads out there." He grinned and pulled open the portal. Sighing, Kari tore herself away from the landscape and peeked through the open doorway. She groaned… *Stairs.*

At least these are leading down.

~Veronica~

The first pink and orange hues of dawn began to glow along the eastern rim of the horizon. The ash from the fire pits in the common room still glowed from the previous evening's crowd. A few guests were face down on the tables, goblets resting askew against the side of their heads. One rather large warrior snored loudly on the floor near one of the three hearths.

Veronica sat at the cleanest table she could find, taking the liberty to re-light one of the pits to warm the chair next to it. She knew full well that Silas and his staff would be doing well to show up three hours from now, let alone at dawn. As far as she could tell, she was the only one awake in the common room. She quietly hung a small pot of water over the fire, and after it had boiled, poured herself a cup of incredibly strong and bitter tea.

"Sleep well?" asked a voice behind her. Magi sat down next to her. "Enough for two?" he asked.

Unstartled, Veronica sat there placidly. "I didn't see you come in. Help yourself, Mage." She sipped her tea, wrinkling her nose. "And I slept fine."

Magi rested his staff across his chair and stared directly at Veronica, cocking his head. He finally broke the awkward pause and said, "Good. Let us finish and head out then. It feels a little warmer, like a clear day is coming. Good day to travel." He sipped the tea and raised an eyebrow. "Well, this should keep us up." He gulped the steaming liquid down like it was nothing harsher than warm milk, the grimace on his face the only giveaway.

Magi then stood and grabbed his staff and travelling supplies. He looked at Veronica. "You fixed yourself up a bit, I see. Ready?"

"If I must. I was hoping to finish my tea a bit more leisurely, if it's all the same to you. We have a long journey ahead; surely a few more minutes by the fire here isn't too much of a delay? Besides, I have news for you." Veronica raised her mug, peeking over top of it while she sipped her tea. *Bracing bitter and piping hot...if this doesn't wake me up, nothing will.*

Magi sat back down. "Do share."

"I have been in touch with my Master. The ring is lost, Magi. I do not know who has it or where it is. I did know before, but that person has, apparently, died." She paused and shifted her eyes to his staff. "You know what I'm telling you is true."

"At least you believe it to be true, yes." Magi reached for the tea but stopped himself, turning toward her. "And?"

"So I am letting you out of our contract, Magi. I can't help you."

"That I'm not so sure about."

"What do you mean? I just told you I don't know where the ring is. It could be at the bottom of the sea! What purpose can I possible serve as you guide? You know where Sands End is. If you truly wish to confront Xaro, then go! You can travel a hundred times faster without me than with me. In a word, you can be across the mountains and walking along the port of Gaust before I finish my tea. Sail for Ipidine if you wish, but why delay by walking with me in tow?" Veronica didn't remember standing up, but she found herself looking down at Magi, whisper-shouting at him.

Curiously, Magi just sat there with a casual smile on his face. "Our contract still stands. You will accompany me, you will not kill anyone, and you will continue to gain 'news' of Xaro's plans and updates on information he may get that pertain to *my* ring. I can suffer the delay if it keeps you preoccupied with something other than murder and keeps me supplied with information. Consider it a blessing that you should steal a ring and then be paid to help recover it."

Veronica sat back down. *Will I never be free from this spell thrower?* She shook her head. "Xaro knows you have this staff. He knows you have me as a prisoner. He will not tell me a thing from this point forward as long as I am with you. You are wasting your gold and your time."

"Like I said—both are mine to waste. And if it ends your killing spree, then I hardly count it a waste." Magi did not, however, deny her accusations of being his prisoner.

"Then why not kill me? Repay me for what I did to you, save your gold, and be about your way. This forced march you are taking me on does you no good!" Veronica finished her tea with one last, bitter swig, looking like she had just swallowed boiled ashes. Straightening her face, she softened her tone. "Magi—I cannot help you. I am a life-ender. It is who I am."

"I think you can help me, Veronica," Magi whispered as he leaned forward. "And I have not given up hope on you. At least not quite yet. Dymetra made you a girl on a farm; the world made you a life-ender." He stood up. "Come. Let's get going. Since you seem so concerned about slowing me down, we'll procure some horses here before we depart; that will speed up our travel west quite a bit." He flashed her one quick, sarcastic glance and turned around to head out the door.

But I like how the world made me. It's what I'm good at. Effortlessly, she pulled the poison dart out of its small stopper where the tip stayed coated in the strongest poison Veronica had ever been able to brew. Magi had his back to her about ten feet away, walking toward the door when she let it fly.

Thunk. The dart should have been buried about two inches into Magi's neck. Her aim, like usual, was flawless.

But a puny dart was no match for the *Shield* spell Magi was apparently surrounded by, given that the dart struck an invisible barrier tight around his body and clattered to the floor, scattering a few droplets of poison.

Time seemed to slow down as Magi turned around to look at the dart and Veronica's outstretched hand, still in midair from the throw. "Though disappointed, I can't say I'm surprised."

He strode toward Veronica, covering the distance swiftly. She was terrified. "Did you think I was foolish enough to let my guard down around you? Know this, Assassin. You *will* accompany me. You *will* get useful information for me. And you *will NOT* try to kill me or escape again. I know you view death as a release. That release will not be granted to you, I promise you that. If you try to kill me or escape—even just one more time—know that I will be your judge and jury alone on the long path west. I think we both understand that parading you back in front of our Queen or one of her city Lords will be a waste of time. And your punishment will be something of a lifetime achievement award for Lionel, Sindar, my father, and your repeated attempts on Strongiron and me. I want to believe there is hope even for someone like you, but even my patience has limits."

Magi put his face up close to Veronica's, close enough for a kiss, but instead he clenched his teeth and balled his fists, whispering, "There are many things in life far worse than death, Veronica. Far worse." He grabbed her arm and yanked her up out of the chair. "Let's go."

Digging her heel in before she was paraded away, Veronica looked at Magi defiantly, "What right do you have to judge me?"

Magi cocked his head, squeezing her wrist ever-so-slightly tighter. "I don't. But I will…and that is all the more reason for you to heed my warning."

Eyes wide, Veronica left with Magi, her head looking around the common room one last time to see if anyone was awake. No one was.

~Kari~

Pushing gently on the door at the bottom of the circular stairwell, Kari emerged from the Staircase to find herself back in Belara's drawing room. She emerged just as Belara was turning around, still dressed in her skin-tight silvery gown. Kari could see the disappointment on Belara's face immediately as they made eye contact.

"That didn't take long. I am sorry, Kari. Perhaps we rushed it?" The True Mage was walking toward Kari casually. "Are you injured?" She looked sincere in her concern, but also preoccupied.

Kari walked through the door to make room for Kyle to follow behind her. "I'm fine, Mistress. More than fine, actually. Do you remember my brother Kyle?"

Belara stopped dead in her tracks. She paused for a second, maybe two, in silence, before chanting a simple anti-*Illusion* spell to unravel false realities. Nothing changed, other than the door to the Staircase fading away to leave a clean wall. She frowned and narrowed her eyes into tiny upside-down crescent moons. "What is going on here, Kari? Of course I remember Kyle. I was there when he was killed." She slowly walked over to Kyle and put her hand over his chest as if he was a statue. She lowered her voice. "Here. The *Magic Missile* tore through him...right...here." She finally looked at Kyle's face but then turned to address Kari. "One went up, and two return. Explain."

Kyle lifted his shirt. There was a circular scar, but it looked faded. "It's me, Belara. I was a guest at Rookwood before Magi...before I died." He turned to Kari. "Let her know that this is no *Illusion*."

Kari smiled. "You prepared me well, Mistress. I *did* make it to the top—I am a True Mage. But I am also a True Cleric. Belara...and I have much to tell you. I've seen God! Everything the old stories say about a True God—everything that I believed when I first heard my prophesy, when I first sought her in Urthrax—it is all true, Belara! All of it! I have never been around such power in my life—Fate took me to her at the top of the Staircase."

"Fate did that?" Belara looked at her incredulously. "Your eyes tell another story."

Kari shook her head gently, placing both her fists over her heart. "I know. It was a gift, Belara. An unbelievable, undeserved gift. But that pales in comparison to Her real blessing. Dymetra answered my prayer to return Kyle to life! I was injured—badly burned. She healed me, Belara. That was when She also allowed me to keep my eyes, too. Just like the Ol' Shakoor."

Belara's own eyes started to twitch ever so slightly. "That's impossible. No one is granted such a privilege. I do not believe you." She backed up. "If you are a True Mage, then *Teleport* into the hallway and come through the real door."

Kari looked over at Kyle. *He looks 17 again—like the day he died.* She searched his face, trying to communicate without words the way siblings sometimes can. In this case, he just smiled and tilted his head toward the door, as if to say *get used to it. You may have more people to convince.*

Kari looked back at Belara and nodded. "As you wish." And then she was gone. Her first *Teleport. The power!* It is an intense surge of energy, *Teleportation.* The making of one's being into nothingness and reforming it in a familiar place requires a significant amount of energy, more than some of her most complex *Illusions.* Electrifying and draining at the same time, yet she didn't have much time to contemplate the sensation. An instant later she was out in the hallway of the castle, and knocked on the heavy, arched wooden door that formed the entrance to Belara's personal chambers.

Belara swung it open, her mouth agape. "But your eyes. *Your eyes!* How did you keep them? Tell me! What spell craft is this? What deal did you make?"

Kari smiled gently. "As I said…there was no deal, Belara. It is a gift, more so in my role as a True Cleric. The white eyes can be…off-putting." She lifted her shoulders a bit guiltily. "She said a True Cleric should be approachable."

"Off-putting? Yes, of course they are off-putting! That is the point. It is a warning—no True Mage should be allowed to conduct their affairs without warning others of their nature. This is— unnatural, Kari." Belara was trying not to curl her lip into a sneer, but it wasn't working.

Kari approached her mentor. "You say 'unnatural'. Perhaps 'unexpected' is closer to the mark. It is a gift—"

Belara interrupted with a wave of her hand, crafting her *Illusion*. The image of Kyle lying in the Great Hall filled the hallway in which they both now stood. His body lay in a massive blood pool, a gaping hole in his chest, right in front of them like they were standing in that room on that very day.

"No, Kari, unnatural is the *perfect* word," she said. "This man, if it is indeed Kyle, is the most *unnatural* thing I've seen. I don't know by what *Illusion* you are keeping your eyes green, but I thought you might at least share the spell with me, given what I have taught you. Get out, and take your brother or this creature or this *Illusion*— whatever trickery this may be—away from my chambers as well."

"You saw Magi return from the dead. The same God, Dymetra, granted Kyle life."

"I never saw Magi die. If he wants to tell stories of ancient gods and show up with a neck scar to explain away his possession of a fancy staff, so be it, but I don't believe in this Dymetra, and I surely don't believe in raising the dead. Not like this."

Kari frowned slightly. "Our general claims to have raised the Elf at the Tower of Dariez. Those are two examples right there. Now Kyle makes three. Surely this must be possible—what other explanation do you have?"

"Strongiron shows up in white armor, looking devout, and I'm supposed to believe he's a True Cleric? Kari, I thought you were smarter than that. You and I craft *Illusions*—it is what we do. Even the goat-herder Herodius questions whether Strongiron's tale is real or imaginary." Belara waved her hand again and the *Illusion* of Kyle's corpse disappeared.

Kyle walked over to fill the space vacated by the *Illusion*. "Belara—that is your name, correct? I can assure you that everything my sister has said is true. Dymetra has brought me back, and my sister is both a Sorceress and a Priestess. She is True. She suffered on the staircase, and I have no doubt that your training helped her through the many trials she faced. I wanted to at least thank you for that. You should be proud of her. I know I am." He reached out to put his arm around Kari.

Belara crossed her arms across her bosom and didn't even acknowledge Kyle's existence. "Go share your story with the Queen. Perhaps she'll be more easily duped. I can't explain this, but I don't believe it, either. Not for one second. I will figure out this abomination, and then you and I will talk again." Even without the benefit of color in her eyes, you could feel the contempt pouring from Belara. "Leave now."

"Yes, Mistress," Kari said sadly as Kyle and she headed for the arched door. "Thank you for your help, Belara. It was invaluable."

As the door shut behind them, Kari heard a muffled scream and the sound of a mirror breaking behind her.

~Magi~

The path Magi and Veronica followed was mostly fields, rolling hills, grassy plains, and some farms; a fairly flat land, largely unsettled between Paragatha and the foothills of the Crystal Mountains on the north side of Lake Calm. No real east-west road existed, just some trails and a few small farms and transient settlements of swords-for-hire. Nobody who saw Magi's white eyes wanted to strike up a conversation, however; they galloped over the land unbothered, and in silence.

The clear day faded into a clear night, and the lack of clouds brought biting cold temperatures. They had made good progress with horses, but it was time to set up camp; a fire was needed.

"I'll build us a fire and get some food cooking. Tie up the horses and let them graze, Veronica." Magi swung down from his deep brown stallion, leaving a trail of his steaming breath visible in the cool night air.

Veronica just nodded, gently pulling in the reins on her auburn horse, which was covered in a mosaic of white patches.

Magi paid no mind to turning his back on her. He would freeze the horse in mid-gallop if she tried to take off. He kept his *Shield* spell on all the time now. It was a bit of drain, and he would need some additional spell components when they reached their first real village or city in order to maintain it, but it sufficed for now.

He threw some spice into a small ring of stones he had gathered, and warm blue fire burst forth from the dirt, warming him immediately. The *whoosh* of the flames caused the horses to nicker, and Magi looked over and smiled.

Veronica. Magi watched her as she lovingly patted down their mounts, talking soothingly to both, laughing lightly to calm hers down when he got a little jumpy by the flames. She reached into her pocket and pulled out a handful of sugar cubes, treating the horses to their desert first.

Surely there is something redeemable about this woman. How does she do it? How can someone so gentle be so cold-blooded? Magi shook his head, trying to think pragmatically. *Even if Xaro expels her from his inner circle, better her to travel with me than take another contract.* He sighed. *I can't stop every killer, but this one is personal.*

Magi looked up at the sky—all the stars were out. It was a beautiful night. He took out a half-dozen small fish they'd caught earlier at lunch. They had stopped at a small stream running off Lake Calm that happened to be gorged with fish. Magi, who preferred real fishing and hunting to over relying on his magic, had a small net in his supplies, and fashioned a rim for it using some dead branches. Half an hour later, he had a dozen small fish, of which they ate half for lunch. Now he took the remainder and strung them on a skewer over his flame.

Satisfied, he looked up to find Veronica taking a seat on the other side of the fire. "Do you have some water that we could heat for something warm to drink?" It was the first thing she had said to him since her most recent attempt to kill him earlier that morning.

"Sure." Magi grabbed some small metal cups and filled them with water from their skins, placing them on flat rocks near the flames. "Give it a moment."

Veronica said nothing in return.

Silence followed. His magical flames didn't crackle like wood. There were no birds nearby, the lake was just barely visible to the south, although the water never stirred anyhow. No coyotes, no animal noises of any kind. When the fish skin started to sizzle, it sounded like a swarm of bees, given the stillness around them. Soon, the whole campsite smelled like flame-roasted fish, which made Magi's mouth water.

"Here. Your three, and your hot water." Magi didn't attempt further conversation, nor did he expect a thank you.

He didn't get one.

"Give me your skin—I'll go fill them up while we're close to water." She shrugged and tossed Magi her skin. "I'm *Teleporting*, but I'll be back in less than five minutes, so don't get cute."

Veronica said nothing, she just stared at him for a long two seconds before lowering her eyes and starting on her second fish. Magi already finished his third piece—he would never leave his food around Veronica unwatched. He said a word...and then he was gone.

Magi looked up from the shore of Lake Calm. He landed at an approachable spot, with a short beachhead that gave him easy access to the water. He could see a tiny blue flame in the distance, representing their campsite. He filled up the skins and then, on a whim, decided to cast a *Far-sight* spell to hone in on Veronica, just to see what she might do in his absence.

He drew a circle in the air, and casting his spell, he focused his *Far-sight* on her, like a sailor's looking glass through the circle he created. And then he saw it.

First one, then two more drops. She put something into *her* cup. And then she drank deeply, tipping her small cup of warm water all the way back until it was gone. Magi bent down to grab the swollen skins, and then he kept looking. *Dammit, Veronica,* he swore. Part of him figured she might try something like this. In seconds, she slumped over.

Magi *Teleported* back to their campsite in a second. "Veronica. Get up, Veronica. What did you drink, Assassin?" Magi looked over at her body and checked for a pulse. Nothing. He felt for a breath—again, nothing. He grabbed the cup she drank from and smelled it. Nothing...odorless. Veronica appeared dead.

Magi looked down at her, laying on the cold ground next to the warm blue flames, still outfitted like a man. He shook his head. "You would never commit suicide, Veronica. All this does is waste time."

Magi balled his hands into fists before grabbing his staff, waiving it over her comatose form. "Assassin—do you think you can pretend to kill yourself, hoping I leave you so that you can awake and resume whatever tasks your foul Master would have you do? Do you think I can't tell when someone is truly dead or not?" He then raised his voice. "Do you take me for a fool? I don't know what kind of black potion you've consumed to mimic death, but I know death when I see it, and this isn't it."

You leave me no choice.

"If you will not agree to simply accompany me without this constant threat of killing me or yourself or running away, then perhaps you are right. Perhaps it is better if I just travel alone. But I will not leave you to wake from this coma only to resume your throat-slashing ways." Magi slowly put his staff down and grabbed Veronica's hands.

Closing his eyes, Magi recalled the spell to summon a giant, floating blade, a wicked curved scimitar—the same one he'd summoned on the Staircase, when he defeated Ragor with it. The arcing sword was suspended near Magi, unattached and unheld, just hovering and glinting blue from the magical fire of their campsite. The blade was more than just razor sharp—it was magically sharp. It had cleaved off both of Ragor's feet in one stroke, bone and all. Holding each hand of Veronica's in one of his, he said a word and sliced both her hands clean off at the wrists in a single stroke.

Veronica's body convulsed, but her eyes stayed shut and her body fell back to the ground with a *thump*. Magi took the two stubs of her arms and cauterized the wounds, sealing them before there was any significant blood loss.

"I am sorry Veronica, but an Assassin with no hands will have a hard time killing anyone again. Consider this your punishment for all the families you have destroyed in pursuit of gold. You don't get to die, at least not by me, and not quickly. Go find your way in this Dark World with no hands. If this doesn't humble you, than nothing will."

He tossed her two hands into the fire, where they slowly burned, causing a wretched smell to fill the campsite as the flesh was consumed. He searched Veronica and removed all her vials, her hidden powders, darts, daggers. Everything. He wrapped them all in a bundle and threw it onto the back of his brown stallion. He then used some water and the hem of her cloak to wipe away all the make-up of her disguise, all the putty, removed the fake hair.

When he was done, lying still by the fire was the athletic, pale woman with jet-black hair he had first seen while travelling with Marik. *Come to think of it, I never did actually see you when you murdered Lionel. Or Sindar. Or my father. Or me.*

"Pity, Veronica. I had hoped you would change your ways. I would have spared you this fate." With that, he let the fire continue through the night, leaving her with the clothes on her back, her food, water, and gold. *I will leave you your gold. You earned it, after all.*

And then Magi untethered his horse and *Teleported* away.

~Queen Najalas~

Kari finished sharing her update to Queen Najalas, Strongiron, Peter, Niku, Simon, Jonathon, and Herodius, who had more or less become a fixture of the Queen's court, given his influence over all the refugees and surprising leadership skills. Kyle stood at her side. They all sat politely, listening attentively to Kari without interruption.

Finally, the Queen motioned to one of her servants, and bread and cheese was brought in, along with fresh ale for everyone except Niku, who drank wine.

The Queen's enormous goblet was the least dainty among them, and she drank without offering so much as a toast to anyone. Jonathon cleared his throat, but the Queen cut him off with a sharp look and a raised hand.

"This is a lot to take in, Kari." The Queen fixed her eyes on the young woman. "This is one of those times when I would greatly like to have Magi and his staff with me in this meeting."

Kari did not say anything, but she didn't look away, either.

Strongiron spoke up. "My Queen," he started. "If I may speak?"

She nodded and took another drink.

"I believe Kari. Who she described could only be Dymetra. No further proof is necessary than her brother standing there, a scar still visible on his chest. No false God can raise the dead back to a living state. Only Dymetra has that power. I have seen and wielded such power myself, and I believe her story. I don't need a staff to know her words are true."

Kari smiled at Strongiron, but again said nothing, just a slight incline of the head before returning her gaze back to the Queen.

Peter, Simon, and Jonathon seemed to share a look. Finally Simon said, "If her word's good enough for Strongiron, it's good enough for me. Well done, Kari."

Simon always looks serious; that is as close to warmth as he typically gets. Her eyes poised over the rim of her goblet, the Queen took in everything, darting from Kari to the members of her council. It was not lost on her that increasingly Peter, Simon, and Jonathon seemed to be forming almost a "pack." Rarely did their opinions on a topic differ anymore. That concerned her. It also had not surprised her to hear Strongiron speak first.

But the largest change she saw, so far, in the people around her was Kari. Her eyes may not be white, but they weren't young-looking anymore, either. She carried herself differently, too.

She carried herself like a woman with power. Not impetuous, bubbling with nervous energy. No—real confidence. She had seen many men and women successfully Climb, and they all came back with that same look, even those who were permanently injured.

Kari emanated the look of a person who could leave and go anywhere, any time. A True Mage.

"Come here," Niku beckoned to her. "I would like to test for *Illusions*, if you'll allow me the courtesy. I don't mean to mistrust you. But that is a fantastic tale, even for one such as me who has lived to see many fantastic things."

"I would expect nothing less, Niku," she replied. "But I appreciate the courtesy. Belara did the same thing, though I don't recall her asking."

"Yes, well..." Niku stammered a bit. He smiled and waved his arm, saying a word. The Queen could tell by their expressions that this wasn't the first time they'd heard it.

The Queen leaned over and whispered to Jonathon. "Go ask Belara to join us. I would hear her thoughts. *Illusion* is her specialty, after all."

"Yes, your Majesty." Jonathon departed.

Niku turned to the Queen. "I see no evidence of *Illusion* here. I know *Illusions* can be crafted to mimic reality in fine detail." He looked over to Kari and extended his arm. "And Miss Quinlan has shown herself to be a truly gifted Illusionist." He smiled, almost condescendingly. "Yet I would find it hard to believe if anyone here would have the power to hide a counterfeit reality from my detection. I am inclined to believe her, my Queen."

He turned back to Kari, his expression shrewd. "I, too, extend my congratulations, though not without a pang of jealousy, I must admit, that I look upon your bright green eyes and consider you now a colleague within our Art."

"Thank you, Niku. You can trust that my story is true. I could not deceive you with spell craft on my best day." She returned his smile. "I doubt anyone could."

Belara and Jonathon had silently approached the group from behind Kari, nearing the Queen, who studied her entrance. *Niku's*

Illusionist stares almost forcefully at the back of Kari's head, as if she could bore through it.

"Yes, your Majesty?" Belara bowed stiffly, and when her hair fell forward, the most pleasant smell of vanilla, roses, and other spices filled the air.

"I understand Kari has told you her story. You trained her, and were there when she started her rite of passage, what you Mages call The Climb. You were the first to see her when she returned. I would like your opinion on this—unlikely tale."

She turned her head to Kari. "I want to believe you, Kari. I truly do. My heart longs for evidence that Dymetra is real, and is joining our fight." She exhaled and set her empty goblet down on the arm of her chair. "But I am also wary of false hope, trickery, and illusion." She motioned for more ale and turned back to Belara. "And that, Belara, is why I wish to hear your opinion."

"I do not believe her." She said it simply. Almost all the men in the room began speaking up, raising their voice. The Queen silenced them with a raised hand and nodded a 'thank you' to her servant for the refilled goblet. *The Miller's spring ale is a fine batch this year.*

"Please. Let her finish." She took a long pull. "Now tell me why you don't believe her."

"I just don't." She waved her hand, and a second Kyle appeared, identical to the one next to her. "Go. Feel him. Talk to him."

The second Kyle bowed low to the Queen. "It is an honor to be here, your Majesty. I never thought I'd see the day when I could return to your gracious Hall after that fateful day."

There was silence in the room. Niku narrowed his eyes and reached out, grabbing the arm of the second Kyle. He gave it a jerk, and the man stumbled.

"Niku! Why would you do that to me?" the second Kyle exclaimed, regaining his balance.

Unsatisfied, Niku cast the same *Disillusionment* spell as he did before. The concentration on his face, the strain was apparent.

The Queen looked over at Belara, who blinked several times. *She strains, too.*

The second Kyle did not disappear. Finally Belara spoke up. "Enough." She waived her hand, and the second Kyle finally vanished. "As you can see, it is not impossible to overpower a *Disillusionment* spell." She looked at Niku, her hands on her hips being the only indication of her strain. "I don't know how she's doing it, but obviously her potential well of power is vast if she can maintain both the *Illusion* of her brother's resurrection and also her natural eye color."

She slowly turned her head toward Kari. "Frankly, I believe you failed your Climb and are too embarrassed to admit it, so you concocted this whole story, even creating this *Illusion*, and further creating the *Illusion* of your *Teleportation* outside my room earlier. I believe you merely disappeared and that you projected an *Illusion* of yourself outside my door, just as I've done here in this room for everyone, mimicking your *Illusion*."

Kari stepped toward her. "Belara—"

Belara cut her off. "I challenge you to a Mage duel. I believe in our Art—I put no stock in this Cleric nonsense. No failed apprentice could hope to defeat me in the dueling circle. I applaud you for the extent and level of detail that you have put into this *Illusion*—humans are notoriously tricky to create. But I would not have you deceive our Queen and this council. Defeat me, with this walking *Illusion* watching, and I will believe you. Nobody would be able to exhaust the kind of energy necessary to expel me from the circle and still maintain this *Illusion* of your brother." She turned back to Niku. "Nobody."

In the brief silence that followed Belara's challenge, Herodius that raised his voice. "This is good, my Queen. I, too, am leery of deception. Let the women duel. Whatever their motivations, the logic seems sound."

All of the eyes in the room turned toward the Queen, who finished her ale. *Magi's staff would be so much cleaner.* She stood up, somewhat impatiently. "The logic may be sound, but the advice is not efficient. This is no time for magical contests and games, Belara. You say her *Teleportation* was an *Illusion*. Fine. Strongiron, Belara, Niku—you will *Teleport—with Kari*, who claims to be a True Mage—to the port down by the water, outside this castle. Kyle, or this image of him, can stay here and talk to me. Surely she can't maintain this *Illusion* and *Teleport in your presence* at the same time? That will take less than a minute. Do it now."

"Alas, your Majesty, a powerful mage could. She could keep this *Illusion* going until she slept." Belara looked up at the Queen. "I assure you, my interest in dueling her is not for pleasure. We can wait to see if the *Illusion* dissipates when she tires. But if you are looking for an *efficient* check, I would drain her power quickly, which is why I suggest a duel. It is harmless, my Queen, I assure you." She looked at Kari. "I won't harm you, apprentice."

Again, Herodius spoke up, this time standing. "I don't pretend to know the ways of a Mage. But I do know people. If I may speak my mind bluntly—"

"When have you not?" chided Peter.

Herodius gave him a look, but there was a slight upturn to his mouth. "As I was saying, I know people, your Majesty. I don't believe this will be a waste of time. Let Belara be satisfied one way or another about Kari's story so we can move on to more pressing matters. An hour to resolve whatever is festering here—spoken or unspoken—will be worth it, and we will all know whether Kari is indeed who she says she is. If she is a True Mage and Cleric, it will greatly even the odds for us."

The men all turned to Herodius. Even Strongiron, who sighed. "I need no proof, but I don't object. Win or lose this duel, I believe her. But Herodius's point is not without merit. Let the women resolve this. I will take her along with me when I leave, regardless."

The Queen stared at her empty goblet, motioning for a third. *There is more to this islander than just revenge, I know it.* "Very well. Prepare the circle, we'll have a duel. Right now."

~Veronica~

Light grey clouds of differing shades filled the sky in a splotchy, overlapping pattern. The clouds were numerous but thin, allowing two or three shafts of sunlight to pierce the cloud cover. One such ray happened to shine directly onto Veronica's face. Perhaps the brightness and the warmth were what finally caused her to stir. Her eyes eventually flapped open, and she rubbed the grogginess from her near-death serum out of them.

Or at least tried to. A massive jolt of adrenaline flooded her system as she saw the slightly blackened skin knitted together at the end of each arm where her hands used to be.

"AHHH!" she screamed, standing bolt upright. There was blood all around the campsite and down her clothes. *"MAGI!"* she yelled. *"MAGI—WHERE ARE YOU!?"*

The True Mage was nowhere to be found. Her water, her foodpack, and her gold were the only pouches around her. However the camp did smell, vaguely, of burning flesh. She looked up and saw several black birds circling overhead.

As the initial shock ended, she plopped back down, her heart still racing. There was no pain in her hands, but she had no memory of what happened either. The last thing she remembered was trying to fake poisoning herself, hoping Magi would leave her to die and ride on, at which point she could resume the task Xaro had set before her. The serum she had was a powerful potion that simulated death by rendering your breathing and heart beat virtually undetectable. She made it obvious that she had poisoned herself, leaving the vial in plain sight.

And now she was horribly maimed. Would an animal do this? *No, why stop at just the hands?* Would Magi? *Of course Magi would—this is his revenge.*

She looked for a note, anything. She couldn't find any messages. She couldn't find her potions or knives either! She patted herself all over with her stumps—there was nothing on her. Clearly someone took all her stuff. *Magi must have done this, I'm convinced. He wanted me to suffer. He threatened me yesterday morning. It's him. It has to be him.*

Veronica screamed again, staring at the magical blue flames that grew lower and lower by the moment as the energy that created them no longer fed them. She went to pull her cloak around her tighter...but could not grab the cloth.

"Damn it!" she swore. *If I had a knife right now,* Veronica thought, *I might just kill myself. I am a life ender. Perhaps it's time I end my own.*

But she had no knife. And she didn't trust herself to bash her head against the ground hard enough to kill—she just couldn't do that. She stared at Lake Calm in the distance. Drowning? Not the death she wanted for herself, either. Besides, she really didn't want to die at all, at least not most. What she wanted *most* right now was to kill Magi—permanently.

And if it takes me the rest of my life to do so, then so be it. To any and all the Gods listening, hear my prayer: "Grant me justice and I will worship you. I swear I will," she uttered aloud, clenching her teeth. She didn't really believe a God was going to help her kill Magi, anyhow. She was on her own on this one.

She saw her horse, still tethered to a nearby tree. First things first; Veronica had to figure out how to untie her speckled stallion without hands.

~Kari~

Niku took the courtesy of relaying the rules to both Kari and Belara, but she wasn't really listening. She had done a few of these before, mostly for fun, at Marik's school. The boys did it quite often, but every so often Kari would throw her name out there, or respond to a dare, or just simply feel enraged enough to want to take her frustration out on something or someone. Usually that someone was her brother, who now was seated as a spectator in one of the main training rooms for the mages who studied in Rookwood. A large, glowing circle, twenty-five feet in diameter, had been magically drawn on the floor.

The object was simple: both mages stand in the circle and cast a force spell to push the other one out of the circle. Since the spells are the same, there is no guile, no skill, no dexterity or quick thinking involved, rather a measure of raw power; one mage simply has more energy to rely on than the other, and eventually pushes the weaker mage out of the ring. But it requires your full effort to push back—the notion that you could cast two spells simultaneously and still win against an otherwise equally paired opponent is laughable. Your *full* commitment to bullying your opponent outside the ring was always required unless you were overpowering a child or something. One mage was typically drained; the other was essentially emptied.

Belara, however, was no child. She would be harnessing the full conviction of her beliefs and unleashing the depths of her energy well against the new True Cleric. Kari did not doubt this for a second.

Furthermore, it was not lost on Kari that Belara had, almost blatantly, just shown herself to potentially be more powerful than even Niku. His spell could not overpower hers to reveal the obvious *Illusion* that Belara created; the Master Illusionist was indeed a formidable True Mage.

If I lose, she may convince others that I am lying. If I win, I may offend her—she is prideful, and jealous of Dymetra's gift to me. That much was obvious to Kari. Belara didn't believe her because she couldn't understand why Kari should get to keep her eyes while she could not. She knew vanity when she saw it. *Because I'm vain myself,* she thought, smiling ruefully.

What should I do, Dymetra? It was an off-hand thought, hardly a prayer. *I'm tired, I just finished my Climb. I probably can't beat her when I'm rested, let alone right now.*

But I can. Trust Me in the simple tasks as well as the big ones, Kari.

The voice in her head was crystal clear and unmistakable, as if Dymetra was standing in the room with her. Niku's voice interrupted her thoughts.

"I said, are you ready, Kari?"

She turned toward Niku, who looked at her somewhat impatiently. She scanned the room and saw everyone from their earlier meeting watching, except Jonathon. Strongiron smiled at her with an encouraging nod.

She looked across the circle at Belara, who was standing calmly about fifteen feet away, well inside the circle. *She looks so poised.* Even Kari had to admit that Belara Kassar was striking in her shimmering silver dress, scattering torchlight everywhere whenever she moved.

"I am ready, Niku." Kari stepped to the line, now equidistant from the perimeter of the circle as Belara.

"Prepare yourselves." Niku cast a temporary, invisible barrier between the two dueling women to keep either from gaining an advantage from casting their spells before the other one did. Both Kari and Belara chanted the same simple force spell, both pushing on opposite sides of Niku's barrier. "Steady....ready, now...*begin!*" he shouted, removing the barrier.

Belara raised her hands as if that would somehow increase the force of her spell, which collided with Kari's and immediately began driving her backwards. One step, then two.

"C'mon, Kari!" shouted Kyle. "Just like we used to do at Marik's! Look at me, Belara—I'm still here. I'm real! Look at me, Belara!"

Belara ignored Kyle. She stepped forward, almost hissing as she exerted herself to drive Kari backwards.

Kari closed her eyes, hands outstretched, fighting against the force of Belara's spell. *Dymetra, strengthen me.*

Out of the corner of her eye, Kari saw the Queen stand up and lean forward, perhaps to get a better look. Soon the rest of the spectators were standing as well.

Suddenly Kari found a source of energy that seemed to come from outside her, flowing through her, but not from her. She managed to take a half-step forward. Belara pushed her arms forward even further, with an almost primal grunt.

Opening her eyes, her arms shaking, Kari took one more step forward. The point at which the two spells met began throwing sparks off everywhere. Kari pushed one more step toward her.

"I'm still here, Belara!" shouted Kyle again. "You can do it, sis!"

Niku gave him a withering look. "Do not distract the competitors!"

For the first time in the duel, Belara took one step backward, grunting again under the strain. And Kari advanced again. She was now past where she had started. She was gaining ground.

Belara sunk her shoulders a little and took a massive, deep breath before unleashing a blood-curling scream: "AHHHHH!"

It was one of the single greatest physical forces that Kari had ever felt. She put one hand behind the other, arms outstretched, as if she was trying to cup a thrown ball. The pressure being exerted to force Kari backwards was extreme and exhausting. Yet despite this, she took another couple steps forward. *I feel like I'm getting tested all over again.*

Belara sank to her knees, her arms still out in front of her, grunting, almost panting. Kari was getting stronger; she could hear the voices of Kyle, of Peter and Strongiron in the background. She thought Niku was saying something as well, but she couldn't focus on any of these sounds, couldn't even turn her head to look their way. She was now almost standing over Belara, who was straining to not fall backwards, trying to make herself small, like a stain glued to the floor.

It was then that Kari smelled it. Or rather *didn't* smell it: she could not pick up even the faintest whiff of vanilla, roses, or any other exotic spices.

"Do you yield?" she asked, her voice measured but steady.

"AHH….N-N-N-NO!" yelled Belara, struggling to stand up, her outstretched palms less than a foot from Kari's. "NEVER!" she shouted.

Such pride. Protect her from injury, Dymetra.

With a deep breath, Kari bore down on her spell, pulling energy from the bottom of her own well and Dymetra's blessing as well. She grunted and pushed forward, her hands touching Belara, sending her former mentor flying out of the circle, slamming forcibly into the padded walls covered with straw behind her. Belara, her dress ripping, slumped onto the floor, disheveled and utterly spent. She lifted her head to look at Kari. *What is that look on her face? Not anger. More like grudging respect.*

"I am no *Illusion*, Belara." Kyle's voice had a soft, conciliatory tone to it, unlike his shouts during the duel. "Everything Kari has said is true."

Kari couldn't tell if Belara nodded or not; the Master Illusionist simply put her head down and was soon out cold. Niku ran over to Belara and began levitating his Number Two mage to take her back to her chambers when Jonathon suddenly entered.

"My Queen," he said. "If the entertainment is now done, I believe you are expecting a visitor tonight. He is here. May I escort you to your chambers for a private meeting?"

All eyes turned to the Queen with curious looks and raised eyebrows. "Thank you, Jonathon," she said. "Yes, you may." She turned to Kari and the rest of the assembled leaders. "We shall regather in the morning one final time before Strongiron departs."

She smiled at Kari. "Impressive, Miss Quinlan. Very impressive indeed."

CHAPTER EIGHT: AGREEMENTS REACHED

~Magi~

Though he was most familiar with Gaust, the city of Nervadine was positioned at the tip of the southernmost of the 'Three Fingers,' and as such made for the shortest journey across the sea. Gaust had a set of marble statues marking the entrance to Lord Corovant's city; Nervadine had a massive wooden wall. Outside the wall were small farms that could hardly be expected to grow more than a single family's needs. A few inns stood outside the wall as well; Magi stayed the night at one called *The Cherry Goblet.* Dawn broke red behind him as he walked out into the mild morning, heading west toward the city gates.

An archery tower was positioned on either side of the gates, which were closed in the pre-dawn air. From behind the folds in his hooded travelling cloak, he looked up at either tower to see arrows trained on him as he approached.

"Who approaches? Show yourself, stranger!" One of the guards atop the tower on his left called down.

"Just a traveler looking to buy passage aboard one of your ships leaving port this day. Nothing more than that." Magi held up his staff in one hand, an open palm in the other.

"City gates don't open for several hours. Come back later." The guard shouted down.

"Your ships will be leaving soon; I doubt they'll depart much later than dawn, which is already breaking. Surely commerce still is valued in Nervadine? Why hold up a harmless traveler?" Again, Magi extended his arms, palms up, shoulders bunched up at this neck.

"If you're truly looking to sail out to sea, another day won't hurt you. Show me the gold that you plan on using to buy passage so I know you're not lying to me."

The irony of the situation was not lost on Magi, given the staff he held. The guards were looking to see whether he was worth murdering and robbing, he could see the truth as clear as the red dawn. He sighed. *We live in such a Dark World.*

After the decision he made last night to end Veronica's career as an Assassin, Magi wasn't much in the mood for killing or maiming or fighting in general. He smiled. "Very well. Here is my gold." Instead, he scattered sand, and put the guards on the tower to sleep.

The wooden bows and arrows falling out of the tower made a modest racket. Magi didn't waste any time. He cast a *Levitation* spell and hoisted himself up and over the wall, landing lightly on the other side. A glance back confirmed least six bodies awkwardly lying against one another and the railings of the watch towers.

Walking down the city's main road was a little eerie at this hour. In Gaust, the city was always alive. Peddlers, merchants, buyers, sellers, beggars, squatters, nobles, tradesmen—the city was a cacophony of sounds and smells. At any hour. Even the library was filled with scribes, writing scroll after scroll.

Nervadine was still. Not empty, but eerily quiet. The only sound Magi heard was a slow squeak from a wheelbarrow full of junk pushed by an old woman. She kept staring at Magi from the other side of the road. Magi looked at some windows as he walked by and saw a few people staring out, but the hustle and bustle of a city was missing.

As he approached the city square, he saw a fish peddler hanging his rather large catch in the first light of morning. He thought about his last experience with Manny in Gaust and decided to walk on the other side of the square. Another merchant, a young mother with a tiny child hiding behind her legs, was unpacking some bolts of cloth.

"Good morning," Magi said, smiling at the woman.

She narrowed her eyes suspiciously. "Can I help you?"

"Not really, although your cloth is beautiful. I'm heading toward the docks. I assume keep following the main city road here to the wharf?" *Why is everyone so jumpy?*

"Get along then." She had a hand on her young daughter's head, the other hand was concealed behind her back.

Magi had learned to keep his cowl up when travelling, as many people were terrified at the sight of a True Mage. But his face was covered in shadow, and yet they still viewed him suspiciously. His curiosity getting the better of him, he pulled his cowl down. "I mean you no harm, I assure you. I'm sorry if my hood is frightening, but I find some are fearful of mages as well. I'll be on my way."

The little girl pointed at his face and started yelling. "EYES! EYES!"

Now all of a sudden the city square awoke. Shutters started snapping shut. People started yelling.

He felt sour breath in his ear, "Best come with me if you wish to live."

Magi turned around and saw the old woman's face next to his— missing teeth and all—with her wheelbarrow full of junk behind her.

Her breath smelled like last night's wine. "Who are you? What is going on?"

"I may be a friend to True Mages, but unless you want to pretend you're a pincushion, we need to leave before every archer in town sends a love note your way. Follow me." The hunched over woman grabbed his arm just above the elbow. *It wasn't the grip of a frail, old woman.*

Magi pulled his arm free, politely but firmly. "I'm sorry, but I don't know your name. I am pretty comfortable taking care of myself. I will ask you again—who are you and what is going on here that has everyone on edge?"

The old woman didn't say anything for a few seconds but simply stared at him, smiling. She had a sore on the right side of her face that her greasy, grey hair hung down over. Her teeth were yellow, and her hands were covered in brown spots. "My name is Daphne. I know a little something about magic and mages. I used to have a son who had the gift. You remind me of him, you do."

Magi cocked his head slightly, gripping his staff involuntarily. *She is a mage herself! An* Illusionist, *but not a True Mage. Her eyes are grey.*

"As to why the people are on edge…they are a playground for the Thieves and Assassins' Guild. They send their recruits from Shoal down here so often that nobody trusts a stranger any longer. The fact that you are a True Mage doesn't help your cause, either." Little flecks of spittle trailed out of her mouth when she spoke. They both ducked into a nearby alley behind some stone buildings. "People end up poor and dead if they talk to enough strangers." She chuckled wickedly.

"But not you." Magi said, looking at her ragged clothes and sagging skin. "Nobody looks to steal or kill you."

She winked at Magi, chuckling softly. "Bah! Who would bother with me, Mage?"

Despite his curiosity, Magi was determined to find passage before all the ships departed for the day. He returned her pleasant smile, trying not to look too fake about it. "Well, I appreciate your concern for my well being, but I'll be on my way now."

"Not one cup of tea before you leave?" She reached up to put a hand on his shoulder. "It is…lonely in this city. It has been so long since I've enjoyed a cup of tea with a fellow mage."

There is something…odd…about this woman. Magi relented. "Very well, but lose your disguise. I see you are a mage as well, and this is a skillful *Illusion*. Show yourself to me—I will know if you are hiding something. Then we will have one cup of tea before I must leave." He then added, "I would like to hear more about this city."

The old woman, hunched over in the alley, looked to her left and right. "Very well." She closed her eyes and with a shimmer the frail, old woman disappeared. Standing in front of Magi was a tall, middle-aged woman, certainly younger than she portrayed, but still beyond the full blossom of youth. Her hair was white, but thick. She stood straight, revealing the outline of a still attractive, though mature figure. She was tall and broad. *In her youth she must have been statuesque.* Her skin was tan and unblemished; her nails painted a deep red to match her lips. The dark skin and white hair was almost as striking as her grey eyes, though if he looked closely, Magi thought he could see flecks of blue. She was tightly wrapped in a violet robe that was so dark it was nearly black, and her boots rose above her knees. She had to be much older than Magi—maybe a *lot* older—but he still found himself gawking at her.

"Better?" she smiled seductively, her teeth full and white; her breath crisp and fresh.

"Much." Magi shook his head, his cheeks hot. He felt a stirring inside himself that was difficult to ignore. He shook his head again, more violently this time. "Actually, I think I liked your *Illusion* better. Why don't you change yourself back; people will wonder where the old woman went and think someone killed her." *It is so difficult being around you! What is the matter with me?*

"Are you sure, Mage? I thought for sure you would find my real self more…interesting. No one will worry about the old woman; nobody sees her." The very air surrounding this Daphne was intoxicating.

Magi found himself unnaturally drawn to this woman; every impulse screamed *get away,* yet instead he found himself walking toward her. Her back was up against the stone wall in the alley. He looked at her boots, her nails, her lips.

He put his head down. Slowly, steadily, he forced the words from his mouth. "I. Think. It. Best. If. I. Leave." He ground the butt end of his staff into the hard-packed dirt alley and pivoted around it, keeping his eyes on the ground. First one step. Then another. He felt a grip on his arm again.

"*You* asked to see *me.* Very well, does this make you more comfortable?"

Magi smelled the foul breath once again and turned his head. The frail, old beggar woman with the wheelbarrow had returned.

Magi took a deep breath, and felt his composure returning. "Yes. I...I did not expect to be so affected by your..." he trailed off.

"Personality?" she offered with a giggle that was loud enough to draw attention. It certainly didn't match the old hag standing in front of him. "Frankly, I'm impressed by your self control. I don't see that in most men, especially at your age." Daphne smirked at him, revealing raw gums in her gap-riddled teeth. Magi didn't say a word, but merely nodded, forcing a polite half-smile in return. He threw his cowl back over his face.

"As much as I've, eh, enjoyed this conversation—I'm afraid I'll need to pass on that tea. I am travelling west, and if I dawdle much longer, I'm not likely to find a ship that's leaving yet today." He looked uneasily at the frail, decrepit woman. "Goodbye, Daphne."

"West? Last I heard, my son was travelling west, but I have no idea where. If you see a Warrior with a gift for spell craft named Xaro, tell him his Mother misses him."

~Queen Najalas~

"Thank you, my Queen," said Silverfist as he graciously accepted a glass of crimson wine rich in bouquet. "This is exquisite; it must come from the west." He smiled. Everyone knew the best wine grew west of the Crystal Mountains.

"Actually, it is Elfish. I don't particularly care for it, but I've heard that wine is your passion, Silver. I hope you enjoy it." The Queen nodded and raised her massive goblet in toast. "To a productive conversation."

"To a productive conversation," echoed Silver. They sat on low couches in the Queen's personal drawing room. Her Mages took turns keeping a blue *Everflame* glowing in a modest fire ring between them, bathing the room in shifting shadows. It was getting late.

"I assume you're wondering why I summoned you," the Queen began.

"Not really. Typically, one reason and one reason only elicits an invitation to me, my Queen. I know you employ a handful of my Guild here in Rookwood, just in case court politics grows a little ugly; I can only assume that the task you have in mind is beyond your confidence in their abilities? Am I correct?" Silver paused, sipping his wine, blinking. "I do believe I have undervalued Elfish wine. Being half-elfen myself, perhaps I am a bit biased against them; this is a marvelous vintage, my Queen."

"Glad you like it. I'll see you leave with as much as you can carry." The Queen rose, uncharacteristically nervous, perhaps from the ale, perhaps from her guest. *Would my husband have sought this help?* She began to pace behind her couch. "Yes. You are correct. I'll get to the point."

Queen Najalas took a deep breath and looked Silverfist square in the eyes. "I want you to find me an Assassin capable of killing Xaro and his lieutenants," she said, taking a long drink from her fourth goblet of ale. She didn't rush to fill the silence between them.

Silverfist lifted a single eyebrow, still jet-black against his reddish-brown skin. His hair may have had a few grey streaks, but the rest of him looked as fit as ever. He finally broke the silence. "That will be expensive."

The Queen laughed. "Money from the treasury is the easiest thing to replace. My question is, who can do it?"

Silverfist ran a single finger around the rim of his wine glass, staring at the blood-colored liquid. "I don't think gold is all that will be needed."

"Land, titles, what? Explain." The Queen sat down on the couch and leaned forward, the low blue flames near the floor dancing silently between them.

"New assassins will work for gold. They have little, and are accumulating their stakes. They'll take any assignments, even death wishes, for a lucrative contract. They are young, talented...and wholly inexperienced for the type of assignment you have in mind."

"I know. That is why I have no interest in the ones on my staff. They *are* young. I tolerate them, knowing that my husband thought it prudent to have someone available should a rival emerge. He was never paranoid about losing power, just...prepared to defend it, shall we say."

"Yes, I knew King Alomar quite well. He is missed." Silver put his head down.

The Queen said nothing at first, but drank her ale. "Yes, well. Elvidor falls to me to rule now, and rule I shall. If I can cut off the head of this serpent that moves against us, I will. Doing so would save many good men from death, many good woman from being widowed...and worse."

Silverfist finished his glass and made a sad face. The Queen pointed to a half-opened bottle sitting on a table close by, to which he helped himself with a nod of thanks. "As I was saying, this will require someone very experienced. Someone who, frankly, probably doesn't need the gold."

The Queen raised an eyebrow herself. "You?"

Silverfist laughed. "Oh, my Queen. You flatter me. But no, I am not the right person for this job, nor would I take it if you offered me the chance to rule in your stead as payment."

The Queen did not think that very funny. She slammed her goblet down on an end table, which luckily was nearly empty, so none was spilled. "Then who? Who do you recommend?"

Silverfist turned around slowly, unaffected by the Queen's outburst. "The only Assassin that might take a contract such as this is Cheyenne." He sat back down.

"Who?" Queen Najalas remained standing, looking down at Silverfist.

"Cheyenne. She is a Master Assassin, of course, but she also has some skill with magic—just enough to be deceptive. She has some Elfish blood."

"This…Cheyenne. Why her? Xaro has at least two lieutenants that I am aware of: a Dark Cleric and an ogre general." The Queen sat back down. "Perhaps more. I know he employed one of your Assassins to kill *my* General. She failed."

"Yes, at least so far. I believe you had captured her. On a separate note, I am curious as to why you would let her go, and relatedly, if you hold our talents in such low regard, why trust me to find you an Assassin for an even more daunting target?"

The Queen smiled and took this opportunity to get up, somewhat slowly, and made her way to the cask for her fifth goblet of ale. *I shall pay for this tomorrow, I know.*

"A fair question. We let your Assassin go because I valued her life less than my Admiral's, whom she was threatening. It is as simple as that. As to why I would trust you with this…I don't. At least, not completely, but I believe in exploring every avenue to divert, prevent, and if necessary, to fight and win a war should war be waged against us. I will not be putting all my eggs in the Black Guild's basket, rest assured about that."

She sat back down with her goblet, a head of rich foam beginning to slide down the side. "But if you are successful in killing any one of those monsters, it will be a boon for us. So I believe it's only prudent to explore a contract." She took a nice, long pull. "I know better than to try and talk you into taking sides. You play both sides for gold; war shall be good for your business, I have no doubt."

Silverfist gave a throaty chuckle. "Prudent? Yes, I suppose it is at that. Very well. You wanted to know why Cheyenne. As I said, only the young typically take political contracts—"

"Like Veronica," the Queen interrupted.

"Ah, yes. Veronica is enormously talented, but in some ways…naïve. She is well-guarded by your resurrected Mage. As I was—"

"Magi?" the Queen interrupted again. "What do you mean, *guarded*?"

Silver narrowed his eyes. He looked like a man who had let his tongue slip. He shrugged. "She travels with him, or did at least. She did not seem to be thrilled with the prospect of continuing to do so. That is all I know." He sipped his wine and changed the subject. "Cheyenne is a tad older, but her elfish blood helps her remains full of youthful vigor—like me. She is a decorated killer, and gifted enough to incorporate some spell craft into her killing. You will need some magic, in all likelihood, to undo any of these three men, let alone all of them, but that's not really the main reason why I would recommend her."

"Then why? I'm beginning to think you are dragging this out to drink all the wine in Rookwood."

Silverfist cocked his head slightly in mock indignation. "Very well. The main for my recommendation is her keen attention to the details of planning a death. She is a student of killing, and a planner of the highest order, who has the ability to convince your targets that she worships their God. Gaining their trust is the only way an assassination at this level can be successful. It was Veronica's plan to gain Strongiron's trust, and she did so. She failed in her execution, however. I don't believe Cheyenne will."

"You are convinced she can do this?"

Silverfist leaned forward, his voice dropping low. "I am convinced she is the only one I would let try. We are still talking about a daunting contract. But Cheyenne…such a *meticulous* killer— she could do this. *If* we can come to terms." He took a large gulp from his wine glass. "Exquisite, really. Do I detect oak, plum and a bit of cardamom?"

She ignored his question. "And what will Cheyenne require as payment for her services?"

Here Silverfist smiled. "The ten thousand gold per kill is the easy part for you," he said. "For a political assassination of this magnitude, however, Cheyenne will want a political assassination in return. The elfs banished her for pursuing membership in our Guild—again, like me. She will want the dead body of their Elfen Chieftain Chocktaw as payment."

"You know that is her price? How do you know this?"

Silverfist just smiled. "Because I do. I know her quite well, my Queen. She will accept a contract for each of these three men. But are you willing to kill your ally? Will you risk war with the Elfs to save war from afar?"

Something was bothering the Queen. "How can I trust her to kill these men if she wishes our ally dead as well?"

At this, Silverfist laughed out loud.

"My dear Queen," he said. "As you have keenly pointed out, the Black Guild takes no sides. We swear no fealty to God or Crown...only our contracts. You know this. At least we are not hypocrites; Tenebrae is filled with men who worship the same God and bow to the same Queen who lie, cheat, and yes—kill one another all the same." He laughed even harder, and indulged in an undainty gulp of his wine. "But I suppose your question is less philosophical and more tactical. You wish to know how will you know the others are dead before you proceed with a plan to kill Chief Chocktaw, am I right?"

"Yes, that is the point of my question. I'm obviously not going to move one finger without proof of their demise."

"Of course. Terms will be proof of the death of the Cleric, the half-ogre, or Xaro himself before you move against Chocktaw. That would only be fair. We will deliver at least one assassination before you deliver yours."

"Fair is not the word I would use."

"Nevertheless, those are the terms. Do you accept?"

Despite even the Queen's unnatural tolerance for good drink, this fresh ale was finally making her mind fuzzy and the room spin. Something told her that this was not a deal she should be thinking about making without a clear head, but she also had other thoughts that seemed more urgent: *Make the deal before he changes his mind! If you delay, you will look weak! Three deaths of such evil men is worth the price of the death of one good man!*

Last thought: *I wish Magi were here with his staff.* But no—this was a decision she would not be discussing with anyone else, council or otherwise.

She shook her head to clear it out. "And if Cheyenne delivers on her end of the contract, but we fail to deliver Chief Chocktaw?"

Silver shook his head slowly. "I'm afraid she will, in that case, likely come after you, my Queen. And if she's successful in killing Xaro, his Dark Cleric, and his ogre General, pardon my bluntness, but I imagine killing you would be no harder." He shook his head very slightly. "My Queen," he added.

She did not say anything for a moment. Silverfist filled the silence after an awkward moment or two. "And one more thing," he said. "If you are thinking about killing her *after* she successfully executes such a high-value contract, be aware that I would be compelled to bring the full force of the Black Guild to bear on Rookwood. There would be no blissful sleep for anyone. You would have avoided a war and sentenced your city to a waking nightmare where death visits your subjects nightly. Do not force me to do that. Many, many Assassins dwell in this town unknown even to you and your spies, my Queen." His voice dropped to a whisper. "We are everywhere."

The Queen sloshed her ale around in her goblet, making it foam again a little. She finally nodded.

"Silver, we have a deal."

~Kari~

After walking her brother to his guest quarters, Kari finally had a private moment to fall on her knees and thank Dymetra for the strength She provided. "I could not have won that duel without You. I pray some good comes of this." Hearing no response, she rose and headed toward her bed when she heard a faint knock outside her chamber door.

A bit late into night for visitors...I wonder if Kyle needs something? She opened the door, but it wasn't her brother standing there. It was Strongiron. Without a word, she invited him in, at which point he wrapped his arms around her, kissing her hair gently.

"I never doubted your story," he whispered.

Kari pulled away from him playfully. "You should have. I *am* pretty good with *Illusions*, you know."

Strongiron curled his lips into a half-smile and shook his head. "So I've noticed."

Kari put both her hands on his stubbly cheeks. "Speaking of *Illusions*, you know *you* were my final test on the Staircase."

Strongiron blinked. "I was? In what way?"

"You tried to kill me. With poison."

The True Warrior blanched and pulled away. "Kari—I would never do that! I...I..." He paused, as if at a loss for words.

I can't remember ever hearing him so flummoxed. It's almost cute. Kari leaned forward. "I know you wouldn't. That is what made the test so insidious. I thought you should know that of all the

Illusions that could have been thrown at me to unravel, *you* were chosen to deliver the poison. Do you know why?"

He spread his arms. "I can't possibly imagine why, Kari. I don't know your magical ways."

She walked over to him and put her arms around his neck. "You may not know a thing about magic, but do you know nothing of women? I love you, Strongiron. No harder test for me could be concieved than to see through a false image of you when I was weakest and needed you the most."

Strongiron grit his teeth. "That is perverse."

Kari laughed. "I won't disagree with you on that point. I just wanted you to know...to know that I love you."

Strongiron closed his eyes. "And I love you, Kari." He opened his eyes. "That is why I am so torn about you accompanying me."

Kari's eyes flashed and she took a step back, crossing her arms. "We discussed this. I thought you agreed that if I—"

The True Warrior held up a hand and walked toward her again. "I said I was torn, not that I was changing my mind. Sometimes the selfish desire is also the prudent one, and believe me when I say that I selfishly want you with me, Kari. But even a fool can see how powerful you've become." He spread his arms. "Don't yell at me for stating the obvious, but the Queen could use you here. Then again...I don't doubt that I will need you more where our path leads."

Kari relaxed a little. "And where, exactly, does our path lead?"

Strongiron tilted his head. "North first, to recall my Lieutenant General. Then west to Adimand. From there...I have no idea." He smiled.

Kari put her arms around Strongiron's waist and rested her head against his broad chest. "I meant, afterward. After the Shield, after the war, where do you think this leads for us?"

The True Warrior gently ran his hands through her silky hair. "Well, for someone who wishes to see the wide world of Tenebrae, I can't imagine a better life than travelling throughout the realm, sharing the truth and wisdom of Dymetra to all who need light in this Dark World."

Kari looked up into his shiny blue eyes in the dim light of her quarters, but said nothing. "That is, if you'll join me when the challenges of the present are behind us?" he finished hopefully.

She gently pulled his head toward hers, kissing him lightly. "I'll think about it," she teased.

~Veronica~

Night had fallen as Veronica slumped in her saddle, dazed and exhausted. The night air was warmer than it had been recently; spring was definitely here. Pinpricks of starlight dotted the mostly cloud-free sky. The few lazy clouds that refused to yield seemed content to float around the full moon, which was large and orange this evening. Veronica raised her head and saw the top of the moon peeking above the clouds. She hugged her horse's neck tighter with her stubby arms as they finally approached her destination.

The journey had not been easy. It took her a long time to find a stone that she could hold between her two stumps to cut the rope that tethered her horse to the tree—she gave up trying to untie the simple knot after endless minutes of pointless fumbling. Finally she got it far enough that she could chew the rope the rest of the way, severing the tether.

Mounting was another challenge, especially with her arms slick with blood and sweat from the exertion. With practice, she had been able to finally haul herself up…only to forget her few possessions still on the ground, like her water and gold. So Veronica had to practice dismounting, which resulted in several spills and a terribly sprained wrist where she kept bracing her falls with one of her stumps. Eventually she figured out how to use the crook of her elbow on the saddle horn to get herself in position to swing a leg over. That took a full day.

She slept the first night on horseback.

After a day of galloping, making her legs ache from squeezing the saddle, she now approached *The Royal Steed* back in Paragatha. There was no point riding after Magi to the west; she wasn't sure she could even survive walking through the mountains without her hands. And she wasn't sure how she could continue with her quest for some mythical shield in a far away land across the sea. She knew she needed to give Xaro an update soon, but she couldn't bring herself to do so. Not yet. Telling Xaro would cause the final curtain of reality to fall, a reality Veronica wasn't ready to face yet. She had no real plan except a few urgent needs: Food, more water, some clean clothes, a bath, a weapon she could use, and some specific potions. And a bed. For one more night at least, she would splurge on a bed, and Paragatha was still the closest city for many leagues.

"Some help, please." She called out to the stable hand, a young teenage boy maybe five to seven years her junior. He was every bit as tall as she was, however, and thicker.

"Miss?" he asked, grabbing the frayed reins. He stared at the blood all over her clothes and her raw wrist-ends, his eyes growing wide.

"Help me down, please." She tried to sound dignified, but her voice cracked.

"Beggin' your pardon, Miss, but I'm not sure I can take a Thief's horse in for the night. You best be riding through to find another inn."

"Please! Go tell Silas that I need to speak to him." Her chocolate-colored eyes begged him.

He looked at her, hugging the dead-tired horse. The stable boy sighed. "Very well." He turned and walked back toward the inn.

She started to doze in the saddle again when Silas finally came out, at least thirty minutes later. "Good god!" was his first comment. "Is that…Miss Sarah?"

He remembers me from my initial meeting with Strongiron…not from a few days ago in my Vernon disguise with Magi. "Yes. Hello, Silas," she began. "I need some help."

"What did you steal, woman?" Silas narrowed his eyes and crossed his arms.

Of course he thinks I'm a thief…no hands. Veronica decided to choose her words carefully. "I did not steal anything, Silas. I was…maimed. By a travelling Thief. He took everything, including my hands. When I awoke, I was covered in blood and bereft of all my possessions, save for my waterskin and a little bit of food and a few coins he didn't find. Can you help me, Silas?" She looked desperate; it was not an act. "Please—I will pay you all that I have."

Silas stared at her. She was hoping he recalled how she befriended Lord Hazelton and his wife Lady Fran—the overseers of Paragatha. She hoped he remembered the look in her eyes when she *commanded* the common room that night, earning a meeting with Strongiron. She hoped there was some small portion of goodness in this man. "I am so tired, Silas… Please?"

He rubbed a hairy forearm across his perpetually sweaty brow. "What do you need, Miss Sarah?

She extended her arm peg from atop her mount. "For starters, help getting down. Water for me and my horse. Food. An apothecary who knows herbs and potions. Fresh clothes. And I will bless you for a bath and a room."

Silas crossed his arms and sighed, staring at the wreck that used to be Veronica's right hand. He wrinkled his nose and finally grabbed it, a bit ungently, and helped her off the horse, who nickered in relief. A nod to his stableboy and it was led away.

"Miss Sarah, I will help you as best I can. And that includes my council. I am going to give you the best advice you will ever hear, and I want you to pay close attention." Silas actually took his hand off her stump and instead softly cradled her jaw, to make sure she was looking at him.

He wouldn't have dreamed of touching me like this before! But Veronica was too tired to jerk away. "Yes?" was all she offered.

"One night. I want you to leave before dawn, out the same way that I am going to take you inside. It is not safe for you to walk through the common room. It is not safe for you in the city *period*. Men will brand you a thief—just as my stable boy and I did—and they won't think twice about taking everything from you. And I mean *everything*. They'll think you deserve it. You're not a fine lady to most, and you're not travelling with anyone to protect you, and you've got no means of protecting yourself. I figured you were someone capable of looking after your own interests when we first met; now you're a wounded animal. Men will surround you and treat you as such. We live in a Dark World, filled with dark desires and darker deeds. If you have no family—and I suspect you don't, otherwise you wouldn't be in my inn, beggin' me for charity—then you know where you must go. Only one place for you will be safe, Miss Sarah."

Tears began streaming down Veronica's eyes. *No...* But in her heart, she knew what Silas said was true. She started shaking her head slowly, choking a sob.

"You must go North, toward Oxen-Pace, to the villages by the Sea of Joy, where the afflicted gather. They live off the charity of Oxen-Pace, but they are safe; nobody bothers them for fear of disease, or rather, because they have nothing worthwhile to steal. You will not last a week anywhere else." He turned his head toward the common room of his beloved *Royal Steed*. "Judging by the crowd in there right now, you wouldn't last the night unharmed in there."

"I would rather die," said Veronica. *Would I?*

"That may come sooner than you think, but I'm not going to be an accomplice. If you want my help, it will be to keep you alive, not to hasten your death. Leave tomorrow and head north. I'd avoid the Lightning Road at night—sounds like you already understand the perils of thiefs and mercenaries looking for work. It will take two to three weeks of hard riding, so maybe three to four in your condition, but that is where you must go."

Veronica wiped her stump across her cheek, the wet tears causing the dry blood on her wrists to leave red streaks across her face. "Okay, Silas. I will head north."

The large innkeeper patted her shoulder gently and wiped the red marks from her cheek with the cleanest corner of his apron he could find. "Let us go inside and see what I have to help you in your travels." He smiled and led Veronica back through the kitchen and up a flight of stairs, his burly arm around her for support.

For the first time since she was a child, Veronica—stiff, tired, and handless—leaned on another person for help.

~Magi~

"Excuse me?" Magi said, pausing to make sure he heard correctly. He knew the woman was telling the truth, but asked again, softening his tone and smiling. An idea was beginning to form. "Did I hear you correctly, Daphne, when you mentioned Xaro was your son?"

"Yes, do you know him?" The frail woman's eyes grew bright. Even her disguise could not hide the joy in her face when she heard her son's name.

Maybe...just maybe. "As a matter of fact, I have heard of your son, and that is why I am heading west. I believe I know where he is. Not too many mages around who are as accomplished as he is with steel, from what I understand. A True Mage and a True Warrior is a rare combination; it takes quite a long time to master multiple disciplines like that. As Fate would have it, I'm actually going to meet him." Magi looked up, wondering whether the woman would get his reference; she clearly wasn't a True Mage.

"Oh! This is wonderful! I haven't seen him since he left with that Ranger, Paul, so many years ago. I occasionally received word. A scroll here or there. Sometimes he would connect with me through a vision, but he never told me where he was. 'To protect you, Mother. I have more enemies now than I once did. Great men always do.' Tell me, where is he? Where over the sea is my son?" She gripped his arm, but it was an excited grip, not a demanding one.

"Perhaps you would like to join me?" offered Magi. "I can't imagine this chance encounter being purely coincidental." *And I won't hesitate to trade you for my ring back. I had hoped Veronica would mean enough to Xaro to be an effective bargaining chip; I could hardly ask for much better than his own Mother.*

The corners of her mouth started to turn upward, then suddenly stopped. She shook her head. "I am not wealthy. I cannot buy passage across the sea. Why would you bring me with you?"

Magi really didn't enjoy lying (especially while holding his staff), and there was a good part of himself he detested for his first thought being to use this woman to blackmail Xaro. Those thoughts, however, were quickly drowned in a chorus of musings that all came back to one common point: *The greater good is served if I have that ring and Xaro does not.*

Magi was convinced Xaro would be unstoppable with that ring, and even if Veronica said he didn't have it, Magi knew he was a lot closer on the trail to finding it than he was. By the time he sailed to Sands End, there was a good chance he might actually have it. *Having his Mother in tow certainly wouldn't hurt my leverage.*

Magi returned Daphne's stare. "If you must know, I am interested in joining Xaro's kingdom. I have heard that he needs good men around him. Showing a kindness to his Mother may help me in his eyes. Gold is not an issue for me; I can buy passage for us both, but I am leaving today—in fact, I had hoped to be in negotiations with a captain already this morning, though this is a fortuitous diversion for both of us. I would greatly enjoy your company—the journey to the other side of Tenebrae is long and lonely. The only thing I ask is…do you have another *Illusion*, perhaps, besides this old woman? Something less—alluring," Magi blushed as he quickly added, "—than your real self, but perhaps a little less off-putting than this disguise. Surely there is something in the middle?" He opened his arms a bit sheepishly.

The old woman narrowed her eyes and straightened the stoop right out of her back until she was nearly eye-to-eye with Magi. He could almost taste the stink on her breath. "You wish to pay for my passage and take me with you, and want *nothing* from me?"

Magi grinned uncomfortably and shrugged. "Uh, just a good word from you with your son."

"And you think Xaro, if he has risen to anoint himself a king, will listen to me—a woman he shows *such* care and devotion to?" She launched a stream of spit through a gap in her teeth against a nearby wall.

Magi swallowed and leaned forward as far as he could stand. "It can't hurt, Daphne."

"Humph! We'll see. You are either a trusting fool, a liar, or both. But I am old. I know I do not look it in my natural state, but I am older than I look. I would greatly like to have a face-to-face conversation with Xaro once again. We have a lot to…" her voice trailed off a bit, "catch up on, and this may be the last chance I ever get." She extended a bony, shaky finger to caress Magi's nose. "As to your terms…I can take any image of any woman you want, young man, but you'll find only the repulsive ones keep the men away. If we are to be on a boat with a crew of men, I expect you'll want me as repulsive as possible if you want to avoid attention."

"What is it about you, Daphne, that makes you so…"

"Irresistible?" She playfully pinched his cheek.

Magi started to sweat. He tried to step back, but found himself already flat against an alley wall. "Er, yes. Good word."

She laughed, but let her *Illusion* slip, and the laughter was light and airy. *Like Kari used to laugh.* "Haven't you guessed? I am an Enchantress. My persona is not a magical spell; it is a part of who I am. I am a decent enough Illusionist as well, as you have seen, but like I said—few men can resist me unless I clothe myself in the most hideous of *Illusions*. Never made it up the Staircase, but I'm fair with a few images. I'm afraid if I 'toned it down' even a little, the men aboard our ship would soon forget their posts and form a line outside my door. Why, given a few weeks at sea, I might even be able to break you down." She grinned her checkerboard smile, pressing her two bony hands against Magi's chest seductively. "Now I have a question for you," she said wickedly.

Magi swallowed. "Yes?"

"What is your name, young man? I only travel across the world with men whose name I know." She winked a wrinkled eyelid at him.

"M—" Magi started. "Michael. My name is Michael, Daphne. It is, uh, a pleasure to meet you." He took one of the hands pressing him back against the wall and shook it. "Now, is there anything you need to retrieve, or can we head down to the docks?"

"All I need is in my wheelbarrow, Michael. Come—I think I know just the captain to introduce you to. I'm quite popular with the sailors."

"Yes. I imagine you are." Magi squirmed away from her and they began walking toward the docks, putting together an easy travelling story to which Magi was only half-listening. His real focus was making sure he ingrained in his own mind his new name, Michael. *If there is even a remote chance that she still communicates with Xaro privately, there is no way I'm going to alert him that I'm coming…and with his Mother, no less.*

~Queen Najalas~

Her council chambers were quite crowded. In the past, she had limited her private advisors to five, heading the same departments that her late husband, King Alomar, had employed. But she felt there were several new positions and tasks that required attention, and good people whose advice and service she could use. That had been her thinking before last night when she'd requested the early morning meeting.

Her thoughts now were far more pointed: *the incessant babbling at this hour is not helping my already pounding head.*

Sighing, she let the small talk continue while pieces of dried beef and freshly squeezed orange juice were served with hot bread, freshly baked. Scanning the room, she saw Herodius pass the bread to Belara, who looked fully recovered from her duel, though she wouldn't sit next to Kari. Peter, Jonathon, and Simon were there of course, along with Niku and Strongiron—the five original council members. The other three were recent additions.

How much should I share of my plans with Silverfist? The thought loomed, uninvited, into her head. Part of her felt guilty for not having even considered their opinions. *Would it matter? Who among them, save for perhaps Belara, would have the guts to make the kind of trade-off necessary to avert this war.* She knew what their advice would be to a person, and having seen how they reacted last time when they unanimously disagreed with her, she was not keen to get into another such debate. *This contingency shall be my burden alone.* How she would manage to kill her friend and ally without involving her small council was a challenge best deferred for another day—a clear-headed day.

Forcing a pleasant smile on her face, Queen Najalas held up her hand, and out of respect they all quieted, nodding their heads. "Thank you for gathering this early. I know there is much to do today, which is why I wanted our meeting to take place first thing in the morning. Hopefully some fresh bread will take the sting out of the hour of our discussion." Several modest claps greeted her ears— even in Rookwood, fresh bread was always appreciated. "Therefore, I will be direct. As you can see, I am expanding my small council to represent an Elvidor War Council. I am adding several positions, and I want everyone fully aware of what each of you is doing."

The Queen took a healthy gulp of juice, which actually made the thumping in her head a little less loud. "Strongiron, as Commander General of our Armies, I authorize you to follow through on your plans to travel North to the plains near Oxen-Pace, where Sir Victor Remington holds command of our Northern arms. Given your decision to relinquish command in pursuit of the Shield of Life, I am ordering you recall Sir Victor to Rookwood where he can take over as Commander General and become a member of this War Council. Is this still your will, General?" The Queen fixed her intense gaze on Strongiron.

"It is, my Queen. Sir Victor is a good man." Several 'hrmphs' caused Strongiron to flash dirty looks around the room.

"I am aware that he is an insufferable lout, a braggart, and brash in his command," the Queen said, "but he wins battles. The man *fights*, and we will need fighters. Bring him to me as your last duty as Commander, before you depart."

"It will be done, my Queen." Strongiron grabbed a piece of tough beef and stuffed it into his mouth.

"Peter—as Admiral, I would ask that you not only fortify our port in Rookwood, but also travel to Plythe. I agree with your previous suggestion, and would like you to build a small, swift-moving fleet of ships that can be harbored in the Sea of Joy and launched to come to our defense should enemy sails come our way. Per earlier discussions, I too am worried about our fleet becoming jammed into our port if the enemy brings an armada with speed, undetected until they are too close to engage. We must have a way of attacking from behind as well, and Plythe is a good launching point."

Peter nodded. "We are in agreement then. Will the treasury support my shipbuilding?" The room looked his way. Every gold crown devoted toward his ships was a gold crown that could have been spent on mercenaries or supplies. War required tradeoffs.

The Queen sighed. "Half of it. Half as many ships, Peter. I don't know that you'll have time to build as many as you wanted, regardless."

"But, your Maj—" Peter began.

The Queen held up her hand and fired a hard look in his direction. "Half, Peter. The kingdom has many needs."

"Then I will make do," he said, as he also stabbed at a piece of beef, grumbling.

"Simon and Jonathon, your excellent service here shall continue. Simon, my only ask of you is to prepare the castle guard on how to fight off invaders. Should our defenses crack, the castle guard will represent our last line of defense. Many of our men have not seen battle except in the open fields—make sure they know how to fight in corridors and on the battlements. Show them the old traps, and get them used to manning the old stations. Speaking of which, these men are old—they come to the Guard when youth has passed them, and far too many are content to drink palace ale and tell exaggerated stories of their glorious youth. They are soft and brittle. Make them hard and strong again, Simon."

The look on Simon's face was horrified at the complaint of his men by the Queen. He pressed his jaws together until his lips formed a thin line. "As you say, my Queen. The Guard shall redouble our efforts."

The Queen nodded and turned to Jonathon. "You, my faithful Steward, know the castle better than anyone. Our stronghold can be traced back fifteen generations. I have no doubt many of my husband's ancestors carved their own history into these walls."

Jonathon just cocked his head.

"As a last resort, I want you to find the secret ways out of Rookwood—the dark paths that descend deep into the bones of the mountain to find the fresh water of Lake Calm on the other side. Legend says that a maze of passages exist beneath the castle. I need you to mark the right path as a last resort of retreat should we have to abandon the castle, but mark it in a way that is undetectable without a key. No one but myself shall order a retreat."

At this, the entire council chamber erupted in a cacophony of sounds. Shouts of "never!" and "death!" and other oaths were made to no one and everyone at the same time.

The Queen stood up and again raised her hands for silence. "I do not plan on retreating; it is imprudent, however, not to prepare for every contingency. Rest assured that we will fight for every inch of this castle, should it be breached, but some of you have wives and children that I presume you would spare capture if possible." She cast a long look at Peter and Simon. "And all of you have those you care about who cannot possibly fight the army that is going to descend upon us. A retreat—for their sakes—is a prudent last option. If we wait to begin exploring her depths until hundreds of undead warriors are crawling around Rookwood, it will be too late."

The Queen sat back down, shaking her head. "No. Jonathon Venerek, my most capable Steward, you shall find a path through the catacombs that leads to Lake Calm. If nothing else, it will also show us a path into our stronghold that must also be guarded."

"Of course, Your Majesty." Jonathon stood and gave a curt bow. "Consider it done."

With a nod, the Queen turned to her head Mage. "Niku," she said. "You have seen some of these undead creatures before. The closest most of your mages have ever come to an actual battle is no more dangerous than the duel we were treated to last night. Their education must be reshaped, Niku. They must learn new battle spells—spells of war. The academic pursuits that many study now must be replaced with training for battle, training under stress. A mage who loses his or her concentration as arrows fill the sky will not be of much use to us in defense of the city. Retrain them, Niku."

The old mage looked at his Queen. Though streaked with grey, Niku's hadn't bothered to oil his normally slick, well-groomed beard, leaving it uncharacteristically bushy. He just nodded at the Queen. *He looks old. Old and tired. I was right to give Belara the next task.*

Queen Najalas then turned to Belara. "Let me start off by thanking you, Belara. You have served me well while Niku was away searching for Dymetra."

The Master Illusionist was dressed today in a skin-tight, emerald green dress. As always, the gown had a head covering that clung to her scalp, forming a bright green triangle at the forehead. She looked completely refreshed, despite her stunning loss the night before. "It is my pleasure to serve you, My Queen." She bowed. The Queen could pick up the scent of vanilla, roses, and other exotic spices from her lithe movements. *I'm sure every man in here can as well.*

"Good. Because more service is required. I would ask that you take on the role of recruiting Mages and Warriors to our cause. I am asking that you go to the Three Fingers and Shith to raise troops for Elvidor's defense. The West has operated too autonomously; it is time they recognize Rookwood as their capital and participate in its defense."

Again, the crowd began to rumble. Several shook their head. Simon, she could hear over the din, was prattling on about "why would they listen to her?" and many more conversations. The Queen raised her arms yet again for silence as she caught Belara's eyes. Even colorless, she could see from the tight lines forming around them that she wasn't happy. *Good,* the Queen thought. *Belara isn't upset because I'm making her travel...she's upset because her peers don't think she can do it.*

"I am picking you, Belara, because I do not want to waste time or money travelling overland or by ship to reach the port cities and villages across the Crystal Mountains. I need a mage who can *Teleport*, and I trust you to be most persuasive in our recruiting efforts. Remind them of their duty, but remember you catch more flies with honey than anything else. We need thousands of swords from across the realm, and Mages, too.

Belara looked at her colleagues with a certain indignation at their lagging doubts. "Thank you, my Queen, for entrusting me with this. I will not disappoint you."

The Queen smiled and turned to Kari. "Kari, you have made it clear that you wish to travel with Strongiron, and it appears you are not likely to slow him down, given your newfound skills." Queen Najalas turned to Strongiron. "I assume you two have discussed this? Is it still your wish that she accompany you as well?"

Strongiron nodded, and smiled at Kari, who barely came up to his neck when they stood next to one another. "I have, my Queen. I would welcome a fellow True Cleric on our journey to share the truth about Dymetra, and to pursue the Shield."

Outwardly, the Queen smiled kindly at them both, but all she could think was: *you could have been a King, Strongiron.* She pushed the thought aside. "Go and recover this artifact—this Shield. May Dymetra bless your efforts and return quickly to Rookwood with it, as I am sure we will need it."

Kari, blushing ever-so-slightly, nodded to her. "We will return with the Shield of Life, my Queen."

The Queen nodded back and couldn't resist stealing a glance at Belara when Kari spoke. *Not quite a scowl, but definitely a frosty look.*

Finally, the Queen turned to Herodius. She tipped her remaining juice back and grabbed one of the last pieces of bread, all of them having had their fill. She turned the hunk of bread over in her hands. "Do you know what this is, Herodius?"

The islander narrowed his eyes slightly, the corners of his mouth turning up slightly. "Bread, my Queen?" He asked it like a question.

Queen Najalas smiled. "That, but much more, Herodius." She tossed it to the islander, who snatched it in mid-air with one hand. "It is *peace*, Herodius. The winter has been devastating to our villages, and I receive word that a march on Rookwood is being planned. I cannot fight a war from without and civil unrest from within. The people of our plains *must* learn how to increase their crop yields, and they must be dealt with fairly, gently, but firmly. I cannot have a revolt, Herodius. I simply cannot. Especially over something like food.

"Therefore, I am asking you to take your best men on a mission of peace, expecting the best but prepared for the worst, to the valleys east and west of the road north, where villages and communities gather. Quell this nonsense of a revolution before it catches a spark, and use your knowledge of farming to educate them. Above all else—we cannot have sympathetic citizens giving comfort to an invading force, and sending my knights for this would likely only provoke or distance them. No...I think the message should come from an outsider, and only one true outsider exists that I trust completely. Will you do this for me, Herodius?" The Queen opened her hands, softening her tone. She saw Strongiron and Kari nodding, Niku and Simon also added their encouragement. Belara just stared at Herodius, curiously biting her lip.

The islander had a stunned look on his face. Pride seemed etched in every feature of his face. He stood up, and when he spoke, he was addressing everyone. "My Queen. It would be an honor for me to do this for you. When the people grow to know you as well as I now do, they won't be able to help themselves but to love you. Leave this to me, and do not give it one more thought. Your mind is needed on other things." He then bowed low and took his seat.

With that, everyone raised their goblets of juice for a toast, with at least one shout for stronger drink despite the hour, which frankly, the Queen thought might actually help with her head, but she never took her eyes off Herodius...

And he never dropped his, either.

~Xaro~

Xaro carefully drew the *Far-sight* spell from the balcony of his bedroom high atop the rebuilt fortress at Sands End. It was especially hot today; it was always hot in the desert, but today was one of those "shimmering" days—so hot that objects in the distance tended to shimmer. Xaro wanted a close up.

He'd heard that *Sheila's Bane* had finally docked. The boat Xaro had been waiting for ever since he felt his connection to Trevor suddenly extinguished. Trevor had been carrying two incredibly valuable objects with him, and he wanted answers.

He had already instructed his men to hold the ship in port, where Xaro would inspect the ship and her crew personally, but then something strange happened. Apparently a man escaped. Xaro didn't recognize him as one of his warriors, and it wasn't like Xaro received guests or visitors. He was limping and hunched over, straining in the heat and occasionally stumbling. The man had to have come from the ship, which means he must have overpowered one of the units that Xaro himself had dispatched to their harbor to hold the ship and her crew. This single, solitary figure was determined to walk right up to Xaro's stronghold, in broad daylight. He was intrigued, and zoomed in for a closer look.

The man was hideous. His face was horribly scarred, his eyes closed or bloodshot, his back was humped. He was deformed. There were members of Malenec's undead host that looked more put together than this man.

Xaro ended his *Farsight* spell with a wave of his hand, and decided to find out who would be so bold as to walk up to his stronghold in broad daylight. He already began to hear shouts from his advance guards calling on the figure to halt. He did not want him killed before he could speak to him, so he *Teleported* out to him.

When Xaro reappeared, a circle of twenty True Warriors were scattered around him and this man, with spears fixated on the stranger, who was already on his knees.

"Your name!" shouted one of his men, Captain Grull. He carried a whip, whereas everyone else brandished a spear.

Murmurings began as soon as Xaro appeared behind Captain Grull, who was facing the man on his knees. Immediately he looked over his shoulder, and his eyes grew wide. "Master Xaro!" he stammered. "I d-did not see you ap-pproach. My apologies!" He bowed his head. "We caught this man walking toward Sands End, asking for you. Do you know him?"

Xaro looked at Grull and his unfurled whip, and then back at the misshapen man on his knees. *Cruelty for the sake of cruelty never builds loyalty.* "I may. What is your name?" he asked.

The figure raised his head, showing the burn marks, scars, his closed eye and his misshapen one. "My name is Tarsh. Trevor said you were expecting us."

The True Mage. Of course. That is how he got past his troops.

The figure struggled to get to his feet, and bowed low to Xaro amidst the threats from the assembled guards. "You must be Xaro. You're the one I've travelled across the sea to meet."

"I am. Trevor did mention that he invited you. Marik also spoke highly of you as well at one point. Apparently, any advisor of mine who speaks well of you ends up dead. I would hear your tale, preferably out of this heat. Can you *Teleport*?"

"I can," Tarsh answered.

"Good. We'll continue this conversation in private. Thank you, Captain Grull, for your attentive service." Xaro dismissed the assembled troops with a wave, then reappeared in his meeting room, along with Tarsh, who followed his *Teleport* trail. Immediately Xaro began pouring glasses of lemon sweetwater for himself and his guest.

"So…as I was saying, both Marik and Trevor have died, yet you somehow survived. Tell me how."

Tarsh took a sip of the sweetwater, and a wave of relief seemed to sweep across his face. "I wasn't there when Marik died, but Trevor told me that another mage, my former roommate Magi Blacksmooth, killed him. We were students at Marik's school. Magi was apparently killed afterword—someone slit his throat and stole his ring—but was later returned to life. Trevor—"

"I know all that. I'm sorry to interrupt, Tarsh, but please—what happened aboard your ship?"

Tarsh took a long pull and wiped his mouth with the back of his hand. "I'm not sure, truthfully. I know that I lifted the boat out of danger when we were caught in the Maelstrom. Soon after that, Trevor and I were in our bunk below deck talking, when there was a knock at the cabin door. I answered, and everything went black. The last thing I remember was a pain in my head. I awoke—I don't know how much later—and there was blood and goo all over our cabin floor, but no sign of Trevor. It was like he threw himself over the edge of the boat."

"Blood and goo?" Xaro asked.

Tarsh nodded. "The room smelled awful. I burned incense for a week. The only reason the rest of the crew didn't throw me overboard was they saw how I had already saved them, and Trevor was unpopular with the sailors to begin with; he always drank all the ale and stole their money when they gambled. All Captain Z and his crew cared about was getting paid for taking us here, and that I could assure them of. As far as they were concerned, Trevor and I had a falling out, and I turned him into a toad or something. None of them messed with me after the Whirlpool, and I kept my distance as well."

Xaro considered Tarsh. No guile filled his words. If this was a lie, it certainly was well rehearsed. Something about the story bothered Xaro, however, though he couldn't quite put his finger on it. Trevor would not kill himself. *Someone killed him.* "So, you did not kill him, or take anything from him?"

Tarsh shook his head. "No. The gold was left in our room, and much of that I used to pay for our passage. Trevor had the ring on when we were speaking. However, he did give me this for safe-keeping." Tarsh took out the Purple Sun jewel.

All other thoughts were soon driven from Xaro's mind as his eyes grew wide with covetousness, staring at the dazzling gem. "Trevor was delivering that to me."

Tarsh held it up. "I will give it to you, but I would like something in return."

Xaro cocked his head. "You would bargain with me for my own treasures? My my my, that little Thief must have rubbed off on you in the short time you spent together."

Tarsh pursed his lips. "It is more of a request than a demand." Tarsh stood up, but made no attempt to straighten his back. "Trevor said you are a real Cleric. That you worship a real God. I would ask that you heal my shattered body and accept my service in exchange for this jewel. I would like nothing more than to wage a war on this world, and on my ex-roommate, who did this to me."

The man wants to be healed. He looked at him—his features were grotesque. "Tell me, Tarsh. Do you know what this jewel does?"

"Trevor said that it can be used to create gold."

"You could be wealthy if you kept this. Even a deformed man can live like a king with unlimited gold." Xaro stood up and slowly approached Tarsh.

"Better a whole man than a deformed king, Xaro. Besides—if I serve you well, I doubt I will starve if you control the supply of gold to the realm. At least, that is the bet I'm willing to make." Tarsh extended the jewel to Xaro.

"Why should I heal you, Tarsh? Surely you must know that I could just take this from you. You walked into an army camp surrounded by an undead horde and tens of thousands of warriors. Why?" Xaro reached Tarsh, but did not take the jewel yet.

"Frankly, it was the only hope I had. If you take it and I end up with nothing, so be it. If you kill me, so be it. As a practical matter however, I do not see many True Mages walking around. I see a lot of swords. Personally, I think you could use me." Tarsh tried to smile, but it didn't look right on his face. More of a grimace.

Is he brave, or just desperate? Can he be trusted? Time will tell whether he can prove his worth to me. Lifting a ship from the Maelstrom shows, at the very least, power, and I can always use power.

Xaro reached out, not to grab the jewel, but to grab his arm. "Kuth-Cergor, heal this man of his infirmities. I ask that you make him whole again, that he may know you are a worthy God, not a false one!" Xaro tightened his grip. "Show him your power, so that he may worship you until the end of his days!"

A gust of wind blew open the balcony doors, and Tarsh dropped his ceramic cup of lemon sweetwater, which shattered on the floor. He moaned as his back began to straighten. Flakes of dead skin fell from his bald head as he felt, for the first time in a long time, new hair growing. Tarsh reached up to feel the long, raised scar down the right side of his face...but it was smooth. And his eyes! He could see from both eyes again. He breathed deep, and felt air filling his young, vigorous lungs.

Tarsh yelled for joy. It was the sound of a young, healthy man.

Xaro let his arm go and stepped back. "Quite a transformation, Tarsh. Kuth-Cergor has shown you his power. Only a God could do this for you, Tarsh." He reached out his hand. "The jewel?"

Tarsh tossed it to Xaro without hesitation, and dropped to his knees. This time it was out of humility, not weakness. "Master," he uttered. "My service is yours, if you'll have me."

Xaro wasn't even looking at Tarsh any longer. Fixated on the jewel, he turned it over and over. "Yes, arise. There will be tasks you can help with, of that I have no doubt. Come—I have been waiting for this."

They headed to the roof, where Krishnan stood next to his potion. He rarely left it save for food and rest, per Xaro's command. "Master?" he said, standing up as soon as he appeared. "Who is this?"

"Krishnan, meet Tarsh. He has brought us a gift." Xaro held up the Purple Sun as they approached the slowly bubbling potion.

"Master!" Krishnan said. "The Purple Sun...the Starburst gem!"

Xaro nodded and handed it over to the alchemist. "Your life's quest, my prayer. Add it, and let us see this miracle."

Krishnan slowly dipped the gem into the cauldron of clear liquid, and released it so that it sank slowly to the bottom. The gem lay at the bottom of the boiling potion, when Xaro resumed his prayer. Krishnan started his chanting. And all of them stared into the depths of the liquid.

Slowly, they began to see a change. The potion seemed to swirl, like the jewel was sucking liquid in from the bottom and spraying it from its facets. It began to glow, and steam quickly obfuscated their view. Krishnan, like so many times before, levitated a series of old pieces of scrap iron to drop into the potion.

One by one they fell, each with an unceremonious "plop", falling to the bottom, where nothing could be seen any longer. The smoke coming from the top of the cauldron now rivaled a brushfire. Yet the mages would not back up.

After a minute, Krishnan drew his chanting to a close. The only sound was the hissing pot, and slowly Krishnan levitated the metal back out.

Emerging from the smoke was an oddly shaped, yet unmistakable, pile of gold. Krishnan dropped it carefully into Xaro's outstretched hands; it was cool to the touch.

A greedy, wild-eyed grin spread across his face. "Let the war preparations begin in earnest now."

Book 2: Crown

CHAPTER NINE: NEW BEGINNINGS

~Victor~

Victor Charles Ethan Remington III curled the thick edge of his flowing mustache around his forefinger as he intensely watched the spectacle. Cross and pile was a game of chance where a gold crown was flipped, and if you guessed which side it would land on correctly, you won the crown. He liked that game. Dice was another favorite game; he kept three cubes on him at all times, even on campaigns. His dice, of course, were slightly loaded to the six side with a few undetectable drops of mercury to unbalance the weight. He also loved chess; it was a game he thrived on, and was known to have two or three games going at once during long periods of leisure.

But none of these pursuits could match the thrill of his favorite gambling pastime: cock fighting.

Two roosters, one large, brown-speckled male and a slightly smaller, orange and red chicken were squaring off in a rudimentary pit cage set up for the barbarism. They set it up next to their camp, northwest of Oxen-Pace, where the Queen's northern army was largely encamped to guard against invasion landing by sea and travelling south down the Lightning Road.

Gathered around the cage were several warriors, some travelling gypsy women, and a Mage. Strongiron had insisted that Victor take at least one mage with him up north; Victor could do without one, but Luther was all right. *For a Mage. At least he's hanging out with the boys at the arena.*

That is what they called the cock-fighting pit: the arena. Luther would use his spells to melt the snow so that they could have their fights all through winter as well. *He has his uses.* Goodness knows Victor and his men needed their distractions through the winter. They were all glad to see the spring thaw.

"Now pay attention, Sheila. The key to betting the chickens is simple: it's not the size that matters; it's the *meanness*. Just like with men. Always bet on the meaner fighter. And that little red one is plenty mean. You watch." Victor leaned over and whispered his wisdom into the ears of a young, slightly plump redhead who appeared content to simply sit on Victor's lap. She smiled and playfully bit his lower ear, flashing haughty eyes at all the other women hanging around the barracks, the camps, and the arena.

The two roosters didn't waste much time. Their combs and wattles removed, the two fierce birds tore into one another as soon as the handlers let them go. The larger, brown gamecock squawked as the leaner red one immediately charged. The pit erupted as the men shouted, jostling the various women who were trying to find a gambling warrior with a fat purse and an unoccupied lap. Ale was spilt. Feathers flew.

The match was over in five minutes. The red gamecock had clawed and pecked the poor speckled one to death in the blink of an eye, much to the dismay of the majority of the bettors. Victor just grinned silently throughout the whole affair, content to curl his mustache.

"Thank you boys—always a pleasure doing business with my fellas." Victor laughed as about a dozen pieces of copper and silver fell into his palms, accompanied by the grumbling of his men. "Cheer up, men. Could be worse. I coulda thrown some of you in there with little red!" He laughed from his belly, and even his troops had to smile at the picture of fighting a gamecock in the arena. "Besides—fresh meat for dinner. Benjamin, skewer that bird up for us!"

A few men cheered; there was always fresh meat on nights when the gamecocks fought. Not a lot, but a few chunks of chicken always brightened the mood. Victor's attendant, Benjamin, who also shared in the cooking duties for the army camp, scooped up the dead bird and headed off to dress it. It was understood that only the wage-bettors would get a skewer of grilled chicken; Victor commanded about a thousand men, but only a couple dozen or so on any given night would gather in the arena to gamble their hard-earned wages. Most meals for the army consisted of rice and beans from Oxen-Pace, a few luxuries from the Queen sent up from the South, and occasionally some exotic fruits from Plythe, a remote port city virtually cut off from central Elvidor by Spookwood. It was easier to reach Plythe by ship than over land, for sure.

Victor patted his coin pouch in satisfaction before snaking his arm around Sheila's waist. "What say we skip dinner tonight?" he said with a wink.

Just then, one of the male gypsies that hung around the camp walked over to Victor. He was large, a couple inches taller than Victor, who might reach five foot ten inches by wearing thick boots. This gypsy was easily over six feet tall and barrel chested. He spoke in a thick accent. "That is my gamecock you killed. You cheat—your bird has spurs. Spikes tied to its legs. I want money for this."

Of course you want money. What else do gypsies want? "Next time put spurs on your bird if you're so concerned. The fight went as it went. You lost. I'll have Benjamin save you a piece so you'll know what a losing *hen* tastes like." He reached out and pushed the man's shoulder out of the way as he walked past, with Sheila still hanging on his arm.

Victor tolerated the gypsies. They were harmless for the most part. Sure, some were thieves, but most were women. He knew that a thousand men camped up north with nobody to fight grew restless. The gypsies would be fools to attack one of his men on so many levels, not the least of which was the fact that his troops were, after all, excellent customers.

But there was something different in this gypsy's eyes. Something wasn't right, and if there was one thing Victor prided himself on, it was his instincts. He wasn't sure what made him turn around; perhaps it was the tenseness in Sheila's grip. But he did.

Silent as a night moth, the gypsy drew a curved blade from his sleeve and was set to bury it between Victor's shoulder blades when he heard Sheila gasp. "Papa, no!"

The man's eyes tracked to Sheila, and in that second Victor turned around with his own dirk drawn. Wiry strong, he grabbed the wrist of the gypsy with one hand and pushed the blade of his own knife against the gypsy's adam's apple. "Are you mad, trying to kill me? Over a blasted gamecock? You are surrounded by a thousand of my men, all camped around here. Who are you?"

Sheila screamed. "Victor—please! He is my Papa! Don't harm him, please!"

He pushed the man away from him. "This is your daughter?"

"It is. She is not for men like you."

"Men like *me?* I am the Lieutenant General of all of Elvidor, Commander of the Northern Army, Knight of Thunder, and heir to the Remington estate. And *I* am not good enough for your daughter?"

The gypsy looked at him, then at Sheila, who shook her head. "Papa, *I* make my own decisions. Me. You do not speak for me!"

The old gypsy dropped his knife, and hung his head. His shoulders stooped before he looked up at Sheila. "I want better for you. This man cares nothing for you, my child. I watch him—he wins at everything because he cheats at everything, always taking what isn't his. I don't want him to treat you the same way, Sheila."

A crowd was now starting to gather at the commotion. His men were looking at him, waiting for a reaction, waiting for orders.

Victor couldn't believe his ears. *This puke of a man just accused me of cheating in front of my men.*

Sheila stepped in between her father and Victor. "Please, Victor—he doesn't know what he's talking about! Let him be. Let's go—you wanted to skip dinner, right? Come with me. He's just an old man, Victor," she pleaded.

Victor shook his head. "Actually, I am hungry now. Both of you—leave our camp immediately. Move on. I'm done with you both. Now get out of here before I change my mind." He flicked his hand dismissively.

Sheila gave her father a withering look, but his face was the picture of relief. He said nothing, he made no move to pick up his knife, and he just grabbed his daughter and pulled her away from the crowd, despite her protestations. Grumblings of "Papa, you fool! He was mine, Papa. For once, *I* could have been the one." His men sheathed their swords as the two gypsies argued into the distance.

Their jokes were interrupted by Luther, who came up to Victor. "Sir Victor," he said. "I've just received word from Niku that we're going to receive visitors. Strongiron is coming."

~Magi~

It started with a simple "Let me help you, ma'am," from one of the sailors as she boarded the plank from the dock. It progressed from there to the captain agreeing to give up his quarters for Magi and his 'mother.' Then followed the best wine on the ship, the freshest grapes, and the leanest beef…not pork, but real beef, seasoned for travel. Magi had had enough when one of the sailors actually offered to give the hideous-looking woman a massage.

"Thank you, but she's a bit too stooped to handle much kneading. We'll just retire for the evening, if that's okay." Magi gently grabbed Daphne's arm and led her below deck to Captain Solomon's cabin. He shut the door and looked at the woman, still wrapped in her *Illusion* of frailty and age. "Has your whole life been favors from unsuspecting men?"

She flashed a gap-toothed smile. "Since I was thirteen, I've always attracted attention. You get used to it." She let the smile fade, and turned more serious. "But it would be nice—just once—to be loved for real. You have no idea how much I envy women that."

Magi arched an eyebrow. "Actually, discerning what is real and what is not is something of a passion of mine. I can see how you would feel that way." He took a seat in a corner chair in the cabin, enjoying the gentle rocking over relatively easy seas. "Tell me about your son. What was he like growing up?"

Daphne sat on the edge of the bed facing Magi. "He started to show at an early age that he might have a gift for magic. He was much stronger than I am; although my strength tends to manifest itself not in my spells as much as in my, uh, gift." She grinned. "It's always on, in that sense. And while it can be tiresome, I'm sure you'd agree that it does have some advantages." She fanned her arm out in a sweeping gesture of the Captain's room, giving Magi a wink.

"But you wanted to know about Xaro. We grew up in Raag-Kaan, off the coast of Oraz. After I had him, I knew we had to live away from people. It wouldn't be good for the boy seeing his mother attracting as much attention as I do. Raag-Kaan is a primitive village, and we were able to live well to the outskirts, in the valleys below the cliffs. I trained Xaro in his youth to harness his magic with the simple spells that I knew while he continued to grow. And grow." She looked at Magi. "Like you, but bigger still. I should have expected that." She looked off into a small candle burning in the corner of the room. "Everything changed when *he* came."

"Who?" asked Magi.

"Paul. The Ranger. He was hiking through Oraz at a time when Xaro was fifteen or so. He saw our cook fires one evening and he came by. Xaro and I lived simply, in a small wood and stone house that we'd built right into a hillside. The man took one look at me and was smitten. And, truth be told, I was lonely too, Michael. Paul the Wanderer stopped wandering for many weeks, content to stay and help us. He taught us farming tips he had learned in Adimand. He helped us fashion better tools. He improved our shelter. And he took Xaro under his wing—taught him to hunt, to track, to fish. He taught him the ways of the woods, spices, herbology, tree and plant life. And while Paul and I grew closer and closer, Xaro was drifting further and further away. His head was full of stories now, and he wanted to see the world.

"I could have kept Paul there forever; he was, shall we say, under my spell. I like to think he would have stayed anyhow. But they don't call him 'Paul the Wanderer' for nothing—he truly had seen every known continent of Tenebrae. When Xaro made up his mind to leave, he insisted that I not accompany him. I don't know, Michael—maybe he was jealous of all the time Paul and I were spending together. But that was the last he and I were close. We had our last fight, and the next day, my boy was gone." She shook her head and closed her eyes, looking every bit as old and frail as her *Illusion* projected.

"At that point, Paul and I tried to track him, but I was slowing him down. I'm not a Ranger. Xaro had taken off on a horse; I didn't ride. Each day he was putting leagues between us, and Paul could tell he was headed toward the mountains. I could not learn to ride at the pace we needed, especially if he headed south toward the foothills of the Hawthorne Mountains. So…I made a choice. I told Paul who I was; an Enchantress. He didn't believe me and wouldn't leave me to go after my son. For him, under my spell, Xaro was probably a distraction. So I lied to him and showed him this image—only I told him this is who he had been living with for months. My other self was the *Illusion*. That is what I told him, and it had the desired effect. He was repulsed.

"I begged him to track down Xaro and try and send him home. I gave him what little gold I had and hoped for the best. He said he would consider it." She opened up her hands. "I had my doubts, but he was only fifteen, Michael. I needed someone to catch up to him. I needed a Ranger."

She steadied herself as the boat rocked, and stood up to pour herself some lemon sweetwater (Captain Solomon had insisted that their room be furnished with the freshest lemons throughout their voyage). "Turns out he *did* follow him. I guess it was a challenge the famous Ranger couldn't pass up. I'd like to think he felt something for me, but I know better." She sat back down. "I received a letter months later, in the form of a scroll. A young man had travelled all the way from Shraal, many leagues to the south, to visit me and drop it off. Paul and Xaro were travelling together, and were boarding a ship to Urthrax, and from there maybe Elvidor. He was going to take him under his wing as an apprentice and teach him how to be a Ranger. Subsequent letters came over the years infrequently. He told me he had climbed the Staircase; he told me about an ancient God. Always short, never any details, never asking about me. Almost like he was obligated. The last time we spoke, was in a vision—he appeared before me using some form of spell; I could talk to his shade. He was so tall and so thick. But he's also a liar."

"What do you mean?" Magi leaned forward. "What did he lie about?"

"He said he climbed the Staircase. But his eyes are still brown. He is not a True Mage, Michael." She sipped her drink and shrugged. "But I do not judge. I have lived many lies, many fantasies. He comes by it honestly, as they say."

There is something missing in this story. Magi was running his fingers through the thick stubble of his chin when it finally dawned on him. "So, where was his father all those years?"

Daphne looked at Magi and didn't immediately answer, though a smile graced her lips as she seemed to relive her memories. "Presumably leading the King's Army. His father was Peace-Arm Orion Tuitio. Xaro may look like me, but he has his father's bearing. Peace-Arm was, after all, a mountain of a man."

~Xaro~

The last week had been a whirlwind. Massive orders for raw materials were placed and secured with good gold; Krishnan was working around the clock to keep feeding formerly worthless deposits of iron ore harvested from the depths of the nearby Ajax mountains into his potion, turning it into gold, then melting and casting the gold into coins. Xaro had an image of Kuth-Cergor emblazoned on one side. His own likeness was on the other.

Lumber, steel, provisions, armaments—the list of requirements necessary to build an armada capable of sailing more than forty thousand men across the world…with provisions to last for months of a protracted siege—it was a never-ending list. He just shook his head when Tar-Tan told him the amount of leather he needed. "Waterskins and travelling armor," was all he said.

This, if nothing else, was where his half-ogre truly excelled. It was astonishing how comprehensive his planning was for this assault, with contingencies for what might happen if they lost half their fleet in the Maelstrom. He thought of livestock. Entertainment on the journey over. Rations. Extra water and salt. Lifeboats. Travelling armor. Battle armor. Back up sails. Boat repair supplies. Medical herbs. Gold for bribes and to hire local mercenaries. Maps and other navigational aids. Oil for fire. Horses. The planning and logistics was endless.

Tar-Tan operated as if gold was not a concern, which it wasn't any longer. So he planned as if they were never coming back to Sands End. *Which is probably right.*

Even the ogre, however, could not place orders or negotiate prices over wide geographies; Xaro had to do that by *Teleportation* or other means. His first week since solving his gold scarcity problem highlighted another problem, this one even more acute: the Xaro scarcity problem. He was the only one who could *Teleport* throughout Ipidine, or communicate with merchants in far-away lands. *At least no one I fully trust.*

The days and nights blurred together, shuffling between Krishnan, Tar-Tan, merchants, and so on. After a week of this, Xaro decided to call a council meeting. It was time for updates and reports. Standing next to him in the flesh were Krishnan, Tar-Tan, and Tarsh. He asked Tarsh to join him, as he had sworn his allegiance to Xaro, and Mages were in very short supply in his camp. He and Krishnan were the only other ones.

Malenec chose to participate from afar. Though he allowed his undead to train with the living warriors, he was becoming increasingly withdrawn. His last spectacle with the wights had nearly resulted in a showdown with his Dark Cleric. Eventually, Xaro knew he must confront Malenec—it was the main reason he pursued the Shield of Life. He would exploit any edge he could gain over Malenec—but for now he needed him.

Next to Malenec's shade was the shimmering image of Veronica. Perhaps it was the light in his council chambers, but she looked different. Thinner, and she was none-too-thick to begin with. Something odd appeared in the way she was seated behind a campfire.

"Thank you all for gathering. By now all of you know, except perhaps our lovely Assassin, that we have been successful in transforming base metals and raw ore into gold. I would start there with an update from Krishnan." He turned to his Master of Coinage.

"Thank you, Master. The production is steady. I have found a sustainable rate of conversion to be roughly one thousand gold coins per day. We are, obviously, spending more than that currently, but that is for the initial raw materials. The coinage is more than enough to collateralize our initial orders, and as you know the shipments from nearby merchants have recently arrived. But our increase in production will announce to all of Tenebrae that we are preparing for war; as I have said before—there will be no hiding our intensions as word spreads of our massive purchases, and our new coins begin circulating in far off cities."

"We are still running at a deficit? Can you create the gold faster?" Xaro asked, somewhat shocked.

"No, Master. I can't. It takes a certain amount of time for the process to complete. But we will not be spending so much forever. Eventually the gold production will catch up and we shall stuff our treasury with a surplus."

Xaro didn't say anything, he simply pressed his lips together and turned to Tar-Tan. "Your update, General? You are the one who is spending all our gold, after all."

Ignoring the shimmering images of the non-present guests, the half-orge turned to Xaro and Krishnan. "I am planning for as many worst case scenarios as I can envision. I admit the plans require much gold. But when you consider we are launching a fleet from the other side of the world, I think we can all appreciate both precision and contingency being incorporated into our attack plans. If I am spending as if we have an unlimited supply of gold, it is only because I know we have an unlimited supply of gold. Should I not buy extra food? What if the siege takes longer than we anticipate? Should I not buy ale? Imagine your morale if you had to be out at sea for months without good drink. Should all our armor be plate and chain? It is more practical to wear simple leather while en route. Should we hire experienced crews, or turn our warriors into sailors? These are the things I must concern myself with. And I can tell you that all is going according to plan."

"When will the spending taper?" asked Xaro.

"Soon, Master. When the shipments start arriving every few hours, and our port is jammed with deliveries, you will know that the spending will soon begin to subside." The half-ogre tipped his head forward slightly and turned back to face the rest of the council.

"I believe I am on record in saying that my troops require no such expense," offered Malenec.

Gritting his teeth, Tar-Tan started to stand up to walk toward the True Cleric, but a wave of Xaro's hand stopped him. He said nothing, and grudgingly sat back down.

"Yes, we have covered this before, Malenec. Since you are so eager to speak, it shall be your turn now." Xaro stood next to Tar-Tan, and put a reassuring hand on the massive shoulder of his General while speaking to flickering shadow of his Dark Cleric.

"I have no update. We gather. We train. I sleep. We repeat. You do not want me to go to Misk, where I could easily expand our forces. But whatever. You feel the need to build an army that you must train, feed, house, arm, transport, and ultimately support. My army requires no training, no feeding, no housing, no arming, no transport, and no support. We could have a hundred thousand undead zombies surrounding Rookwood already, but please, continue with this course so that we can give that hideous queen all spring and all summer and all fall to prepare her fortress while you buy wheat and corn by the bushel. The only part of this plan that encourages me is knowing that as your men die from one cause or another heading across the seas, that I will be there to ensure their bodies are not squandered. Eventually, they all shall end up with me. I take it as a lesson in patience that Kuth-Cergor is teaching me." Malenec sat in his private barracks, his shade facing the group, seated with his arms crossed.

One day I shall take great pleasure in ripping that impertinent tongue clear from your throat. "Yes—your objections have been noted. The undead are not without weaknesses of their own, Malenec. I have no intention of rehashing this again."

He turned to Tarsh. "Young Mage, I have not given you a task yet, but I shall soon. Until then, I want you to study with Krishnan. Learn what he knows about metal changing, and let us see if we cannot increase the gold production rate by the two of you working together."

Tarsh nodded. "I already have begun studying with him. I will continue to do so." He glanced at Krishnan, who inclined his head in acknowledgement.

And now my Assassin. Let me give her a cover story for the others. "Good. And now, Veronica…I am most interested in how you are progressing on your efforts. You may recall when we last met privately, you were planning on trying to leave Elvidor?"

Veronica seemed to be only marginally paying attention, but she snapped alert when Xaro said her name. "Yes, Master?"

"Your update?" Xaro said, eyebrows raised.

Her shimmering image exhaled, and it was a loud enough sigh that everyone heard it. "Master, I—" she began, her words catching. "I've been injured."

All eyes were steadily focused on the image of her sitting cross-legged behind a campfire, obscured from the neck down by the flames. "How so, Veronica? What happened?" Xaro seemed genuinely concerned.

She closed her eyes and held up her hands…or rather her wrists. Both hands were missing. There was a piece of flint crudely strapped to her wrist, and a metal striker strapped to another. "I don't remember what happened. But I woke up like this." Xaro locked eyes with her and knew immediately what she didn't want to say to the rest of the group: *Magi did this.*

Xaro didn't say anything immediately, his mind racing. The first and overarching thought he had was that he had underestimated Magi. *If he is capable of this, perhaps he's not as soft as I thought. I would have bet good gold that he would have let her go, or turned her over to the Queen. I did not expect this.*

Veronica had been talking, but Xaro only now started listening. "—heading north now. But I wish to come back to Sands End. Will you help me? You can heal me, can't you?"

Gone was the supremely confident Assassin. Seated in front of him was a broken woman. Even if Kuth-Cergor healed her for him, would she ever be the same? And further, if Kuth-Cergor wouldn't heal her, she would end up with Malenec. *No, it is a kindness to keep her from that fate. Besides…a woman with no hands, travelling alone all the way across the seas to rejoin us when we are preparing to head to where she already is? That is a waste of gold, and would only expose her to a set of imprudent dangers sailing across all of Tenebrae.*

"No, Veronica. Stay on Elvidor now. When we come into power, I will look for you in the Valley of the Afflicted. Perhaps I can heal you then, my God willing. Until such time, I release you from my service, and from all contracts. Go find a new life, Veronica." He shook his head. "Such a pity."

There was a bunch of cross-talk as the others started asking questions about how could she not know what happened. Tears streamed down her face; she seemed to shudder. Before she could say another word, Xaro cut her out of the meeting, and her image vanished. They all turned to Xaro, who held up his hands to silence the others.

"Obviously something has happened to Veronica. Even the best Assassins sometimes develop powerful enemies, and based on her escape from the Queen, I expect this is the Queen's justice. No matter, it would have been ideal to rob the Queen of her General, but I am confident that Strongiron and the rest of them will fall because Kuth-Cergor will see to it. An Assassin without hands is not going to further our goals, so I offered her the humane option of staying with other cripples. Unable to protect herself, she would not survive the long sea voyage to Sands End. We will move on."

Through some shrugs and a few head nods, it was Malenec who Xaro was looking at when he spoke, whose his image just stood there, unmoving, wearing a dark, greasy smile.

~Kari~

The day dawned bittersweet. A warm morning greeted a cool reality; Kyle and she were headed in separate directions.

The final preparations made after yesterday's meeting with the Queen, Kari rose early to say her final goodbye to her brother. She cherished every free minute she'd had with him, often just sitting quietly next to one another, watching falcons soar and dive from their aeries around the mountain stronghold. Inevitably, Kari would broach the topic of him joining them. Predictably, Kyle gently refused. Today was no different.

"But Kyle, I've barely gotten to spend any time with you. Won't you reconsider? Just come to the northern outpost with us. You can just as easily head west from there." Kari had her hands on her hips. They were in the stables, where Kyle was getting ready to mount up to leave.

He checked his saddle buckles one more time, then sighed before turning back around. "Kari, we've discussed this. Elsa needs help, too. You will be fine. I'll miss you too, sis. Besides—I would just slow you down. You and Strongiron can *Teleport*, or whatever it is you Clerics do—"

"Pray," she helped.

"Yes, well, you two can pray your way north in a blink. I'll just hold you up. My path lies west of the mountains, and the best way through is the *Elf's Bane* Pass, which is near the southern end of the range." Kyle smiled softly at his sister. "C'mon. Last time." He extended his arms and wrapped them around his sister tightly. "I love you, sis. So proud of you." He gave her one final squeeze before separating. "Take care of yourself."

Kyle effortlessly swung himself over Granite, his beautiful grey stallion with coal-black patches. *He always was an athlete. And a show-off.* Kari wiped a single tear away as she giggled.

Kyle smiled at her, winked, and pushed his heels into Granite. "Yaah!" he shouted, as the horse darted forward, kicking up some dust. He began the long ride down the ramps and through the various gates that wound down from the mountain.

"Goodbye, Kyle!" she shouted after him, the sound of metal horseshoes striking rock still ringing in her ears. *Will I ever see him again in this life?*

A wooden door creaked open near the back of the stables. She turned to see Strongiron standing there. The early sun, low on the horizon, shone directly into the stables. The sunbeams hit Strongiron's pristine, white armor perfectly. Standing there, framed in light, he looked the very picture of goodness.

"Everything all right, Kari?" he asked. "Were you able to say your goodbyes?"

"We did. I was hoping he would come with us. I miss him already." She walked over to Strongiron and grabbed his massive hand. She could feel the rough callouses where he still trained regularly with his giant sword.

Strongiron smiled and ran his free hand through her thick tresses, combing it away from her eyes. "It is time we gathered our packs and made our prayers to leave as well. As for Kyle, I wouldn't worry too much about him. He will be okay, Kari. He goes with Dymetra's blessing to help a prophetess who loves Her. She still cares for this world—a point worth sharing with others."

She snaked an arm around his waist. His armor was cold, but it felt strong. *Unyielding—like the man who wears it.* "I know. I'm not really worried about *him*." She looked up into his ice-blue eyes. They were the color of a glacial crevasse, and if she stared at them long enough, she felt like she might just fall in.

Strongiron leaned in and tenderly kissed her lips, whispering, "I'm not worried about you, either."

~Veronica~

The former Assassin had always preferred the night. It was like a favorite blanket or a trustworthy friend. She hated it now.

The night meant work. The simple task of dismounting, tethering her horse, building a fire, and pulling apart her travel gear for food and water was a grueling chore that she dreaded. Just *existing* was impossibly hard—but she adapted. Veronica always adapted.

She learned to stop around small trees or bushes over which she would loop her reins. Dismounting ended with shoulder bruises initially, but it did not take long for her to master a technique of balancing on her stomach and swinging a leg over to land lightly on her feet. She left her pouches loose, and would use sticks and twigs to 'flip' contents out, or she'd just dump them all out and deal with repacking in the morning. Building a fire was almost impossible; but one night she did manage enough of a spark by banging a piece of flint against a rock into some tinder at the base. That was the night she felt Xaro's tug. She knew this day was coming.

Dismissed. She was dismissed. *You were a fool to think he would heal you anyhow. You failed him.* She should have taken Silver's advice. She should have killed Magi. *I tried,* she reminded herself. *Then you should have travelled with him and helped him defeat Xaro.* Betray Xaro? The thought repulsed her. Xaro had given her very first contract. Had praised her. She had a purpose—felt like she was contributing to something bigger than herself.

I could never have helped Magi defeat Xaro, but I should have played along. Waited for a different opportunity. On and on her thoughts went, night after night, as she traveled north. Always second-guessing herself. With each night, the battle to survive began anew.

Fortunately the nights were becoming warm enough where a fire wasn't completely necessary. She was cold with only a blanket, but she wouldn't freeze to death. At least, as long as it didn't rain. The few times it did look like rain, she usually could find some woods or some large rocks to provide a modest shelter.

Wet, thinning, and sore, she began to smell the salt before she saw the Valley of the Afflicted. The Sea of Joy must be close, and she knew the community was nestled into a valley bracketed by steep, rocky hills on one side, and the sea on the other. The terrain began to change as well. The gentle, grassy hillsides were giving way to cracked dirt and rock. And in the distance, she saw white water splashing against rocks.

Long shadows covered the valley as the setting sun fell behind the hills to the west. Veronica licked her lips, cracked and bleeding from having to chew through so many things. She didn't really trust her eyes in the queer light, but she thought small shapes moved in the shadows.

Veronica patted the neck of her horse with her blunt stump as gently as she could, cooing into its ear. "If we are meant to die, here is as good a place as any. You're a better horse than I deserve; I'll grant the Mage that, at least. Walk me into the valley." She pushed her heels into its ribs, and the horse moved slowly forward.

The distance to the Valley shrunk, and the sound of water hitting the rocks could now be heard. She could see that many small caves and overhangs were available for makeshift homes. On the ground were lots of small baskets.

As she approached, she saw the people were almost all covered from head to toe. *The Dying Disease.* Most turned and walked away before she even made it over the last hill. One man, however, slowly approached. He leaned heavily on a staff.

Cresting the hillside, Veronica now saw the full encampment of the valley. There had to be over a hundred bodies lying around, maybe closer to two hundred. But the first thing that hit her wasn't the number of afflicted.

It was the smell.

The Valley reeked of death and approaching death. If she'd had more food in her stomach, she would have retched. Even her horse needed extra coaxing to continue stepping down into the valley. In the end, she dismounted about as gracefully as possible, hooked the reins into her elbow, and tried to lead her skittish mount forward.

The approaching man dropped his staff and held up two hands in front of him, both wrapped completely. Veronica stopped and waited. The man bent down to grab his staff, stumbled slightly, but regained his balance and continued to approach. When he was about fifteen feet away, he stopped. The only thing uncovered on the man was his eyes. From this distance, they could be any dark color.

"Good evening," he said, somewhat muffled. "Why have you come to this place?"

Veronica swallowed hard, her throat scratchy. "I—I have nowhere else to go." She held up her arms.

"You are a Thief?"

"No. I am a—wounded traveler." *That is true enough.*

The eyes seemed to crinkle slightly, but Veronica couldn't be sure at this distance. "Your horse—I would not bring him into our midst. There is no food for him, and he will find the smell unpleasant. I'm afraid it would be best if you unpacked him and let him go free. If you plan to stay, that is."

Unpack my horse. Veronica gave a little laugh, knowing she probably looked deranged. "Yes. I plan to stay if I may." She turned around and started to look back at the buckles in her saddlebags containing her remaining gold, provisions, and clothing. She began pushing up on the straps with her stumps, moving close to the horse to try and bite the widening loop.

"May I help you?" The man was standing behind her, close but not on top of her.

She hung her head. "I would be grateful."

The man waited for her to step aside and then he proceeded to unharness everything, occasionally grunting. Veronica couldn't be sure, but based on his twitching eyes, it looked like he was in pain. After a minute or two, the relatively simple task was done, and Veronica's bags were on the ground. She hooked her elbows into the straps and easily picked them up.

"Thank you so much," she said. "I will pay you what I have for the kindness."

The man gave a muffled chuckle. "Your gold has little value to me, but I appreciate the gesture. No—I thank *you.* It is a gift for me to be able to help you. Nobody ever wants help from us."

"Us?" she asked. "Who are you?"

He leaned on the staff, and Veronica could see damp bloodstains through the cloth covering his fingertips where he was manipulating the buckles and straps. He kept his distance still, but he gestured to the valley below. "We are the Afflicted. The blind, the deaf, the dumb, the lepers, and the cripples come here. We live off the charity of others, some from our families, but most from the kindness of Oxen-Pace. We help each other, but our visitors are few. It has been months since someone new has sought to make refuge here. You are most welcome to live out your days, however long they may be, in peace with us."

He slowly began walking down the back of the hill toward their encampment. The horse didn't dawdle to say much of a goodbye; it bolted with a frenzied nicker.

Veronica easily caught up to the slow-moving man. "Well, thank you again. What is your name?"

The man didn't stop, just looked over his shoulder at Veronica. "Garin Massilon."

~Queen Najalas~

"Herodius," the Queen began. "Your men are assembled, I presume?"

She had given him the assignment yesterday to quell the unrest in central Elvidor. Night had fallen, and the Queen had asked him to a private dinner before he set out the next morning.

"They are, your Majesty." He was carefully slicing a piece of roasted pheasant that had been prepared with a spiced orange glaze and aromatic rice. The Queen regarded him with amusement; he looked like he wanted to lick his fingers and then chew on the plates.

"Be at ease, Herodius. You look tense. Please, enjoy the meal—it will be one of the few good ones you are likely to have any time soon." She rose and turned her back to him as she helped herself to a fresh goblet of ale from the small keg she kept tapped in the back of her private dining room. *Just in case I get thirsty late at night,* she thought with a wicked grin that was very unlike her, which no one hardly ever saw. She smoothed her thin lips to project her normal, cool demeanor. "Ale, my friend?"

Herodius was already on his feet. "Please—allow me," he said, aghast that the Queen was serving him.

"Relax, Herodius. You make me nervous." She laughed lightly and handed him a second glass. "My arms and legs still work; I can fetch a couple of drinks without much trouble, I assure you." She patted him on the shoulder as she walked past to take her seat.

Herodius followed her lead and sat back down, although he still looked ill at ease. "Very well, my Queen. I'll try to…relax." He raised his glass slightly, offering a modest toast. "To the task at hand."

The Queen stared at him for a second or two more than proper, a warm smile spreading across her face. "To the task at hand, and more so, the hands that perform the task." She nodded and clinked his goblet before tipping it back without hesitation.

Herodius looked somewhat embarrassed and did his best to smile back, but his face still looked a little wooden. *Stiff.*

"Ah, that is fresh. A good batch from the Miller to fit the changing seasons. I find his Spring Ale to be my favorite." She stared at the foam in her goblet before locking back in on her guest. "Do you know the real reason I chose you for this task, Herodius?"

"Because I am an outsider, you said?" He shrugged, but kept his eyes on her. "A good farmer?"

"An outsider, yes. A farmer, yes. But think about it a little more. Why not just send some knights to make an example of the rebels and be done with it?"

"Because you are kind, my Queen. You wish no harm to come to these people." Herodius was still slicing off thin layers of tender, fatty pheasant to dredge in the pool of spiced orange glaze on his plate.

"Hah! You don't know me very well. I am fair, but kind is not a word often pinned on me. No…this isn't really about the uprising of peasants." She kept her eyes on him while taking another long pull.

"My Queen?" He looked confused.

"This is about *you*, Herodius. I want you to succeed in turning the tide on this little rebellion because I want you to consider becoming a Knight. Should you succeed, I will talk to the three Orders—Thunder, Thorns, and Blood on your behalf. I imagine the Thorns and Blood, in particular, will be interested. They represent Loyalty and Sacrifice, respectively. You will, of course, need to earn your mark as a True Warrior as well. But with everything you've been through already, I imagine passing the Warrior's Test will be child's play. I will have one of my Warriors devise your test."

Herodius put his silverware down. "Why do I need to be a Knight, my Queen? I am happy to be a simple man from the Uncharted Isles. Of what value is a title to me? It will not give me back a thing that I've lost, so I don't understand, your Majesty. Why can't I serve you just as myself?"

The Queen put her goblet down slowly on the table before lifting her eyes to face him. "You can serve me, Herodius, just as you are. You cannot serve Elvidor, however, without a title."

Herodius blinked a few times, saying nothing.

Are the wheels turning? she wondered. *Must I come right out and say it?*

"Elvidor needs a King, Herodius."

Chapter Ten: Deception and Confession

~Magi~

Like a restless mob gathering before a fight, the seas picked up on Daphne's news, causing the wooden hull of the *Water Ghost* to squeak noisily in the awkward silence that followed. There was no lie in Daphne's statement. After a few seconds, Magi became aware of the dumbstruck look on his face and tried to play it off with a cough and a smile.

"Some wine before we turn in?" he asked, turning his back on her to give himself a chance to rearrange his face into its boring mask of polite attentiveness.

Brothers? he thought, his mind spinning. *How can it be that Xaro and Strongiron are* brothers*?*

He pushed a half-dozen questions from his mind and sat back down, offering Daphne a sturdy wooden cup of good wine, not bothering to have heard whether she wanted any or not.

"Thank you," she said, watching him with her head cocked. "Everything all right?"

"Yes, yes. You just…caught me a bit off guard with that news." Magi half-smiled. "The Tuitios are a well-known family, having served Kings and Queens in Elvidor for several generations. If it's not too personal, I would be curious as to how you and Orion Tuitio met."

Daphne leaned back in her chair while Captain Solomon steered the *Water Ghost* through choppy seas. Her wine sloshed around in her wooden goblet. She looked at Magi and smiled slightly. "It was nothing, really. I was young, and had not studied *Illusion* yet. I knew I attracted attention, and for many years I craved it. Made me feel powerful, actually."

She sipped and continued. "People said I was blessed by the Goddess of Beauty, the Goddess of Love. It grew tiresome in Raag-Kaan, especially with the women. I was accused of every problem they had with their men, and it drained me. I was not happy there. After a few years of men throwing themselves at me and women gossiping about me, I decided to head east, toward Kekero. I'd heard it was full of fighting pits, training new warriors. To me, it sounded like a place where I could have my pick of any man I might choose, given my…talent."

She sighed. "I was so very wrong. It wasn't my choice at all. Orion ended up challenging half the men there to duels and fights and wrestling contests—all to impress me. A few took up his challenge, and I believe he may have even earned his Mark as a True Warrior fighting several men at once, with me as his prize. He was just so...taken by me." The ancient, wrinkled face in front of Magi actually giggled.

"In the end, there was no stopping him. He bested all others from the moment I showed up. He was so tall, Michael. I can still smell the leather on him from his armor." She stared into her cup, swirling the wine wistfully before looking up at Magi again. "That was the first time I realized how lonely I would end up."

"Lonely?" Magi pulled his chin. "I'm not sure I completely follow."

The old woman smiled sadly, and when she did, it was very convincing. For a moment, Magi thought she actually was as old as she looked. "I had to leave within a week, Michael. Orion was constantly getting in fights over me. It wasn't safe for me, and therefore it wasn't safe for him. That was when I decided to learn a little magic—I had some talent with it. I figured I must have some in me to be an Enchantress, right?" She winked. "But my prophesy made clear that the Staircase would not be in my best interest, so I contented myself to master a few practical *Illusions*, and that was it."

"How did Orion take your leaving?"

"I don't know. Relieved, I imagine. At some distance the effect wears off. I left him in the middle of the night. He had been fighting for three straight days, and was cut and bruised all over. We had a short time together, but…" She paused and stared into her wine again. "We made the most of it. Xaro became my life shortly after that, until Paul showed up."

Does she know about Strongiron?

"Do you know that your son has a brother?" Magi asked. "I've heard he's part of the Queen's army, not unlike his father."

"Yes, I've heard of Strongiron. He's the General, I believe. Who lives in Elvidor who hasn't heard of Strongiron? He's known even west of the mountains. If he's half the man his father was, the Queen's army is in good hands."

"Have you ever talked about Strongiron to your son?" *This is the question I really want to know.*

"No. Why would I, Michael? He is nothing to me, and in the few minutes I've had over the last fifteen years where I actually spoke with him, I assure you that Strongiron was not a topic of conversation." She narrowed her eyes. "Why do you wish to know so much about Xaro and his past? Just how do you expect to join his kingdom, if indeed he is building one?"

Magi shrugged. "He's lived an interesting life. Clearly, so have you. I have no agenda here. You're just not used to having a conversation with someone who doesn't want something from you."

Daphne laughed. Standing up, she dropped her old woman *Illusion* to show her beautiful, mature form. The effect was immediate, making Magi's heart began to race.

She strutted over to him and bent over, pressing a hand into each of his thighs, lifting her head to stare directly into his white eyes. "Michael, I am not stupid. *Everyone* wants something. I just haven't figured out what you want from me yet."

With a slight squeeze and a playful smile, she pushed herself back up to her full height. "But I will."

~Xaro~

The look on Malenec's face when Veronica pleaded to join them in Sands End was almost wolfish. *Ravenous.* The thought of turning the former Assassin into the walking dead seemed to be almost intoxicating to his dark Cleric. Almost as if he knew Xaro couldn't heal her, and he would get his chance to claim another. Now back in his private chambers, Xaro was disgusted by his naked lust for more power.

Why should I be? Would I feel so different if the power to raise the dead had been granted to me? Xaro pushed his upper lip into a half-sneer. *Yes. I would be different.* Xaro wanted to rule. *Zombies are not subjects; they're more like...dolls.* At least, that's what Xaro told himself. In reality, he had a hard time separating the undead from Malenec's growing power. If he could build his own undead army, would they follow his orders if Malenec countered them? Would they be loyal to the Dark Cleric that created them, or simply respond to the strongest, most faithful Cleric of Kuth-Cergor? *We never studied that in Dariez...*

Malenec didn't want to govern a people; he wanted to enslave them. *Surely that is not your will, Kuth-Cergor? Surely you are using him to usher in a new age, where the conquered worship you, and I rule at your right hand?* Zombies didn't worship anything. What would be the point of conquering Tenebrae if not to be worshipped?

Xaro was contemplating these things when a knock sounded on his door. He did not have a Steward for Sands End; the entire fortress was run mostly by former islanders and True Warriors. Xaro thought it ridiculous to turn an able-bodied man into his servant. He wanted them all fit to fight.

"Enter," he said.

"You asked to see me, Master?" said Tarsh.

"Ah, yes. Come in. Shut the door." He beckoned the True Mage over.

Tarsh entered, walking over to stand in front of his new Master. Books were stacked everywhere from floor to ceiling, and several scrolls lay half-curled at his reading desk. The room smelled strongly of lemons and clove. "I came as soon as I could, Master."

"Good. Sit down, Tarsh." He gestured to a chair opposite him. "I've been thinking about how I can best use your skills."

"I am learning the art of metal changing, Master. I hope to help Krishnan increase our rate of production."

"That is not the task that I have in mind for you."

Tarsh frowned slightly. "Master?"

"Did you see Veronica earlier this evening? She was the Assassin that killed Magi." Xaro sipped his bitter lemon water; he didn't feel like sweetening it tonight. He offered Tarsh a glass, which he politely accepted.

"I did. I had never seen her before. It's a shame the Queen caught her." Tarsh took a sip and wrinkled his face; clearly the sour was unexpected, especially after the sweetwater he was accustomed to having with Xaro.

"I don't believe the Queen caught her. Would it surprise you to hear that she was travelling with Magi?"

Tarsh's white eyes widened slightly. "It would, Master. Why would she do that?"

"She did not have a choice. I believe Magi overtook her and was travelling with her for some reason, likely to try and gain information about me. Magi thinks I have something of his—the ring you and Trevor were going to bring back before he disappeared. Anyhow, something must have happened that led Magi to knock her unconscious and cut off her hands. I would not have expected him to do that, but—"

"He would. You saw what he did to me." Tarsh's face was stern as he interrupted.

True, but he was also not quite himself when he did that—the Scroll of Tralatus saw to that. "Yes, well, as you say. It is the only reasonable conclusion I can draw. The Queen would have killed her for attempting to kill her General. And while it is true we live in a

Dark World, I highly doubt random gypsies or vagabonds would cut off her hands and leave her horse. Besides—only a True Mage could have stopped the bleeding before she died. It was Magi, I am convinced of it."

Tarsh began rubbing the backs of his hands, almost brandishing them like weapons. "Just say the word and I will hunt him down for you, Master. Nothing would please me more."

Xaro smiled. *His vengeful spirit will be put to good use some day.* "That is not the task that I have in mind for you either."

Tarsh stopped rolling his hands together and stood up. "Then what, Master?"

"I would have you pick up the task that I had assigned Veronica. A private task. A critical one. She was to pursue the Shield of Life for me, starting her search on Adimand. Have you heard of the Shield of Life?"

The True Mage sat back down and leaned back in his chair. "Once. When I went to receive my Prophesy. The Shield belonged to an ancient cleric, if I recall."

He looks a little disappointed. "You are correct. It is a unique object, Tarsh. Powerful. The Shield of Life is one of the Artifacts of the Ancients. Legend has it that it is a shield that the great True Cleric Windomere wore into battle. Windomere was a contemporary of Quixatalor. It is said to protect the bearer from prayers derived from Kuth-Cergor."

"Why would you want to protect yourself from Kuth-Cergor, Master? He is our God, right?" Tarsh expressed genuine confusion.

"Yes, of course he is our God. And bringing his power to bear against Elvidor and the rest of Tenebrae is our plan. I would prefer it if the Shield was not comforting our enemies." Xaro stood. "That is the task I set before Veronica, and which I now set before you. Go to Adimand and see if you can find and bring me the Shield of Life. Tell no one else on the council of your plans; tell them during our group updates that you are travelling to negotiate raw material contracts for me, or pursuing rare spell components, as I cannot be everywhere at once. You and I will discuss your real task in private. Do you understand?"

Tarsh looked up at Xaro. He slowly nodded. "I will do this, but I would much prefer to track down Magi for you, Master."

Xaro grinned as he extended a hand to Tarsh, who took it. He then put his hand on the other man's shoulder when he stood up. "And you will. Why waste gold and time trying to track him on another continent when he surely plans to sail here? Rest assured that if he lives when you return, you shall have your revenge, and if he dies before you return, I will let you dance on his bones until they are trampled to dust."

~Veronica~

"The salt spray. It helps, doesn't it?" Garin asked.

He sat on the rocky beach, staring out at the Sea of Joy. He had his own blanket near Veronica, but not too close. He never got very close.

"Helps with what?" Veronica asked. One of the Afflicted had tied a leather strap through the handle of a spoon, and then tied it around her wrist. She could eat soup and rice with it—staples from nearby Oxen-Pace. Just to be able to scoop something up to her mouth was a blessing she would never take for granted again.

Garin chuckled, and it sounded like the most genuine laughter she had ever heard. "The smell. Down here by the water, the salt masks the smell a bit, don't you think?"

"Ah. Yes—very much so." Veronica looked over at Garin, and could see his smile in the crinkle of his eyes—the only part of his face exposed. She laughed a little herself. "Although, frankly, it doesn't take long until you get used to it, does it?"

"Not very long at all." He turned his head toward the Sea again. "It is aptly named—the Sea of Joy. Sitting here has brought me much joy, I must admit."

"How long have you been here?" Veronica asked as she scooped up some undercooked rice.

"Many years…most of my life, actually. I developed the disease as a teenager. My younger brother first began to notice it. When it became clear I had the 'dying disease,' they separated us. I was sent north to this community. My mother came once or twice the first couple years I was here, but it was a long journey, and eventually, she stopped coming. My father never came; not even once. He was a noble, and I'm sure he couldn't bear the shame of having a leper for a son. What would the other nobles think?" He told the story plainly, without sarcasm or bitterness.

"Didn't that bother you?" asked Veronica.

"For a spell. But over time, I met a wise man here—a dying man—who shared a piece of wisdom with me that I've never forgotten. He said 'holding on to bitterness is like drinking poison hoping it will kill your enemies.' I've always liked that piece of advice…I've shared it often enough that some here probably attribute it to me." Garin chuckled again, making all the rags and bandages wrapped around him jiggle. "But it's true. I don't hold anything against my family. In a way, it is better that they don't see me like this—better that they remember me as the strong sixteen-year-old than what I am now. Besides, I would feel terrible if they got sick on my account from visiting."

How does he just switch off the resentment like that? "Well, perhaps over time some of that will rub off on me. But for now, my bitterness fuels me."

Garin didn't reply, just sat there quietly as the sea crashed over the rocks to break upon the craggy beach. The high tide now pushed the water only a few feet below them. "So, what did you do to get your hands cut off, Veronica?"

She had a lie all ready to go. *After travelling with Magi and his damn staff, it feels good to be able to lie again! I'm good at it, too.* But for some reason, the words died on her lips. Looking out over the water, she wasn't sure what she had to go back to, anyhow. Maybe nothing. *So what's the point?*

"Garin, I—I'm not a very good person. Not like you. I don't think I deserved this, but…" she trailed off, the truth dying in her throat.

"Well, if you ever feel like talking, I'll be right over here most days. Blanket to your right." He looked over at her, and she could see softness in his eyes.

"If I told you, I don't think you'd like me very much," was all she could think of saying.

"Who says I like you now?" His eyes crinkled again, though. "Then be someone else. This is the one place where your past doesn't really matter, Veronica. Nobody cares if you're a Thief, a cheat, or even a killer. We have nothing you could exploit. Even our lives are more trouble then they're worth. If you don't like who you are, or were, then change. You'll find we're a pretty adaptable lot." He winked at her.

Veronica smiled politely, but shook her head the more she thought about it. "I don't really believe you, Garin. If you knew half the stuff I've done, you wouldn't be sharing your food or helping create utensils I can use. Trust me, I'd be repugnant to you, and there is still a price for me to pay for opening up to you."

Garin started to get up. "Very well—if you say so, but you are hardly the first Thief or Assassin to find themselves in the Valley of the Afflicted, and nobody is shunned here."

Veronica blinked up at him. "What makes you think I'm a Thief? I told you, my hands were not taken for thievery."

Garin bent down. "Then you are a murderer. It must be one or the other."

Veronica shook the spoon off her arm so she could stand up and put each stub on her waist. "Why must it be one or the other?I just said I was an injured traveler."

"Perhaps. I suppose you might have gotten too close to a forge and had your hands burned off. Or to an ax-man gathering the first wood of spring. Or a cruel victim of fate, having your hands bitten clean off by wild animals. Or simply in the wrong place at the wrong time when gypsies passed on by." Though Veronica couldn't tell for sure, she thought he was smirking. "But I doubt any of that is true. It's quite unusual to see someone who isn't born maimed survive a maiming. I've seen many people bleed to death here from cuts a fraction of the size of losing their hands. Yet you somehow managed not only to live, but to get on a horse, find provisions, and ride many leagues. That kind of training…that type of resilience gets hammered into you from the Guilds. I'd bet the rags on my face that you were either in the Thieves' or Assassins' Guild."

Veronica stared at him, speechless for one of the few times in her life. *He is sharp, this one. Oh, what the heck—what does it matter anyway? Nobody's coming for me.* She sighed. "You're right. I am an Assassin. I lost my hands by a rogue Mage who thought I needed…thought I needed a comeuppance, I guess you could say."

Garin sat back down. "Go on. What did you do?"

Veronica couldn't look into his piercing eyes. So she gazed out over the Sea of Joy, and reflexively reached to pull a cloak tighter around herself with hands that would never grip anything again. "I've killed many people. Took money for it. I…even killed the Mage who did this to me. At least I thought I had. I tried to kill the Queen's General. I even threatened to kill her Admiral in order to escape. I—"

"Her Admiral?" Garin interrupted. "The Queen's Admiral? His name wasn't Peter, by chance?"

Veronica turned to him. "I believe it was. I didn't kill him, though—just held him at knifepoint. I only took him hostage to bargain for my freedom. It worked, but in the end that Mage caught up to me and eventually maimed me. Why do you ask?"

She heard Garin exhale slowly, but forcibly enough that the dirty cloth over his mouth quivered and blew outward. "Last I'd heard,

Peter had risen quite high in the Queen's Navy. It sounds like you nearly killed my little brother, Veronica."

The islander did not say anything immediately. His eyes were soft, but he finally shook his head. "Your Majesty," he began. "I am flattered, but I am no King. I am not worthy of such an honor. Your people—"

"*Our* people, Herodius. You have been here long enough to stop with the distinction."

"Perhaps, but I am not from Elvidor. I am a refugee! I have no land, no title. How could I possibly rule?" Herodius was still shaking his head, and he started smiling. "You are testing me, aren't you?"

"Yes, I am. But I already told you the test—put down the turmoil, settle the people, and solve our food shortage. I'm not lying, Herodius, Elvidor needs a King. I have watched you in my court for many months—you are far more than a refugee. Men follow you and respect you. That is why I have you on my small council. I'll grant that you are right when you say you have no land and title...but I can change that easily enough. What I cannot do easily is take a soft noble and turn them into a warrior king. What I cannot do easily is take a selfish lord and teach them how to serve and govern. What I cannot do easily is take a fool of a man and give him wisdom. And..." She paused, gripping her goblet a bit too tightly.

"And what I cannot do easily is provide Elvidor an heir on my own."

Herodius rose and walked to the Queen, dropping to one knee beside her. "Surely you can have your pick of men, my Queen? If all you require is a good and virile man, surely there are any number of suitors better fit to be King?"

The Queen laughed tightly. "You might be surprised. I don't have the same 'effect' on men as, say, Belara does."

Herodius gently took her hand. "I would take a real woman over the *Illusions* of the mind any day. And I doubt I am alone in that view, my Queen."

For the first time in many years, Queen Najalas felt her cheeks flush from something other than ale. She cleared her throat. "Herodius...don't make any decisions right now. Go to the plains, and do this task for me. If you are the man I think you are, the people will require little convincing of your quality. Consider it, and we will discuss it further when you return. I just want you to know…" Her voice faltered.

"My Queen?"

She cleared her throat again and gently put her free hand atop Herodius's. "I just want you to know…I'm not trying to take the place of your fallen wife. We've both suffered losses. Perhaps we need not grow old alone, Herodius. Perhaps there is something here that we both can share."

Herodius stood up. "I will quell the unrest for you, My Queen, but I have one more question. If the Mage with his staff were still here, I'd like to know the truth on this one." He regarded her for a long moment. "Are you asking me to be your King because you think I'm capable…or because I'm available? I still find it impossible to believe that you would choose me from all the other men who would love nothing more than to be King of Elvidor."

The Queen sipped her ale and looked over the top of her goblet at the tall, dark islander. The months of proper food had restored his muscular frame. Setting her goblet down, she stood and without hesitation put her arms around Herodius and kissed him deeply. She felt his hand tighten behind her in the small of her back.

Slowly, the Queen gently pulled away. "You can think whatever you want, Herodius. There is not just one reason why I am asking you to do this. Perhaps I'm selfish. Perhaps I want a man next to me who never sought power in the first place. Perhaps I've looked at other men and found them all wanting, or they've looked at me, and all found me wanting. Is it not enough for you to know that I respect you, trust you, and desire you? Is it not enough that I've chosen *you*?"

Herodius caressed her cheek with the back of his hand. "You see something I never did."

"That is part of your charm, Herodius."

"And your bluntness is part of yours, Najalas." He smiled and kissed her again.

~Victor~

It was unusual for his commanding officer to arrive for an inspection. Victor pressed tobacco into his pipe bowl and reached over to a fire pit for a light. He had walked among his men, done his own inspection of their barracks. A little armor polishing here, a bit of blade sharpening there—he wasn't about to go crazy because

Strongiron was coming. This was a northern camp just emerging from winter…not the tidiest of places.

Regardless, Victor hadn't risen through the ranks because his armor was shiny, anyway. He had risen precisely because it was not. Victor fought hard and lived hard. *The way a man ought to.*

Puffs of blue smoke billowed from his smiling mouth. His men were good. They would be ready in a few weeks, whenever Strongiron arrived. The camp might not be the cleanest, but he always took care of the basics: shelter, fires, food, scouts, disease removal…and most importantly, training. One thing Victor did—he drilled his men repeatedly. He was constantly coming up with new ideas on how a northern attack could be mounted,and threw those scenarios against his troops in mock battles and various drills. They were lean, hungry men. *Always bet on the meaner fighter.* His soldiers were mean.

A knock on his door pulled his attention from a detailed map spread out on his table.

"Enter," he grunted.

Luther, his True Mage, stepped in. "Commander, General Strongiron is here, along with his guest."

"Guest?" He looked up, pulling the pipe from his mouth.

"A young lady, Sir. Her name is Kari. Kari Quinlan."

"Hmmm." Victor bit down on his pipe stem and puffed while he thought. "How did they get here so quickly, Luther? I was not expecting them for several weeks? Was Niku late in giving you notice?"

"I…will leave that explanation to them. Will you see them now?"

"Yes, I suppose I will have to. While I entertain our guests from Rookwood, do me a favor and see if you can't use your magic to clean up our camp a bit, will you? I don't care if it's a little untidy, but we still have a few men walking around with chicken blood on their armor."

"I'm not sure if that's the best use of my skills, but I will do what I can, Commander." Luther left before any further orders could be given.

A moment later, Luther reappeared at Victor's door. "Presenting the True Warrior, Sir Strongiron, Knight of Thunder, Commander of the Realm, Bearer of the Ancient Crest of House Tuitio, and his guest, Ms. Kari Quinlan."

Strongiron entered Victor's office, gleaming in the most pristine armor Victor had ever seen. Following closely behind was a stunning young woman wearing simple leather armor and comfortable traveling pants. Between Strongiron's white armor and Kari's bright green eyes, Victor's gaze kept darting between the two. Both were unusual in their beauty. *Out of place up here.*

He rose and walked over to Strongiron, offering a quick show of allegiance—fist over heart—followed by a warm grasp of his hand. "That's some kind of mail, Commander." He smiled, clutching his pipe in his teeth, then turned to Kari. "And to what do we owe the pleasure of your presence, Miss Quinlan? I'm afraid if you stay very long up here, the wandering gypsies will fall into jealousy or despair or both, for none can hold a candle to you." He reached forward to kiss her hand.

Kari's eyes flickered to Strongiron, but she didn't jerk away.

Strongiron laughed. "Some things never change, Victor. Save your mouth for your pipe and your poetry for the gypsies. But I'll take a mug of ale, if you're looking for something useful to do."

Victor straightened and looked at Kari. "And you, Miss Quinlan?"

Kari smiled. "Wine, if you have any. And please, call me Kari."

"Benjamin!" Victor yelled. "Ale for two and wine for the lady." He gestured to a couple of comfortable chairs opposite his table, and walked around it to take a seat himself, trailing a plume of light blue smoke behind him.

"So, Strongiron—I must admit, this is a bit of a surprise. I'm glad for it, however. Unexpected inspections keep men vigilant. You may find our camp to be a little less tidy than you'd like, but I doubt you'll find a group of warriors more ready for battle. We prepare like an attack is imminent, General." Victor took his mug of ale off Benjamin's platter and raised it to his guests in a silent toast.

"I didn't come for an inspection, Victor, though I'm sure your troops are well trained. They always are." Strongiron took his mug and held it low.

Victor had already pulled his pipe out and was ready for a large swig when Strongiron's words stopped him in mid-drink. "What do you mean? Then why are you here?"

Strongiron smiled, and stood up. Kari followed suit silently. Now Strongiron raised his glass. "I came to promote you personally, Victor. You're being recalled to Rookwood as the new Commander General of the Queen's Army."

Victor was still seated, staring up at the towering man in front of him. Strongiron dwarfed Kari, who was basically Victor's height. His battle against the three Steele brothers to earn his mark as a True

Warrior was legendary. He had a way of getting men to run through walls. Victor could not see himself reporting to anyone else.

He put his mug down and pushed his pipe back in. "All right. You have my attention. But before I leave the north, you want to explain to me what in all of Tenebrae you're doing? I mean no disrespect, but before I toast a promotion, I'd sure like to know where my Commanding General is going, why you're dressed in a steel bedsheet, what you're doing traveling with this beautiful young lady, and how in all the Gods' names you got here on horseback in two or three days?"

He took his pipe out of his mouth, grabbed his mug, looked to the side over his shoulder and blew the suds clear off the top of his ale before drinking deeply. "Don't mind me, I'll just shut up and listen."

~Magi~

The cold salt spray was bracing. Magi stood at the extreme front of the bow, looking at the wood-carved figurehead of a two-fisted skeleton bobbing up and down with every wave, silently screeching at the sky—the moniker of the *Water Ghost*, presumably. It did not take long for his travelling cloak to grow soaked, his damp, reddish-brown hair dripping onto his shoulders. *At least my cheeks are no longer hot.*

A couple days had passed since Daphne dropped her disguise alone with him, and Magi found himself looking for groups of sailors to congregate with. It had taken all his will to tear himself away from her and leave the room. He would have succumbed to her charms already…if he didn't have secrets to keep, and didn't trust himself under her beguiling influence. That—and then there was Kari. He still had feelings for her that he hadn't quite sorted out yet, but they existed, and needed expressing.

"There she is, if you've not seen her."

Captain Soloman had come up behind him, and was pointing to the south. Far off—but unmistakable—was a black swirl of churning water: the very edge of the Maelstrom. "We'll be steering clear well north of her, I assure you that."

Magi nodded.

"None of my business, but I'd be curious to know why you and every other trading vessel seems keen to go to Sands End. Just an old, abandoned castle on the edge of a desert. Before we left port, there were rumors already building among the seafolk that gold was flowing from that ruined fortress. Now you and the old woman want to head there. You heading for the gold, too?"

Magi curled his fingers around his staff before turning to face the Captain. He smiled. "In a manner of speaking. I've heard similar tales and decided to have a look. Most people could use a good mage, and this good mage could always use a little more gold."

"Then why drag your mum along, if I can ask?" He narrowed his eyes at Magi, but that was the only hint of aggression. "She makes me and the rest of the crew…nervous."

Nervous. That's one word for it. "She wanted to come. Is there a problem?"

Captain Solomon looked at Magi's pure white eyes, and frowned. He reached into his pocket to pull out his pipe and tobacco, but the salt spray kept dousing his tiny flame before he could get it lit. He grunted. "No, there's no problem. You brought a damn siren aboard the *Ghost*, but other than that, no problem at all."

Magi smiled. "You know about that." He cast a tiny *Glowball* and lit the captain's pipe for him.

Captain Solomon smiled and nodded his thanks. "'Course I do... Feel an unnatural stirring every time she walks by. Don't know how you stand it. Well—you're prolly immune, I suppose. I just wanted to see who was calling the shots heading over to Sands End. Is your mum using you, or are you using her—that's what I wanted to know."

"Why do you care?"

Captain Solomon exhaled sharply, filling the space between them with wispy grey smoke. "Because I mean to throw her overboard if she keeps distracting the crew. Ever since you left her room, she's been walking the decks. My first mate left the damn wheel to dote on her, and before you know it we're headed right for the Great Whirlpool. Sirens are a menace on land; they're death on the sea. If you can't keep her *occupied* and away from my men, I swear on the mast of the *Ghost* that I'll see her as fish food. Her bones can charm the sharks as far as I care. That gonna be a problem?"

Magi looked at the Captain. "I do not want any harm coming to my mother."

"Then keep her off the deck! Surely that's not too hard for a True Mage to understand." He puffed a few more grey clouds, staring at Magi while the spray continued to shower them as they crested each wave.

"I'll see what I can do, but if any harm comes—" Magi stopped. He felt his body start to tighten and could see from the look on Captain Solomon's face that his pulse was quickening.

"Harm comes to whom?" said Daphne. She was disguised as the disgusting old woman, which helped, but did not alleviate her allure by any means. "I've been looking everywhere for you, Michael."

Biting down on his pipe stem, the Captain was gripping the railing. "Miss Daphne! You'll catch your death in this sea-spray. Let me personally walk you down to your quarters, help you warm up a bit…"

Magi put his hand firmly on the Captain's shoulder. "Thank you, Captain, but I'll see to it that she is taken below and warmed up. Come along, Mother. Grab my arm."

Daphne grabbed Magi's arm, and the heat from her touch bloomed on his cheeks. He looked back over his shoulder to see the look on Captain Solomon's face. *Jealousy…or relief?*

~Veronica~

"I didn't know he was your brother," was all she could think of saying.

"Does it bother you now that you know he was?" he asked.

"I—I—" she stammered. "Threatening him was the only way I could escape, Garin. It was nothing personal. Besides…I thought you said you weren't all that close with your family."

He turned back to the sea, shaking his head. "You don't really get it, do you Veronica?" He slowly started to get up from the beach.

"Wait. Where are you going?" Veronica called.

"To my cave. I do not desire your company any longer." Garin pulled his rags closer around him and began walking away.

Veronica sprung up to stand in front of him. "Wait! I told you that you wouldn't like my past. You said this was a place where it didn't matter, but the minute I share a few words, you immediately run away. Well, fine. Go. Run away. I've made it this far on my own, and I'll make it further still."

Garin reached out and poked his finger into Veronica's chest, startling her. She knew that lepers hate touching people, and almost never do. "I'm not leaving because of your past."

"Then why?" she asked. A small smudge of blood was visible where the tip of his finger had pressed against her tunic.

"I'm leaving because of your present. Because you don't care. The Afflicted survive for however long they survive because we care about one another. I helped you earlier because I care, but I can see that you do not. No remorse is evident in your voice, no sadness, no guilt. You are full of self-pity over the loss of your hands when you should be full of guilt over the loss of your victims' lives. Perhaps I was too quick to extend a hand of friendship here." Garin shook his head and started to walk around her.

"Wait! Just…wait a second. I do care." She stared at his eyes— the one uncovered part of his face, hoping for…*for what? Garin is right. What do I care? When has anyone in this world cared about me?*

"This Valley is littered with the bones of men and women whose deeds were far worse than yours, I'm sure. Some die with friends, some die alone. Follow me," was all he said.

He led her in silence, walking slowly away from the sea up toward a rocky plateau near the edge of the valley. After walking for quite some ways, he stopped and sat down on the edge of a cliff, his feet dangling over. From this point, looking down on the valley, you could see nearly the entire community.

Finally, he reached out and pointed down below. "There. Describe what you see."

His bandaged finger pointed toward a woman who dismounted from her horse. She was shouting something, but Veronica couldn't make it out. Finally a single figure came out to her; this person was also covered in rags and used a single crutch; they were missing a leg. The woman and the crippled person talked for a few minutes, never getting too close, then she placed a basket down before taking several steps back. The figure picked it up with their free hand as the woman mounted her horse and began trotting away. The figure hobbled over to a stone table and began emptying the basket; it looked like food. Several other Afflicted began coming out of their caves, and the figure gestured to them to come and sit down. Soon five or six of them were eating from the basket left by the woman.

Veronica described it all, but Garin just looked at her. "Let me tell you what you're *not* seeing. That one-legged person is the son of Lord Arrington from Shoal, far off to the west—from the Three Fingers area. His name is Walter. He had a brother, Lionel Arrington, who was killed by an Assassin. Losing his brother so senselessly drove Walter mad for a spell that he took to killing as a way to cope with his grief, I imagine. Only his killing days were short-lived; he soon developed the disease and had to have his leg amputated. He could no longer walk among people—he was outcast. Walter Arrington, the noble's son, turned Assassin, turned cripple.

The woman on the horse would have been one of Lord Pendleton's servants. Lord Arrington sends gold every year to Lord Pendleton of Oxen-Pace, and Lord Pendleton ensures that plenty of food is brought to Walter every couple days, as well as food for the community at large here."

That name, Lionel Arrington, rings a bell. "Why are you showing me this? What is your point?"

Garin's voice rose slightly, with an edge. "He's younger than you, but in many ways far older. You see a figure sharing food. He is a noble's son and could eat his fill, unlike nearly anyone else here. But he doesn't. He sacrifices so others might have a few more morsels. Like you, he's had seemingly everything taken from him: his wealth, his title, his brother, his health, his mobility. Like you, he was a murderer. Yet he gives freely of the one thing he has in surplus: his food. Do you still not know why, Veronica?"

She shook her head.

"Because unlike you, he cares." Garin stared at her, and she could see his eyes narrowing. "And he does not wish to die alone."

Veronica slowly, almost imperceptibly, nodded. "I don't either, Garin. I'm sorry about your brother. I was just trying to survive." A single tear slid down her cheek as she finally began to let her conscience creep back into her mind after keeping it walled away for so long. She shuddered. *I know what I must do next.*

"Garin, I have one more favor to ask. Will you introduce me to Walter?"

His voice softened. "Yes, I can do that. May I ask why?"

More tears welled up in her as she began to cry in earnest for the first time since her own parents were killed. "Because," she said between choked off sobs. "You aren't the only brother I've wronged. *I* killed Lionel Arrington, and I need to make amends."

~Tarsh~

The trip from Sands End to the southwest edge of the Great Isle was a relatively quick sail. Tarsh packed light; he could live off the land, and frankly he wasn't sure what he might find, where he might have to go, and who he might meet. Rather than pack for every contingency, he chose to pack for few and rely on his magic. Most mages travelled this way. *Why scale a mountain if I can levitate over it?*

No port or shoreline was available on the Great Isle, at least none that were mapped. The island was uninhabited, so far as anyone knew. *So far as anyone knew.* Tarsh's plan was to challenge those assumptions. Someone somewhere knew where Windomere was buried. The legend, which was all anyone had to go on, told of the Shield of Life being buried with the Ancient True Cleric. The fact that others had searched and not found the grave only made Tarsh (and Xaro, for that matter) more convinced that it was an overlooked group of people that held the knowledge of where he might be buried. Maybe the Great Isle, which *technically* was part of Adimand, held the key. Perhaps it *wasn't* uninhabited. In any event, Tarsh planned to find out.

The ship could only get so close to the shoreline, which was an endless line of craggy rocks and stone formations that would like nothing more than to dash a ship into splinters. Indeed, wood planks and nets dotted the coast from ships that failed the test of tidal knowledge. "Here you depart," was nearly all the dialogue Tarsh had had with the tradeship captain Xaro had hired. "The Strait of Blinter is where we're headed next."

Small sack in hand, Tarsh verified his spell components and *Levitated* off the top deck of the boat to the nearby shore, offering little more than a nod goodbye.

After spending so much time in the desert, the change in landscape was welcome. Forests and rolling hills seemed to fill the land. He would have *Levitated* around the entire isle, but for two problems: it would drain him immensely—who knew what type of magic he might need, and more importantly, he needed to look for signs of settlement, tombs, cemeteries, burial mounds—something. He couldn't say what, but he knew his best chance for finding clues wasn't a hundred feet in the air.

So he hiked, keeping a map of his journey to avoid walking over the same places multiple times. Occasionally he would *Levitate* up over the canopy to look for clearings where settlements might exist and noted those as well.

After five days of searching the isle, he came to one obvious sign of human settlement: The Forgotten Land Bridge. Whether it was built to flee to the isle or from it, was impossible to tell. Regardless, he almost missed it.

Camping near the northwestern coast, the tide went out near sunset. Tarsh roasted a pungent fish over his *Everflame*, accompanied by some lovely, fresh herbs. A gibbous moon, close to full, began to show its face. Gradually, the rock formation of a bridge could be seen, and it stretched *forever.* Tarsh stood up and cast a *Farsight* spell to attempt to focus on the endpoint of the bridge.

"My god, it would take more than one tide to pass over that." He spoke to the sound of breaking water pulling out to sea. More and more of the bridge, which had no rails, could be seen. The greenish-grey rock surface looked slick from seaweed and slime. It was smooth, and there were some sea crawlers on top that found themselves stranded by the quick change in water level. Massive stone support pylons anchored the span at regular intervals. Tarsh was no sailor, but he could see now why ships bound for Ipidine from the east had to navigate the Strait of Blinter to the south; he wasn't sure a large ship would pass over that bridge, even in high tide.

The next morning, the bridge was gone—covered once more by the sea.

Tarsh sighed. After noting the location of the Bridge, he began pushing inland, to the east, with much of the Great Isle yet to explore.

He hadn't taken five steps before his muscles began to seize on him. Thirty seconds later, he toppled over like a stone statue that had been tipped on its side. He could not shift his eyes, could not move at all, not his tongue nor his feet…but he could still use all five senses. He saw what looked like four or five pairs of sandals approaching, each covered by the hem of brown robes.

"Proventus shall be greatly pleased! No sacrifices are better than magical blood. Our crops this spring shall be doubly blessed, will they not?" A voice floated above him.

"Most assuredly."

"Indeed."

"Without question."

Tarsh lay on the ground, unable to move or speak, wondering what had just happened.

CHAPTER ELEVEN: CHANGING ONE'S TRAJECTORY IN A DARK WORLD

~Herodius~

Herodius paused at the crest of a small hill from atop his beautiful grey mare. Behind him were thirty mounted islanders, leading a long line of supply wagons. A couple Rangers travelled with him as well, mainly to help with navigation and small game hunting along the route.

From the hilltop, the plains of central-eastern Elvidor opened up, with the Lightning Road cutting through the gentle, rolling hills. He looked at the ground spread out before him—it looked rich. The winter snowmelt had dampened the soil, and he could see for several leagues good ground unhindered by rocks, rivers, or excessive vegetation. This was prime farmland.

With a wave of his hand, he beckoned the rest of his group down the hill and toward the sprawling valley. An hour passed before the land began to rise again, with another rolling hill approaching. Only this hill was not unoccupied.

A dozen men on horseback, wearing mismatched armor, came into view as Herodius rode up the second hill. Behind the men on horses were at least a hundred other men, all brandishing crude weapons: clubs, stakes, torches, hammers, bows, and some swords. Dozens of arrows were trained on his lightly armed men.

"Whoa!" Herodius yelled. He signaled behind him, and one of his fellow Islanders raised the white banner of peace. "Greetings. I see this is a vigilant community—I can appreciate that in these times. It is a Dark World, as they say, but we mean no harm and, in fact, may be of some help. I am Herodius." He cautiously dismounted, keeping his hands in sight the whole time, and led his mare forward.

The dozen men rode up to Herodius, most brandishing spears or long swords. A particularly dirty man with a filthy beard snarled at him. "A toady for the Queen if ever I saw one. She enslaving island folk now, too?" He started laughing, but the points of their spears were far too close to inspire humor; Herodius's mare was getting spooked.

Herodius firmly but calmly stroked his horse's neck to settle her. His own men were approaching fast, but he held up his hand to slow their gallop. As his horse steadied, he looked at the dirty man who spoke. "I am Herodius—my men and I are neither toadies nor slaves. But I have been sent to offer some aid. Who is the leader here?"

One of the men on foot walked between the horses to approach Herodius. "We have no leader. We're free men." He wore a heavy leather vest, with a smock down his front. His right arm was noticeably larger than his left, and he carried a hammer.

Blacksmith. Herodius nodded. "Just so. Is there a council of elders or some smaller group that represents the interests of so many? I would prefer not to shout across the valley if I can avoid it." He smiled, hoping to break the ice.

The man in leather just narrowed his eyes. "Tell me what you have to say, and perhaps I'll pass it along to the rest."

By now the Rangers that had accompanied Herodius were each training an arrow on some of the mounted men surrounding him. His fellow Islanders had quietly drawn steel. He could feel the tension sizzling in the air.

"Very well, but first, can you tell me why you're gathered here to greet us armed for battle? You obviously saw us coming." Herodius kept a firm hold on his horse with one hand, stroking her behind the ears with the other.

"Obviously."

Herodius looked at the man in leather, growing annoyed, but keeping his emotions in check. "I have heard that you and your neighbors here have some grievances."

The man in leather looked at the mounted men around him and slowly started laughing, twisting his smock. "Grievances? Grievances? Ha! You hear that boys, he says we've got *grievances.* Tell me, Islander, who told you that?"

Straightening his back, Herodius carefully said, "No one in particular. The winter has been difficult for many, and the plains are no exception. I come bearing grain from the Queen, which I will show you how to plant for maximum yield, if you are willing. Tell me, what is your name?" Herodius extended his hand, hoping to plant a seedling of trust.

The man in leather ignored it, leaned in close and whispered to Herodius. "So let me see if we understand each other." He then turned around and started yelling so that all the men closest to the hilltop could hear him. "The Queen steals our gold so we can't buy good grain, then sends us back a bunch of second-rate seed led by a damn island-dweller to teach us how to farm, from which she'll steal even more, all while our children die of starvation, so that the privileged few in Rookwood can drink the grain that should be our bread. Does that sound like Royal Aid to you?"

Angry shouts and mocking laughter filled the hillside. His mare was beginning to grow skittish again, and Herodius had to tighten his grip on the reins to keep her from pawing the air.

"More like a Royal Raid!" shouted the man in leather.

Taking a deep breath, Herodius shouted for quiet. "Good Men of the Plains! Listen! Our Queen has heard your plight. I have been asked to provide you with aid—this grain is good, and I assure you that the techniques we use to farm our islands will help you greatly on the fertile grounds around us. Put down your weapons—we mean no harm; the grain we bring is for planting, and we will gladly share it all. Let us help you, and if there are other concerns you have, I give you my word—I will bring them directly to the Queen myself."

The man in leather scratched his chin and looked back over his shoulder at his mounted men, nodding here and there. He turned back around and gave Herodius a warm smile...right before he swung his large hammer into the Islander's side, crushing his arm.

"Ahh!" he shouted, crumpling to the ground as the air around him filled with hooves, dust, and arrows.

~Veronica~

Garin waited for Walter and his companions to finish their small meal before forcing his bones to stand and support his weight. Veronica expected him to berate her after admitting killing Walter's brother, but he didn't. Once her first tear started to fall, others came, and she could no longer hold them back. She strained to control her sobs, and began shuddering as wave after wave of killings flooded her mind:

The Ranger
The Fighter
The Dwarf
The Cook
The Gypsy
Magi
Magi's father.

And there were others—the entire family of the man who killed her parents, plus all those during her Tests. When she added them all up, she had the blood of at least a dozen souls to her name.

Strongiron was the only one I couldn't kill. Magi...just wouldn't stay dead, but I killed him, too. He counts.

214

As Garin silently rose, Veronica reached out her left stub to him. She wanted to hold his hand, but the gesture was pointless. He just stared at her.

"Garin," she voiced between her tears, trying to regain her composure and wall her emotions back up.

"Yes?"

"I—I…" She didn't know what she wanted to say or how to say it.

Garin wouldn't help her. The silence lingered.

Veronica took a deep breath and shuddered again. She did this twice more, until she could exhale cleanly. "I wanted to say that I don't know how to apologize for my past. How does one apologize for what you are? I'm a life-ender; it's what I've been trained to do, and it's the only thing I've ever been good at. I feel…*empty*. Terrible and empty, but I don't know what to say or do. I have no goals. I have no hope. I have no *hands!*" she screamed. "And you're right, I probably don't deserve them. They just killed people. It would have been so much easier if Magi had just killed me. I can't—"

"This is a more fitting punishment, Veronica. Death would have been easier for you, but this affords you an opportunity. You were made into a killer, but I don't think that's how you were born. You can do more than that."

"What can I do, Garin? What can I do now?"

For the first time in a long while, he smiled at her. She could tell from the crinkling around his eyes. "You are not sick. Your legs and back are strong, unlike most of ours. You are young and…fit. I imagine your previous profession required as much. Surely our camp could benefit from someone like that. You can carry things on your back, especially water, to the sick and sedentary. Why don't you start there?" He shrugged and began leading her down from the cliff-top toward Walter.

Veronica blinked, staring at Garin's back. *Contract-killer turned water-fetcher.* And yet the chance to be needed again filled her with energy. She fell in behind him. "Where are we going?"

"To see Walter."

"Now?"

"You have a more pressing appointment?"

Veronica shut up and walked down the long, winding slope toward sea level, where Walter was seated at a stone table. *What do I say to the brother of a man I killed?*

When they reached the other end of the table, Garin stopped. "Hi, Walter. Veronica is new to our community. She wanted to meet you."

The man looked up. He was slim, like his brother, and had the same general hair color. Veronica never saw Lionel's eyes or face; she had snuck into the Great Library in Gaust and had slit his throat and was gone before anybody knew what was happening. She came and left that room like an arrow loosed at close range. Dark brown hair was all she remembered.

Not that it would have likely mattered if she was trying to compare features. Looking at Walter, he had an ugly lesion on his cheek that should have been covered, but wasn't. His forehead was cracked and flaky, like dried fish scales. He smiled, and a tooth was missing…one of many that looked to be on the verge of tumbling from his raw gums.

And yet there was a warmth to his smile, despite the deformity. "Welcome, Veronica. I would have saved you some food if I had known—I'm sorry. You're probably hungry, aren't you?"

"I—no, thank you. That is kind of you, but Garin has been helpful to me. I wanted to—" She stopped, her throat catching. *What do I say?*

Walter raised his eyebrows expectedly. If his forehead had been any drier, it probably would have crumbled right there, but he just smiled patiently.

"I wanted to tell you something."

Walter nodded. "Please, be at ease. What is troubling you?"

"I killed your brother," she blurted. "I…I am—I was an Assassin. I didn't know him, or anything about him. My deeds have cost me these." She held up her missing hands. "And yet they can't make up for what I've taken from you and many others. If you wish to strike me, to banish me, to kill me—I needed to tell you what I'd done when Garin told me who you were. I am so very sorry, Walter. I can't take it back."

She no longer tried to keep her tears in check when they came again. She wasn't shaking any longer, but her eyes were like fountainheads, and the tears followed the previous tracks that seemed to have been carved down her face from earlier. She could no longer look at Walter's face. She hung her head and watched the tears cascade in large drops onto the edge of the stone table when the tracks dead-ended at her chin.

Another awkward silence ensued, with neither Garin nor Walter saying a word. Finally Walter broke the silence, and Veronica picked up her head. "How can you be sure you killed him if you didn't know him?"

Veronica shook her head. "It fits. I killed a Ranger in Gaust. I found out his name later, when I…killed another man. It was him. He had your build." She finally wiped her greasy face with her sleeve. "I wish it wasn't."

"If it hadn't been him, it would have been someone else's brother or husband or son. You killed a noble's son and a leper's brother. What do you want from me? Forgiveness?" He laughed, and the warmth of his earlier demeanor vanished like a flame under water. "In this Dark World? Surely you are not looking for that."

Veronica stared at Walter thickly. *What do I want?* "No, I'm not looking for forgiveness. I don't think I'm looking for anything. I just…I just needed you to know I'm the one who did this to you, and that I'm sorry, and—"

Walter interrupted. "*You* didn't do this to me. The bloody disease did, but I've killed people too, sweetheart. And let me tell you—the disease is not my penance. My leg is not my penance. It just happened, and I got it. That's it. There's no deeper meaning than that, though it stopped me from killing, and I'm not angry anymore because I've learned how to do little things that are needed. Maybe you will, too, but we're not going to be friends, and I won't have the food my father pays for shared with his son's killer. So you can eat the other stuff and whatever scraps you find. As for banishing you…that's not for me, or anyone else to do. Stay as long as you want; leave if you have someplace better or safer to go, but you don't need to sleep with one eye open—Walter Arrington is not going to come after you for revenge, if that's your fear."

It isn't what I fear, but now I wonder why not. She looked at him with a tilted head. "Why not? You've killed before, why not take my life? Is it forbidden here?"

Garin and Walter both laughed grimly. "Forbidden? Hell, people die every week here, half by their own hands. No, it's not forbidden. I doubt Garin would stop me if I wanted to kill you, even if he could."

"Nope," agreed Garin.

"I won't kill you because you should have to live like this, just as I am."

"Without my hands. My penance."

"No, I told you—I don't look at it like that. Not anymore. I used to, until I eventually figured it out. I didn't lose my leg because I killed some wayward knights. I don't think that's how it works at all.

217

I ended up here, of all places," he said lifting his arms, "and it changed me, which I think is the point. Not punishment—but transformation. You probably gotta go through a lot of guilt and bitterness first, though. You see, these people need my father's support, and now that I'm one of them, they have it. A noble from the other side of the mountains wouldn't give two bent coppers for this place otherwise. They need me more than I've ever been needed by anyone anywhere else at any point in my life. Don't get me wrong—I'd leave here if I could, but I can't, so I've found a way to make do, and it's a life of value. Maybe you'll find your way, Veronica. I dunno, though…you look like the type of Afflicted that'll throw yourself off a cliff soon enough." He got up and began hobbling away awkwardly, pivoting off his good leg first, and then swiveling forward on his single crutch.

"Wait! Why do you say that?"

Walter spun around on his crutch to face her. "Because you look like someone who hasn't been needed for anything except dealing death in a long, long time. Might be a bit much for you to bear."

~*Tarsh*~

The whole world seemed to be bouncing up and down, swaying to and fro.

Tarsh couldn't stretch out, his legs still bent in mid-stride, frozen in place, like a freezing spell had been cast on him. Several rough hands picked him up, and he was carried for a short distance, making his field of vision shift with every step.

"On the cart," said a voice.

The rough hands lifted Tarsh up over his shoulder and then tipped him over and poured his stiff body onto a low box cart, unconcerned apparently with how he landed. His fall was broken by his elbow and his nose, or perhaps it was more accurate to say his elbow and nose were broken by his fall. Regardless, not so much of a grunt passed his lips.

I have found people, at least.

The rough wheels rumbled over the forest floor as he was carried away from the coast and inland. Tarsh was situated on the cart so that his eyes faced the floor of the cart; he couldn't see anything, but he felt every bump and could smell the forest.

"Our fields have not been good for years. Proventus has not been pleased with our sacrifices."

"Yes, but the blood of the White Eyes is magical! A more acceptable sacrifice is not possible. Our fields will yield good grain once more. You will see, Trimba."

"Why should our fields be so broken, when the traitors across the bridge produce so much? It is not fair."

"They sprinkle their fields with the blood of White Eyes. You mark my words, the Fertile Plains are fruitful because they are more faithful to Proventus. They are giving him magic, and he is blessing their ground. We give him spoilage; the fault is ours—we have lost touch with the old ways, but this traveler is a sign."

A rather large bump caused Tarsh's whole body to shift, and he could feel a small animal crawling on him as he now lay to one side. He could see the forest floor rolling past him. Apparently they were on a rough path through the forest floor. It was springtime, and wildflowers struggled for light through the overhead canopy.

"The northern druids *are* traitors! You talk of the old ways, Omar. We *do* keep to the old ways. The *magic!* Remember, that is why we are on the Isle. So we could keep to our ways."

"Trimba, we keep to some old ways, but not all of them. Too many have passed into myth…"

"Omar speaks wisely, Trimba, Tonight we shall rekindle some of the old ways. Tonight, Proventus will be sated. Tonight, we shall see the land restored!"

"Yes!"

"It will be so."

"But the full moon is nearly here; should we not wait until then?"

Tarsh listened closely, but the squirrel or other small animal crawling all over him made it increasingly hard to concentrate. The silence did not last long.

"Yes, Trimba also speaks wisely. The full moon will only increase the significance of our sacrifice. We should wait two more nights."

"Will the herbs he ate keep him at rest? White Eyes are tricky. We do not want him free."

"Our herbcraft is strong, Yar. He should be at rest for quite some time."

"That is good, Saalal. We want the traveler to be still, we surely do. Some say they disappear like smoke in a windstorm with a word."

Tarsh listened to more general agreement, processing what he'd heard. *So, four Druids have captured me…apparently a splinter group of the Druids that tend the great crops of Adimand in the Fertile Plains. They must have poisoned or cursed some of the herbs growing around the coastline that I used for the fish. Stupid. I should know better. That must be why Marik always had his students travel with Rangers.*

But how much did I really eat? Very little, in truth. The Druids are known for their skill with plants and trees, yet this group must think that my blood will somehow help their crops grow. Another group creating their own god to suit their purpose. If they only knew of Kuth-Cergor, a real God, perhaps their crops could be improved. Or perhaps, if they travelled across the bridge and tried to learn what the northern Druids are doing in their fields...perhaps that would help.

It doesn't matter. They're convinced my blood is the key, and it won't matter one bit whether they're right or not if I'm bled like a hog and cooked till my bones ash over.

They came to a stop, and Tarsh could tell from the sunlight striking his face that they had come through the forest and were in a large clearing. Four pairs of hands lifted him, this time much higher, and set him on something very cold, hard, and smooth. They shooed away the animal before it could nibble on his neck. From his new vantage point, he looked to be about four or five feet off the ground. More druids in brown robes were starting to approach.

"Brothers! Sisters! Two nights hence, at the next full moon, our prayers have been answered! Proventus has given us an acceptable sacrifice—a White Eyes! His blood shall be shed on this altar and scattered on our fields as in the old days. Saalal, Trimba, Yar, and I shall watch over him. Do not touch him; leave him as he was presented to us. Do not defile Proventus's sacrifice. Come harvest, our yield will be glorious, and food no longer scarce. Our children shall eat, and our old shall live to the fullness of their days! Rejoice in our good fortune! Rejoice in the faithfulness of our people! Rejoice in the blessing of Proventus!"

Tarsh heard several excited shouts. One man entered his field of vision. Whether it was Trimba, Yar, Omar, or Saalal, he could not guess, but he dutifully took his post at one quadrant of the altar upon which the True Mage had been laid.

Two nights. Tarsh had never concentrated on moving his tongue harder in all his life.

A miserable, cold drizzle shrouded their ride in a gray curtain. Large, pregnant drops burst atop Victor's bald head as he bounced around in his saddle. He rode next to Kari, with Strongiron a few feet ahead, on horses from the Northern Army. His head hurt, not so much from the raindrops, but information shared the night before. It was a lot to take in.

A Cleric? A "True" Cleric, no less, whatever the hell that means. Bother. He almost didn't recognize his Commanding Officer. *At least I can't miss him in that armor...would have been useful camouflage in winter. Now he just sticks out like jester in a grave.*

Victor smiled and shook his wet scalp, running a gloved hand across his scratchy face. He hated shaving, but he hated a beard even more, so he just seemed perpetually scruffy, maybe shaving once a week. Usually when a gypsy started complaining, he might... If he liked her.

"So, how did you and Strongiron meet?" asked Kari, riding next to him and shouting over the steady raindrops and the *clippity-clop* of their mounts.

Victor turned his head to look at her. *If the gypsies looked like her, I might just settle on one. By all the Gods real and imagined—she is divine. Those light green eyes!* Victor just smiled at her. "We met in Shoal." He thought about saying more, but left it at that.

Kari returned his smile, but when he didn't offer anything further, she continued making conversation. "So...Shoal. Were you from there originally? I grew up in Fostler."

"Then you have me to thank for your safety," he boasted. Victor straightened a bit in the saddle. "Did Strongiron ever mention my role in leading the defense of Fostler from a water-borne raid of ogres, cut-throats, and various swords-for-hire? No? Shortly after my appointment in Shoal, I started surveying the inlets. They were ripe as a means for a quick-strike landing for a force to penetrate into the knuckle-area of the Three Fingers, capable of terrorizing the villages on the interior. It had happened before, so I stationed some scouts and within a month of the spring thaw, when the iced-over channels near the coast began to melt, sure enough, we had a raid. Not a skiff with a few bandits, mind you, but twenty boats—"

"You said ten the last time I heard that story, Victor," Strongiron called over his shoulder with a chuckle.

Victor looked over at Kari and winked. "It was a damn lot of boats, Kari, pardon my language." He cleared his throat, raising his voice a tad. *"Anyway,* if I may continue, General—as I was saying, a multitude of boats came in under cover of fog and landed several hundred of the meanest, nastiest looking, murderous wretches you'd ever set those pretty little eyes on. I only had a small group of warriors under my command at the time; King Alomar never could stretch too many resources west of the mountains."

Kari just rode politely next to Victor. "You fought them off, I imagine?"

"Fought them off? Hell, we rained flaming arrows down on those barbarians until they were throwing themselves back into the icy water. I bet 200 men burned and 200 ogres drowned. We had the high ground staked out, and the ones that weren't lit up like torches scattered and then trampled by the cavalry I had strategically placed to the north and south. They couldn't make it east to Fostler from their landing, and they couldn't go north or south into our mounted troops, and west just dumped them back into the inlet. We recovered more metal from their armor than a blacksmith could hammer out in a year, and salvaged the boats for the crown. King Alomar himself made an appearance west of the mountains to personally knight me while my commander here sponsored my admission into the Order of Thunder." He shouted up to Strongiron, "Wish you could have seen it, General! It was an efficient, devastating defense."

Strongiron looked over his shoulder, smiling and shaking his head. "What my lieutenant lacks in modesty, he makes up for with gusto, Kari." He looked over at Victor. "Better for you that I wasn't, Victor. I came to give you Thunder, not steal it."

Kari raised a single eyebrow. "Well, it is a comfort to know that Elvidor's defense will be in such capable hands during our travels. Have you ever lost a fight?"

Victor mopped his bald head in a pointless effort to dry off, and his expression changed. He didn't say anything immediately, when Strongiron piped up, "I can't think of one battle that didn't end in victory."

My General parses his words to keep his promise to me. About our first meeting. Damn that man— he's impossible not to like.

Victor swallowed a small lump and cleared his throat over the din of drizzle and hooves. "About men under command and this whole quest of yours...I still don't get why you'd turn over command of the entire army at a point when you say war is imminent to go hunt for a relic a world away. Meaning no disrespect, General, but that's not what a True Warrior does. I don't like reporting to others. You're the only commanding officer worth a spit in this whole damn land. Pardon my directness, but now you want me to take my cues from the widow—"

"That's enough, Victor," said Strongiron, firmly but gently. "You will show our Queen the respect she deserves." He slowed his horse slightly, until he slid back between Victor and Kari, and looked over at the grizzled soldier. "Would it surprise you to know she fought for your appointment?"

Victor smiled. "No, of course it doesn't surprise me, old friend. Who else would the two of you pick?" Tilting his head to one side, he made a mocking gesture of removing an imaginary hat and bowing while still bouncing up and down in the saddle. "I am, of course, a servant of the crown." He straightened up and let his expression turn serious again. "It's not that I am unappreciative or frankly undeserving. I just don't understand why you would leave. Clerics and Gods and Windomere's Shield—bother! Together we can crush any foe that even *dreams* of taking Rookwood."

"Not any foe, *old friend*. This one will require…more." Strongiron smiled and spurred his horse forward, toward the east.

"Why this way?" Victor hollered over the sudden sound of hooves. "The road to Rookwood continues south. This takes us to—"

"The Afflicted," Strongiron shouted over his shoulder. "I would have them hear the same truth about Dymetra as you have."

~Herodius~

"*BREAK THEM!*" he heard the man in leather yell. Herodius was on his back, one arm shattered and the other reaching for his sword before any further blows rained down on him.

The hammer came down toward his chest, but Herodius saw the long arc and rolled out of the way, though it was agonizing to curl over on his arm. The hammer landed with a *thud* into the softened ground and sunk into the early-spring muck. Herodius scrambled to his feet and drew his sword. He looked at the man in leather yanking on his hammer handle and considered running him through, but paused. *Elvidor needs a King, Herodius.* The Queen's words kept coming back to him as he looked at these rag-tag men attacking his force with pitchforks, hammers, and rolling pins.

Thirty islanders trained for battle against a hundred bakers and farmers. He looked around quickly to get his bearings, and already saw the ground lumpy with fallen bodies, arrows protruding from them. *This will be a slaughter…am I to be a butcher King?*

Herodius gave a shrill whistle that his steed recognized. Sheathing his sword, he used his one good arm to swing himself into the saddle, then rode in front of his Rangers.

"Stop this madness!" he shouted. "All of you—*listen to me!*" He drew his sword and pointed it at the man in leather. "The next swing of that hammer will cost you your arm and your livelihood, so consider your place, blacksmith. I will separate it from your shoulder myself."

"With one good arm? I'd like to see that. You don't threaten me. You don't threaten *us*. We're free men, and you just kill in the Queen's name. Kill with arrows, kill with taxes, kill with starvation! All we know is death from the crown." He held up his arm. "Here, islander. Here is my arm. Take it if you wish. You can't kill and maim us all."

"Actually, that's not true. We can. Look around you. Who lies dead or dying on this wet ground? *Your men.* You are not fighters— you are desperate. I know what that is like. I am desperate, too."

"Har! *You*—look at the food wagons you bring. You lived well this winter, holed up in your little mountain fortress. *We* are starving! Aren't we, men?" He looked around and waved his arms. A few of the men were wild-eyed and gave token shouts of agreement. "Desperate...we are *determined!*" He reached down and grabbed the hilt of his hammer.

Herodius rode forward and swung his long sword down, slicing off the man-in-leather's arm right above his elbow.

"Ahh!" the blacksmith screamed. *"You damn Islander! You—"*

Herodius shouted over him, "I will be *HEARD!*"

He turned to Mikel, his best friend and a fellow refugee who escaped enslavement to flee east with other islanders. "Tourniquet. And gag him." With a nod, Mikel swung down from his horse and began the painful process of stemming the waterfall of blood pouring from the man's forearm.

Circling on his steed again, Herodius raised his voice to everyone on the hillside. "Men—listen to me! Put your weapons down. We will not strike further if you do not attack us, but I cannot allow you to attack our envoy. You claim you lack food; so why attack us when the Queen provides seed? You claim you are starving; so why attack us when we are here to show you techniques that allowed us to farm in small strips of land on our isles? The Queen hears your petition; you greet us with raised weapons.

"This fool-of-a-man has crushed my arm as if he was shaping metal. Only my extreme forbearance kept me from separating his head instead of his arm, so hear me: *The next man who raises his hand against us will end up fertilizing these fields with the rest of your fallen neighbors.* Do not tempt me on this!" He sheathed his sword and gingerly put his good hand over his upper arm that was bruised, broken, and bloody. He winced, but swallowed it quickly, mumbling, "As they say…an arm for an arm."

Someone in the crowd shouted, "What will you do with us?"

Herodius rode his horse up to the man, parting the sea of terrified humanity. "What I just said: our plan all along was a mission of peace. This is grain we brought for you. Will you accept the Queen's gift of food and help?" Several murmurings could be heard.

The man in leather flapped open his eyes, somewhat deliriously, and shouted above the buzz: "Don't take it! It's poison! They're trying to kill us!"

Herodius flashed a hard look at Mikel. "I thought I said to gag him."

"I'm not sure he could breathe," Mikel said with a shrug, though he quickly began stuffing the guy's mouth with cloth.

Herodius shouted one more time over the din. "Hear me, men of the plains! The only poison here this day is the filth coming from this wretched man's mouth! Do as you will, however; other villages will appreciate the grain and knowledge more." He spun his horse around, causing several men to jump out of the way as he cleared a space around himself. "I will ask this only one more time: will you accept the Queen's gift of food and help?"

The same man who'd spoken up early worked his way forward. He looked to be in his fifties, with thin hair and a thin face. He stood up straight, and though he had dark bags under his eyes, they were still brown and sharp. "What is your name?" he asked.

"Herodius Cromwell. We come from the Uncharted Isles, where a terrible enemy enslaved us and slaughtered our families. We and some others escaped, and fled to Rookwood, seeking refuge from the Queen. She graciously provided that and more. Your pleas do not fall on deaf ears; you have to know that travelling during the winter is difficult, especially with such heavy wagons, but we do come on a mission of peace, I assure you."

The man reached up and extended his hand. "I might not speak for everyone," he glanced at the man in leather, now bound and gagged, "but I speak for enough. We accept. Show us what you know."

Herodius shook his hand, and heard a few cheers as the islanders shared their water with the men of the southern plains. Herodius smiled through the pain in his arm and slowly rode over to the man in leather, where he dismounted.

He looked at the man, clutching the bloody bundle of soaked rags at the stump of his arm. He appeared to be on the verge of blacking out. "You're lucky," Herodius said quietly, leaning in. "By rights you should be dead for insurrection and inciting a riot, let alone attacking me."

The man in leather gave a low, throaty chuckle. "No, actually *you're* the lucky one, islander. Wait until my brother finds out what you've done. He'll fill your head with a lifetime of nightmares, and then you'll wake and wish you were back asleep. He's coming, and death follows him everywhere. The Queen's days are numbered. Have been ever since our King died." His eyes started to roll back in his head.

"Who is your brother, blacksmith?"

The man in leather flapped open his eyelids one more time, delirious and on the verge of losing consciousness. "Malenec." And then he was out.

~Tarsh~

All the telltale signs were present: the growing buzz of mosquitoes and their infuriating thirst for his blood; the stifling heat and humidity causing sweat to pool at the base of his back; and the most obvious indicator of them all—a still wind that hung stagnant on the morning of Tarsh's first day slowly grew into a steady breeze by evening, then windy overnight, and finally as sundown approached on the second day…forceful winds and overcast skies.

A thunderstorm was approaching the Great Isle, and Tarsh still couldn't so much as blink his now dry and burning eyes. The first peal of thunder only confirmed what he could sense all around him.

"Trimba, the full moon is behind the clouds. Do you think we should hasten the ceremony?" said a voice Tarsh thought was Saalal's, but he wasn't sure.

"I say no. I say this is an encouraging sign from Proventus. He brings us water—water for our crops, but more so to cleanse the altar. Let the blood of White Eyes spill down the altar and mix with the water poured directly from Proventus's basin. This is good, and as it should be. The moon is full behind the clouds; we do not need to see it for its power to be at peak. We open his body in an hour. Tell the village, and let the storms come!"

As if to underscore Trimba's point, a jagged lightning strike filled the clearing with light, which must have hit the nearby coast, just on the other side of the forest. The immediate thunderclap caused the altar to vibrate.

Hearty agreement followed. *At least I have a few more minutes. I never thought I would survive the Staircase and Magi's cruelty to end up a human sacrifice. Can this world grow any darker?*

Tarsh could hear the trees around the clearing begin to sway in earnest as grey twilight became an angry, black night. Trimba, who was positioned near Tarsh's head, pulled a severely curved knife out of his robes and held it in front of the mage's eyes.

"I know you hear and see all, White Eyes. I know you are awake, and I know you feel heat, cold, and pain. I want you to know that I will try and kill you quickly, so that your blood does not spoil. This is the blade I will use—first on your throat, then your wrists, and finally your legs, but I will be gracious to you by starting with the throat. With luck, you may be dead before we get to your legs. I want you to know that your sacrifice will feed a great number of my people, perhaps for a generation, if Proventus is pleased. For that I thank you, White Eyes."

Tarsh, of course, said nothing. The shiny blade looked terrifyingly sharp. It was curved so tightly that it looked like it might fit snugly around half his neck, more like a massive fishhook than a knife. The idea of the point on that semi-circular blade dragging across his throat was horrifying.

"Like the great Druids of old—the ones only remembered by the nomads far away, beyond the northern mountains—we will reconnect with our ancestors tonight. The death of one steeped in the Black Art will spell life for many who practice the Green Art." Trimba smiled and patted Tarsh's cheek.

More and more villagers had gathered, and the now the rain began to fall in earnest. A figure Tarsh thought of as Omar turned around to face the crowd as the rain came down harder. He said a few strange words, and red flames sprung up from a ring of torches that surrounded the altar. Clearly some form of Druidic magic, because the rain did nothing to affect the flames. The crimson light bathed the faces of his captors and cast dark shadows everywhere. Another dangerously close bolt of lightning was followed by a peal of thunder, which brought the meeting to order.

"Brothers! Sisters!" Omar was shouting to the crowd gathered in front of him. "As we have said, we captured this traveler on our isle not two nights ago. How fortuitous that we've only had to wait two days until tonight's ceremony under the full moon!

"We have all seen our crops wither further year after year. Our northern brothers want nothing to do with us; they leave us to starve while they charge us the same as everyone else for the fruit of their so-called Fertile Plains…much of which they send to distant lands while we struggle in our hunger. They have forgotten from whence they came. *We*, however, have not.

"Tonight, under the shower of Proventus's overflowing basin, we shall offer a worthy sacrifice. Year after year we burn our failed crops, believing that will be a suitable offering to a god. Why would we think that is so? What god wants vegetables riddled with disease, or fruit trees dying of pestilence, or maggoty harvests? We have kept the first-fruits for ourselves, and denied our god his due. That is not the old ways. Our ancestors taught us that the land must be rekindled, that the sower and reaper must prove their worth if Proventus was to bless them. And there is no greater sacrifice than a full-fledged White Eyed mage, a man guilty of nothing but existing. The magical blood of an innocent cannot be overstated, my brothers and sisters. Proventus *must* bless our fields once they are soaked in this man's lifeblood!"

Out of the corner of his eye, Tarsh saw the red flames from the ring of torches flare, with a bolt of lightning that seemed to punctate Omar's speech. Again, the altar shook, and the torrential rain now pounded everyone mercilessly as the storm reached a crescendo.

"Trimba!" Omar shouted over the downpour. "It's time."

If I could just move my tongue! Tarsh concentrated every bit of his being on getting his tongue to say the words that would *Teleport* him away. Frozen to the roof of his mouth for two days, all he could feel in his mouth and throat was *dry*. The irony was not lost on Tarsh as he was being soaked from an epic spring thunderstorm.

Trimba held the long, shiny blade above his head, and the crowd began chanting something strange that Tarsh couldn't recognize and tried to block out. Something like *Provo-Na-Meni! Provo-Na-Meni!* Seeing the scarlet light dance off the hooked blade only whipped the crowd into more of a frenzy.

"Proventus be praised that our crops be raised! Bless us so we can grow that which we sow!" Trimba roared to his fellow villagers before slowly turning around.

Trimba turned around to look at Tarsh with a feverish glint in his eyes as he approached. "Thank you again, White Eyes," he whispered, slowly raising the blade up high once more for all to see.

It was then that Tarsh felt a familiar tingle in his arm. *Xaro! He wants to talk!*

Trimba brought the blade down close to his neck, preparing to draw it straight through, sure to slice windpipe, voicebox—everything.

Tarsh swallowed hard, preparing for his death. *He swallowed hard...*

"*Lamuae!*" he croaked even as he felt the initial prick of a blade. The True Mage *Teleported* away from the altar to the place of his initial landing, far on the other side of the isle, and immediately pressed his hand to his throat. *Only a tiny spot of blood.*

The tempest was not quite as strong here, but it was still raining, and the temperature had dropped. Tarsh tried to stand but couldn't; his entire body was stiff, and his legs were still largely asleep. He could blink again, however, and could get some moisture back in his mouth.

Xaro's spell must have activated my body, or woken me out of the effects of those cursed herbs from the Druids. He lay there in the mud, exposed, sore, and still vulnerable—but never so happy to be so miserable in his life.

"Guess I better give Xaro an update," he said, thrilled by the sound of his own voice, as he cast a rudimentary healing spell to try and address his throbbing nose and crooked elbow.

Chapter Twelve: Wine and Water, Sand and Flame

~Belara~

Belara stared up at the old, ornate sign in the heart of Shoal: *Finest Livery*. She never passed up an opportunity to add a new, curve-hugging dress of the latest exotic color to her repertoire. In all of Elvidor, this was her preferred place of business. Belinda and Miranda never failed to take care of her, maintaining all her measurements, right up to the tight-fitting hood. She often *Teleported* here for new clothes and took the opportunity provided by the Queen's assignment to have a custom dress made of rich violet, accented by shimmering silver thread along the edges. That, however, was not the main reason she stopped at the *Finest Livery*.

She was here for a meeting.

Walking down the stairs, she came to a cozy meeting room bathed in dim, soft light from a handful of heating lamps. The intoxicating aroma of heavy incense filled her nose from a bowl in the corner glowing with several smoldering embers.

Seated in a large, well-cushioned chair was a muscular man with dark skin and thick, black hair, just barely touched with gray. He swirled a glass of wine that almost looked black in the dim light.

Belara nodded. "Silver. It's good to see you again."

He smiled back. "Cheyenne—I'm glad you came. Please, have a seat. Wine?"

"Of course."

Silver reached over for the handle of an opulent jug, from which he poured a glass of wine before topping his own goblet off. Belara took the glass and watched him return to his chair.

"It has been quite some time since I've been called by my Guild name." She sipped the wine. "Good to see your tastes have only gotten better with age, Silver."

"My taste is not the only thing in this room that has aged well, my dear." He also sipped the wine and narrowed his eyes. "I have a reason for you to emerge from your semi-retirement."

Belara laughed. "Of course you do. I wouldn't be here if my curiosity wasn't piqued. Let me guess—your client is dissatisfied with the work of that amateur Sarah or Veronica or whatever her name is, and would like me to finish the job on Strongiron. Is that what you're going to ask me to consider?"

Silver didn't say anything immediately, but he walked across the room to the corner where the incense burned and breathed deeply. "I find that the sense of smell and the sense of taste are very closely related, at least for me. Don't you agree?"

Same old Silver. Fine, we'll go at your pace. "Actually, they are very closely related indeed. It is impossible to make a convincing *Illusion* of taste that does not also incorporate smell. They are interwoven, my friend, but I digress. I believe we were talking about a contract?" She raised a single eyebrow, which had the effect of framing her white eye in a far more menacing fashion than she intended.

"Would you?" Silver asked, turning his head to regard her before returning to his plush seat. "Would you come out of retirement to kill Strongiron?"

Belara smiled. "I knew it. While it is true he seems to have changed in powerful ways, I ultimately believe this newfound faith of his will prove to be a sham, like the belief in any god. Though killing him would have been much easier had I been contacted earlier; I could have joined him on his little expedition instead of Niku, and it would have been child's play to pick him off. Now, it will be harder, but I would consider it because killing him helps me with *my own* goals."

"And what, my dear, would those be?"

Belara put her goblet down. "I have the same goal I've always had, Silver. Even when I was here. I wish to be the best, and to rule. That I take commands from an ugly, plain woman with no talent is asinine. In the end, you will see—the gods will leave their Clerics like they've always done; the Warriors will run themselves into each others' swords, and even the Thieves and Assassins will be mere tools of the ones with *real* power: the True Mages. *We* will put this world right and usher Tenebrae out of the Darkness that covers us like smoke from an endless fire."

Silver slowly nodded. "And you would make yourself a Queen to replace the one who sits in Rookwood? While I may be a tad skeptical of mage-rule, I can certainly lend my support to having an Assassin on the throne. That has many...possibilities." He winked at her. "But alas, no, that is not the contract that I'm here to offer."

Belara shifted in her seat and spread her hands. "Very well. Then who, and why do you want me?" *The man was clearly enjoying this.* She grabbed her goblet again and took an impatient swig.

Silver sighed. "Always in such a rush. Still no time for the finer things, I see. Very well. The who will explain the why. That ugly, plain, and untalented Queen of yours has taken out a contract for Xaro, his half-ogre general, and Malenec, his dark cleric. Only a True Mage could stand a chance with that contract. Terms are ten-thousand pieces of gold per kill…along with the head of Chief Chocktaw, which the Queen will see to."

Belara nearly spit up her wine from laughter.

"Our precious Queen has decided to assassinate her enemies, and will sacrifice an ally to do so. Perhaps I give her too little credit. But tell me, Silver—why ask for the head of Chocktaw?"

He ran a finger around the top of his goblet with a sly grin. "I told her you were part Elfish, and upset that they rejected you for joining the Black Guild."

Belara rolled her eyes, but the affect was lost on Silverfist completely. Instead, the slight movement of her eyebrows and tightening around the corners of her mouth were more chilling than engaging. "As if there are no Elfish Assassins. Please. The woman must have been in her cups."

"Quite."

"How fortunate for you that Magi wasn't seated next to the Queen during your discussions, brandishing that damned staff of his. I've seen for myself the power truth has on people. So, what is the *real* reason you wish the Elfish Chieftain dead, besides the obvious fact that she will likely turn to you and ask for a discreet contract to keep up her end of the deal?"

His grin shifted into more of a smirk as he slowly took a long drink from his goblet. "Simple, really. The Elfs provide stability throughout the Southern Border. If we can create conflict between Rookwood and Thalanthalas—well—the opportunities for our Guild increase dramatically, wouldn't you say? War from overseas, war on your doorstep, revenge on everyone's mind. If you sell death, what better way to create demand for such a service than war, chaos, and betrayal, my dear?" He reached for the jug of wine to top off his goblet once again. "Now, the real question is, what will *you* do?"

Belara shook her head. "No, the real question is what I *won't* do. And what I won't do is board a ship to find a man an ocean away, holed up in his stronghold, surrounded by his army, preparing to attack Elvidor. He and his followers will come here. And when they do—"

"You will kill them."

"I will look at them as they pass through."

Silverfist narrowed his eyes. "So, you do not accept the contract?"

Belara slowly shook her head. "No, Silver. Not quite. You may never collect the gold from the Queen; her resources are already depleted from preparing for war. And this war is one—if I am to believe what Niku and Strongiron have reported—the Queen will have a very difficult time winning. And with no offspring, the throne will pass to the conquerors. I hear Xaro is a True Mage; that can only be an improvement over the unskilled, homely widow. No…I have a better plan, Silver—one that may create more contracts for you, more gold for both of us, and more magic and power behind the throne, including mine. In that regard, I believe our motives and plans can be aligned."

"You have my undivided attention, Cheyenne. Planning and attention to detail were always your gifts. What will you do first?"

Belara raised her goblet and gently clinked her glass with Silverfist's. "I will do exactly what the Queen sent me here to do, of course. Recruit."

~Veronica~

Hauling water was a two-person job, and that was a significant improvement in efficiency for the camp. The water was plentiful, but most of the Afflicted couldn't carry more than a cup, and many hardly moved at all, too embarrassed or weak or both. Sometimes friends would make a "water run," but that often took several trips. Multiply that by about a hundred or more people, and water distribution was a daily struggle.

Veronica changed that. Garin could lift a large barrel onto her back—there was a special pack one of the stronger Afflicted had used until he became too weak. A manual stopper was on the bottom, and a person could pull the makeshift lever that uncovered a tiny hole that allowed water to run out and into a cup, a bath, a pot, or even a pair of cupped hands.

Veronica easily carried the fifty-pound water barrel on her back and shoulders; she had always been extremely fit and strong. She just needed help getting the barrel onto her back and buckled on, and then needed someone to fill it up pail after pail until it was near overflowing.

Delivering the water was easy enough; it felt good to use her back and leg muscles. The gratitude was…overwhelming. She was amazed at how frail so many of them were. The chance to wash their hands or face in private, to heat water for themselves, to drink their fill without waiting in line for a tiny cup from the well…the outpouring of appreciation was more emotion than had ever been expressed to her in her life. She found herself smiling and crying nearly every afternoon as she got to know the colony. The children got to her the most and almost always broke her down.

She became known, fittingly, as simply "the water girl." It took only a week before even Walter began asking if she'd like to share some of the "better" meals that came from Lord Arrington via Oxen-Pace. She gladly accepted; the smell of cured meats and fresh vegetables was simply too much to pass up.

She was seated with Walter and Garin one afternoon when they all turned, picking up on the same sound simultaneously. "Horses," she mumbled. They could just make out three riders rounding a hillside and coming toward them in the distance.

"No doubt our numbers will soon grow. A Dark World will always need a place where the Afflicted can congregate in peace." Walter shrugged and nodded to Garin. "You are, unofficially of course, part of the welcoming committee." He smiled, but made no other movement.

Garin slowly pulled himself up, grumbling something about "lazy nobles" as he hobbled toward the riders. Veronica couldn't make out their faces yet, although one appeared to wearing some sort of white armor. She wasn't sure what that meant, but it had a way of drawing her attention. The other riders were smaller.

Soon Garin reached them, and they stopped their horses. From this distance, she still couldn't quite make out their faces, but it looked like one was bald, and the other was…female? She strained her neck further. Was that a beard on the large one in white? A beard, a quick flash of ice-blue colored eyes…

Strongiron! He's here! Several thoughts ran together at the same time for Veronica:

Why is he here?
Is that Kari with him?
If I kill him, will Xaro take me back?
Could I still kill him?
Would I still kill him?

Other thoughts circulated as well. In the end, she let her mind wander, but asked Walter if he would reach behind her back and pull her loose-fitting hood over her head, completely covering her face in the black shadows of its folds. Walter looked at her and did so, but said nothing. He could probably guess what she was trying to hide from. Soon, she felt a hand on her shoulder as the three horses and Garin approached.

"Would you let the others know that we have some visitors from Rookwood?" Garin asked. "I would alert them, but you move much faster than I do. We'll be down by the beach, near the caves, so that our brethren don't have to walk very far. Let them know that a friend has arrived, and would like to speak to us all."

Veronica was grateful he hadn't used her name, and nodded before departing. She took less than thirty minutes to round up several dozen Afflicted and have them gather at the edge of their cave dwellings, the others being too sick or tired to listen. One only knew they were listening at all by the light of flickering campfires, as almost none made their way out onto the beach proper. *We Afflicted love to stay in the dark.*

Veronica sat close to one of the fires, her face still hidden in shadow as she saw Strongiron walking toward the caves, away from the waves that constantly licked at the sand. She could see Kari clearly now, who also approached the colony on foot, both having tethered their mounts up the hill. The bald man stayed in his saddle, a firm grip on his reins.

Strongiron stopped about fifteen feet away from the cave openings at the base of the cliff. "Thank you for your time. My name is Strongiron, and I know many of you suffer greatly in this Dark World. I have good news: Dymetra is real, and She is the One True God. Hope for a better life than this is real in the next. I have seen Her. She—"

A decaying tomato struck Strongiron's shiny, white armor, leaving an ugly red and brown splotch on his breastplate. He turned to see Walter balancing on one leg, his crutch on the ground and another piece of rotting fruit in his hand. "Come to preach about the Gods to the suffering masses in your pretty armor? Get out of here, charlatan! Do you think any of us have faith in a God that would do this to us? Save your words for the outside world. There is no God, and your words of hope and faith are a fool's gambit for a desperate soul."

Strongiron made no attempt to wipe his armor clean, but he approached Walter gently, unthreateningly. "What is your name?"

Walter hopped to keep his balance. "Stay away from me, knight. I know your type."

Strongiron slowed down, but still approached, his arms extended, palm outward. Kari was beside him. "I mean you no harm, I assure you. This is Kari Quinlan. I am Strongiron Tuitio. We are True Clerics, and we serve Dymetra. I wanted to simply let you know that She exists."

"Why would I believe you? Do the sea gods grant us easy food? Does the rain god water our soil? Does the sun god keep us warm but not hot? What about the god of healing—does she remove our disease? Do the gods of wood and iron grant us plentiful fruit and useful tools? Does the god of money free us from poverty? NO! The only reality we have is *this!*" He tore open his bulky robes to reveal sores all over his torso. "Take your God-talk and leave, *'True Cleric,'*" he said mockingly.

Several muffled sounds seemed to indicate agreement, as many of the Afflicted shook their hands toward him in a dismissive way. Several others now held small stones.

"I told you this was pointless," said the bald man as he rode up. "These people will not listen to your sermon, General. I don't think you'll find attentive ears elsewhere, either. Dymetra is such an *old* God; you're invoking myth and legend, Strongiron. Come—we're wasting daylight. If you're set on this transition, let's get to Rookwood and do this."

Strongiron looked at Kari, then back at Walter, though he addressed everyone on edge at the front of their caves. "We will leave now. I am sorry to have distressed you. I will pray for you." He turned around to leave.

"Wait."

Strongiron turned back around. Veronica stepped out of the shadows, and with the exposed stumps of her arms, she pushed her hood back, revealing her face to Strongiron and Kari.

He sucked in his breath slightly. "Miss Sarah? Or Veronica? What are you doing here?" Strongiron looked at her, staring at her missing hands.

"Why I'm here doesn't matter. I suppose it's because I tried killing the wrong person." She shook her head, blinking, trying to keep her eyes from watering. *Control your emotions, Veronica!* "As you can see, I've paid dearly for my crimes, and yet I don't suppose I can ever pay dearly enough. It doesn't matter. I am here now, and I just wanted to say I believe you, Strongiron. I have heard of Kuth-Cergor, and I know powerful people who swear he exists, and if he exists, then I have to believe Dymetra does, too. And…" She swallowed a lump. "And I just wanted to say that I am sorry for accepting a contract on your life, Strongiron. I tried to kill you, and I never even knew you."

"Magi did this to you, didn't he?" Kari asked.

Startled to hear his name, Veronica turned to her and nodded. "I think so. I was asleep, but…it had to be him. I had tried killing him and running from him. He warned me he would do something like this. I—I didn't listen."

Kari's eyes narrowed, and she looked at Strongiron, who sighed and said. "Our friend anoints himself judge and jury, apparently." He turned back to Veronica and stepped toward her. "Why are you telling me this?"

"I don't know. I just wanted you to know. I have much to make amends for, and no way of doing so. But it makes me feel better knowing you know. That—and I wanted you to know that I believe you. I don't know about the other gods, maybe they all exist, but Kuth-Cergor and Dymetra must. If She is as good as you say, I don't know why She allows our plight, but maybe I can lead a better life next time. I don't know. I just—have to believe in something." She lowered her gaze.

"As I said, a fool's gambit for a desperate soul!" cackled Walter.

Strongiron stared at him, and at the growing chorus of cynicism from the rest of the colony. Setting his jaw, he grabbed both of Veronica's wrists. And then he shouted.

"Dymetra, hear my prayer! If this one is truly Yours, I ask that you forgive her deeds and transform her heart. If she is Yours, and if You have something for her yet to accomplish in *this* life, than I ask You to restore her hands, Dymetra! Let all the Afflicted see the power of the One True God. If it is Your will, let Veronica's hands serve Your ultimate purpose for her life!"

His voice boomed off the cliff face, and the sea itself seemed to roar in response. Half-terrified, Veronica's eyes widened as she looked up into his determined face. Her wrists began tingling. She stared down at them as new flesh began to grow from her scarred stubs. A thumb. Then her four fingers, one after another. She wiggled them and gazed at the seamless point where moments before, her arms had ended in darkened stumps.

Now she had two unblemished, ivory-colored hands. Even her nails were flawless.

Strongiron released her wrists, and she rubbed them, only now aware of how tightly he'd been gripping them.

Veronica Edgewild held up her hands and turned to look at the faces of the Afflicted, many of whom were gasping "…water girl…" in amazement. It did not take long for one to yell, "Heal me next!" She could sense them pressing closer, surrounding Kari, Strongiron, and her. The bald man's horse began pawing the air as the diseased bodies and their stench began getting too close.

Had this all happened even a few weeks ago, Veronica thought this would have been the ideal time to kill Strongiron. *An Assassin always honors their contract. I'm a life-ender, that's all I've ever been good at.*

That wasn't her plan now, however. Killing was a skill she had, not a defining characteristic. No, Veronica knew the moment Strongiron completed his prayer exactly what she had to do next, as if Dymetra Herself had given her a direction.

And who's to say She didn't?

~Tarsh~

"*Fennatulum,*" said Tarsh.

The shimmering shade of Xaro slowly appeared underneath some scrub brushes near the rocky coast of the Great Isle. The steady, gray rain caused his Master's image to look as though it were behind bars.

"Tarsh, I see it is raining where you're at. I hope I reached out to you at a good time?" Xaro asked.

"The best, actually."

Xaro smiled, blinking his plain brown eyes before continuing. "Given the weather, why don't we proceed quickly with your update? How does your search for the Shield progress?"

Tarsh had managed to rub the stiffness out of his legs before beginning his conversation with Xaro, and now sat cross-legged in front of an *Everflame* burning atop a pile of stones, looking out over the rocky cliffs, his back against some thick underbrush. He took a deep breath before answering.

"I am on the Great Isle, Master. You were right…it is inhabited. By Druids."

"Really now? Druids. That would make some sense. I know there are many practicing Druids on Adimand. Perhaps they migrated to the Isle over time."

"Or perhaps they migrated *from* the Isle. These Druids kept to old traditions, Xaro—very old traditions. I am ashamed to admit that I was captured, and nearly killed. I think your spell triggered something to help free my paralyzed muscles."

"How did it happen?" His tone was factual, not judgmental. For that, at least, Tarsh was relieved.

"I'm not sure, but I think they poisoned me. I ate some herbs that caused my muscles to seize up—I could not move anything, including my tongue. *Especially* my tongue. It wasn't until I felt you reach out that I finally was able to speak, and not a moment too soon. They were ready to bleed me out, believing my sacrifice would somehow bless their struggling crops. As soon as my tongue was loosened, I *Teleported* away. The last two days have been wasted, unfortunately." Tarsh rubbed his thighs again. "What else can you tell me of these Druids, Master? Besides that they are good with plant life...I can assure you they are more gifted than that."

Xaro gave a modest snort of agreement. "They are certainly not without their gifts. In general, Druids can bend the four elements to their will. They work with fire, water, ground, and air. Their spell craft is similar to a mage's; it is based on an incantation, sometimes with spell components and such. The Clerics derive their power from prayers, and while Druids fashion themselves as Nature worshippers, we know that Kuth-Cergor grants prayers...Tenebrae does not. They are essentially mages who study nature. It does not surprise me that they raised the Forgotten Land Bridge or mixed poison herbs together. This is their craft, but you should be able to defend yourself against them."

Xaro's image appeared to shake its head, but it was difficult to read his body language in these conditions. *At least the temperature is warm...a cold rain out in the elements, even with an Everflame, is miserable.*

His Master continued. "Nevertheless, Druids can be very crafty, Tarsh. I've suspected some dwell on the Great Isle, but I am surprised to hear they are still clinging to their old superstitions. Blood sacrifice to grow better crops? That would be a tragic waste of magical blood, for sure."

Something unsettling lingered about Xaro's first thought being the preservation of his magical blood, but Tarsh couldn't follow up on it before the other man continued.

"Most Druids have knowledge of plant life that would embarrass all but the most seasoned of Rangers. You must be vigilant for further traps and snares. They may continue to track you. The very leaves behind you can be their spies."

Tarsh peered over his shoulder before turning back toward Xaro's rainy image. A stray branch seemed to sway in the wind. *Or is it just mocking me?* "I will certainly avoid fresh herbs, Master."

"You must do more than that, Tarsh. Much more, if you are going to explore the Isle further. I expect they already know where you *Teleported*, and the roots of nearby trees may wrap themselves around your throat while you sleep. If your blood is what they want, choking you to death and moving your body for whatever pagan rite they envision will hardly inconvenience them. You need to safeguard your camp, and you need to get off that Isle as soon as possible. Have you seen any signs that might point to Windomere's tomb? How much of the Isle have you explored?"

Tarsh missed the last part of Xaro's question. He had cast a *Shield* spell around himself as soon as the elder mage started mentioning 'trees may wrap themselves around your throat.' "Excuse me, Master, I didn't catch your last question?"

Xaro crossed his arms and leaned forward. "Just tell me what you've seen and heard."

"Well, the Isle has no beach, no ports that I could find. Whatever the Druids eat here, it all comes from whatever they can grow or kill. The only connection to the rest of the world that I can find is the Forgotten Land Bridge. Just like your map indicated, it is exposed at low tide and covered in high tide. From the bits of conversation I heard, it doesn't sound like these Druids care much for their brethren on Adimand who oversee the Fertile Plains."

"Interesting. Did they say why?"

"Probably jealousy. The Druids here spoke much talk of 'old ways'—I don't know Xaro. Seems they do things differently on the Fertile Plains, and the Great Isle Druids resent their crop yields."

"Indeed, I'm sure they farm much differently. They probably have better seeds, better land, and perhaps even better spells with which to nurture their crops as they share information across the wide world of Tenebrae. When Kuth-Cergor comes to power, the Fertile Plains will provide food for the entire realm, Tarsh. Just watch what a real God can do, but I am getting ahead of myself. Anything else before you move north?"

Tarsh thought for a moment, running his hand through the wet mop of new hair atop his head. "I have seen no signs, Master, on this Isle. It is all forest, hillside, and cliff edges, with some flat fields scattered throughout. I've seen no ruins, no other civilization." He paused. "The only other thing I recall from my ordeal was that my captors mentioned Old Druids, remembered by the nomads north of the mountains."

Xaro uncrossed his arms and stood. "The Fertile Plains of Adimand are *south* of the Shembolt Mountains."

"That is what I recall as well, Master."

Xaro pressed his palms together as if praying, holding his hands to his lips. "Perhaps the Old Druids are really Old Clerics…the two Arts are fairly similar. One worships God, the other Nature. I would suggest you leave immediately for the mainland, and seek the nomads north of the Shembolt Mountains to see if there are any who may have heard of Windomere's Tomb."

"As you wish, but I will need to cross the Forgotten Land Bridge. I doubt I could *Teleport* across it during high tide."

"Yes, best not to try…messy things happen to mages who try *Teleporting* over large bodies of water." Xaro sat down. "Let us speak again soon, Tarsh. The army looks nearly ready. The armada is nearly built. Soon we will need to launch, and I do not wish to recall you before you have recovered this Artifact. Be quick in your search."

"Of course, Master." *My two days unable to move did not help.*

"And Tarsh—take further precautions than a *Shield* spell. It will not protect from vines entangling your feet, for example. If you are held down by aggressive vegetation while a dozen Druids come to find you…a single *Shield* spell will not protect you very long. Be quick *and* smart." And his image vanished.

Tarsh blinked, looking down at the patches of wild grass and weeds around him. *Were those always there, or did they just pop up during my conversation?*

The True Mage immediately increased the protective spells surrounding his camp, burning everything living around him, and decided to stay awake until low tide, when he would *Teleport* back across the Isle to cross the Bridge.

Curling his lip into a snarl, he almost hoped the Druids would come for him again. *Almost...*

~Herodius~

The tall, lean islander watched as Mikel cauterized the massive wound left on the blacksmith's missing arm. Herodius wanted him kept alive, and that meant cleaning the wound, cauterizing it, and stopping the bloodflow. The tourniquet helped, but the man's arm at the bicep was massive. Slicing off his arm had nearly knocked Herodius off his horse. Had his blade been duller, it would have. As it was, with Herodius's own arm crushed, he felt a bit dizzy himself, but he needed to know some things.

The controlled flame applied to the man-in-leather's arm woke him up immediately.

"*Ahhh! What are you doing?*" Sweat poured down the blacksmith's face as he strained against the thick leather straps and ropes restraining him as he lay on the flatbed of one of their wagons. His eyes looked like they were about to pop out of his head, and his teeth looked like they were about to splinter from his clenched jaw. He also smelled like a man no longer in control of his bowels.

"Purifying the wound, blacksmith. The worst will soon be over." Mikel applied the heat again, and the hillside reverberated with a blood-curling scream that caused everyone—islanders and rebel-peasants alike—to pause. His head fell to one side and he was out, again.

***

Hours later, Herodius watched as the maimed man stirred again. The wound was angry, but dressed. He had the blacksmith resting comfortably in the home of one of the villagers, and had water drawn. He held out a cup as soon as his eyes fluttered open.

"Drink," Herodius said.

The man-in-leather drank.

"What is your name?"

"P-Palinor," stuttered the man-in-leather, weak from his ordeal. "Why don't you j-just kill m-me?"

"Because I want you to tell me about your brother. About Malenec."

Palinor tried to smile, but his mouth never really moved; only his eyes softened. "Why do you care? Does he bring the dead to your sleep, too?"

Herodius shook his head. "No, but he is a threat to my Queen. *Our* Queen, though you do not appreciate how good you have it. You speak of your brother like he is a demon. Would you like him to gain power over all of Elvidor? He means to attack us, with others. Even if you view our Queen as uncharitable, surely you can recognize the horror life would be like under his rule?"

"He comes, I know it. He cannot be stopped. And when he finds out that you have cut into me, he will see your pain increased tenfold. You have no idea what he is like." A fit of coughing came over Palinor, and he drank more water greedily.

"Then tell me. What was he like growing up?"

Pushing himself into a sitting position with his one arm, he looked at Herodius. "Why should I tell you anything? You have cut off the arm that wields my hammer. How will I earn enough gold to even pay for the seed that your precious Queen now sells to us? How will it get planted? I have one arm!"

Herodius, truth be told, had never intended to slice off the revolutionary's arm, but the man was inciting the crowd against the Queen. Against the *crown. Elvidor needs a King, Herodius. Settle the people…*

"I am in position to do one of two things for you, Palinor, if your answers are satisfactory," he replied. "I will provide you with enough gold that you may buy grain for many seasons to come, and to hire a servant to help you with the planting and harvesting that my men will soon be instructing. Or, if you prefer a second option, I will kill you quickly if living a life one-armed is too much a burden for you to bear. Your choice. But either way, first I would have you tell me about your brother."

Palinor leaned back against his hay pillow, pursing his lips. "Hardly much of a choice, Islander. Very well. We grew up in these plains, not far from Paragatha. We're twins—not the look-alike kind, but same birthdays. He was the smart one; I was the big one. He left our village after his God-day."

"God-day?"

"That's what I called it. You have to understand, Malenec has always been obsessed with power. 'There is no power higher than a God's, Palinor. Surely at least one exists.' He was always saying stuff like that. I thought for sure he'd go try and become one of those white-eyed mages, the way he liked to read, but he always scoffed at the idea. 'Why limit myself, Palinor?' He used to mock me when I started swinging the hammer. 'Only a fool earns his bread with his biceps. You should read more.' I said 'Yeah? Well bring your fancy books over here and let's see where the real power is?' Anyhow, when we were young men, he wanted to take a trip to Paragatha. That was the day I started to call his God-day."

"What happened?"

"You ever been to Paragatha? Place is crawling with God seekers of every kind. We must have visited thirty or forty temples, shrines, and statues. My brother prayed to every damn one of them. And then he came to *his*."

"Whose?"

"Kuth-Cergor. You gotta understand, we'd been praying for two days to wood gods, iron gods, gold gods, love gods, food gods—you name it, Paragatha has it—and nothing was happening. Finally he prayed to this crumbling statue of this ancient god, Kuth-Cergor. Hell, I thought he was a fable or something until I saw the actual statue. Now I've never told another soul this, but it answered. The damn stone answered! I was there. As clear as the pain in my arm, I heard a voice from the ancient statue that said, **'You will be one of my chosen. Go to Urthrax, and I will see you learn my ways.'** I'll never forget his God-day. My brother, the elitist, the bully, the lazy scroll-reader—Malenec left home two days later. That was ten years ago, at least."

"When was the last time you spoke to him?"

"Oh, I don't speak to Malenec, but he sure speaks to me. Seems that way at least. Legions of his followers fill my head every night, as if to amuse himself. And their message is clear: *Soon.*"

The wheels were already turning in Herodius's head. "Thank you, Palinor. Your life need not end here with pain and infection. More skilled healers reside in Rookwood. Come back with me, and I will grant you an audience with the Queen herself." He reached into a pouch and sprinkled some bright green leaves into some water that had been simmering over a fire. "Drink this. It will not cure the pain completely, but it will help enough."

"Or poison me."

"If I wanted you dead, you'd be dead. Come. Drink up." Herodius smiled as warmly as he could.

Palinor drank, and soon his expression relaxed as the pain became no more than a dull throb. He narrowed his eyes. "Thank you, I think. Now tell me, where is my gold, and why do you want to take me to see your Queen?"

"To give you a job, Palinor—a very, very important job. One that will provide you with more gold than a year's worth of hammering on an anvil."

~Magi~

The harsh sand—even the heat—felt good. After weeks and weeks at sea, it felt great to stand on ground, even sandy ground.

With his staff in one hand, and Daphne on the other, Magi led her up the beach, past the port, and into the dunes. Sands End stood atop a small mesa, one of the highest points in the desert, and could easily be seen while still far out to sea. The entire desert opened up around them.

Magi's plan was, in a word, fluid. There was so much he didn't know. He had no idea whether Xaro had recovered the ring by now. He had no real idea what Xaro looked like. He was gambling that the other man had no real idea what *he* looked like—having last seen him as an infant, when the would-be ruler took Magi from his father and handed him over to be raised by Marik. He had no idea what

Xaro's relationship with his mother was really like, and therefore didn't know whether she was a bargaining chip, or a nuisance.

Perhaps most importantly, he had no idea what would happen if Xaro tried to take the Staff of Wisdom. *Would it work for him? Would it expose me?*

In the end, he had a simple story that Daphne could both believe and corroborate: Magi was a True Mage for hire, heard rumors of a growing power in Sands End, and wanted to learn more. He had heard about a True Warrior named Xaro who was purportedly building an army. Surely an army of warriors could use the skills of a True Mage as well? That was the extent of his interest. While looking for passage across the vast sea, he'd stumbled across Daphne in Nervadine, found out she was this Xaro's mother, and offered to take her to see him, for karma, or goodwill, or both. *All basically true.*

Of course, he would be introduced as Michael. From there…he would just have to play this thing by ear and hope he could find his ring before his cover was blown, but if it came down to a fight, Magi would be ready. *Unless he's wearing the ring. Not much I can do against a True Warrior impervious to my magic.* He thought about how useless he had been against a wolf without his magic in his final test on the Staircase. And Xaro was a thousand times more powerful than a lone wolf.

A large man walked toward them as they left Captain Solomon and the ship behind to be unloaded and searched. This man wore sandals with leather straps that crisscrossed up his calves. He was shirtless, and his bronzed torso was shiny from the heat and the walk from the top of the mesa. Two wide straps of leather also formed a large 'X' across his chest before looping over his shoulders. Two scabbards were held by those leather straps in place against his back, the hilts of two massive swords poking up behind his head at menacing angles. Small cuts and scars covered his body like a patchwork quilt. Reaching behind his head, he drew one of those swords effortlessly as he approached.

"You two!" he shouted. He had a handsome face with a low, scratchy voice that didn't quite fit. He pointed his sword at them as he came closer. "Your captain said you wanted to see the Master of Sands End. State your business."

Magi started to step forward, but Daphne—still disguised as an old woman—clutched his tunic sleeve and pulled herself in front of him to face the bare-chested man. "Tell your 'Master' that his beloved mother is here to pay him a visit." She closed the gap between her and the guard surprisingly quickly.

The man's face changed completely, and his sword quickly went back into its sheath. He gazed at her sheepishly and flashed an awkward smile.

"Yes ma'am! Why don't you accompany me *personally*, and I'll be glad to take you to him for a private meeting. You must be thirsty after such a long voyage. Can I get you some fresh lemon sweetwater? Xaro has it made with the finest lemons from the plains of Adimand. Won't be any trouble at all."

"No, but thank you. My friend and I would simply like a private audience with my son as soon as you are able."

"Yes, of course. Here, take my arm." The giant man turned over his shoulder and looked back at Magi with—*what? Smugness? Disdain?* Magi nodded politely, and let the brainless oaf escort Xaro's mom. After a few steps, Daphne glanced back over her shoulder and winked.

The path wound up the mesa through a series of switchbacks, with a large guard tower flanking each turn. They were manned, and Magi could see how the path up to Sands End was a gauntlet of exposed land for any number of arrows, catapults, and spells to rain down at every turn. *It would also be a harrowing escape should a quick retreat to the sea be necessary, if he couldn't Teleport.* He kept moving, making a mental note that he would likely leave on his own.

The mesa flattened out near the top, and the wide expanse of the desert could be seen in all its barren majesty. Wave upon wave of hazy light reflected the same scenery and color back from three directions: brown sand to the east, north, and south. Behind him lay the sea to the west. Magi sighed from the exertion of the climb and wiped the salty sweat from his forehead. It was flowing so freely his eyes stung.

And there, atop the mesa, was the fortress of Sands End, like a king's mausoleum in the center of a graveyard.

The castle was imposing. Harsh angles of black stone stood in contrast to the brown world around it. Magi could only make out one gate. The only thing surrounding the fortress was a trench of some sort; Magi couldn't see what might be inside it, but he doubted it was anything wet. Water evaporated quickly here.

The fortress itself wasn't, however, the most imposing sight: Xaro's army was. Thousands and thousands of warriors were training in the hot sun. Down the back of the mesa, in the desert proper, was an endless sea of ringed pits, where the sand had been compacted or hardened. Warriors, islanders, and even some ogres were drilling with swords, shields, spears, javelins, etc. Magi couldn't fathom how many men he got a glimpse of, but the army was multiples of thousands. Maybe forty or fifty times a multiple.

And to one side, circling several of the pits, were other men, but they weren't quite right. They just stood there, and there features were distorted, almost decaying, but they moved. *Of course…the undead.*

"Follow me," grunted their guide, though he was quick to soften his tone with Daphne.

"Xaro? Son!" Daphne, still disguised as an old woman, disengaged from their guide as she recognized her son's profile. She quickened her pace as an enormous, barrel-chested man clothed in a loose-fitting white shirt turned away from some type of ogre at the sound of her voice.

Good God, he's as large as Strongiron. Maybe bigger. The ogre was larger still, of course, but as humans go, this was one of the largest men Magi had ever seen. Brown hair curled down to his shoulders, framing his square jaw flawlessly. The man watched as the woman raced toward him with a look of surprise—*aghast?*—on his face, before he ripped his gaze away from her to look directly at Magi.

It was Xaro. Magi knew it with certainty. He could see the white eyes behind his plain brown ones, though no one else—even his own mother—could see past the *Illusion*. This was indeed the man who had taken him from his parents and gave him over to Marik. The man who commissioned the attack on him, his parents, and god knows who else. *The man who sent his minions to steal my ring…not once, but twice.*

With that thought, Magi's white eyes flew to Xaro's uncovered hands, knowing his line of sight was imperceptible behind his own colorless orbs. He sighed ever so slightly. *Unadorned*—Xaro's fingers were devoid of jewelry. Disappointed, Magi put a modest smile on his face and continued toward Xaro, ever watchful.

Daphne had slowed and finally stopped about five feet from her son, with Magi catching up. The ogre left with a curt nod and a few last hushed sentiments, leaving Xaro facing Daphne and Magi. Before he could open his mouth, she was speaking again. "I see you've been busy, son. What are you doing?" She had both palms open and arms spread wide, covering the entire operation. "Who has filled your head with thoughts of war?"

"Pleasure to see you, too, Mother, and wholly unexpected. I hardly recognized you in this disguise. I would keep it while you are here, if I were you." His soft brown eyes narrowed slightly, as he flitted between her and Magi. "I see, however, that your peculiar charms have landed you an escort." He turned to look at Magi. "Had you not been travelling with my mother, I would never allow an unguarded True Mage so close to our camp. But let me guess—you have no idea why you felt the need to escort this old woman, but felt compelled to do so nonetheless. Am I right, Mage?"

His guess is probably a better lie than the one I had built. She'll never play along, however.

Daphne's voice interrupted Magi's thoughts. "Not everyone is mindlessly susceptible to my charms, Xaro. Michael here actually found *me*. He was looking for you. To join you. I came along for the ride. He's a finer Mage than you ever could have been."

Magi cringed inwardly. *I asked for a kind word, not for you to insult your own son!*

Xaro's plain brown eyes seemed to study every inch of Magi's face. He stayed silent and just moved his eyes along Magi's head, measuring him up. Finally, he said, "I see. Michael, you said your name was? Why don't you come inside out of the heat? Perhaps we can see whether you might be suitable for my army." He smiled and grabbed his mother's upper arm, a bit too formally. "Both of you, come inside with me. We don't get many guests here. We shall dine tonight."

Perhaps Magi was just being paranoid, but it certainly seemed like Xaro's eyes stayed glued on his staff during the entire walk into Sands End.

~Tarsh~

Dawn broke on the Great Isle, with heavy, thick fog that covered everything as if the clouds themselves had descended. Tarsh scratched the sand out of his eyes, cursing himself for falling asleep. *This grey curtain might as well have been a baby's blanket.*

He stood up, the *Everflame* from his campsite glowing a hazy blue. However, any further than two or three feet beyond the light—nothing. The entire Druidic village could be aiming their woodland spells and throwing knives at him less than ten feet from where he sat, and he would never see them. He squinted, but saw nothing.

His magical enchantments protecting his campsite must have held. He had cast a *Shield* spell not only around himself, but also around about a five-foot perimeter where he sat (slept), in all directions, *including* the ground. He was essentially in a bubble— just him and his blue *Everflame*—though that perimeter *Shield* was going to dissolve when he *Teleported*. Ever since Xaro's warning about roots growing up out of the dirt to choke him, he was taking no chances; he would coat the very ground around which he stood. This sapped his strength a bit though, more magical than physical, after maintaining that spell all night long. He had no idea what time it was; even the sun was obscured by the fog.

It must be low tide. It must. He took a deep breath, and *Teleported* to the Forgotten Land Bridge, across the Isle, back to where he was originally captured. He materialized into more fog, and cast another light spell to try and cut through the impenetrable grey, but his light just seemed to get swallowed up, almost like the fog was unnatural. *Unnatural...*

Without warning, Tarsh fell into a pit at the foot of the Bridge, straight through an illusion of solid ground. He screamed as he plunged ten feet, landing in a heap on the dirt before he could cast any type of *Levitation* spell.

Four darts, one from each side of the pit emerged with a simultaneous *whoosh* as he stood up. All four struck his torso— chest, ribs, and back—and fell harmlessly to the ground, unable to penetrate the *Shield* around him.

"I know you're out there!" he shouted. "If I catch you, rest assured I will make you part of your own fog." He slowly *Levitated* up and out of the pit, rotating around like a cork rising from a wine bottle.

Though really growing tired, he spun with arms outstretched and brought forth fire from each palm, engulfing the surrounding area in huge arcs of orange-red flame as he rotated faster and faster.

He heard muffled screams from within the fog, and saw some objects (people?) burning, but he didn't stop. More and more fire bathed the shoreline and surrounding water's edge, until the grey fog itself started to become consumed by the flames. Faster and faster Tarsh whirled, a fiery tornado, until all the fog was gone.

He finally relented, and could now hear the sea crashing against the breakers and cliffs that formed the foundation of the Great Isle. No more screams...

There were, however, a dozen Druids strewn about the area where the Bridge connected Adimand and the Great Isle. Their bodies were black and smoking, and the air reeked of salt and death. Large, black birds were already descending for the feast of a lifetime.

He looked over at the tide, which was still low. Whether it was falling or rising from its current level he couldn't tell and didn't plan to sit around and gauge it; he'd levitate if the water closed over the rock span. And if he couldn't muster that, he'd swim if he must.

After a deep breath, Tarsh carefully placed a foot on the railless Bridge, testing his traction. It was slick, but wide enough that he felt he could move quickly across if he stepped lightly. He took another step and then paused, looking back at the charred bodies behind him with one final thought: *this is nothing compared to Magi's fate, should I be fortunate enough to encounter him again.*

CHAPTER THIRTEEN: LOVE KINDLES, HATE SIMMERS

~Victor~

Victor pulled thick, white chunks of grilled fish off a long stick he was using as a skewer and handed a piece to Kari, who was seated next to him. Across the small firepit sat Strongiron, his armor no longer pristine white, but still a beacon against the surrounding night. The three of them sat in silence, broken only occasionally by the subtle movement of their horses, or the crackling flames as a bit of fat dripped into the fire.

The silence was driving Victor nuts. Finally, he broke it. "You have to stay now. You know you do."

"Give it a rest, Victor. For the third time, I am not staying. We'll finish our ride back to Rookwood, and then Kari and I depart. We'll stop in Paragatha on the way back—it is only fitting that the city of Windomere rekindle their knowledge of the True Clerics."

Victor stood up. "No, I will *not* give it a rest! You *healed* that woman—I watched her hands grow back from stumps! Your greatest value is in battle, Strongiron! Imagine a plan where you are a roving healer, bringing strength to our wounded while they crash upon our swords like waves against the shore. Not only would Rookwood be impenetrable, but we could expand! Yes—to that rock Oraz, or Urthrax across the straits, or even across the ocean! Strongiron—I could devise a plan to keep you safe while you performed your spells. I'm telling you, we would be invincible!"

Kari stood as well and pointed a finger at Victor. "First of all, they are *not* spells. We pray. To a God—to *the* God. She has a name, it's Dymetra. When you are done dreaming of conquest, I would suggest you consider praying to Her as well. Humility might be in order for you.

"Secondly, our task is given to us by Dymetra. If She wanted us to scoot from injury to injury on some pitched battlefield, She would have told us. I imagine if we tried such a thing, we would fail utterly. Her world, Her plan. Even our faith has limits…we are, after all, mere humans. You saw that, unfortunately, as well today."

Victor had seen how some of the Afflicted were healed; others were not. Exhausted, the three of them had to gently, but forcibly, break through the mob of Afflicted to leave. He was curious about that. "Why could you not heal all of them?"

Kari softened her voice just a little. "As I said—our faith has limits. Great concentration, confidence, and energy are necessary to heal even one person. We healed dozens, many with terrible injuries and grave suffering. Even if Dymetra willed that all in the colony should be healed, we can't do it alone. Your ambition that Strongiron and I race around a battlefield dispensing new arms and legs and healing stab wounds and burns is just plain fantasy, Victor. You are a more pragmatic general than that, I assume." She sat back down and grabbed her full skewer of fish.

Victor remained standing, looking down at both of them. "Indeed, I am pragmatic. It is my *pragmatism* that compels me to insist that at least one of you remain behind for the good of our defenses. If you can heal only one man that would otherwise die in battle, is that not enough? Do both of you need to go on this fool's quest across land and sea to dig up Windomere's bones? If Strongiron must go, then fine. Surely *you* can stay behind, Miss Kari. Unless there is some reason you feel you must accompany him that I am not aware of, hmm? I'm sure your god wouldn't look too kindly to any *selfish* motivations, would She? Not while Rookwood suffers?"

Strongiron narrowed his eyes. "Sit down, Victor, and shut up. I'm not going to tolerate your insinuations much longer, and it already has been a long enough day for us all."

Kari's eyes flashed as she looked up at Victor and added, "Strongiron and I will be departing as planned, Victor, in hopes that Rookwood will not suffer. Your strategy is flawed, and your heart is selfish. You know what I see? I see a man who would gird himself with a True Cleric for his own safekeeping. You have no intent of letting us roam the battlefield. In your heart, when you saw what we did today, you were thinking how advantageous it would be if one of us were by your side the entire time. Strongiron vouches for you as a tactician; perhaps you are. All I see is a small coward."

Victor drew his sword with a furious scream and approached her when his feet froze, Kari's mouth moving silently. His arms stiffening, his grip on the hilt of his sword was being pried apart like stiff clamps slowly being widened. The sword fell to the ground with a *thud*, its blade scattering campfire coals skyward.

"You would draw your sword against me, Warrior? I should have you stay up all night, frozen in your stance *right there* so you may contemplate your temper, and my words. Do not test the limits of my forgiveness again, Victor." Kari stood up to walk away.

"Enough. Kari, release him. Victor—if you ever draw a blade against my friends again, I will feed you to the birds and find a new General. You are not irreplaceable. No one is, save Dymetra. Consider yourself lucky. Lucky…and *warned.*"

Kari turned around and said a few words of prayer, and feeling slowly began to return to Victor's legs and arms, his neck and tongue. He sat back down, dragging his sword away from the fire to cool off before sheathing it. He rubbed his arms and legs. "What did you do to me, woman? And why should I consider myself lucky?"

Kari smiled at him, but it conveyed no warmth. "You are lucky your friend holds your talents in such high regard; I would have left you to bathe the Afflicted until you learned some humility. In fact, I have prayed for your humility to increase as you take on the leadership of the Queen's army. Apparently, Dymetra plans to bring you along slowly. She's far more patient with you than I could ever be, but know this: She will get your attention eventually, Victor, however She sees fit. Just like Veronica. That I can guarantee you."

Victor grunted. *It's all just magic to me, Gods be damned.* "And where did that pretty little killer go? She cut out of there pretty quick when that mob of disease started hemming us in."

Kari looked over at Strongiron, who stared right back at her, as if they were sharing some kind of hidden conversation. Finally, she shook her head. "I don't know…but I can guess."

~Queen Najalas~

It took a significant amount of patience for the Queen to let the man rest. Herodius had personally escorted a one-armed man back to Rookwood, and the journey clearly had not been easy—for either of them. While it was true that some of the best healers in Elvidor were at Rookwood, they were hardly clerics. At least not *True* Clerics. No, she had access to the only True Clerics seen in Tenebrae for hundreds of years, but they were off fetching Lieutenant Generals and chasing buried treasure. Herodius and this Palinor could have certainly used their help. *Bother. Not likely the last time I'll think this.*

As it was, Herodius's arm, while salvageable, would not likely ever bend correctly again. The elbow was shattered, though he could still wiggle his fingers and rotate his shoulder. That was at least something.

By the time he reached Rookwood, Palinor was part lunatic, part delirious, part insurgent, and completely sick with infection, despite the cauterization. His situation was far more dire, and several Mages immediately began their spellwork, rudimentary as it was. Niku himself bent his will to the task of ensuring Palinor's recovery once Herodius made clear to the court that this was, in fact, Malenec's brother.

The hours passed slowly, but Palinor's fever finally broke, prompting Niku to give his blessing to Queen to meet with the one-armed, former blacksmith. Palinor came to her formal meeting room, where she met with her Small Council. Everyone was there…except Strongiron who, according to her last report, was headed back already with Victor. Herodius was seated next to Palinor, and they appeared to be speaking to one another amicably enough. *An arm for an arm, I guess.*

"So. I invited our guest, Palinor, a blacksmith from the Interior Plains, to join us this afternoon. I trust you are feeling better?" asked the Queen.

"Still short an arm, and waiting for my gold, but other than that—yes, I suppose I am getting better."

"Jonathon? If you would, please." Queen Najalas nodded to her Steward.

Jonathon stood up and handed a small but full bag of gold coins to Palinor. "As promised, Palinor. More is available if you would serve the crown further."

Palinor bit into the side of the pouch to hold one drawstring and used his free arm to uncinch the bag. Reaching in, he drew out a fistful of gold pieces. "What more do you want? I've told you about my brother."

"You have told us about your childhood, yes, but you say that he sends dreams to you. Do you see him in these dreams?"

"Of course, but they're just dreams. Nightmares, really. I struggle to remember the feeling of a proper night's sleep. But I see him in my dreams, nearly every other night, always surrounded by walking dead. I've seen him so many times, I even recognize one of the zombies he seems close to. Calls her Genevieve. Disgusting…I do not recognize the brother I grew up with."

"Where is he when you see him?" The Queen stood and helped herself to a mug of fresh ale. "Some ale for you?"

"Aye. I don't know where he is, but it's hot, and I see sand. I often see him by a seashore, surrounded by several undead creatures, praying at night. Sometimes I can hear his prayers."

The Queen handed a foamy mug of ale to Palinor, smiling. "And for what does your twin brother pray? You told Herodius you were twins, correct?"

"Aye. Damn, this is good. Now you see why we are so upset— what with you hoarding all the good grain and ale." He took another long pull, and wiped his mouth with the edge of his shoulder-stump arm. Simon stared at him ominously. "Beg your pardon, Your Majesty. He prays for all sorts of stuff, mostly he keeps asking some god whether it is time or not. He keeps telling this Genevieve '*Soon. We are leaving soon.*' He also prays for more whites, whatever that means. I never did understand his ramblings."

Niku looked over at the Queen. "Wights. He is praying for wights. A stronger undead creature than the zombies we have faced. They are intelligent, and they cause unbearable pain with their touch."

Palinor's eyes grew big, and he took another gulp of ale.

The Queen turned back to him. "I am curious…do you think he is communicating with you, or do you think you are merely observing him without him knowing?"

"I don't know. Growing up, it's not like we could read each other's minds. I guess I've heard about some twins that have a magical link or something, but I never got into any of that nonsense. This is fairly new—maybe the last year or so. I can't imagine he'd try and show me this stuff unless he wanted to scare the hell out of me, keep me up all night, that sort of thing. But then he's cruel like that, so maybe he's found a way to send me these images just for his amusement. I hate him. Never did an honest day's work on our farm, no respect for our animals. I once caught him cutting apart a dead pack horse 'just to have a peek at the insides.' That's Malenec. No respect for life, no respect for death. But if he's found a way to bring the dead back to life, the numbers I've seen…"

"How many?"

"Thousands, Your Majesty. Thousands."

The Queen sneered, and it made her plain face even uglier. She could care less. She finished her cup and was getting ready to refill it when she stopped and looked at Palinor. "Thousands. Hmph. Tell me—have you ever tried communicating with Malenec? Do you think he sees your surroundings in his dreams?"

Palinor chuckled. "Aye, I've tried 'communicating', all right. Spent many nights convinced I would take control of my own nightmare and beat the hell out of my twin, but I never could. Take control, that is." He finished his mug, shaking his head. "'Course, I could never beat him up as a kid either. Too damn quick, and then he got into spells and scrolls, and I'd likely end up cursed or worse. And as for him watching me…I'm not sure my brother knows how to dream, to tell you the truth. Hell, he might not even sleep anymore, for all I know. In my visions I always see him in the sand, on a dune, or down by the beach surrounded by his minions. Except when he's alone in his room. Occasionally when I see him there, he's staring at his hand."

"His hand?"

"Yeah, he wears a ring underneath a glove. I can see it clear as this goblet in the flickering torchlight. Silver, with a black square on top and a green gem embedded in it. He seems real protective of that ring."

Niku inhaled sharply, stood, and with a curt nod to Queen Najalas, left. She nodded at Jonathon, and he produced a second bag of gold and extended it to Palinor.

"What? Did I say something important?" He took the gold with a smile, exchanging it for his mug, which he handed to Jonathon to refill.

~Tarsh~

The water was rising. The fog was gone, and the sun shone down on him from a perch far higher in the sky than he'd hoped. *Midmorning, sprinting toward noon.* He tried to quicken his pace, but he had slipped twice already. The Bridge was about three feet wide, but it was slicker than an oily snake. Eons of algae and decomposed fish mingled with salty water put a nice shine to the smooth stone.

Tarsh reckoned he was roughly halfway across when the water began covering the Bridge, lapping all the way up to his mid-calf. He could still see the stone under the rising tide, but the force of the choppy whitecaps made each step treacherous. After another slip that nearly swept him into the sea, Tarsh dropped to all fours and began crawling as fast as he could. Salt water spray stung his eyes; he felt like a crab.

Should I even try and Teleport? The thought had occurred to him. He well knew the perils of *Teleporting* over water; yet small bodies, like rivers and streams, were never an issue. *Wouldn't Teleporting over the path of the Bridge to the mainland be akin to Teleporting over a long, narrow puddle?* He smiled as a particularly large wave drove water into his shoulder. If he were to take a chance at *Teleport*ing, the time to do so would have been when land connected the Great Isle and Adimand, when the Bridge was completely visible. Not now.

"Yow!" he yelped as he put his hand down on something sharp. He pulled his hand up and saw bits of jagged seashell stuck into the fleshy part of his palm. The cuts weren't deep, but they bled all the same. The saltwater stung, but he cleaned it as best he could, and kept crawling gingerly forward.

The waves began to pick up even more, and now crested at eye level while down on all fours. Tarsh couldn't stand; he could barely move forward. His hand was throbbing, and the bridge was now impossible to see in the swirling water. He had to feel his way forward.

Not going to make it like this. How could anyone cross this thing on foot? Tarsh waited for the next wave to pass over him, and set his mind on *Levitating* up and out of this soup. He had enough strength left for this, he believed.

"*Subvolo!*" Tarsh incanted.

Another wave smashed into him, and Tarsh was knocked halfway off the Bridge, completely submerged. His fingers clung to the far edge, with his feet floating behind him.

What is going on? Controlling his thoughts, holding his breath, he incanted silently once again: *Subvolo!*

Nothing. Not a hair on his head even tingled with the spell.

Straining, he threw one leg up over the Bridge and hauled himself up. He quickly poked his head above the roaring water to gulp some air. The water was rising fast, and crawling was no longer an option. He tried to think; he knew he had enough to lift himself out of the water. This didn't make sense.

More water crashed over him, causing Tarsh to flatten himself onto the Bridge to avoid getting swept away once again. He couldn't think deeply—the first thing that came to mind was building a wall of ice to stop those waves. A freezing spell should do nicely here. He cast it to his left, hoping to build an icewall that would, if nothing else, give him time to think.

No ice came forth; only more water, higher water, more waves battering Tarsh yet again. His feet and hands couldn't maintain their purchase on the Bridge this time, and he was sucked into the undertow, pressed down into sea that quickly went from clear to blue to black.

He tumbled over and over; up was down, down was up, with salty blackness everywhere. Blackness…with trickles of red droplets.

Normally, Strongiron reveled at the rare opportunity to banter with other knights, share a few stories, and hoist a pint or three with regular folk in the common room of a fine tavern such as *The Royal Steed.* The inn buzzed when he walked in, accompanied by Victor and Kari. The awkward hush abruptly ended almost as quick as it began, when some of the knights in the back from his Order—Thunder—gave a welcoming shout and began to come forward, each one looking to be the first to salute, buy his first pint, or both.

Strongiron, however, was exhausted.

He smiled at the adoring crowd, and then looked over at Victor, who slowly stroked his mustache, staring intently at the General-turned-Cleric. Strongiron didn't say a word, but Victor gave the slightest of nods. The Lieutenant General wasted no time leaping atop a nearby table, unencumbered with the heavy armor Strongiron bore.

"Friends! By now you have heard the words of our General in your temples and shrines this afternoon. If not, come gather around, and in exchange for a mug or two in trade of Silas's good ale, I will recount Strongiron's words, but let our good General rest this evening. He has travelled long—longer than any here, I venture to guess—and a warm bed calls. I regret that, alas, you will have to take your entertainment from me this evening. Then again, despite the difference in our size, I daresay I can hold every bit the ale our beloved General here can, and perhaps a pint more!" Those gathered laughed as Victor grabbed a mug from the table he was standing on and lifted it in a toast for the room. He took a gulp, leaving a bit of foam on his flowing mustaches. "Why, I remember when Strongiron and I were in the Three Fingers…"

Strongiron felt Kari tighten her grip on his hand. Taking the cue, he meandered through the forest of backslaps, salutes, and toasts until he reached Silas, the innkeeper. He smelled of roasted goat, spilled ale, and sweat. Mostly sweat.

"General, it is always the highest honor for you to favor my humble inn. To what do I owe this pleasure?" Silas rubbed a hairy forearm across his forehead.

"The pleasure is ours, Silas, but as Victor said, we are passing through on our way back to Rookwood, and I would like a room for the night."

"Of course, of course. Are you sure you won't stay down in the gathering hall for a spell? My patrons always delight in hearing from you, General Strongiron."

Kari stepped forward. "As much as we would like to keep your guests entertained—and keep your bar active—we desire rest. It has been a long, long afternoon. I'm sure you understand."

Silas blinked and took a quick step back. "Beggin' your pardon, my Lady. Of course, of course. The Lieutenant does not come often, but he seems more than an entertaining fellow in his own right. Come. Follow me." Silas turned sharply, almost plowing over one of his barmaids in the process. "Excuse me, pardon me," he mumbled without stopping.

Strongiron saw Kari grinning as he led her behind Silas. *The woman could disarm a dwarf of his beard if she so desired.* He flashed Kari his own grin as they headed up two flights of stairs.

"'Tis the only room left, I hope that's alright?" asked Silas. "I'll find your friend a room once I know who is likely to sleep in their cups downstairs. If he drinks as good as he boasts, I have no doubt he'll outlast many patrons tonight." Silas said nervously.

"This is fine. Thank you." Strongiron reached for gold, but Silas waived him off. "The crown is always welcome at the *Steed*." He bowed, mopped his forehead again, and left.

Strongiron and Kari entered the room, bolting the door behind them. The sound of laughter could only dimly be heard, and the room smelled clean enough. The aroma of roasted goat and sage wafted up from the kitchen fires below. Strongiron exhaled deeply, and sat down. "I was hoping for better results."

Kari walked over to a couple of large candles set on either side of the bed and lit them both. They provided the only light in the room.

"We shared the truth; not everyone will believe the first time they hear it." She sighed softly, rubbing the back of her neck. "Your armor looks blinding in this low light…it shines as if the light is drawn to it." She stood in front of him, placing a hand on each shoulder. "Though I think you should remove it. Precious few times in our travels will you be able to safely remove your armor. It must be heavy, and besides…you could use a wash." She wrinkled her nose playfully.

Strongiron grabbed her waist, placing his hands just above her hips, his eyes sparkling. "A wash, huh? And I suppose after all our travels you smell clean as winter's first snow?"

Kari moved her hands to cup the stubble on both cheeks, bending down to move her face closer. "My dear general, you have no idea what I smell like. I can smell like roses if I wish." She flashed her eyes mischievously, and Strongiron immediately inhaled deeply the scent of sweet, red roses.

"Or perhaps you prefer something more exotic?" She pushed her hands through his hair.

Strongiron smelled lavender, lemongrass, and a hint of...*was it clove?* His sense of smell was not his strongest attribute—not by a longshot. Not that it mattered. Strongiron felt his emotions stirring, and he stood up. He ran one hand through her hair as he leaned in to kiss her. "About that wash..."

A loud knock on their door separated them with a start. "Strongiron!" It was Victor's voice. The General narrowed his eyes as he slowly turned toward the door. "Strongiron!" Victor called out again with another pounding on the door.

Strongiron slid the wooden bolt and opened the door. "What is it, Victor? Surely Silas could keep you in ale for one evening of storytelling?"

Victor put his hand on Strongiron. "My friend, we must leave. Tonight. Your work this afternoon has not gone unnoticed. More than one knight from our Order has informed me that the mob gathers and approaches. Some to hail you, others to denounce you or worse. If we do not slip out tonight, by morning the *Steed* will be surrounded by both followers and deniers alike. You and Miss Kari may *Teleport* away, I suppose, but if you wish to arrive in Rookwood—the three of us together—it must be now. Unless you wish to pray your way through in the morning..."

~Magi~

It had been weeks since fresh meat and vegetables had been set before Magi, but truly it felt longer. His mouth watered at the sight of such an opulent spread.

"Michael, try the plum glaze on the roasted lamb. I have them shipped weekly from the fertile plains of Adimand—the finest gold can buy." Smiling slyly, Xaro raised a glass of wine and proceeded to explain at great length how it paired with the meal in general.

The meal was perhaps the finest Magi had ever eaten, better than the grandest feast the Queen would have had prepared in Rookwood. *The world may be starving, but somehow the desert becomes a paradise.*

Soon the lamb was cleared…and replaced by succulent duck breast accented with more sweet citrus from the Adimand. The food was endless.

"Son, where are you getting the gold to eat like this? The entire city of Nervadine should eat so well!" Daphne, however, was hardly shy as the plates came her way.

Xaro did not answer immediately, but beamed smugly over the rim of his goblet. It was only the three of them. Frankly, Magi was surprised he had even been invited. He would have thought Xaro would prefer to catch up with his mother alone.

"I have done well enough, Mother. We do not eat this way every night, I assure you, but it seems only right to celebrate having not seen you for so long."

"That was your decision. You left with that Ranger, and that was practically the last I've seen of you, save your shade." She drank deeply of the wine in front of her, and Magi could swear her "old woman" *Illusion* was starting to break down. He couldn't see any degradation yet…but he could *feel* it. He shifted uncomfortably. He looked at his host, who seemed completely unstirred by his mother's nature. *Perhaps it doesn't affect one's own flesh and blood?*

Magi stood suddenly, clearing his throat. "Thank you, Xaro. You are a gracious host, and a better meal I'm not sure I've ever had. I'm sure you two have a lot to catch up on. If you would excuse me, I'd like to take my leave to give you two your time together. We can discuss our business in the morning, if that is all right with you."

"But Michael, it's still early, and I have a dessert that you must try—a Mage that works for me has perfected the art of cooling cream until it thickens, which he mixes and sweetens with fresh strawberries. You will not find a finer end to a meal anywhere in Tenebrae, I assure you. Besides, I would like to hear more about your travels, and your interests in my army, if it's all the same. My troops will occupy much of my day tomorrow. Come—dessert first, and more wine." With a word, he *Levitated* the massive jug to refill Magi's goblet. "My mother says you are quite the mage, but I am not without a modicum of magical talent myself." He smiled again, that same charismatic smile that Magi found infuriating. "Please—stay a while. I have nothing private to say right now to my dear mother."

The last thing Magi wanted was to be around Daphne at the moment. Xaro, yes. Daphne…not so much. He smiled gamely. "If you insist, I'd love to have another glass with you." He held it up in a silent toast before sitting back down, while a scoop of ruby-red iced cream was placed before him.

Xaro sculpted a spoonful off his plate and closed his eyes while savoring the taste, as if in ecstasy. "Divine." He then began gesturing with the spoon while he talked. "So. What I am most fascinated by is your staff, Michael. I've never seen one like it before. Where did you get it?"

"A magical supply shop on the outskirts of Nervadine, actually. Little more than a handy walking stick, really," Magi replied.

"Hmmm. Quite a stone to put atop a walking stick."

"Yes. Quite." Magi sipped his wine, wetting his lips but drinking little. He finally dug into his own dessert, and had to agree—it *was* delicious.

"May I examine it? It is quite unusual."

"I've never let another hold it, Xaro. Being practiced in the Art, I'm sure you understand a Mage wishing to keep his craft private. I would no sooner let a stranger read my handwritten scrolls or handle my spell components. I mean no offense, of course."

Xaro kept his eyes on Magi, kept the same easy smile. "None taken." He maintained the stare just past the point of awkwardness before finally shrugging. "So, you heard about me, and wish to 'join.' Tell me what you have heard, and what you think you're joining. I am most curious."

"Rumors of power rising in the West. Gold, men, some sailors even say spirits answer your call. I figured I'd take a look myself if you're building an army. A True Mage can be a boon to any army."

"They can also be a threat." Xaro narrowed his eyes, his smile vanishing as he leaned forward in his seat. "You travelled across the sea, past the Great Maelstrom, on a whim that 'power is amassing in the west,' hoping to trade spell craft for gold? Is this what you honestly expect me to believe? Most men run away from war, not toward it."

Magi allowed his own sly smile to spread across his face. "Mercenaries do not. We live in a Dark World, Xaro. Not many lords are hiring, and festival tricks don't spin much gold. War always does. Why is that hard for you to believe? Surely I am not the first man to knock on your door, asking if you need help? If your vision is conquest, I think I could help your troops. You will find I am a fairly skilled Mage."

Xaro stroked his square chin, running his forefinger and thumb through the day's stubble, pressing so hard that he was squeezing the sides of his cleft together. He stood up. "That is a splendid idea, Michael. Let us have a mage duel. Tomorrow morning, first light. I would like to see how strong you are. If you are as strong as you say, perhaps we can use another Battle Mage."

Daphne's old woman *Illusion* had all but dissipated, the wine clearly affecting her concentration. Magi was terribly uncomfortable. He kept shifting his eyes over to look at her thick, white hair, the red nails, the flecks of blue in her grey eyes... His desire for Daphne was beginning to crowd out every other thought. *Focus!*

His head spun with passion; he couldn't think straight. He had to get out of here. He was still processing what Xaro had just said, but he couldn't think through the several competing ideas in his head. He went with his gut, clearing his throat. "Xaro, I would be honored, of course, but is this truly fair? I am a True Mage, after all. What would it prove for me to push you from the dueling circle?"

Xaro didn't answer immediately, but let his smile once again return. "Actually, it would prove a lot, Michael."

That was when Magi felt a tingle...and it wasn't from Daphne's real appearance, either.

~Queen Najalas~

"They have arrived, Your Majesty." Jonathon Venerek, her capable Steward, announced.

"I will see them yet tonight. See that they are refreshed, and I will meet them in my private drawing room in a few minutes. Thank you, Jonathon." The Queen called from her private chambers and proceeded to walk over to her washing bowl. When she heard her Steward's fading footfalls, she turned back toward her bedroom. Herodius was framed there, shirtless.

"Herodius, you heard Jonathon. Strongiron has returned. I want you to join us, but you must come through the drawing room. Wear your armor—at least the breastplate." She dipped her hand into the water. It was cool, having lost its heat throughout the day, which suited the Queen just fine; she splashed the crisp water over her face, bracing for her senses to clear. The day had been long, full of questioning Palinor, when the ale seemed to flow freely. And it had been a short evening with Herodius, where the interruption of her former General's return was one of the *only* events Jonathon would have announced. She dabbed her face with clean linen.

"Najalas—" Herodius began as he walked over and snaked his one good arm around the Queen's waist from behind her while she washed her face.

She spun to face him, pressing a long, white finger against his lips. "Shh." She smiled, but her eyes were all business. "Soon, there will be no need for pretense, Herodius. Soon, Elvidor shall have a King. We have discussed this. It would be imprudent for there to be any doubt as to the legitimacy of any future son we may raise, and you must have a proper title if you are to govern the people— Herodius the islander will do nothing but invite rebellion from every noble in Elvidor with a little gold and a few swords. No. You *will* be knighted, Herodius. I will grant you land, and you shall be my husband. For the good of the Kingdom—"

"And what about the good of the Queen?" He flashed a warm smile, and pressed his forehead gently against hers. The Queen dropped her hand from his lips to rest on his smooth chest, and she could feel his heart thumping aggressively.

"The Queen *is* good." She looked up in the islander's dark eyes and curled her thin lips in the most seductive smile she could muster. Reluctantly, she pushed herself away. "But the Queen is, unfortunately, busy. Now please, go—get prepared. I want you to be ready to greet Strongiron and our guests tonight. I anticipate a very long night still, but this is not an update I wish to delay until morning."

Herodius sighed, but stepped back. "Tell me, Najalas. Do you ever slow down to enjoy a moment of peace?" His voice wasn't perturbed or annoyed. He sounded genuinely curious, even playful. "Did your former husband, King Alomar, ever become accustomed to your pace?"

My husband... Half a dozen thoughts and memories flooded her senses at the sound of his name: love, disappointment, respect, anger, passion, frustration…too many to fit into a tidy response.

"Running a kingdom requires more 'pace' then farming an island, Herodius. Tomorrow waits for no one." She immediately regretted the words before she had even finished.

His face hardened. "I see. Thank you for the lesson, *my Queen.* I hope I execute all my duties as well as you do. That is clearly the meaning of life, after all." He turned and left without another word.

The Queen started to call after him, but stopped herself. Instead, she looked at her reflection in the mirror. Her limp hair hung damp and flat around her face. Her skin was too pale, her eyes too dark, her nose too thin. *For me, duty is the meaning of life. Leave the romantic pillow talk and slow mornings to the bards and poets. War is coming, and Elvidor will need a hard Queen…and King.*

She cupped her hands into the water basin once again, throwing water against her face furiously as if she was trying to remake it through splashing. After several fistfuls of water, she straightened her back with a garbled, frustrated yell. Dripping, her dirty blond hair was sopping wet, along with the rest of her face. *My duty.*

She ripped the linen off the side of the basin with a *snap* and toweled off her hair, fetched a clean cloak that could be wrapped tightly around her in the process. Finally, she proceeded toward the drawing room, but not before stopping to pour herself a goblet from the bitterest barrel of ale in Rookwood that she kept for just such moods.

We each have a duty, she thought as she drank deep, *and mine is no less than to protect our land and our people...whatever the cost.*

~Magi~

"Malenec. The ring is possessed by the Dark Cleric, Magi. I have seen him in person; his power is unlike ours. He will be protected from your greatest strength while you are vulnerable. Do not throw your life away needlessly, Magi. We need you back in Rookwood." Niku's shimmering shade cut quickly to the point.

Magi had finally been able to take his leave of Xaro and head to his quarters, at which time he accepted the message from Niku. His message was succinct. *Malenec has the ring.*

"How do you know, Niku?"

"He has a twin brother, Palinor, and the brother's dreams are tortured. Malenec wears gloves everywhere, but occasionally he takes them off in his room while alone. Palinor often sees him admiring your ring."

"That's it? Hardly much upon which to base a claim, Niku."

"I know. But I wanted you to know nonetheless. Have you arrived at Sands End?"

"I have."

"And have you seen Xaro or Malenec?"

"I had dinner with Xaro this evening, actually."

"Really? By chance could you strike? The death of either one of them would be a huge advantage, you realize?"

"I can't strike until I know he doesn't have my ring, or know where it is. I know he's not wearing it on a finger. But if he knows where it is, I must know that before I kill him."

"I've told you where I believe it is. If you can kill Xaro, you may be able to end this war before it begins." Niku's hands were balled into fists. Magi always knew him to be more cautious. *He must truly be worried.*

"Perhaps a chance exists. I duel him tomorrow morning. We shall see how that goes. I would prefer not to have to fight my way through a horde of both undead and live men on my way back to the docks, hoping a ship is getting ready to leave, but if an opportunity presents itself, and I am reasonably sure he does not have information I need, I will certainly try and end this, Niku."

"Why are you dueling Xaro?"

"It's a long story, but mostly it is his ego. That, or he doesn't believe I am who I claim to be. I fear he may have recognized my staff."

Niku's image was silent for a few seconds, arms folded across his chest. *He looks older,* thought Magi. *This conflict is aging him.*

Finally Niku's shade spoke. "Be careful, Magi. This is a dangerous game you're playing."

He nodded to the fading image. "I will, Niku." Then the shade was gone.

Two related thoughts ran through his head. *I need to confirm whether Malenec has my ring before first light tomorrow, and if so...I need to kill Xaro in the morning.*

~Tarsh~

Surely a spell was written to allow a mage to breathe under water. Had to be. Probably even a simple one that young mages could master, well before they Climbed. Tarsh was sure it existed.

He just didn't know it.

Minutes stretched into one gulp-and-dive drill after another. Tarsh would poke his head above water, gasping for breath. He'd open his eyes and see a wave hurtling toward him. He'd suck in as much air as he could and dive a few feet down. The wave would pass overhead, and he'd spin around in the undertow for half a minute, maybe longer, before he could vaguely see a patch of light somewhere in the distance. He'd swim toward it, breaking the surface of the water, sputtering once again. He'd open his eyes and see a wave hurling toward him...

Tarsh was getting exhausted. Already he had swallowed enough seawater to make him thirsty. His elbow and nose still hurt. If only he could stop and *think.* He couldn't concentrate, couldn't call to mind any spells, and still couldn't figure out why his previous attempts had failed.

Of all the ways I thought I'd die, drowning was near the bottom. Surely I wasn't restored just to die like a swollen fish?

Another wave, another dive, and another underwater scramble toward light. He spotted a shimmering strip of brightness, and began kicking toward it.

And then the strip moved. The strip of white made a tight circle, and began diving down toward Tarsh. It wasn't the surface of the water that he was seeing move...It was a shark.

Tarsh had never seen one before, but had heard sailors talk about them while at sea. The descriptions were always the same: white belly, black eyes, sharp teeth. 'Yeh don' want to fin' yerself face-to-face w' one of dem, trust me Mage,' was basically how it went.

Well, Tarsh was now face-to-face with a shark. The speed of the animal was breathtaking. It honed in on him at ramming speed, mouth open, with a clear intent to fillet the first part of his body it could latch onto. There was no time to think—Tarsh just reacted as the head of the beast launched toward him. The first spell to come to mind was his electric hands—the same spell he used to defeat Magi an eternity ago in Marik's Tournament. He thrust his fingers toward the beast's head without thinking and cast the spell.

Lightning crackled when he touched the shark, and a flash of light seemed to encircle them both. The great fish thrashed violently, with a single tooth snaring on his robe, ripping it and slicing open his arm. All around Tarsh, fish began to float down past him, still and slowly sinking. He took his hands off the shark and watched it slowly drift downward, too. It was an eerie scene as clumps of dead fish bounced off him on their way to the sea floor. As the spellcaster, Tarsh was immune to the electric effect, but the salt water must have carried the current well beyond his intended victim.

He couldn't ponder this any further; by now his lungs were on fire, and he kicked to the surface, exhaling bubbles furiously as he swam. He punched through the surface and immediately started gasping, though another wave soon crashed over his head again. On a whim, exhausted, and at the end of his physical and magical endurance, he tried to *Levitate* again. *If my Shocking Hands spell worked, perhaps...*

Like the ship, he lifted out of the storm, Tarsh slowly lifted himself above the water, above the waves. The free air—the sweet, *dry* air! Unencumbered with the practical worry of swallowing the sea, he could finally fill his lungs...and cough up the water that had invaded them. What's more, he could float high enough now to get his bearings.

Tarsh could no longer see the Bridge, but could see both Adimand and the Great Isle; he was much closer to the mainland. He had no idea how far he had travelled east of the Bridge, but if the soreness in his muscles could be translated into leagues, he was far away indeed.

Slowly, Tarsh *Levitated* north and westward. He glided over the choppy seas, close to the water but not touching it. The mist from the cresting waves sprayed his legs. Onward he floated, until he came to the mainland. In the distance, he could see a fair-sized city.

Tarsh lowered himself and gently set down. The solid ground underneath his feet was never more appreciated. It may have only been early afternoon, but he was utterly spent. More than food, more than water, more so than even heat, given how waterlogged he was— what Tarsh needed most was sleep.

Drenched in seawater, he found an unusually large cherry tree and curled up at the base of the trunk to doze. The scent of sweet cherries was intoxicating. The fruit was ripe and plentiful. He was too tired, but on the outer edge of his consciousness he was aware of other smells nearby, too. Exotic smells. Berries, lavender, spices, even Mikenese melons—everything was here. Soon he slipped into the world of dreams…

…only to be awakened moments later by two figures standing over him. Dazed, unrefreshed, and still rubbing sleep out of his eyes, he saw sandals and the brown hem of their robes and groaned.

CHAPTER FOURTEEN: CAPTIVE HEART, MIND, AND BODY

~Strongiron~

"Victor Charles Ethan Remington the Third," Jonathon formally announced Victor.

Strongiron couldn't help rolling his eyes as Victor strode through the doorway to the drawing room and knelt before the Queen with a flourish. He looked over at Kari, who shared a private half-smile with him. They were both tired, but if the Queen wanted to meet at this hour, then meet they shall. He looked at her face—at her remarkable, piercing green eyes. *Would my heart stir if I were staring into the face of a True Mage's snowy eyes?*

"An honor to see you again, my Queen." Victor's voice filled the small room, and brought Strongiron out of his reverie.

"Victor, arise and be comfortable. Enough pageantry. Drink, anyone?" The Queen nodded for Jonathon to bring glasses, took a seat, and gestured for everyone else to do likewise. "The hour may be late, but there is much I would like to know, and some I would like to share. First, I trust Strongiron has briefed you on your appointment during your journey here?"

"He has, my Queen."

"And you accept?"

"I do—it is an honor, your Majesty." He paused and narrowed his eyes, leaning forward. "But if I may speak plainly—"

"You may, and you must," Queen Najalas interrupted.

"Yes. Very well. Strongiron or Kari should not leave. I will command the army, but one of them should stay at Rookwood."

Kari started to stand, and Strongiron put a gentle, yet firm hand on her shoulder. She brushed it off and stood up anyway to face Victor, eyes flashing. "We have discussed this. Did you forget your lesson on the road, Victor?"

"I remember the conversation, but I think we took two very different lessons from it." He turned to face the Queen. "Your Majesty, these two worshippers bring healing—*true* healing—to people. I saw them *regrow* hands! I saw them cure the Dying Disease from the Afflicted! I saw—"

Peter stood up. "You visited the Afflicted?" He turned to Strongiron. "Did you find him? Did you see my brother Garin?"

Victor kept talking over Peter. "*True* healing! Imagine a defensive position—"

Kari started shouting, "Our mission is to—"

Herodius looked over at Kari. "You re-grew part of an arm?"

Jonathon was holding a large pitcher, staring at the crowd.

Strongiron slowly shut his eyes, took a deep breath, and re-opened them to look over at the Queen, who, unsurprisingly, had similarly closed her eyes and was tenting her fingers against her temples with one hand while clutching a goblet with the other. When she opened them, she was looking at Strongiron, she looked worn. Her eyes seemed to almost plead with him, *if you won't be King, will you do me this one favor and shut everyone up?*

Strongiron stood. His armor was no longer gleaming white, but was splattered with dirt and mud and god knew what else after weeks of travel, but when he stood, everyone quieted, even Victor. He almost seemed too big for the drawing room.

"Enough. The Queen deserves an orderly discussion, for there is much to process. Although I think she realizes that Kari's and my own course are set, she still deserves to hear your argument, Victor. We shall all speak, but perhaps not all at once. Jonathon, I'll take that glass now, if you please."

Strongiron sat back down and made a simple gesture to Victor, the universal sign of *the floor is yours.* He sipped, and immediately fought back a cough. *She's into the bitter ale tonight, I see.*

"My Queen, as I was saying, Strongiron and Kari have shown marvelous healing prowess that the realm has not seen in centuries. Allowing them both to pursue this shield is, in my opinion, folly. I would insist that one of them stay behind that we may incorporate their talents into our defense strategy. Surely Simon and Peter see the prudence in this course as well?"

Simon and Peter said nothing, but did tilt their heads slightly.

"Victor, do you not think that I've made that wish known as well?" The Queen looked at Strongiron and Kari again. "Kari, I ask you again, will you not stay?"

"No, my Queen. My mission has been put before me by Dymetra Herself. We shall depart as soon as practical, I have no doubt."

The Queen turned back to Victor. "You see? What would you have me do? Throw them in the dungeon?"

"Your Majesty…they are still your subjects! Surely you will not allow this defiance—"

"They are my subjects, but they follow a *God*. I appreciate your update and your willingness to assume command. Now here is *my* command for you: concern yourself with the defense of Elvidor without Strongiron or Kari. Perhaps they will return before we are attacked, but you must be prepared regardless."

"God. Pish-posh. You don't truly believe that, do you my Queen?" Victor sat back down.

"How do you explain this 'marvelous healing,' if it does not come from a True God?" The Queen set her goblet down and leaned toward him.

"Magic. Just another form of arcane magic, that's all." Victor folded his arms and leaned back. "But Elvidor will be defended vigorously, regardless of our healers. You can bet on that."

"I am." Picking up her goblet, the Queen sipped again, waving her hand dismissively at the notion that magic was the source of their ability to heal. She left Victor to his thoughts and turned to her Admiral. "I believe you had a question for them, Peter?" She gestured back to Kari and Strongiron.

"Garin—my question is about Garin. Did you see my brother in the Valley of the Afflicted?" His face shone with an almost painful hopefulness.

Strongiron walked over and put a hand on his shoulder. "We did. Your brother gives his regards, Peter. He is well now. Kari was able to heal him before we left. He is staying to help some of those we could not heal, but I imagine he will find his way to Rookwood eventually to reconnect with you. Or perhaps you may be able to connect with him in Plythe when you leave. Have you obtained the resources you need?"

Peter didn't even acknowledge Strongiron's question; building boats was the furthest thing on his mind at the moment. He just turned to walk over to Kari, and hugged her. "Thank you. Thank you, Kari." Tears of joy traced a path down his cheek, and when he disengaged, he called Jonathon over and hoisted a full mug. "With the Queen's blessing, I would like to toast Kari. For Garin…I cannot begin to thank you enough—"

"Thank Dymetra, Peter," Kari said gently.

"Yes. Of course—Praise Dymetra!"

They all drank, even Victor, who waited for the shouts to die down. "As I said, all the more reason one of them should stay. Disease comes to the battlefield, too."

Kari whipped her head around, but Herodius put a hand up before she could fire back. "Kari…tell me about the hands Victor claims you regrew. Is that possible?"

"I'll let Strongiron address this question, as it was his prayer."

She looked at him as he nodded and stepped forward. "Anything is possible, Herodius. I know you and I have not always seen eye-to-eye when it comes to our faith, but yes, Dymetra saw fit to forgive and heal even the worst among us. I healed the lady Veronica, who some here knew as Sarah. She was the Assassin that took the contract on me. Apparently Magi caught up with her, and while it's unclear exactly what happened, she's convinced he sliced off her hands and left her to fend for herself." Strongiron shook his head. "And I must admit her story rings true in my ears. She attempted to kill Magi; perhaps he had had enough." He opened his palms to Kari and shrugged.

"It does fit him, I am sad to say." Kari walked over to Herodius and looked more closely at his arm.

Strongiron continued. "She believed in Dymetra. She showed genuine remorse. Whereas the entire Valley wanted nothing to do with the one True God, Veronica did. I prayed for her healing, and it was done. Her courage to step forward allowed many formerly faithless, dying people to be healed, to have hope for the first time since the beginning of their disease. The entire Valley owes her a debt."

Herodius stared at Strongiron. "You healed the assassin who tried to kill you? Why?"

"Forgiveness. I do not think she poses a threat to me or our realm any longer."

The Queen now stood up. "How can you be sure? Forgiveness is one thing, but so is Justice. Why would you heal such a killer? Surely Magi took her hands to keep her from slashing any more throats. His judgment seems the wise one, yet you are the True Cleric! Why, Strongiron?"

"If the decision to heal her was unwise, then Dymetra wouldn't have allowed it, my Queen, and if Magi hadn't cut off her hands, then no dramatic healing would have been possible at all, and Garin and the others would have simply run us out of the Valley to remain Afflicted. You must have a little faith, your Majesty. I don't pretend to know how it all works out, nor should any of us." He looked over at Peter, then more pointedly at Victor.

Mumbled agreement percolated throughout the room before Niku raised his voice.

"I have an update as well. We believe we have learned the whereabouts of Magi's ring of magical protection—it is purportedly in the possession of the Dark Cleric Malenec. I have notified Magi of this through the communication of our shades. He is in Sands End currently, and I believe he may try to kill Xaro and recover his ring tomorrow."

Though rarely used, Magi cloaked himself in an invisibility spell. Stealth was paramount tonight. He peered outside his window from his guest room at Sands End. The night was hot; he suspected every night was hot in the desert. Clouds obscured the stars and moon; only the sporadic campfires from the training grounds below cast any real light.

Magi assumed that Xaro would have Mage-guards stationed near his door. He may be a "guest," but the banter from this evening proved that at a minimum, Xaro was suspicious. He wanted to see the staff, and Magi had no idea what would happen if he grasped it. He had also unhesitatingly challenged him under the pretense that it was to prove his worth for his army. *There's no way a journeyman Mage would defeat a True Mage; it is a pointless duel, and he knows it. What's more, he knows I know it.*

The only reasonable conclusion was that Xaro suspected he was dining with Magi Blacksmooth, not Michael Mother-keeper, and a duel would surely confirm that.

Unless I lose on purpose. What if I let him win? Put forth just enough of a showing to impress him, but not enough to cause him to suspect I might be who he thinks I am...

Magi shook his head. Even if he knew where to draw that line, he wasn't sure he could stop himself. First, for the practical reason that Xaro might be unleashing so much force that he would need every ounce of his strength not to get blown inside out. Second, for the emotional reason that if he got the upper hand against Xaro, he seriously doubted he would ease up against the man who oversaw his mother's murder, his father's hardship, and the tainting of his very soul. He further considered Niku's prescient words: *"If you can kill Xaro, you may be able to end this war before it begins."*

No...if he got the opportunity, he absolutely planned on killing Xaro in the morning.

Whispering a few words of magic, Magi leaped from his window, fluttering down silently with the aid of another spell to break his fall. Stealthily creeping toward the edge of the mesa, he looked down at the surrounding fighting pits, forges, and armories. Down by the sea was a crude stone hut that seemed oddly out of place with the surrounding landscape, which were mostly shifting dunes. A path from this dwelling wound upwards toward the pits and the base of the mesa, and it looked well-worn, but that was the only sign that it was connected to the industry of war that surrounded Sands End.

However, the undead surrounding the hut gave it away. As Magi looked closely, he saw that the dunes kept shifting because the zombies hid there, buried under the sand. Hands and feet stuck out at odd angles, and sand was constantly spilling one way and getting shoveled back on top by others. *Malenec must be inside.*

Magi had to know for sure if he had the ring. The challenge was how. The easiest would be to ask him, of course. Armed with his staff, he'd know for sure, but that obviously wasn't going to work.

He could try and sneak inside the abode, looking for an obvious bulge underneath the cleric's gloved hand. Unfortunately, he also knew there were thousands of undead loyal to Malenec—far more than what he saw or even suspected hiding underneath the nearby dunes. They could be under the sea, in the pits, even in the desert…and they would smell him, even if he was invisible. Had he studied *Illusions* a little more fervently, perhaps he could mask his scent…but that was not the case.

He thought about fighting his way inside, but if Malenec had the ring, he did not like his chances of killing him before he was consumed by a horde of zombies.

Ultimately, he decided the simpler the plan, the better. Still invisible, he dared not get any closer than he was already. Grabbing a few grains of the plentiful sand, he readied one spell. Grabbing a pinch of cinnamon, he readied another.

With clear line of sight to the door of the stone hut, Magi cast an *Everflame* into one of the nearby dunes.

The undead began screaming immediately. Sand collapsed everywhere as the air began to fill with the stench of rotting, burning flesh. The fire quickly caught, and frantic zombies began running everywhere, bouncing around and spreading fire to one another in a mindless dance macabre.

The door flew open, and a figure dressed all in black burst into the melee of blue flames. Magi cast his sleep spell with the full force of his magic—enough to put a small village to sleep, had there been anyone else in the path of his spell.

The figure in black stood there, very much awake with his arms raised to the heavens, and a magical downpour opened up, quenching the flames.

Magi *Teleported* back to his room in Sands End. He was now sure of two things: *That man cloaked in black is Malenec the Dark Cleric, and he has my ring.*

His head spinning from one idea to the next on how he might retrieve it, he finally closed his eyes and tried to sleep to recoup his strength for the morning's duel with Xaro. He would need all the energy he could muster.

~Queen Najalas~

Several thoughts swam through the Queen's groggy head. She listened to the scuttlebutt and chatter in the room from Niku's bombshell update, but unlike her subjects, she wasn't fixated on how Magi might prevent war. Not directly. Somewhat guiltily, her first thought was that she might not have to kill Chief Chocktaw to fulfill her end of the contract with Silverfist if Magi killed Xaro first.

On the heels of that thought were the words of her former General, with whom she was annoyed. *Faith? Have a little faith?* The Queen narrowed her eyes at the room, indignant. *Do they not remember that I was the one who commissioned their expedition to Urthrax? That I first believed in the old elf's council regarding Dymetra? That I supported Kari when she first wanted to see the world and chase her own prophesy like a child with wanderlust?* The hour was late, but the Queen found renewed vigor from Strongiron's preachiness.

She stood up. "I find it interesting that you would lecture me to have faith. Let us not forget that it was *my* faith that sent you to find your calling in the first place." Eyes flashing, the Queen stared long and hard at Strongiron.

He opened his mouth to speak, but shut it just as quickly. He then stood up and inclined his head. "Forgive me, my Queen. I meant no disrespect." He sat back down and sipped his ale, returning the Queen's gaze over the lip of his own goblet.

"What's done is done. You healed the Assassin. If she comes after you again…" The Queen hardened her voice. "If she comes after you again, it's on your hands." She sat down and looked over at Niku. "What did Magi say when you notified him of our suspicions regarding Malenec and his ring?"

"He has his doubts. We did not have much time. He appreciated the update. Obviously, I had no idea to question him about Veronica or anything else. As I have said, he was preoccupied with a duel he has with Xaro in the morning."

Strongiron looked at Niku. "This brother of Malenec's…Palinor. Can you rouse him and bring him to me? I would like to question him myself. If he is lying, perhaps there is time to get another message to Magi before the morn."

Herodius stood up. "He is likely awake. I will bring him." The tall islander left.

Niku shrugged. "I suppose Magi's staff would come in handy here, but regardless whether or not you believe Palinor is lying, he fights Xaro tomorrow. He may have a chance to end this before it even begins. I encouraged him to try."

Victor cocked his head. "What the hell is a duel? You mean this guy has a chance to kill their leader this morning? He better level his—"

"Victor," interrupted Niku wearily. "It's not that simple. Xaro may be one of the most powerful mages in Tenebrae. Magi is admittedly strong, but he's still a new True Mage. Besides…I worry that he may not kill him if he thinks Xaro can help him recover his ring."

Standing up, Victor thundered. "Ring? What ring? We're really talking about a piece of jewelry? See, this is the problem I have with you mages! Here we have a golden opp—"

"Victor!" This time the Queen interrupted, and he fell silent. "This ring is magical, given to Magi long ago by his father is my understanding, but beyond its sentimental value, it has military value as well that you should well heed: whomever wears the ring is impervious to magical attacks, and I *know* the value of magical combat is not lost on my Commander-General. We must assume that one member of the invading force will be impervious to our battle mages."

Victor began twisting one of the ends of his mustache. Puffy, little bags supported his still-bright eyes. "I see," was all he said. Sitting back down, he looked at Jonathon and asked for a glass.

Herodius and Palinor returned, and all eyes spun around to look at the one-armed former smitty.

"Palinor, thank you for agreeing to meet with us. I know it is late. My True Cleric, Strongiron, wanted to speak with you, and it is time sensitive."

The one-armed man looked at Strongiron in his filthy white armor and laughed. "Strongiron? The former general of our land? That must be some promotion. What God do you follow?"

Strongiron walked over. He extended his left hand as a courtesy to Palinor. "I am Strongiron. I follow the one True God. Her name is Dymetra. I understand your brother is Malenec the Dark Cleric?"

Palinor didn't immediately shake, but slowly he took the big man's hand. "Yes. I don't know anything about a one true god, but I can tell you he worships Kuth-Cergor, if that means much to you."

"Tell us about your dreams."

Palinor shrugged. "It's like I've already told the islander and your Queen, in my dreams I see him surrounded by the dead. He speaks to them as if he knows them. I've seen him kill and make more creatures."

"Is he aware that you can see him?"

"I don't know. I doubt it…he would torment me if he knew. My nightmares are never personalized. They're not about *me*. They're always about *him*, but they're terrifying nonetheless, and I don't scare easily. Malenec and I have that in common—neither of us scares easily. Although…"

"Yes?" Strongiron pressed.

"Before Herodius woke me up, I had an unusual vision. I saw fire, and his creatures crying in pain. And I just caught a glimpse of his face before I woke up. For the first time in my life, I saw Malenec was frightened…of something."

The entire room looked over at Niku, who said nothing.

Kari stood up and walked over to Palinor. "My name is Kari Quinlan. Thank you for sharing your visions. They have a ring of truth to them." She smiled gently and, unbidden, put her hands on the stump of his arm. She closed her eyes and lifted her chin to speak.

"Dymetra, You have brought us insight into our enemy's plans a world away, and we thank You. If it is Your will, I would ask that You heal this man's arm; make him whole. In so doing, let him come to know You, that there is only one True God, and You are Her."

Everyone leaned forward as the air around his arm began to pulsate and shimmer. Palinor's eyes grew wide as he watched his own arm begin to grow from its stump, first bending at the elbow, then the wrist, and finally each finger.

"My arm!" he gasped. "My arm! You beautiful girl! You have healed my arm!" He kept flexing his elbow, twisting his wrist, and balling his hand up into a fist. Tears of joy burst from his eyes as he threw his arms around Kari. "God bless you! You healed me!"

Shouts for Dymetra rang out as the Queen looked at the room in stupefied silence, blinking slowly. She had just watched Kari regrow the equivalent of a man's sword arm. She could feel Victor's eyes boring into her, and she finally returned his penetrating stare. She couldn't help but think, *he just may be right.*

~*Tarsh*~

"I'm sorry, but did we startle you?" asked a brown-robed man standing next to Tarsh, underneath the ample boughs of a spectacular cherry tree. Next to him was a brown-robed woman.

"A bit." Tarsh was still thoroughly depleted, but he still had a knife on him, concealed in his sleeve, against his forearm. *A Mage's last spell*, some called it.

"Our apologies! It's just, quite *unusual* that a True Mage should make it across our wee little span. Quite an accomplishment as well, and you look like you could use a comfortable bed, perhaps some tea?" said the man with a gentle smile.

"Linar, I think he might want something a bit stronger." The woman winked at Tarsh.

The man in brown looked down at his sodden clothes and chuckled. "You may have a point, Prithi. I believe I would, too, were I in his sandals!"

Tarsh shifted his eyes between the two of them, which they couldn't see him doing anyhow, and considered them. They were dressed *exactly* like the Druids on the Great Isle. "I'm sorry, I'm not used to the hospitality of Druids in these parts. You'll have to excuse me if I'm a little—reserved. Who are you?"

The two of them looked at one another and sighed. "I see our southern brethren are still caught up in their old ways," the man said. "Let me guess—were they hoping to introduce you to their god, Proventus?"

"If by introduce, you mean cut me open and sacrifice me to him, than yeah—that was their intent."

The woman put her hand over her mouth. "Ghastly!" She shook her head.

The man extended a hand toward Tarsh, who was still seated on the ground, his back against the tree. "My name is Linar. This is my wife, Prithi. We are farmers. Druids, yes—but we broke from the pagan worship of Proventus—or any god, for that matter—long ago. It is what separates us from those heathens to the south. Come, let me help you up and show you the hospitality of our Fertile Plains."

Tarsh hesitated, but slowly reached up to grab Linar's hand. "So, you don't believe in any gods?"

"Bah!" said Prithi. "Heavens, no. Farming is a *science,* good Mage. We use our Art to manage the acid balance of the soil, to influence the weather, to cross-populate seeds, to treat diseases, to restore nutrients by crop rotation, to fertilize, to harvest properly— the True Druids quit praying to gods long ago and started focusing on what we could control. I assure you, there will be no prayers or sacrifices to Proventus or any other god. You may sleep well tonight."

The cherry tree that served as his brief canopy was actually just the first in a long line of fruit trees that stretched beyond his sight. They began walking between many rows of them, away from the city and the sea toward the fields. The land was flat, and from this vantage all Tarsh saw was tree boughs and trunks. But the smells! The air brimmed with cherries, but other fruits as well. Mikenese melons, figs, peaches…the scent of fresh fruit was intoxicating.

"How did you separate from the Druids of the Isle?" Tarsh asked.

"It is a rather simple tale, really." Linar turned down one of the other rows and began leading them toward a village in the distance, if the rising smoke was any indication. "Religious differences. As you can probably tell from our complexion, most Druids come from Elfish descent, but over time we comingled with other races. At one time we all shared a worship of similar gods—"

"Which ones, if I may ask? Kuth-Cergor, perhaps?"

Linar raised an eyebrow. "That fairy tale? Unlikely. We would have worshipped Proventus to bless our fields, and other gods for virility, for iron, etc."

"But then we grew enlightened, we progressed," Prithi offered.

"So, you give thanks to no god for the original seed that grows?" Tarsh asked.

Linar stopped. "All that exists in nature has always existed, my friend." He smiled and continued walking. "Regardless, the Southern Druids did not seek knowledge the way we did; they did not embrace our discoveries. We agreed to split up, and in truth, we even gave them the best land. Believe it or not, the soil on the Great Isle is even *better* suited for growing than our Plains."

"Yet they turned it into a forest." Prithi tried not to curl her lip, but failed.

"Forests are beautiful, too, dear."

"Yes, if you wish to feed squirrels."

Tarsh changed the subject. "Is that when you built the Forgotten Bridge?"

"Indeed it was. We built it using our Art, raising the stones from the very bones of Tenebrae to take root on the sea floor, high enough for us to cross, with some difficulty, during low tide. What you did, however, was remarkable."

"Why is that?"

"True Mages who employ magic to try and cross are thwarted, as I'm sure you discovered. We wanted only Druids to cross. We, who can influence the elements—the plants, the tides, the weather—the Forgotten Land Bridge is our gateway to share knowledge with our brethren, should they ever decide to come around. To see *reason* as plain as the noses on their faces."

"Apparently they haven't." Tarsh ground his teeth together.

"No, apparently not," Linar agreed. "That is why your crossing is so remarkable. The Bridge absorbs power that doesn't derive from the Druidic Art. You should have been washed out to sea…it is a rare Mage that has the fortitude to battle the elements as you have done, and to somehow rise from the ocean like a hovering eagle! We watched from afar how you battled—it was spectacular, young man."

"Tarsh. My name is Tarsh Minster."

"A pleasure to meet you, Tarsh, and once again, well done."

"So, once I was away from the Bridge, I could cast spells again?"

"Yes. Though as I've said, there are few Mages, True or otherwise, that could cast anything in the rolling sea. Now, if I may…a question for you. To what do we owe the honor of your visit? Most visitors and traders for our crop yield come through the port of Kalimoran, or through the city of Munty-Whash behind us. You certainly chose an unusual point of entry."

Tarsh considered. Given their openness, he figured it was harmless, and potentially helpful, to share his mission. "I am exploring Adimand, if you wish to know the truth. I am looking for an artifact…one of the Artifacts of the Ancients, though I doubt you put much stock in such things, given what you've told me of your faith. I have heard that Windomere, an Ancient Cleric, came from Adimand. I am searching—"

"For his Shield. You are searching for the Shield of Life," Prithi finished. "It is said that the Shield is 'Light as a feather, yet as heavy as a stone…as plain as the noon-day sun, yet as hidden as the noon-day moon.' Yes, Tarsh, we indeed have heard of the Shield."

This time Tarsh paused his steps and put a hand, gently but firmly, on Prithi's shoulder. "Do you know where it's buried? Can you point me there?"

Linar and Prithi exchanged a quick glance that was almost imperceptible. Prithi took Tarsh's hand in hers, one underneath and one placed softly on top of his. "Young mage, the Shield is a myth, I'm afraid; a fairy tale of olden days. I would not send you on such a hunt."

Tarsh removed his hand and put it on Linar's shoulder instead. "What of you, Linar? Can you share anything—rumor, myth, or otherwise?"

Linar sighed. "True Clerics are myths as well, Tarsh. There never have been, because there are no gods...at least none worth worshipping." He took a deep breath, "But—the famous figure you named, Windomere—it is said he came from the Dusty Plains north of the Shembolt Mountains. Very desolate up there, as the Fertile Plains get all the good weather, but if you wish to dig graves for this mythical man, start there. Just know that you will be digging one for yourself in the process."

~Magi~

"It is time, Mage."

A guard pounded on his door to make sure he was awake. The desert sun had not yet risen, but a softening hue to the east foreshadowed the breaking dawn.

Magi was already wide awake; he had hardly slept, his mind racing with ideas, plans, and implications. "Coming!" he shouted as he rose from the hard bed. A basin of seawater was in his room to splash on his face. He was still full from the meal last night, and parched. Taking a quick swig from his waterskin, he grabbed his staff and left his room.

Two guards flanked him, with two Mage-guards behind him. He doubted a single Mage-guard could control him, but two? *Possibly.* The fact that four men were tasked with "escorting" him to the duel was not lost on him.

They led him down a winding set of stairs that eerily reminded Magi of The Staircase. The normally dry, desert air began to feel thick and stale from the crowded torches hanging on the walls. Natural light gave way to flickering flames with each passing step. Smoke hovered in the stairwell like a sticky film that couldn't be avoided.

The descent, thankfully, did not take long. One of the warrior escorts slid two heavy wooden bolts back, and then pushed the old door inward. The acrid smoke from the stairs seemed to sense an escape route and *whooshed* through the door ahead of Magi.

"In here," gestured the warrior, coughing.

Magi entered a large room, with surprisingly high ceilings. The oblong room was ringed by stone rooms, each with bars on the door. *This is no 'training room'...this is a dungeon.*

"Michael! So good of you to come this early. How do you like the magical proving ground? Like the pits above for our True Warriors, this dueling circle is where I like to test our would-be Battle Mages." Xaro's word echoed off the rock walls as he gestured to the circle glowing in the center of the chamber. The four guards that had escorted Magi either left or had never entered the room in the first place, leaving Magi alone with Xaro.

He lies. Not one Battle mage has he 'tested' here. He cleared this out specifically for me. Magi gripped his staff, his suspicions confirmed: Xaro didn't buy his cover last night any more than he himself bought Xaro's, brown eyes and all. *I wonder if he knows Malenec has my ring...*

"It looks...subterranean is the word that comes to mind, Xaro. I am curious why you train your mages here—wouldn't the pits up above be as equally effective for testing your mages as they are for your warriors?" Magi approached the circle, but did not step within it.

"It's cooler down here, and since we don't have need for prisoners here at Sands End, it seems a waste not to make productive use of such space. Do you enjoy history, Michael?"

"Indeed I do."

"This Keep was built by a True Warrior from another age, the legendary Ajax, after whom the mountains to the south are named. This chamber was built on the bones of prisoners, and the mortar strengthened with the blood of criminals. Legend has it that Ajax was particularly merciless on the treacherous. Men who stole or killed or disobeyed his commands would be dealt with swiftly and effectively...but the disloyal—he reserved this holy space for them. It is said that no bodily torture could compare to the mental anguish one suffered inside these cells."

"Charming story."

"Isn't it, though? I have not had a reason to imprison anyone here, but I would be lying if I didn't admit that I was a little curious what the Shackles of Ajax held for their victims."

He's certainly telling the truth now. "Plenty of foot soldiers above us if you want a guinea pig. Why are you telling me this, Xaro?" Magi was growing impatient.

"No reason, really. Just sharing a bit of history. And I would never subject my troops to such a fate unnecessarily."

Again, he tells the truth...or at least half the truth. His reason for the story was intimidation, but he wouldn't just lock anyone up down here.

He would, however, lock up Magi.

"I appreciate the yarn. Let us do this while the morning is still young. Last chance—it is your decision, obviously, but if you prefer not to engage in this spectacle, I will understand. True Mage to True Warrior, I would not test my sword fighting skill against you; you needn't test your spell craft against me."

Xaro smiled. "I relish the chance, Michael. Step into the circle and let us begin."

Magi returned Xaro's cocky smile with one of his own. He looked around; they were completely alone. Not a soul stirred down here. *A better chance to kill this wretch will never present itself.* He stepped into the circle.

Xaro followed. They faced one another in the twenty-five-foot circle, about fifteen feet apart. Both Magi and Xaro had about five feet behind them.

Xaro raised his hands. "We shall begin on three. One. Two...Three!"

The room erupted in sound and literally shook as the *Force* spells collided. Sand shook free, sifting down the walls in powdery bursts. It must have felt like an earthquake to everyone in the fortress above.

Magi was playing for keeps. His spell was so powerful that he would force Xaro's flesh into the stonework behind him, adding his blood to the gallons that Ajax had famously spilled when he built this Keep. He had not dug into his potential well this deep since his battle on the Staircase.

Xaro, however, was unmoved. Tendons began to stand out on his neck like the iron bars on every cell door, but he held his ground. Yelling, he leaned forward.

Magi could feel the power emanating from this man. He had never seen another man equal his own energy. He could be tricked, like with Ragor, or bewitched, like with Marik...but this was raw power against raw power. He kept looking at Xaro's face and neck strain, and he could feel the muscles in his own neck growing taut.

Slowly, gradually, Xaro's eyes began to lighten…not lighten, but shrink. The whites of his eyes were consuming his brown irises. Soon they were brown dots…and then the *Illusion* vanished completely. *Pure white, like every other True Mage.*

Magi swallowed hard and leaned in, teeth clenched…and he took a step forward. All the hate he had for this man poured into his spell. *Killing my mother. Destroying my father. Forcing me to live with Marik. Living a lie. Corrupting my soul.* The reasons to hate this man fueled a rage that he channeled directly into his spell, holding nothing back. He would not drive him out of the circle or even into a wall. Magi would liquefy the fiend.

Eyes wide, Xaro took a step back. Any more give now, and he would be flung through the rusty bars into the cell behind him, sliced like a block of cheese. He began to yell.

Sensing the moment, Magi pressed forward in one final surge. "Die, you son-of-a-bitch!" He stepped forward again.

Falling to his knees, digging his toes in at the very edge of the circle, Xaro screamed "My God! Kuth-Cergor, save your Cleric!"

A loud *crack* of thunder filled the dungeon, reverberating against the stone, causing more sand to shake down the walls. The torches everywhere blacked out, plunging the chamber into the deepest darkness imaginable.

Magi was lying on his back when a *Glowball* approached. He was too exhausted to get up, but he saw Xaro's sweaty face reflected in the bluish-white light. He felt around for his staff, but it wasn't anywhere close. He tried to cast a *Shield* spell, but it was no use.

For the first time in Magi's life, he was empty; he had no energy left with which to cast a single spell.

The light from the *Glowball* was finally close enough to show Magi lying clear across the room, well outside the circle. Xaro was holding the Staff of Insight.

"Magi Blacksmooth, it has been a long time since I last saw you." Xaro was leaning heavily on the staff, gasping for air. "I must admit, I had hoped to become—reacquainted—under different circumstances."

~Queen Najalas~

The celebration of Palinor's healing and conversion stretched toward morning, when sleep finally came. The exhausted Queen excused herself and collapsed into bed, her throat dry and head pounding. Mid-day greeted her only when her timid attendant plucked up the courage to call her name. *No doubt on Jonathon's urging. The Queen's duty never sleeps.*

By the time she had bathed, her small council had already gathered for dinner. Strongiron, Peter, Niku, Simon, and Jonathon were all seated informally, as was the newest member of her council, Victor. She had also asked Kari and Herodius to join them, and to her surprise, Belara had returned from her travels as well. A simple meal of bread, cheese, grapes, and dry meat had been laid out for the group.

She stood up. "Last night was quite the spectacle. I dare say that many of you also embraced a late start to your day." The polite chuckles and tired nods confirmed that they all felt somewhat miserable. The Queen flashed a weak, yet sarcastic smile at the room. "It is, however, time to turn our attention to several key items. The first order of business I would like to discuss is Herodius. Will you step forward?"

Herodius rose to his full height, easily pushing himself up from the table with his newly-healed arm, thanks to Strongiron's efforts last night. He had a questioning look on his face, but he was grinning, and he didn't look quite as dour and as hard as he had been yesterday evening. *Good...I had never meant to insult him in the first place*, she thought with relief.

"Herodius Cromwell, most of us here today have heard your story. One last time, I would like you to confirm the following deeds. Are you the man who led a slave revolution against our common enemy to the West?"

Herodius raised his eyebrows as if something was just now dawning on him. "Your Majesty—"

"It is a yes or no question, Islander." She was grinning playfully for all to see, however.

"Yes, I am that man."

"And did you rescue 9,000 islanders in that rebellion?"

"I did."

"And did you lead them, short on food, on ill-constructed sea vessels unfit for rats, past the Great Whirlpool to seek refuge on our shores?"

"Nay, your Majesty. I may have been admiral of our rag-tag fleet, but I'll take no credit for that journey. *That* was a miracle." He nodded slightly toward Strongiron.

"Well said, we can agree on that," the Queen acknowledged. "But were you also not the man to put down the rebellion in the very heart of Elvidor, the plains of our central valley?"

"I am, my Queen."

"At great cost to you? Your arm was crushed in that rebellion, was it not?"

"It was. Yet the faith of your clerics and another miracle has healed me."

The Queen looked at Victor, her General, and Strongiron, her Warrior-Cleric. "By your standards of testing, would you not say that this man has surpassed the requirements necessary to receive the mark of a True Warrior? Or is it necessary that I throw him in a pit with some animal to kill for you to be convinced?"

Victor stood up, not waiting to hear what Strongiron might say. "He is True enough Warrior for me. He fights, and fights well. It shall be my privilege to brand him myself."

Strongiron looked up at Victor and slowly nodded.

"Good. I had your Mark prepared in advance, knowing you both to be reasonable men." The Queen stretched her lips into a thin smile and nodded at Victor, gesturing to one of the fire pits in the corner. A pair of thick leather gloves lay near a branding iron that, unbeknownst to anyone, had already been resting in the fire for some time.

Herodius stood stoically as Victor slipped on the gloves and fetched the red-hot branding iron. As he approached, Herodius held out his right arm. "My left arm bears the mark of what I've lost. My right shall bear the Mark of what I've gained."

Victor nodded. "I'm a man of few words, Herodius, but know that I'll take up arms with you anywhere. Let the world know from this day forth that you are a True Warrior." He pressed the oval encircling three parallel lines of differing lengths into his upper right arm.

Herodius narrowed his eyes, but that was as close to a wince as he would allow. The sweat pouring off his scalp and the puffy scarring of his flesh were the only outward signs of pain. The small group cheered, and Victor raised both his branding iron and (mercifully) Herodius's left arm to chants of *"Her-oh-DIUS! Her-oh-DIUS!"*

The Queen smiled, letting the pageantry continue for a moment longer before raising both arms to still the room. "And now, it is my turn." She stared at Herodius, whose eyes were watering. From the pain of the brand or the outpouring of support, the Queen didn't know. *Probably both.*

"Kneel, Herodius. For the bravery, leadership, and skill you've shown, your fellow warriors recognize you as one of their own. For your might, loyalty, and sacrifice, *I* recognize you as a Knight, as is my authority to do so. But to which Order shall I assign you? You are mighty, and you are loyal; this is true. I find, however, that it is your sacrifice, Herodius, that best embodies your Knighthood. Therefore, arise Herodius Cromwell, True Warrior of the Valley, Knight of Blood, Keeper of the Grain, and Lord of the Central Plain!"

More shouting and clapping ensued, particularly from Simon, Peter, Niku, and Jonathon, who had all spent the most time with Herodius. He did not, however, rise.

The Queen stared down at him, his eyes glistening. Amidst the background noise, she mouthed to him, *"Arise, Herodius."*

He just shook his head, and spread his arms wide to quell the commotion. "Your Majesty," he began. "I will accept your most gracious gifts of title and land, but there is still a greater gift I seek. Najalas…accept me as your husband, and together let us share the burden of planning for the hard days ahead. I already love you as my Queen. Now, let me love you as my wife."

Silence. The room fell completely silent. The Queen looked up, and all eyes were on her, mostly in shock. *Men don't ask a sitting Queen to marry them in public. Especially newly minted knights and nobles...*

Time seemed to slow as she sought out faces in the crowd. Niku had a single eyebrow raised. Peter looked sheepish. Victor looked so serious, like protocol had just been completely subverted. Kari looked excited. Curiously, Belara looked…detached. She was wearing her trademark cowl, this time reddish-orange. Her arms folded across her chest, she almost looked like some kind of impatient phoenix.

Eventually the Queen's eyes found Strongiron, as if she somehow felt like she needed his approval. Which was silly, of course—she was The Queen. Her word was law; the only approval she needed was her own. *And yet...*

When she found his deep blue eyes, his face softened into a warm smile. She blinked and returned to look at Herodius, who was still at her feet, staring up at her expectantly. "Arise Herodius. You shall be King of Elvidor, and I shall be your Queen."

His face broke into the widest smile she had ever seen from the Islander, as he stood up and kissed the Queen in front of her entire court.

Peter was calling for ale to be brought and toasts to be made, and as Queen Najalas gently pulled back from Herodius, she shouted above the din. "We shall need more than ale, Peter…we shall need a True Cleric to bless and marry us."

CHAPTER FIFTEEN: DEALS MADE

~Tarsh~

In the end, the hospitality of the Northern Druids won out.

Waterlogged, cut and battered, exhausted physically, drained magically—not to mention hungry and thirsty—Tarsh talked himself into at least one day's delay at the offer of bed, warmth, food, drink, and treatment. *Besides, they must know more old stories of Windomere, whether they believe them or not.* The argument for haste disintegrated like straw on the fire.

He was led to a guest room off the gathering hall in one of the many village farms dotting the Fertile Plains. The room was small but clean, with cool water for washing, and more brought for his thirst. Clean brown robes were brought for him, and fresh fruits (Mikenese melons!) and lean strips of roasted meat 'for a late snack.' Lastly, an old Druid came by with both a greenish-grey salve and a lighter green paste.

"What are those?" Tarsh asked.

The grizzled Druid had long, black hair that contrasted with his long, white goatee. He held out the salve. "*Sanitor* tree sap, which we harvest ourselves. Useful for cuts and bruises, such as you've sustained." He then held up the light green paste. "This is a special herbal blend made largely of *pillafer* leaves, blessed by nature herself. You must consume this paste so that it cleans your insides from sickness."

"You want me to eat…that?" It looked thick and difficult to swallow.

"Yes. It is good for you, Mage. You may trust our knowledge of herb-lore. If we wanted to harm you, we would not have bothered to offer you our hospitality this night." He said it factually, patiently, but not overly-friendly.

Tarsh took a finger and swished it into the thick, green concoction. It had the consistency of soft clay, and felt gritty. He put it to his nose and took a deep sniff. *Minty.* He cast an eye at the Druid. Despite Tarsh's lack of pupil or iris, the aged-man in brown seemed to know he was being looked at suspiciously. "It's all right, I assure you," he said again, this time with a faint smile.

Tarsh pushed his finger past his lips and half-chewed, half-swished the semi-solid around in his mouth. *Not terrible. Like overripe fruit, only without the sweetness.* It definitely tasted medicinal. He continued eating the rest of the paste. "Thank you," he offered.

The crusty Druid finished applying salve to his neck and arm, among other sores, and left with a slight bow. Linar poked his head in a little while later.

"You are well? Is there anything we may have overlooked?" he asked in that same gentle voice.

"No, thank you. All is well. I am tired, but your people have shown me much kindness."

"Excellent. Rest tonight, Tarsh Minster. Tomorrow, we shall talk over breakfast, when you are fully refreshed." Linar bade him goodnight and left him to his thoughts.

He thought about contacting Xaro, but as yet he really didn't have much more of an update. The plan was still to get to the Dusty Plains, and really, staying here in the Fertile Plains would only be looked upon as a delay, despite what his body was telling him. He decided to hold off on any updates until he had made legitimate progress. That decision made, he stretched out on the luxurious feather-stuffed bed. Sleep came soon enough…

***

The next morning, Tarsh woke and felt more refreshed than he had since the day Xaro first healed him from his ailments. The Mikenese melons, the salve, the *pillafer* paste, the food, water, warmth, bed—everything contributed to his restored vigor. He felt like he could take on Magi, Xaro, or even Kuth-Cergor himself.

He strode into the gathering hall to find it brimming with people. Forty or fifty men and women, all seated at long tables, were feasting like at a royal wedding. Breakfast potatoes covered in spices, ham smothered in a pineapple-clove glaze, sausages sizzling in skewers, dripping over a large fire pit, freshly sliced tomatoes with thick slabs of cheese, eggs prepared in every way imaginable…it was a spectacle. *For breakfast?*

"Ah, our guest! Come down, come down." Linar waved him over. "Please—sit here. What can we get you, Tarsh? You'll find nearly everything you could hope for to fill your belly in advance of your quest."

"Thank you. I must say…I've never known such plenty as this. Do you always eat this well?" Tarsh came over and sat down.

"Very nearly so. The fruits of our hard labor, you see." Linar said with a gleam in his eye.

"I see. Science, you said?"

"Exactly. *Science.*"

Tarsh sat down and helped himself to the feast. He couldn't imagine starting for the Dusty Plains with a better send-off. "So, Linar," he began. "Is there nothing else you can tell me of this mythical man I'm chasing? I would love to hear your fables, even if that is all they are to you."

Linar patted Tarsh on the shoulder before he stood to address the entire hall. "Friends, our guest here is searching for Windomere's Shield. He wishes to hear our thoughts and learnings on the matter. Who would share their mind with our guest the Mage?"

A man in the corner stood and said, "send him off with poison to drink, in case he wishes for a quick death rather than wandering forever in the desert."

"He's a True Mage...he'll *Teleport* back to our fields b'fore he dies of thirst, but yes, give him the poison regardless, to spare him the frustration!" Several at the table next to this Druid began guffawing with laughter, banging their forks onto the table.

"What's a True Mage want with a Cleric's Shield, anyhow?"

"Might as well dig for gold in the Shembolt Range."

"Or water in the Dusty Plains. Probably just as likely."

More laughter ensued, which was getting on Tarsh's nerves, despite the Druid's hospitality. Finally, he put his fork down and stood, holding his arms up to silence the group.

"Good Druids," he began. "I know you are a faithless bunch, and that you look at my quest as mere foolishness, but that is only because I know something that you do not. I know that God exists; I've been healed of injuries that an ocean of *sanitor* salve and *pillafer* paste could not possibly treat. I was healed by a real cleric, who was a vessel for Kuth-Cergor to take mercy on me. Furthermore—"

Several gasps were uttered as he invoked Kuth-Cergor's name. Tarsh raised his voice to get their attention back.

"*Furthermore*, I know that at least one of the Artifacts of the Ancients has been rediscovered. The Staff of Wisdom exists, and I have it on good account that it is blessed to do what the old stories claim: it reveals truth to the one who possesses it."

More gasps, and even louder whispering.

"*Therefore*, if the one exists, I am willing to bet that the others exist as well. I will find it. Those old stories that you've heard and discounted, I would hear them now myself, if you would give me this one last kindness before I depart, and leave you as you were."

Linar stood up and motioned for quiet. "Now, now, everyone, please. Your manners. We are not savages, like our cousins to the south. This Mage, if nothing else, has shown remarkable fortitude to cross our Bridge. No one but Druid blood has crossed it for centuries, and very few Druids have attempted to cross in nigh a generation. Perhaps this is an omen?"

A man whom Tarsh recognized from the previous night stood up—the old Druid with coal-black hair and a long, white beard. "There is no omen, Linar. He is a talented Mage, perhaps, but a treasure hunter like many who have come before, but I will share the fable we have all likely heard, little good it will do him, though."

He turned to face Tarsh. "Young man, this cleric of old was rumored to have wished upon his death to be buried in the place of his birth, which many think was from the nomadic tribes of the Dusty Plains. Over the years, the Druids have co-opted the story, with many claiming the one you call Windomere as the Greatest Druid of All Time. He is likely the Greatest Ghost of All Time, but you have your convictions. If you say *True* Clerics now exist, far be it for any of us to convince you otherwise. It's your life—just don't try too hard to convince *us*, either." He wagged a finger at the young man, narrowing his eyes.

"Proof—we would need proof, of course. You would need to bring us this Staff and show us the power of a True Cleric in all their ancient glory to convince these old eyes, and I daresay I speak for us all. We gave up on counting on gods for our crop yields long ago, and we sent away those who clung to those silly beliefs, in case you're wondering what our cousins to the south are doing there in the first place. All we've done is shown you traveller's mercy; all they did was try and sacrifice you for this god nonsense." At his, he waved both hands dismissively, and his fellow Druids nodded and began echoing his sentiments in muted tones throughout the room.

The old Druid raised his hands to bring back some semblance of order and quiet so he could continue. "So, leave our midst in peace. Go on your way, chasing old stories and making new ones. Be forewarned, however—the few nomadic tribes that still exist are said to be fierce, and unkind to strangers. The land is hard, and food will be scarce. We'll help pack your supplies, but most that go searching the Dusty Plains end up contributing to its dustiness with their very bones—even those with the gift to *Teleport*. That place is not hospitable, and you may find yourself bereft of your magic at inopportune times. You have been warned, and our fables have now been shared." The old man pointed a crooked finger that wouldn't fully straighten, and then sat back down.

Tarsh nodded, first to him and then at the general group in the gathering hall. "Thank you—for the food, treatment, and information. We indeed will part friends of a different mind, but I will take your council under advisement. I would, however, share one final piece of information to all of you. Have you found the market for your food to be increasingly good?"

Linar looked up at Tarsh, a single eyebrow elevated. "As a matter of fact, yes. The gold has been good of late."

Tarsh smiled. "You may choose to believe or not to believe, but Kuth-Cergor, the god whom I follow that you disavow, has blessed our efforts, and it is my Master, a True Cleric, who has spun gold from common metal. He is buying up your food, and you are all benefitting, whether you believe it or not. A day may come when your belief—your *worship*—will indeed be very important. Know that I won't forget your kindness. You will have an advocate in me. When the time comes, you may find that you need one." He bowed his head and started to leave the hall.

The old man stood up once again. "The Druids, you will find, are not moved by godly threats."

Tarsh turned around and smiled, knowing how creepy a True Mage looked whenever they cracked a grin. "And you will find, my friends, that my Master never makes a godly threat."

He bowed once again and left the hall with a full belly and a firm direction.

~Xaro~

It did not seem to work.

He hadn't expected it to, not really. But he had hoped.

Lying in his bed, still tired from his duel with Magi several days ago, Xaro had finally built up his strength enough to recolor his eyes back to their regular, old brown. *At least that is something.*

He then reached over and curled his large hands over the Staff of Insight, lying on the bed next to him.

He felt nothing special. No tingle. No visions. *Nothing.*

Of course, Xaro did not need the staff to know that he was facing Magi Blacksmooth in the duel. Who else in Tenebrae could match his power, according to his very own prophesy? He had suspected it might be Magi the minute he saw the curious staff. *Besides, Veronica warned me he was coming for his ring.*

He ran his hands greedily over the smooth shaft, as if he could will it to work for him. Yet the only wisdom or insight he felt was conspicuously his own.

It's Her *Staff...what did you expect?* Xaro sighed and slowly pushed himself up from the bed. He had never felt more depleted of energy in his life—*that*, more than anything he might have gleaned from the Staff, confirmed his suspicions that the man chained to the wall in Ajax's Shackles deep within his dungeon was none other than Magi Blacksmooth.

The Staff would never impart wisdom to a follower of Kuth-Cergor. That was disappointing, but unsurprising. What bothered him was far more personal, and he didn't need a magical staff of truthtelling to be honest with himself:

Magi had *won.*

Xaro had *never* lost a contest of magic. He had never lost a contest of steel. In fact, Xaro rarely lost at anything. Yet this man—a boy on the green side of twenty years old—had nearly killed him. His power had been seconds away from overwhelming Xaro. He would not have been pushed out of the circle; he would have been pushed *through* the very walls, with bits and drips scattered into the far reaches of the desert. Once Xaro's resistance gave out, Magi wouldn't have been able to stop his spell even if he had wanted to do so—he was simply pushing too hard to stop quickly enough.

Not that he would have anyhow...he knows too much. Too much of what we tried to do, and too much of what we mean to do. Kuth-Cergor had answered his prayer; that was the only reason Magi now found himself stripped and chained in the dungeon while Xaro rested and reflected in the comfort of his room.

He walked across the room to pour himself a glass of lemon sweetwater, which helped him get his strength back. He would need it soon; it had been some time since his last update, and he would need to cast his complex communication spell in order for Tarsh to attend, and it was critical that he do so. Part of Xaro wanted to turn Magi over to Malenec straight away, to bind his soul as one of his undead servants, but he thought Tarsh ought to have the right to kill him. Rather, he *wanted to give* Tarsh that right. Only a few gifts could he offer a lieutenant that would engender more loyalty than handing a tormentor over to the tormented. A weakened Magi should be no problem for Tarsh to kill, and Malenec could take it from there. A plan that for once, even his Cleric agreed.

Xaro stretched, rolled his neck, and loosened his muscles. He was finally starting to feel like his old self again. He turned to look at the small pile of Magi's belongings: his boots, clothes, and cloak; all his bags and pouches of various spell components (some of which Xaro was quite impressed with); his dagger—a well-worn hunting knife that Xaro could also appreciate—it reminded him of his old mentor Paul, who some called The Wanderer. The plunder of which he was most pleased, however, was a handwritten scroll he had carefully unraveled to reveal the word *Tralatus* scribbled across the top.

Magi had made a copy of the very curse that Marik had used against him!

The thought tempted Xaro. Now that he saw the type of power Magi commanded, the thought of him joining their cause was intoxicating. It always had been intoxicating—that had been his original plan, after all. And now, to have the means to try again dropped right into his lap…

Xaro carefully rolled up the scroll and tucked it away in a protective case. Would *She* really raise him from the dead with his soul vulnerable to the same spell? He doubted it. He could think of a better candidate on which to use the scroll—someone that would be a boon to his efforts and crippling to the Queen's. Someone that, by rights, *should* look up to him. Someone his assassin had also failed to kill…

~Queen Najalas~

"It just might work, my Queen." Victor stroked his mustache thoughtfully. "If common sense won't reach them, if military sense won't reach them, if a Royal Edict won't reach them…then perhaps they will bow to the will of the people." He raised a small, ceramic pipe to his lips and puffed deeply, blowing rich, bluish-grey smoke into the small council room presently occupied by the Queen, Herodius, and Victor.

The Queen shrugged her shoulders. "Perhaps it may, but I doubt it. They are Clerics—*True* Clerics, Victor. Dymetra would need to redirect their efforts." She quickly held up a hand before her new General could scoff. "I agree with you, for the record, but I am convinced Dymetra exists, my friend. You would do well to come around to that same conclusion. I just think Strongiron, and particularly Kari, are letting their obvious desire to travel together to cloud the way they interpret Her will. Surely our God would not want both Clerics to depart us?"

Herodius rubbed his arm absentmindedly—the same arm Strongiron had healed. "My Queen—"

"Najalas. Learn to call me Najalas in public, Herodius."

"Yes. Of course. Two days is not long enough to break old habits, apparently." He grinned a bit foolishly at his bride-to-be. "Let me say that I do not think this is the best plan. To me, the risks outweigh the benefit."

Victor puffed audibly. "Your logic?"

Herodius set his glass down, which was filled with nothing more interesting than fig juice. "The goal of this union is, in part, to provide a legitimate heir. That is not to say I don't love you, Najalas. I do. But delaying our wedding six months in order to plan a royal wedding seems to be an expense we do not need, and a delay we certainly do not need. It is a second marriage for us both. Come—let us not delay this wedding simply to allow distant lords to attend. Let us legitimize our union, which can be blessed by Strongiron, and then they can be about their business, and we…we can be about ours."

"Hmmph. I can see your motivation." Victor scowled until he caught the Queen's poisonous look. "I do not have to call him 'Your Majesty' yet, do I?"

"You see? This is the political advantage that lies in doing this properly, dear. A large wedding, well attended, with Strongiron in his Clerical role, bestowing the blessing of the One True God and declaring you King of Elvidor for all to see, all kneeling before you…it will accelerate your respect and establish your authority, my dear. You cannot go from island refugee to knight to King in two fell swoops. The people need time to get behind the news, but perhaps more importantly, if the attack happens while the wedding is being planned, we shall at least have a True Cleric here at Rookwood to protect us." She set her goblet, *not* filled merely with fig juice, down as well.

Victor nodded, fanning blue spoke everywhere.

Herodius stood up. "Najalas," he began. "I do not think it prudent that we give up what we want most for what we want right now. You said yourself, 'Elvidor needs an heir.' The priority is the heir; the priority is *not* having a True Cleric babysit Rookwood. Come now, we are not that defenseless. I understand better than most the allure of this new power we've discovered, but what if they *still* refuse to split up? What if we make the announcement, set the date, and the Clerics leave anyhow? All we will have done would be to cast illegitimacy on any heirs borne prior to our wedding, which is what you are most hoping to avoid. I think—that your drink is thinking for you, Najalas." He regretted saying it as soon as the words came out.

"I won't point out what is thinking for you," she fired back without hesitation.

Victor chuckled, his teeth clamped down on his pipe stem. "Ah, your first spat. How charming." He shook his head, but stopped suddenly, pulling the pipe out of his mouth to puncture the air with his points. "You know, it would not take much of a rumor, Your Majesty, to make the people think the True Clerics were leaving, and that Dymetra was once again turning Her back on her people. If Strongiron, or Kari, won't delay their trip for six months to officiate a proper royal wedding, I'm fairly certain we could stir up the people against them. Abandonment is a powerful emotion, my Queen." He slowly tucked the pipe back into his mouth.

"This is madness!" Herodius said. "Forget this scheming, my Queen. The people will flock to Dymetra when they hear the testimony of men like Palinor. Already his heart burns for this ancient God. We need the people united. We need them to believe in something bigger than themselves! Stirring up discord and disharmony would make our fall to Xaro and his general that much easier. Why are we even discussing this? Better to lock one or both of them up and *force* them to stay than to offer up such a flimsy excuse as a wedding, with the threat of slander as a blackmail gambit to fall back on." He threw his arms up in disgust. "What is this really about, Najalas?"

Queen Najalas let the silence hang in the air between the two of them, staring intently at Herodius. *This is about protection, My Love. The people need the protection of God's own ambassador. Victor here needs protection for our troops. You and I need protection if we are to actually raise an heir. But the one who really needs protection—the reason I so desperately want a True Cleric close by—is to protect my friend Chief Chocktaw. From me. Someone must make right the wrong I have committed myself to do.* She finally sighed and broke off her stare.

"Husband-to-be…you make fair points. He is right, Victor, we are kidding ourselves. We have asked them both numerous times, and their answers have both been resolutely no. Already they make their final preparations. It would be a luxury to allow the people the anticipation of a wedding knowing that our Kingdom teeters on the brink of war. I would have Strongiron conduct our wedding before he leaves, and we will announce the marriage afterward far and wide through our network of Mages. All who wish to travel to Rookwood to pay homage to the new King may do so. If the worst of the gossip revolves around a 'rushed' wedding, well, I for one have survived far worse than that."

Smiling, she reached out to touch Herodius's cheek. "As iron sharpens iron, so will you make a good King, Herodius."

~Magi~

The feet. Tonight, it's going to be the feet.

"Hello, Magi." Ragor Stri faced him in Marik's annual Magic tournament. The entire village of Brigg had turned out, as they always did, to see the students compete. Proud parents mingled with excited shop owners and farmers who milled about, trying to get a decent view of the Tournament Square. Only the faces in the crowd weren't brimming with a natural excitement; they had a macabre look to them. Of course, the faces here always had that look—sunken eyes with those crimson shadows, like the kind you find staring at someone across a blazing campfire in the dead of night. The faces were always the same—familiar, yet twisted.

"Hello, Ragor." Magi seemed to recall fighting the thick boy before, but he couldn't quite grasp the memory; it was like trying to hold smoke. He didn't think he'd fought him in the tournament, but such facts didn't seem to matter in this place where memory, dreams, and reality comingled into an endless, hazy nightmare. He would fight him here. He vaguely felt the tingling in his feet grow sharper.

Ragor approached nonchalantly, almost sauntering across the square to the moaning cheers of the crowd. Magi would make short work of this. He would create a fireball that would silence his mockers and boil Ragor's blood inside his own skin. Somewhere deep inside, Magi thought his foe might deserve such a fate, but again, the details eluded him. They always eluded him these days.

He reached for the cinnamon. Magi was sure that was the component he needed. Except he couldn't find it—he couldn't find any of his pouches. In fact, Magi was standing there in a soiled loin cloth and nothing else. He turned his head and saw Kari pointing at him, the shifting red shadows making her face longer, more hollow. But her eyes were still green flames, and they were laughing. Her other arm snaked around Tarsh...

Magi had seen enough. His missiles required no components. He would put a hole through Ragor. Something told him that he knew exactly how to do it. That would stop this mockery.

Except...he couldn't quite remember the spell. He knew he knew it; he just couldn't connect the dots, like a man who suffered a blow to the head and has to learn how to write again. The spell danced just beyond the edge of his mental reach.

Ragor stood a few feet away from Magi, grinning wickedly. His features were equally distorted by the eerie, red glow that seemed to fill this place with shifting shadows, but he was as thick as ever. He raised his hands, and Magi suddenly felt himself lifted off the ground, hovering parallel to the floor of the tournament square, his feet chest high to Ragor. A curved sword appeared out of thin air, hovering between them. Dawning began to fall on Magi as the blade began to whirl like a giant propeller.

"Shall we go feet first?" Ragor bellowed to the crowd. "What say you?"

The crowd started to cheer, and several began to chant, "Ray-gor! Ray-gor!"

He walked around the blade's arc to stand next to Magi's head, where he slowly leaned in to whisper sour breath into his ears: "Go on. Cry for mercy. Cry like I did to you."

Magi's eyes grew wide as he slowly drifted toward the spinning sword, unable to curl up his legs or move in any manner. He felt his pinky toe get sheared off before the rest of the pain came, as Ragor fed him into the whirling blade like a holiday pig to get thinly sliced. Magi tried to scream as he watched the inches shorn off his height, but Ragor had frozen his tongue, too. But not his eyes or neck; those worked perfectly well.

The sour breath was back in his face. "Every night..."

"Every night is different, is it not?"

Magi's eyes opened at the strange voice. His heart was racing, and he was covered in a fine layer of sweat. The desert heat didn't penetrate this far underground, apparently; he was cold, sitting here on the stone floor. Time had quickly lost meaning for him; day and night were indistinct here. His world consisted of sleep and wakefulness, and both were nightmarish. He looked down at his naked feet. They were still attached, but the pain he had felt was unquestionably real. He looked down at the rags around his waist. They were soiled anew. Looking down at his intact feet, he thought that was a fair trade.

"The visions. They differ nightly, do they not?" The voice repeated with less patience in the tone.

"Who are you?" Magi asked. He stood up, hoping to test his feet and tighten the damp undergarments around his shrinking waist.

Both arms were shackled to the wall, but he had enough room to push himself into a standing position. The chains securing each wrist were anchored to the back wall of his cell and crisscrossed his body. They screeched painfully when the heavy links rubbed against each other.

"I suppose there is no harm in telling Magi who I am, Genevieve. What do you think?"

Magi didn't hear a word, just the sound of slowly shuffling feet. His mind was still struggling to connect the dots. *There must be two people close by. Three? More?*

"Yes, Genevieve. Quite right. I agree." Beyond the iron bars of his small, six-foot by six-foot cell, a man stepped out of the shadows alongside…someone or something.

Magi's eyes still were not good in the darkness below…*where am I again? Sandy plains?* He could barely focus on the here and now, and the here and now was a cell with a man asking him about visions.

Slowly his eyes adjusted to the dimness, and Magi could make out a tall, thin man standing on the other side of his cell bars. His goatee was sharp and a bit shiny from a generous amount of oil, like his dark hair, which had also been slicked and pulled back into a ponytail. The man placed two gloved hands on the bars of Magi's cell and pressed his face close enough to see the stone-gray color of his eyes.

"I am Malenec. My friend here is Genevieve. She greatly wishes to kiss you, but alas, I don't think this is the right time for intimacies. As for you, I already know a great deal about your background, Magi Blacksmooth. I know that you killed a few of my army with your fire the other night to draw me out of my home. And I think I know why. What I do not know is what it feels like to be shackled in Ajax's dungeon. From the look of you, I imagine it is quite exquisite."

Magi shook his head, trying to scatter as many cobwebs as he could. He took a deep breath to try and calm his heart. He was sure the name Malenec held something important. His feet still throbbed, but at least he could wiggle all his toes. He stepped forward, drawing the short chains taut with a grating squeal.

"The visions come when I sleep. They are never 'exquisite.' The only blessing is that it is hard to sleep. If you free me, I can promise you more gold than you could ever spend." Magi smiled, albeit feebly.

The mirthless laugh Malenec returned was a sound so painful that Magi knew it would later be turned into the subject of its very own nightmare.

"Gold? Magi, if you knew how little gold mattered to me…" Malenec drew his laughter to a sudden stop, turning to the woman who stood in the shadows near him. "He offers us gold, Genevieve. Now here sits a man with no grasp of his situation."

Magi yanked on his chains, and not for the first time, by the look of his bruised and bloody wrists. "Tell me what you want! I can offer you a great many things." He tried to sound commanding, but he knew the tone in his voice came off as desperate. He *was* desperate.

Malenec turned his attention back to Magi, pressing his face close to the bars. "Young Mage, there is *nothing* you have that I cannot take. *Nothing*… and that includes your very soul." He turned around and began walking away.

"Then why not kill me now? Be done with it, then!" Magi yelled.

Malenec turned back around. "Believe me, I would love nothing better than to let my dear friend Genevieve put her hands on you. Alas, the pleasure of killing you has been promised to another, and on this I actually agree with Xaro. However—" He paused. "Perhaps I can do one small favor for you." He was too far away for Magi to make out the look on his face, but his tone seemed cheerful. "May Kuth-Cergor help you fall asleep whenever you tire, Magi."

"No!" Magi yelled, trying to grab the bars of his cell that were just out of reach. The last thing he heard was that same mirthless laugh coming from the Dark Cleric as he drifted to sleep.

The chest. Tonight, it's going to be the chest…

~Tarsh~

Looking up at the purplish-peaks of the Shembolt Mountains, Tarsh paused to consider his approach. An urgency drove him; he could feel it, but couldn't name it. The information he received from the Northern Druids had filled in a number of gaps for him. He'd suspected that Windomere was indeed an ancestor of the nomadic tribes that wandered the Dusty Plains, and that he was buried somewhere past those sharp peaks. In the fading twilight of a long day's ride, it was uncanny how symmetrical the mountains were. *Like dark teeth protruding from Tenebrae's jawbone.*

Fortunately, he would not need to *Levitate* over them. At that height, the drain on his energy would be significant, even for something as light as himself, but the mountains did not separate the

North and South of Adimand quite as completely as the Crystal Mountains bifurcated Elvidor along East-West lines. The Shembolt peaks gracefully descended toward the eastern shores, leaving a wide swath of relatively tame terrain across the range.

That was where Tarsh stopped now. He was riding a horse he'd bought in Munty-Whash, and he wanted to give the animal one last night of good grazing before heading into Dusty Plains. Using a *Farsight* spell, he could see the changes in landscape on the horizon: grass-to-dirt-to-hardpack. Swirling dust devils could be seen in the great distance, and there was nothing beyond the hardpack he could see even with his spell craft. *Desolate.*

The horse would eventually die—quickly if the hardpan was a salt flat, less quick, perhaps, if it was more rock/clay with a few shrubs...but taking the horse in there was to kill it. He was prepared for a few weeks of searching; a month at the most if he rationed aggressively. The more ground he could cover in the first week, the better.

He nibbled some dry meat, took a sip of water, and packed the rest up. *Time to train the body to make do with less, I guess.* The central question he kept coming back to was the approach. No man, mage or otherwise, could search the entire Dusty Plains. Not on horse. Perhaps on the back of a wyvern, maybe...but Munty-Whash was fresh out of trained wyverns for hire. He smiled at the thought.

No...I'll need to Levitate. *A birds-eye view will be my best bet. Now that I've travelled through Munty-Whash, Teleporting should be less dangerous; I can always go back there.* The horse had allowed him to conserve some energy while getting this far, but the humane thing to do would be let it go free instead of taking it into the desert. *If I'm going to try and cut down the amount of ground to explore by levitation, there's no point to keeping the horse anyway. How heavy can this Shield really be, anyhow?*

The *only* thing that gave him pause was the warning from that old Druid...something about his magic not working at inopportune times. *Like on their bridge. How many other magic-absorption traps might I encounter in the Plains?* A horse might yet have some value...

Long mountain shadows slowly gave way to the first stars of night, as he enjoyed the small campfire. The sound of falling scree behind him broke his thoughts. Whipping around, Tarsh saw small, loose stones and dust sliding down a nearby slope in the foothills. Three small figures were in the distance, atop a ridge. One of them must have triggered the rockslide.

Nomads! Tarsh immediately sprang up. "Hello there! I say, are you hurt?" he yelled up to them.

No response. No movement, either.

Tarsh stepped toward them, cupping his hands to this mouth. "I say! Can I help any of you?" he called again.

They were pretty high up, far away, and dressed in gray that blended into the mountain backdrop quite effectively. Only his strong eyes even spied them. He thought he saw the tiniest flicker of movement between them, but wasn't sure.

He shouted up one final time. "Greetings! My name is Tarsh. May I help you?" He waited another second or two, and then decided to *Levitate* up toward them.

Up he rose…until the air itself seemed to get heavier. It felt like the very air was pushing back on his *Levitation* spell, making it harder and harder to rise. *What is going on?*

He poured more of himself into the spell, drawing on the same energy reserves that had once lifted an entire boat out of the Maelstrom. Slowly, but resolutely, he continued to rise. Beads of sweat quickly formed and begin tracing paths down his scalp, cheeks, and neck. He could finally begin to make out their faces.

They were boys. Three, small boys to be precise—the oldest of which could not have been more than twelve or thirteen. He lowered himself onto a large, flat boulder that seemed more stable than the other stones, anchored to the side of the foothill. The air continued pressing down on him from all sides.

"My name is Tarsh. I saw the scree give way and wanted—"

"We're not supposed to speak with outsiders. Especially White Eyes," said the tallest of the three. They kept their eyes on him, but continued picking their way carefully across the ridge.

"Wait! Perhaps you could then help me instead?" The air around him was crushingly heavy, which made no sense. *Shouldn't air get lighter the higher one travels?* "Please, young men. I mean you no harm. Just a question or two from a weary traveler?"

They paused, and again the oldest boy took the lead. "White-eye words can be tricky. We know your kind. Good bye!" And the three of them began picking their way along the ridge with surprising agility, their gray robes all but disappearing against the rocky backdrop.

With supreme concentration, Tarsh pushed back on the air that was literally trying to squeeze his body into pulp and dust, put a *Shield* around himself, and cast his own freezing spell on the third and smallest boy bringing up the rear. The boy dropped like a stone, his head narrowly missing a sharp, rock outcropping.

Immediately, the air began to lighten—so much so that Tarsh nearly flew upward, not realizing he was still trying to *Levitate*. *Interesting. Druid children.*

He quickly rose to stand next to the fallen boy, who had landed on his back and was staring up into the star-studded sky. His face was frozen into a picture of abject panic.

"Now that I have your attention," Tarsh began, "I would ask my questions and receive fair answers. You needn't fear me, but I will not hesitate to freeze all of you here in the mountain shadows and leave you for wolves if you try and squeeze the air out of my lungs again."

The oldest boy stuck his chin out, but it was quivering. "What have you done to Eben?"

"He will be fine. Do you three belong to a tribe?"

The other two said nothing.

Tarsh sighed. He didn't want to intimidate these children, but that urgency he felt kept snapping in the back of his mind. "All I want to know, quite simply, is the location of where Windomere, a renowned True Cleric of old, is—"

"He was a Druid."

"So, you have heard of him?"

The older boy slowly nodded.

"Do you know where he is buried?"

The boy swallowed hard. "No. But my father does."

Tarsh's eyes lit up, and it was a shame nobody could tell. "And who is your father?"

"He is an Elder."

"Will you take me to meet him?"

"I am not supposed to talk with outsiders. He is a great distance away. I cannot."

"Can you carry your two friends?"

"My brothers? Why would I carry them?"

Tarsh cast another spell and froze the second brother, who also fell over, sliding to a stop next to the still form of Eben. "Because that is the only way they're getting off this mountain unless you take me with you."

~*Xaro*~

A week into Magi's captivity, Xaro finally decided to deal with the problem. Felling Rookwood and conquering Tenebrae to usher in the Age of Kuth-Cergor seemed to pale, at least immediately, to the problem his mother was causing.

She tried to keep to herself, but that wasn't always possible—not unless Xaro wanted to lock her up as well. Even as an old hag, Daphne attracted unwanted attention. The strong-minded were merely overly polite, but still cloyingly accommodating. And the weak-minded—they were…persistent. Some would say *insistent* in their pursuit of her.

Eventually Xaro had to assign her a bodyguard. Except he was preciously short on female bodyguards, which is to say the bodyguard proved more of a problem than a solution. And this was when his mother was making a concerted effort to *dissuade* her new admirers.

Sirens, however, don't dissuade attention forever—deep down, they all craved it. His mother probably couldn't help herself, but it didn't make it any easier when she sashayed into his Great Hall, demanding to see Michael. His enchantress mother was hardly disguised as a withered prune of a hag…

***

"Hello, everyone. I pray I'm not interrupting an important meeting?" Daphne purred.

She had barged into the Great Hall, with several True Warrior guards standing dutifully behind her, each with a more stupid-looking grin on his face than the next. Her dark blonde hair cascaded over her shoulders like amber honey, resting softly behind and around her bare shoulders. She wore a bright red, strapless dress that clung to her curves like wet silk, falling mid-thigh. Her desert sandals had straps that crisscrossed halfway up her perfectly tanned calves.

She looked all of nineteen or twenty.

Xaro stood, but his mother spoke just as quickly. "Now now, no need to get up. I just had a quick question for the men of your court. You see I've been unable to find my escort, Michael, and I was hoping one of the good men here would tell me where he's hiding." She walked over to their meeting table, adjusting the top of her dress as she leaned forward. "I would be *most* grateful if any of you boys could help me find him."

Predictably, three captains all stood up and shouted he was being held in Ajax's dungeon, and would she like him to personally escort her? Heck, even Tar-Tan, his enormous half-ogre Commanding General, stood up and started to extend his hand to Daphne. Xaro was reminded at that moment that Tar-Tan was, in fact, only *half* an ogre. He looked over at Malenec, who interestingly seemed amused at the interruption, but unstirred.

"Enough," Xaro said. A couple men paused before turning back toward Daphne and her gossamer dress. "I said *enough!*" he shouted, this time shooting blue flame from his palms. "Come with me." He marched over to his mother, forcibly grabbed her upper arm, and pulled her away from the table and his men.

***

Seated alone with his mother after the episode in his Great Hall, Xaro stared at her, his eyes narrow. "I thought we had an understanding. You are a foolish woman, Mother."

"We did have an understanding. And then you took away the one person with whom I could speak. I am a prisoner in this God-forsaken desert sand castle!"

"Michael was not who you think he was. He's a killer, Mother. He is being locked up before he can do any more damage. A week ago he tried to kill my Cleric in a fire, and burned several men in the process."

"Men? You call the zombies that hover around that Cleric of yours *men?* I may not know much of war, but one thing I do know much about is *men.* I assure you, those creatures are no more men than I am."

"Soldiers, then, if you wish to be exact." Xaro stood and walked to an open balcony, where a sea breeze blew a puff of moist coolness through his window. He stared out over the pits to the water in the distance. "Now, you must leave."

"Leave? Where would you have me go?"

"Away. I don't care where, Mother, but if you are capable of exhibiting such an astounding lack of judgment, then you must leave. Our understanding was that you were to assume the countenance of an elderly, ugly woman, keep to yourself, and in return you may stay. I—"

"Our understanding was that I would have some access to you."
Xaro turned around at the interruption. Daphne stood up and reverted
to her middle-aged form, with thick white hair. "You are *my son!* I
came to…to spend time with you. I know full well that your mind is
preoccupied with war, which I do not understand, but would look
past for an opportunity to reconnect with you after these years. An
opportunity to…"

Daphne slowly raised her arm and pointed a finger toward her
son's chest as she approached him. "Let me tell you one thing I
won't be doing: *leaving.* If you aim to take over the world, then I *will*
have a role in your empire, son. You owe me that."

Xaro blinked. "You want…a *role*? Just what kind of role do you
expect to have?"

Daphne smiled, cocking her head. "One that fits, my son. The
King's Mother, for one, but I will settle for The Cleric's Siren, or the
Mage's Escort, if my role in your court falls short of what I
deserve—*what I'm owed!* You see, I have plans too, and if you think
you have to be the epicenter, then you are as foolish as you are
power-hungry. So let me speak plainly for your consideration. If you
try and marginalize me, or send me away, then I will align myself
with your enemies, and you may find my…talents, quite the obstacle
to your conquest."

"My enemies, you say?"

"Xaro, your mother is not a fool. I see how Michael and Malenec
interact with you. I am not blind; they are no friends of yours."

"Yet you would make them friends of yours, Mother? For
what—the promise of a *role* in *their* kingdom? And you consider me
the foolish one."

Daphne jabbed a stubby finger into his chest. "You have no idea
what it is like growing old alone, son. I walk streets, begging for
handouts, picking through garbage on some nights, seducing bakers
for food on others. *I deserve better! I will have better!* By whatever
god you pray to, I swear I will force you to kill me if I am not given
a place of purpose—of *power*—in your kingdom. I am not on your
side, or Michael's. Certainly not your Cleric's. Just know that my
peculiar—and not insignificant—talents are at anyone's disposal
who can elevate my life. I would prefer to wield power behind your
throne…but if you try sending me away, I will wield power behind
another's rule. *Son.*"

Xaro stared at the middle-aged woman in front of him. Calling
her bluff would be the easiest thing in the world to do; he certainly
didn't fear his mother joining forces with Malenec. *And Magi will*

never be in a position to challenge me again. No, his mother's threat was about as sharp as a clay sword.

What struck him was the passion. Xaro had always assumed that his father had provided the regal stock that destined him for leadership. *Perhaps I am selling my Mother short.*

He gently took her hand away from his chest and held it between each of his own. "Mother. You are right. You *do* deserve better. But I will not have you ingratiating yourself with my Cleric. As you say, his company is only fit for the soul-less. That is not a place for you. As for this Michael—you don't know him. His name's not even Michael. Its Magi, and he came here to kill me, Mother. The only reason he brought you here was likely to use you as leverage against me. Separating you two was a necessity, and it remains a necessity. I won't have him filling your head with lies and promises to turn you against me, nor can I allow you to comfort him, given your stated willingness to sell yourself to the highest bidder." Xaro smiled as Daphne ripped her hand away from his.

"How dare you—"

Xaro laughed. "That is what you have implied, dearest Mother. You may not be selling your body, but you certainly seem more than willing to sell your—how did you put it? Your *peculiar, not insignificant* talent?" Xaro gestured at Daphne to calm down. "Alas, Magi will stay here to answer for his crimes in a place you would not enjoy visiting. However…" Xaro grinned. *Perhaps I won't have to waste that wonderful scroll on my half-brother, after all.*

"What?" she interrupted his thoughts.

"However," he continued, "Perhaps a simple business proposition can be reached between the two of us. You have a point; I *can* make use of your talents, Mother."

Daphne fumed still, arms across her chest. "What are you thinking?"

Xaro approached her, putting a hand on each shoulder. "I want you to travel ahead of my army. To Rookwood. Disguise yourself however you best see fit. I have tried unsuccessfully to assassinate my half-brother, your *stepson*, of a sort. If I cannot remove him with an Assassin's contract, perhaps I can eliminate him with a stepmother's love. Your *peculiar, not insignificant* talents ought to bring him to his knees. After all, your charms worked on our father. Do this, and when I come into power, you shall sit at my table, join my Small Council, and serve as the Royal Mother, answering only to me. I only ask this one task of you—distract my half-brother, however you can. Will you do this for me?"

Daphne uncrossed her arms, and slowly her image returned to the smoldering twenty-year old in the clingy, red dress and the honey-colored hair. "We have a deal, Xaro."

"Good. Prepare to leave in the morning."

CHAPTER SIXTEEN: THE BEST LAID PLANS...

~Queen Najalas~

Over the next week after the Queen's private meeting with Herodius and Victor, it became obvious to all that a rushed wedding and the crowning of a new King in Elvidor required a little more planning and time than Strongiron would have liked, but a great deal less than Victor had hoped. Like most affairs of the crown, compromise often ruled the day. The date was set a month out—the first day of summer—to allow some lords, nobles, and country folk alike to travel to Rookwood for the festivities.

Queen Najalas considered all the detailed planning required to host such an event. Despite her strong desire to keep the crowning of a new King in Elvidor small...she was forced to admit that such a notion was pure folly. Kings came into power one of two ways: by sword, or by womb. Her best scholars could not find a single example where one ascended through *marriage*. It was, by definition, unprecedented. She sighed. *I surely hope Jonathon is up to the planning of such a spectacle.*

Looking around the room, the Queen brought her expanded small council to order, including Belara, Kari, Victor, and, of course, Herodius. *The time is approaching when this will be* our *small council. Yet I am the one still calling the meeting.* She made a mental note to continue to encourage Herodius to begin acting in a more kingly manner. *Perhaps he will assume more leadership when it is formally bestowed upon him.* She hoped that would be the case, and sighed again.

"Friends, there is much to discuss. I know our conversations of late have centered around planning a wedding, but there are tasks of war that I have laid before each of you, and now is the time for a full and proper update. Let us begin with you, Peter."

Peter was arrayed in a white tunic and blue trousers, with a sash that bore the five-mountain crest of Rookwood. He removed his plumed hat with a low bow. It was garb more fitting for a Grand Ball or the launch of new vessel. Her former husband, King Alomar, also preferred informal attire for their small council meetings, but that never stopped Peter from his Fair Day best. *"My admiral could make a peacock jealous,"* was a favorite saying of his. *He could indeed,* the Queen thought with a small smile.

His voice brought her attention back to the room. "I have designed *small* ships, my Queen. I am trying to stretch our gold with smaller ships but greater numbers. My plan is to build mage platforms at the bow. A Battle Mage on every ship, plus some other True Warriors. I've also commissioned a boat rammer that should crack the hull of any wooden vessel. We won't have large boats, but they'll be fast, and we'll have Mages on the water."

"How many boats?" asked the Queen.

Peter looked down. "Three hundred."

"Against a force of 30,000 men, and who knows how many undead?"

"My Queen, it is all we can build with the gold we have. Keep in mind that we don't need to match Xaro's naval force; we only need enough to defend our port. Three hundred ships, armed with Mages—the port will be *secure*, my Queen!" Peter slammed his fist into an open hand.

"There are other landfalls, Peter. You cannot guard our shoreline with three hundred ships."

"Stro—Victor, I mean, will defend us from overland attacks from the north. The mountains guard our western flank. And Chief Chocktaw and his elfs have always watched our southern border. I am concentrating our sea resources on the east."

Chief Chocktaw and his elfs have always watched our southern border. She cringed inwardly, and hoped her face remained inscrutable. She called for a goblet.

Victor stood. "We have good men to the north who will fight, but I am making Rookwood the priority. Knight commanders reside in the Three Fingers, and I am allocating some men to coordinate with Lord Jamison in Shith in fortifying the Elfsbane pass. As Peter can attest, we've sent some Warriors across the sea to join his shipwrights in Plythe. Let us be honest though among ourselves here, if nowhere else—the priority is Rookwood. I can no more guarantee the safety of Oxen-Pace as I can Paragatha. We have 15,000 fighters, of which perhaps 14,000 are True Warriors, and around 1,000 are True Mages. I've deployed no more than 2,500 outside of Rookwood and her surroundings." He paused, and when no one spoke up, he finished his thought. "Elvidor will burn, your Majesty."

The Queen slowly closed her eyes and then slowly opened them. "Perhaps not, General. Perhaps not." She did, however, reach for the goblet that had been set before her. One rarely left her hand these days, it seemed. "Jonathon?"

"My Queen," he began. "You asked me to find a path out of Rookwood. I have done so. The catacombs that wind through the bowels of this mountain often lead to pitfalls, drop-offs, falling gates, and some other traps that are equally deadly. Kings of old went to great lengths to guard their backs during a retreat. Even the faded maps left behind were filled with misinformation. That said, I have found the singular path that will lead to fresh air on the shores of Lake Calm. It is a two-day hike underneath the mountains."

Peter turned to Jonathon, "And how will our wives and children make it out if the way is fraught with danger?"

"It will be difficult, Peter. Even with me leading a group, there are no guarantees. I have left a glow pebble at most of the forks; they will glow in the dark when given the right word, but that is hardly foolproof, and even then there are some traps to still avoid. I dared not leave any hard signs; that would defeat the purpose. My best guess is that we will have one shot to retreat, and one shot only, relying on my memory to lead the effort." His update also culminated in a restless silence, which he also broke with an uncomfortable conclusion: "I doubt we will be able to leave in waves."

"Well, we certainly can't empty the entire castle in single-file! You will need to share your keyword that lights up the glow pebbles." Simon had his hands on his hips, staring at Jonathon as others quickly began murmuring agreement.

Jonathon held up his hand, and he stared at Queen Najalas. "To whom shall I share this information, my Queen? Besides you, of course," he hastily added.

The Queen smiled. "I trust all of you. I will give the retreat orders, should it come to that, but Simon is right—we *must* be able to leave in waves. What is the word, Jonathon?"

Jonathon looked at everyone in the suddenly quiet room. He shrugged and nodded at the Queen. "*Aduro*. But remember, there are other traps to avoid besides following the wrong path. I had to prod the floor ahead of me, for example, the illusion of at least one false floor ran down the center of a passageway in the underground cave system. I tried to leave a glow pebble in front of these types of traps as well, but whoever is leading an escape must be prudent in their retreat. My walking stick plunged through the illusory floor without warning, but it was solid on each side of the hole. A mob of us running for our lives would surely plunge through unaware."

"*Aduro*," Queen Najalas repeated, marveling at how close she had come to losing her Steward on what she thought was a harmless reconnaissance mission. "Thank you, Jonathon. Your return, unscathed, means a great deal to me. Hopefully we won't need your pebbles, but it is good to know that they are there."

"I found one more thing, my Queen." Jonathon was looking down.

"Yes?"

"The *Terraemotus.*"

Puzzled looks abounded as her small council looked at Jonathon, and then back at the Queen. She looked sternly at her Steward. "We will not use that under any circumstances."

Peter leaned forward. "And may I ask what a *Terraemotus* is?"

The Queen looked at Niku, who nodded wearily. She spread her hands wide. "As you may guess, more than stone anchors Rookwood into the mountain. Great magical forces were combined with stonemasonry to erect such a fortress as this, held in place by the *Terraemotus.* Pulling the lever, which can only be done by the hand of the Crown, will sever those ties. The mountain would shake Rookwood off like a flea from a dog, and half of Elvidor would likely feel the quake as this castle crumbled and plunged into the city and sea below. As I said...we will not use that."

She let the uncomfortable silence hang in the air before turning to Belara. "And how has our recruiting progressed?"

"My Queen," she said, bowing respectfully in her rich, brown dress that stuck to her curves like a strawberry dipped in chocolate. "I have recruited many Mages to our cause. One hundred and some, all of whom Peter has requested in Plythe to form the backbone of his naval defenses. They come from every city, town, village, and several wandering mercenaries as well."

Herodius looked up. "So few?"

Belara smiled sardonically. "It was not an easy sell, Islander, considering that they all see the same outcome ahead that we do: the land be damned as long as Rookwood stands. This is our destiny, as General Victor spelled out so succinctly. Our people sense this, know this. They will not commit even more of their precious resources to defend the crown when their own communities and families need safeguarding." She opened her hands and looked at the Queen. "We were lucky to raise more than a hundred mages, and I daresay few others could have been more persuasive."

"Oh I don't doubt that," the Queen added. "A thousand would've been nice, that's all." She exhaled and turned now to Simon, but she couldn't stop wondering whether any of her council would soon consider Herodius more than an Islander. "Share some good news, Simon."

The Captain of her Guard nodded slightly. "We have begun training again, my Queen. The vigor of youth may have departed many, but I assure you they are all rediscovering their muscles. These are not staid drills or ceremonial pomp we have been training for. We have been preparing for battle, in tight, around corridors, using our knowledge of Rookwood to offset a disparity in numbers, should it come to that. The men are growing lean; even their food and ale have been rationed."

"And the ramparts? How fast can they be mustered?" Herodius asked.

Simon bristled and stepped forward. "Fast enough. The Queen asked me to prepare, and so I am preparing. Are you questioning my leadership?"

All eyes turned to Herodius, especially the Queen's.

Herodius stepped forward and put his hand on Simon's shoulder, smiling to break the tension. "Nothing of the sort, Simon. I assume that your first priority was and is to prevent invaders from breaching our walls, but are preparing for the worst—room-to-room combat—in the event that they do. No one questions your leadership. I simply wish to know how much *time* we have from giving the order to muster until the archers have arrows nocked at the wall." Strongiron and Victor both nodded slightly at his words.

Simon narrowed his eyes at Herodius, but did not disengage from the smiling islander. He did turn to Victor, Peter, and Niku. "I would think that we should have advance warning of an attack, be it from ground, sea, or magic, rendering a muster timeframe moot." He turned back to Herodius and, after a quick glance at the Queen, softened his tone. "But, to your question, the Guard can be at the wall from wherever they are in the castle in under nine minutes."

"See that they can be at their posts in under seven." Herodius withdrew his hand and walked back to stand next to the Queen.

"Seven? To what purpose? Who are you—"

"I am your future King, Captain. While I would hope our brethren can indeed provide us the warning you desire, it may not come. Minutes mean lives. No one in this room is more qualified than I am to speak about attacks in the night without warning, and the value of knowing exactly where to go when called, to arrive there quickly, and to know what to do when you get there." He held up his wrist, where the tattoo *1X5Z9* was still visible to all. "*No one,*" he repeated.

Simon hesitated, and then bowed. "As you wish."

The Queen was hoping for some acknowledgement, a simple 'Your Majesty' would suffice. *But that would be inappropriate until he is formally crowned, I suppose. Baby steps.* She was encouraged that Herodius was beginning to strike a commanding tone—*the tone of a king.*

"Thank you, Simon," she said, filling yet another awkward silence in an evening of disquieting updates. "Herodius is right, we should be prepared for every contingency." She finally turned to Niku. His hair and beard were properly oiled for the meeting, but the puffy bags under his eyes told the real tale. *The man's energy is low. Does Herodius see it, too?* "Lastly, my dearest Niku. Tell us how your mages are preparing for battle."

Niku pushed himself up from his chair like a bent sword getting worked over by a smith, unfolding his back slowly to stand at his full height. "My Queen, the mages are getting trained, some for their sea platforms, some for the ramparts, and some for the field with Victor. All are learning battle spells, but that is not my main update." His voice cracked a little as he spoke.

The Queen and her expanded council said nothing, but inched closer to the True Mage, leaning forward to hear better. In that moment, she saw Kari reach for Strongiron's hand.

"It is with great disappointment that I relay to you that Magi has passed beyond this realm. My shade cannot reach him, which can only mean that he has died."

~Malenec~

Night fell quickly in the desert, and a solitary figure in white stood in sharp contrast to the deepening black sky that draped everything from the mesa to the sea. The figure approached a small dwelling that, in better light, bore the mark of fire. "Come in."

Daphne entered the Dark Cleric's spartan quarters, dressed in a loose white dress that fluttered scandalously in the hot summer breeze. Amber hair fell flawlessly about her shoulders, resting on thin white straps, one of which had slipped down her arm.

Daphne looked twenty again.

She jumped as the door creaked shut behind her, shrouding the dark hut in shadow and candlelight. She spun around to see Genevieve staring at her with an empty face and a rotting hand pressed against the door.

"I thought we were to meet alone," said Daphne.

"We are. Pay no attention to Genevieve."

"Difficult not to, given the smell." Daphne wrinkled her nose.

Malenec simply smiled. His face looked eerie in the dim light. "A gifted *Illusionist* such as yourself should have no problem masking an objectionable scent." Seated himself, he gestured to a nearby chair. "Sit."

Daphne let out a long, nearly inaudible exhale, and did *not* sit. Instead she walked up to Malenec. "I would prefer to stand." She leaned over the Dark Cleric. "I won't be long."

Malenec inclined his head to look directly into the siren's soft, brown eyes. "Very well. You wanted to speak to me. Speak."

Daphne let a slow smile simmer on her lips as she placed her hands, uninvited, on his shoulders. "Tell me, Malenec. Tell me what you plan to do with Xaro when the fighting is over. You may find I am more an ally to your interests than a hindrance to your plans."

The Dark Cleric allowed the awkward silence to linger to the point where her sultry smile began to fade. Genevieve shuffled her feet across the room, but made no move. Finally Malenec reached up to return her touch by gently caressing her cheek.

"Daphne…such a sweet, sweet child, really. I suppose there is no harm in sharing my plans with you. Xaro will not long survive this war, I'm afraid. But you knew that, else you would not have asked if you did not suspect my intentions. Tell me—what is your interest in seeing your son destroyed?" He grabbed a handful of her hair and yanked her down to her knees.

"Ohh! You're hurting me!" she screamed, her *Illusion* quickly fading.

Malenec stood. "Unless you're spying on me for him. Tell me why I would trust you—his mother—to help me?" He pushed her away, and Daphne fell back, her eyes watering.

She looked up at him. "Why aren't you nice to me, like all the other men?"

Malenec laughed. "Your charms are like a soiled loincloth to me. You will never be as beautiful as my Genevieve." He motioned to the zombie by the door, who approached Daphne with a greedy, slobbering hiss. "Now tell me, why did you come here?"

Daphne scampered to her feet and pressed herself against the opposite wall, away from both the zombie and Malenec. "To make sure I took care of myself! I swear—Xaro does not know I am here. He is sending me away to kill my stepson, Strongiron. If you kill Xaro, I want a place in your kingdom. I'm tired—so very tired—of begging for food, for attention. I thought, maybe, if you were interested…" she let her eyes dip as her voice trailed off.

Malenec walked over to her, putting his gloved hand under her chin. Daphne was back to being middle-aged, and she shook at his touch. He looked directly into her eyes. *She fancies herself a future Queen—or Queen Mother—if the cards fall differently.*

"Indeed, I believe you. And I *am* interested…"

He shifted his eyes to Genevieve, then back to Daphne. "I am most interested in your soul."

Only the dead and Malenec heard her screams.

~Tarsh~

As it turned out, the village was indeed inland. It had been over a week of switchbacks to make progress through the sawtooth mountain range, travelling further inland along the Shembolt Range, gradually tacking westward. Tarsh effortlessly *Levitated* the frozen bodies of Eben and (as he soon found out) Uriah behind him, but the physical exertion was significant with only a few carefully orchestrated stops each day for food and water. He had intended to pass the time walking and talking with the oldest brother, Zachary.

He spent it mostly walking. And huffing.

The footing was tricky on the mountain ridge, and Zachary did not appear to be particularly interested in engaging in much conversation. Whether that was to allow Tarsh to concentrate on keeping his brothers from banging into rocks or simply out of loathing for the True Mage, he wasn't letting on. Tarsh suspected the latter...and could care less.

"Zachary," he began for the umpteenth time one morning more than a week into their hike. "Tell me again about your father, the Elder."

"As I've said, he is a True Druid, more powerful than the likes of you."

Teenage bravado…I am not so far removed from such thoughts myself. Perhaps a different track...

"I see. A True Druid? May I ask what separates an acolyte from a Master in your Guild? You are no doubt aware of the rigors of our Staircase, I assume?"

"We've heard of it."

"Your Tests must be challenging indeed. Please, tell me more. I assure you again, I mean no harm."

"My frozen brothers beg to differ."

"Come now. You three combined your might to nearly crush my lungs. I am a simple Mage on a wandering quest, and instead of kindness, you greeted me with malice. I defended myself with my considerable talents, but I have shown no ill will toward you or your brothers. You are all unharmed, yes?"

"My father will answer your questions."

Tarsh sighed and let the matter drop for the moment, as the terrain was finally changing. The path along the ridge snaked downward into a narrow canyon, with steep walls to either side. A small offshoot of the path led behind an immense boulder that connected with more stone up top, forming a crude archway. Zachary took this path, which curled back around and downward at such an angle that steps had been formed to ease the descent.

As they rounded another corner, trees and bushes began to appear, as well as the sound of trickling water. *Telltale signs of habitation.* When he had looked out to the hard-flats of the Dusty Plains, water would have been a serious problem. He soon saw a steady stream of water running down the mountain, gathering in a clear pool at the base of this little valley tucked between the mountains, with the desert beyond.

Gasps and shouts rose as soon as they saw Tarsh and Zachary, with his younger brothers floating in still form behind them both. Tarsh had his *Shield* still, but was wondering what other protection he might need in a camp full of Druids. *God knows what a handful of them did to me last time.*

Taking a chance, he immediately released the children, setting them down gently.

"Thank you, Zachary. I appreciate your help." He turned to the villagers rushing toward the dazed children, held up his hands and started to shout. "I come in peace! I have seen the hospitality of Druids, and I seek a simple council with—"

A ring of fire materialized around him, neck-high. The flames were close enough to catch his robes on fire—the ones he was given by the friendly Druids from the Fertile Plains. He stamped out the hem of his robe and extended his *Shield* to counter the fire.

Nothing is ever easy.

With a word, he lifted himself above the flaming circle, and floated in their midst. He cleared his voice loudly once again. "My friends! I come in peace. I have shared the hospitality of your brethren of the Fertile Plains, Linar and Prithi, if you know them. I seek only—"

A fierce blast of wind blew Tarsh straight back out of the air and slammed him into the mountainside. His *Shield* spell held, keeping him from major injury, but it hardly felt good to be nearly splattered against a rock wall, landing headfirst. He started to stand—

A shower of head-sized stones was hurled his way. A more proper stoning could not have been conceived. The small boulders rained down on him, testing the limits of his *Shield*. Some were flung so hard that they crumbled inches away from his face. Others split nearly in half against his magic barrier.

I'm beginning to think they really don't *like outsiders.* Tarsh was on one knee, his arms reflexively in front of his face. *This is ridiculous.* Grabbing a pinch of sand, he prepared to put most of the village into deep sleep. He tossed the sand—

The stream of water that poured down the mountain was diverted and flushed the airborne sand into mud droplets before he could utter the simplest of spells. Tarsh screamed in frustration as the water was re-diverted back onto him. Like the rocks, the water seemed to hit a pane of glass inches from him, scattering in all directions.

Enough!

Closing his eyes, Tarsh brought down an *Air Hammer* on half the mountain, and *Lightning* on the other. An explosion of rock erupted where the force of his *Hammer* spell came down, and brown-robed Druids ran in all directions as a huge chunk of rock split off and tumbled down. Many were then struck by lightning from the bolts that seemed to come from nowhere and everywhere all at once. It was chaos as seven, then eight, soon ten and more different blue-white bolts scorched the hidden oasis.

Unsurprisingly, the jet of water and barrage of mini-boulders ceased. Tarsh stood up, straightened his back, and addressed the village in a clear, booming voice: "*I will speak to your Elder, and I will speak to him* now!"

A middle-aged woman looked up at him. Zachary was kneeling next to her; his eyes bloodshot and filled with hate. "He is dead by your hand, White Eyes," she said.

That was when he felt the familiar tingle in his arm. Xaro wanted an update.

~Xaro~

Xaro brought the sparring partner assigned to challenge him to his knees before he realized his mother had already departed. She was to leave at first light, aboard the *Sprayquest,* bound for Elvidor

319

with enough gold to see her passage all the way to Rookwood. He frowned; he was so caught up in his rituals that he never saw her off. Sneering, he shoved the weaponless warrior to the dust.

"Why wasn't I summoned before my mother departed?" he bellowed.

"Because the last man who interrupted your precious training nearly lost a hand. If you are so concerned though, I can assure you she departed uneventfully. I saw her off myself, and she bid you farewell."

Xaro didn't need to turn around to look at the face to whom the voice belonged. *Malenec.* He turned anyway.

"You saw her leave and did not come get me? I—"

"Let us not pretend there was genuine emotion on either of your parts. This is a woman you haven't seen in years, and one you sent away, presumably with a task in mind. She said it would be done. The boat was leaving at dawn, and you cared *so much* that your silly swordplay began precisely when it always does. You should thank me that I happened to be up, walking after my morning prayers. She left safely, and the crew will not bother her." Malenec began walking away. "You can never be the son she remembers, nor the son she wants. And camp was unsafe with her in it. For her especially." Malenec wasn't threatening, but his voice was so damn cold that it irritated Xaro even more than usual.

Xaro fixed his gaze on the Dark Cleric walking dismissively away, outfitted in loose black robes, despite the early morning heat. His favorite zombie, Genevieve, was always close. "Come here. It is time we palaver once again as a small council." Malenec paused and slowly turned back around, nodding slightly.

With a simple prayer, they both *Teleported* to a small antechamber within Sands End, where Tar-Tan and Krishnan were already waiting. With a word and a cloud of black powder, the shimmering image of Tarsh joined them. He appeared in a nearby chair, looking dusty and disheveled. *His real update will come later...*

Xaro poured himself some lemon sweetwater and offered the pitcher to his assembled council. Malenec and Krishnan each poured themselves a glass, while Tar-Tan saw fit to drink the rest straight from the pitcher. With all the gold in the world, importing lemons was no longer an extravagant expense. Xaro pursed his lips and sent a servant to go make more.

"My thirsty General, now that your lips are wet, why don't you grace us with your update first?" Sending his mother halfway around the known world this morning had put him in a feisty mood.

Tar-Tan rubbed a rough forearm across his mouth in satisfaction before beginning. "Master, our preparations are nearly complete. The boats are built, the crews bought, the supplies packed. Our men are nearly trained." Standing, he unrolled the large map of Tenebrae and spread it along the table in the center of their council meeting.

He continued. "You may recall that our plan is based on siege. For this to work, all avenues of escape must be choked off. As before, our armada shall be divided into four divisions. Malenec shall lead a march with his...*followers*...in an attack on the Elfs. Both he and I shall head for Shith, with my troops taking a northern route to hem in the Elfs. He shall move through the forests, flushing them out, killing them or using whatever unholy rites he plans on performing. Now Xaro—"

"My rites are hardly unholy. I could say that the union of ogre and man that produced *you* is far more unholy than any prayer for undying life which our God may grant at my request."

Two small, beady yellow eyes narrowed as Tar-Tan took a step toward the Cleric.

"Leave it alone. Both of you." Xaro let tiny bolts of lightning to crackle between his fingers to emphasize his impatience with the banter. "Finish your update, Tar-Tan. I want to know *when*."

Slowly, the half-ogre turned back to Xaro. "The timing is no longer dependent on my efforts. I assume you wish Tarsh to command the fourth division—our sea attack at the port of Rookwood. You will still lead the march from the North, and we need to leave before fall if you wish to avoid a winter march. My desire is for Tarsh to return by the start of summer, within the next month, whereby we can launch our armada. You and he will have the furthest to sail; I would have you depart sooner than the puppeteer and myself."

Xaro caught Malenec's upper lip twitch at Tar-Tan's dig, but he said nothing.

"This is good news. Very well done, Tar-Tan." He looked at Tarsh's flickering shade. "You look...a bit haggard, my friend. Tell me, how goes the negotiations? Will you be able to return within a month?"

"Master, I believe so. I've uncovered some new traders whom I believe will be extremely valuable. If their goods are not what I expect, I will begin my journey back. With favorable seas, I can be back from the nearby coast of Adimand to Sands End inside of a week, should you need to recall me early. I look forward to serving in whatever manner you prioritize, Master." Tarsh bowed his head.

"Surely the priority is coming home to lead the division. I can't imagine spices or exotic fruit from Adimand is worth any delay." Malenec raised an eyebrow.

"Some specialized spell components specific to this region may prove invaluable to our efforts. I wouldn't expect anyone but a True Mage to fully appreciate the opportunity." Tarsh pushed back immediately.

"Indeed. I will set our priorities, Malenec." Xaro nodded at Tarsh. "Thank you—carry on for now. I will tell you when to return, unless you find the ingredients we've discussed." He now turned to Krishnan. "Speaking of True Mages, what is the state of our financial affairs, Master of Coinage?"

Krishnan stood up. "Our spending has—finally—begun to taper off. I begrudge your General nothing; his spending has been pertinent, but extensive. We have a large debt, but our trading partners currently feel confident that they will get their gold. We may not fully pay off all our debts until we add the wealth of Elvidor to our treasury. As long as we don't run out of iron, we shall not run out of gold."

Xaro found it hard to believe that they were in debt, given an unlimited supply of gold, but this didn't seem like a pressing problem at the moment. "Good. Keep looking for ways to increase production."

He sighed and spread his hands. "Production isn't the issue, but yes, I will continue to do everything in my power to keep up with our consumption."

Xaro narrowed his eyes, but let the matter drop. Finally, he turned to Malenec. "Do you have anything useful to add to our discussion?"

"Nothing that I haven't already said. Genevieve and I are bored. We are ready. By the time you are ready to commit us to a course of action, we'll be on cooler seas and frosty ground. It won't matter to me, but I daresay your other troops will find it harsh. Never fear though; I will be there to scoop up anyone who succumbs to the elements due to the slowness of this plan and will grace them with immortality." His Cleric smiled, and the entire room felt chillier as a result.

"Yes, I know you look forward to nothing more. We *will* depart before mid-Summer. Tarsh...I will talk to you soon on how to prioritize your efforts." Xaro started to dismiss everyone when Malenec cleared his throat.

"What about *your* update, Xaro? I'm sure some of us in particular would love to hear about the guest you've got chained to Ajax's Shackles in the dungeons?"

Xaro did not immediately reply. He'd intended to tell Tarsh privately; the fewer the people who knew Magi was a prisoner the better. Had Malenec not confronted Xaro shortly after the duel, having already visited him and seen him with his own eyes, he wouldn't have told his Cleric either. *Trust is not something I heap on anyone in this room. Least of all Malenec.*

"We have a prisoner. The fire that started several days ago was kindled by none other than Magi Blacksmooth. Our former associate appears to have been right. Apparently he was raised from the dead, and he seemingly came here on his own for his own purposes. Perhaps for justice—at least how he sees the world in his own mind. His efforts were predictably futile, and he is chained in our dungeon. When you return, Tarsh, you shall have your vengeance on him before we depart. But *first*, I need you to procure the rare spell components we have discussed, which I'll prioritize for you separately."

All eyes turned toward the shimmering image of Tarsh. Even though the image was distorted somewhat by the flickering and wavy sheen of the spell, everyone could see his eyes narrow into white slits. He had balled up his fists as well.

"As you wish, Master. I cannot think of a better send-off to war than to christen the moment with his blood. Thank you for giving me the opportunity, Xaro. This news hastens my efforts. I await your next call." Tarsh bowed his head solemnly, and faded out.

Tar-Tan looked at Xaro. "Are you sure it's wise to keep him alive, Master? Can he not just *Teleport* away?"

Xaro looked at the half-ogre. "No, General. He cannot. The shackles are better than Mage-guards; he won't be able to cast a spell while he's chained; Ajax had them wrought specially to hold True Mages with whom he…disagreed." Xaro allowed a half smile to creep up one side of his face. "Truth be told, it won't be much of a fight when Tarsh returns. An aggressive mouse might kill him one toenail at a time."

Everyone chuckled darkly except Tar-Tan. "Then let us pray that Kuth-Cergor fills his cell with aggressive mice. The man is a menace to our efforts."

"Dead? Are you certain?" The Queen's question echoed through the chamber as her voice cut through the silence following Niku's bombshell.

"Yes, my Queen. He is beyond my reach. I can only assume his duel with Xaro ended unfavorably. It is not hard to imagine that he tried to kill the man, given all he was put through, not to mention our encouragement to do so. He must have been found…wanting." He turned to Kari. "I know that he was…a friend of yours at one point, despite the curse that afflicted him. I am so sorry for your loss, Miss Quinlan."

Kari pulled her hand from Strongiron and crossed her arms over her chest. "The only magic battle I've ever seen him lose was when someone cheated. He is so powerful in his Art, Niku. I can't believe he's dead. I just can't."

"Kari, it's not like Xaro wouldn't cheat to win, especially if he knew who Magi was," Herodius said gently.

"This is hard news, Niku. Hard to digest, harder to accept. Weren't we told that Magi had been *groomed* by Kari's former teacher—in the most foul way imaginable—to serve Xaro? If he is dead…" the Queen trailed off.

Niku finished the Queen's thought. "It is because Xaro was threatened. Yes, it is the only thing that makes sense. As Kari has said, he would have given Xaro all that he could handle. He was emotionally invested in the man's death. I suspect Xaro realized it would be impossible to convert Magi, now that the curse was broken, so he killed him. By any means necessary."

The Queen looked around the room and saw several heads nodding. She held her head up high, her chin jutting out.

"Well, then he is no longer with us. Unfortunate that Dymetra sent him back only to see his life wasted chasing a ring, but we must move on. He is not the first good man to suffer and die under the shadow of war, and he won't be the last. What concerns me is that this fiend now possesses his Staff."

"I do not think it will help him, my Queen." Strongiron spoke up for the first time since hearing the news. "It is a blessed artifact of Dymetra; She will not grant Her wisdom to Xaro, I am sure of it. For him, it will be just a pretty stick."

"Let us all pray that you are right, Gen—Strongiron." She looked at Victor and smiled ruefully. "As I was saying, let us pray you are right, my Cleric. God help us all if one of you were captured and subjected to an interrogation if the Staff *did* work for him."

After more murmuring, she dismissed the group. Victor exited first, wearing a grim mask as he departed. Strongiron and Kari left next, followed by Belara, who wanted a moment of their time for something. Then Jonathon, Peter, and Simon left, each looking more determined than the next. Finally Niku filed out, shuffling slowly. *War is a young man's game.*

She turned to Herodius, who now shared the room with her. "This is a bad omen, my dear. He was the one who came bringing hope. If he could not defeat Xaro…"

Herodius stood up and walked over to the Queen, wrapping his arms around her. "My hope never came from Magi or his Staff. In fact, I haven't had any hope until the last few months."

Queen Najalas looked up into his dark eyes and ran her thin, pale fingers through his curly brown hair. She flashed him the kind of knowing smile that only comes from someone fishing for a compliment that they know will be given. "And what, pray tell, has given you hope these last few months?"

She was not disappointed. "You, my Queen. You are the source of my hope…and my fear."

She pulled back slightly, cocking her head. "Fear?"

"As I have said before, a man can have no hope unless he fears something to lose." He kissed her in full, and she let him.

~Xaro~

Alone in his bedchamber, Xaro once again summoned Tarsh's shade to join him. The black dust was scattered, creating first the outline that was filled in by the True Mage's image.

"Tarsh."

"Master."

Greetings clipped short, Xaro focused the conversation. "My intent was to tell you about Magi privately. You did well controlling yourself with the news. I do not want anyone else to know your quest, which you have done well to keep secret."

"It is as you wished, Master." Tarsh nodded slightly. "And again, I thank you for keeping him alive until I return. I greatly wish to see the look on his face when I bring an *Air Hammer* down upon *his* skull. Let *his* bones twist into a monstrosity. Let *his* muscles protrude in odd places. Let *his* skin crack and sizzle from my fire. *Then* we shall see how powerful Magi Blacksmooth is. *Then* we shall see how much his God truly loves him. He will leave Sands End boneless, Godless, and soulless, Master."

Xaro did not interrupt. He just smiled and let his lieutenant go on. *The man's got more passion in his fingertips than Marik had in his entire being.*

Finally, when Tarsh had finished his rant, Xaro continued. "And you shall have your chance, young Tarsh. He will be no match for your newfound skill, I promise you that." He let the smile linger on his face another second or two before a deep breath. "Now then, to your *real* update. Where are you, and what have you found?" After a short pause, he added, "And you look terrible. What is going on?"

Tarsh smiled wearily, and related his tale of crossing the Forgotten Land Bridge, his meeting with the "good" Druids (at least to his way of thinking) in the Fertile Plains, and his recent encounter with the boys, and his demolition of the village in defense of himself. "If I look a little drained, know that I am taxing my resources greatly in pursuit of this Shield, this ancient artifact. I *Teleported* to a small clearing, away from the village, to answer your call for our private counsel, Master, but I am unsure how to get this village to cooperate. They have done everything in their power to destroy me before I even *begin* to have a conversation with them. Now that I have killed their Elder, I doubt they will offer information to me freely."

Xaro said nothing, but tapped his cheek with an extended index finger. "Druids are a mercurial bunch. No central Guild exists of which I'm aware; knowledge has traditionally been passed down from generation to generation. I must admit…I did not expect such hostility toward us Mages."

"I am open to suggestions. I did not aim to destroy them, but they know where Windomere was buried."

"I'm thinking." *Raising their Elder from the dead would be quite a trade-off to offer in exchange for information, if only he had such a skill. Alas, even Malenec could only animate a walking monster. Sigh...* "How many do you believe survived?"

"Most of the village. Some men, women, and children were killed by the rock fall and lightning storm."

"And how are you holding up? I mean magically."

"I am well enough, Master. A little tired, but I can cast anything."

"Here is what you should do, Tarsh. Protect yourself to the greatest extent possible. If you are facing an entire village of Druids out for your blood, little chance survives for you to win a fight alone, and I cannot *Teleport* there across the open sea, nor waste a month sailing to you and back. Make one last effort to reason with them, and if that fails…" He trailed off, opening his hands.

"I know. The children."

Xaro nodded slowly. "Until you are convinced that no one in that village will tell you what you need to know—regardless of your ruthlessness—unfortunately you must press their resolve. Yes, the children. Let the villagers see the price their sealed lips will cost them. First, however, approach them with honey. I will lend my prayers to your efforts; Kuth-Cergor may yet bless this quest of ours with a bit of good fortune." He nodded, and dismissed Tarsh without another word.

~Tarsh~

As Xaro's image blanked out, there was a sharp rustle in the nearby shrubbery. The late-morning light was approaching its noon zenith, and the shadows were sparse. He thought he caught a little movement, so he stood. "Who goes there?"

A small figure that looked like a walking bush stood up. The camouflage was as good as any *Illusion* he had ever seen. "Who are you?"

The bush faded into the complexion of a boy he recognized— Zachary. He had a murderous look in his eyes. Tarsh cast yet another spell of protection around himself…just in case there were others nearby.

"Were you spying on me?"

Zachary stepped forward. "I came to kill you. You murdered my father."

Tarsh held up his hands. "No, I defended myself. Your father's death was an accident. I have told you repeatedly that all I want is information on Windomere's burial chamber. Yet all you and your clan have done is attack me for being a True Mage. Your hatred runs deep. Why?"

Zachary took another step forward. He stood about five feet away from Tarsh; had they been next to one another, he might have come up to his chest in height. Yet his up-turned chin was defiant. "Your ancestors *corrupted* Windomere! He might have lived forever, had it not been for your kind's involvement. My father said that the darkness of this age grew from the ambition of White-eyed mages. He always said that Windomere made a pact with an ancient mage that sealed his doom and robbed him of his immortality. He said to *never* trust the White Eyes!" He narrowed his eyes and pointed a finger at Tarsh. "And nothing I've heard or seen this morning would cause me to believe differently."

"You are very courageous to approach me by yourself. I take it you heard my council with my Master?"

Zachary said nothing.

"Let me assume that you know I have committed to harming no one further—*if* you tell me where Windomere is buried. Let me *also* assume you know that I will begin torturing the children of your clan if you and the rest of the villagers refuse to tell me what I wish to know. That torture can begin…with you." He held his hands slightly apart, so that mere inches separated each finger. Blue-white lightning crackled and jumped from each finger, left-to-right and back again.

Tarsh stepped toward Zachary. "Are you *sure* you do not know where Windomere is buried?"

The boy's eyes grew wide, and he started to take a step back…but his feet were frozen in place. Tarsh took another step forward, and the lightning changed from blue-white to deep violet.

"Scream, if you wish. Try and run or punch me. Call on plant, wind, or water. Bring forth your fire and stones. Right now the only two people who can hear one another are you and me, young Zachary." Tarsh towered over the boy now, whose lower lip quivered uncontrollably. "For the last time—do you know where Windomere is buried?" He was reaching his hands out to grasp each side of Zachary's head.

"Please! Stop! I'll show you."

"So you *do* know?"

Zachary nodded, crying.

"And you are not lying to me now?"

He shook his head violently. A small puddle at the boy's feet indicated that he was scared enough to tell the truth.

"Then lead the way and behave, young Zachary, and you may live to be Elder yourself one day."

CHAPTER SEVENTEEN: LIES, PLAGUE, AND FATE

~Belara~

"Thank you both for joining me." Belara poured Kari and Strongiron a cup of tea, the aroma of which was sweet oranges from the Fertile Plains, mixed with ginger and mint. "I know our Queen prefers something a little stronger, but I thought you both might enjoy some mid-afternoon tea, instead. I see you are a couple now?"

The bluntness of her question seemed to embarrass Kari slightly, as she withdrew her hand somewhat suddenly from Strongiron's. "Is that why you asked us to join you? A bit of court gossip?" She smiled, but a slight edge lined her voice.

Belara sipped her tea and winked at them. "No, I'm not much for court intrigue. Just observant. Be at ease, Kari. You've already bested me in a duel—I hardly wish to get your hackles up." She absently picked a long, brown, stray hair off her peach-colored dress. "Actually, I asked you here because I have an idea, and seeing as you are now a couple…I thought it prudent that you both hear it.

"When I was recruiting True Mages for our Queen on the other side of the Crystal Mountains, I came upon many villagers. I believe you may find willing ears to your preaching—many who are seeking God thirst for a positive message. The winter was harsh west of the mountains. If you can bring healing back to your hometown of Brigg, for example, I think you would find many who would follow Dymetra. Take, for example, your former classmate who now runs the school that your previous Master left behind—Serenity, I believe her name is. I spoke with her in my journeys, of course. I also think your brother Kyle would love to see you again, Kari, before you head to Adimand on your quest after the Crowning."

Belara studied Kari's face when she mentioned Brigg and her brother. It softened considerably.

Strongiron cleared his throat. "Why do you think we would find fertile ears, and what are you suggesting? I must stay here for the month to aid the plans, given my role in the ceremony. Every few days more nobles arrive, some obscure and some of note, all of whom nevertheless require an audience with me. I don't complain, however, except in the unfortunate delay. I've found many of these visitors quite receptive to my message of hope. For the next month, I shall have quite a number of evangelical opportunities right here in Rookwood."

Belara smiled and sipped her tea. "Surely, though, you wouldn't begrudge your lady the opportunity to spread her wings and to try her own hand in spreading the same message west of the mountains? Especially if doing so allowed her to see her friends in the village from which she came of age, let alone to again see the brother that Dymetra raised from the dead for her?" She turned to Kari. "Unless that is of no interest to you? Just an idea I had for a way you could spend the next month, seeing some of the villages and cities west of the mountains for yourself."

Kari looked at Strongiron. "It would be wonderful to surprise Kyle, dear. I've never seen Shoal or Nervadine and only passed through Gaust. Perhaps the Ol' Shakoor might even have some words of wisdom that might aid us in efforts in Adimand. I can *Teleport* back in plenty of time for the marriage and the Crowning. What do you think?"

Strongiron rubbed his stubbled chin with his thumb and forefinger; it sounded like a whetstone giving a dull blade its edge back. He furrowed his brow slightly, but the beginning of a smile showing in the little crinkles around his icy blue eyes. "It's your decision, Kari. If this is Dymetra's will, you will be in no danger. And if it is not...then I pray for your enemies." He smiled in full now, and retook her hand without resistance.

Kari's own green eyes sparkled with excitement. "I think your idea is excellent, Belara. Thank you for suggesting it. I will go. Kyle will be stunned!" She reached over and gave Strongiron a light kiss on the cheek. "I'm sure you'll keep Rookwood on the right path in my brief absence, won't you, dear?" She giggled, and then looked over at Belara, who watched pleasantly, legs crossed, cupping her tea. "Sorry, I was getting a little carried away. Come, Strongiron. You can help me pack."

The True Warrior and True Cleric rose to his full height, the hem of his white robes barely touching the floor. "Of course, my dear." He bowed to Belara. "Until our next meeting, I presume." He turned politely to leave.

"Indeed, Strongiron. There will be no shortage of meetings this month, I'm afraid. Take care, Kari. I think your escort would much rather trade places with you!" More seriously, she added, "Tell Serenity I said hello."

Kari turned at the door and nodded. "I will, Belara. Thank you again for the idea. And one more thing—the tea *Illusion*, it is fabulous. I must recreate it myself for guests on the road."

Strongiron looked queerly at his tea and snorted, shaking his head in amusement as he watched it turn into simple water right in his cup.

A slight blush appeared on Belara's olive-toned cheeks, but she smiled. "Careful—you mustn't reveal all our secrets, my dear."

As they left, however, only one thought on occupied Belara's mind: *Thank any God listening that I got rid of the Illusionist.*

~Tarsh~

Tarsh was beginning to wonder whether he would ever walk on flat land again.

Already he had spent more than a week hiking up and down steep mountains carrying two bodies in stasis behind him, defending himself from a village onslaught, gaving an accounting to an impatient Master, and taking a child prisoner. Zachary, stumbling into his midst alone, (at least as far as Tarsh could so far tell) was the best stroke of luck he'd encountered in a month. Throw in his escapades on the Great Isle, and he was seriously running on empty—physically, mentally, and perhaps most important, magically.

And yet he persevered. Not for Xaro, and certainly not for an old shield—an object with which his Master was peculiarly obsessed. No. What drove Tarsh to drive Zachary was the newfound knowledge that the singular source of his intense hatred was chained in Sands End, and the only thing standing between him and sweet revenge was the quest for this ancient artifact.

He had tied a piece of rope around the boy's neck like a dog collar, which he could electrify without taxing himself too much. A few early jolts quickly got Zachary's attention; no 'behavioral issues' surfaced in days. Sleep spells ensured the boy didn't try to run during the night.

The only close call had come during the third day. They'd passed a few spruce trees while climbing through one of the mountain passes, and Tarsh grew nervous when the trees seemed to sway. Only it was more like a twist…*like a person craning their neck to get a better look.* On a hunch (and with Xaro's warning about plants doing the Druids' bidding), Tarsh cast an invisibility spell and a muffling spell around them both. A Druid search party from the village appeared an hour later, passing by, calling out for Zachary, who was still, silent, and concealed. The Druids moved on.

The constant spell casting was taking its toll, however. Tarsh was no longer sure he had the strength to *Teleport* in a pinch. He needed a few days of uninterrupted sleep…days he didn't have.

"How much farther until we reach the catacombs, Zachary?" Tarsh asked. As bad as he felt, the boy looked worse. Zachary could call water down the mountain to quench their thirst, but he was unaccustomed to forced marching day after day, living on dried rations. Furthermore, an ugly, black, circular ring-scar had also formed around his neck from the electric shocks Tarsh had sent down the rope early on to emphasize the seriousness of their journey. "If this is some charade, I will—"

"No charade. The entrance is not far now." He answered weakly, desperately. "As we descend."

The shadows appeared quickly in the mountains, and twilight rushed into night. The two had descended for a long time down a series of tedious switchbacks, often on a path no more than three feet wide, with a sheer drop of a thousand feet on one side. Tarsh didn't fear falling; he was pretty confident he could still *Levitate*, but that didn't make the vertigo-inducing drop-off less intimidating. He eventually cast a couple *Glowballs* to safeguard their footing until they finally reached a flat area. The crescent moon hardly lit up anything in the mountains.

That was when Zachary made his first unprompted comment: "We're here." He pointed to a cave at the base of the plateau. The switchback they had been following continued downward toward the Dusty Plains.

Tarsh pushed his *Glowball* to the cave mouth, and even sent it inward a little bit. He could see nothing unusual.

"No marker? The greatest True Cleric—excuse me—*Druid*, who ever lived is buried here, and there is no sign? No ruins? What type of trickery is this?" He let some blue-white lightning crackle in his hand, ready to send it down the rope as a reminder to the boy.

Zachary flinched, slipped and skinned his knees on the loose rocks. "Please! No more. No tricks! I don't know why nothing is marked, but this is the place! We come here once a year as soon as we can walk…it is our pilgrimage. A Druid inside guards the tomb. Maybe he will answer your questions. That is all I know. Please Master Tarsh, please no more! I'll be good, I swear. I'm not lying— all truth. No tricks." He was clutching the rope, tears mixing with the dirt on his face to give him a smudgy, pathetic look.

The children. Let the villagers see the price their shut lips will cost them.

Tarsh exhaled and saved his magic. "Very well. No tricks. A Druid inside, you say? Then we shall both enter, and if *he* attempts to stop me in my quest, it will be *you* who suffers alongside him." He gave the rope a firm but short jerk. "Lead the way."

"Tonight?" Zach asked as he quickly scrambled to his feet.

Tarsh didn't bother to reply. He just pointed to the cave and sent both *Glowballs* in ahead of them. Zachary ducked his head despite the easy clearance.

Inside, the cave walls were smooth, as if polished by water. Knowing the Druidic gifts, perhaps they were. The cave floor began to descend as well; they were walking into the heart of the mountain.

Fifteen minutes of slow descent culminated in a spacious room, perhaps twenty feet square, with a firepit in the center that corralled dancing blue tendrils of an *Everflame* spell. Murals adorned each wall. On the first was the scene of two young men bent over a piece of parchment. The writing on the parchment seemed to glow, or at least reflected the light of the *Glowball*.

The second was clearly a picture of a city. In the foreground was the entrance, lined with columns, and in the distance in a corner of the mural was a five-spired castle in the mountains. It was a beautiful-looking stronghold, but the city in the foreground was absolutely pristine.

The third mural depicted a path made of brightly colored stones that rolled gently over a few hills to a small dwelling in the background. Lions and sheep were painted on the grass, oddly lying together.

The fourth mural was behind them, on the wall next to the opening through which they came. It showed an irate woman in white with her hands rolled up into fists. Cowering at her feet was an old man, both arms thrown over the top of his head.

"The Hall of Consequence," said a familiar voice behind Tarsh.

He spun around, involuntarily jerking Zachary by the throat. The *Glowballs* quickly flew forward to illuminate the owner of the voice. Tarsh immediately recognized the speaker. *The bright green tunic, loose trousers, ridiculous hat…*

"You!"

"Me!" the man in the silly hat shouted back.

"What are you doing here?" Tarsh took a wary step forward.

"Just passing through. Slow day on the Staircase. And you? Tsk, tsk…I thought your eyes had healed over after your Climb. Surely you can tell the difference between a boy and a dog?" The funny-looking man waved his hand, and the rope dissolved. He walked over and hugged the boy. "Go comfort your mother." He snapped his fingers, and Zachary was gone.

Tarsh ground his teeth. "You fool. That boy was my leverage past the Druid guarding the object I seek."

Fate curled his lip at Tarsh. "It takes a serious intelligence deficit to call Fate a fool, considering I know everything, or nearly so, but then, I've never been much impressed with your mental acuity.

"No 'Druid' guards Windomere's Shield of Life...only me. The Druids draw their own conclusions when their Elders venture into the Hall of Consequence once a year. Far be it from me to rain on their parade; everyone likes to take pride in their identity, don't you think? If they fancy thinking that Windomere was a Druid and his tomb is guarded by a Druid, well then, that is the least of my concerns."

Tarsh just stood there, facing the man who'd refused to heal his facial scar the first time they met—a scar that Xaro, however, did heal. That was all the proof he'd needed as to where the *true* power lay. He steeled himself for a final confrontation.

"Very well. If you are all that stands between the Shield and me, then fight you I will!" He began to supercharge a ball of purplish lightning, dancing in his hands.

Fate just sneered. "As I said, you never struck me as a genius." He snapped his fingers again, and Tarsh's budding ball of electricity fizzled with a puny little *pop*. "The tragedy is that, unfortunately for you, it is your *brains* that will be required for you to leave here with the Shield. I will give you one clue, and then you must choose the Shield."

Tarsh narrowed his eyes. "What clue?"

Fate just smiled. "Follow me to the actual burial chamber and you shall hear." With that, he tipped his multi-colored hat forward, gave Tarsh a mischievous wink, and actually *skipped* through the mural on the far side of the room, right between the columns.

~Belara~

Peeking around a large tree, Belara took one last look in a small mirror she always carried to make sure her *Illusions* were up to her standards. Her skin tone was almost the same, but she'd darkened it about two shades. She had also broadened her nose slightly, raised her cheekbones, left her lips unadorned, and made her hair short and oil-patch black. She dressed humbly, in a comfortable gray robe that fit loosely. Of course, there was nothing for the eyes. Even a skilled

Illusionist couldn't hide her status as a True Mage. *But Kari could.* A shiver of jealousy passed over her like a hot wind, and was gone just as fast. *She's a young girl, untouched by reality in this Dark World— let her have her secrets and tricks. I certainly have mine as well.*

Subsequently, all her disguises required her to be a True Mage of some sort. Or blind—but most people assume folks who wore blindfolds were really True Mages trying to conceal themselves, so that bit of deception was pretty much useless. Fortunately, Belara had many aliases, each to suit her own purpose and agenda, and confining her list of identities to True Mages was not terribly limiting.

Satisfied with her appearance, she tucked her mirror back into her robe and conjured up the most perfect imitation of a grouse call, which were native to Filanthalas. She could have used her lips to make the call, but she preferred to exercise her magic.

In fact, she figured to get plenty of magical exercise today.

Cherokum, an elven scout for Chief Chocktaw, emerged from a nearby copse of trees where he'd been hiding. He carefully looked around, and seeing that they were alone, raced over to wrap his arms around her.

"Galihali! I've missed you." He kissed her all over before catching himself. "I'm sorry—it's just been so long. Forgive me. Your message said it was urgent and that you needed to meet in person." He couldn't help but let a sly grin creep back over his face. "Of course, I'm hardly complaining."

When he saw that she was not responding with her normal exuberance, he finally relented and straightened up with a growing frown. "What's going on?"

Belara gently pushed him away so she could look into his eyes. She put on her most serious, most grievous face. "Not here, dear. The trees hide much more than just you and I, my love. You must arrange for a private meeting with Chief Chocktaw. I have some news, but—"

"A private meeting with our Chief? Come, what is this about, Galihali? Is it about Niku? You know how proud our Chief was when you were accepted into the mage guard at Rookwood. Few elfs are so close to the throne."

"No…it does not concern Niku. In fact, it concerns Chief Chocktaw." Belara leaned in, hooded her eyes, and bit her lower lip.

Cherokum put his hands on her upper arms and lowered his voice. "In what way?"

"Please, Cherokum. I must see our Chief!" *A little shake here, perhaps a single nervous tear for added effect…*

At her shiver, he wrapped his arms around her as if she was cold. "Whisper your news in my ear, and let me help decide how to approach our Chief. You know I would never hurt or betray you, Galihali." He carefully ran his thick fingers through her short, black hair, kissing her forehead.

"Promise?" She lifted her chin, eyes glistening.

"Swear to the Gods of our forefathers."

Belara tried to smile, but let her head fall again. "I can't look you in the eyes—the news is just so evil." *And, amazingly, true!* She slowly stood on her tiptoes to bring her lips to Cherokum's dark-colored ears, where she carefully cupped her hands.

"The Queen is going to attempt to kill our Chief," she whispered. "I overheard it myself as she was talking to an Assassin."

Cherokum grabbed Belara by the shoulders and pulled her in front of him again. "What? Why would she do that, Galihali? This makes no sense. The alliance between Thalanthalas and Rookwood spans centuries. On the eve of war? No. You must have misheard."

Though her eyes really couldn't flash, she could certainly furrow her brow to express the proper amount of displeasure. "This is why I did not want to bring this to you. You know nothing of what I've heard. I thought you trusted me."

"I trust you, Galihali, to keep our love a secret. But this—this will plunge us into war! It makes no sense."

"I heard what I heard. I don't know why the Queen would hire an Assassin against our Chieftain. Who can say when a ruler gets drunk on power? Is it so hard to conceive that our Queen might be making a deal of some sort? Would it *truly* surprise you if some grand bargain had been struck to save her precious mountain castle by sacrificing our woodland home? What is Thalanthalas to her? Would she trade a piece on her gameboard for an enemy's piece she more highly valued?" Belara stepped forward, raising her voice into a whisper-shout.

Cherokum stared at Belara for a pregnant second. "Are you sure about this, Galihali? It will be the death of us both if you are wrong."

"It will be the death of our Chieftain if I am right." *Unblinking eyes, unwavering voice.*

Cherokum let out a long exhale. "All right. I will take you to Chief Chocktaw. Gods be with us if there is any truth to this, Galihali. May the Gods—old, new, fake, and real—be with us."

Sometimes the best-laid plans were the easiest to shred. That was how Kari felt.

Intending to spend roughly a week in each "finger" of the coastal cities, the plan she formulated called for a few days each in Nervadine, Shoal, Gaust, and Briz. She would then spend a little longer in Fostler to see her parents ("I'm a True Cleric *and* a True Mage, Dad!"), perhaps even longer still in Brigg catching up with all her friends, and spend the remainder of her time visiting her brother Kyle with the Ol' Shakoor. She could envision bringing multitudes to know of Dymetra, all while seeing a bit of the wide world and enjoying the company of those closest to her as well. She would then *Teleport* back to Rookwood with a couple days to spare before the wedding to help Strongiron, who was consumed with the preparations for the Crowning of a King. It was a *wonderful* plan.

Just one that wasn't meant to be.

This was the thought running through her head as she knelt before Black-John, the smitty from Brigg she'd grown up watching at the village's forge. She could still see his leather vest soaked with sweat, even in the middle of winter, the steam curling off his head so thick it looked like the man walked beneath his own personal raincloud. The muscles in his right arm bulged fatter than most men's legs, yet only unformed steel had a reason to fear good ol' Black-John; a gentler giant might not exist in all of Tenebrae.

Now, lying on his side, blood trickling from the corners of his eyes and nose, he didn't much look like a gentle giant. He looked like all the others: victims of plague.

Her twentieth prayer that day stemmed some of his bleeding. He looked like he would live to see the next morning at least. *Please Dymetra! Grant me more strength!* Black-John wasn't cured. The children she prayed over earlier that morning, however, were—she always started her day with the children—but at least the smitty's face looked peaceful. The coughing had ceased, and his breathing seemed steady if still shallow. *He may suffer ill dreams, but he should live to see another sunrise.* This was her ninth or tenth day in Brigg…they were now running together. In the time since she had arrived, she had probably slept twenty-four hours in total. Her energy was fading, and consequently her prayers were becoming gibberish.

"Come Kari. Take a rest." It was the voice of Serenity. Marik's school had been turned into an infirmary. Most mages who could *Teleport* had long since left; most students had fled as well. Some stayed, however, like Serenity, to brave the outbreak and offer what comfort and care they could. Some spells were helpful in slowing the spread of the disease, but the mages had no real healing skill. That fell to Kari when they saw what she could do.

"I cannot, Serenity. I see Melanie Goodwin lying there, and the woman was old and frail before I left. I have to help her." Wearily rising, Kari slipped on some blood on Marik's stone floor before catching herself.

"Nothing can be done for her any more, Kari. Please—rest properly tonight so that you may provide hope to those healthy enough to see you in the morning." She reached out her hand, and Kari took it. She *was* exhausted.

They walked outside, where the hot, sticky night was made even hotter by the central bonfire being used to burn the dead in a crude attempt to keep the plague from spreading. The smell was retch-inducing, and the women walked quickly past it to arrive at Serenity's home, formerly Marik's. Serenity insisted Kari stay there while she helped her hometown with this crisis. Kari plopped herself down into a chair as soon as the door was shut to the stench outside.

"Water?" Serenity offered.

"Wine, if you have it." *Let me sleep like a rock this night.*

Serenity smiled and brought two goblets out. "I don't want to keep you up—please turn in whenever you wish, Kari, but I do want to thank you for all you're doing. You are single-handedly saving this village."

Kari smiled wanly. "Dymetra saves this village. I'm Her hands and voice, that's all."

Serenity nodded politely, but said nothing further. *She doesn't believe, and I'm too tired to preach. So be it.*

Kari changed the subject. "When did you first notice the outbreak of the plague, and why didn't you notify Rookwood?"

Serenity crinkled her eyebrows into a frown. "Your colleague from Rookwood blew through here, looking for volunteers to support its defense. Some of the *men* left with her; she was…convincing." There was an unmistakable edge to her voice.

Convincing is one way to put it. "That would be Belara. She was the one who encouraged me to come here and speak with you."

"Yes, that was her name. The plague came after that, and some who were not inclined to leave their homes to defend your precious Rookwood changed their tune when the first drops of blood began leaking from our eyes. Soon only a handful of True Mages remained behind to tend to so many, and our magic does not seem to work. At least not fully. *Yours*, however, is extraordinary." Her voice began to rise. "As for help…if I thought the crown cared for us in the west, perhaps I would have asked for help. You know as well as I they do nothing for us on this side of the mountains. The crown asks for our scarce money and our best swords and our most skilled mages—all at the *slightest hint* of war—but let the *reality* of a plague come to our village, and see what help comes back our way! None, of course. But do you know what our practical little Queen *would* do? She would ostracize us and send magical messages throughout all of Elvidor—perhaps all of Tenebrae—telling everyone to avoid Brigg. Our own villagers can do as much when they flee to four winds. Frankly I'm surprised you came at all, surely word has reached Fostler by now?"

Kari shook her head. "I had not heard a word of this, Serenity." *Please don't ask if I would have come if I had known.*

Serenity swirled her wine, staring at Kari while the pregnant silence between them grew uncomfortable. She finally sighed, perhaps exhaling her ire. "I am sorry for my rant. It is just so frustrating to be this isolated. I am thankful that you are here. As I said, your power—at least when you are fresh—is extraordinary. You must share your spells, Kari. How are you saving so many?"

So many…but not nearly enough. "As I have said, they are not spells, but prayers. I would gladly share my knowledge, but it is Clerical in nature."

Serenity sipped her wine. "Perhaps when this outbreak is under control, you can teach me more."

Kari nodded through heavy eyelids and set her wine aside, disinterested. She rose to head to her guest room when she stopped just as suddenly.

"Serenity, your eyes are bleeding."

~Belara~

Belara softened her tone and took his hand, allowing herself to be led. They passed through the river with the brightly-colored pebbles to emerge on the outskirts of Thalanthalas. Of all the cities and villages Belara had visited, Thalanthalas was one of her favorites. The old magic practiced by the elfs, what some called Druidic Arts, resonated with her. The strong smell of cedar filled the air on this side of the river, along with the muted scent of sweet berries that her practiced nose easily caught.

They passed by the scentless *cicutorum* bushes, which Cherokum gave a wide birth. One prick from the thorns causes unquenchable thirst, leading to inevitable death by drowning. Up the stone path they walked, with Cherokum waving occasionally to out of sight elfs that Belara knew were watching them. Massive trees framed either side of the path leading to the woodland city.

As they passed between the two towers that marked the main gate, Cherokum turned to Belara. "I don't know if he will see us right away. I will tell him it's urgent, but then every request for his time is urgent. How long can you stay, Gali?"

Aw, he's using my pet name. "An hour, no more. I have a friend covering for me in Rookwood, believing this to be a 'short visit' to see you. I did not want to wait for my day off; I came right away, but soon I must *Teleport* back to Rookwood." She put on a disappointed face. "I'm afraid I won't be able to stay this time, Cherokum." She quickly turned serious once again. "Chocktaw. This visit is about him, my dear."

The elfen scout shook his head, but smiled nonetheless through tight lips. Whatever he was about to say, he seemed to swallow the words and led her through a series of rugged hallways, often with trees growing right in the middle of them. They arrived at Chief Chocktaw's private room, where Cherokum asked the guard to announce them.

"The Chief is not seeing anyone this afternoon."

"Please tell him that we have an urgent message from Rookwood," Belara said sweetly. "One that must be delivered in person."

"You are here on the Queen's authority?" The guard raised his eyebrows.

"Absolutely. Whatever our Chief is doing, I can assure you it is less important than the news I bear." Belara, still disguised as Galihali, stepped forward and gently pressed her hands together in the universal gesture of pleading. "Ten minutes—can you tell him I need ten uninterrupted minutes?"

The guard shifted his eyes from Belara to Cherokum, his mouth tight like he was sipping vinegar. "Wait here."

Cherokum and Belara stared at one another in silence, him with a *well, we gave it our best shot* expression on his face. Belara was already preparing to put the guard (and Cherokum) to sleep in order to break into the room. The *real* Galihali, who was a Mage Guard under Niku, was already going to die in all likelihood. *What's a ruined love affair when you're going to be (falsely) accused of instigating a border war anyhow?* Belara liked Galihali…thought she was a hardworking, competent True Mage. Young, perhaps, but skilled. And most critical…she was an Elf. When it got right down to it, Belara needed an elfen True Mage with access to the crown in Rookwood, and that was a population of one. *Tough break, Gali.*

"You may have ten minutes," said the guard upon his return.

Belara smiled broadly and nodded, the pinch of sand finding its way back into one of her inner pouches. Cherokum clapped the guard's shoulder with a word of thanks and followed Belara into the private audience parlor of Chief Chocktaw.

The room smelled of light incense and spiced wine. *Silverfist would love this,* was Belara's first thought. There was a tinkling on her left from a fountain. A beautifully sculpted woman poured an endless stream of water over a single, brightly-colored flower. Belara turned away from the statue; for some reason, the fountain made her nervous. She stepped forward and knelt before Chocktaw.

"Ker-Tok," said the Chieftain. The curved, floor-to-ceiling windows began to darken until they were opaque, but several *Glowballs* replaced the lost light. "Arise and welcome, Galihali. You as well, Cherokum. Please, sit, enjoy some wine and make yourself comfortable." The Chief, however, remained standing and faced them both. "My guard said you had an urgent matter from the Queen to discuss with me?"

Not much for the usual regalia today, I see. She rose and passed the wine to Cherokum; this was hardly a time to pour herself one. *Maybe tonight, if all goes well…*

Cherokum looked at her with big eyes. He was trained as a scout, and Belara imagined he would be nearly unflappable. He took the wine and poured himself a generous glass, but the tiny beads of sweat at his hairline and saucer-sized eyes told the real story: *he's an absolute wreck.*

Belara stood up and plunged right in. "Chief, I bring you terrible news. I have heard that our Queen plans to kill you."

He stared at Belara for a second or two, clearly trying to process the information. He pushed his chin outward a bit; it made him look haughty and superior. "And why would she do that? Is she worried what kind of gift I may bring to her wedding?" If it was a joke, nobody cracked a smile. He stepped forward and put his hand on Belara. "Tell me how you came to know this information."

"I was on duty just outside the Queen's very own parlor when I heard her mention the word *Elfs.* She was alone with an out-of-town visitor who I did not recognize. Being Elfen myself, I—"

"You eavesdropped on our Queen?!"

Belara hung her head just long enough to appear properly shameful before sticking her own chin in the air defiantly. "Yes, Chief, and a good thing my curiosity was roused. She was talking to an Assassin!"

Chief Chocktaw shook his head. "Galihali, you must be mistaken. Queen Najalas is more than our Queen; she is a friend. But more so than even our friendship, she is smart. *Prudent.* Of what possible value to her would my death bring?"

Belara put her hands on her hips and stayed silent for a moment or two, letting the question marinate between them. The posture was calculated, for sure, but one she hoped would lead him to his own conclusion. Finally, she said, "For only one logical reason, Chief."

He narrowed his eyes severely. "You think she's made some kind of *deal* with this monster from the West? That is insane, Galihali. I cannot believe that."

The hook is set, the fish is tiring, now for one good snap of the line. "I couldn't either...but perhaps you will believe this."

Belara reached into her robes and pulled forth a small, smooth ball roughly the size of a lemon.

Cherokum stepped toward her. "You have a Memory Ball?"

Belara nodded. "All Mage guards carry them. Our role is to record the petitioner's requests and the discussions and decisions made by the Crown, unless we are instructed otherwise." She released the ball, and let it hover in the air between the three of them. She turned back to face Chief Chocktaw. "Would you see the recording on it?"

"I would...but how did you get it?"

"I did not like what my ears were hearing outside the Queen's parlor. So I pushed this Memory Ball into the room as unobtrusively as I could. You have to understand, Chief, I realize this is treason. My first loyalty is to my people. Up until recently, it has been a great source of pride to represent our people in Rookwood as a Mage guard for our Queen. This conversation has changed all that for me."

She knelt one more time. "If you are not convinced and wish to hand me over to our Queen, I will accept your judgment, but I pray that you will at least treat this information with great care, for I know she is playing you false."

"Show me."

Belara rose and touched the floating Memory Ball, which opened like an egg split cleanly down the middle. The two half-spheres folded up, and an image and voices began pouring out, filling the space between the three of them. It was exactly like the Queen's private sitting room, although the angle showed only the bottom half of one man who was seated and one woman who was seated as well. The conversation began in mid-stream.

"—I assume you're wondering why I summoned you." The voice of a woman who sounded identical to Queen Najalas.

"Not really. Typically, one reason and one reason only elicits an invitation, my Queen. I know you employ a handful of my Guild here in Rookwood, just in case court politics grows a little ugly; I can only assume that the task you have in mind is beyond your confidence in their abilities? Am I correct?" A pause. "I do believe I have undervalued Elfish wine. Being half-elfen myself, perhaps I am a bit biased against them; this is a marvelous vintage, my Queen." The voice of a man. Belara gauged Chief Chocktaw's and Cherokum's facial expressions; neither seemed to recognize the voice.

"Glad you like it. I'll see you leave with as much as you can carry. Yes. You're correct. I'll get to the point."

The Queen's voice continued. "I want you to find me an Assassin capable of killing Xaro."

"That will be expensive."

"Money from the treasury is the easiest thing to replace. My question is who can do it?"

"I don't think gold is all that will be needed."

"Land, titles, what? Explain."

"New assassins will work for gold. They have little, and are accumulating their stakes. They'll take any assignments, even death wishes, for a lucrative contract. They are young, talented...and wholly inexperienced for the type of assignment you have in mind."

"I know. That is why I have no interest in the ones on my staff. They are young. I tolerate them, knowing that my husband thought it prudent to have someone available, should a rival emerge. He was never paranoid about losing power, just...prepared to defend it, shall we say."

"Yes, I knew King Alomar quite well. He is missed."

"Yes, well. Elvidor falls to me to rule now, and rule I shall. If I can cut off the head of this serpent that moves against us, I will. Doing so would save many good men from death, many good woman from being widowed...and worse."

"As I was saying, this will require someone very experienced. Someone who, frankly, probably doesn't need the gold."

"You?"

"Oh, my Queen. You flatter me. But no, I am not the right person for this job, nor would I take it even if you offered me the chance to rule in your stead as payment."

"Then who? Who do you recommend?"

"The only Assassin that might take a contract such as this is Cheyenne."

"And what will this Cheyenne require as payment for her services?"

"The gold of ten thousand per kill is the easy part for you," the man said. *"For a political assassination of this magnitude, however, Cheyenne will want a political assassination in return. She will want the dead body of the Elfen Chieftain Chocktaw served up to her as payment."*

"You know that is her price? How do you know this? Why would she want Chief Chocktaw dead?"

"Her reasons for wanting the Elfen Chieftain dead are her own, but I know her quite well, my Queen. If you let your feminine imagination run wild, perhaps her reasoning will not be so hard to grasp? Regardless, she is the only one who could reasonably get close enough to the man you are targeting. I can speak for her; she will accept a contract for Xaro. But are you willing to kill your ally? Will you risk war with the Elfs to save war from afar?"

"I will not move against the Elfs without proof."

Low laughter.

"Of course. Terms will be proof of Xaro's head before you move against Chocktaw. That would only be fair. We deliver one assassination before you deliver yours."

"Fair is not the word I would use."

"Nevertheless, those are the terms. Do you accept?"

A pause. The woman stirred and stood up finally, and as she did so, her face came into view from the angle at which the Memory Ball had been recording, the unmistakably image of a very pale, thin-lipped Queen Najalas. She had walked over to where the man with whom she was speaking was sitting, and extended a hand.

"We have a deal."

The imagery faded like smoke before a gust of wind. The shells of the Memory Ball closed, and Belara reached up and gently grabbed the small sphere. Chief Chocktaw snapped his hand out and grabbed her wrist.

"I will keep this," he said.

Belara looked up at the leader of the Elfs. His grip on her wrist was like an iron shackle, and the cords in his neck could be seen pressing against the sides of his dark flesh. His eyes were smoldering. *The man is irate…and the fish is in the boat.*

"You may keep it, Chief, but it will only open at my touch. My Memory Ball, my touch—that is the way the magic works. If you wish to confront the Queen—"

"No. Not yet. But—"

"Then let me make a suggestion. Let me return to Rookwood with it, and I will gather more evidence. You take the precautions necessary, and begin planning your response, my Chief. If and when you wish to confront her, I will be ready with it."

"You do not have another one of these?"

"I do not. Having one would raise suspicion at a minimum, and get me demoted to the point of uselessness at the maximum should I go to Niku asking for a new one. The Memory Ball does not leave a Mage guard's posession…not if they wish to remain part of the guard."

Chief Chocktaw slowly relaxed his grip, releasing her wrist. "Very well. I have much to consider. For now, your idea makes sense. I will communicate with you via Cherokum if there are to be different arrangements made. Until then, return to your post in Rookwood, and consider yourself a spy for your people until…"

"Until we battle." Cherokum spoke up, his eyes blazing. Whether in rage over the Queen or with pride for his beloved Gali, she could not tell.

"It will be as you command, my Chief." She nodded and then turned to Cherokum and gave him a sad smile. "Would that we had more time, but I must return." She put her lips to his forehead and kissed him gently, pulling away quickly and modestly before he might embrace her again. "I will keep you updated, and we shall see one another again soon."

With a bow to the Chief, Belara *Teleported* away, laughing to herself the whole way. *I wonder if he is spinning through all the women he may have known to try and guess which one might be 'Cheyenne'…*

CHAPTER EIGHTEEN: GIFTS FOUND, LEFT, AND GIVEN

~Queen Najalas~

For Victor, the days moved too fast. For Strongiron, they moved too slow. For the rest of her court, and the stuffy nobles from out-of-town, they also moved too fast. "The preparations will never be complete for a wedding such as this!" or "We'll never get there in time!" or "If we only had more time to explore the splendor of Rookwood!" Such was the sentiment of most.

But for Herodius and the Queen, the days were interminable. An urgency charged her desire to be coupled with her husband-to-be…physically, emotionally, and politically.

When the morning of her wedding finally came, a feeling of relief, not anxiousness, enveloped her like a warm, salted bath. Usually of a mind to let the royal primping slide for her daily sessions in court, today would be different. Today she would stand before all of Elvidor (at least those who could travel or *Teleport*) as a widowed Queen for the last time. Today she would acknowledge a new King. And tonight…perhaps she would finally create an heir.

At this, she did feel a bit of anxiousness.

"Are you nervous, my Queen?" asked one of her two attendants timidly. "It is good to see you smile so."

Queen Najalas looked at the young woman who was arranging her gown—a simple white affair that was elegant, but not ostentatious. She was the only one who liked it; everyone else wanted one with a longer train, more jewels, more *flourish.* The Queen overruled them all, and had this one made instead. *Practical.*

"Nervous? No, not nervous. I am excited for the people, however. This is a momentous day for Elvidor that will give everyone a chance to celebrate after a terrible winter; a welcome distraction for many amid the rumors of war that haunt us."

The young woman nodded demurely and kept running a needle through the hem, making a final adjustment, when a knock sounded on the heavy wooden door of the bedchamber.

"My Queen, you have a visitor." It was Jonathon's voice, not one of Simon's Guards.

"I am sure I have many visitors this day. They will have to wait, Jonathon." She sighed. A request from Jonathon usually meant some Lord or Lady from out of town wanted a moment with the Queen.

"Have them visit with Strongiron, if you please." He had been invaluable in this capacity.

"My Queen, you will want to see him. Alone."

The two attendants stopped what they were doing and looked up at their Queen, awaiting instruction. She looked down at her dress and in the mirror at her face. The top hung about her slender bosom unflatteringly, and her eyes and cheeks lacked color. *Not that extra time spent painting my face will do much to improve it.* She tightened her lips. "Go on, ladies. I won't be long. If my Steward deems it important enough to interrupt your work on a day like this, than it must be important indeed."

The girls stood, bowed low, and prepared to exit as the Queen called out to Jonathon to send in this guest. When they were alone, it was obvious why her Steward allowed him an audience. He was carrying a gift box, exquisitely wrapped in colorful paper. The ribbon and bow were silver.

"Your Majesty," said the man with the gift.

"Silver," said the Queen. She was anxious now. Quite anxious indeed. "I did not expect you at the wedding."

"Nor should you. I prefer my celebrations to be of the quiet variety. The pageantry that will unfurl in a couple hours is a little too...*public*...for my liking. Nevertheless, I would be remiss if I didn't at least extend to you my congratulations." He walked toward the Queen, chiseled as ever, wearing a tunic that clung to his torso and a leather vest covered with pockets. He knelt before the Queen and offered his gift. "For you."

The Queen took it. "Thank you. Herodius and I look forward to opening our gifts on the morrow. Is there—"

"Open it now, my Queen." It was not a request.

She stiffened. Heart racing, she said nothing in return to the head of the Black Guild. The paper crinkled slightly under her fingers. The bow was beautiful. She narrowed her eyes and handed it back to him.

"Open it yourself for me, if you would have me see it now."

Silver smiled, and it was a greasy-looking smile. His hair was only lightly threaded with grey (silver?), and was slicked back. "Of course. As you wish."

He took the box and pulled the end of the bow effortlessly. The covering came off the plain wooden box, which was latched but unlocked facing him, with hinges on the other side facing the Queen. Silver lifted up the top of the box to look inside. "For you." He spun the box around and handed it to her.

Inside was exactly what she expected—what she both hoped for and most feared. It was a human head. The smell hit her before the visuals, but she didn't flinch.

"Is this Xaro?" She would have recognized Malenec, and the head was clearly human, not ogre.

"Indeed it is. Your war with this man is likely averted. Cheyenne did not stick around for the after-effects, but my eyes in his camp tell me that it is in complete disarray. He held them together because they feared his God. Nothing quite says that God has abandoned you like the severed head of your leader. Their forces may scatter to the four winds, my Queen."

She looked at the head. Its eyes were white. "Strongiron said Xaro had brown eyes."

"Indeed he did…while he lived, he disguised them with spell craft. Once he died, they became white like every other True Mage's." Silver pointed at the box. "Of course, I would encourage you to share this news with your small council. Let Strongiron confirm his identity."

"And the other two? The Cleric and the Ogre?"

At this, Silver came forward and gently shut the lid of the box while it was still in her hands. "Yes…but now we come to the point. The gold I will take now, but your additional contracts will not be fulfilled until you can show me similar proof that Chief Chocktaw has been slain. Unless…"

"Unless what?"

"Unless, of course, you wish to give me the contract for the Elfen Chieftain as well. I have other assets that are close to the Chief, and I can satisfy your end of the contract with Cheyenne without you having to become, shall we say, entwined?"

"You knew this would be the choice I would have to make at the beginning of our discussion." She curled her lip distastefully.

"It did strike me as the most logical outcome, yes." *Again with the greasy smile.*

The Queen took the box and set it in the far corner of her room. "Of course you did. Very well. So be it. I will convene a meeting of my small council. *If* the head is confirmed, you shall have your contract for…for Chief Chocktaw." Her mouth dry, she could hardly breathe. The room felt small. Stifling. She poured herself a glass of water, wishing it were anything stronger.

"When can I expect our business to conclude? As I said, I do not plan on attending the festivities. I would like confirmation today."

"Today is quite busy, Silver, in case you haven't noticed." *God, my crown for a pint right now!*

"Indeed, it is. A decomposing head in your bedroom is hardly an elixir for romance, and I worry that the passage of time might cause you to reconsider the nature of our agreement." He pointed a slender finger at the Queen and took a bold step toward the corner where she stood. "Today is a good day for confirmation, Najalas. It will take less than two minutes for Strongiron to tell you that is Xaro's head." He stopped and folded his arms across his chest. "I'll wait, my Queen."

Impertinent...what? Scoundrel? This whole situation was her own doing, and she knew it. If that *really* was Xaro's head, if he *really* was dead...there was a lot more to celebrate, frankly, than a wedding and a crowning. *Is the death of one good man against all—stop it.* Queen Najalas shook her head, not at Silver, but to clear her own thoughts. She wasn't going to allow that line of thinking to meander through her mind today.

She walked across the room, ignoring Silver. "Jonathon!" she called out. He came at once. "Assemble the small council. Ten minutes, in our meeting chambers."

"As you wish, my Queen." He turned on his heel and made haste, picking up on the urgency of her tone and request.

She turned and walked back into her bedroom, where Silver had leisurely seated himself. The Queen stared fiercely at him as she strode across the room and picked up the box. "Wait here. You shall have your confirmation within the hour, Silver."

"Always a pleasure doing business with the Crown, your Majesty." He bowed his head, but the Queen was already walking away, her mind going in a hundred different directions: *Xaro, Strongiron, Silver, War, Chocktaw, Elfs, War again, Wedding, Herodius, King, Heir.*

Ale.

~Kari~

Will it happen to me? Will I get it? Could I heal myself? Could Strongiron heal me? Should I call him and ask him to help me?

These were the thoughts occupying her right up until the day of the wedding, and with each passing day, the idea of exposing her beloved to this horror grew less appealing, and she knew why, in the quiet moments of honesty that she shared with herself: partly to protect him, but mostly to protect *me. If I contract this disease while working to save this village, at least he will be clean and fresh enough to perhaps save my life.* Oh, she told herself that he was busy…or that she shouldn't waste her energy contacting him…or that she shouldn't expose him to the disease. She had a parade of excuses, but deep down she knew that it was her own selfishness that kept her silent. Kari Quinlan wanted to save this village *on her own*, and she wanted to make sure someone clean could *save her* if, in the end, it came to that.

Another week of prayers, and the True Cleric did save most of Brigg. Serenity lived; despite her fatigue, her prayers were strong enough (or perhaps the disease was still in its infancy in her) to cure her. Black-John, however, did *not* see the next sunrise, nor did Melanie Goodwin. Brandon Gains stayed in Brigg and lived; Horace Packard abandoned his farm.

Much work was left to do, but she desperately wanted to see her brother and the Ol' Shakoor before heading back to Rookwood. Rising early on the day of the wedding, she made her farewells to Serenity, Mr. Gains, and the others brief. Much was still left to rebuild, much to heal, and much to preach, but her time in Brigg needed to come to a close if she wished to be present at the crowning of a new King. That, and about a week's worth of sleep would be useful before her and Strongiron set out for Adimand. Lengthy goodbyes at this stage would only cause further delay, and yet it was mid-morning before she was finally able to *Teleport* to the edge of the woods leading to the Ol' Shakoor's isolated cabin.

She knew she was procrastinating by proceeding with a visit to Kyle and Elsa, but she wanted to see them, had *planned* to see them. Even though her ability to *Teleport* made distance over land moot, there was something about being *this* close to her brother that felt logical to surprise them with a visit. *Ah well, what's one more day? One afternoon, really—it's not like we would leave for Adimand any earlier if I headed back to Rookwood now. I'd just spend extra time getting ready, which is laughable. I am still an Illusionist after all, am I not?*

Kari shrugged as she materialized near the clearing of the woods, where she was immediately struck by the sound of rushing water. Mist had congealed from the massive waterfall spray formed from ice melt that started its sheer descent from high atop Kraggentop and culminated in a large pool that eventually joined the Elomere River. *Home. This reminds me of home.* Even though she'd spent her early childhood in Fostler, she couldn't help but think of Brigg as home, despite Marik's treachery and the recent devastation of the plague.

Contrasting the fresh horror and imagery she'd just left with the pristine, just-as-I remember-it view of the falls from Kraggentop stirred her to the point of weeping. This voyage to the cabin was one of those traditions that would always evoke strong feelings of home. *Even for a girl who wants to see a bit of the wide world.* She blinked the dampness out of her eyes, shivered away the goose pimples, took a deep breath, and walked toward the misty cabin.

The door opened before she could reach it, and her brother emerged. Fit as ever, his blond hair perhaps a little longer than she remembered when they last separated, he turned toward Kari.

And stared at his sister through pure white eyes.

"Kyle!" She started running toward him and opened her arms wide for a hug, which he welcomed with a warm smile.

"It is good to see you, Sis. Elsa is inside preparing some refreshments." He hugged Kari tightly.

"Refreshments? Were you expecting company? I meant to surprise you two!" She pulled an arm's length away and gave him a playfully shocked look.

Kyle chuckled. "Prophetesses are hard to surprise, Sis. She doesn't see *every* future occurrence, and some things can change by sharing information, obviously. That is the point of young mages hearing their own prophesies, after all. Shaping the future."

Kari let her smile drop and turned serious. "So…she was focusing in on my coming?"

Kyle put his arm around her and began leading her toward the cottage. "No. But I was."

"*You?*" They reached the open door and walked in, still in conversation. "I see you have Climbed. The eyes look…good on you, dear brother."

"They look like they're supposed to look: terrible and terrifying," he replied. "But yes, I've Climbed. It probably doesn't surprise you that my study is in the Prophetic Arts."

"We make a good team." The smooth voice of Elsa, the Ol' Shakoor, drifted in from the adjacent sitting room.

Kari turned and quickly found Elsa, sitting peacefully next to a pitcher of cloudy lemon-sweetwater and a platter of small finger pastries—little biscuits coated with a white, citrusy frosting. She approached her and placed her hands on the other woman, who immediately stood up and embraced Kari, though she looked past her. *Still blind.*

"It is so good to see you again. You look fantastic," Kari said.

"Yes, well, Kyle tells me that my cat-eyes are still flecked with gold. I may look the same to you, but alas, nothing looks the same to me!" She smiled at what was clearly an old joke between the two of them. Kyle groaned audibly.

Kari sat down and made herself at home, helping herself to one of those tantalizing biscuits. "So, you two are a team now?"

"More than a team. He's my husband, and I taught him everything he knows," said the Ol 'Shakoor with a wicked grin.

"And I tell her everything I see," replied Kyle, winking for Kari's benefit.

Husband? "You're married!?" she exclaimed. "Why didn't you tell me!?"

Kyle slipped his hand into Elsa's. "We just kept it quiet, Sis. Few know I've even returned to Tenebrae. Just a quiet ceremony between the two of us. We meant no slight."

Elsa looked in the direction of Kari's exclamation, almost directly at her this time. "We would gladly take a blessing from one of Dymetra's True Clerics, however, if you're so inclined."

Kari stood, trying to sort through a cacophony of emotions: surprise, guilt, indignation, anger, joy...and a touch of sadness. "Yes. Yes, of course I would bless this union. It was, after all, in response to your prayers that Dymetra sent my brother back. May Her blessing shine upon the both of you until the end of your days." She swept the room in a flourish with her hands before sitting back down, somewhat embarrassed.

The Ol' Shakoor smiled. "No dear, She sent Kyle back because of *your* request. You're Her Cleric, after all."

Kari tilted her head, but didn't argue the point. She turned back to her brother. "You're really a prophet now, Kyle?"

He nodded somewhat solemnly, reflecting his sister's mood. "I am. Not quite to Elsa's level, but she helps me interpret what I've seen. I've gotten much better; to the point where I know we've saved several students a lot of misery by informing them of their fate should they Climb."

Kari sighed softly. "Did you see the plague coming to Brigg?"

Kyle's eyes widened. "Plague?" He looked at his wife, who looked equally stunned.

"I did not," said Elsa.

Kari nodded. "Many are dead, Kyle. Black-John, Melanie Goodwin. I saved as many as I could...I have been there for two weeks. Even my faith is not inexhaustible in the face of so much sickness. That was worse than the Afflicted."

Kyle shook his head slowly. "We had no idea…we weren't attuned to Brigg, I guess." He looked up at Kari. "That does explain why you look the way you do."

"That bad?"

"Pretty much, Sis. You look…well, awful."

She laughed a little. "My big brother's a True Mage, a married man, and now a prophet as well…yet as tactful as ever." She shook her head, but there was pride in her voice. "I"ll need some time to get used to those eyes, though."

"Alas, I guess only the women in my life get to have their cake and eat it, too," he said it nonchalantly, enough to stun Kari immediately.

She stared incredulously at her brother for his insensitivity. *Your wife gave up her eyesight for your best friend!* "I think your wife gave up her 'cake,' dear brother," she said with an edge.

Elsa put a warm hand atop Kari's and another atop Kyle's. "We're long past that, Kari. I don't look for offense where none's intended." She patted Kyle's hand. "Pour your sister and I some of that refreshing sweetwater, will you, my love?"

"Absolutely." He poured the drinks and looked up at his sister. "Of course I meant no offense. Don't you think it's amazing, however, that the only two True Mages I've ever met who kept their eye color are sitting next to me: the two most precious women in my life? The fact that you both have the most stunning eyes to begin with is just proof positive that Dymetra must care for beauty as well. At least, that's my story, and I'm sticking to it."

"Flatterer." Kari relaxed, however, and sipped her drink. *Astonishingly cold, given the temperature outside.* "How does this stay so cold?" She asked absently, speaking more to herself as she stared at the glass.

"Kraggentop water," Elsa answered. "Always cold, but there is more on your mind, I believe."

Indeed there was. While it's true she wanted to see Kyle, at least one other reason remained for her to delay her return to Rookwood. She put her glass down and leaned forward.

"Elsa, I would like to heal you. All this talk of your eyes only underscores it. Your sacrifice has never sat well with me since I became a True Cleric. It isn't fair that you should suffer for the kindness you showed Magi."

Elsa gave a gentle sigh. "My dear, since when is fairness promised to anyone?" Before Kari could answer, the other woman held up her hand and continued. "You may pray for my eyesight, and

I would be thrilled if it was returned, but I do not think that prayer of yours will be granted, regardless of your faith. It was a price I willingly paid, and one I have not regretted one day since Kyle came to join me. I count my blessings, child, and you should, too. I may not see the present, but how many can see the future? I may not walk alone in the woods, but that just means I am never lonely. I may not pour lemon sweetwater from my pitcher, but I can afford to import the lemons from across the world. I am still a True Mage, my dear, and a powerful one at that. You may pray for my eyesight, but Kyle sees well enough for the both of us." She put her hand back atop Kari's. "I would pray for you and Strongiron instead."

Kari straightened her back. "What do you mean?"

Now it was Elsa who leaned forward. "Pray for haste, Kari. I sense there is great danger in your delay."

~Tarsh~

Illusion. Seeing Fate skip through the mural reminded him of the power of *Illusion*, which naturally reminded him of Kari. *Where are you now?* he wondered. *If you could see me now, see how powerful I've become...* In both a personal and professional sense, in his mind he was still competing with Magi.

The thought of torturing him to death, of *proving* to Kari that he was superior to Magi in every possible way spurred him forward. He pushed his hands effortlessly through the mural and followed Fate into a smooth tunnel behind it.

"Come come, don't dawdle. Mages everywhere are lining up to meet me while I give you a grand tour of these catacombs. I'd hate to make their Climbs any longer than they already are."

"Somehow they'll manage." He moved in lockstep with Fate, their crisscrossed shadows dancing on the cave floor from the glowballs spaced at regular intervals. "Tell me—is that mural always an *Illusion*?"

"Of course not. The way to Windomere's tomb is sealed…unless you have a guide like me."

Tarsh put his hand on Fate's shoulder. It wasn't threatening, but it wasn't a friendly grab, either. "Then why are you helping me?"

Fate turned his blue-grey gaze on Tarsh. "I just am. As I once told you, there may be hope yet for your endpoint." He delicately picked the mage's hand off his shoulder the way a man might pick a moldy slice of cheese off his sandwich. He continued his brisk walk down the tunnel.

Tarsh again fell in next to him. "So the Druids can't come this far? To see the Shield, I mean. Has anyone come this far?"

Fate spread his arms wide, but didn't slow down. "The entire Shembolt Mountain Range is a burial chamber for Windomere, young Tarsh. A bit of history, while we descend.

"After Windomere and Quixatalor received their punishment from God, they—"

"Which one?" Tarsh asked. "Which God?"

Fate turned toward Tarsh, slowing only slightly. "The God. Dymetra, of course."

"People worship many Gods," Tarsh countered.

"So I've noticed." He continued. "Their punishment was severe, having to—"

"What did they do?"

Annoyed, Fate stopped to face Tarsh. "Didn't that Master of yours teach you anything? Actually, now that I think about it, I suppose it makes sense that he might gloss over a few details in this story. Still, we're only talking about the most famous Archmage and High Cleric of all time. Nothing particularly noteworthy or anything."

Rolling his eyes, Fate continued walking. "Anyhow, they created a terrible scroll—using their combined power, they sought to change human nature. They sought a means to 'flip' a person's moral center, if you will. The affects were, predictably, disastrous. Their punishment was a greatly shortened life.

"Near the end of his life, one of Windomere's last prayers was the creation of these Mountains—the Shembolt Range. He had studied with the Druids, having been raised here, and knew of their love for the four elements. Paragatha of Elvidor may claim him as their own, but when it was time for him to die, Windomere sought to be buried in the homeland of his childhood, here on Adimand. He lifted these mountains from the heart of Tenebrae itself; that's why the peaks are so symmetrical. You humans have such a limited creativity when the scale becomes so large. Anyhow, his tomb is encased under the mountains, protected forever from those who would seek to desecrate his bones or steal his secrets."

"Or his Shield?" Tarsh asked.

"Especially his Shield. It is one of the Artifacts of the Ancients."

"Yet you are leading me to it."

"Correct. See, spend some time with me, and you get smarter, young Tarsh. Like magic."

"And you know my intent is to take it and give it to my Master, and he does not serve your God."

"Xaro. Your Master's name is Xaro, and the one he serves is Kuth-Cergor. I am Fate, Tarsh. You can use names…I do know them all." He smiled and pointed up ahead to a widening of the tunnel. "And here we are…Windomere's burial chamber!"

Tarsh rubbed his hands through the hair made possible only through Xaro's blessing. He was missing something; he knew this didn't add up. The mural would have been a solid wall to anyone else. The idea that Fate was *leading* him here made this feel like such an obvious trap that had it been anyone *but* Fate, he probably would have smote them, turned back, and taken his chances wandering the Dusty Plains. It was infuriating. He decided to take a different tack.

"Would you have led Veronica down here? Since you are the world's biggest know-it-all, I assume you know that she was Xaro's first choice to find this Artifact."

"Indeed. That's a great question. Pity that I'm terrible at answering hypotheticals; in my line of work that could take all of eternity." Flashing the fakest smile imaginable, he nearly power-walked into the large cavern. "Behold…the entrance to the heart of these catacombs."

Tarsh looked. It struck him that it was circular…perfectly circular. *Like it was created instead of forming naturally.* The room was essentially a giant dome, with craggy stone walls lit by *Everflame* spells. In the center of the dome was a small lake, and near the center of the lake was a fountain.

A marble platform stood a foot off the surface of the water, anchored by a pillar that plunged into the lake. Atop the marble dais was a man on his knees, face uplifted, with his hands spread open, and palms up. Four thin streams of water shot forth from each palm, forming eight magnificent arches that landed near the edge of the lake at evenly spaced points along the compass. This created what looked like a bird cage made of water. What was so creepy about the effect was its near silence: not a splash or hardly a ripple. The jets of water pierced through the lake surface as a pin might slide through a cushion. Tarsh couldn't hear so much as a drop until he strained an ear at the very edge of the water.

On the far side of the cavern, facing the man in the fountain, was another statue, hidden in shadow. This one also looked to be white marble, and Tarsh recognized it from the mural in the Hall of Consequence. This was Dymetra again, only here She was not depicted as angry. Her arms were spread wide, and there was a slight smile on Her face. Eyebrows tented upward made Her face serene.

And lining the walls in a ring around the entire cavern were shields. *Dozens and dozens of them.* Tarsh stopped counting after forty. They were all unique—different sizes, different shapes, different materials. Some ornate, some plain. Some emblazoned, some sigil-less. All worn; some worse than others.

"So, here we are. Isn't this exciting? I can't wait for you to see how this turns out!" Fate rubbed his hands together.

Tarsh ignored him. "You said I would get a clue."

"Yes, and so you shall. Are you ready? Here it is:"

> *"I am lighter than a feather, yet heavier*
> *than a stone. I am as plain as the noonday*
> *sun, yet as hidden as the noonday moon. I*
> *am the Shield of Life."*

"There you have it. Pick the right shield, Tarsh, and it will serve you well." Fate took his hat off with a flourish and swept his arm in a circle around the entire cavern.

"And if I pick the wrong one?"

"Well, they're all good shields, Tarsh. They're just not all *the* Shield. The imposters may not provide the kind of protection Xaro is looking for in the heat of battle. And that would be such a shame."

"I imagine you would cry big tears over that."

"Bigger than you can well imagine."

"And you guarantee that the Shield of Life is here? This isn't some trick?" Tarsh was beginning to piece something together…

"Yes. That's the last question I'll answer about it though. But yes—the Shield is here."

Fail in the heat of battle…cry big tears. "And you can't lie to me?"

Fate cocked his head. "I never lie, Tarsh."

Tarsh nodded and began to walk around and look at the shields. The first was oval. Bronze…it looked like a quality shield. The next more rectangular, with a dragon emblem. The third was encrusted with emeralds in the center. The fourth was a simple wood buckler. And on he looked.

It was odd to be alone with his thoughts for the next half-hour or so, but Fate followed him around the dome silently. *Almost reverentially.* Without his constant japes, Tarsh could think. He was convinced the key to finding the shield was getting to the heart of

Fate's motivation. *Why would he lead me here if all other Shield-seekers throughout history were turned away?*

Only one answer endured: He wanted Tarsh to select the wrong shield.

He *needed* Tarsh to select the wrong shield. This other God, this Dymetra, must see the same thing Tarsh sees—the gathering power of Kuth-Cergor. If She can use Her puppet Fate to help plant a false shield in Xaro's hands...*that* is why She allowed him access.

She expects me to fail.

"I know why you led me here." He turned to look at Fate.

"Figured it out, have you? Well, illuminate me as to my reasons."

"Your God has all but given up on Tenebrae. She sees the coming kingdom of Kuth-Cergor, and She grows desperate. She wants me to plant a false shield in the hands of my Master, hoping to dash his hopes when he needs it most. You expect me to fail, but I will not."

Fate wasn't reacting with sarcasm this time. If anything, he looked uncomfortable. Finally, he said, "Then make your selection. Your only one."

Tarsh quit looking at the shields on the wall. These were all decoys, of that he was convinced. The *real* Shield of Life would have been buried with the True Cleric, and this burial chamber was missing one key thing: a body. That meant there had to be another room, unless he was under the water?

He came to the statue of Dymetra. He looked around for buttons and levers, carefully probing to see if there were further *Illusions. I wonder if the statue itself might be a door? Why else would it be here?*

Tarsh cast his *Levitate* spell, and slowly picked up the statue and set it down four or five feet away. Behind it was more stone wall. Disappointed, he went to *Levitate* the statue back in place when he felt a draft. Reaching for the smooth wall, he went to touch it—and his arm passed right through.

Illusion! Tarsh walked through and found himself covered in gossamer spider webs inside a small room, again lit by *Everflame.* He raked his face and hair to try and rid himself of that uncomfortable feeling, but his attention was soon drawn to the stone sarcophagus raised off the cave floor on a black marble dais. He could sense Fate behind him, though he never bothered to look over his shoulder. Creeping on his toes, he approached the coffin.

Before opening it, he scanned the room. No shields donned these walls. The shelves, however, were crowded with figurines, books, and scrollcases innumerable. Picking a tablet from one of the shelves, he could make out the following: *Let death cover me like ice, and let ice cover my death.*

Tarsh shivered. *Come to think of it, it* is *cold in here.*

He placed his hands on the edges of the stone that sealed the coffin, carving eight little ridges in the undisturbed dust from the fingers on each hand. "I am guessing that you never expected me to get this far, Fatum." He turned around to see the look on Fate's face. How pleased he was when it looked so glum.

"You may surprise me yet, young Tarsh. And that is not easy to do."

Tarsh turned around to *Levitate* the top of the stone away from the coffin, more energized than he had been at the top of the Staircase, more so than when he rescued *Sheila's Bane* from the eye of the Maelstrom. Power unimaginable seemed to radiate from beneath the stone lid.

Lying there, perfectly preserved, was the body of Windomere. *At least it looks like the fountain and the other murals.* He looked old, but not a spot of decomposition. Atop his breast was indeed a shield. Round, inlaid with white that looked like ivory, the edges were gold. No emblem...just a plain, white shield.

Plain as the noonday sun, hidden as the noonday moon. Well, the shield was indeed plain compared to most of the others, and it was certainly better hidden by far. He reached down and picked it up.

Lighter than a feather, yet heavier than a stone. It *was* light. Incredibly light—so light that a wooden sword might shatter it, let alone a real weapon. Yet the *burden* of carrying the Shield, knowing you were the only one truly protected from Kuth-Cergor prayers (and all the responsibility that might follow)...that burden *was* heavy. He turned around to look again at Fate., whose eyes were downcast. *It all fits.*

"This is my selection. This is Windomere's shield." Tarsh soaked up every bit of energy that seemed to be seeping from Fate, adding to his own exhilaration. "I've found it!" he yelled.

"Go then. Go and use the Shield. You can *Teleport*." He fixed Tarsh with a long stare. "And so can I."

"WAIT!" Tarsh yelled. "This is the one, right? It must be!"

Fate didn't immediately answer. He just cocked his head and sighed. "Perhaps I've misjudged you. Goodbye for now, Tarsh Minster." And he was gone.

You damn well misjudged me, you little freak. You and everyone else. Guess I was smart enough to find your relic after all. Tarsh prepared to *Teleport* to the port city of Kalimoran when he stopped. He walked out of the crypt and back into the cavern where shields lined the cave wall like works of art. A smile creased his face as he left a final surprise—a gift—for any who might follow after him, hunting for the Shield. Satisfied, he whisked himself away, daydreaming of his triumphant return to Xaro…and envisioning his next (and final) meeting with Magi.

~Queen Najalas~

Victor, Strongiron, Peter, and Simon arrived immediately. Jonathon next rounded up Herodius, who entered the room in mid-conversation about bad luck to see the bride on the wedding day before the ceremony. Jonathon was waving his hands dismissively in a way that twenty-four hours from now he probably wouldn't. *He better not, not to the King. Still, this was no time to cling to island superstitions,* she had to admit. Last came Niku, who shuffled in stiffly.

She looked at the seven men seated at the table around her. *Seven men, all serving me. This may be the last time I call the council to order.* While the burden of her rule felt like a mountain atop her bones, there was a part of her—a small part—that relished the power. Seated around her were likely the seven most powerful men left in Elvidor, and yet they had dropped everything to meet with her in ten minutes. She took a long pull of her goblet of ale to savor this moment, knowing that it was less about savoring and more about trepidation that stilled her tongue a moment longer. She was scared that the head might be a fake, *but I'm petrified that it's not.*

"Thank you for convening on short notice, especially today. I would not have assembled you all if the need was not great. Let me get to the heart of this quickly.

"A while ago, I arranged for an assassin to try and eliminate Xaro and perhaps his lieutenants as well. I kept this council to myself; I did not want any of you distracted, nor did I want to give you false hope. Your full attention on our war preparations was, and still is essential."

Several gasps ensued, and Victor leaned forward as if he was about to say something, but the Queen shot him the *I'm not finished* look and he leaned back, holding his tongue.

She continued. "Today, I have been offered proof of Xaro's death, complete with rumors that his western army is now leaderless…which brings me to my point." She had placed the box from Silver on a pedestal behind her, and she now took and placed it on the table with the latch facing her. "Number one, I wanted all of you to know that this plan of mine has been running parallel to your efforts. And second, I wanted you all to be witnesses to the verification of Xaro's death. Strongiron, I believe, can identify him. I am told that this is his head." She clipped her words matter-of-factly, the way a baker might recite an old, familiar recipe.

She flipped open the box, spun it around, and slid it across the table. The smell was immediate, and the men all began to gasp, grumble, and gossip while she took the opportunity to take a *very* long pull on her goblet.

"My Queen—!" Strongiron exclaimed as the head thumped against the sides of the box when it came to rest at his seat.

She did not give him a chance to finish a thought, and brought the chatter to a stop by slamming her goblet down on the table. *"Is that Xaro's head?"* she shouted over everyone.

All of the men save for Niku and Victor (who were seated adjacent to Strongiron on either side) stood up and walked behind the True Cleric to get a look inside the box. Strongiron rolled the severed head over so that it was staring up out of the box, its final expression one of pain and loathing.

"The eyes are white," he said.

The Queen nodded. "Yes. Apparently the magic he used to conceal his True Mage status fails upon his death, and his eyes revert back to the color they ought to be. At least, that is what I was told."

Strongiron looked at Niku, who slowly nodded. The old mage spoke. "That would make sense." He leaned forward, almost putting his entire head inside the box with the bloody mess, looking at something. "My Queen, if I may. I would call Belara. Let her inspect this for *Illusion*. It looks very real to my eyes, but let someone trained in her Art verify the auth—" He started to cough. "Authen—" He straightened. "I think water…" More coughing now, and everyone was looking at him.

"Niku? Are you all right?" asked Strongiron.

"Water…help me…" He grabbed his left arm and collapsed.

"Niku!" the Queen yelled. "Strongiron—help him!"

The True Cleric was already on his knees, scooping the old mage up like an autumn scarecrow that had toppled in the wind. He gently laid him on the table and began praying for help, for healing, for restored energy.

For Niku's life.

This can't be happening, not on my wedding day! Xaro's head lying next to Niku's body on the same table. "Jonathon! Water, quick! And Simon…go find Belara!"

Victor was looking fiercely at Strongiron, hanging on every word, like a man with gold riding on a miracle. Herodius had come around to the head of the table and put his arm around his Queen's shoulders. Peter held Niku's other hand, adding his amateur prayers to the powerful ones Strongiron was sending to Dymetra. Seeing Her work in his brother's life had been all the convincing the Admiral needed to believe.

Seconds flitted by, grouping into minutes. Jonathon came with water, which they pressed against his forehead, sprinkled on his face, and dribbled onto his lips. The water beaded and slid down his neatly oiled beard; he was certainly ready for the evening festivities. Breath, however, did not return to his body.

Strongiron looked up just as Belara entered with Simon. "Your Majesty, Niku Whitestone is dead."

"What?" Belara quickstepped to the table, and Strongiron stepped aside. "Surely you can heal him like the others!"

The Cleric's eyes were glistening; one good blink and the floodgates would open. He resisted and looked at Belara tenderly. "His time is done. Dymetra has taken him, and She will not release him back to us. His heart has beat to its conclusion; I cannot bring him back to his youth anyhow, and no grievous injury, even if healed, would add years to his life. He is just…done." The last word was a whisper, and indeed the blinking and dam bursting in Strongiron's eyes begun. "He is at rest now."

Stunned silence ensued; Belara just stared at her mentor lying on the table. She reached out and gently closed his eyes.

Herodius gave Najalas a shoulder squeeze. "Belara," the Islander who would be King began softly.

"Yes?" She looked up, and clear tracks from her own tears were running from her white eyes down her cheeks.

"Speaking for our Queen and for all of us, we need you to do two things, if you are willing and able."

"Yes?" she repeated.

"We asked you here before Niku's collapse. His last advice to this council was for you to verify that the head in that box is not an *Illusion*. Gruesome as this meeting has become, it is vital to our war and defense effort that we know for sure whether that is a real head. Niku trusted your skill as a Master of *Illusion* to spot any trickery."

"Would that we had Magi and his Staff for this," offered Peter to no one in particular.

Belara ignored Peter and looked inside the box. She sniffed, just like Niku did. She then pressed her fingers into the cheeks, into the eyes. She listened closely as she ran a fingernail against one of the teeth. "Which True Mage is dead? This isn't..." she trailed off.

What is your opinion, woman! The Queen leaned forward, her hands balled up into fists as if she could hold the stress inside her and keep from exploding by tightening her grip. "Is the head real, Belara?" She tried not grit her teeth when she asked.

Belara looked up. "I don't think we need Magi and his magical stick for this one. That is one very real, very severed head. It's Xaro, isn't it?"

The Queen and everyone else turned to Strongiron. "Yes. That's him."

Nobody cheered. Nobody celebrated. *Which is proper. If they knew the price I agreed to pay, they'd probably stone me right here. We'd have three dead bodies at this table.*

Herodius walked around to Belara. "Which brings me to the second request. Belara Kassar, on behalf of our Queen and all of us assembled here, will you accept the position of Head of Magic, and continue the work that Niku began, using your talents to prepare our mages for battle and to cultivate their minds in the way of your Art?"

He no longer waits for my guidance or rulings...but he honors me still with his choice of words. Not "for King and Crown", but "on behalf of our Queen." Finally a fitting leader...one even I can follow.

The Queen joined Herodius, slipping an arm around his waist, and smiled at Belara. "Elvidor needs you, Belara. We need you. Xaro may be dead, but Malenec and his ogre are not. There is no guarantee that we will now have peace. We must be ready. Our mages must be ready. Will you accept?"

Belara stood up with what can only be described as a *hungry* look on her face. She closed the lid on the boxed head with a resounding *snap*. "It would be my honor, my Queen." She looked over at Herodius, and for the first time since she entered the room (perhaps now that the box was closed) the Queen picked up the telltale scent of roses, vanilla, and some other exotic spices that followed her everywhere. "I accept, my King."

CHAPTER NINETEEN: JOY...AND PAIN

~Belara~

Belara Kassar waited patiently for the Queen to return to her parlor. Her *Illusion*ary disguise as Silverfist, the head of her *other* Guild—the Assassin's Guild where she was known as Cheyenne—was flawless. Her *Illusion*ary disguise as Galihali, one of the Mage guards, was flawless. And her *Illusion* of Xaro's severed head, right down to the details of every lock of hair, was an absolute masterpiece. It was a shame there was no one talented enough in Rookwood for her to apprentice, and a travesty that no one would progress her talent for creating an *Illusion* that could travel so far away from the spell weaver, as was the case with the head while she sat patiently in her own chambers. After the Queen left, Belara *Teleported* back to her own chambers where she dropped her *Illusion* of Silver. She correctly assumed the Queen would summon her, wanting someone to verify the head was real. Such a pity there was no one around to fully appreciate the skill of maintaining an *Illusion*ary head in one part of the castle while *Teleporting* somewhere else.

Well, truthfully there is someone talented enough, but she has chosen a different path. Keeping Kari away from Rookwood while the head was inspected was imperative...if she could tell that the tea was fake, she would have picked out the flaws in the head for sure. *Too many details to get them all perfect upon close inspection.* Introducing the plague to Brigg's water supply and encouraging Kari to visit Serenity may have been her most brilliant stroke of all.

Belara *Teleported* to the Queen's parlor after accepting the royal appointment following Niku's unplanned—yet convenient—death. She had just resumed her disguise when her thoughts were interrupted by Jonathon announcing the Queen's return. Her Majesty strode into the parlor, at least one goblet of good ale in her already, with noon yet to arrive. Belara stood up and bowed low.

"My Queen," she said, mimicking Silver's voice expertly.

"Silver." She handed him the box. "The death is confirmed, and you have the contract for...Chocktaw." The word came out of her mouth haltingly. "Be discreet. Take the head and your gold with you. Rookwood has nothing to do with these deaths. *Nothing.* Only my small council knows, and they will tell no one. As far as Elvidor is concerned, we prepare for Xaro as if nothing has happened, for until we see Malenec and his ogre, this Tar-Tan dead as well, we must assume they will continue with their warmongering."

"We take pride in our discretion, of course." Head properly tilted, nodding *just so.*

"I would ask for more than discretion, Silver. Do me one favor on this contract. I ask for mercy. A painless poison of some sort— please. Chocktaw is a good man. He does not deserve to suffer for this grand bargain."

Belara allowed a moment or two to pass, weighing the request. "Alas, you are talking about the leader of a nation. We must take our opportunities as they present themselves, but if multiple options exist of equal risk, we will pursue the path of least suffering. That I can promise."

Queen Najalas just closed her eyes and started rubbing her temples. "Go, Silver. Our business is concluded. I have a wedding to prepare for."

"Certainly, my Queen. Thank you, as always. Until we can be of service to you again, or have proof of the Cleric or the ogre's early demise, I bid you farewell." One final bow, and Belara swept out of the room.

When she was alone, she *Teleported* back to her own quarters, removed her *Illusionary* disguise of Silver, let the *Illusion* of both head and the box fade away into nothingness, and began to laugh. *War from the west led by a leader you think no longer lives, and war with an ally who now treats you as an enemy. Rookwood will surely fall without the Elfs, and when Xaro claims the throne, he will surely need a dark Queen...*

And in the meantime, with Niku's passing, I'm now Head of Magic for all of Elvidor and on the King's small council as well! Belara was not prone to extended laughter or giddiness, but truly— this day could not have started out any better, *and sometimes you just have to enjoy the moment.*

~Magi~

The hands. Tonight, it's going to be the hands.

A dark sky shrouded the campsite, the kind of clouds that preceded a windstorm. A clear night sky could be refreshing, uplifting even. Not this deep grey. The whole world felt oppressive, like darkness itself was embodied in those clouds, pressing down on Tenebrae. On their campsite. On Magi.

The normal blue flames from an Everflame *spell were replaced by the scarlet blaze she created herself. The last five minutes progressed at the pace winter sap thaws, with no communication between them.*

Just the steady shrrrrrrrik *of stone sharpening steel.*

"Veronica!" Magi shouted. "Please. Be reasonable!"

Shrrrrrrrik.

Magi looked out at the landscape…he knew the place. To the south lay Lake Calm, behind him, to the east, was Paragatha, where he had just left. He was headed west, toward the Crystal Mountains.

Was headed west. Presently, he felt like he was headed to hell.

He was seated on the hard ground with a large stump between his legs. Bolted to the top of the stump were shackles, special shackles that prevented him from any form of magic. He recognized these manacles, but could not remember from where. The fetters had no play in them; there was not enough chain length for him to reach a standing position, even if he bent over. His wrists were effectively glued to the flat of the stump three-quarters of the way down his elbow.

Shrrrrrrrik.

"Veronica!" he screamed. No bird cawed, no insect buzzed. Just the feeling of the sky pressing down on him from above.

The woman finally stood, apparently satisfied by the sharpness of the long blade. She was pale, but the scarlet fire cast a red glow over her features. In another world she would have been pretty; here she looked wicked, even more so when she smiled, shadows dancing across her face.

"Such a shame for a mage to lose his hands. Tenebrae is unkind to the handless, Magi. It is a Dark World, such a Dark World indeed." Her voice dripped with empty sympathy.

"No. No! Please no! Not my hands…I promise I won't hurt you. I swear. My magic, please. I can help you, just…not my hands, Veronica. PLEASE!" He could taste the sweat running into his mouth.

She just kept approaching, walking leisurely around the campfire until she was on her haunches, eye-to-eye with him, with only the stump between them. "Your pleas for mercy warm my heart, Magi. They really do. I've changed my mind."

Magi's white eyes softened as a sheepish, hopeful smile spread across his face. "Really? Thank you, thank you!" He started to weep, his head down and shaking between sobs.

"Yes, yes. There now." She placed her left hand under his chin and lifted his head back up to look her in the eyes. *"You shall have mercy, Magi. Instead of sawing your hands off slowly, I will cleave them off cleanly like this."*

Her right hand drove the blade down on his wrist—

"Shh!" came the whisper from the dark. "Quickly now!"

Magi opened his eyes. He was drenched in sweat, but then he was always drenched in sweat. *Every morning.* At least, he came to think of whenever he woke up from sleep as morning. In reality, he had no idea what time of day it was. He stayed awake as long as he could, knowing the misery that awaited in his dreams.

He rubbed his wrist…*he rubbed his wrist!* He looked around and saw he was still in the small cell somewhere in the bowels of…*of where? Sandy something.* But he was no longer shackled to the wall—his wrists were free. Bloody, bruised, but free.

"C'mon. We don't have much time!" A voice…a voice that seemed familiar. *If I could just think straight for a minute or two…*

"Who are you?" he asked.

A figure approached, carrying a bundle of something. Slowly his eyes were able to focus in the scant light from a few distant torches. A woman's voice…but a man's face. Tall, thin, short black hair, holding something…

"Veronica? Is that you? What are *you* doing here?"

She threw him the bundle. Clothing. "Paying off a debt. Put those on—I can smell you from across the desert. The last trading ship departs this morning. We'll have time for a deeper discussion later. If you wish to leave this place, then get dressed, turn yourself *Invisible*, and meet me down by the docks. I am already disguised, and avoid attention quite well when I've a mind to do so. I *will* be on that ship. Move your bones!"

Magi's mind was slowly catching up to his hands, which were already ripping his waistcloth off and stepping into some heavy travelling trousers, high boots, and a blessedly fresh tunic. "My staff. The Staff of Wisdom—I cannot leave here without it. And Malenec has my ring!"

Veronica put her hand under Magi's chin in a manner that gave him *deja vu* whiplash. "Listen to me very well, Magi. I will only say this once. We. Do. Not. Have. Time." Her tone was steady, and her lips emphasized every word.

She continued. "If you wish to continue your hopeless quest to retrieve these trinkets, be my guest. My debt to you is paid. We—"

He slapped her hand away from his chin harder than intended. "Those are not 'trinkets'! Do you realize what I can do with those objects? I can *end* this war! I—"

She grabbed the scruff of his tunic. "No, Magi. You can't. We all have lessons to learn, and perhaps yours is this: you can't do this alone. Not with ten staves and ten rings. Tenebrae needs *you*—not some special objects. Dymetra will give you what you need, but if you insist on pursuing your own agenda, then your fate will be your own. I did not travel halfway around the world across land and sea to free you from this cell, only to watch you throw your life away on a fool's errand. I am leaving now. I've arranged for our passage on the last merchant ship, provided we get away from here before your next feeding, when all manner of alarms will be raised." She lightened her grip and instead put a hand lightly on each shoulder.

"Will you come with me? Are you strong enough to *Teleport*?"

Magi knew time was short, but something about the absurdity of her rescuing him seemed to break through to him. Leaving the Staff of Wisdom and his Ring of Protection behind was, however, a hard pill to swallow. Perhaps Veronica's invocation of Dymetra is what softened his stubbornness. *Or perhaps I just have so many questions for this woman that my curiosity eclipses my desire to retrieve those objects. Who knows?* In the dark, his face was inches away from hers; he could smell the sea in her hair. Peripherally, he saw her hands...her smooth, wholly attached hands. He closed his eyes, took a deep breath, and said the first thing that came to mind:

"Yes, I can *Teleport*. This hole in the desert may have drained me, but my well is hard to empty. If I follow you Veronica, I want to know how you got your hands back."

She graced him with a half-smile. "Despite your best efforts, you mean? Come...there will be time for all that later. For now, there are some bodies you can *Levitate* out of the way for me before you *Teleport* to the docks. Stay invisible, and follow me aboard the *Cornucopia*. It's the last trading vessel, and it is leaving *now*."

~Tarsh~

Boats. Ships galore, ready to be launched from the shores of a desert. *So this is what an armada looks like.* Every spot in the port of Sands End was occupied, and new launches had been built beyond those. Only a single channel was left—one way in, one way out. Tarsh watched as a solitary supply ship caught favorable wind heading out to open sea, the Endless Waters of the West. His ship,

The Bridgewater, was a small schooner designed for navigating straits to bring raiding parties close to shore. He'd made good time from Kalimoran, and *The Bridgewater* flew with ease through the crowded channel lined with heavy ships. The short journey to Sands End took less than three days.

Tarsh could still hear the exuberance of his Master's voice when he contacted him in Kalimoran to tell him the news and show him the Shield of Life…

"You found it? You have it? Show me! *Will you look at it…Kuth-Cergor has favored you and I, Tarsh Minster, truly he has! When our war is done, I shall have an exalted position for you in my empire. Your revenge on Magi is but a taste of the reward I have in mind for you when our conquest is at an end.* Well done.*"*

"Magi is still alive, waiting for me?"

"Indeed. My guards confirm his sleeping screams. Come with haste—find a fast ship. We feed him, but his strength ebbs. The Shackles of Ajax are a taxing punishment…"

That update had been three days ago. Now, this very afternoon, Tarsh would *finally* have his revenge.

He wore the Shield strapped to his back, under a heavy cloak. No one paid it any notice. Once the schooner was close to land, Tarsh didn't bother to wait for any tie-ups to disembark; he *Teleported* to the fortress atop the mesa on Sands End. Materializing in front of Xaro's private chambers, the guards were expecting him. He was shown in immediately.

"Tarsh!" said Xaro, who was alone, looking out from a balcony that overlooked the harbor below. "Welcome home…good to see you again." He walked over and clasped his hand in a show of informality.

Tarsh nodded, disengaged and took one step back, allowing room for a proper kneel down. He had envisioned this moment for days now. With a sweep of one hand, he brushed the cloak to one side and pulled the Shield off his back with the other. Rays of sunlight slanted in through the open balcony and struck the ivory circle perfectly. *Am I seeing things, or does the Shield appear to glow?*

"Master," Tarsh began, "Behold the Shield of Life, brought from the grave of Windomere by my hand at your command. Take it—I give it to you."

Xaro did not wait long to snatch it. "Well done, Tarsh. You have served me and my Master very well indeed." He slipped it over his arm. "How very light this is…"

"I found it so, too."

He moved his arm around, with the Shield strapped over his forearm. Tarsh knew that Xaro, as a True Warrior, had probably worn many shields. He seemed to move fluidly. "Not exactly the type of protection I'd want between my skull and a battle-axe, but against dark prayers and magic, I imagine it has no equal."

Tarsh still wasn't sure why Xaro would need such protection, but he swallowed his inquiry, for a far more pressing subject was on his mind.

"And now Master, I would ask that you take me to see Magi. I would like to see him without delay, if possible."

Xaro stopped playing with his shield to look at Tarsh, who was still on bended knee. "As you wish. I see no reason to drag this out further."

He carefully took off the Shield and slipped it into a box at the foot of his bed. Runes carved into the box glowed at his command and gesture, and again upon the lid closing. *A Warlock's Chest,* Tarsh thought. *Only the owner can get inside.* He had heard about these, but hadn't seen one. *Quite expensive…but then gold is nothing to Xaro, or any of us any longer.*

"Come. We shall talk and walk down. The dungeon is not far." He left the room, and Tarsh followed him.

Tarsh came quickly to the main topic in his mind. "Master, you say that Magi is weakened. Do you know how much?"

Xaro looked over at Tarsh with an eyebrow raised. "I fought Magi myself when he was at his peak…a battle into which I would not send any of my mages, especially ones I value as highly as I do you." He put a reassuring arm around Tarsh as they walked. "Krishnan is right; the man is a menace. He is confined by the Shackles of Ajax, and they prevent him from casting a single spell. I will tell you this: after what he has endured for the weeks he has been our prisoner, I doubt he would have the strength to make so much as a spark even if I *did* release him to fight you directly. But I will not do that. Have your final words with him as you see fit, and then destroy him such that the only remnants of his visit to Sands End are two arms dangling from Ajax's most wonderful Shackles."

The corners of Tarsh's mouth began to twitch upward as he tried to temper his enthusiasm. *Enthusiasm…or relief?* "Nothing would give me greater pleasure, Xaro. *Nothing.*"

They rounded a corner and came to a spiral staircase that descended. Xaro stopped at the top, looking around. "Hmm. There should be a guard here." He headed down, and the air quickly became greasy from the accumulation of torch smoke. His pace was a little quicker, two steps at a time.

The descent didn't take long to reach the bottom, especially when compared to the endless Climb that this staircase mirrored. Still, they had corkscrewed their way down a hundred feet before coming to a mammoth, double-bolted door. Xaro again paused. "Something is wrong, Tarsh. Another guard should be at this door." He turned to him. "Prepare yourself," was all he said. Xaro had already crushed a small marble and cast a *Shield* spell for himself before he lifted the bolts with another spell.

The oblong room on the other side was vast, and the stone wall along the outside was segmented at regular intervals into cells. Lots and lots of tiny caves, with vertical bars covering the openings. Xaro cast a massive *Glowball* to light up the entire dungeon. He walked— *nearly ran*—across the floor to a cell on the far side of the cavern.

Tarsh could see inside the cell before he heard Xaro scream: four men, dead. Their throats were all cut. And Ajax's wonderful shackles were empty. Bloodstained…but *empty.*

Magi was gone.

Xaro turned to Tarsh. "I swear to you by the power of Kuth-Cergor, we will find him, and you shall have your revenge, Tarsh. Whatever treachery unfolded here, I promise I will unravel it."

Too stunned to speak, Tarsh just nodded. *Magi is gone.* His carefully planned speech, the spells he would use to torture him, the final killing blow…he'd had it all worked out.

Magi is gone.

"Tarsh!" Xaro snapped, bringing him back to the present. "We shall council with the others immediately. If he is still on our grounds, we will find him. If not…"

Tarsh focused his eyes on Xaro, who had balled his hands into fists.

"If not, the time has come for our launch. The time has come for war."

~Herodius~

Apparently, one month was, in fact, enough time to assemble the entire continent of Elvidor. Looking out over the assembled crowd, it sure felt that way to him.

After much debate, Herodius himself decided that the ceremony should take place in the outdoor theater, away from docks, and in the heart of the city. Some (most notably Simon) advocated that the

Great Hall should be used in the mountain fortress, but looking at the mass of humanity below the stage, that idea now seemed laughable. No rooms were large enough to hold all the citizens and all the pilgrims who wanted to witness Strongiron place the crown upon his head. If you asked Herodius, this was a wedding first and a crowning second…but for everyone else, perhaps including even his Queen, it was the other way around.

They want me to lead them. On the precipice of war, and it falls to me to push us one way or another. He had never sought to be King, but then he never sought to be an Elder for his people on the Islands, he never sought to lead a rebellion, never sought to lead thousands across the sea on haphazard rafts, he never sought to put down an insurgency.

That is why you must lead, said a voice in his head…not his, but his bride to be. That is what she'd said many times during their precious moments of privacy…*you must lead.*

He scanned the crowd from atop his perch on stage. Normally wide-open fields where commoners could gather for a bit of comedic or tragic art to escape the drudgery of reality were now filled with thousands of Elvidorians. Over the last month, Herodius had met many—at least those he could see closest to the stage. Strongiron truly had been a godsend this past month, helping entertain nobles, answer questions, smooth over concerns, and most importantly, gain support. If a more well-liked, more well-respected man or woman existed in all of Tenebrae than Strongiron, Herodius had yet to meet them. People respected the Queen, but they adored Strongiron. Herodius may not have always appreciated his True Cleric's newfound faith, but he couldn't argue against it any longer. Not after Palinor; not after his own arm. Miracle healings aside, he had a chance to see first-hand how he moved among the people these last few weeks, and he was convinced the man was blessed: *nobody* built trust with the people like he did.

And in moments, he's going to confer that trust onto me. It was a heavy burden, but one Herodius embraced.

"Nervous, your Majesty?" Strongiron broke his train of thought. He stood next to him as they awaited the arrival of the Queen.

Herodius smiled. "A bit, my friend, truth be told. Just a bit."

"If I may…" started Strongiron in a whisper.

"Please. Speak."

"Wave to the crowd. You'll feel better, and it will give them something to cheer about."

Herodius chuckled. *Yes…let's wave a little.*

The crowd roared as he threw his hand into the air confidently. He began picking out specific faces in the crowd: Lord and Lady Hazelton from Paragatha; Lord Jamison from Shith; Lord Kensington, formerly of Kekero, who now made his home in Rookwood; Kari, who'd arrived just this afternoon from her trip out west, Jonathon, Simon, Peter, Victor, and Belara—his go-forward small council, and even Lord Corovant, all the way from Gaust (and dressed impeccably), had managed to sail halfway around the continent just to show up for this can't-miss event. There were, of course, countless others in attendance as well. The only notable absence was Chief Chocktaw, who sent his regrets; he was apparently under the weather. It was odd, however, that the stand-in for the entire Elfen nation was not Lady Elyn, his daughter, but Galihali, one of Belara's mage guards. Herodius liked Galihali, but it was a curious appointment; she wasn't exactly a 'state official.' *Something perhaps to run by Najalas tomorrow…*after *the wedding.*

Behind him, trumpets began to blare, announcing the Queen's arrival.

Oohs and *aahs*, gasps, and even a few squeals began to compete with the brass fanfare as the Queen *Levitated* over the crowd. She stood on a small disk, with her white dress spilling gracefully over the back. Slowly she rotated, just above the crowd, but low enough for all who made the journey to get a view of the Queen-turned-bride. Her mages lined the outside of the crowd on either side of the stage and easily kept her floating above the delighted cries and pointing fingers.

She has never looked more beautiful. The Queen may have been plain-faced every day prior and since, but she was anything but plain this day.

The mages gently lowered the disk to the stage, and Herodius's bride stepped lightly off it to stand opposite of him, with Strongiron facing the gathered crowd between them.

"You look beautiful," he whispered.

The Queen smiled. "Thank you, my King." Her eyes sparkled mischievously in a manner that was so out of character for her that all Herodius could do was grin back.

"Elvidorians," Strongiron said to the crowd. His voice carried beyond them off the stage, yet to Herodius it sounded normal. "This day we come together for a great occasion! We gather to witness not only the union of this couple, but the Crowning of a new King!"

All the work of the last month could now be heard in the roar of the crowd. *Now I see why we took the time to build this trust, these alliances, these noble relationships—it was for this support.* What felt like an hour-long cheer was condensed into less than a minute, and Strongiron let them voice their pleasure—even encouraged it with his arms.

Finally, he drew the shouts to a close and continued, turning to the Queen. "My Queen: Standing before your people, your King, and Dymetra's watchful eye, will you commit your life to Herodius as his wife, bear his children if you are so blessed, and lead your people through feast and famine alike?"

"I will indeed."

The crowd roared again, and a smiling Strongiron again motioned for them to tamp down their enthusiasm.

"Herodius: Standing before your people, your Queen, and Dymetra's watchful eye, will you commit your life to Najalas as her husband, welcome an heir to this throne if you are so blessed, and lead your people through feast and famine alike?"

"I will, 'til breath leaves this body."

Now Strongiron let the crowd's momentum build. He plowed ahead, his voice rising over them. "Then as the True Cleric of the True God Dymetra, I bless this union, and to Najalas, I give you Herodius…"

The crowd began to reach a frenzy, many of whom had been in their cups since morning.

"And to Herodius, I give you Najalas!"

The pitch was at its crescendo. Herodius drew Najalas close and kissed her heartily.

"And to Elvidor, I give you your King! Long live King Herodius!" With that, Strongiron lowered the King's Crown onto Herodius's brow.

"LONG LIVE KING HERODIUS!" echoed the crowd, reverberating off the mountains behind them.

Book 3: War

CHAPTER TWENTY: A TIME FOR TRUTH

~Magi~

The scroll...it had to be the scroll.

Magi stood at the rail near the bow of the *Cornucopia*, enjoying the fresh air and salty spray after what felt like an eternity in the dungeons at Sands End.

He'd spent the first day below deck; it had taken nearly a day just to put some distance between the armada of ships gathered around the desert fortress—a day which Magi spent almost entirely asleep, indulging in warm, comfortable dreams that didn't end with a painful torture scene.

Finally, they were able to head east, and were clear of Xaro's navy which had to have consisted of a thousand sea vessels. Magi did not want to be spotted...not with the naked eye, not with a *Farsight* spell. He had spent weeks below ground; another day or two out of the sun wouldn't kill him, especially given his need for blissful, uninterrupted slumber. Besides Veronica, only the Captain knew who he was, for which Magi was grateful.

That did not, however, stop him from jumping up like a schoolboy on the first day of study break when Veronica came and got him.

"Coast looks clear, Magi," she said, beckoning him to join her on the top deck. "Why don't you come up, and we'll talk a bit."

"Splendid idea." He led the way up the steps and hardly looked over a shoulder.

Now, as he leaned over the rail listening to the waves break against *Cornucopia's* wide hull, he kept coming back to that thought. Every one of his questions for her came back to this assumption: *someone has another copy of that scroll, and used it on her.* It was the only thing that made sense to him.

"So..." he began, admittedly lamely.

"So," she echoed, standing next to him at the rail, watching the bow rise and fall over each successive wave. Her jet-black hair was shiny from the spray, and her facial features restored; she had ditched her disguise, and her face was as creamy-pale as ever, but something different gleamed in her eyes, Magi thought. They were still that doe-brown color, deep and rich, but they looked softer to him. *Of course they do—she did just save your life.* He shook his head and chuckled quietly.

"What is it?" she asked. "What do you find amusing?" She flashed that same smile he saw when they were leaving the dungeon.

"Nothing, really. I'm just laughing at the absurdity of this...I'm not sure where to begin...I have so many questions. I guess the biggest one I have is simply this: you've changed. I mean, you've *changed.* The only thing I've seen capable of such a transformation is the Scroll of Tralatus...the one used on me, of which the only copy, I believe, is still in Xaro's possession now, along with my staff and ring. Do you remember anyone reading such a scroll to you?"

Veronica was looking at Magi, shaking her head. "It wasn't a scroll, Magi. I told you—I owed you a debt."

Magi chuckled again. "Hah! A debt? Surely you know I took your hands from you...what debt did you own me?"

The Assassin turned away to look out over the water. "I took your life once, and attempted to take it many other times. I attempted to kill your friend, Strongiron, many times. And the amount of successful contracts? I've killed dozens and twice that number again. You were right, my hands are killing machines, and by taking them, you put me on a different path. Perhaps unwittingly, but a different path no less.

"The brief version of my story is that Strongiron took mercy on me, and through his God, Dymetra, he healed my hands in front of the entire Valley of the Afflicted, where I was living after you maimed me. And I thank you for that...had I never been maimed, I would never have come to see the distinction between Dymetra and Kuth-Cergor. That was my debt, Magi."

"Which is now paid in full?" he asked.

She turned back to look at him, eyebrows elevated. "I would say so, wouldn't you?"

Magi smiled. "So...what now? We go back to trying to kill one another?"

Veronica relaxed, and again Magi was struck by the softening of her features. "You're not the one I want to kill."

"Who then?" It was Magi's turn to raise his eyebrows.

She sighed. "Who do you think? When you cut off my hands, all I wanted was to come back to Sands End to see if Xaro could heal me. He has healing powers—I've seen them. You should see what your 'friend' Tarsh looks like after Xaro blessed him. But Xaro wouldn't ha—"

"Tarsh? What about Tarsh?" Magi interrupted.

"He has joined Xaro. Effectively replaced Marik."

"I thought I had killed him," he said with a sigh of relief in his voice.

"You may wish that you had, should he ever meet you. I was there that day when you crushed his body, remember?"

"Pretty hard not to." Magi stuck his chin out, showing the angry white scar along his throat. *Courtesy of yours truly.*

Veronica reached out to touch Magi's scar; it was a gentle touch, and he allowed it.

"I am so sorry about that." She paused. "Do you believe me?"

Magi looked at her wrists—wrists that bore no scar whatsoever. *Why is she scar-free while I am not? Were we not both healed by the same God?* He reached up and clasped her slender hand into his, holding it loosely. "I want to believe you Veronica, but I don't fully…not yet. Not without my Staff." He let the hand go.

He then took a step toward her, however, and put a hand on each of her shoulders. "Perhaps that's a crutch of mine, as you said. My 'trinkets,' as you put it. Perhaps you *have* turned to a new season, as they say. But how could you be sorry for killing me? Was I not a consolation prize to your Master at the time for your failure to kill Strongiron?"

"Yes, but—"

"And, if we are going to be honest with one another over the next month we have at sea, then I can at least admit that I owe a debt to you as well. I would never have been cleansed of that cursed scroll had you not freed my soul from my body. Nor would I have brought back Quixatalor's Staff, either."

"Quix—who?"

"Never mind. I guess I'm trying to say we both have had debts cancelled. We'll just have to earn one another's trust a little at a time."

Veronica, though six feet tall, still had to look up a few inches to meet Magi's snowy eyes. "A little at a time," she agreed.

~Xaro~

Eager. From Tar-Tan's beady little eyes, to Malenec's impatient countenance, to Tarsh's frustration, his three remaining lieutenants were *eager.* Eager for war. Even Krishnan looked interested in a change of venue; Xaro would not leave his Master of Coinage behind.

"My friends, it is time. Tarsh has returned successfully with the spell components I sent him to find on Adimand. However, before we leave, I need to tell you that Magi has apparently escaped."

Krishnan sucked in his breath. "What?"

Tar-Tan frowned, while Malenec, sucking his teeth, curled his lips into a sneer. Tarsh shot him a glance at the sound.

"You had one of the most dangerous mages chained in our dungeon, and instead of killing him, you let him fly from his cage like a sparrow released in the wild. How fortunate we are to have you as our leader." Malenec's contempt poured out like body odor.

Xaro leaned forward across the table until his face was uncomfortably close to his Cleric. "We all agreed to give Tarsh his due, and to that promise I still hold us all. Nobody let Magi 'fly away'—he had help. Four dead guards were lying in his cell." He slowly unfolded his massive, meaty index finger to point at Malenec. "And when I find out who, *or what*, aided his escape, my wrath will be unquenchable."

Malenec did not so much as blink at the finger in his face. He slowly opened his gloved hands up with a shrug. "If you are insinuating that I contributed to this little escape, I would remind you that this man attacked me several weeks ago, killing several of my undead warriors. How were these guards killed, may I ask?"

Xaro, once again, picked up on Malenec referring to 'his' undead warriors. He let this one slide. "Their throats were slashed."

"Well, if I was a logical man, I would consider that whoever helped this man probably did not have any Druidic, Clerical, or Magical prowess. Surely they would have used such means to get past the guards without raising a sound, if they could. You are looking for Warrior, a Thief, or perhaps an Assassin."

The other two were looking at Xaro, and he leaned back, withdrawing his finger. "Perhaps, but I don't rule anyone out until more information is clear. An *intelligent* man, working his own agenda, might do anything to create a desired impression. Regardless, the man is gone."

"I told you he was a menace." Krishnan rubbed his hands together nervously.

"He is one man. What can he do against us?" Tar-Tan spread his enormous arm in a wide arc.

"He may yet still be here. We need to search for him! What if he was too weak to *Teleport*…he could be hiding right under our noses in this very fortress." Tarsh stood up, smacking a fist into his open palm.

"I agree. Malenec, your undead can sweep the castle for him, can they not?"

The dark cleric ran his thumb and index finger down his angular jawline, pinching his goatee. He fixed Xaro with those stone-cold grey eyes, rimmed in black. "Of course, Xaro. None could do it faster. Can I assume then that you trust I had nothing to do with this colossal screw-up?"

"You can assume that I know how to deploy *my* resources effectively," he shot back. He turned to Tarsh. "That said, I do not think we will find him. He could *Teleport* anywhere on Ipidine, and be on a boat anywhere." He turned back to Malenec. "Although, *logically,* he will likely return to Rookwood. When we meet next, I imagine it will be with the winds of war all around us."

He looked at all of them in turn now. "How soon can we launch, Tar-Tan?"

"Per our discussions, you and Tarsh must leave in the first two waves. You have the furthest to sail, with you marching to Rookwood from the North, and Tarsh taking his division into their port. The fleet is ready."

"How long will it take for us to do a final sweep of Sands End for Magi?" Xaro asked.

"I have already given the order. You see, all I need to do is *think* it, and they obey. Your fleshy army should be so responsive."

"Kuth-Cergor help me, but you try my patience. *How long?*" Xaro had ceased to care about the open hostility between him and Malenec in front of the others.

"Hours, maybe less. We have thousands of zombies systematically crawling through the castle as we speak."

Xaro just nodded. "Very well. Tarsh, prepare your things. You and I shall launch at first light tomorrow. Tar-Tan, you and Malenec shall leave afterward, upon *your* command."

"And if we find Magi tonight?" asked Tarsh, still holding out hope.

"You must kill him immediately and feed his soul to our colleague in black over there," he said, jerking his thumb in Malenec's direction, who just sat there with the tips of his fingers tented, nodding with a smile.

It had been a *looooong* time since she had felt like a woman. Not a Queen. *A woman.* Last night had carried over to this morning, and that is exactly how she felt in Herodius's arms: a woman.

Up in the mountains, a morning that started with sunshine and a cool summer breeze was a good day. On rare occasions, the wind blew out of the east, and she could catch the faintest hint of salt in the air; usually a precursor to storms. As the first rays of sunlight cut through the small window in the private room high atop the mountain fortress, she could smell the sea.

Still, she kept her eyes shut, part of her wondering whether last night was a dream. *Is he really here? Is there a King in my bed? Am I no longer alone?*

Eyes closed, her thin lips pressed into a private smile, she knew last night was no dream. She could feel it in her body. Her mouth…her bosom…the small of her back…her hips. Everything felt tired and invigorated at the same time. *Like a frozen waterfall thawing into a cascade all at once.*

She rolled over and allowed herself the girlish pleasure of cracking open one eye. Her King was lying on his side, staring back at her.

"Good morning, my love," he whispered. "Are you awake, my Queen?"

Her smile betrayed her sleep as a sham. "Indeed. If our nights are to be like the last, we may need afternoon naps, my King." She reached out and rested her pale, white hand against his reddish-brown barrel of a chest. She inched closer and ran her fingers through his curly brown hair, which had grown long. *What a beautiful man he is…*she wanted to start kissing him again.

Instead, he took and kissed her hand before slowly rising from bed. He went to a standing basin and splashed water on his face before reaching for a robe; a simple grey robe, no more fancy than what a farmer might don to start his day. *Which is what he is—was,* she corrected quickly.

"I see Elvidor's new King has not lost his industriousness. Not even the day after our wedding." She hid her personal disappointment behind a playful, almost flirty tone, which was quite out of character for her. She ached for more of him.

Herodius looked at her with his own mischievous smile, one she did not recognize. *Good. Perhaps we'll both act like fools for a while.* But his smile slowly faded.

"Alas, I imagine the work of our day will not wait on our love; our love must wait on our work." *Not the most romantic sentiment she'd ever heard across pillows.* She nodded slightly, and rose to fetch her own robe.

"I can only imagine the petitioners today at court. With every noble in town, we're likely to be regaled with stories of thievery, lover's quarrels, drunken shenanigans, land disputes, and the always pleasant griping over crown taxes. You'll forgive me if another few minutes in bed with Elvidor's new King seem a more pleasant way to break in the day." She dipped her hands into the cool water and slowly rubbed the sleep out of her eyes, allowing the sleeves of her robe to get wet.

"Well, when you put it like *that*…" Herodius again flashed a boyish smile she had not seen before this morning. *But I love it…it's a smile meant only for me.* Again, it was fleeting; as quick as he flashed it, the smile was gone. "There is something, Najalas, that I do want to ask you about before our day takes on a life of its own."

It appears husband will take a back seat to King, at least this morning. "And what is that, my love?"

"I wanted to ask you about the Elfs. Did you not find it odd that Chief Chocktaw did not send *anyone* to the wedding from Thalanthalas? They let one of the Mage Guards represent them…I find it peculiar that our staunchest ally did not send *a single* representative. I mean, if that dandy, Lord Corovant from Gaust, decided to sail halfway around the continent to be here, *surely* our friends and neighbors would send someone, given their proximity if nothing else. I find it troubling, do you?"

Whatever desire she felt for Herodius shriveled up inside her like rotten fruit in the desert.

I cannot tell him so soon. Not yet…what will we he think of me? However, he had a point. It *was* troubling. Surely Silver could not have completed the task so quickly? They would have heard if something had happened to Chief Chocktaw while in route. No, that contract could not have been fulfilled between her meeting and the Crowning; there wasn't enough time. Which meant—

Oh God! What if he chose not to come because he knows? What if Chief Chocktaw knows? But how?

"Najalas? Are you all right?"

She sat down and shook her head. *Too early for ale, much too early, but if I have to share this with my husband now, a goblet would make the telling so much easier…* "No Herodius. I'm not. And I have a feeling you won't be in a few minutes either."

"What do you mean?"

"Lost in the whirlwind of last night was Xaro's head in a box, Herodius. As I said earlier, I hired the services of a skilled Assassin to try and eliminate him. I did not, however, share with the council the price." She raised her head. *I will look him in the eyes when I tell him. I will not hide from this.*

Herodius tilted his head, the air coming out of him in one long breath. "My Queen…don't tell me…"

She stood up. "The price for Xaro was Chief Chocktaw—and some gold. I authorized the contract after our meeting, once Xaro's death was confirmed by Belara and Strongiron. They could not have killed him before the wedding, I don't believe. He would have been in transit, and he sent his regrets a day or so again, saying he was ill. I agree that someone, most likely Lady Elyn, should have been escorted here in the Chief's absence. I can't be sure Herodius— perhaps there is another explanation—but the simplest one is that the Elfs somehow know about my dealings with the Assassins, and are not coming close to Rookwood. I pray I am wrong."

Herodius closed his eyes, and kept them closed for what seemed like an eternity of seconds. Finally the Queen walked over to where he was sitting. "Say something, Herodius."

He opened his eyes. "This was a terrible decision, Najalas, one that may cost us everything, you do realize that?"

I do, but I don't want it thrown in my face by a man who's been King less than 24 hours. Come rule this land on the cliff of war for years, and then judge my actions. Her eyes were starting to fill with anger as she drew her lips into a thin line. "I did what I thought would keep us from war."

He shook his head. "I doubt it will keep us from war. At best, our enemies may have an open border to our south; at worst, they may join them, or we may find ourselves fighting them concurrently. What possessed you to—"

"Do not lecture me now, Herodius! You have graced the throne for less than a day. I am opening up to you here because…because I need your help. I need you to help me share this burden. What is done is done! We don't know what the Elfs know, but we must prepare for some contingencies. Perhaps they know nothing. Perhaps they suspect something but can prove nothing. And there is a chance that to them, Chocktaw will die of an accident, and you and I may attend his funeral with the truth buried in our hearts. A burden comes with the Crown, Herodius. Sometimes that burden is paid in gold; sometimes in secrets kept."

Herodius softened his eyes, nodding slightly, but his lips were still taut. "Yes, I understand what leadership is, and what it is not. A throne does not make the leader, my Queen. It is the other way around." His words slapped her harder than a hand ever could. "Tell me this one thing, and then we will turn our attention forward, as we must. Do you regret this decision of yours? Even a little?" he added, his tone softening.

The Queen sighed, uncrossing her arms and spreading them wide. "Why do you ask me such a thing, Herodius? Of course—I've not made a harder decision. Now let me ask you this, husband-of-mine: Is the life of one good man worth preventing the deaths of thousands?" Her eyes were moist, but defiant.

Herodius finally stood up and approached her, taking her hands in his as he looked down into her glistening, mud-grey eyes. "It is, my Queen. One good man's life *is* a fair trade, provided that he sacrifice it himself. It was never yours to barter away."

He bent down to kiss her gently on the forehead, and that was when the tears began to pour.

~Strongiron~

Finally…the day arrived—not the day of the wedding or the crowning.

The day of their *departure.* The new General had been fetched, the villages visited, the Afflicted healed, the western cities placated, a plague contained, nobles wined and dined, sermons preached, new clerics trained (Palinor had developed quite the passion for Dymetra), and the minor business of officiating a royal wedding, complete with the crowning of a new King, was complete.

Yet for weeks, the same urgency that hung over Kari had been needling Strongiron in the background as well. *Finally*…they were ready to depart.

Yet now that the day had arrived, a feeling of trepidation stole over him as he looked at the small council of which he had been a part for so long. Excitement, sure…but also trepidation. Peter and Simon looked…*stretched;* worn, as if from too much worry. Victor was dour; his views had certainly not changed. Even Jonathon, who was more fastidious than most, seemed anxious. And Herodius and the Queen looked exhausted. Perhaps it was just their wedding night, but Strongiron doubted it. Nothing was radiant about either one of them…more *haggard* than anything else, really. Only Belara looked to be unaffected by time, worry, drink, or lack of sleep. She wore a long, cherry-red dress with a matching cloak and cowl that fit snugly everywhere, right to the triangular point in the center of her forehead. As always, she provided the scent for the meeting: vanilla, roses, and other exotic spices hung in the air.

I may never see all of them together again. He could not shake that sense of foreboding, though he did his best to tell himself his friends were just tired. *Nothing more than that.*

"When do you think you will return?" asked the Queen, breaking his thoughts. Out of respect for the festivities last night, Strongiron and Kari had agreed to wait a full day before they left for Adimand. Actually, hearing what Kari had just been through in Brigg, and seeing how exhausted she was had made a day of sleep a necessity. Perhaps it was the contrast of the Queen standing next to the richly tanned new King, but she looked even paler than usual today. *And stiff. Perhaps her love of the goblet is catching up to her—maybe that's it.*

"I do not know, my Queen. Adimand is a vast land. All that I know is the belief from the old Clerics who trained me is that Windomere is buried in the Dusty Plains, and that he may have had the Shield with him. We will travel across the wide arc of land and sea on the wings of our prayers, but who can say what we will find when we reach his burial plot? We will return as soon as we can."

"We know the danger of staying away too long," added Kari.

"Do you now?" returned Victor, his mustaches jumping. Kari ignored him, letting her glare do the talking. As recent as an hour ago, he was still lobbying to keep one of them in Rookwood.

"We will return as soon as we have this Artifact, my Queen." Strongiron said. "Until then, be vigilant. Victor has a good plan to keep Rookwood, if not the entire land, well defended. Belara has taken over well for Niku, and Peter's navy is ready. Jonathon has plotted an escape route through Rookwood should the worst happen, and I am sure our allies, the elfs and Chief Chocktaw, are well prepared along our southern flank. And…we now have a worthy King as well, your Majesty." He nodded to Herodius before turning back to the Queen. "The defensive plans you have set in motion provide a level of protection few could assail, my Queen. Take heart in your men, your women. Trust them, and trust your judgment. Rookwood, and by extension Elvidor, is in more than capable hands. Kari and I will join you again as soon as we can."

No huzzahs nor shouts of agreement arose. *Perhaps that's fitting; I am not, after all, delivering a speech to men preparing to die on a battlefield. God help me, but I hope I'm not...*

"And what will this magical shield do for us when you bring it back?" Asked Belara. "Refresh my memory."

"This shield combats dark prayers. It will help us against the Dark Cleric Malenec, whose power comes from The Other One."

"Kuth-Cergor," added Kari.

"His name is Kuth-Cergor." Strongiron nodded.

"Protects us, or protects just you?" continued Belara pointedly.

"I…do not know. There is much about the Shield I do not know."

Victor narrowed his eyes. "As someone who has been accused of trying to plan for ways to save my own skin, I think the Mage's question is relevant. What good is this shield to *us* if it only protects you?"

Kari's eyes flashed, but Strongiron put a calming hand on her shoulder, squeezing it more than lightly. He stepped forward. "If you think for one minute we're leaving to try and obtain some object to save ourselves—"

"That is what Magi did, am I not right? Now this all-powerful True Mage is dead," Victor interrupted. "How are your actions much different?"

Kari shrugged Strongiron's hand off her shoulder and strode right up to Victor, where she grabbed his tunic. "We are doing this for Rookwood, for Elvidor, and for all of Tenebrae. If you can't get that through your pebble-brained—"

"Enough." Herodius stepped between Kari and Victor. "Enough," he repeated, tired but firm. "The Crown does not question the direction you've been given. Stress builds in all of us as we wait for spells, steel, and spirits to rain down from our enemies. We will *not* be torn apart by this stress, for that is all it is. We *will* stand together, even when we are separated, and we *will* protect this land. The Crown *will* protect Elvidor, and any artifact we find that helps even one of us to withstand our foes is an artifact worth pursuing.

"Go with the blessing of the King and Queen, Strongiron Tuitio and Kari Quinlan. Go and find the Shield of Life."

~Magi~

It may have been a simple piece of fish, but to Magi it rivaled the meal he shared with Xaro. Freshly caught, lightly sautéed in the galley with shallots and herbs, and served over hot, fluffy rice, it was such a welcome delicacy after the rat meat he'd lived on for weeks.

"Where did you learn to prepare fish like this?" Magi asked. "This is wonderful, Veronica."

She smiled. They were dining alone in Magi's small but comfortable quarters. The *Cornucopia* was a trading vessel that shipped food from the Fertile Plains all over Tenebrae; there were lots of vegetables aboard, but the quarters were tight.

"I watched the cook on the way over. When you've lived off tree bark and squirrels, you appreciate a decent meal, and he was kind enough to show me how to hold a pan over a small blue flame he maintained. He's a mage, but not a True one. Come to think of it, I don't even know his name. Everyone just calls him Blue, since his claim to fame is keeping a controlled blue flame aboard without burning a hole in the ship. Anyhow, he showed me." *Was there a little color in her cheeks?* "I'm glad you like it."

They were slowly passing through the Strait of Blinter, and hopefully would be heading out to open sea again soon, well south of the ever-present Maelstrom.

"Have you been able to get in touch with Rookwood, Magi?"

He shook his head. "I have not. My connection was only established with Niku—and that connection appears to be lost. I cannot reach them."

"What does that mean?" Veronica put her food down.

"I think…that Niku is dead. That would be the only reason why I couldn't get in touch with him."

She accepted this without even blinking—just a tilt of the head before she resumed flaking off a piece of her fish. "I see. He was old, but powerful."

"Yes. Which means we'll be coming unannounced."

"All the more reason I'm glad to be arriving with you." She smiled. "I highly doubt the Queen will welcome me back after my stunt with Peter if you didn't vouch for me."

Magi gave her a sly smile. "So, you are using me. You're buttering me up with this fresh, moist, succulent fish so that I put a good word in for you with the Queen. Is that your end game, Assassin?"

"Perhaps…"

Magi chuckled, but then he looked at Veronica more seriously. "Why do you want to go back? You could have cleared your conscience by rescuing me and drop me off anywhere in the Three Fingers. I can *Teleport* back to Rookwood on my own, and you can start your own life. Why go back to Rookwood? You saw the force that is going to attack."

Veronica returned his look and nodded. "I've spent a life killing people for gold. Before this, I worshipped nothing but a contract. You are one of the few people on Tenebrae that can relate to this, Magi, but when you've been given a second chance—a second pair of hands, in my case—I would rather kill for Her. I don't know how I'll be able to help, I'm not as gifted as you or Strongiron, or…or your other friend, Kari." She paused briefly. "But the one talent I do have I think can best be put to good use in Rookwood. I can't explain it, but that's what I feel. I'm not asking for gold, or even a pardon. I just want a chance to stop Xaro and his men."

"Because he wouldn't heal you?" Magi asked gently, pushing food around on his plate.

"No. Not really. Because Tenebrae is already dark enough, and I don't want it to grow any darker."

Magi nodded. *Good enough for me.* "There is one piece of information that I truly was hoping to pass along to Niku. I'm sure Strongiron has long since left for the Shield, but he should know who he's facing in Xaro."

"His half-brother." Veronica casually finished the last bit of fish on her plate.

"You know?"

"I do. It's one of the reasons Xaro had me target him. Perhaps the main reason. How did you find out?"

"I put it together in talking to Xaro's mother. She's…different."

"Where did you meet his mother?"

He retold the story of meeting Daphne, including her being a siren. Veronica raised her eyebrows. "Hmm. Interesting. That explains quite a bit. However, it may be best that Strongiron doesn't know. He may have to kill Xaro…why make it harder for him?"

"I will kill Xaro," said Magi.

"Not if I get to him first," she replied. "Besides," she added with a little smile. "You had your chance."

Magi opened his mouth, pointed a finger, and said…nothing. Absolutely nothing. He put his hand down and clamped his jaw shut. *So this is how it's going to be. Very well…game on.*

~Xaro~

Malenec's private horde of zombies did *not* turn up any trace of Magi, nor did Xaro expect them to. *Flew to parts unknown on a Teleport spell once he regained his strength.* When they met again, there would not be any delays in his death, waiting for Tarsh or anything else. Krishnan had been right; the man was a menace to their plans.

Dawn broke hot over the desert, the first rays seeming to light up Sands End all at once from high atop the unprotected mesa. Xaro had hardly slept, his mind going over a hundred details involved with the launch, but it always came back to two key questions that gnawed on him like carrion returning to an old kill: *where is my ring, and will this shield work?*

Someone had the ring; someone stole it from Trevor and killed him. He had long since searched Tarsh and his quarters and confirmed that he did not have it; Xaro was at least convinced of that. Perhaps a sailor aboard with some magical ability had enough to cast a simple *Darkness* spell, blind Tarsh, knock him out, and then kill Trevor in a bloody struggle, disposing of the body overboard. It was not so hard to believe that he might have flashed the ring drunk one night, and if a sailor felt swindled, perhaps they took the ring to try and get their stake back. The bottom line was that Ring of Protection could be on some sailor, or more likely, sold to gypsies on the black market in any port city. *It is likely gone forever.* He might have been able to take Rookwood on his own with that ring.

A shaft of sun pierced the open window facing the desert, and landed on the large rectangular chest at the foot of his bed. Xaro walked over and spoke the words that would allow him and only him to open the Warlock's Chest. Inside were four items: The Staff of Wisdom, the Shield of Life, a copy of the Scroll of Tralatus, and a book. He reached in and pulled out the book.

Sitting down, he opened up *Ancient Artifacts* and thumbed to the section regarding the Shield of Life:

> *While no picture of Windomere's famous Shield survives, it is said to provide the bearer a level of protection against dark prayers. Blessed by Dymetra, it was a gift to Her High Cleric against spiritual attacks of any and all forms. It is unknown whether the Shield's power can be extended to protect others beyond the Shield-Bearer.*
>
> *The Shield of Life is one of three so-called...*

Xaro shut the old book harder than he intended. He never *really* expected the Shield would work for him—not really—but he held out a glimmer of hope that perhaps the Shield would be different than the Staff of Wisdom. He walked back over to the Warlock's Chest and looked down at that magnificent staff with its cold, dead stone atop. No truth would be revealed to Xaro by *Her* Staff, and apparently no protection would be afforded by *Her* Shield, either.

He pulled the Shield out, again marveling at how light it was. *I could probably bend this into scrap metal if I tried hard enough.* Xaro narrowed his eyes and considered testing it nevertheless. *Just to be sure.*

"Kuth-Cergor, your authority is unrivaled. Show me that your power extends beyond your adversary and Her puny shield. I pray that you etch your name into the soft metal of this frail defense!"

Inside the shaft of light (which now fell on the white of the shield), dust began to swirl into a tight spiral the size of quill. The cyclonic finger of dust slowly descended against the ivory-looking surface, causing a screech that Xaro was sure would rouse any men still in their bunks. A few quick strokes later and the first unmistakable letter appeared in the shield: *K*. Seconds later, the name *Kuth-Cergor* graced the surface of Dymetra's Shield of Life.

It was as he expected. Not necessarily a fake, just not a shield that would protect *him* from any "dark" prayers, at least "dark" according to *Her* followers. *Heck, the shield couldn't even protect itself.*

He put the book and the shield back in the Warlock's Chest and sealed it again. One had to be a follower of Dymetra in order to receive the use of Her blessed artifacts. Part of him hoped that *maybe* the Shield would work as long as he believed She existed, but clearly that wasn't enough. No matter. This complicated his plans, but he would adjust.

In the dawning of the day of his war launch—in the quiet, private stillness before the armada took to the sea—he thought about this new wrinkle. That Malenec must die shortly after Rookwood fell was not debatable. He would use him for just as long as he needed his undead army, but under no circumstances would he allow an army of undead souls *loyal to him* to share power. He had hoped the Shield would provide him with an unassailable defense when he and his True Cleric clashed. That would have given him a definitive advantage—a comforting thought, given that Kuth-Cergor clearly had some affection for Malenec; that is why he blessed him with the highest level of skill, but not Xaro himself. Protecting himself against Malenec's prayers—prayers to the same God he worshipped himself, no less—was a desire that he would never voice out loud, however.

And yet, am I not a True Warrior? A True Mage? A True Ranger? A True Assassin? And this close to being a True Cleric myself? Surely I can find another means to kill this man after our victory against the rulers of this age; surely Kuth-Cergor's marginal favor cannot close such a gap in talent?

Which drew his thoughts back to Magi. Grudgingly, Xaro again would admit something in the privacy of his own thoughts that no man would ever hear him utter: he knew he was *not* the most powerful mage in Tenebrae…but he had met the one person who was, and that mage now ran free. *Kuth-Cergor helped me when I faced him, perhaps he will help me again with Malenec…or at least let us battle as equals, unaided, and let the better man triumph to serve at his right hand…*

The beginning of a plan was forming in his mind. He would need help; Malenec will likely be protected by thousands of zombies, and who knows what other soulless creatures that he might hatch in the heat of battle with the East. But maybe, just maybe…*especially with the power of the Scroll…*

Xaro began putting on the light travelling armor he intended to wear for the launch—black leather. His men would load the Warlock's Chest and the rest of his remaining items designated for the long voyage east. Inside was a reference book along with three items of incalculable power, only one of which he could use. *At least my enemies can't use any of them against me, either,* he thought as he left his room to make ready for the departure of his massive armada. He left his fortress at Sands End, perhaps for the last time, and gazed out over his army from high atop the mesa.

One thing Xaro appreciated about their desert stronghold: day and night did not gradually appear. When dawn broke, it might as well be noon; when night fell, it might as well be past midnight. Staring out toward the sea, even at this early hour, his men were up. They were ready…the day had come.

Xaro gave a word of thanks to Kuth-Cergor, and then stepped clear off the mesa, arms outstretched. He floated in the air above his army and the array of boats beneath them, his black cloak snapping in the hot wind. Then he amplified his voice.

"Men," he shouted, hovering above the tens of thousands assembled for war. "Look around you. Look well, and mark this moment forever in your mind's eye. Look at the face of the man standing next to you. Look at the color of the ground beneath your boots. Can you smell the salt in the air? Do you smell the sweat of battles yet to come?"

Several shouts began to build, and some men began clanging their swords against their shields. He continued, slowly rotating so that everyone could see his face as he spoke.

"Men! Hear me well. Today is more than a boat launch, more than a battle cry. Think bigger. Mark well the taste of the air, the feeling in your stomach. Will there be conquest? Will there be land? The fortunes of war? Yes, and more so!"

Two columns of fire began to swirl upward from his palms, stretching up like flaming tornadoes drilling into the sky. His voice rose and deepened, and the men were no longer banging their swords and shields. Many fell to their knees and covered their heads; others stared dumbfounded at Xaro's irradiated face between those spinning columns of fire. The heat coming from those columns was *intense.*

"Today we do more—*so much more*—than go to war! Today, we usher in a *New Age*! Let this day mark the end of the current age— the Age of Any and No God—and mark the dawning of the New Age…the Age of Kuth-Cergor!"

With a roar, he clapped his hands together, and the flaming columns combined and ripped a window into the morning sky that was black and dark and empty. The hole in the firmament seemed to swallow the fire like deep well swallows light. Then the fire stopped. Xaro was still hovering over the armada, hands pressed together and eyes uplifted in prayer.

Silence filled the field as everyone stared at the tear in the blue. Xaro knew that those who joined him from the pits of Kekero had seen this before, and they knew whom he had just summoned. *You never forget the sound of his voice…which is the point.*

A moment later, that voice erupted from the gaping hole: "*You fight for me. Honor me and my appointed leaders, and I will fight for you. None can stand against me. I am Kuth-Cergor, and I am returning soon.*"

The hole in the sky closed with a deafening thunderclap, causing even these hardened men to cover their ears. Xaro pointed to his massive armada. "To the sea, Men! Take ship for the dawning of our New Age! May Kuth-Cergor bless us with wind at our backs! *To Elvidor and War!*"

Chapter Twenty-One: The Dance of Life and Death

One lonely tumbleweed bobbled along the hardpan, carried along on the slightest of stale, dusty breezes. Strongiron turned to look at Kari, whose eyebrows were raised. Nikron was not a city, and it wasn't a village.

It was a building.

They walked toward the lone building, which looked like a hotel or tavern of sorts, containing two levels. To the right of the batwing doors was a chalk circle, inside of which was a pile of bones that glared white in the sun. A single black bird pecked at them, but there was no smell whatsoever.

Strongiron paused. "Well, we made it."

"I'm not sure what I was expecting, Strongiron, but it wasn't this." Kari turned in a complete circle. "It is desolate out here. When we prayed for safe travel to Nikron, I was picturing Gaust, or at least some of the villages we visited on our way back with Victor." She looked at the pile of bones in the circle. "This is something else."

Strongiron nodded silently, thinking. "Tell me again the difference between *Teleporting* with magic versus the way we do it, by praying?"

"Well, when a True Mage *Teleport*s, they are using science, my dear. You have to have visited the place and picture it in your mind; otherwise you may *Teleport* inside a tree or a rock and immediately die when your body is reformed. *Teleporting* over large bodies of water is also an issue; something in the science causes you to diffuse away.

"Our prayers are different. We pick a spot and trust Dymetra to place us where She would safely. We can visit unknown places such as…this, for example."

"That's what I thought. So, this, apparently, is the extent of Nikron."

"Apparently."

Strongiron drew his sword, more out of habit as a True Warrior than anything else. "Let us go explore it, then." He looked over his shoulder and grinned at Kari before striding onto the deck and pushing open the doors, with Kari close behind him.

A thick layer of fine dust coated everything in the common room, which looked empty at first, save for a middle-aged man seated at a table with two scantily-clad women—too thin by far— one on either side, pawing at him. At the sound of the doors, all three looked up. None said a word, but the two female drifters took one look at Kari and hissed. Their lips were dark, dry, and cracked.

"New customers," said the squat, fat man behind the bar at the back of the common room. On the shelf behind the bar were several brown jugs. Strongiron took a closer look at the man's face: dark skin, bald head, pure white eyes. *A True Mage.*

Strongiron walked to the bar, sniffing the air. He couldn't smell anything out of place; in fact, if anything, the bar smelled remarkably clean. Just dusty. "I say, good man, can you tell me if this is Nikron?" He sat down on a chair, but kept one eye on the three patrons to his right, his sword still in hand.

"You're speaking to him. Name's Nikron, and you don't give a damn about my last name and I'm not inclined to share it neither. How's your coinage?"

Kari had seated herself at the bar next to Strongiron, and now stared at the True Mage warily. "A bit presumptuous, aren't you? How do you know what we want, or that we want anything at all?"

"Lady, there's only one thing anyone wants, and only one place to get it, and I happen to be the only one that sells it. My magic elixir," he said, waving a hand at the shelf behind him. "Nikron's finest water, and the only water you'll find for miles and miles in every direction." His face was smugger than a gambler with all the cards. "Coinage? Prices are up everywhere…one jug'll set you back five honest pieces of gold."

Kari stood up. "Five gold pieces? For *water?*" Her fingers began to twitch, as if she might send this guy into his own personal nightmare of *Illusion*. Strongiron gently put his hand on her shoulder, encouraging her to sit.

He dug into his coin pouch and took out ten pieces of gold, making sure this Nikron character saw that the pouch was still bulging. "Two jugs for two thirsty travelers, and perhaps some information?" He tried to slide the gold over to the back of the bar, but his hand ran into an invisible wall. "What's this?"

"Protection. Against any and all thieves, assassins, druids, and scoundrels of all types." He smiled wide, and Strongiron could now see he was missing at least three teeth. "I'm a simple man. We all have our gifts. My forte is *Shield* spells…*Shields* of all kinds. Spent my life experimenting with 'em, perfecting 'em against all types of attacks, keeping 'em up at all times, widening 'em, penetrating 'em at *my* command. You don't live in an outpost in the middle of a desert situated over the last remaining spring of cool, clear water very long if you can't protect it."

Kari scowled at him. "So you have access to drinkable water, yet you charge people exorbitant rates for what springs freely from the ground?"

"*Magic Elixir*, sweetheart. Life-giving *Magic Elixir*." Again with the gap-toothed smile.

"You disgust me."

Strongiron leaned forward. "So, how are we to exchange our gold for your 'magic elixir,' Nikron?"

"Leave your gold right there." He said a few words, and the coins disappeared. Behind the bar, Strongiron heard a tinkling sound. Nikron bent over, picked up a coin, examined it, bit into it, nodded, and tossed it beneath the bar again. Two jugs disappeared off the shelf and reappeared on top of the bar, on the other side of the *Shield* spell. "Like I said, I'm good with protection spells. Lots of tricks."

Kari smelled the water. "How do we know it's not poisoned?"

The fat man was sweating, and he mopped his bald head with a wash rag that he also used to wipe the dust off the bar. He shook his head. "You don't. But poisoning my customers wouldn't be very smart. I'd like another ten pieces of gold from you sometime later."

Something struck Strongiron about that. "Why is it so expensive, Nikron?"

Whenever he smiled, his dark jowls seemed to jiggle a little. He shrugged. "Near as I can tell, someone must have struck a gold vein, because it's been flowing everywhere lately. I spend more on my supplies—my spell components are bit more involved than crushin' a marble, if you know much of the Art—so I have to charge more as well. Gold's lost a bit of its value and stuff's expensive, so it would seem." The man stopped mopping the bar surface from behind his invisible *Shield* and pressed both hands into the wood. "But somethin' tells me you don't want to really talk about gold or the price of my elixir. Lookin' at your white armor, I can tell coinage ain't much of a problem for you. You and your lady over here got a purpose about you. What're you two doing here?"

Strongiron glanced briefly at Kari, who sat there staring at Nikron with her arms crossed and eyes narrowed. He turned back to the proprietor. "Perhaps it's not a coincidence that we've come across someone who has spent so much time studying *Shields*. We're looking for one in particular ourselves. Have you heard of an ancient

True Cleric named Windomere? It is said he possessed a great shield—the blessed Shield of Life—purportedly buried with him. Do you know anything about such an artifact?"

Nikron pulled a jug of water off the shelf behind him and drank straight from it, spilling half down the front of his shirt. "I might have heard a thing or two about such a tale. Another ten gold pieces might jog my memory a bit."

Kari immediately stood up, smiling sweetly. She reached below the bar where the bartender couldn't see her hands, and brought up ten sparkling gold pieces, which she made a show of dropping, one-by-one, onto the surface of the bar, each coin clanging against the wood with a heavy *thud.* "You seek to protect yourself from thieves, yet it appears the only thief here is *you.*" She sat back down, wearing a smile that was anything but charming.

Strongiron stared at Nikron pleasantly; he carried all their coins himself. *My shrewd little Illusionist...*

Again the gold disappeared, with the sound of it tinkling into some massive, hidden chest behind the bar. He reached down, grabbed a coin, looked at it, bit it, and satisfied threw it back in with the others. "Like I said, what good is poisoning you two when there's more business for us to conduct?" His lips peeled back in an oily smile, and Kari couldn't help but wrinkle her nose.

"It's been quite some time since a traveler has sought old Nikron out for advice on that Shield. I'm old, even for a bald dwarf!" He laughed, and grabbed his water jug for another long pull, wasting more down his tunic. "Here is what I can tell you about all that. What you see here—the Dusty Plains—it wasn't like this when Windomere lived. These plains were fertile, every bit as fertile as the plains south of the mountains. Nikron was one of many cities and villages throughout central Adimand, and it's long been said that Windomere was born here. Some say the water that comes from our little spring is a lastin' reminder of his birthplace. Heck, we might be standin' *right over* the spot the little tyke was welcomed into this God-forsaken land! Har!"

He took another gulp and continued. "That all changed when he died, o'course. Legend has it he used his power to raise not just a tombstone, but *an entire mountain range* to cover his grave. You can't see 'em from here, too far away, but straight-away south are the Shembolt Mountains. You can't miss 'em; they look like a sawblade—perfectly uniform peaks. I've heard old druids drunk on fermented nectar say that 'shembolt' is a corruption of 'saw blade,' or vice versa. Who can say? But them peaks are eerie, no two ways about it. I've *Teleported* all over Adimand, collecting my needs, and every time I get close to those mountains, I don't feel right. I do believe he had himself buried underneath those mountains, someway somehow. Those crests are cursed. Something guards them, keeps them, *protects* them. Good reason nobody's ever found that Shield— you two ain't the first to look, and ain't the first to hear this ol' story.

"Anyway, you prolly figured out the rest. Pullin' mountains up from the bones of Tenebrae must have caused the biggest land-quake in history. Changed the climate and the land. Now we have Fertile Plains to the south and Dusty Plains to the north. That's a kinder way for mapmakers to say life below and death above, if you ask me. But so it is, and has been for a thousand years.

"As for me...my family staked out this spring long ago, and we keep it still. A little oasis in the desert—a waystation for the weary traveler."

"A thieving station, where desperate men exchange gold for a few drops of water to quench their thirst." Kari continued in the same tone of voice.

"We all have to make a living."

"You have enough gold already to live like a king."

Nikron leaned forward. "Aye. And who's to say I'm not?" He didn't grin this time, but there was a glint in his eye.

Suddenly there was a thump behind Strongiron, and he turned to see the two lady wayfarers running out the door, one with a water skin, the other with a small pouch. The man had fallen over in his chair, a large thorn protruding from his neck. Strongiron jumped up and ran over to the man.

Nikron just shook his head. "Don't bother. He's good and dead. Those thorns are loaded with quick-acting poison."

"You saw the whole thing while our backs were turned, listening to your story, and you said nothing? What kind of man are you?" Kari was standing herself now, somewhere between furious and incredulous by the look on her face.

"Lady, I sell water for a living. Common sense you have to carry in here with you. A man who sits down next to two of those harpies gets whatever Fate deems prudent." He splashed water onto his hands, rubbing them together. He began casting a spell that Kari recognized, and the body was *Levitated* off the floor of his bar, slowly floating toward the front doors.

"What are you doing with the body?" asked Strongiron.

"What I always do. Add it to the bone pile with the rest..."

In the week or so since Strongiron and Kari left, Herodius second-guessed his decision *multiple* times, but always came back to his wife's point-of-view: telling the small council would only undermine the Crown's authority, shame his Queen, and distract them all from their pressing preparations.

But something else troubled him as well: *if the Elfs know the price the Queen paid for Xaro's head, they must have found out from the Assassin's Guild...or someone from our court overheard, which means there is a traitor in our midst.*

He was sitting next to his Queen in their drawing room, alone. The morning had broken cooler than the last week; perhaps the summer's zenith could be put behind them. The pitcher on the table between them was filled with warm water, and they were eating hard biscuits with a few berries. The plains were still learning how to grow fruit in the summer months, and the yields had been small.

They had received no word from Chief Chocktaw in a week.

"Najalas," Herodius began. "You know we have to find out what the Elfs know."

"I know." She nibbled on a biscuit, and pushed it aside.

"The thing is...I can imagine how the Assassins might betray us. I don't know how anything else makes much sense."

His Queen tried to smile with her thin lips, but it came across more pained than anything else. "You've not been on the throne very long, my love. The Assassins value their contracts like mother birds protect their eggs. I grant that it's possible, but unlikely. More likely the Elfs don't know a thing, or, worse—someone in court has found out and betrayed us. That is why I did not want to tell our small council; I trust them all, but..." She sighed.

"Yes, I still respect your instincts, especially when your head is clear."

She looked up, her eyes narrowing dangerously, but Herodius held up his hand. "Not now. I'm not picking a fight with you this morning, Najalas. We need to make a decision. Someone must travel to the Elfs, and if we are to keep our secret yet to ourselves, I believe we have only three choices."

The Queen sipped a little water. "Go on." She sipped a little more. *She looks tired.*

"You can travel there, I can travel there, or we can send our Mage guard, Galihali. I would not send Belara—she would ask too many questions, or offer to conduct a meeting of our shades. Those telepathic meetings cannot be conducted without involving at least one mage here and one mage there, both of whom would then be present for our conversation. When we are ready to involve others, that may be an option…but for now I would prefer a direct conversation, and Galihali will follow our orders without question or delay.

"Before you say a word, I'm not sending you, my Queen. I know how guilty you feel, and I understand you want to make this right, but I'm *not* sending you—not alone, and not with a guard detail, even if we were to make up a reason for you to travel to Thalanthalas again to placate Simon."

He expected a fight from his Queen, but instead she sipped her water and simply said, "Okay. I would not wish you to travel there, either."

He watched his Queen carefully; she seemed more passive than usual. He continued. "To my thinking, a great risk surrounds our travel until we know what the Elfs know. They may kill us, make it look accidental, and call the score even. If we wish to avoid a tedious and delicate dialogue with Belara, I think the obvious move is to send Galihali, who can *Teleport*, back to her homeland. I've heard she is in love with one of the Chief's scouts, and likes to see him anyhow. Let her visit the Chief, bring our greetings and concerns for his welfare, and report back to us what they say. We don't have to tell her a thing; we only need to ask for her Memory Ball upon her return. There is a good chance that the Chief will not ask for it when she greets him; he may not know that we use them."

"Surely you don't expect her to ask her own people whether they are plotting against us!?"

"Of course not. We'll have to pick up on the tone of his voice, but if we tell Galihali to ask the Chief specifically about his recovery from the fever sickness, his answer will tell us much."

The Queen slowly started nodding. "It was never communicated to us from which sickness the Chief suffered that prevented his attendance to the wedding. If he acknowledges that he's doing better from the 'fever sickness'—"

"Then there is a good chance he's lying, yes. Which is a good indicator that he knows he's got a price on his head, which means we must confront the situation directly."

"And if he corrects her and says it was something else, then perhaps he really is telling the truth about falling ill." She took another sip of water. "The plan has one flaw, however. What if

Galihali is the traitor? If one is in our midst, surely the only elf at court is a good place to look."

Herodius looked at the Queen and nodded. "I've considered this, and I admit it's not a foolproof plan. If she *is* the traitor, she would likely agree to go, report to her Chief, and would turn off her Memory Ball. If she returns but has nothing recorded, perhaps that also tells us much. Again, we're drawing conclusions on imperfect information, I realize that. Two minutes with Magi's Staff would solve much, but it is as decent a plan as I can conceive that allows us to stay here and tell no one."

The Queen stood up and looked very tired indeed. "I agree, my King. Staying here and telling no one is paramount." She grabbed the edges of the table as if to steady herself.

"Najalas?"

"I'm fine." She smiled and for the first time that morning looked genuinely happy. "Perhaps more than fine. Your Queen is with child, my King." She promptly turned to walk quickly toward their privy, one hand on her abdomen, the other over her mouth.

~Magi~

A welcome breeze began to fill their sails, straight from the west. Several sailors commented that it was a bit unusual this time of year, but the seasons seemed to be turning slightly; Magi was glad for the heavy cloak he wore above deck, for the morning was chilly, and the stiff breeze and water mist made it feel even cooler.

Veronica stood at the rail next to him. He noticed her hair was a bit longer than when they had travelled across the central plains of Elvidor. *Still as black as a raven.* She must have sensed he was staring, as she turned to him and smiled.

"It's getting cooler," she said. She was wearing a dark green, leather-padded vest and brown breeches. *Lionel would have approved.*

"Perhaps this is autumn's turn." He moved a little closer. "I can go get your cloak if you're cold?"

She laughed lightly. "Oh, I'm a bit hardier than that. Just a brisk morning." She looked at him squarely. "I did, however, want to share some more information with you, and talk about your plan."

"The last time I made a plan, I ended up in shackles. My current thinking is get to Rookwood and figure out where their defenses need bolstering. To be honest, I haven't gotten much further than that yet."

"Well, my plans haven't exactly turned out, either, but this much I know: Xaro is splitting his invasion into four groups. Two groups, one led by Tar-Tan the half-ogre, the other led by Malenec, will land in Shith and then split to invade the Elfen woodland home of Thalanthalas. Have you ever been there?"

"No—can't say that I have."

"It is beautiful, Magi. Stunning, really. I was shipwrecked and saved by the Elfs in what seems like a different life. The dwellings are woven into trees and the forest…a truly magical place that will be overrun by those undead zombies to the south and hemmed in by Tar-Tan and his men to the north. The Elfs will be left with a terrible choice: burn their own city to purge the undead, abandon their homes, knowing that many will die fleeing and fighting their way out, or stand and fight, knowing that their entire civilization may be wiped out. A single scratch by one of Malenec's creations is death for the Elfs."

"Why attack them in the first place?"

"Xaro does not want a path west for Rookwood…he is planning a siege, and conquering the Elfs is paramount to cutting off any possibility of retreat behind the mountains. Xaro will come down from the north. I'm not certain, but I imagine the fourth division will be led by Tarsh via the sea, coming in to the port of Rookwood."

Magi ran his thumb across his stubbly cheek, thinking. He had shaved off the wild beard he'd grown during his imprisonment, but hadn't quite taken to the clean look. He shaved when his whiskers got a little unruly, but that was about it.

"If we could somehow surprise them in Shith…"

Veronica raised a single eyebrow. "You would need an army, Magi. Don't even think about going it alone again."

Before he could answer, a huge gust of wind picked up and blew steadily, sending Veronica's silky hair streaming behind her. One of the sailors passed next to them, muttering. "Grateful for the push, but it's an odd gale to be blowin' outta the west without a storm cloud in sight, ain't it?" He shook his head and continued to follow his orders to unfurl a sail from one of the masts.

…an odd gale…without a storm cloud in sight. Magi spun around, the spell on his lips mid-turn. He cast a *Farsight* spell, and dialed in as far as he could behind the *Cornucopia.*

On the distant horizon, Magi saw land sliding over water. Only he knew it wasn't land; it was Xaro's armada, propelled by a fierce zephyr that was only now reaching them.

"Full sail!" he shouted. "All speed ahead if you value the ship, Captain! In fact, I will add my own wind to the ill breeze that nudges us forward. If you value this timber, tell your men to sail this floating fruit basket faster than it has ever been sailed before. All of our lives depend on it, for the winds of war hasten behind us, and they are gaining."

~Strongiron~

Nikron was right about one thing: you couldn't miss the Shembolt Mountains.

Long, slanted shadows began to grow as Strongiron and Kari stood facing the massifs to the south, though they had no idea how close they were to either coast of the vast continent of Adimand. As far as they could see, to the east and to the west in front of them were mountains—uniform, monotonous, and sharp. Strongiron was struck by the unmistakable image of a gate: a tall, wide, spiky gate. That's not to say there weren't foothills as the hardpan gave way to some rifts and undulation, but if you had a long enough sword, Strongiron was sure he could balance it on the tips of each peak, stretching it across the width of Adimand.

"You head east, I head west, we meet in the middle?" Strongiron joked.

Kari rolled her emerald eyes. "I have a better idea. We start exploring in the middle together. If I was going to cover myself with an entire mountain range, I'd bury myself in the center. Wouldn't you?"

He cocked his head to one side, slowly smiling. "Actually, yes, I think I probably would." His face turned serious. "Let us pray for protection—for a *Shield* before we enter the foothills. Nikron spoke of danger."

They prayed, and a light *Shield* encased each of them. Strongiron drew his sword, forever a slave to his training, danger or not. They hiked along a stony path that began climbing around a small hill. The path continued, slowly snaking steadily upward.

Abruptly, Strongiron paused. He turned to Kari and whispered, "Do you hear that?"

She nodded. *Water.* Strongiron put a finger to his lips.

They moved quietly now, a skill Strongiron found greatly improved whenever he wore his white armor from the Clerics. It never seemed to squeak like his typical knight's armor. Not that his stealthiness mattered; Kari had cast a sound-muffling *Illusion* as soon as he put his fingers to his lips.

The narrow path twisted further and further around the large foothill, until it crested and began to descend into a narrow canyon. The sound of flowing water could be heard more distinctly now, near a branch of the path that led between a rock wall and a boulder, with cracked stone forming the top of an ancient-looking natural archway. They proceeded in the direction of water, silent as spiders on a web. The path fell away quickly into stairs. Rounding a corner revealed a spectacular valley, lush and green, a *real* oasis in this hard land, unlike Nikron's outfit miles to the north.

Something was odd, however, about this beautiful gem hidden in the folds of the mountains. A dozen scorch marks marred the ground in random places, and seven bodies were lying flat on altars, surrounded by men and women, all dressed in hooded, brown robes.

Strongiron heard Kari gasp, and he knew why immediately. Those weren't altars. They were funeral pyres. Shiny wood was poking out underneath the bodies in all directions, and a woman was speaking, cradling fire in the palm of her hand. *She is a mage of some sort.*

One of the brown-robed men in the crowd spotted Strongiron and Kari on the hillside, descending into their village, and began pointing and shouting. Both Strongiron and Kari held their hands up, palms facing outward. The woman who was holding fire in her palm approached, and as she did so, the fireball changed color from blue to violet to red, growing in size.

"Come no closer, strangers!" she shouted. "Enough evil has been brought upon us by outsiders in recent days. I will rain fire down upon all our heads before I let another foreigner come into our midst."

Strongiron and Kari both stopped, but kept their hands up. "We mean no harm."

She sneered. "Of course you don't. Nobody means anyone harm in this Dark World, do they? Especially large, hulking brutes covered in armor, brandishing swords."

Kari spoke up. "You speak truly. I will grant you that. You are wise to be mistrustful. We do indeed live in dark times."

"Fair words and flattery will not soften my heart. Not when we have lost so much. I will say this one time only: if you value your life, turn around and leave."

Strongiron slowly nodded, sheathing his sword. "Very well. We did not come to interrupt your ceremony. I pray to the One True God

Dymetra that you have peace in your heart, and perhaps tomorrow will be a better day for you. Farewell."

"What did you say?" said the woman. "You worship Dymetra?"

"We do. She has chosen us to be Her Clerics—*True* Clerics—the first new priests of hers in centuries. We bring healing and knowledge of Her to Tenebrae. Have you heard of Her?" Strongiron asked.

She slowly walked toward both of them, the flame in her hand still crackling. "Old stories. This is the land that gave birth to the most powerful Druid in history. So powerful that when he died, he took his God with him!" Several in the crowd shouted in agreement at this. "We haven't seen Her since. We have a painting of your God in one of our caves, but that is all. Where was your *one true God* days ago, when one of the White Eyes murdered my husband! Tell me, where is your God in that?"

Kari turned to Strongiron, and he was sure she was thinking the same thing he was: *Oh God, are we too late? Has someone else stolen the Shield?*

Instead, she took a tentative step forward toward the woman, looking her in the eye. "I truly am sorry for your loss. Was your husband a kind man to you?"

She blinked at the odd question. "Kind? He was our Elder! None fairer, none wiser among us, yet no better than the other six who were killed by lightning—bolts right out of the sky! For all I know, the White Eyes asked your God to smite our village for him. Why do you want to know if he was kind?"

Kari was now standing directly in front of the woman. Strongiron also approached gently, with no sudden movements that might set off a spark with this twitchy woman. He could see the redness in her light grey eyes. *Sad eyes.* He patiently waited for Kari to answer her question, though he knew what was coming.

She held up her hands. "As my friend has said, these are healing hands. Show us your husband's body, and let us offer a prayer to Dymetra. You can then judge for yourself where She is in all this. As to my question, I simply feel better knowing that the man I shall bring back to life will appreciate his wife and treat her kindly."

Gasps could be heard throughout the crowd as Strongiron watched the woman's mouth slowly form a very round 'O'. Before she did anything rash with that fireball, which was now orange, he spoke over the growing discontent.

"I said we would leave you in peace, and we shall do so. But my friend offers a gift before we depart, and we ask nothing in return.

You have nothing to lose. Let us pray, and if nothing happens to those you have lost, you may ridicule us, and see that we leave chastened before you resume your ceremony. Or, we can leave now, and you will proceed to burn these bodies according to your custom. As the widow of your leader, I would leave this decision to you, my lady. We have already troubled you this evening far more than you bargained. I would only say this—are you not even the least bit curious whether we are genuine? I swear we will not lay a hand on any of the bodies; we would not desecrate your traditions. Look at us, *look at our eyes.* You can trust us."

He was careful not to say, *because neither one of us are True Mages.* That would be a lie, of course, and a Knight of the Order of Thunder—let alone a True Cleric!—wouldn't lie. *I might leave a bit of information out, that's all...besides, wasn't Kari given a special dispensation regarding her eyes from Dymetra Herself specifically to build trust?*

"Very well. Come this way and say your prayers. My husband is the last body."

The crowd parted out of respect for the widow, and they followed her to the last and largest funeral pyre in the line of seven.

"What is his name?" Kari asked.

"Dimitri."

"And your name, my lady?" Strongiron followed up gently.

"Yelena."

Kari smiled and then turned to Strongiron. He extended his hand to her and gave her a look that said *your idea, your prayer. You lead this one; I'll try the remaining six.* She nodded, as if she comprehended.

She said a simple prayer, "Dymetra, if it is your will, raise this man Dimitri back to life. If more work remains for him in Tenebrae, reunite him with his body, fully healed, that he may once again be a comfort to Yelena and to his village at large."

Strongiron echoed her prayer request, asking for the others to likewise be raised, to show Her power, Her presence. He had never tried to raise six people from the dead at one time, and he could feel the energy flying out of him. Whatever *Shield* he had earlier was gone now, completely overwhelmed by the enormity of this prayer. Sweat poured out of him. He looked over at Kari, and she, too, looked a little drained.

"Kari..." he said feebly. His knees buckled, and he slipped. She ran over to him, helping support him. The villagers were screaming something, but the whole world had gone hazy. He could barely think straight, he was light-headed.

The last sight he had—or thought he had—was of seven bodies sitting up, swinging their legs off the oiled wood to jump down off their pyres. He heard lots of shouting, but couldn't tell whether in joy, fear, or anger.

The last face he saw was Kari leaning over him as she gently laid him down on the ground. *Is she calling my name?*

Then everything went black.

~Belara~

Well, that didn't take long.

To be fair, Belara never considered that the Islander and his toad-of-a-wife would assign Galihali a *mission*. She figured it would be Galihali's love for that scout (*whatshisname?*) that would send her back to the Elfs, and thereby necessitate her elimination. She grudgingly had to admit, at least to herself, that it was sharp of them to send her in person to gently inquire about the Chief's health.

Not that it mattered. From the moment she'd impersonated her, Belara had put the Mage guard under a death sentence; Galihali was walking dead. As the Head of Magic in Rookwood now, she was keeping extremely close tabs on the young woman, waiting for the right time to put 'Cheyenne' to work. *Now, if I can make her 'accidental' death look a tad suspicious, that would* really *push the Elfs into a tizzy. They may declare war on Rookwood before Xaro even arrives...*

"You wanted to see me, Mistress?" Galihali entered Belara's chamber, shortly after her private meeting with the King and Queen. Belara looked at the soft-spoken Elf maiden, with that rich brown skin, modest face, and hair so black it looked like Lake Calm at midnight. Galihali nervously tightened the belt around the traditional grey robes of the Mage guard. It was quite a feat to be that young to Climb and serve the Crown in that capacity. *Perhaps Niku needed a token elf...*

"Thank you for stopping in on short notice, Galihali. Please, sit down." Belara smiled at her and poured two glasses of wine from a large carafe situated on a nearby end table. She took a glass and handed the other to the slender woman. "I trust no one saw you enter?"

Galihali shook her head slowly. "None that I saw, Mistress, as you requested." She looked down, gripping the goblet with both hands. "May I ask why you wanted to see me?"

"Of course, of course. Relax, Galihali. Nothing to fear here. I take it Niku never took the time to meet with you one-on-one? Is this the first time you've been in the Laboratory?" Belara smiled sweetly, swirling her wine.

Galihali seemed to take a deep breath, but she returned Belara's smile with one of her own, appearing relieved. "No, I can't say I've ever been allowed in here, and he never summoned me for a meeting, here or anywhere else. Now, twice in one day…" She stopped, sipping her wine.

"What do you mean, twice?" asked Belara.

The young Elf did not respond immediately, and did not look Belara in the eye, either. Belara continued, filling the lingering silence. "I summoned you to encourage you, Galihali. I've been watching your training closely. It isn't easy for a woman, especially so young, to achieve so much in this Dark World. To be a member of the Crown's own Mage guard…very impressive." She leaned forward. "What's troubling you, Galihali? You look more nervous than a slaughter-hog before festival!" She laughed lightly. "Who else summoned you today?" *Who else indeed?*

"I'm really not supposed to speak of it, Mistress. The King himself asked me—"

"Come now, I'm on the King's Small Council. Perhaps I can help…"

Galihali started to sweat, and dabbed her forehead with the loose sleeve of her robe. "Very well. His Majesty is worried about my people. Our Chief, Chocktaw, has taken ill, as you know. He could not travel to attend the ceremony, and I've been asked to *Teleport* there to see…him."

"To see Chocktaw…or *your friend*?" asked Belara, a wicked grin slowly spreading across her face.

The color rose in the young Elf's cheeks, bold enough that even her deeply tanned skin felt hot. In fact, her *throat* was hot. "H-how do you know about Cherokum?"

"My dear, am I not a woman? I know what love feels like. Your periodic 'visits,' though quite discreet, do not get past me. One of my many responsibilities is to know where all the Mage Guards are, Galihali. Be at ease here. Your secret is safe. I know quite well the *power* of a woman's passion."

Galihali took another gulp of her wine with shaking hands. "Thank you for understanding, Mistress. I…I feel like I should get going if there is n-nothing else?" Her voice kept cracking. "I don't feel that well all of a sudden, and should probably not delay the King's command."

Belara stood up. "Oh, I think you'll delay his command quite a bit, actually."

Galihali dropped her goblet, the sweat now running freely down her cheeks, mingling with droplets of white foam escaping the corners of her mouth. "Miwstess…?" she mumbled, before falling to her knees. It was the last thing she ever said.

Belara just continued to swirl her wine. *Another moment or two for the poison ought to do the trick.*

The young maiden fell to her side, clutching her throat, and died. 'Cheyenne' lamented that while no contract was in play, in the end, she looked at Galihali's death more like investment protection. If she was invested in war, chaos, and ultimately the Queen's Crown beside a new King, then she couldn't have Galihali *Teleporting* to visit the Elfs facing questions from her lover about a previous visit the young maiden never took. *No, that wouldn't do, not at all.*

She verified the Elf was dead, poured the wine back into her 'special occasion' carafe, cast a spell of *Invisibility* over the body, and *Levitated* it out a balcony window and hurled it down the mountain, causing small rocks to bounce down after it. By the time she removed the body's concealment, Galihali's shattered, half-decomposed, vulture-pecked corpse would look *awfully* suspicious lying in the middle of the woods.

The only Elfen representative in court, a powerful mage guard no less, mangled in the foothills…*By god, in his quest for answers or justice or both, this Cherokum fellow might well lead the Elfen charge himself.*

~Magi~

Climbing a small platform near the stern of the *Cornucopia*, Magi gave himself over to his Art, breathing in that heightened sense of his environment with every spell.

First, he cast a *Shield* spell over the bow of the ship. At the speed they were going to move, he knew he needed something other than the thin hull of a trading ship to take on the waves. Their ship would be punching through, not gliding up and down the crests and troughs.

Next, he needed wind. They were already feeling the effects of the wind Xaro was bringing behind them to propel his armada furiously through the open water. He would add to it with a gale of his own, filling the sails until the ropes and knots screamed with tension.

And finally, his third spell would lift the boat—not out of the water per se—that would divert far too much energy and do little to increase his speed. He wanted to ride high along the surface, grazing the sea as he punched through the relentless waves. He did not want to *sail* to Rookwood; he would *slide* across the vast ocean, like flat steel across ice. Magi may not have been able to *Teleport* to Rookwood, but by God, he would get there quicker than an arrow if he could.

When he set these spells in motion, he could feel the enormous vibration in the water from the armada far behind him. He picked up the smell of bird droppings from a flock of distant gulls searching for easy meals in the distance. He even heard the churning from the Maelstrom, far off to the north. But mostly his senses were filled with Veronica, who stood next to him, guarding him throughout his casting. He didn't need his heightened awareness to pick up the modest scent of berries with which she bathed, or the reflection of sun off her dark, wet hair. He could also feel the deep rhythm of her beating heart, and it thrilled him.

A week blew by—literally, as Veronica stood sentry, bringing some food and water when needed. Outside of occasional breaks and a ration of four hours of sleep per night (mainly to recharge himself), he kept the spells humming. The *Cornucopia* raced past Raag-Kaan, through the Strait of Holstine, and around the Elfen homeland of Filestalas. Magi finally stepped down from the platform to cast another *Farsight* spell, peering as far into the distance behind him as he could before they started a more northerly tack.

Nothing. Magi could not see any signs of the armada as far back as (what he guessed was) the western half of Elvidor. *We've put some water between us and them.*

He closed the spell and took a long, deep breath.

"You look awful," said Veronica, who was never far from him these days. She had been his lifeline the last week, with food, water, mandatory breaks, and protecting his sleep. He looked up and just grinned, raking his damp hair with his fingers.

"I say! Never passed over the water like that in all my years at sea, Master Blacksmooth! A fine job you did, fine job indeed. Why, we skipped along the water like a greased stone! That was somethin',

I tell ya. Somethin' this here Cap'n won' soon ferget!" Captain Leonard said as he thrust his hand out for a shake. "Say, ya don' suppose ya could maybe teach ol' Blue how do that, do ya? I could triple my profit if I moved like this on every trip! 'Course, I'd cut Blue in, ya know, fer the effort and all…"

Magi took Captain Leo's hand good-naturedly, gave it a hearty shake, but shook his head. "Captain, those spells all running concurrently would tax any True Mage, let alone your cook, who does quite well just where he is. What's more, you may find the fees for a good Sea Mage deplete whatever extra gold you earn pretty quickly when your speed is motivated by business versus necessity— which is what drove our need for haste. Nevertheless, I thank you for the kind words and hospitality. Your ship has earned every piece of gold you were promised. Just a few more leagues, and we should be close to the port of Rookwood."

"Not before you rest, Magi. You need a full day, at least, before we're thrown back into the plans and politics in the capital." Veronica grabbed his arm and forcibly began pulling him away from the rail and the other sailors, who would have been more than happy to sit on deck and jaw with him all afternoon. "I'm sure you understand, Captain."

"Aye, aye, o'course! Harder workin' mage ain't never seen in all my years floatin' on the sea. Take yer rest, 'bout time my crew got used to sailin' proper again. Har! Man yer posts, boys. Set a course…"

His voice trailed off as Veronica led Magi below deck to his small quarters and shut the door behind them. "Like I said, you look awful." She handed him a cup of water and some hard cheese, dried meat, old bread, and mixed berries. "Here…you need to eat."

Magi took the plate and set it aside. "Why are you doing this?"

She stopped and looked straight at him. "Doing what?"

"Guarding me. Helping me. Feeding me. All of it. Why are you being so nice?"

He wasn't quite sure if she was blushing or not, but she flashed him a sly little smile. "Maybe I'm just a nice girl."

Magi laughed out loud, hoping he wouldn't offend her. "You are many things, Miss Edgewild, but a nice girl is not at the top of your list."

Her eyes sparkled in mock outrage, but her smile never faded. She crossed the tiny cabin in three steps to stand next to him, arms folded across her chest. "Maybe my list has been recently reshuffled."

Magi put a hand gently on each shoulder. *She is so tall, and so...dangerously beautiful.* "I'm serious, Veronica. It's like I don't recognize you. Why are you doing this?"

Veronica put her arms around his neck and kissed him with a sudden passion that nearly knocked Magi into the wall behind them. But he let her, and then some.

She looked up at him with hungry eyes and said, "You ask stupid questions, Magi. Some things aren't that complicated. I don't know who's waiting for you when we get to Rookwood, but I'd like to make sure you remember me."

Magi leaned closer. *She's intoxicating...* He whispered, "How could I forget the woman who killed me?"

"You mean who saved you?"

"That too..." as their lips met again.

CHAPTER TWENTY-TWO: THE TEARING OF A VEIL

~King Herodius~

Father…I'm going to be a father again.

The thought was never too far from his mind over the next few days. A future prince—or princess—would be welcomed into the kingdom nine months from now…if the kingdom still stood. He galvanized his will toward ensuring that indeed it *would* still stand, and that brought his attention squarely back to the matter of the Elfs. He needed them, and thus he needed to know if the relationship had been poisoned by his wife's ill-advised gambit.

He looked over at her across their private chamber. She was lovely to him, standing by a window that overlooked the sea far below. His Queen was wearing a gossamer white, silken robe—loose-fitting and comfortable and nothing that anyone would ever see her in, save her maidservants and himself.

The nausea was hardly constrained to the morning, but thankfully it was infrequent. What's more, she always seemed to have a burst of energy right after a trip to the privy. Though it was long past midnight, now was one of those times.

"Herodius," she started, turning toward him. Pale as she was, he thought she looked radiant. *Like a star, not a ghost.* "I've been thinking. We probably need to prepare to tell Chocktaw."

He started to object, but she talked over him. "Hear me out. Galihali has been gone now nearly a week. I realize it may take time for her to get an audience with the Chief, but I have a feeling something is wrong. At some point, I think I need to tell him."

"That you hired someone to kill him? What would you do to him if he came to you with the same news, Najalas?"

She sighed, but kept her lips into a taut, thin line. "I would hold him. Question him further, but I would hold him, with orders to kill him if anything happened to me. And I would prepare for war."

Herodius was nodding patiently while she spoke. "Of course you would—I would do the same. We've discussed this. I will not let you travel to Thalanthalas, even if you were not carrying the heir to the throne. It is too dangerous. We must be a bit more patient, my love. Let the information come to us; let this play out further, and then we'll react based on facts, or at least good guesses. This I can tell you with certainty: you will *not* be travelling to the Elfs. If it comes to that, we will use Belara to call a meeting via her spell craft, or I will travel there in your stead."

She walked toward him, and put her arms around his neck lightly. "That crown has made you terribly bossy, *Your Majesty*," she playfully mocked. "If I actually wanted to leave to do this, do you think I would listen to your command?"

He broke into a sheepish smile, and placed his large hands against the small of her back, around her slender waist. "I suppose it was more of a strongly-worded suggestion."

She leaned in to kiss him, pulling his body closer; he gently began running his thumbs against her silken robe. She whispered gently into his ear, "There is something about a King protecting his Queen that just—"

"Your Majesties!" came a shout from outside their private chambers. Jonathon's voice.

Queen Najalas closed her eyes and let her head droop, clearly annoyed.

"The Queen is still not feeling well, Jonathon. This is an hour for rest; we will meet in the morning," yelled Herodius, though the moment had passed. His Queen was already untangling herself from his embrace, grabbing a heavier robe and a long cape.

"I understand, Sire, but I have unsettling news that should not sit. Perhaps then a moment with you, my King?"

Herodius and Najalas exchanged a look. She did not wait for him to yell back an answer.

"Jonathon, give me a moment, and we will both see you in our drawing room shortly." The Queen said with a raised voice. She threw on clothes more befitting an audience, but quietly she said to Herodius, "Must be important for him to shout through walls himself, rather than send a messenger."

Herodius just nodded. He helped his Queen tie on her cape, which was stitched together with brightly-colored fur and covered her completely. "A bit warm for this still," he said.

"It's quick and presentable," she said impatiently. "Come, King of mine. Let us hear this news."

They met Jonathon in the adjacent room; he stood and bowed when they entered. "Your Majesties. Forgive my intrusion."

Herodius gestured to the chair and they all sat down, the King and his Queen on a small couch with their Steward facing them. "It is fine, Jonathon. What is this news?"

"There has been a murder, or a suicide, my King. A body was found outside Rookwood."

Herodius spread his hands and leaned forward. "Murder and suicide happen every day, Jonathon. You know that. We live in a Dark World, one that grows darker by the hour it feels on some days." He shook his head briefly. "A tragedy perhaps, but hardly news—"

"Who was it?" the Queen interrupted.

"That is why I wanted to bring it to your attention, your Majesties. She was a member of your court: Galihali, the Elfen Mage Guard."

Herodius slowly turned his head to look at his wife's face, which was growing paler by the second. *Like a ghost, not a star.*

Jonathon continued. "You see the unsettling nature of this news? This could not be an accident—not with a *Levitation* spell so readily available to someone of her caliber. Furthermore, it was an open secret that she was in love with an Elfen scout; she disappeared from court all the time to visit him. I suppose a spurned love affair might make one leap to their death, but she was a *True Mage*, my Queen. What kind of True Mage opts to kill themself by jumping off a mountain? It's possible, I suppose. As you say, it is a Dark World."

"That would leave…" The Queen's voice trailed off.

Jonathon nodded. "Murder. Killing a True Mage Guard, a member of your court, and throwing them down a mountain is no easy task, your Majesty." He turned to look at Herodius shrewdly. "She may have taken her own life…but if someone killed her—let me just say that I thought this news warranted an interruption, my King."

"Who else knows?"

"Many. Peasants, likely stumbling home from a night at the tavern, found the body in the foothills below, just outside the city hours ago, and word travelled fast. By now the other Mage Guards know, so I assume Belara would know, assuming she was awoken as well; though, I haven't spoken with her or any other Council members yet. I wanted to bring this to your attention first." He spread his hands open. "Perhaps this is nothing more than a love affair gone sour."

Herodius scratched his chin. *You don't believe that, and neither do I. This was no lover's quarrel. There is a killer—and most likely a traitor—in our midst.* "Thank you, Jonathon. Call a council meeting in an hour—yes, even at this late hour. We will discuss this further as a group at that time."

~Kari~

The last week or so had been quite a celebration for the Druid conclave nestled into the foothills of the Shembolt Mountains. The village had their Elder back, and Dimitri had spent much of that week telling everyone about Dymetra, with whom he had recently met.

"So, She gave us all a choice," he thundered to a crowd outside Kari's hut. "She says, 'My Clerics are asking this of Me—that I should send you back to Tenebrae—and I will grant them this miracle if you promise Me two things, Dimitri.'" She had heard him tell this story three or four times now, as more and more villagers came to hear their Elder speak, but it never got old. Every time she heard him tell, it brought a smile to her face.

"What did She ask you to do?" inquired a young girl from the assembled crowd.

After a pause, Kari heard a log *crack* on the campfire as if on perfect cue. *Dimitri sure knows how to spin a yarn. He has a certain flair for it.*

"I'll tell you. I was on my knees, unable to even look up at Her. I only saw light spilling into my field of vision on the floor, but I heard Her voice, clear as you hear mine right now. She said, 'Help my clerics, and teach your village about Me, that I am real. Teach them that I am Wisdom, I am Protection, and I am Justice. Tell all who will listen about Me when I send you back to Yelena, Uriah, Eben, and Zachary."

Outside, Kari heard the *oohs,* she heard the *ahhs.* Then: "And that is exactly what I am doing now."

"Your friend…is he feeling better?" asked Yelena, who poked her head into the hut to check on Kari and her ward. Strongiron was lying down, sleeping. They had cleared out a small hut for her to lay Strongiron after he'd blacked out from the exertion of his Resurrection Prayer. *Six at one time…too much.*

He had, however, begun to get up throughout the week, and was certainly getting stronger, but he still needed rest—sleep, water, and food, pretty much in that order. Kari tended to him while getting to know the village. Yelena, in particular, was someone to whom she grew close almost immediately. The woman had transformed from a bitter, suspicious, fireball-wielding Druid to a compassionate friend who drew and heated water, prepared food, and watched Strongiron when Kari herself needed a break. *Raising a beloved husband from death will do that to a woman, apparently.*

"He grows stronger every day. Thank you, Yelena."

"I'm not surprised—he has a good name." She walked over to sit down on the other side of Strongiron's body, across from Kari, while the crowd shouted in favor of something her husband said outside.

"Your husband…he seems to be fully recovered," Kari said with a warm, genuine smile. "If he keeps this up, we might have to make him an honorary Cleric as well."

"Oh, I am sure you will. I'm quite serious—the man burns for Dymetra, and he has ignited the whole village. If you don't make him an apprentice, he will find a way to get trained himself. Dimitri has never lacked for passion, Kari."

"I can tell." She patted Strongiron's cheek with a warm piece of cloth. "Our mission will take us back east soon, but we will gladly share what we know, and can leave behind plenty of material to help you grow your faith."

"Your mission for Windomere's Shield."

"Yes. That is what we are searching for."

"You are not the first, you know." She had a sad smile on her face, and had the look of a woman offering condolences. *Like we have already failed, or died trying.*

"I know that others have sought it, but how many *True Clerics* do you know have searched these mountains for Windomere's Shield?"

Yelena's face brightened a little. "None, actually…until a week ago I would not have believed that True Clerics even *existed.*" She looked around the small hut and lowered her voice, like a girl whispering secrets to another. "You know, I may be able to help you."

Kari involuntarily squeezed Strongiron's hand as she leaned forward. "How? Do you know where he is buried?"

"Every year we make a pilgrimage to the catacombs, which are really a network of caves that descend into the bones of these mountains. The place is sacred to us. We are forbidden to take any outsiders there, but…"

Kari released Strongiron's hand and reached across his broad chest to grab the other woman's hands in her own, gently but firmly. "Yelena. If you can help show us the entrance, saving us the time of having to search every crack and crevice of these mountains…"

The woman looked Kari in the eyes. "My husband says we are to help you—says that Dymetra Herself gave him that command. If you can put breath back in his lungs, then perhaps that is a sign that you are to be trusted. I have to warn you though, a crafty Druid with timeless features guards the body someway, somewhere. He does not bother us, for we do not seek the Shield. I can't help you with him, but I can lead you to where the catacombs start. From there, you'll be on your own."

"*We'll* be on our own," corrected Strongiron, who happened to have both eyes open now.

"Master Strongiron! You are awake!" Yelena looked at him and clapped her hands together.

"I am. Just needed a little rest and meditation after that last prayer. Took a little out of me, that's all."

A little? You've been in and out of consciousness for a week! "Did you have a nice rest, my dear?"

"Just resting my eyes." He tossed Kari a wink of those maddeningly bright, crystal-blue eyes. "Besides, I think I've been babied enough for awhile. I feel great, and I think we should delay no longer." He sat up and looked at Yelena. "When can we leave?"

"It is at least a three-day hike to get there, and a strenuous one. I will need a day to prepare…and I will talk privately to Dimitri. He may want to join us, or…"

Kari frowned at Yelena, but said nothing.

"Or he may try and forbid it. Those are really the only two ways that conversation will go. But I must tell him if I'm to be gone for six days or more."

"And what if he forbids you to lead outsiders to this place?" asked Kari, unable to keep a modest edge out of her voice. *Please don't make me remind this man that he owes his life to us…*

A wide smile spread across the Druid's face. "Then the three of us will have to be discreet in our journey. You two can manage that, I presume?"

~King Herodius~

"Follow me," he said to his Queen. Herodius walked briskly out of the drawing room and into the corridor leading to the Royal chambers. A few late-owl passing knights paused to salute him; he ignored them or dismissed them with a wave.

He passed the Great Hall and passed the Small Council room, where he would be assembling with the council in an hour. His jaw was set, and his Queen was hustling to keep up, but she offered no complaint. A curved stone wall protruded into the main corridor, with an archway leading into the grand cylinder. Above the archway was a sign that read *The Crown Showeth Mercy*—the first tower of Rookwood's five spires.

He passed the Tower of Mercy and kept walking.

Mages and the advancement of their Art filled the next section of Rookwood. More than a few grey-robed Mage Guards whispered to one another as Herodius and Najalas strode through the castle silently but resolutely. They all snapped to attention, many bowing, but the King just nodded or waved without slowing down. On he walked, past several quarters, mage barracks, laboratories, dueling rooms, and the Royal Library as well. All seemed quiet. Eventually he came to another curved wall fashioned lovingly with beautiful stone. This one also protruded into the hallway, with an archway opening cut into it. Each tower was unique in their masonry— different colors and definitely different-sized rocks. The sign above the opening to the second spire read *The Crown Wieldeth Power.*

They passed the Tower of Power and continued down the corridor.

The sounds of early-morning cooking for the preparation of a large-scale breakfast filled this section of the castle, with the unmistakable aroma of roasting pork filling the hallways. Magical fires burned low over pits high in the mountains where working mages, old knights, and talented peasants all worked tirelessly around the clock to keep the castle inhabitants fed. Herodius felt his mouth begin to water as he got a strong whiff of rosemary while passing by one of the kitchens. Several hallways branched off the main corridor to lead down to various storerooms. The one leading to the King's ale room was always guarded—a standing order from his Queen. The older knight straightened into a salute the minute he saw them both striding his way. Herodius again just nodded, but he heard his Queen say, "Good morning, Hector," as she walked past, her bright fur cape *whooshing* behind her. On they walked past the kitchens and the dining halls, some large for castle inhabitants, others smaller and more intimate for visiting nobles. The corridor continued to bend and meander as it conformed to the irregularities of the mountain cliff face upon which it had been built.

Not long past the cooking and eating area, they came to another curved stone wall that jutted out into the hallway. The third cylinder was smoother than the first two, with light-colored stones. They came to the archway, and the sign above this one read *The Crown Demandeth Truth.*

"Follow me, Najalas," he repeated, and turned into the middle spire of Rookwood, the Tower of Truth.

The towers consisted largely of a spiral staircase cut into the stone. Niku had always said that the towers were built in part to resemble *The Staircase* that all of them were forced to climb, which was unsurprising, given the blend of stonecraft and magecraft that went into the building of such a fortress as Rookwood. Herodius had heard the stories of how interminable the Climb was for mages who sought to be true masters of their craft; thankfully the Towers of Rookwood, while tall, did not go on forever. However, by the time he and his wife reached the summit, she was breathing heavy, and a fine sheen of sweat covered him as well.

He took a deep breath, and cast his eyes to the east, with the entire world seeming to fall away from him in the wee hours of the morning. The fortress gave way to the mountainside, the mountain gave way to foothills, the foothills led to the surrounding city, and the city ran down to the sea. And the Endless Sea of the East…went on forever.

Turning his gaze to the north, Herodius was high enough to see a few fires marking the city of Plythe in the distance, across the Sea of Joy. He could not see his new navy, but he knew they were out there, somewhere. The mountain air felt quite cold on his damp forehead, especially at this hour. He wiped his brow on a sleeve.

"I apologize for bringing you all the way up here, my love, but I do not trust our privacy any longer."

"Nothing to apologize for, Herodius. Your concerns are my concerns. But let us now talk quickly before we meet with the small council. You do not believe Galihali killed herself, do you?" asked the Queen as she caught her breath. "I certainly do not."

"Not for one minute. Jonathon was astute in that this was no accident either; no True Mage dies from a fall unless they're unconscious, exhausted, or already dead. Only a fool would believe a mage guard fell to her death shortly after we set her up on a quest for information divination with her own people…with Chief Chocktaw."

"Agreed. She was murdered, Herodius." She said it matter-of-factly.

"And that is why I wanted to speak up here. The Mage Guards have memory balls, and who knows what other means to listen and see what we wish to keep private. Not for the first time have I wished Magi and his Staff were still with us, may he rest in peace."

Queen Najalas sighed slightly, and pulled her cape more tightly around her as a gust of wind whipped at her hair.

"My Queen, as much as it pains me to say this, we must assume there is a traitor in our midst. If not a traitor, then someone who was motivated to kill Galihali…and I hardly believe it has anything to do with her love for an elfen scout."

"I've been worried about the same thing, my love. When the Elfs failed to show up—"

"They know. We must assume they know," he finished, smacking a fist into his open palm for emphasis. "I don't think we need a mission to Thalanthalas to confirm our worst fears. Chief Chocktaw knows."

"But how?" asked his Queen.

"That is the question. Killing Galihali would likely require either a surprise confrontation…or someone she trusted. I just can't imagine someone taking on a mage guard directly and keeping the battle quiet."

"An Assassin, then?"

"Likely. But for now, before we meet as a Small Council, I think we should use the same approach we were planning on using on Chief Chocktaw: misinformation. We need to catch the traitor in a lie."

"You really think the traitor is a member of our Small Council? Surely not Simon, nor Peter. And Jonathon—"

"We cannot trust anyone fully from this point forward until we know whether an Assassin was hired to kill Galihali, and if so, who, and most importantly—why. That must be our first step, I believe. Do you agree, my Queen?"

She stared out over the waist-high rock wall that served as the railing, pressing her hands into the smooth stone. Distant, white-tipped waves crashed endlessly on the shoreline of the great port of Rookwood—the only part of the sea she could see in the night. "Yes. I think you are right on this. Our second priority though, which cannot be delayed much further, is to notify Chief Chocktaw. I am inclined to set up a meeting of our shades, facilitated by our respective mages, to share completely my…my folly and our suspicions. Doing so may be the only hope we have of convincing them to help us." She turned to look at Herodius, who reached out his arms to hold her tight.

He gently pulled away to look his Queen in the face once more. "It may come to that, but I would feel much better about opening up to the Elfs once I have a bead on our traitor. If we are right, then someone fed them information, which in turn has led to the Chief's distancing himself from us. Identifying the traitor prior to a discussion with Chocktaw serves our cause well, if we could."

Suddenly the Queen's eyes grew big, and she pulled even a little further away from him. "Herodius, what if *Galihali* was the traitor? What if someone killed her *for us,* and tried to make it look like an accident? What if someone is trying to protect us, acting on their own to keep us plausibly ignorant?"

Herodius smiled, but his eyes looked sorrowful. "Such fortune seems unlikely in this Dark World, but as Magi once said to us, it is not a hopeless one. We shall see, my love. In less than an hour, we shall see…"

~Luther~

Serving Victor as his singular 'battle mage' required a form of discipline akin to a ship's cook: trapped in one spot, depended on by everyone, appreciated by few. When Victor was promoted, Luther entertained a glimmer of hope that the new Lieutenant General and Commander of the Northern Army would be different—a man with a more sophisticated appreciation of the contributions of mage-craft on the battlefield, perhaps…a man who would, at a minimum, order more mages up north to help lighten the burden on Luther.

He was disappointed.

Oliver Creighton, Knight of Thorns, was a copy of Victor, and—as his knighthood indicated—fiercely loyal to the man. The only difference Luther could tell between the two men was that Oliver, half-a-head taller than Victor, would never have beaten the General in a fight; he wasn't *quite* as mean, and he didn't cheat *quite* as much. Beyond that, Luther's days were filled with the same monotony: help Benjamin prepare food, help Benjamin clean up, mix healing salves for everyday cuts and bruises, *Teleport* here-there-everywhere for armloads of supplies, and open a communication link to Rookwood for occasional updates. Menial tasks more befitting an apprentice, or even a journeyman…*certainly not a True Mage.*

Well past midnight after another night of cock-fighting and drunken revelry (an occurrence of increasing frequency, given Victor's departure and the news that Xaro had been killed), Luther once again found himself putting out *Everflame* spells and tidying up camp. Oliver expected the camp to be clean and orderly for their morning drills, and he expected Luther to 'put his magic to good use.' Working the night shift was Luther's time, it would seem. He sighed in the stillness; even the frolicking gypsies had finally gone to sleep.

Looking to the north across the black sky, he went about his duties. Armor was scrubbed with cleaning spells, clothing stitched with sewing spells, water boiled for the morning. He kept looking to the starless sky. *Not even the moon shines tonight.*

Something was odd; the moon had been out earlier. Casting a *Farsight* spell, he looked to the southeast...the distant twinkle of a few fires shown where Oxen-Pace lay slumbering under a star-filled sky. Swinging his spell back to the north, he saw only an empty sky...not even a cloud.

Not even a cloud...if not clouds, then what obscures the heavens? He slowly shifted his telescopic spell across the sky to pinpoint the edge of where the blackness began to conceal the constellations. Slowly his white eyes grew less oval and more round: the darkness was moving south, toward them, and *fast.* He could see now that it wasn't just the sky that was being painted black—a *wall* of blackness, like a tidal wave, was coming forward. He could see now that landmarks on the horizon were disappearing as the wall accelerated toward their camp. They had just minutes before it arrived.

"Arise!" Luther shouted, amplifying his voice. *"Arise, men of the north!"* He immediately rekindled all the *Everflames* he had just put out, and the camp was awash in blue light.

Lieutenant Commander Oliver pushed open the door to his quarters and emerged shirtless, wearing only small clothes. Luther was running toward his cabin, his cloak billowing behind him in the night air. "Mage, what in all that is holy are you *screeching* about—"

"Sir!" Luther cut him off. "Behold, to the north. An ill spell approaches us, darkening all in its wake. I strongly recommend you muster the army. Nothing good comes from that spell in the middle of the night, Commander."

Commander Oliver looked to the north; even to the naked eye, the wall of black could be clearly seen now, like a dust storm that filled one's vision. He turned back into his cabin and said, "Leave," to a red-haired gypsy, groggily waking.

He grabbed Luther's arm. "Awake all the men, now. Can you create a light to shine through that...that *black cloud?*"

"I will try, sir." And Luther ran off to wake the entire camp with thunderous cries. He then cast a quick *Shield* around himself on instinct as much as anything else. If asked, Luther would have guessed it would take an hour for the men to be awoken, dressed, armed, and mustered, given the nightly festivities. To Oliver's credit, his men would have been ready in half that time.

Unfortunately, the darkness fell on the Northern camp within fifteen minutes, plunging everything into the thickest form of night anyone could ever remember. Buckling armor became laughable in the dark, and even the *Everflames* were reduced to glow pebbles.

"*Solis!*" cried Luther, standing on a rock platform that overlooked the eastern flank of Commander Oliver's thousand men. *Surely the light of the sun will reveal what lies hidden in this ill spell.* He held his hands over his head, a foot or so apart, and an intense ball of light grew to fill that space. He slowly pulled his arms further and further apart, allowing the 'sun' to grow ever larger until it rose from his hands and began to float into the darkness.

What he saw from his perch were 10,000 shadows, swords drawn. In the near distance, behind the army, was a *Levitating* man, palms forward in front of him pouring darkness from his hands like two chimneys spewing smoke. As the magical sun from Luther passed near to him, he turned his head toward the fellow mage and smiled. He opened his mouth and spoke in a voice so loud it seemed to come from everywhere all at once:

"I will let your little light shine above only briefly. I want you all to see the final doom of your days, and know that the architect of your end is my face: Xaro. With the falling of our first sword, we hasten the ending of this Godless age and christen the dawning of a new age—the Age of Kuth-Cergor! Let my face be the last you see, and let his name be the last you hear!"

The next sound was not the clang of steel-on-steel, but the tortured cry of a man suffering from steel-on-flesh. Soon the lone cry was joined by others as Xaro's swords fell on men still scurrying for armor.

Luther began hurling *Lightning Bolts* from both hands…for light as well as maximum damage. He tried to take out the obvious mage in the back, but his bolts diffused harmlessly around a *Shield* that seemed quite formidable. For every five men he killed, fifty of Commander Oliver's were run through. He could hear some steel clanging now, but still far too many death cries.

"Luther!" cried his Commander. "Protection! Give us time to armor ourselves! By whatever God you worship, *protect us Luther!*" Two heavily-armed men were on either side of Sir Creighton, and he was fighting gamely in a leather vest and a pair of breeches, hastily thrown on.

Luther turned and cast the largest Shield spell he thought he could muster, using his mind to fold and bend its edges around his army, while leaving the invaders unprotected; a dome spell would have been easier, but useless now that it was hand-to-hand. Sweat was pouring from Luther—he was tiring.

Battle-axes and halberds rained down on this intricate *Shield*, the blades getting blunted mere inches away from skulls. The blows continued, drawing more and more of Luther's energy out of him. Most of the men were able to put on helms and grab bucklers, but few had time to truly buckle chain or plate armor. The first sword breached Luther's *Shield* over a distant warrior who lost an arm from a particularly vicious stroke. Luther fell to his knees.

"I cannot keep this large of a *Shield* up!" he shouted. He stepped down and hid behind the rock upon which he had been standing. His *Shield* faded, and the cries resumed. The few seconds he had afforded his army only gave the invaders a chance to nearly surround each man. *They were being slaughtered like...like roosters in a tight cage.*

An exhausted man stumbled toward him; his arms and legs were cut to ribbons, and he was using his sword like a cane as he limp-ran toward the mage. *Commander Oliver!*

"L-Luther," he mumbled. "*Teleport* to Rookwood. Tell the G-General. Tell V-Victor about Zar-oh. Go. *G-go!*"

A glowing missile, undoubtedly from the *Levitating* mage, struck Lieutenant Commander Oliver Creigthon in the neck, pitching him forward onto the ground and leaving his head swinging on a hinge of bloody flesh.

Luther didn't waste another second; he was more than convinced his work on this battlefield was done. He *Teleport*ed to Rookwood just before the rock he was hiding behind exploded from another of Xaro's blasts.

~King Herodius~

Three low, oily torches bathed the Small Council chamber with flickering light. The room would have smelled like smoke had it not been for the Head of Magic. Last to enter, the general scent was transformed from dank and smoky to vanilla, roses, and other exotic spices. Belara, clothed today in a shiny lavender gown and cowl that clung to her like wet paint, took her seat next to Simon.

Herodius stared at the mostly groggy faces and drooping eyes of his recently-awoken council: Simon, Peter, Jonathon, Belara, and Victor. The thought that one of them, or anyone else (*Galihali?*) could be a killer or traitor turned his stomach. Not for the first time did he wish Niku or Magi were still alive, or that Strongiron or even

Kari were still here. *Good* people, people he *knew* he could trust…even his beloved Queen could not always be trusted in her judgments.

He looked over at Najalas's pale face and smiled. *That's not fair to her and you know it—at least she* eventually *confided in you. Still…*

Herodius turned back to the five men and one woman sitting around his table. Shadows danced across their faces from the three torches burnt low. *Much rides on your choice of words…sometimes it takes a liar to catch a liar.*

"Thank you all for agreeing to forego the last couple hours of sleep so that we may council together," began the King. "By now, you have heard that Galihali has been murdered."

Victor looked at Simon and Peter. "The Elf? A Mage Guard? Did you know this?" he asked them both.

Simon nodded. "I heard an hour ago."

Peter looked shocked. "I had not heard. Murdered?"

The Queen nodded. "That is our initial thought, yes."

"Why do think she was murdered?" asked Belara.

Victor turned to her. "So, you had heard that she was dead as well? Are Peter and I the only ones finding out this minute?"

Heads generally nodded in agreement, and Belara turned to Victor. "I heard just a few hours ago as well, when some of the other Mage Guards woke me to tell me that her body had been found." She turned back to the Queen. "Again, you do believe she was murdered?"

King Herodius answered. "At the moment, yes. What else could it be? Mage Guards are not easily thrown off the side of a mountain, Belara."

"Of course not, my King, but she was rumored to be involved with another Elf back in Thalanthalas…perhaps a lover's quarrel?" she offered.

The Queen laughed at this. It was such a rare sound, like an Assassin's apology, that it immediately drew everyone's attention. "A lover's quarrel? Do you expect me to believe a woman that powerful would throw her life away over some *man?* Please, Belara. Would you?"

Some of the eyes shifted uncomfortably to King Herodius, who sat there stoically. Belara answered, "No, of course *I* would not—my Art is my soulmate. I was simply raising the possibility. That is all."

"Which is why our investigation continues," said Herodius, leaning forward. "Fortunately, we were able to retrieve her Memory

426

Ball from her corpse. Once we replay it, we shall know for sure what happened." He leaned back to survey the room.

Jonathon sat silent, barely nodding. Victor and Simon were exhaling. Peter was frowning. Belara, however, blinked. It was only a second, but she stared at Herodius…and blinked.

"Where is this Memory Ball, your Majesty?" asked Peter. "Did you bring it for Belara to open?"

"I have dispatched an emissary to Chief Chocktaw. Since Galihali was the singular Elf in our court, I wanted him or his designees present when we opened it. If she was murdered by someone in the castle, I would want to give him the opportunity to mete out his people's justice."

"Is that—wise? Surely we should play it first before we trouble him to come all this way?" asked Belara.

Do I detect an edge in your voice? Herodius wondered. "Perhaps, but I would not want another leader to question whether the ball was tampered with or not—especially when the outcome under consideration is murder. This way there is no chance of a cover-up. After all, we only want the truth. Galihali surely did not deserve this fate," he finished smoothly.

Belara pressed her point further. "But Sire…if this deed was a suicide, I can't imagine asking the Chief to come all the way to Rookwood just to see a lonely Elf maiden launch herself down the mountain?"

The Queen leaned forward. "As discussed, Belara, we are confident that did *not* happen."

One of the torches was obscured and nearly winked out as a large shadow blocked the light. Seven heads turned at the flickering torchlight to find a young man standing there in midnight-blue robes with a matching cloak that would have been a rich ensemble had they not been splattered with dirt and blood. He nearly collapsed, but managed to fall to one knee.

"Luther?" exclaimed Victor. "What in the blazes are you doing here?"

The exhausted mage acknowledged Victor with a weary salute before turning back to his King and Queen. "Your Majesties. Forgive my unannounced intrusion, but it is most fortuitous that you are already awake and assembled. It grieves me greatly to tell you that our Northern army is completely wiped out. We have been attacked, and our enemy heads south, toward us even now."

King Herodius stood up, peppering him with questions. "So the Ogre comes, does he? Or is it the Dark Cleric? How many? How far away? What happened?"

Luther tilted his head quizzically. "I don't know about an Ogre, my King. Nor do I know what a Dark Cleric looks like, but he said his name was Xaro. He must have had 10,000 men…we never stood a chance, Sire."

The Queen now stood up. "Did you say their leader was Xaro? What did he look like?"

Peter jumped in before the mage could answer. "I thought Xaro was dead!"

Luther framed his white eyes by lifting his eyebrows in modest surprise. "I assure you, the man I *Teleported* away from five minutes ago was very much alive. Tall, wide—built a bit like our former General Strongiron actually, with curly brown hair. He got close enough for me to see the cleft in his square jaw. I couldn't see the color of his eyes, but they weren't white—I can assure you that. Yet he was *Levitating*, casting *Shields* and *Missiles* and spewing *Darkness* right out of his palms! His invading force out of the north swept into our camp shrouded in the blackest of black fogs, unlike anything I have ever seen. By the time alarms were raised and our men armed, their swords were already upon us. I can't explain how they could see while we were blind, but he's a True Mage if ever I've seen one."

"And you swear that this man is alive, Luther?" asked Victor as he stood.

"On my life. Whatever report you received about his death was wrong."

The King, Queen, and five more sets of eyes—including Luther's—converged on Belara…but she was gone, *Teleported* away to parts unknown before anyone could say a word.

~Magi~

Two days of mostly sleeping did wonders for Magi's energy level. Dawn broke fair as the *Cornucopia* drifted near the port of Rookwood, which was strangely blocked by thirty war ships spread out in a line across the seaway entrance.

"Don' recall a damn blockade cuttin' our means to the docks. I don' suppose this has anything to do w' that armada chasin' us halfway aroun' the world, do ya?" said Captain Leo, pointing to the ships ahead of them.

Magi and Veronica were on either side of him, near the helm. "I think that's a safe bet, Captain," said Magi. "If I may offer you some advice to go with our gold?" He gestured to Veronica, who handed the Captain a very large, very heavy sack of coins.

"I'll take any advice yer offerin'." Leo pulled open the drawstrings, peeked inside, and nodded.

"Sail as far away from here as you can. I'll *Levitate* Veronica and I to shore. Don't even try to enter the port; even if they let you, this is not likely a place you want to be. Find your fortune elsewhere, Captain Leo, and may fair seas carry you far."

"Aye. War's not good fer trade, not when men are just as likely to kill, steal, and sink as they are to make a fair exchange. If yeh come outta this to the good, I'll trade wit yeh any day, mage. An' yeh too, darlin'." He winked at Veronica, jangling his sack of coins a bit.

"Thank you, Captain," she said, smiling. She turned to Magi. "I'm ready for a lift whenever you are."

He nodded, clasped hands with the Captain one last time, and cast his spell. All the crew on deck watched Magi and Veronica slowly rise off the boat, and begin to float out over open water toward the shore of Elvidor, near Rookwood.

"Farewell, Master Blacksmooth!" shouted the Captain. Veronica waived at the crew and boat, dwindling in the distance behind them.

The first arrow fell just short of them as they were a hundred feet from the docks.

"What the—" said Veronica.

Magi was already casting a *Shield* spell around them both just as a flurry of arrows began to boink off them. Below them, he could hear shouts and calls for mage guards. A dozen grey-robed figures began to pour out of a guardhouse.

"Rookwood has become a bit less welcoming, wouldn't you say?" Magi said to Veronica. "I'd rather not try my luck taking down a dozen guards, but I'm not *Teleporting* away and leaving you if they're firing arrows at anything that moves."

"I'm glad to hear that, because I'm pretty sure if I enter this city alone *in the best of times* my life is probably forfeit. Now…"

"I'm not leaving you in the city. We'll land and I'll try to reason with the guards. Hopefully Simon is still in charge."

"Better him than Peter…I can't imagine he wants to see me again."

He took a quick scan all around from his lofty height. The city looked desolate, save for guards, soldiers, a beggar or two. Maybe everyone was hiding indoors, but he doubted it. *Something's happened.*

Magi lowered them onto solid ground, whereby they were completely surrounded by a dozen mage guards, four or five swords, and another half-dozen archers. The combined force of the mage guards would drain his *Shield* in no time.

"We come in peace! Please—we need to see Queen Najalas. We have urgent information about the attack. Where's Simon, or Jonathon? I was a trusted member of the Queen's Small Coun—"

"Magi?" It was Simon.

"Simon! Dymetra smiles on us still. Will you please call off the attack?"

"Prove to me it is you."

"What did you say? Prove to you it's me? What are you talking about, Simon?"

"Show me your Staff."

Magi turned to Veronica. "I—I don't have it. Xaro does."

"Hmmm…that is unfortunate. Mage guards! Break down his *Shield* and apprehend him until we decide what to do with this imposter."

"Wait!" Magi insisted. "I am *not* an imposter! I can prove it. Would an imposter know Peter's guilty secret of how he murdered a sailor to protect his career? Would an imposter have sat in court listening to petitioners complain about the quality of ale? Would an imposter have chased down Veronica, the former Assassin who attempted to kill General Strongiron several times? I was linked to Niku—our shades could communicate, but that connection was broken…I can only assume that he is no longer with us. Would an imposter know all this? Would he, Simon?"

The Captain of the Guard sheathed his sword and held up a hand to the assembled troops. "No, I don't suppose an imposter would, Magi." His face broke into a smile and he strode forward to hug the other man. "We thought you were dead. Niku couldn't reach you, and has since died, and well…lies have run deep lately."

Magi pulled away. "I nearly was. In retrospect, it was folly to attempt recovering that ring on my own in the first place. Xaro captured me, and I will spare you a description of the dungeon into which I was thrown. Needless to say, no magic could reach me there." He flicked his head toward Veronica. "But she could…and did. I would be dead, if it weren't for her."

Simon looked at Veronica as if recognizing her presence for the first time. He shifted his eyes back to Magi with a look of cold irony. "I thought you were dead because of her."

"Yes, well, we can have that philosophical discussion long into the night, but time is precious and fleeting. Will you escort us to the Queen? Veronica has detailed information about Xaro's attack plans, and time is of the essence."

"Indeed. His plans are already in motion, it appears. The north has fallen."

Veronica grabbed Simon's arm reflexively. "That means Xaro himself has landed. Malenec and Tar-Tan are not far behind, and Tarsh sails here as we speak."

Simon looked down at the hand holding his forearm, causing Veronica to withdraw it self-consciously. "Forgive me. I didn't mean to grab you."

"No, it's not that. I was just marveling at your hands...not so much as a scratch. So it is true that Strongiron healed you? Regrew them completely?"

Magi put his arm around Simon. "I promise we will catch up on all this, but now...the Queen?"

Simon nodded. "Yes. Of course. Follow me." He led them through the city and up the great causeway that led to the entrance to the fortress. Magi was in no mood to climb steps or wait for lifts; he cast another *Levitation* spell and soon was in the small council room with the others. Impatient as he was, he would have *Teleported* if he didn't think it prudent for the three of them to arrive together.

Jonathon filed in first, followed by Victor. The Queen entered, holding Herodius's hand. Last came Peter, who did not take his eyes off Veronica. Magi thought his hands kept straying dangerously close to the dirk sheathed on his belt.

"My Queen—" Magi began.

"And King," added Najalas gently. "Herodius is King, Magi."

"Your Majesty," Magi corrected, bowing with the slightest impatience to his new King. *You can call yourself Emperor for all I care, but can we proceed?* "If I may cut to the quick—Veronica, who I know has committed grave crimes against the Kingdom in general and members of this court in particular, has valuable information regarding Xaro's plans. If you ever trusted my judgment of character, trust it now: on my life I swear to you that this woman is no longer a threat to your crown or your people, my King. I beg you hear her out, and let us discuss how to address this information when it is combined with what you already know."

"Your Staff confirms this?" asked Herodius.

"No, my King. The Staff of Wisdom is in Xaro's possession. But I would not be here if it was not for her, and I cannot think of any reason why she would do that."

Peter stood up. "To gain our trust, of course! So she can betray us later, when the stakes are higher. Let us not forget that our enemy was patient enough to invest *eighteen years* of lies just for the privilege of betraying you, Magi. Surely you, more than anyone else here, are the least susceptible to such schemes and facades!"

Magi watched as Jonathon and Simon both started nodding at Peter's sentiment. He started to say something when Veronica put her hand on his shoulder to quiet him, as if to say *my turn.*

"You are right, Peter, that I am trying to gain your trust. I have a long way to go—furthest with you, I know. I am so sorry for threatening your life…it was all I could think to do at the time with the tools that I had." She walked to the front of the room slowly, hands in front of her where they could be seen by all, so she could address the entire group at once.

"Let me share what I have heard. You can debate it, act on it, or ignore it as you see fit. After that…Strongiron saw fit to forgive me for trying to kill him, which I did not deserve any more than I deserve this court's mercy. If you wish to imprison, beat, or kill me—I throw myself on the mercy of the King's judgment, and I will accept my punishment without protest or recourse, but hear me out; at least use what I know to protect yourselves from Xaro as best you can."

Peter sat down, with a gesture to King Herodius. "Very well. Speak, Veronica. What do you know?"

Veronica nodded, and told them of Tar-Tan's war strategy, that four divisions would converge on Rookwood from the north (Xaro), the sea (Tarsh), and behind them, through the Elfen lands (Malenec and Tar-Tan).

Victor stood up first when she finished. "My King, I don't know this woman, but I do know that when I saw her last, she didn't have hands. If this intelligence is true, we cannot let them lay siege to us. We have already allowed too many citizens to take refuge in the fortress; our food will not last a month, let alone past harvest. We cannot hope to hole up in here…we must take the battle to them!"

Jonathon turned to Veronica. "Why did you leave to Sands End after Strongiron healed you?"

"You may find this hard to believe, but I owed a debt to Magi. For killing him…and, in a way I don't expect you'll understand, for saving me as well. Strongiron may have healed my hands, but Magi saved me by taking them in the first place." She blinked back tears that had begun to swell in her light brown eyes. "Anyhow, I knew he was headed to Sands End, so I travelled there as well." She stifled a small chuckle and looked at Magi. "Of course, I didn't know the mess you had gotten yourself into."

Herodius pursed his lips. "Victor, I believe your council is prudent. If we assume this information is true—" He looked at Veronica. "—then I would say it is imperative that we keep open a path behind us to escape, and to the sea to resupply us. Peter, what do you think of moving a portion of your fleet forward to engage this Tarsh and their armada before our port is bottled up?"

The Admiral narrowed his eyes. He stood up to look at a large map of Tenebrae. "Again, assuming we can trust this…this *killer*—" He stopped in mid-sentence; Magi was staring at him. They all were in fact. Peter cleared his throat audibly. "We've all made mistakes. Grave ones." He looked down at the map again, swallowing hard before continuing. "*Here*. I will position the fleet here—between Ilbindale and the southern coast of Elvidor. The seas narrow a bit, there are shallows, and some of the advantage in their greater numbers will be moot. I will try and stop Tarsh there…but I will leave a tenth of our fleet behind to guard the port, and plug it as a last resort."

Herodius nodded. He joined Peter at the map and looked over to Victor. "Based on how swiftly Xaro was moving south, along with our reports from Oxen-Pace, they will sweep over the central plains in no time. If we can stop his advance *here*—" He pointed to Paragatha. "—that would be our last stand before they join forces around Rookwood."

Victor nodded. "Agreed. Paragatha is where our armies shall meet, and where his shall fall."

Finally, the King turned to Magi and Veronica. "The Crown could still use your services, Staff or no, Magi."

Magi glanced at the Queen, who was rubbing her belly. She stopped as soon as his eyes fell on her. "I came back to serve, your Majesties."

Queen Najalas stood. "Will you go with all haste to the Elfs, Magi? Tell them everything—in fact, there is more than we've discussed yet here that I would have you say. The King and I will brief you. What I ask is that you protect Chief Chocktaw, and use your magic to turn back this undead horde that is about to descend upon them."

Magi nodded, putting a hand on Veronica's shoulder. "We will depart as soon as you brief us on the particulars."

Herodius straightened his back. "No. Not her. She stays here."

Magi frowned, forgetting the courtesy of a title. "Why, Herodius?"

"She threw herself on my judgment. Very well. I don't have time to punish her or waste manpower guarding her. My ruling is that she should experience what Rookwood experiences—for good or for ill, but also for a more practical reason would I keep her close. You boasted once to this court that you knew the ways to the west underneath and through the Crystal Mountains. Was that a lie?"

"No, your Majesty. I do know the way."

"Then you shall be the guide that leads our people there, should it come to that."

Chapter Twenty-Three: Alliances New and Old

~Malenec~

"Look, ogre. Watch, and be amazed." Malenec sneered at Tar-Tan, who was bent over a map of the shallows near Shith. Their plan was to bring the boats in close to a wide swath of beach along the southern shoreline. That beach was now blocked with a handful of ships—nothing that could defeat the approaching armada, but it would inconvenience them greatly if the shallows were plugged with downed ships. Malenec sailed on his own ship, but he *Teleported* over to confer with Tar-Tan once he spotted the blockade. *Better that I act now before the beast does something stupid.*

"Tell me your plan, Cleric. What are you doing?" Tar-Tan asked. "Sinking the boats will cause a lengthy delay if we have to row onto the beach."

"Yes, well, that depends entirely on *where* the boats sink, doesn't it?" Malenec said, his goatee framing a snide little grin. He turned his head toward the blockade so fast that his ponytail slapped the side of his neck. "The fool Lord Jamison thinks to protect his city with four or five boats. But there is no protection against the dead."

He stood on a platform normally manned by a sea mage and spread his arms wide, lips moving silently. Soon a large ripple in the sea began to emerge, spreading like a crack in the ground during an earthquake. Water rushed in to fill the gap, and the rip was propelled forward, toward the boats guarding the beach.

"What are you doing!" shouted Tar-Tan again from the helm, but if Malenec heard him, he ignored him.

Soon, far off in the distance and well out of range, the first ship in Lord Jamison's pathetic defense began to sway back and forth, port to starboard, as the first ripple in the water reached it. Tar-Tan scowled up at the Cleric and ran forward to get a better look.

Hundreds of arms were lifting the boat up onto the surface of the water until the hull seemed to be just skimming the surface…and the boat was floating out of formation, toward the armada. Out to sea.

Soon more zombies could be seen crawling up the sides of the ship, grabbing anywhere they could get purchase, scrambling up netting and anchors to reach the deck, all while the ship was moved into deeper and deeper water. Tar-Tan could now see the second boat begin to rock back and forth.

Ten minutes later, Malenec had a hundred more undead soldiers and Tar-Tan had five more boats. He floated down from his platform to stand next to the half-ogre. Malenec was a little drained from the exertion, a condition he would never let on to Xaro's pet General. Instead, he just raised one of his long, thin eyebrows and swept his hand at the sandy horizon.

"The beaches are now safe for your fleshy soldiers, ogre. Let us hope none of them drown in your landing. The conquest of Shith I leave to your men. We depart for Thalanthalas—do try to keep up." With that, he *Teleported* away—not to his ship, but to the shore. He held up both hands to the sky.

"To me!" he shouted.

The sea began to foam near the beach, like it was boiling underneath. Rising up through the foam were hundreds of hands, then decrepit-looking heads—swollen and misshapen—followed by decaying bodies. Wave after wave of zombies began filling the beaches of Shith, spreading out like a human shell to mark the outskirts of the great Elfen forest of Filestalas. Thousands upon thousands, ten-deep, fanned out to cover the western edge of the forest as they all emerged from the water, having walked across the sea floor from Sands End. Only one stood apart and next to Malenec: Genevieve.

A subtle flash of color caught Malenec's eye in the periphery of his vision. Kuth-Cergor had answered his prayer for a shield, plus he wore the Ring of Magical Protection still. He moved slowly to turn around.

"You and I both know your Master has no intent to rule this world," said a voice behind him.

Malenec finally had his head turned toward the voice of the man behind him, a short, barrel-chested Elf. He looked young, wore a yellow cloak, and sported a gold loop earring in his left ear.

White eyes. "And you are?" Malenec asked. "I don't believe we've met."

The young man kept his distance. "I am Pilanthas, and I see much. I know what kind of world this will be if your Master wins."

Malenec narrowed his thin eyebrows to a point above his nose. "Then you are misinformed, Pilanthas. I have no Master." He took a step forward, toward the elf.

Pilanthas held his ground. "Yes, you do have a Master, Malenec, but I am not talking about Xaro. I'm talking about Kuth-Cergor. And as I just said, he has no interest in ruling Tenebrae."

Malenec paused his approach. "So. You seem to have used your Art to glean some information. How foolish of you to come out here to meet me. One silent thought from me, and I can have 40,000 undead destroy you, one scratch at a time. What is it you want?"

"Your attention. That is all. I want you to see your future. Your colleague Xaro wishes to rule, but he doesn't really understand the will of Kuth-Cergor, does he? He's not as close to your God as you are, is he?"

"No…I suppose not."

"Then heed what I tell you now: Look around you, Malenec. You are surrounded by the undead. Kuth-Cergor's vision for Tenebrae is not one of worship; it is one of death…or rather *undeath*. When every last living being's soul is trapped, that will mark the beginning of Kuth-Cergor's reign. There is no outcome where you are King, no future where you, not even Xaro gets to govern. There is only undead, and when the last living thing submits to your will… Kuth-Cergor will turn on you. That is your path, Malenec—a grey world of soulless bodies, forever in limbo. I just thought you should know." The squat Elf brought his hands together in a sudden flourish…and disappeared.

Malenec stroked his chin down the sides of his long face, feeling the oil in his goatee. He turned to Genevieve. "The Elfen spellcaster was right about one thing, my sweet. Xaro is a fool if he thinks Kuth-Cergor will let him rule. The dead shall rise again, and they will rise at *my* command. I *will* rule, and all *will* worship Kuth-Cergor." He turned to the east. "Starting with the Elfs."

Closing his eyes, raising his head, he pushed one silent command out to his army—the tens of thousands poised to plunge into the forest: *forward and kill all*.

~Magi~

Teleporting to the location closest to Thalanthalas with which Magi was familiar turned out to be the edge of Lake Calm. From there, he was an *Invisibility* spell and a day's walk to the gemstone river that served as the gateway to the Elfen capital.

The Queen had told him the whole truth—right down to her poor decision to engage one of Silverfist's Assassins. The *Illusion* of the head, Belara's assumed treachery…all of it. He was further told the secret of how to enter Thalanthalas, by plunging himself into the river. He was advised to muffle his sounds, as well as to cloak himself in *Invisibility*; the Elfs were likely on high alert for intruders.

They were indeed. Rising from the waters to gaze on the fair city, the trees were lined with archers, and True Warriors stood at attention along the stone path that wound its way up from the riverbed to the Golden Towers that marked the entrance to the fortress. Elfen True Mages were atop each tower. *Magical detection spells may be woven in front of the gate.*

Unfortunately, time was too short to test this, and not knowing the fortress layout, he couldn't risk *Teleporting*. He walked slowly between two sentries, tip-toeing out of habit. No alarms sounded as he passed, silent and unseen, underneath the True Mages staring down from atop their perch. He carefully wound his way through hallways, looking for Chief Chocktaw. After fifteen minutes of wandering, he came to a small meeting room with a guarded door. He could hear voices inside.

"Chief, she is dead. I am sure of it. This can only mean that the traitors have found out that we asked her to spy on that murderous Queen! We *must* act now! Grant me a small force, Chief. I beg you. Let me go to Rookwood and demand answers. We cannot—"

Magi had heard enough, and the guard outside had already flopped forward into his arms, asleep from a simple spell. Reinforcing his own *Shield* spell, he opened the door and walked into the room.

Only two were present, and both were looking at the suddenly open door. Magi revealed himself.

"Before you say a word—I did not come to harm you. My name is Magi Blacksmooth, and I come as a friend, with much information. I am sorry that I had to sneak in here, but I must speak to the Chief on a matter of great urgency, and I understand that any visitor seeking an audience, especially coming from Rookwood, should not be trusted in the current climate of misinformation. Given the brief conversation I overheard, I can only assume you are referring to the Elfen True Mage Guard Galihali. I would share what I know and what I suspect of her death, if you will hear it?"

The Chief rose from his chair. "I have heard of you. Not long ago the entire realm was searching for you as a murderer in the Queen's own court. Have you now decided to try your hand at killing in my kingdom? No man has ever found this fortress uninvited. The Queen, it appears, can no longer keep secrets. Whatever mischief you are planning on behalf of the Crown, know that we Elfs have long memories, and we will pay back any evil you commit this day on every generation of Blacksmooth henceforth. Mage Guards!" he yelled.

Magi sighed. "If you mean to capture me, then I will be brief. The entire forest is about to be overrun with an undead horde. They will march through the woods until they descend on Thalanthalas, and it will only take one dead elf raised by the Dark Cleric Malenec before the entire army knows how to locate the city. Xaro has landed and is already moving south; he has wiped out the King's northern army near Oxen-Pace already. Another force shall attack Rookwood by sea, and the fourth division will hem you in north by Lake Calm, cutting off your retreat from the zombies that are soon to move through the forest. You do not have much time to prepare. I was sent to help."

The other man tilted his head and laughed, almost shrilly. "You say a horde of undead creatures means to attack us, and the Queen— in all her benevolence—sends us a *single mage*. I am awestruck by her generosity."

Magi spread his arms. "I don't claim to be enough help on my own; in fact that is a recurring lesson that evidently I am slow to learn. I am not without skill, however, and I know how to destroy these zombies: fire."

The Chief shook his head. "Why should we believe you? The Queen has betrayed us!"

Magi looked down. "You are not wrong, Chief, but you are also not right. May I share the truth with you, and let your heart judge my words?" Three mage guards appeared. "I will stay as your captive willingly if you do not believe me. There is no need for any of us to waste our energy fighting one another."

The Chieftain approached Magi. "Speak."

He shared everything that the Queen had shared with him—the clandestine meeting with the head of the Assassin's guild, her reluctant, ale-induced agreement to his price; the *Illusion* of Xaro's death and the likely betrayal by her Head of Magic; the suspicious death of Galihali—everything.

"The Queen deeply regrets everything that has transpired. Should we escape this war, she vows to make amends to you personally and the Elfen people in general." Magi finished, and let the silence hang in the air. He knew the Mage Guards behind him were poised to wrap their encasing spells around him with the slightest nod from the Chief. He looked over at the other man; his eyes were glistening.

"Your words ring true when I match them up to our recent conversations. You say Belara was a Master Illusionist? She could have presented herself as Galihali that day with the Memory Ball, could she not have, Cherokum?"

The other Elf nodded. "She was...distant, that day. I thought it was the news she bore, but perhaps, especially upon hearing this…"

A flash of movement shimmered in the corner—the telltale signs of a *Teleportation*. A short Elf, hooded and cloaked in yellow, materialized out of thin air. All eyes were drawn to him. He pulled down his hood to reveal a young, handsome face.

"Pilanthas!" said the Chief with a sense of awe. "Eldest and wisest among us—to what do we owe such a visit?"

"The day has come when I can no longer stand aside, detached from the events of our time, my Chief. Not when such a great evil moves against my own people. All prophets pay a price for their silence; mine is my youth. Though I shall age quickly from this day forward, let me spend whatever days I have left fighting."

The Chief walked over to grasp Pilanthas's arm in a friendly embrace. "So Magi speaks the truth? He says—"

"I know what he said. Yes—he speaks truly. Especially the part about being short on time. I just left Shith, where tens of thousands of these foul undead have already plunged into the western edge of our forest. They do not sleep, eat, rest, disobey, or die. We have two days to prepare."

Cherokum looked up. "If you know what he said, then you can see the future. You are a prophet…so prophesy! How does this end for us—for your own people? Tell us, Pilanthas!"

The young elf looked around the room, addressing them all. "This can end many ways. I can't tell you which string Fate will pull. I know most endings are unkind to Tenebrae, for it is a Dark World."

He walked over to Magi and put his arm on the shoulder of the tall spell caster. "However, someone once said it is not a hopeless one. Isn't that right?"

Magi placed his hand on the prophet's shoulder with a smile as well. "It most assuredly is not."

~Belara~

The Master Illusionist *Teleport*ed back to her "other" Guild headquarters—the one underneath a simple storefront owned by two sisters called *Finest Livery*. Belinda and Melinda outfitted Belara in some dresses more conducive to travelling, including a camouflage-colored ensemble that virtually disappeared in heavy foliage, helping the True Mage conserve her energy for more important things than concealment. For her purposes tonight, she donned plush black mage robes embroidered with silver thread to form a series of runes to the untrained eye. A learned True Mage would recognize the runes as protection spells woven directly into the fabric.

She then headed downstairs to the Assassin's Laboratory and picked out a few interesting poisons, and a small knife that was attached to her forearm. She also stocked up on food and water; her days in the castle were over.

At least under this regime.

As usual, Silver was in his private meeting room. He enjoyed the confines of his office when he wasn't sneaking around Tenebrae, checking on contacts and contracts. He was alone, adding the smell of his own personally blended tobacco smoke to the heavy aroma of incense he kept burning over coals in a corner. Not even Belara's fragrant hair could cut through the heavy aroma that hung over the room like a blue fog. He saw her enter, and his eyes lit up.

"Cheyenne! Radiant as ever. Come, sit. Wine?"

Belara wrinkled her nose. "Good to see you too, Silver. I won't be long." *How does the man breathe in here?* "I came to restock some things, and thought I would let you know that discord has been sewn between the Crown and the Elfs. I've led the Elfs to believe the Queen has taken out a contract against their Chief, and—"

"She has," interrupted Silver with a playful wink.

"Yes. Furthermore, the Crown believes that the Elfs know of this contract, and that they no longer trust the Queen."

"Which, is also true," added Silver with a nod and a raised wine glass in a mock-toast.

"Indeed, and all I've done is told the truth, for the most part. Up until recently the Crown believed that Xaro was dead, which triggered the Queen to execute a contract with you for Chocktaw."

"But I haven't met the Queen recently," Silver said, narrowing his eyes before softening them as understanding spread across his face. "Cheyenne, you impersonated *me*? How clever. I assume you had to fake Xaro's death somehow?"

Belara nodded, but still kept one foot in the room and one foot in the doorway. The stench from all that flavored smoke was making her eyes water. "Indeed I did. The details aren't important. I just wanted you to know for the sake of the Guild, that the ruse is up. The Queen knows Xaro is alive, and also knows that he is marching on Rookwood as we speak. Your next visit to Rookwood is apt to be a painful one. I would steer clear, and consider moving your assets as well."

"Noted." He sipped his wine. "And you?"

"I'm going to find Xaro, somewhere on the Lightning Road."

"Surely you're not thinking of actually *taking* the Queen's contract, now that you've made a mockery of it?"

"Of course not. I have my reasons." She turned to leave.

"Cheyenne." Silver rose. "You aren't taking sides in this conflict, are you? You do not have to take the Queen's contract, but *I* accepted it for the Guild, which means it is still valid and awaiting execution."

Belara turned around, a cold smile drawn upon her face. "Thank you for the reminder. I'll be sure to let Xaro know that you'll be sending one of your finest assets against him."

And like the blue smoke wafting through the doorway, she was gone.

~Xaro~

Somewhere near the central plains of Elvidor, well south of Oxen-Pace, Xaro made camp. His night raid of the northern army was a near obliteration. *Except for the mage. They had a True Mage up there, and he Teleported away before I could kill him.* The only blemish on an otherwise perfectly executed attack: his Art blinding his foes; his God allowing his own men to see. *What could stop such a lethal combination?*

He picked the last piece of stringy meat off some fatty bird one of his men knocked out of the sky for him. His troops were on marching rations, but grilled mystery bird was on Xaro's menu tonight. He absentmindedly held the small bones up to the single candle he had burning inside his otherwise dark tent. He sighed, longing a bit wistfully for the comforts of having your own castle. The food production at Sands End had spoiled him a bit in recent weeks. He tossed the tiny bird bones onto the floor.

The disappearing mage was a problem. A small one, but a problem nonetheless.

A successful siege of Rookwood depended on bottling up the inhabitants, which depended on all arriving at the major axis points of the fortress at roughly the same time. Once the fighting started, word would travel; word always travels. He just would have preferred *not* allowing a True Mage with *Teleportation* spells to accelerate the news. Little doubt existed in Xaro's mind that Rookwood now knew he was coming.

And in the end, is that so horrible? If the fortress emptied, and the Crown scattered, wouldn't it be just as easy for his four armies to pick them off? Easier, perhaps. And if they stayed and readied their defenses, how much extra time has this bought the castle? Three weeks? Two, perhaps, if Paragatha falls quickly? The Queen's preparation may change the timing of her fall, but it hardly changes the inevitability of it.

His tent flap suddenly came open and a gust of wind nearly snuffed out his only candlelight. Xaro stood up, drawing his short dirk instinctively.

The tent flap slowly began to close itself, and a woman in black robes stitched in silver suddenly appeared. She pulled her hood down to reveal a thick head of black hair spilling down to her shoulders. Xaro immediately picked up an unusual scent of roses, vanilla, and some other spices that he couldn't quite place. And white eyes…

He cast a spell of *Paralysis* over the woman. She started to speak, but Xaro wanted no part of any words that might spill over her tongue. After some mild resistance, he found himself having to put forth a little more energy into his spell casting. The silver runes on her robe caught fire, and the woman began to scream, but she was held fast now by Xaro's spell and her voice died in mid-shout. The threading quickly burned out, leaving her robe in tatters, with burnt pieces of cloth falling off her to reveal beautiful olive-toned skin underneath.

"How did you get into my tent?" Xaro asked, approaching the half-naked woman standing in front of him, knowing full well she couldn't answer him.

The woman was, of course, a statue.

He took the sharp edge of his dirk and sliced away a piece of cloth covering her belly, which was hanging by mere strands. "Who are you?" he asked softly, more to himself.

Nothing from her.

He ran his knife against more frayed cloth that was dangling over her shoulder, cutting it away as well. "Why are you here, I wonder?"

Not even a bead of sweat could build on her temple in this state.

Xaro stood in front of her, his rough, square jaw splitting into a wicked grin. "Only a fool would try to meet with me, unannounced, past my guards, in the middle of the night." He took the cool blade and let the single candle light fall against it, leaving a long shadow across her face. "My curiosity over these three questions is overriding my common sense, I suppose. What I *should* do to you would stop your blood cold and leave you begging for death. But again…that curiosity of mine. So I will let your tongue move, but know this: the first spell that comes from your lips will cost you your tongue, and the rest of your body will be forfeit soon after. Now that we have an understanding," he moved his dirk to rest firmly against her cheek. "Tell me how you got in here, who you are, and why you're here."

The woman swallowed, and only her mouth and throat moved. Her forehead and eyes were still rigidly fixed, as was the rest of her body. "I *Teleported* from Rookwood, my name is Belara and I was formerly the Head of Magic for the King and Queen, and I'm here to tell you their defensive strategy." She appeared ready to say more, but she stopped there.

Xaro never moved his knife. "Why?"

"Because I want you on the throne."

"Why?" His blade didn't budge.

"Because the Queen and her Islander are weak."

Xaro took one step back, keeping the dirk high, no longer pressing it against the corners of her mouth. "Islander? What are you talking about?"

"The Queen remarried. There is a King on the throne now as well—the same Islander that led the revolt against you. I came to warn you. Your converted army may not fight for you if they see him on the throne."

She has a point. While nine thousand or so escaped, many thousands of my army are the remnants of Tar-Tan's island raid. Hope of returning to anything resembling their old life has been beaten out of them. Why give it wings?

He slowly lowered his short blade. "Why do you think the Queen and this Islander are weak, Belara?"

She swallowed again. "Because they have no talent. Not like you…or myself. I would rather see a True Mage on the throne, especially one that is favored by a real god. That the Queen and her pet should rule people like *us* is laughable. I came to help you in any way that I can."

Xaro narrowed his gaze at her tattered clothing barely keeping her decent. "And what price do you expect for such service?"

Belara still could not move her eyes, but she was able to curl her lips sensually.

"Release me, and I'll be glad to show you what I want, Xaro."

The good news is that Dimitri would not even *think* of forbidding his wife, Yelena, from showing Kari and Strongiron the path to the opening of the catacombs.

The bad news is that Dimitri would not even *think* of allowing them to leave the village a day later, or even three days later. He insisted that they teach the village and the Elders simple prayers for healing, for light, and especially for protection. He wanted detailed accounts of history, from Windomere to the present day. And of course he wanted camaraderie—for seven straight days there was a different festival, one for each resurrected villager—where their families cooked for everyone.

Not even the Afflicted took to Dymetra with such zealousness. As guests of honor, it was impossible to turn down one family after having celebrated with another. Frankly, an extra couple of days were probably worthwhile for Strongiron's recovery anyhow. After nearly two weeks in the remote village, however, his body had zoomed straight past recovery and into sluggishness. *My bones need to move.*

They finally set out for the trek to the entrance to the catacombs. Both Dimitri and Yelena served as their guides, leaving their children under the watchful care of fellow Elders. The walk was refreshing, and reminded Strongiron that he was a True Warrior as well as a Cleric. Over a series of sawtooth ridges they climbed, the cool mountain air filling their senses with the smells of autumn's approach.

The path through the uniform crags did not become tedious until late on the third afternoon, when they began to gradually descend a series of switchbacks down the backside of one particular ridge. The gradient was so steep that the path felt more like a shelf hugging the side of the mountain. Single file they lumbered, Dimitri in front, followed by Yelena and Kari, with Strongiron behind. His massive frame spanned the narrow ledge in some parts, with a thousand foot drop-off serving as a constant companion.

They rounded a corner and came to a widening plateau. The sun had already fallen behind the nearby peaks, and what little light came to this plateau was already brushed aside by lengthy shadows.

"The sacred entrance to the catacombs which you seek," said Dimitri. Had he not pointed it out, Strongiron would have walked right past it in the grey twilight. He prayed for something a little brighter, and tossed a *Glowball* near the perfectly camouflaged cave entrance.

"This is where we part, Master Strongiron. You have taught us the truth about the Gods of this Age, and we will pass on that which we now know. I have seen Dymetra myself, and am living proof of Her existence. Go into the cave with our blessing. I hope you find that for which you seek. The catacombs are sacred to the Druids, and are guarded by us. You will meet another inside; perhaps you will gain his trust as well."

"You're not coming inside with us?" asked Kari.

"No, Miss Quinlan," replied Dimitri. "Dymetra Herself said you two should proceed alone."

"She spoke to you?" asked Strongiron. "What else did She say?"

Dimitri walked over and hugged the large True Warrior. "Only to make sure you get there quickly. I would have had you stay in our village a month had I not felt rushed!" He smiled. "We still have much to learn, but you have left us much to study, and ponder. How foolish we have been, worshipping our Elementals, but enough of that! Are you sure that you will not come back to our village when you finish your quest here? We would welcome you back as a King, you know."

Yelena did not wait for Strongiron to answer. She put a hand on her husband's shoulder. "Dimitri, you know their work will take them back to distant lands. We've occupied them here long enough."

You don't say. Dymetra Herself encourages haste, and yet we celebrated for a week before leaving, now ten days ago. The sense of urgency Strongiron had been feeling turned into something far worse with Dimitri's passing words—a feeling like swallowed lead. One look at Kari and he knew she felt it too: *Dread.*

"Unfortunately, we won't be able to visit again for a while, Dimitri. If we are successful, then Windomere's great Shield will be needed back east, in Rookwood. If we are unsuccessful, then we must either keep looking, or will have died inside these mountains. Either way, our paths must separate here, but I will never forget the hospitality of your village and the fervor of the Druids." Strongiron clasped his hand and then moved to hug Yelena, who was already crying as she separated from Kari.

"You gave me Dimitri back. I can never repay you, Kari."

"You never have to." She quickly moved to say her goodbyes to Dimitri.

"Farewell, Strongiron Tuitio! Farewell, Kari Quinlan! We shall see one another again, in this life or the next!"

Strongiron inclined his head before turning around to face the cave entrance, still illuminated by his little ball of light that made his white armor glow as he approached. He put one arm around Kari and drew his sword with the other as they both plunged into the near darkness. He turned to Kari and whispered, "I fear that we have tarried too long in our mission."

She paused and reached up to put her hand on his bearded cheek. "I'm just glad you weren't hurt."

He gently took her hand in his. "I am not sure a prayer for others can harm us, my love, but I am so glad to have you with me." He paused, staring intently at the light reflecting off her green eyes made all the more exotic in the surrounding dark. "Whatever happens in here Kari, I want you to know that I love you." He wrapped his free arm about her waist and kissed her, feeling her fingers gently comb through his long hair to clasp around his neck.

"I love you too, Strongiron. I think I have since the moment I first saw you in Court." She kept kissing him, kept pulling his neck down toward her own.

I could lose myself in your eyes forever. I could kiss you and hold you close to me forever. I could shed this armor and—

Slowly, the *Glowball* drifted away from them both, of its own volition, deeper into the cave. The darkness began to close in around them both, and they reluctantly pulled away from one another to move back into the light, sharing a queer look.

"I guess no time abounds for love at the moment," said Strongiron, a single eyebrow elevated. "I think we are meant to follow."

Disappointment flashed across her face only briefly, before she set her resolve with only the faintest of sighs. "Then let us find this Shield and be done with this mission, my love."

~Magi~

"So, what do you suggest?" asked Chief Chocktaw, turning to both Magi and Pilanthas.

Pilanthas turned to Magi. "I am no military strategist, and I can predict no clear path forward. Now that I have entered into events by corroborating Magi's word, my visions grow ever cloudier, like blood poured into a shallow stream. I will lend my magic to whatever purpose you need, but at present, would not even try to paint a credible picture of the future."

Chocktaw, his scout Cherokum, and Pilanthas were all staring at Magi. *Battle planning is Strongiron's forte…I fight alone.* The thought no sooner crystallized in his mind when Veronica's voice immediately filled his head next: *We all have lessons to learn, and perhaps yours is this: you can't do this alone.* Magi took a deep breath—

"Chief!" someone shouted, right before an elfen guard burst into the room. "My Chief, I apologize for the intrusion, but reports are coming in of a massive force of…*creatures* racing through Filestalas. Our scouts have peppered them with arrows, and nothing slows them down. Reports vary, but it is a massive number, Chief. I've heard four thousand, I've heard eight thousand. What shall we do?"

Chief Chocktaw slowly turned from his guard to look back at Magi. Four sets of eyes were now looking at him.

"Fire. It is the only way, short of a Cleric. Pilanthas—you will come with me." He turned back to the Chief. "How many elfen warriors do you have in Thalanthalas?"

"Two thousand, perhaps."

"Send them north to fight the half-ogre. Your mages and druids—they will come with me. We will need to form two lines, one of steel and one of flame. Between them your people may flee west, toward the Crystal Mountains."

"Sir, what ogre? And what is this talk of fleeing?" The guard turned back to his Chief. "Chief Chocktaw, who is this mage—"

Chief Chocktaw held up his hand, turning to Magi. "Fire? That will destroy the forest!"

"It will." Magi let the silence that followed do the talking.

Finally, Cherokum spoke up. "This is our homeland. Your plan is to evacuate. Thalanthalas is not without its defenses. Why, the river alone—"

Fools! Magi slammed his fist on the table. "You do not understand, and I cannot wait for you to come to grips with what is happening. Let me paint this picture for you. One. Last. Time. Eight or nine *thousand* zombies are running through your forest as we speak. One dead elf is all the Dark Cleric needs to know that the river hides your city; he will simply raise the body and probe the dead elf's mind for whatever secrets he holds. The undead are tireless killers. This is not a mission of conquest; it is a mission of genocide. Every elf that dies increases their numbers while lessening yours. You have two choices: you can wait for them to overrun your walls and *all of us* will die from their scratches and bites, or you can set up a wall of flame, destroy your forest and abandon your homes, and perhaps only *some of us* will die.

"Those are your two choices. To the north lies an entirely different army, one led by a half-ogre who serves as General. They mean to destroy you and bottle up Rookwood from behind the mountains, cutting off any chance of escape. Our only chance is to carve out a path west, along the edge of Lake Calm. Xaro is *counting* on your pride. He is *counting* on you staying in one place, caught between an undead anvil and the ogre's hammer. We—"

"Father!" Magi watched as a stunningly beautiful elf also barged into their meeting. She was one of the most striking women Magi could remember seeing.

"Lady Elyn?" said Cherokum, his eyes wide. "What is it?"

"There are *thousands* of decaying bodies approaching our river!" She looked around the room at the assembled men before her, each focusing on Chocktaw. "Father—Chief, what do we do?"

Chocktaw nodded at Magi. "All Druids and Mages are to follow this man, and are under his command until further notice. Alert our Warriors to muster with all haste at the northern field, prepared for war."

~Kari~

The tiny ball of light that Strongiron had prayed into existence floated a few feet ahead of them. Kari walked next to him, on his left and away from his sword arm, resisting the girlish impulse to hold his hand in the dim cave. She cast a *Glowball* of her own, and sent it to illuminate the walls, which she found surprisingly smooth, like polished glass. After ten or fifteen minutes of walking progressively downward, she thought she saw a pinprick of light in the distance.

"Do you see a light ahead?" she asked.

"I do. Blue, I think. One of yours."

She knew what he meant: magical. *Everflame.*

"We should keep our eyes open for this Druid," she reminded him. Strongiron nodded, but said nothing.

Sure enough, the cave opened up into a decent-sized, rectangular hall. In the room's center was a firepit with blue *Everflame* flickering, easily the source of light they saw earlier. Their attention, however, was not centered on the mysterious flame; it was drawn to the murals depicted on the four walls. To their left was a picture of two young men creating a scroll with incandescent ink. Opposite her and Strongiron was a picture of a city they both recognized.

"Paragatha," uttered Strongiron under his breath. In the quiet, his voice still echoed.

Kari nodded without thinking. "Windomere's home, if not his birthplace."

They turned to their right to look at the next wall, and Kari immediately sucked in her breath. *I've been there!* The third mural depicted a path made of curiously sized stones of different shapes that fit together like a child's puzzle. At the end of the path in the scene's background stood a bridge spanning a stream…and opposite the bridge was a gate…and beyond the gate…a small dwelling.

Only Kari knew better. That was no small dwelling; *Dymetra lives there.*

Scanning the room from left to right, Kari turned to look behind them. When she saw the picture of Dymetra incensed at the old man, both her and Strongiron instinctively fell to their knees.

"Dimitri and the other Druids are right to treat this place as sacred, my love." She turned her head to Strongiron. "They may not have understood what they were seeing, but there is a solemnness to this place."

"Indeed there is, Miss Quinlan. It is called the Hall of Consequence for a reason."

Kari stood and turned around, recognizing that voice immediately. "Fate."

Strongiron stood up and also turned around, his sword still drawn. He did a double take at the odd-looking young man before shifting his eyes back toward Kari. "You know this man?"

She smiled and nodded, never returning Strongiron's gaze. Instead she approached the strange little fellow in the bright green tunic, too-large yellow hat, and loose trousers that tapered into a pair of calf-high leather boots. "I never imagined I'd see you again until my time on Tenebrae was drawing to an end."

"Yes, well, who's to say it's not?" He smiled, and it seemed genuine enough, but he wasn't exactly coming forward to hug Kari like a long-lost friend. What's more, she couldn't tell whether his ominous greeting was meant to be lighthearted or not. *You could never quite tell anything with Fate.*

Strongiron rather loudly cleared his throat as he approached, carrying his sword casually—but at-the-ready. He did not extend his hand in greeting to the stranger, but simply said. "I am Strongiron Tuitio. May I ask who you are?"

"How very polite. Why don't you tell him, Kari? Seeing as you and I go *way* back…" he said with a smirk and a wink.

She could feel, more than see, Strongiron tense at his words. She turned to him and finally looked him in the eye. *Those beautiful, ice-blue eyes...* "This is Fate, Strongiron. He sits atop the Staircase that all mages must climb if we are to become True Mages. He promotes us, and transforms our eyes. In my case, as I've shared, I was taken to meet Dymetra, which is when I became a True Cleric, like you my love. Fate is the one who took me to meet Dymetra."

"Can we trust him?" he asked Kari.

At this, Fate laughed. *Guffawed* even. "Trust me? Strongiron Tuitio, you are such a gem. As if *I* was an actor in *your* grand play. How truly quaint of you." A chair suddenly appeared out of nowhere, and Fate plopped himself down into it, dangling a leg over the armrest. "Please, do tell me how it all works out. I'm *dying* of suspense here."

Strongiron opened his mouth, but Fate cut him off again, pulling his hat off to reveal a head of rich brown, curly locks. "Now think it through, think it through. Don't rush—I want all the details. Take your time; it is the one thing at which you two are *truly* exceptional."

Kari cocked her head toward the man seated in front of her. "You're the Druid Dimitri warned us about, aren't you?"

Fate laughed again. "Why is it that every powerful person these villagers hear about *must* be a Druid? Talk about a blind spot!" He hopped out of his chair, which disappeared when he did so. "I suppose to them I come across as a Druid; we certainly have had a few interesting conversations about the elements. I let them believe what they want."

Kari took one step forward. "But you know the truth. You took me to meet Dymetra! You know there is only Her. Yet you say nothing to the villagers who come here year after year?"

Fate slowly approached, and she could almost feel Strongiron growling, but he took no step toward her. Drawing uncomfortably close, Fate lowered his voice, but he might as well have shouted. "They would not have believed a word from me, even if I were so inclined to tell. Not my call, of course, but I can always tell what lies down a given path, for I am the path maker. I assure you, nothing short of raising their Elder from the dead would have gotten through to these stiff-necked people.

"Now then," he continued. "Do you really wish to question my means-to-an-end, or shall we get on with your assigned task before all that you cherish is ash and rubble?"

Strongiron stepped toward him. "What do you mean, 'ash and rubble'?"

Fate turned to Strongiron and back to Kari. His voice never wavered. "Elvidor is burning now, Strongiron."

~Magi~

A line of True Mages and Druids stretched across the great forest of Filestalas, maybe a mile apart from one another, cutting diagonally from the southeast to the northwest. The True Mages were few in number; most Elfs eschewed magic for a life studying the Druidic Art of shaping the four elements. Given Magi's battle strategy, however, the Druids were as serviceable as any True Mage.

The front of the massive wave of animated flesh could be seen moving through the trees, snarling and dropping bits of decay in their wake. Even the trees, which could be controlled by the Druids, put up a resistance to having their limbs come in contact with the undead. Had the forest known that soon it would be ash, perhaps the trees would have submitted more readily to the Druidic will; a few heads were knocked off by swinging branches, some roots rose up out of the ground to tangle feet. In the end, these minor delays allowed the True Mages and Druids to get into position, but they barely slowed the advance.

Magi was stationed just before the river, in the center of the line in front of Thalanthalas, and would cast the first spell. One did not need to be a Druid to appreciate the cost of this defense. Every tree that died today would be a tragedy. Every soul that would become tethered to the unholy Cleric, however, was an abomination on so many levels.

Magi closed his eyes, and began to lose himself to his Art. This would be no ordinary *Everflame*, which simply heated and burned. He would call forth a wall of scorching fire that incinerated everything in its path.

That same moment of heightened clarity enveloped him like a cloak. Malenec, in the distance, was exhorting his creations forward. Hundreds of carrion birds were circling above the canopy. A mile away, Pilanthas was staring at the back of his hand, noting the emergence of his first aging dark spot. Then the magic flowed.

The ground began to shake, and a crack split open in front of Magi, spreading out in both directions to either side of him. Hot gases spewed out in a long blast that screeched like a pot whistling over hot coals.

And then came the flames. The fierce, volcanic, red-orange flames.

A perfectly vertical wall of molten lava was pulled straight up out of the crack in Tenebrae itself, higher than the highest tree in the Thalanthalas. Like a veil of water flowing down smooth rock, only instead of flowing down, the molten rock flowed *up*. Like building a wall by starting with a center segment, the fire began to spread in both directions rapidly as the crack expanded. Soon mages a mile away on either side picked up on the crack and powered it further, creating shrieks and explosions and thunderous roars as the ground itself was split. They harvested the hot core of Tenebrae like it was nothing more than a crop of potatoes.

The trees in the immediate vicinity never caught fire; they were vaporized, as were the zombies. Magi and the rest of the Mages protected themselves and the Druids with a *Shield* from the heat; otherwise they would have been bone powder, too. Even so, they could not keep up this wall and shield forever.

Magi pushed.

The wall of lava "jumped the track" of the crevasse they had opened in the ground and began cutting across the entire width of Filestalas, with the trees in its path exploding from the approaching heat. The hot air was soon filled with tree splinters that ignited into thousands of fireballs that blew westward, lighting more trees on fire. The air was ablaze, and the undead were getting cremated by the hundreds every minute.

"South! Bend the wall to the South!" Magi screamed, more telepathically than audibly; nothing could be heard over these distances, especially with the trees boiling in their own sap. He thought he saw Malenec frantically commanding his zombies to head south to pitch themselves over the cliff and into the Strait of Holstine. Magi wanted them hemmed in; if he had had enough True Mages and Druids to encircle them all, he would have.

As the wall moved further away from him, he saw the desolation left behind. The air shimmered from the intense heat, but it didn't matter. Nothing but gray ash could be seen. Some of the ash still had an orange glow, but for the most part everything was a hazy gray. Not so much as a green leaf was left in the wall's wake. Angry, he channeled his fury to push the wall out further, incinerating every living—and *unliving*—thing. *You will pay for this, Malenec.*

Suddenly the skies opened up, ripped apart much like Magi had split the ground. Lightning began to crackle, jumping across the sky chasm. A hideous, enraged roar shouted down from the heavens as rain began to pour forth as water from a pitcher. The deluge spilled onto the wall of lava, sending enormous clouds of steam and fog into the air. Between the ash, wood, heat, steam, fog, fire, and rain…nobody could see anything.

They could all hear, however, a voice above the hissing sound of water striking fire. ***"How dare you threaten my Cleric. As I snuff out your fire, so shall I snuff out your souls."***

The wall began to dissolve. Everywhere the skywater fell, the wall of flame was extinguished with an angry hiss. Magi knew they were exhausted; he was growing weary himself, but the Druids would fight on for their people, mustering to the north to engage the fight with their warrior brethren.

When the rain pelted down on Magi's section of the wall, he couldn't help but resist. *Snuff my soul out, will you?* Stubbornly, he began pouring his energy into raising his lava wall against the unholy downpour.

"Stop."

The voice only barely registered.

"Magi, let it go. This is not your fight." *Pilanthas.*

Magi turned his head to look at the Elf. His hair was now heavily streaked with gray, and his formerly smooth face now exhibited the telltale wrinkles of middle age. *The man must be making up for lost time—he's aging a year a minute!*

"What do you mean, Pilanthas?" His concentration broken, Magi felt his wall dissolve in the deluge as if it was made from salt. Steam filled the air with angry hisses.

"As was foretold to you by yours truly many moons ago, this is beyond your ability. Save your remaining energy for the rest of this day; taking on Kuth-Cergor now does nothing for your cause. Look around you. Thousands of souls have been freed as their undead bodies were burned. You have done well today, but more is required."

Magi scanned the landscape as the last bits of wall were indeed 'snuffed out.' Miles and miles of forestry had been transformed; he could see Lake Calm in the distance to the north, and the cliffs overlooking the sea to the south. Not a twig stood between the two edges of the horizon. The river, completely dried up, no longer offered a hidden gateway to Thalanthalas, which now stood out starkly against an ashen backdrop.

The center of Filanthalas had become another Dusty Plain.

"Are there more undead? Where is Malenec?" Magi asked, his eyes stinging from either the smoke or the sight.

"I saw the Dark Cleric leave the field after he called to his god for help. However many undead are left, they will find him if they escaped our wrath. If he came with ten thousand, only a few hundred are left at most, and only those that he managed to drive south before we cut that route off. As I said—you did well today, Magi, but more is required. From us both."

"Back to Rookwood, then?" he asked. *To Veronica.*

"I would recommend north; perhaps that is where Malenec has gone. More mischief goes on there regardless—much more. What good is securing a path west for refugees if Xaro's men cross Lake Calm? As you can see, the trees no longer offer much in the way of cover."

No. No they do not.

CHAPTER TWENTY-FOUR: THE SPRINGING OF TRAPS

~Tarsh~

Really, it was like a puzzle.

Staring out at the array of Royal ships protecting the port, Tarsh focused on one detail common to all the warboats: a platform for a Sea Mage. *I may not be an Admiral, but I know a fair bit about magic at sea.*

As he led Xaro's armada around the coast of Elvidor, bearing north along the shoreline toward Rookwood, he saw the defensive formation. The ships were strung out in two long, curved columns that intersected at the port of Rookwood like a "V," creating an ever-widening channel. Tarsh thought the boats looked like cat whiskers spreading out to sea.

The point was obvious: make approaching the port a gauntlet, though he suspected the greater goal was to protect ships that might wish to *leave.* In this, Tarsh had an advantage; he needn't defeat his enemy so much as keep them bottled up.

The puzzling aspect to all this was *what to do with the mages.* He outnumbered the boats that made up the "whiskers" six hundred to maybe four hundred, though he knew they had reinforcements a few days away in Plythe, if necessary. While he had some Sea Mages as well (counting himself as one aboard his flagship, which bore the Fate-tempting name *Stormrider*), he probably did not have as many; it looked like nearly each of the King's ships had at least one, and he had around a hundred sprinkled amid his fleet. Sailing between the arms of the 'V' would expose his boats on both sides, and while he unquestionably had more men and more boats, he doubted he had as many Sea Mages. *That* was the problem.

He thought about just sending *Missiles* from his mages from distance, but he could see the ships had shimmering *Shields* around them. His mages would deplete themselves before cracking enough *Shields* to damage many boats, and a quick test of a water-borne *Missile* confirmed that the shields went all the way under the sea to protect from mast to hull.

He thought about *Teleporting* aboard one of the ships. *Teleportation* was likely the only spell that could get behind the *Shield* without overpowering it…but at great risk. He could visualize the deck—no chance he would emerge inside a piece of wood or something, but the greater problem was any momentary disorientation. He, or any of the Sea Mages under his command, would be woefully outnumbered once they appeared in the midst of the crew. All it would take was a quick sword, or more likely a quick spell, to thwart his efforts. *And besides, those Sea Mages wouldn't even have to lower their Shields to cast a Sleep spell, Lightning, or Missiles at a strange mage who materialized in their midst within the cocoon of their precious Shields. Too risky by far.*

He thought about opening up a thundercloud; the rain would raise the water level, but hardly damage a *Shielded* boat. Lightning? Again, like with *Missiles*, his Sea Mages (outnumbered maybe four-to-one) would run out of energy well before his enemy did if he had to concern himself with trying to break through a bunch of *Shields*. *Levitate* the boats, like he did with *Sheila's Bane*? It had drained him to *Levitate* one boat, and he didn't have enough mages to move all those heavy boats. As long as the *Shields* were up, those boats were well protected.

However…those Sea Mages (or archers) couldn't really launch anything at *his* armada either as long as their *Shields* were up, but that wasn't their point at the moment. They would undoubtedly lower them to fight off an attack if a boat with precious cargo was trying to escape the city. *Precious like a King or Queen.* Outside of protecting an escape channel out to sea, Tarsh doubted they would attack superior numbers.

Xaro had updated him earlier that morning, based on recent intelligence he had apparently received. He knew all the boats were here, save for some that might set sail from Plythe, but that might take a day or longer to reach a sea battle near the port of Rookwood. As far as Tarsh was concerned—what he saw is what he faced. *What's the best way to bottle them up, as Xaro commanded?*

His mind kept turning over ideas on how to sink the boats, but given the weight and the resistance—both natural and magical—it would fiercely drain his mages to try pulling and keeping those ships underwater. He couldn't match them mage for mage and didn't want to get into a battle that would hinge on which mages had more power anyway. Tarsh felt good about his own well of energy, but he wouldn't make claims about many others. *Think! There has to be a way of pushing a floating cork into the bottom of the bottle!*

Or…*drain the bottle and let the corks sink?* Why not attack the very water upon which the King's precious fleet floats? Why not push the water from under the boats into the city itself, flooding Rookwood while the royal navy settles on the muddy sea floor, protected in their little shields a hundred feet down? He pictured hundreds of boats resting on their sides, sunk halfway up their hulls in sediment and sludge. *Like coffins in a swamp.*

Moving the water had one distinct advantage: the Sea Mages could not protect each ship *and* the water upon which they all floated at the same time. *And by the time they realize the* water *is the target of enemy spell craft, they would have to drop their Shields to attack or counter us, exposing their own boats. At which point...*the plan was coming together quickly in his mind. His only question was whether his Sea Mages were strong enough to move that much weight. They would need to drain a pie-wedge of water, push it into the city, all while keeping the rest of the sea from rushing in on three sides until the King's fleet grounded. He counted on the majority of the crown's Sea Mages to focus on their boat *Shields* and not the water; he would need every ounce of strength from his own mages to pull this off even without active resistance, and even then he wouldn't be able to hold back the water long.

He relayed his orders through the network of mages he had across his fleet and began repositioning his armada to strike. Slowly his warships began fanning out into a massive arc, surrounding the "cat whisker" formation of the King's fleet like a lid, though far out of any archer's range. Tarsh watched as his ships closed the opening of the "V." Truly, if he did nothing else but drop anchor and keep their desired water escape route plugged, he would effectively support the land siege for some period of time.

Eventually I'll need supplies, too, though, in order to control the port.

He cast his *Farsight* spell from the platform high atop *Stormrider*, scanning the enemy fleet. Waiting. Watching. *Surely they won't allow us to sail in front of their precious sea channel to open water?*

The boat at the tail end of the curved line of the southernmost "whisker" lowered its *Shield* as the Sea Mage aboard began a new spell. Tarsh did not wait to see what was being cast. The *Lightning* spell was on his lips, striking the unshielded boat square on the main deck. The accompanying thunder filled the sky, rising above the normal din of waves crashing against ship hulls. Wood chips and splinters filled the air surrounding the struck boat. Tarsh called forth a second bolt, one meant to rip the ship in two.

The bolt struck a hastily cast *Shield* spell surrounding the lone sinking boat, and the lightning diffused around the entire vessel and into the sea, illuminating the whitecaps that slapped against the leaky hull.

So, the Sea Mage lived. He cast his *Farsight* once again to peek at what was happening on deck. Several sailors were dead or unconscious, and a robed mage was bleeding from his head. Having reestablished the *shield*, it looked like he was trying to move the boat back to port while the remaining sailors bailed water furiously. Clearly they were trying to save the crew and possibly the ship, but the Sea Mage was laboring mightily.

Tarsh smiled. *Is this the best the Crown can produce? I lifted an entire boat out of the* Maelstrom *to set it back on course!* He did not think any other boats would lower their defenses after *that* spectacle. He took another look at the wounded warship struggling to make it back to port from the far end of the line, even with the wizardly push. He doubted their chances. *Just too much open water to cover.*

With a nod to the *Stormrider's* captain, Tarsh's smile spread from haughtiness to outright excitement. *Let me take care of some of that water for you...*He cast the spell that set the wonder in motion.

The triangle of seawater bounded by the King's fleet on two sides and the (crust of pie) warships under Tarsh's command on the third, began to roll toward port. The sea level at the point of the port on the shores of Rookwood quickly rose and water began pouring into the city, flooding the outer portions. All of his Sea Mages were concentrating their combined *Levitation* to force that pie-wedge of water clear out of the sea and onto the mainland, while keeping the rest of the ocean water from rushing in. Sheer walls of water began to form along the three sides as everything—ships, rocks, fish— *everything* began to sink to the bottom of the sea inside that triangle.

The wounded ship limping its way back to port seemed to realize what was happening sooner than the others, lowering its *Shield* yet again to attempt a counter force spell to "hold in" the water.

Tarsh immediately sent a finishing bolt of purplish *Lightning* down upon it, this time striking the platform directly. The mast fell over this time, and a massive crack began splitting the boat apart. Several bodies were in the water now, or were soon jumping into it. *One less Sea Mage to worry about.*

Luckily, no other boats mounted a resistance to the movement of water. The lone boat he struck "sunk" in five minutes, but the rest of the sea had drained ten minutes later, revealing that same ship lying in pieces on its side, mud halfway up its hull.

The entire King's fleet now rested along the sea bed, too horrified to lower their *Shields*, yet trapped regardless. All of the ships lay at odd angles, their weight sucking them further and further into the muck a hundred feet down in some places, *Shield* or no *Shield*.

His mages straining to hold back the sea, Tarsh waited a moment longer to take in the spectacle. With a word, they released the water, which fell upon the trapped boats, cocooned in their little *Shields*, with a roar that could be heard on the other side of the mountains. The ocean collapsed on the boats that were now held fast to sea floor. The royal navy was crushed under such a weight in mere minutes. Only the Sea Mage's shields kept the boats from splintering.

Mission accomplished. Sea-bound escape from Rookwood was no longer an option.

~Queen Najalas~

"My King!" shouted Jonathon. "The city is flooded! Shall we lower the bridge?"

The Queen looked over at her husband, who barely registered the interruption from their Steward, shouting behind them. At her husband's request, Queen Najalas had accompanied Herodius up to the fourth tower, observing from this lofty perch the unfolding sea battle and chaos below. Together they saw Xaro's ships enclose their own. Herodius had expected that they would rain fire, missiles, and other wicked forces to break apart their naval defenses; she was not so sure. When she saw Xaro's Sea Mages begin to *drain the sea*— she wished her husband had been right. They had been prepared for *that*. For sinking ships and mass flooding? Not so much. They watched in horror as a single ship tried to defend the city (and the Crown's fleet), only to be struck by lightning twice. When the water collapsed back upon her marooned fleet she felt sick to her stomach, and knew it had nothing to do with her pregnancy. The sound of that rushing water etched a permanent memory.

Her husband finally addressed Jonathon. "I see that water fills the streets. We told everyone of the coming war. Surely the people left when they could?"

She knew very well many, in fact, had *not* left. And so did Herodius.

Jonathon shook his head. "They cry at the bridge, my King, begging for it to come down. The city is covered in water twenty to thirty feet deep in some places. They have no homes anymore, sire."

Dump a hundred feet of seawater on land, and that will happen.
She glanced over at the scowling face of her husband, who continued

with Jonathon. "Have you asked Simon about our defenses? If we lower the bridge with Xaro's men out there…"

She looked over the waist-high wall of stone—a balcony of sorts at the top of the tower—and could see the bridge from where she stood. The mountain upon which Rookwood was anchored rested on a plateau of land. A deep, mammoth crevasse yawned between the surrounding foothills and that plateau at the base of the mountain. A long pathway twisted from the other side of the naturally occurring land-crack through the modest foothills down to the city and beyond to the wharfs below.

Spanning that magnificent defense was a single bridge that the Crown could raise and lower. *The entrance to Rookwood from the east.*

The water had not risen to the bridge beyond the lazy foothills; instead, it was spreading out (and stagnating) over the city below. From the Queen's vantage, it was obvious that Rookwood, the city, was built inside an enormous, geographic bowl, a bowl Xaro's sea mages had just filled with harbor water.

Jonathon cleared his throat. "I have spoken with Simon. Xaro's army is camped north of the city, on the outskirts of Paragatha. Their ships now encircle our port—but they do not appear to be disembarking or making for our shore. As for the Elfs…we have no word yet. The world on the other side of these mountains is opaque to us. In short, I do not believe our enemy is at the bridge yet, your Majesty."

Perhaps he needs a gentle reminder. "Herodius." The Queen tenderly placed her hand on his shoulder. "We sit watching this war from the Tower of Protection."

Far below, the entry to the Tower bore a sign that read *The Crown Provideth Protection.*

Herodius smiled at his Queen, placing his own hand atop hers. He nodded. "Let the remaining people come. Feed them, dry them, warm them. The Queen is wise. What point is there in ruling if we cannot protect our subjects? We cannot protect everyone, but those we can, we must try. Lower the bridge, Jonathon."

"Immediately, my King." Jonathon rushed back down the tower steps, clearly pleased with the decision.

"He's a good Steward," Herodius said, turning to face his Queen.

"You're a good King," returned Najalas.

Herodius let a polite smile briefly light his face before turning serious once more. "We need to go find Luther. Every other True Mage is either with Victor, Magi, or stuck in the seabed that used to be our port. We need updates, my Queen. Come. Let us head back to our council room and have Luther summon their shades or *Teleport* to them for news."

After a dizzying descent from the Tower of Protection, Queen Najalas and her King plopped into their less-than-ornate thrones, with only Luther seated across from them. Everyone else was obviously engaged.

Herodius dispensed with all pleasantries. "News from the battles, Luther. What have you heard?"

"My King, my Queen," Luther nodded stiffly. He was dressed in dirty travelling clothes that reeked of smoke. "Magi has preserved Thalanthalas—"

"Oh thank God!" breathed Queen Najalas.

"—at great cost," he finished. "A third or more of the entire forest of Filestalas has been utterly destroyed. The city now rests on a plain of ash."

"And Malenec and his foul horde?" asked Herodius.

"The Dark Cleric lives. He *Teleported* somewhere. His zombies…Magi thinks the vast majority are dead. Some may be left alive—or rather animated—but most were consumed in a wall of flame and molten rock that he and the Druids summoned."

"And the Elfs?" asked the Queen.

"No longer hidden in their forest homeland, as the magic of their river is now dust. Many are cowering inside their homes; the warriors and fighting druids are preparing to face off, potentially, against the half-ogre on the south side of Lake Calm." At this they both turned to look at Herodius, whose face was a mask of stoicism. The Queen thought she saw the corners of his mouth tighten slightly, but then they usually did at the mention of the half-ogre.

Luther continued. "Victor and his men will engage Xaro and his northern army just north of Lake Calm, near Paragatha."

"What of Peter?" asked the Queen.

"He has fewer than twenty boats still floating, all from Plythe, and certainly not enough to harass the armada arrayed against us in the Sea of Joy." Luther held open his hands. "So he has decided to take his men and sail to the inlet near Paragatha to try and flank Xaro's army, hoping to catch them between his men and Victor's. The port is a lost cause."

"We must keep our western escape route open, then. Through the mountains." Herodius was matter-of-fact.

Luther nodded, biting his lip slightly. "Your Majesty—to that point—there is one other thing you should know." He paused to verify the King was looking at him. "About the half-ogre. When I visited Magi, they were scouting for battle. They believed that Tar-Tan—I believe that is his name—leads an army for which many of your countrymen—from the Uncharted Isles—are fighting. If they knew you were on the throne…" he trailed off.

"Of course! They would turn on that yellow-eyed slaver faster than you can draw a sword! How fast can I get there?"

"You would have to ask Jonathon for sure—he has scouted the short cut through the back of the mountains, but my guess is less than a week. Perhaps in time for this battle, I'm not sure. Magi and the Elfen Druids could use rest after their defense of Thalanthalas, and I doubt they will attack Tar-Tan if he is willing to wait as well. Furthermore, Magi and Victor are speculating that after failing with the zombies, the half-ogre may be contemplating sailing across Lake Calm to pin Victor down from the south, flanking his army with Xaro from the north and Tar-Tan from the south. They may all be converging in Paragatha. We just don't know yet, but a modest delay will do our side well. If you abandon the ships that are stuck at the bottom of the sea, our Mages at least could *Teleport* away to join Victor."

"If the Mages leave those boats, the men aboard will surely die. Those Shields are the only thing keeping the boats from getting crushed at the bottom of the sea." Herodius shook his head.

"Yes, your Majesty. They will die, but right now you have hundreds of mages guarding useless wood, sire." Luther spread his hands wide.

"Wood and men, Luther."

"If you will allow, sire, those men are already dead. Our Sea Mages will eventually run out of energy, the shields will weaken, and they will be destroyed. Or they will simply starve—no one is resupplying them; the city is under water, your Majesty. My fellow mages are guarding wood and corpses right now, my King, but they could make the difference in a battle at Paragatha, if they have any energy left at all. *You* could make a difference in that battle, as well, if the enemy sees you as King." Luther let the silence linger, and then concluded. "If we leave now, I believe you can still influence the allegiance of some of their warriors."

The Queen looked at her husband's eyes, and knew he would go. She put her hands in his. "Go. Let them see who is King, and then we will see against whom they raise steel." She turned to Luther. "Inform our Sea Mages to abandon the boats. You are right, Luther. Neither the men nor the Sea Mages can assist us at the bottom of the sea…may Dymetra have mercy on their souls." *How apropos that our enemy wins a battle by draining the Sea of Joy right in front of us.*

Herodius looked over at the command given by his Queen, and nodded agreement with heavy shoulders. "Luther, find Jonathon after the bridge is lowered. Have him make the arrangements. He will lead me through the catacombs. You must stay here and keep my Queen apprised of everything."

"Yes, my King." He bowed to his Queen and *Teleported* away. Perhaps she imagined it, but Najalas thought she saw him mouth a silent *thank you* before departing.

Herodius turned toward his Queen, who was still seated in her throne. "I will return, you know I will."

"Of course, my love. You have a prince to help me raise."

"You know it's a boy?" he asked with a genuine smile.

"Call it intuition." Even with her thin lips, she beamed a warm smile back. "You had better go and make some of your own preparations. I'm going to visit Palinor and ask him for a blessing; you know he's been studying all the scrolls he could get his hands on from Strongiron."

"Indeed. A blessing would be wonderful, my love." Facing her, he gently pulled her up from her seat and wrapped his arms around her tightly. "I love you, Najalas. You will be safe here."

No one is truly safe anywhere, and you know it. Instead of saying a word, she kissed him in answer, deeply, before finally separating. "Go, before I threaten to join you on the battlefield."

He nodded, giving her forehead one final kiss. "My love." He turned and left.

Alone now, the Queen sighed. *If you were born for one thing, my love, it was to rally men to you.* She turned to leave when a curtain moved to her left. She looked over her shoulder as a voice spoke.

"Ah, we meet again. The fortress here is just how I remember it, minus the cold water, shackles, and rag in my mouth, of course."

The face took her a minute to recognize, but the voice was immediately familiar. Somehow, some way, Malenec the Dark Cleric was back inside Rookwood.

And staring right at her.

~Strongiron~

"Elvidor burns? What is happening back home? Tell me!" said Strongiron.

"Tell you what? War comes to Elvidor. This you already know. War is nasty business, my friend. It brings fire, it brings floods, and it brings death. Why the sudden concern, my White Warrior?" The sarcasm oozing from Fate's mouth was so heavy Strongiron could almost *see* it. Kari put a hand on his shoulder, but he shook it off to slowly walk toward the silly-looking man.

"*Sudden concern*?" he said through gritted teeth, approaching Fate like he was stalking prey. "My heart is and has been *filled* with concern for Rookwood, for Elvidor, for all of Tenebrae! That is why I am here instead of fighting alongside them all. I am trying to be obedient, but I am a Warrior at heart, and when you say 'Elvidor burns,' I would like to know what you mean!" His face was a foot away from Fate's, who never flinched despite Strongiron's spittle-laden rant.

Fate cocked his head, blinking his blue-grey eyes back at Strongiron. He removed his floppy hat and mopped his face before setting it back upon his head at an angle. "You're quite right, Strongiron. I suppose you are *trying* to be obedient—you're just failing miserably. Do you even remember the last thing Dymetra told you when She commissioned this quest of yours?"

"She said She would accompany me as long as my faith in Her was strong." He was sure of that. "She has lived up to Her promise, for here we are."

"Hmm. I believe she also said '**Do Not Delay Unnecessarily.**' Do I need to recount your perpetual procrastination, or can we agree that haste has *not* been your overarching objective since you left the Tower of Dariez all those months ago?" Fate waved his hand and his comfortable-looking chair, fat cushions and all, reappeared directly behind him, in the middle of the cave. Without as much as a peek behind himself to verify the seat, he plopped back down, crossing his legs leisurely. "By all means, time is nothing to me, so let me know if you wish to pursue this Shield or engage in frivolous debate."

This fop of a man! Strongiron took a deep breath, composing himself. "May I ask questions while we walk?"

Fate stood up, and his chair disappeared once again. "Certainly. Now follow me." He proceeded to walk straight into the mural on the back wall—the one depicting the columned-entrance to Paragatha—and continued walking right through it.

Strongiron glanced over at Kari, a single eyebrow raised.

"I would have found that *Illusion*," she said, a little sharply, her arms crossed.

"I never said a word."

"You didn't have to."

Pick your battles. "Oh, let's just go already." He plunged through the *Illusion* and saw the floppy yellow hat bouncing around as if worn by a man in desperate need of a privy.

"Come on, come on! Let's pretend the world isn't crumbling around your ankles, and make haste," Fate chided, pushing his hat to the other side of his head as he continued skipping down the cave, their way dimly lit by *Glowballs.*

Kari plunged through next and joined Strongiron, and they both hustled to catch up to him. "Are we too late?" asked Strongiron, who was struggling to keep up without breaking into a light jog.

"Too late for what?" returned Fate.

Always a question for an answer with this guy. Dymetra, why are you torturing me with this gatekeeper? He exhaled another deep breath. "For Elvidor? Can you tell me specifically what is happening, battle-wise, at this very moment?"

Fate shrugged. "I suppose I could, but then I hate to *push* you down a path. I prefer to build the paths and let you pick them yourself. Too much information may propel you away from your commitments. And I prefer *not* to be the architect of such transgressions, because ultimately that just creates more work for myself in the long run. You know how that goes."

No. I have no idea how that goes, actually. Another sigh, swallowing his frustration. "Yes, we wouldn't want you engaged in our petty quest any more than necessary. Surely a few updates on Elvidor will not unduly influence our future decisions? You don't think we would come *this* close to our goal only to fly away back East at the hint of trouble, do you?"

Fate considered this, and the look on his face (at least his profile, given his walking pace) was that of a man lost in thought. *Like a man processing dozens of scenarios.*

"Very well," he began. "You make a fair point. If you hear these updates and abandon your quest, well then, that is just a different path, after all. As it is presently, Xaro has already slaughtered your Northern army and camps patiently outside Paragatha. Victor is there as well, preparing to attack. Has he learned patience yet, Strongiron? Will you have to save him again? This we shall see."

Kari looked at Strongiron. "I thought you said he has never lost a battle?"

Fate looked smugly over his shoulder. "Tell her."

Strongiron shrugged. "I never said he didn't lose a battle; I simply said we always won, which, technically, is true. Victor can be…impetuous. He fights, though. More battles are lost from inactivity than they ever are lost from moving too quickly. Long ago, during one of his earlier battles against raids in the Three Fingers, I was bringing up reinforcements, but Victor didn't wait. The division under his command was decimated, but once I brought up reinforcements, our victory was secured. That was years ago, though. He has improved as a Field General many times over since then." *At least, that is my hope.*

Fate stopped, turned around, and leaned forward. "But you're not sure, are you? Such a maverick, marshaling the entire army in defense of Rookwood…it does call into question your choice of him, now doesn't it?" Fate lightly tapped his fingertips together. "Alas, you wish for an update, not speculation. So onward. Victor may be reinforced by Peter, who sails for Paragatha from Plythe, or he may not…depends on whether or not he waits. Meanwhile Magi and Pilanthas—so sorry to see him turn his back on prophesy, he was such a good one—they have killed thousands of zombies to momentarily protect the Elfen homeland of Thalanthalas. It only cost them half the entire forest. Pity they couldn't kill *all* the zombies, however. I suspect great harm is still possible from that quarter. And Malenec escaped as well; he is terrorizing your Queen even as we speak."

"What?" yelled Strongiron

"Yes, a terrible turn of events for her. Malenec is in Rookwood right now, alone with your Queen. I can't imagine this ending well for her, frankly. Actually, that's not quite true. Given my responsibilities, I actually *can* imagine a path or two that might end amicably for your Queen. We'll just have to see what happens."

Strongiron stood there silently blinking, mouth agape.

Kari narrowed her eyes at Fate. "Where is Herodius in all this? What of the Small Council?"

"I suppose you want all the details then? Very well. As I said, Magi and Pilanthas are aligned with the Elfs to protect their homeland…and more practically, to secure an escape route to the West from Rookwood. They are facing Tar-Tan, who you know is Xaro's General. Magi and the Elfen Druids are all fairly exhausted from their confrontation with Malenec's horde, however. Quite iffy, if you ask me. Herodius and Jonathon are navigating their way under the mountain with a small retinue that will ride out to meet Magi and the Elfs on the shores of Lake Calm. You see, there are Islanders still fighting for the Ogre; your King hopes to rally them with a show of the Crown."

"Surely his brethren won't fight for that slaver?" Strongiron asked incredulously.

"Ah, but are they still slaves? Xaro has unlimited gold, dear Cleric. Many of those men have drowned their grief in any number of vices, paid for lavishly by a man who appears to summon God from his fingertips. Careful on how you judge them; they may have had one life ripped from them, but those who could not escape with Herodius coped with their remaining life as best they could…and Xaro has not been stingy when it comes to promoting 'good morale' among his men. Still—it will be interesting to see how they react to Herodius arriving on the scene as King. One has to imagine they all believe he probably died trying to escape their bondage. Of course, there's no guarantee Herodius *will* arrive. That is why Jonathon is leading the company through the catacombs under the mountain. Many problems may obstruct their navigation enroute…lots of balls in the air for yours truly to juggle." Fate exaggerated his workload with a sweeping wipe of his brow.

"You'll excuse my lack of sympathy for your plight," Strongiron remarked.

Fate smiled but ignored him. "As for the rest, you may be curious to learn that Veronica is in Rookwood as well. Remember her—the young Assassin upon whom you took pity?"

"Of course we remember her. She tried to kill Strongiron, Magi, Peter—what's she doing in Rookwood?"

"Ah that is a lengthy tale, but your grace saved more than her hands that day. But by saving her hands, she also saved Magi's life. He brought her back to Rookwood with him, where the Queen has given her the task of leading a retreat, should it come to that point. She was with Simon at the bridge, listening to the citizens cry out 'Protect Us! Protect Us! The city floods, we have nowhere to go! Lower the bridge and let us in!' when Jonathon passed along the King's order to lower the bridge. Luther, whom you may remember as Victor's Battle Mage from the North, appeared shortly thereafter with another order for Jonathon from the King: lead him out of the castle through the mountain so he could rendezvous with Magi and the Elfs."

Oddly, something tightened in Kari's stomach with this update, but she ignored it. "And where are they now?"

"As I said, Jonathon and Herodius are under the mountain, and oblivious to Malenec's presence, if that is what you are wondering. Veronica is in a tower, also oblivious. Luther is communicating with other mages."

Strongiron closed his eyes and his head drooped. "Anything else?"

"Only this: your Queen is also with child."

The True Cleric's eyes popped open and wide. "An heir?"

Fate didn't say a word, merely an almost imperceptible nod.

Kari looked at Strongiron. "What do we do? Why don't we *Teleport* now and confront Malenec?"

Strongiron looked at Kari, and he looked at Fate. *This is exactly the choice you knew we'd have to make.*

Kari continued. "Surely we can disrupt him? Two True Clerics against one? Plus my *Illusions*, your steel? We cannot let her die! We can *Teleport* right back here to this very spot!"

Fate shook his head. "Alas, you cannot. You are here only because I am your guide. I can take you past the Hall of Consequence once, and once only. If you leave, you won't be able to return."

Kari looked at Strongiron. "We could split up."

Strongiron narrowed his eyes at Fate, but then turned to Kari and softened them with a head shake. "I don't want to separate, Kari. Forgive me, Dymetra, but I won't let you fight Malenec alone—"

"And I know little of shields," she conceded.

Strongiron stared into her deep green eyes. "And...I don't want to...to lose you." He finished, turning back toward Fate, tightening his grip on his sword involuntarily. He didn't draw it. "You are a fiend."

"I am a timeless watcher of events, Strongiron. I am no fiend, but I am no angel either. Make your choice, and be quick about it, for time *does* impact all of you."

Scowling, Strongiron asked, "At least tell me this: Are we the first ones here? Have there been any others that have come this far?"

Fate shrugged. "You are hardly the first on a quest for Windomere's Shield. The greater the relic, the wider the search."

"I mean recently?" Strongiron asked patiently, gritting his teeth.

"What is recent to me? As I said, time has no meaning to me, Strongiron, given the *leisurely* pace at which you progressed to this point, however, well...let's just say that it would not be hard to imagine your adversaries in this world demonstrating more urgency."

Strongiron grabbed Fate's forearm and stopped. "So we *are* too late? To recover the Shield?" he clarified.

Fate gently disengaged himself from the True Warrior. "I see we are back to one of your first questions." Fate looked at them both soberly, and raised a single finger. "You *are* late. That much is true.

Whether you are *too* late is not my call. Now do we carry on, or are you leaving?"

Strongiron looked at Kari strained face. He grabbed both her hands in his and offered a simple, three-word prayer: *"Forgive us, Dymetra."*

"Carry on."

"Then let us do so." Fate began walking again, and set out down the cave briskly. "Your destination is up ahead."

Strongiron and Kari hustled to fall in behind, and noticed the tunnel they were in expanding. Up ahead the lighting changed; in lieu of the soft luminescence of *Glowballs*, blue *Everflame* could be seen flickering through a wide opening.

It only took a minute or two for them to come upon the end of the cave tunnel, which yawned open into an enormous cavern. Amazingly, eight streams of water silently arched through the circular dome, radiating from a statue of a penitent man to pierce the surface of a vast underground lake. The formation looked like a birdcage of water, albeit compressed from above to form arches instead of vertical bars, and yet, hardly even a tinkle of sound.

Mounted on the walls along the cavern was every shape of shield imaginable. "There must be over a hundred…" Strongiron said under his breath. "Surely there is a clue of some sort?" He turned to Fate. "Fate?"

The odd little man was, however, nowhere to be seen, nowhere to be heard. The question of *where did you go* was left unvoiced as, with a sudden rumble of stone, the cavern collapsed on them both.

~Victor~

Two days. Too long.

Peter had some reinforcements from Plythe headed his way, but in two days this battle would be over, or rather a full-on siege of Rookwood would be in play. In his mind, Victor had a small window. He heard what Xaro had done to the northern men formerly under his command: *slaughtered them.* Black clouds rolled from Xaro's fists to obscure the field, spooking man and beast alike, and his army had torn the northern troops apart like soft bread from an oven. *We will* not *line up on a wide field to clash spells and steel, I assure you that.*

Besides, how many men might Peter bring? At best, several hundred. *If all goes according to plan, I'll drive Xaro's disoriented army straight into Peter's reinforcements. And what do I gain if I wait?* Victor considered, and came to same conclusion no matter how many times he revisited a delay: Xaro would move out of Paragatha long before Peter could flank him, not that a hundred tired sailors on forced march would be of much use in organized battle anyhow. And the Elfs? Magi and the Elfs appeared to have their hands full on the other side of Lake Calm dealing with Xaro's pet ogre. Hopefully they could keep the half-breed from flanking *him.*

All the more reason to strike first. All the more reason to *raid.*

The mid-afternoon shadows began to slant, and Victor whispered to the young mage crouching next to him. "It's time, Edward. Alert the others." He liked the True Mage with curly, golden hair who hailed from Brigg. He was a heckuva lot more entertaining than Luther the Laconic.

The mage winked at Victor. "Call me Nugget, Sir. Edward was my father's name, and he was a bastard." He disappeared to communicate the order in his mysterious ways.

Victor then turned to the other, older man standing next to him. The man's rosy cheeks and healthy gut, which, spilled over his well-worn breeches all but screamed his occupation. "Are they ready, Ronbar?"

The amiable miller nodded, wiping sweat from his forehead. "Yessir, Cap'n! I mean General!" he corrected. "A hundred casks."

"Good. Start moving them."

Ronbar smiled nervously and turned as quickly as his belly would allow, walking fast down one of the hills that overlooked the Godly City. "And Ronbar," Victor called out after him. "Move them *casually.* Nothing too close to the camp. Let *them* spot *you.*"

Ronbar mopped his forehead again, gave another curt nod, and proceeded down the path like a man racing against diarrhea. *What has it come to that the Kingdom of Elvidor may rest in the hands of a Brewmaster?* Victor sighed and lit his pipe.

Twenty minutes and a bowl of tobacco later, Nugget reappeared. "The mages are in position, General. We're carrying more white marbles than an oyster farm."

Frowning, Victor stroked his mustaches and blew a cloud of blue smoke at the young mage. "White marbles?"

"Never mind. For our spells." Nugget waved his hand. "Point is—we're ready for your plan."

"Good." He pointed toward Paragatha with his pipe stem. "And you saw fit to start the rumor?"

"King's ale, moving toward Rookwood, *'just in case there's trouble from the approaching army.'*" The mage split his lips in a wide grin.

Victor nodded. *Surely Xaro's men will take the bait? Everyone* knows *the Queen likes her ale…it would only be fitting for an army preparing for a lengthy siege to deny their foe her liquid comfort. A hundred full casks of 'the good stuff,' enroute and barely guarded…*

"Can you do that telescope spell? The one that looks far into the distance?"

Nugget snapped his fingers brashly. "Focus on the caravan, I presume?"

Victor murmured, "mmm-hmm" with his teeth clenched on the clay pipe. Nugget cast the spell, and Victor peered through the circle, focusing on a trade route where the wagons loaded with ale were being drawn *slowly* through Paragatha.

Already, he saw men wearing fine armor beginning to surround the line of carriages. He saw swords drawn. Ronbar was at the front, and Victor, aided by the spell, could see the flop sweat shining on his neck and staining his armpits. *Indeed it has come down to this.*

The armed men were laughing, and he saw Ronbar ordered onto his knees. Another man threw a towel at him, nearly guffawing. Still another man—this one in chestnut armor standing over the Miller— produced a goblet. He walked over to the nearest cask and uncorked it, filling it to the brim with fresh, foamy ale. He walked back over to Ronbar and stood over him again, glass raised.

The warrior then thrust the goblet into the hands of the Miller, who was still cowering on his knees with a towel over his head.

Ronbar turned his head to the hill where Victor and Nugget were spying from a distance and appeared (through lens of the spell) to be looking straight at them. Victor couldn't tell whether he was crying or sweating, just that he was scared as hell. The moment passed as quick as it came, and he turned back to the chestnut-clad fighter and smiled nervously before he drained the cup like an old pro.

The assembled raiders seemed quite pleased. They even helped the Miller up, albeit roughly, before redirecting the entire caravan north. Several men produced goblets and didn't wait for the ale to make it back to camp before sampling.

Ronbar seemed to be asking for another glass as well before the tail end of the wagon train moved behind a building and out of view of the telescope.

Nugget closed the spell. "Looks like the trap is sprung. Plan is still nightfall, General?"

Victor shook the embers out of his pipe. "Deep night, in the wee hours. Give Xaro's army plenty of time for the ale to make its way around camp. He brewed it strong, with a blend of *cicutorum* in the grain to boot. One mug, and they will be unable to *stop* drinking. The Miller will now likely pass from this world in a haze of drunkenness, but if Fate favors our cause, Xaro's men will die this very night at the point of our swords as we arrive as uninvited guests to their impending, pre-siege party."

Chapter Twenty-Five: Of Spell and Stone

~Magi~

Magi had no idea that Malenec stood face-to-face with his Queen at this very moment, or that Strongiron had sprung Tarsh's cave-in trap. His focus was on Tar-Tan's army, which was camped near the southeastern shore of Lake Calm, on a small inlet such that water bounded their troops on two sides, to the north and to the west. East of the half-ogre were the foothills leading to backside of Rookwood. *The only escape west for the Crown, should it come to that.*

South of that army was the formerly thickly wooded forest of Filestalas, now a scorched, barren plain. Magi, Pilanthas, a hundred or so Elfen Druids, and perhaps five times that number of archers were gathered a mile away, some tucked behind hills, but most woefully exposed, given the lack of foliage. Both forces could see one another in the mid-afternoon sun.

"Pilanthas, can you predict their course of action? What does the near-term future hold?" Magi asked.

The wizened elf looked like a man out of time. He had a mouthful of teeth an hour ago; his cracked lips now revealed gaps. That didn't stop him from smiling at Magi—albeit a warm, sad smile.

"I can't see five minutes into the future any more, lad, but I don't think we need to. Logic ought to provide us with whatever insights we need in lieu of prophesy, Magi."

"Then by all means, reason away."

Pilanthas was using a charred limb as a walking stick, and he leaned heavily on it to move toward a flat rock where he could face Magi. The two of them had *Teleported* to a hill dangerously close to Tar-Tan's camp for a better look.

He took a deep breath that rattled around his lungs like a bag of nails etching glass. After a short coughing fit, the ancient elf declared, "I'm dying. I'm dying, but I'm not quite dead yet."

Magi said nothing, just nodded slowly.

"The way I see it, Tar-Tan would be attacking us if he had many mages. I suspect he is trying to decide whether to head north to support Xaro by flanking Victor in Paragatha, or to try and wipe us out and secure the mountains behind Rookwood. *Logically*, I imagine he did not plan on needing many mages; he had a Dark Cleric and a zombie horde. That should have been more than enough.

His mages are with Xaro or with Tarsh, who, we know from Veronica, was picked to lead the sea assault."

"If you are implying that we should attack, surely you realize our Druids are exhausted, Pilanthas."

"Yes, and you probably are too, though you're too proud to admit it. What you need is *time*."

Magi bristled. "I have plenty of energy, but at the risk of stating the obvious, *time* is the one thing you seem to lack."

Pilanthas's new beard had already grown thin and wispy. Still, he raked his fingers through it as best he could. "I am the least of your concerns, but yes, I am implying that we attack. Not with Druids, however. I agree, they need to recover. They are little more than straw dummies for arrow practice at the moment. You and I must protect them—protect them all—to give my people time to recover. That's why I recommend that you and I attack them."

Magi lifted a single eyebrow, but before he could say a word Pilanthas continued. "And as you indelicately reminded me, time is not on my side, so I recommend that we attack them *right now*."

"The entire army? You do see they have at least some mages with them capable of putting up some type of *Shield*? What spell craft do you have up your sleeve, Pilanthas?"

Pressing the butt-end of the gnarled branch into the hilltop, Pilanthas stood. "Those shields protect them from a hail of arrows or a cavalry of Elfen Warriors. If our Druids weren't depleted, I'd try and break it. If you were fresh yourself, I might suggest *you* try and break it. Given the situation, I think our best shot is to *Teleport* behind their *Shield* before they decide whether to attack us or head north to attack Victor."

"And when the two of us materialize in the middle of an army camp a thousand or more strong?"

"I will use whatever energy I have left to protect you. You will use whatever energy you have left to put them to sleep. A simple *Sleep* spell takes very little energy as you well know, and it can affect vast numbers of people. If you put most of their mages to sleep—perhaps even the ogre—our Elfen Warriors ought to put the sleeping men to rest for good."

"And while I cast the *Sleep* spell—"

"I will *Shield* you from whatever comes your way."

"You're talking about a spell powerful enough to put a *thousand* or more men asleep over acres and acres of their camp."

"I would have you burn the camp or bring lightning down on all their heads if I thought it would take less energy. You can push a simple spell like that far, Magi."

"If we get close enough."

"If we get close enough," Pilanthas echoed. "Again, every second we delay robs me greatly, so let us do this *now*, while I have some life-force left to guard you during the protracted spell." He reached out his hand, which was blotchy with brown spots and webbed with dark blue veins across the back.

With a grim nod, Magi took the old elf's hand and *Teleported* into the midst of a lovely conversation, mid-camp.

"—I'd like to see the look on one of them nature-lovers' face when I slide three feet of *this* up their spine!" The mercenary gripped his broadsword so tight his forearms shook beneath a heavy leather gauntlet.

"Forget the damn elfs. We should head across the lake—the real fight is there. Besides, I heard rumor going around from one of our spell-throwers that Xaro's army is awash in ale. Good ale, too—a whole load meant for that drunken Queen. North is where the ogre should take us."

"Bah, we could wipe out the rest of the—hey, who are you? What are you two—"

Magi wasted no time. Fistfuls of sand were pouring between his fingers as he cast the mother of all *Sleep* spells. The familiar slowing of time at the apex of his spell casting washed over him, and his heightened senses brought him the pungent aroma of body odor from the mercenaries all around him. He could still hear the ground sizzling where the volcanic fires had been snuffed out by Kuth-Cergor. He saw the dagger slowly rotating toward his head, aware that someone nearby had thrown it, but not which one. He ignored it, would not even flinch or blink, even if it arrived point first at his eye. Either Pilanthas would protect him or he would not; instead, he focused on pushing his *Sleep* spell *out*.

The dagger was knocked out of the air by some unseen force, and the *Sleep* spell radiated out from Magi in all directions. Without thinking, he grabbed more sand from his pouch, and dug deeper, willing *Sleep* everywhere. If he could send all of Tenebrae into a dream state, he would.

The men close by fell easily, keeling over. No more daggers would be thrown from that motley crew. Lost in his Art, he could hear the thumps of bodies falling over in the camp.

A True Mage stumbled toward Magi, fighting off the weariness with some type of personal *Shield* spell. Clearly groggy, the mage cast a bolt of lightning well wide of Magi. Pilanthas struck him down with a lightning bolt of his own, but he was on his knees, breathing hard.

Magi redoubled his efforts, recalling the same force of will he had used a handful of times before. Deeper and deeper he went into his well of energy, going further into a dreamlike trance himself. *Sleep—everyone will sleep, and I will crawl out of here.* Let the Elfs come and burn them while they all dream.

Magi was lost in his spell, lost in his own power, pulling energy from the reserves of his reserves. Behind him, Pilanthas's life finally gave out, and the old elf tried to give Magi a warning—tried to say goodbye, really—but Magi never saw him. His eyes were closed to the world around him…all he saw was sand and sleeping bodies as wave after wave of his spell pulsed from him.

His self-induced trance was interrupted by the point of Tar-Tan's enormous, two-handed blade as the general drove it clear through his belly, right up to the hilt.

Blood gurgled on his lips as Magi's eyelids flew open to focus on the groggy, yellow eyes and the sour breath of the large half-ogre standing nose-to-nose with him.

"Your sleepy-time spells don't work very well on me, mage." Stumbling forward, he twisted the wide blade, rounding the hole he had just created. "It is far beyond your time to die, and few deaths are as painful as a blade through the gut." Tar-Tan ripped the sword out as he stumbled sleepily first to his knees, and then face down.

Magi immediately collapsed, holding his ruined gut. He was truly exhausted, bleeding, sweating, and screaming in agony. Between his own cries, he heard Tar-Tan's muffled chuckles.

"You will be dead before I awake. Pity I won't see you suffer, but oh will it fill my dreams…" His head *thumped* against the ground; the general finally succumbed to sleep.

Magi couldn't speak. White-hot pain blotted all words from his mouth. He closed his eyes, letting his tenuous hold on consciousness also slip away, with a final thought of Dymetra. *Of disappointing Her…*

~King Herodius~

His wife would be safe inside the castle. *Far safer than the battlefield*. Luther would keep her apprised, and the supplies they had could last for months, even with refugees. The mountain stronghold would protect her, and she would protect the realm.

Herodius saw the light of a smelly torch ensconced along the wall illuminate his forearm. Most of it was gauntleted, but he caught a glimpse of the edge of a scar he would always carry: 1X5Z9. The "9" was still visible, near the elbow.

He told his Queen and Jonathon that he would try and rally his fellow Islanders to fight for the Crown. In the quiet of his own thoughts, he would at least be honest with himself: he wanted a chance to kill that half-ogre. For the memory of his first love, for his former life, for his new life, for his homeland, and for the freedom of his new land: Tar-Tan must die.

"*Aduro,*" whispered his Steward. A small pebble, no larger than the smallest fingernail, began to give off a faint glow. "This marks the entrance to the secret way through the mountains to the west. No torches remain from this point forward; we must carry our own. I have tried to mark the paths that I could, but…the way is tricky. It may take us up to two days to come through."

"We must emerge in less than one. Hours count, Jonathon. We must travel with haste through this maze. I will follow you."

His Steward grabbed a lit torch and handed him a few spares. "Step where I step. We will go as fast as possible, I assure you my King." Without further chit-chat, Jonathon turned and began scampering down one of several well-holes (the one with a glow pebble slowly fading back to grey) at the base of the mountain.

The wood ladder they descended had seen better days, and the creaky sound coming from each rung did not instill confidence. Herodius was about to ask about a safety rope, but he bit his tongue. *You'll have to accept some risk in exchange for speed.*

Below him, he finally heard Jonathon's boots fall on solid ground—a welcome sound after listening to each rung groan like a bent tree branch right before the *snap.* Herodius looked below and saw the yellow light spreading out in a circle where Jonathan rested fifteen feet or so beneath him at the bottom of this "well." His Steward waved him forward impatiently. The last rung before the ground did, in fact, give out, and Herodius fell about four feet.

"My King—are you hurt?" Jonathon extended a hand to help him up.

Herodius took it. "I'm fine, Jonathon. Could have been far worse. How do you expect to lead a retreat down such a hole?"

Jonathon was already moving forward. "Mages, sire. *Levitation* spells. Anything else will be most difficult for thousands to move through. The path was not designed as a retreat, my King. At least…not for the masses."

Herodius curled his lip in a snarl. *A path meant only for the Royal family to flee, perhaps.* "Carry on," he said, swiping invisible spider webs out of the way as he went.

Jonathon's torch began to highlight their surroundings. To their left was the rough wall of a dry cave, with veins of different minerals snaking through the rock. At the bottom of the chute, the path forward narrowed into little more than a ledge, as the right side of the path dropped off into a crevasse that swallowed all light. Herodius could not see the other side of the crevasse, let alone the bottom. "You may just as well have led me to the abyss."

"There is but one path through. Please watch your step, Your Majesty."

The ledge narrowed until it was a foot—no more than two— wide, and began to curve downward. Ahead, Jonathon kept whispering *"Aduro, Aduro"* every few steps, clearly looking for something. Finally there was a tiny glimmer of light, halfway up the left side of the cave wall, in a little nook by a large crack in the wall. The path continued forward.

"This way," he said, stepping sideways to shimmy through the crack in the wall.

Herodius stared at his Steward incredulously. The crack looked like a natural fissure, not a path leading out of the mountain. It could not have been more than two feet wide at its narrowest. *No way a man—let alone one wearing armor—could walk straight through.* He turned to his side and shimmied his way through the opening as well, shoulder first. The sharp rocks scratched the back of his thighs, and the confined area quickly filled with black smoke from the torch.

"This is insane, Jonathon!"

His Steward kept shuffling forward, and eventually the crack in the rock widened into another narrow cave, albeit one they could at least turn around in and face forward. Jonathon looked back over his shoulder to check on Herodius.

"There are many difficult traverses, my King. We *are* moving quickly through, howev—"

A steep pit, camouflaged as merely a cave floor, engulfed Jonathon and he fell ten feet into the trap with a sickening yell.

"Jonathon!" shouted Herodius. "Are you okay?"

Their one lit torch still burned brightly in the corner of the rectangular pit. Jonathon clutched his ankle, trying not to howl in pain and mostly failing. Looking down from above, Herodius could see the obvious; Jonathon's foot was not supposed to point that way.

"My foot, sire. It will not bear me, even if I could climb out of here. I missed this trap in my haste." He screamed *"Aduro!"* in agony.

A tiny glow pebble shone at Herodius's feet, right before the *Illusion*.

"Oh Jonathon," Herodius said. "Can you reach me?" He stretched out on his belly and lowered a hand, knowing full well it was pointless.

"My King," said Jonathon. "Step back." Herodius did, and his Steward crawled along the bottom of the small pit, screaming, until he reached his torch. "Here!" he yelled, tossing it up to his King. "You must go on."

"I'll go back, get help for you, Jonathon. I cannot leave you here in a pit in the dark! That is madness!"

"The bottom rungs of the ladder leading up have shattered, and I wouldn't trust that wood regardless. Navigate carefully, my King. Speak *Aduro* every other step. Test your footing at all times. Go and bring a mage back if you wish to save me. I have water, I will live for a while. Even if you could lift me out, I cannot travel on my own." He began to cough. "Not if the path was paved. You see my f-foot."

"Jonathon…"

His Steward shook his head. "Go. Go now. While you can make a difference—for the war and for me. Remember, *Aduro*, my King."

Herodius did not feel like a king. He felt like a farmer from the Uncharted Isles. *I should be planning harvest around the weather, taking in the open sea air.* Down here, the air only stirred when a bat flapped its wings.

"I *will* come back for you, Jonathon. Have faith!"

"Always, Your M-majesty." He leaned his back heavily against one of the pit walls, still clutching his ankle, rocking back and forth.

Here I am imploring my Steward to have faith. Do I? Herodius carefully walked around the edge of the pit, putting Jonathon's stifled wails behind him. He set his jaw forward.

"Aduro," he whispered.

Screaming for help would have been logical. So would running away. Queen Najalas could do neither, but it wasn't a dark prayer that stilled her voice and legs.

She was stunned to see him standing there.

"Quite a bit different, this meeting, no?" Malenec continued. "Your Mage guards have all been repurposed and scattered to the four corners of our battlefield. And your Knights—where are they? Call them."

The Queen found her voice. "What are you doing here?"

"I should think that fairly obvious, Najalas. Already your rule crumbles around you. We have been given the sacred task of ushering in a genesis; this Godless age shall pass like clouds before the gale! The new age shall be a God-fearing one, and all will submit to Kuth-Cergor. You, my sweet Queen, are of the past age. You have no place in the new one, and so I must, regrettably, remove you from your throne." A greasy smile spread across his long, narrow face. "Somehow, I will manage."

"If you kill me, I will be the world's greatest martyr. You have no idea how far men will fight for a murdered Queen."

At this, Malenec's smile erupted into downright laughter. "*A martyr?* You truly are a gem, Najalas. An out-of-touch gem, but a gem nonetheless. My how you overestimate your popularity! Do you honestly think the people will rally around your corpse? Not that I would even give them that chance in the first place. You will never be a martyr, because you will never die. Perish the thought. Let us ponder whether your men will raise Rookwood's colors for an undead zombie-Queen who wishes nothing more than to rip, tear, and eat." Malenec began a worship ritual, raising his black-gloved hands skyward.

"You will do nothing of the sort, brother."

"Palinor!" yelled the Queen.

Malenec turned around to see his brother dressed in a simple white robe, cinched at the waist with a fine piece of yellow rope. "Dear brother…I was wondering why I no longer could pay you a visit with my loving visions. Clearly you have chosen to worship a creature disinterested in Tenebrae."

"Dymetra has a keen interest in this world, Malenec. And She is no creature. The same cannot be said of the beast you call God."

"As much as I would love to entertain your newfound interest in theology, I'm afraid the blacksmith's opinion must yield to the True

Cleric's." He formed a large 'O' with his hands, which he held up to his mouth. "In the name of Kuth-Cergor, let flame lick your flesh!"

The Dark Cleric blew through his hand ring, making a jet of red-black flame roar from his hands, racing toward Palinor. Queen Najalas screamed.

Palinor extended his left palm into the incoming fire stream. His hand began smoldering, and the smell of burning flesh filled the room. Pain lines creased his face, and the tendons in his neck bulged.

He did not withdraw his bloody and charred left hand, however, nor did he scream. Instead, he raised his right hand and threw a soft ball of white light at Malenec, little more than a child's soap-bubble. It fell on the Dark Cleric and quickly expanded to encase him in a translucent cocoon.

"What did you do to him? What are doing here? Your hand!" The Queen's thoughts tumbled out like hay from rafters.

Palinor was clearly straining to imprison his brother. "I can't…hold him long…my Queen. Forget my hand… At the King's request…I came to bless you—so consider yourself…blessed. Now *run!*"

The Queen blinked…and then ran. Her hands involuntarily went to her womb, which hadn't begun to show.

She burst out of the council room and turned toward the front of the castle. *Simon will know what to do! My Captain of the Guard has more pressing matters to address than lowering the damn bridge.* She quickened her steps, rounding a corner into a long stretch of hallway. The Queen looked up and saw—*thank God!*—Simon approaching her in the distance.

He was moving strangely, however. *Stiffly.*

"Simon! Quick! Palinor needs help. Simon?"

The man walking toward her had dead eyes, and his pale flesh had already begun to show telltale signs of rot. Several doors burst open near him, and out poured more undead guards under his command.

His *former* command. The Queen could see the obvious; these men were now under Malenec's command. Rookwood had been breached.

She turned on a heel and ran as fast as she could the other way, toward the Towers, and the rear of the castle. Her lungs began to burn, unaccustomed as they were to the exertion. The Queen stole glimpses behind her. The castle was eerily quiet, and her footfalls sounded like drumbeats on the stone. She couldn't *see* anyone behind her…but she knew they saw her. They were *coming.*

She raced past the first Tower, the one representing the King's Mercy. Neither Herodius's, nor her own, mercy came to mind, however. *Dymetra, have mercy on me, my husband, my people, my—*

She ran through the stitch that developed in her side. Soon the second tower came into view, its entrance bearing the sign: *The Crown Wieldeth Power.* She mouthed a silent prayer, wishing that true for her husband, bemoaning that she didn't feel very powerful herself.

Queen Najalas pressed onward as if the whip was at her back. Past the third tower, where not-so-long-ago she had counseled together with her husband up those very stairs in the Tower of Truth.

Still she ran, stumbling but never falling, until she came to the fourth Tower—the Tower of Protection. *The King Provideth Protection* was carved above the doorway that she had left what seemed like a lifetime ago. Here she paused to take a breath, wondering *how did I fail to protect my people? Is that not one of the most important jobs a King or Queen has?*

She did not dawdle long. One foot in front of another, she again quickened her pace, rounding another corner until she spied the entrance to fifth and final tower of Rookwood. Above its entrance read the sign *The Crown Giveth the Law.*

In other words, the Crown's word is final.

King Herodius wasn't here, but the Queen had an idea of what Mercy, Power, Truth, Protection, and Law looked like under the present set of circumstances.

"My Queen?" a soft voice asked. "Are you alright?"

Queen Najalas turned. It was Veronica…and she was not a zombie.

~Nugget~

Victor stared into the distance, stroking his mustaches aimlessly. He sighed, tapping his second bowl of tobacco ash against a rock. "Edward," he called, not bothering to turn his head.

"You can call me Nugget, General," reminded the True Mage.

"Edward," Victor continued, turning around. "You said you once roomed with Magi. Can you speak with him from here? I very much need to know what that Ogre is doing on the other side of the lake. Before this evening, while light still graces us, I would know whether our flank is at risk. Can you do this for me? I've seen Luther summon a shade or two in his day, and I dare say you're more clever by half than that boring sot ever was." He felt the bowl of his pipe.

Satisfied that it was cool, he started to jam a third pinch of tobacco into it.

Nugget shook his head. "I wish I could, General. The last I saw of him was when he left our village to seek his prophesy. From what I've heard, things got pretty weird for him after that. I'm just glad he's on our side. He *is* still on our side, right?"

Victor lit his pipe and let smoke begin to curl forth from the corners of his mouth. "Yes, yes. The Queen trusts him, so that's that. Why can't you communicate with him?"

"I don't know. I don't think he's dead, but he's not...how shall I say this...he's not *answering.* I can summon the shade of another mage to speak with them over distances if they agree to join the spell—to link up. I can give a charm to a non-mage that does the same thing, basically. Magi and I are not linked, and he is not answering my request to confer."

Victor took the pipe from his mouth and pointed at Nugget with its stem. "Then *Teleport* to their camp and ask him in person. Hell, I'd sail there myself if there wasn't an army between me and them. I need information, Edward. And I need it *before tonight*. Do you understand?"

"Completely, General." He nodded, smiling as nonchalantly as he dared. *Nothing like Teleporting blind into the middle of an army camp on the eve of battle.* He did look on the bright side: at least he would see Magi again. The Most Famous Mage In Tenebrae had already left Rookwood for the Elfs when Nugget showed up there, fresh off his Climb and ready to fight. Instead, Victor had taken the sunny young mage with him.

"One more thing, *Nugget*," said Victor, smiling now himself. "Don't screw this up."

"Of course not, sir." Nugget chuckled under his breath...and was gone.

He reappeared on what he hoped was the Elfish camp. One look around at the deep brown skin tones told him he was in the right place. By the looks of it, there force was small. A hundred Druids seemed to be resting, and maybe five hundred archers were either spread out or propped up on trees and rocks, heads listing to one side.

"My name is Nugget," he announced. "I come from the Crown's army at the North side of Lake Calm seeking information. Who is in command here?" he asked. "Is Magi Blacksmooth here?"

"Sir Mage, I am—for now—in command. My name is Cherokum." The young elf kept yawning. "I speak with the Chief's authority. Magi *Teleported* with our brethren, Pilanthas, into our enemy's camp, which you can see in the distance if you look closely. We await his return, for now." He stifled another yawn. "Forgive me, stranger, but the camp is groggy. We had quite a fight earlier, but we incinerated an entire infestation of the unholy, the undead. You can see for yourselves the cost of such a burn." He made a sweeping gesture at the dry, cracked soil that hours ago had been the lushest forest on Tenebrae.

"I see. And how long has Magi been gone? You said he and Pilanthas *went alone?*"

Cherokum nodded and said, "Thirty minutes, give or take." He stretched his arm.

Something didn't feel right to Nugget. Thirty minutes was an *eternity* for a spellcaster to sustain a spell. If Magi was out to reconnoiter, he would have *Teleported* back by now. If he was attacking, surely he would coordinate something with more than just the two of them?

Would he? Magi never lacked for self-confidence.

And what was all this grogginess around camp? Your enemy stands a mile away, and your soldiers are *napping?* Victor would have skinned them alive if he knew his flank was being watched by a bunch of codswallop Elfs counting sheep.

What in the name of all that is holy is going on here?

"Cherokum…can I get close enough to Tar-Tan's camp to get a look myself?"

"Follow me." He rubbed his eyes roughly and moved his leaden feet forward, toward a hillock. They crested, and Cherokum led him behind an enormous boulder. "Down there, in the distance," he whispered.

Nugget peered around the stone and frowned. He didn't see anything moving. He cast a *Farsight* spell for a closer look. A couple men stood outside; they looked like guards.

They were lying on the ground. Some even had swords drawn.

Nugget frowned some more. *This wasn't an army camp…it looked more like a burial mound waiting for the mound part. Everything was still. Nobody tended the fires. Heck, nobody was* standing.

"Cherokum, I need to see what has happened there. Magi should have returned. Nothing is moving down there. I will return soon."

The elf smiled weakly and patted Nugget on the shoulder. "That's what he said, too." He shook the sleepiness from his face and simply said, "Good luck, Mage. Be careful."

For the second time in less than ten minutes, Nugget *Teleported* to a strange camp. This time, however, he immediately cast a *Shield* spell upon his appearance.

The entire camp looked dead; no one seemed to stir. He approached one of the bodies, carefully, eventually bending down, ready to cast anything if the man stirred.

He did not stir, *per se*. But Nugget quickly realized that this army wasn't destroyed—at least not yet. They were asleep! All of them. And then it dawned on him: *Magi must have cast a Sleep spell to do this*. Ingenious. To put an entire *battle-camp* to sleep…only Magi could have dug that deep. He dug so deep that the effects of his spell must have diffused over Cherokum and the rest of the Elfs. *Good God, that is powerful!*

But why didn't he come back? Nugget's worried feeling intensified; he started tearing through tents and temporary shelters.

"Magi?" he mouthed in a loud whisper. *"Magi?"*

Faintly, ever so faintly, he heard something. Someone snoring. He tore open the next large pavilion tent and saw an enormous half-ogre awkwardly sprawled on his stomach, snoring loudly.

Next to him, in the corner, lay Magi, face pale, sitting with his back against the canvas side, clutching his stomach. Blood trickled through his fingers, but Nugget saw his eyelids drift open.

"Magi! What happened here? How bad are you hurt? It's me, Nugget!" He raced over to Magi, who was already damp with both blood and sweat, burning up.

He tried to speak, but struggled, shivering. He kept trying to say over and over again "C-c-c-c-" but he could never finish the thought.

Nugget did not waste another second. They might not be able to heal him, but they sure as heck would be able to make him comfortable. *And they owe him.* "Magi, we're going to Thalanthalas. We're going to see the Elfs and their Chief."

Silently, he carefully *Levitated* Magi's body, wincing as the other mage tried not to scream. From underneath, Nugget immediately saw the problem: blood dripped freely in long, sticky strands as he lifted his former roommate several feet off the ground and guided him clear out of the tent. In the distance, with no trees and few hills to obscure the view any longer, Thalanthalas stood like a mecca in the desert.

"I doubt you have the strength to *Teleport*, and I can't *Teleport* you, so I'm going to transport you the fastest way I can think of, Magi. Just *hang in there!*"

Nugget took a deep breath and put his hands on Magi's feet. He aimed his damp head at Thalanthalas, the Capital of the Elfs, which stood just at the tail end of his line of sight. And with the fiercest wind spell he could cast, Edward Sheldon "Nugget" Klingelman gave his friend a mighty push.

~Queen Najalas~

"Thank Dymetra!" said the Queen, pushing air through her lungs like billows before the fire. "We have no time, Veronica. We must leave; Rookwood has fallen, and they are coming."

The Assassin took a step back. "What are you saying, my Queen? Who is coming? Xaro is here? Because if he is, I would just assume see him—"

"The undead! Those foul creatures made by that foul Cleric. He cornered me. I would be one myself, had it not been for Palinor. But Simon! My Captain!" She dropped her eyes. "My friend…"

"How far behind are they?"

She took one deep breath and snapped her head back up to look Veronica in the eyes. "Minutes. We must leave now. Jonathon left a path—I know where it begins." Before Veronica could object, debate, or delay, the Queen forged ahead, past the fifth tower. The Assassin fell in step easily beside her.

They moved with haste, picking up a few torches along the way. Queen Najalas led them through a large, damp cellar, and in the back were a series of well holes that stared up at them from the floor like great, black eyeballs. Waving their torches over them did nothing to illuminate their depths.

"*Aduro*," whispered the Queen. A small pebble began to glow near the fourth hole. "This way."

She put her foot on the nearest rung when Veronica stopped her. "Let me go first, your Majesty. I do not trust the wood in such a place as this."

Queen Najalas nodded. "Very well, but be quick. I would rather break my neck in a fall then have my neck fall into the clutches of those that follow us."

Veronica spied some spare rope used to bind casks and dropped a line down, frowning when she didn't hear it hit bottom. She fashioned a retrievable knot on the other end around some of the bricks in the well wall, and grabbed on tight. "Keep tension on this rope, my Queen; it releases on slack." Down she went, rope in one hand, rung on another, holding her torch between her teeth.

There is no way I can do that, not even with horse teeth. She observed as the glow pebble faded back to grey. She then watched Veronica nimbly maneuver in the shaft, half-climbing, half-swinging down. Far below, she saw the light begin to spread and escape the bottom of the shaft. The Assassin had reached the bottom.

Alone at the top, the Queen spun her head around. *What was that?* She thought she heard shuffling feet. She strained her ears for a second, but the blood pumping through them created a deafening *thump-thump*. She literally could barely hear herself think. Veronica was shouting something, but she couldn't hear a word. The undead— the Dark Cleric's zombies—were *close*. She could smell them, she was sure of it.

She shone her light on the little grey pebble and kicked it across the room.

The Queen swung her leg over onto the top rung, which creaked like an ancient rocking chair. Closing her eyes to steel her courage, she focused on one, clear thought: *better my baby die from a fall then get turned into a night creature along with his Mother.*

She could not balance the torch in her mouth, nor could she rappel down the chute, so her choice was between rope and light. She chose the rope and dropped her torch to the bottom, hoping Veronica would step out of the way. Everything went dark in the shaft around her. Rope in her left hand, rung in her right, she slowly felt with her toes for the next step down.

The damp wood began splintering almost immediately, and the first rung that broke was barely a few from the top. The rope held, and though her left palm was getting raw, she caught herself. A few feet later it happened again, and she screamed before catching herself a second time, ripping away more skin.

"Najalas!" Veronica called up, her voice echoing in the well. *"Light steps! Let the rope bear your weight!"*

Her left palm was bleeding now, and another slip would be the end, she knew. Gritting her teeth against the rough cordage grinding into her flesh, she found herself learning to rappel out of necessity, bracing her feet against the side walls. The light at the bottom finally began to brighten from a pinprick to a soft glow…to a person holding a torch.

"My Queen!" called Veronica, maybe ten feet below her. "The rope runs out before the bottom. Be careful on the last few rungs, they are weak and many are missing."

As if on cue, the Queen heard the *snap!* before she felt her stomach rising into her chest for the third time. No rope was left to grab either, and her arms flailed.

"No!" yelled Veronica, dropping her torch as she tried to get underneath the falling woman. Queen Najalas fell on her like a sack of grain thrown off a roof, and together they rolled into the cave opening at the bottom of the well. The slack rope fell beside them, gathering itself in a tangled mess.

"Veronica?" coughed the Queen.

"Your Majesty," Veronica wheezed in return. "Are you hurt?"

"Are you?" she answered.

Veronica slowly sat up. She was sore and scratched all over. Her tunic had caught on a rough stone, slashing it open, but nothing seemed broken. "I'm ok...I think." She pushed herself up, grabbing one of the lit torches to better survey herself and the Queen. "And you?" she repeated.

"I am fine, and I have you to thank for my life." She sat there in a cloud of dust staring up at the pale Assassin. "And to think there was a time not long ago when you would have taken my life for a few pieces of gold; now you throw yours to the wind to protect me. These are strange days, Veronica."

"We all have a purpose, my Queen. It just takes some of us longer to find ours." Veronica extended a hand to her Queen, helping her up. "Are you sure you can walk?"

Before she could answer, they both turned to the well, where a low moan began to build, growing louder and louder, until a zombie crashed in a heap at the bottom of the well, landing mere feet away from them. It fell on its head, snapping the neck clean in two. The head rolled to a stop next to the Queen and Veronica, face forward.

The clouded eyes still moved, staring first at the Queen with loathing before darting to Veronica. She gasped.

"Oh my God—*Trevor?*"

Recognition briefly flickered across the face of the disembodied head, tinged with—sadness, perhaps? The Queen stared at the scene unfolding in front of her, speechless. *You know him?*

Her thoughts were broken by another wail, followed by a thumping body and another cloud of dust. The head stayed on this one, but the body was twisted like scrap metal from the fall. And then another thump. And another. The well was raining zombies.

"Run, your Majesty! They are making a human ladder!"

The Queen did not need to be told twice; she had no interest in ever seeing the rotting face of her Captain of the Guard up close. So they ran…until the path narrowed. It was now far too treacherous to race ahead; the path was barely two feet wide, and the abyss to their right made the well they had just descended look as deep as a puddle. They walked with purpose, hissing *"Aduro!"* impatiently while casting glances over their shoulders at the zombie pile sprouting up the hole, back up the well.

Along the narrow path, the faint glow of a pebble marked a rather large crack along the cave wall, but the path continued forward.

The Queen stopped, pointing at the fissure. "There, Veronica. You first—through there. Hurry."

Veronica raised a questioning eyebrow, but the glow pebble clearly seemed to mark the rather natural-looking cleft in the stone. She turned sideways and began to wiggle through. "As you wish. It will be tight, Your Majesty. Step in right behind me."

The Queen nodded. "I will. You just keep leading the way, Veronica. I'm going to cover our tracks a bit." She waited for Veronica to squirm a little further along before she took the glow pebble in her bloody hand and tossed it over the ledge.

She then continued down the path, with haste. She had to move quickly now, lest Veronica turn back. *I may not be able to save everyone, but I might be able to save* someone.

The ledge widened at a dead end, and the cave floor spread out once again. She waved her torch around looking for something…something King Alomar had shown her long ago. Something she would have shown Herodius, eventually. Against the far wall was a rock pedestal, waist high. There was nothing ornate or suspicious or even noteworthy about the rock at the back of the cave.

The *Terraemotus*.

Her thoughts were interrupted by the howls of zombies. *They've made their ladder; they're coming for me now.*

Before she could talk herself out of it, Queen Najalas strode up to the nondescript rock. She shone her torchlight upon the surface of it, wiping away a fine layer of dust. With a closer look, the rock pedestal *did* look curious. It was oddly flat and smooth on top, and when she looked closely, a faint inscription could be read:

> *The Crown is Mercy*
> *The Crown is Power*
> *The Crown is Truth*
> *The Crown is Protection*
> *The Crown is Law*

Thus, the true hand of the Crown holds up
the World...or lets it fall.

The growls were now echoing off the cave wall and into the chasm behind her. She whipped her torch around and could see the shadows beginning to dance at the edge of her torchlight, looming larger. Time was nearly out.

She turned her back to the approaching horde and focused on the small crevice atop the pedestal, which upon close inspection roughly resembled the shape of a hand, with five tiny cracks spider-webbing from a larger one. Queen Najalas closed her eyes and stuck her left hand—the one raw and bloody—into the crack. She felt a small, smooth stone—it felt like a gem. An *icy* gem; the jewel was freezing. She wrapped her fist around it nonetheless.

I'm so sorry she thought, though she wasn't apologizing to anyone in particular. She heard the undead break into the clearing; the smell of their rotten flesh wafted over her like shallow graves in mid-summer.

She opened her eyes. "Goodbye, Herodius," she said. "I shall see you again." She felt the hot breath of the nearest zombie on her neck. "But I shall see Alomar first."

Queen Najalas pulled the stone free from its cradle.

Chapter Twenty-Six: The Last Nightfall

~Victor~

At his camp on the outskirts of Paragatha, Victor looked up from his map when he heard a thunderous tremor in the distance, toward Rookwood.

"What was that?"

~Xaro~

Allowing his men a night of good cheer—courtesy of the Queen's confiscated ale—before he commenced his siege, he turned his back on Belara when he felt the mountains to the south rumble.

His face drained of color as he turned back to the Illusionist. "I pray that isn't what I think it is…" She shook her head questioningly and *Teleported* away.

~Magi~

Teeth chattering, arms folded over his mortal belly wound, Magi drifted in and out of consciousness as he arrived in Thalanthalas. He was only vaguely aware he was hovering off the ground, and he thought he heard a familiar voice. Just as he was entering a doorway he heard a distant roar, like a mountain cave-in.

His eyelids snapped open, and he turned his head toward Rookwood.

~Tar-Tan~

The General stirred, but kept snoring.

~Peter~

The Admiral guided his small reinforcement fleet ever closer toward the sandy shoreline of a small bay due east from Paragatha. Far into the distance, near the horizon, he heard the reverberations of thunder echoing across the sea. He stroked his chin, frowning. "Nothing good comes from a sound like that," he grumbled.

~King Herodius~

"*Aduro!*" he shouted, finding another pebble. He turned toward the tunnel when everything around him began shaking violently. Dust from the ceiling fell thick all around, obscuring the light from his low-burning torch.

"Najalas?" he whispered. *Something is wrong.*

~Malenec~

Trailing somewhat leisurely behind the main group of undead, he followed their trail of dead bodies from room-to-room throughout the castle, raising a new horde as he went. His main force had been decimated in the fire, but a few had survived, and they had hidden in the water flooding the city. When the gates were lowered, they came. Malenec had directed them to overcome the guards, including their captain, and the citizens quickly changed their minds about running into the castle for protection as dozens of zombies broke the surface of the floodwaters all around them. After securing the drawbridge, Malenec turned his attention to finding the Queen.

Now he turned to Palinor on his left, his brother and one of his newest converts. "That was quite a fight you put up, little brother. But in the end you only delayed the inevit—"

An ear-splitting rumble cut him off as large cracks began to snake down the walls.

Frowning, Malenec narrowed his eyes for a moment before turning to his right, a place of honor reserved for Genevieve. "Goodbye, sweet Genevieve. Your time is at an end." He said a quick prayer and *Teleport*ed away, right before the ceiling collapsed above where his brother, Genevieve, and he had been standing. The floor gave way, and the undead and anyone else still alive in the castle were crushed as it hurtled down the mountain.

He never did say goodbye to Palinor.

~Veronica~

"Jonathon!" she said, offering her hand to pull him out.

"It's no use. You must go on. King Herodius went on. Leave me, and try to help him. Use the word '*Aduro*' to light your path.

"You don't understand. The Queen is right behind me, and so is a horde of those foul, dark zombies. They will devour you."

"Then kill me and save me that fate. I cannot walk—my ankle is shattered." Jonathan held a light to his foot, which looked swollen even from ten feet away.

Veronica balked at the idea. In the back of her mind, she could hear Silver's voice: *You're a Life-Ender. It's the only thing you've ever been good at.* She shook her head. "I don't want to kill you Jonathon."

"Then send me down some poison, if you have some to spare, and I will make the choice for you. Please—I do not want to be alive when the zombies crawl into this pit."

Veronica took a small vial from an inner pocket and turned it over in her hands. Sighing, she gently tossed it to him. "A drop in your water will suffice, Jonathan. May Dymetra have mercy on you."

He caught it and held it in front of his eyes. "She does." He uncorked the small bottle.

Just then an enormous earthquake rocked everything, and Veronica nearly fell into the pit on top of Jonathon. Dust and small stones cascaded down on them, and the cracked wall leading to the other section of the mountain completely caved in upon itself. The opening was now a dusty rock pile.

"Queen Najalas!" Veronica screamed.

Jonathon closed his eyes and tossed back a swig straight from the vial.

~Tarsh~

The first roar from Rookwood caused everyone to stop and look up. From his vantage point out at sea, Tarsh saw a spectacle for the ages.

Like a cataclysm, the mountain seemed to shake the castle off its moorings. One by one, the great Towers began to crack and fall, splitting in two and then shattering into a million stones as they tumbled down the mountain. The entire fortress began to crack and slide, showering the surrounding village with an avalanche of debris. Already flooded, the massive amount of rock, dirt, wood, and stone that flew down the mountain began sending the filthy water, filled with flotsam and jetsam, back into the sea.

Tarsh didn't even bother to try and stop it; he was transfixed by what he was witnessing.

The castle, along with the entire mountain face just tore off and avalanched down, pulverizing the city of Rookwood into sand.

Tarsh closed his eyes. *I pray Magi wasn't in there. I am owed revenge, and it is for me to exact.*

~Queen Najalas~

As she pulled the gem from its setting, she spun around, waiving her torch in front of her in an arc. The nearest zombie caught fire and immediately screamed, backing away. Yellow light began spreading from the egg-sized gem in her palm, covering the walls, floor, and ceiling. The light did *not* spread to the crack in the wall that Veronica had passed through; that was the line, King Alomar had told her long ago, that marked the protected tunnels under the castle. Everywhere else the light touched, however, began to crumble like dry wood burned to ash.

The first stone struck the Queen in the temple, and she was glad for that kindness. The undead never touched her, as they were crushed right along with her. She never felt the weight of the castle falling atop her, nor did she feel herself hurled down the mountain to the city below.

When she opened her eyes, she found herself lying on a stone path. No two stones were the same shape, yet they fit together with amazing symmetry. On each side of the path was a grassy knoll, covered with pastel wildflowers that filled the air with a scent of pure bliss. She looked down the path and saw a man approaching. It was a familiar face.

Dark complected, with a black goatee that made him look terrifying when angry and mischievous when smiling, he strode up to her, offering his hand to help her stand up.

"Alomar!"

King Alomar helped his former wife stand and hugged her close, his handsome face split into a warm smile that was anything but mischievous. "Come, Najalas. Let me welcome you and show you Paradise…"

~Veronica~

From the time she was a small girl, one thing had always been true of Veronica: she was a survivor. Her training in the Black Guild had only honed those instincts. She quickly accepted that the Queen was dead—no one could have survived what happened on the other side of that crack in the cave wall. Her ears were still ringing; her very bones were still vibrating. She felt as if she had been trapped inside a massive church bell that had rung for an interminable number of minutes. The very roots of her teeth hurt.

She also knew, instinctively, that the Queen had died on her own terms, by her own hand. All Veronica could muster was a silent prayer to Dymetra, the One who saved more than her hands, as she pulled herself together and moved on. She called down to Jonathon in the pit one last time, and found him slumped over, her empty vial lying next to him.

She moved on. She was a survivor.

Somewhere in between whispers of "*Aduro!*" and shouts of "Herodius!" she became aware that time must be moving forward again. She drank her water. She made water. She probed for traps and looked for signs. Obvious places under the glare of torchlight showed dust recently disturbed. She was on the King's heels.

This is worse than the cave through the Crystal Mountains. I'd kill Zender all over again for one honest map. The constant doubling back, cautiously looking for pits, *Illusions*, spring traps, blow guns, sticky patches—not to mention countless insects that undoubtedly were poisonous—it made minutes seem like hours, and hours seem like days. The mental fatigue was the worst.

"Herodius!" she called out again, as she did every so often, in case he was within earshot. Nothing.

On she trudged until she saw light up ahead. Not sunlight, unfortunately, but lit torches—enough to hurt her eyes. She approached the end of the tunnel she was in and came to a tiny clearing, a small cavern with eight paths proceeding from the "central station." Veronica groaned.

"*Aduro!*" she yelled. Four glowstones lit up, including one at her feet. She was entering from one of the eight tentacles.

Great. Three choices…they can't all *be right.* "Herodius!" she shouted. Silence answered.

Sighing, she carefully walked into the center, heading for the path directly across from her, which had a glowing pebble on the ground. As soon as her foot stepped on the square, she immediately was spun dizzy, dropping her torch.

Stepping off, she looked at the fading pebbles in confusion. *Which is which?* She could no longer tell which path she had entered from. Behind her, a tiny glowing stone twinkled out.

Twenty-five percent chance? She took a deep breath, picked up her torch, and walked through the opening.

Ten feet from her, unconscious, was King Herodius.

"King Herodius! Are you hurt?"

No response. She put her ear to his mouth and heard faint breathing. His lips were cracked, and there was a gash along his head. He was lying awkwardly next to a sharp rock.

She held her torch higher…they were in a cave that was *littered* with sharp rocks. Like weeds in a garden, the rocks *almost* looked like plants. They were *everywhere*, and the cave floor was shiny. Veronica leaned over the King's body and gently rubbed the ground next to one of the rocks with a long finger. *Slicker than lamp oil.*

It did not take a genius to figure out what happened to the King. The challenging part now was how to rescue him. *How to rescue us.*

She carefully put a few drops of her dwindling water in his mouth and applied a healing salve made from *sanitor* trees to his forehead. Every Assassin carried a few supplies with them.

It took a while, but eventually his eyes peeled open. "Veronica?"

"Yes, your Majesty."

"What are you doing here?"

"Trying to find you. To help you get through. It was Queen Najalas's…" she stopped.

"Where is my wife? What happened back at the castle?"

Veronica did not drop her eyes. Time for a proper mourning would come later. She looked at the waterskin they now must share. "She died, my King. I am sorry for your loss. I don't know for sure what happened, but we cannot go back. The way is sealed. Our only path is forward, and we are dangerously low on water, of which you are already sorely lacking. Are you able to stand?"

Herodius closed his eyes, looking like a man who wanted to cry, but lacked the tears. He let his head drop, rubbing his forehead. "I grew to love her, you know."

"I know you did. I wish I could do more, your Majesty. If I could trade places with her, I would."

King Herodius looked up. In her torchlight, he stared at the "9" branded into his forearm, above his gauntlet. Veronica saw him nod. *You're a survivor, too.*

She stood up and helped him stand. "Is your head ok? Don't venture any further back…the path is slicker than winter's first ice."

"So I've noticed."

They both walked back toward the opening. *Toward the spinner.*

Veronica had an idea. She took out the rope she had saved from their earlier descent. "Stay here—hold this." He nodded, immediately picking up on her plan.

She let the rope out and walked into the center of the tiny clearing carefully…and was immediately twirled. She never let go of the rope, stepped out of the clearing to a new path. "*Aduro!*" The four pebbles lit up…and she wasn't on a path that led to one.

Clearly Jonathon must have tried several paths here, and maybe used pebbles to mark the ones he tried, and simply forgot or found it too problematic to pick up. Regardless, she had to believe one of the four paths led onward. She stepped back into the center, spun again, and found herself on a glow-pebble marked path. She inspected it…and immediately found a shelf above her head loaded with massive rocks. She carefully backed away, picking up the pebble. *One less option to consider.*

Again onto the spinner, and luck was on her side as she ended up on another branch leading to a marked opening. This one looked promising. The air felt thinner. *Fresher.* She took a few steps inward, curving the rope into an 'L' shape with Herodius holding the other end two branches away.

Far in the distance…she saw a pinprick. It was still dark, but a lighter shade of darkness. Natural darkness. *Starlight!*

"This way, Herodius! Follow the rope in when you spin."

A minute later, a very wobbly King grabbed hold of her shoulder to steady himself. She looked at the gash on his head. She knew that last spin would be murderous for him.

"Sit, my King. We both need rest."

Herodius shook his head. "I'll rest when I feel fresh air stir against my face. Let us be rid of this treacherous cave once and for all."

Veronica couldn't help but smile. "As you wish." She started forward, but his hand, which had not left her shoulder, tightened slightly. "Your Majesty?"

"Thank you, Veronica. I would not have made it through without you."

Veronica finally let her stress climb up her throat, and swallowed hard. Her eyes were moist, and she made no attempt to stop her tears. "Then it is to Queen Najalas we owe a debt of thanks. She is the one who saved us both."

Together, they walked out of the catacombs into the night air, facing west while the dawn still slumbered.

~Xaro~

Surely Rookwood stands. Surely my throne still awaits. Xaro had pictured himself on the throne of Rookwood—the Seat of Elvidor, and for practical purposes, the Sovereign of Tenebrae—a hundred times since he left Sands End. Every vision, every dream, every plan culminated the same way: Xaro on the Throne, Rookwood a Temple for Kuth-Cergor, and the people everywhere worshipping his God and following their Ageless King...

Laughter and cheers had begun again outside his pavilion tent, bringing him out of his reverie. He looked at his own wine goblet and sneered, pushing it aside. *I told Captain Finkus one pint—no more than two. Did they not just hear the explosion? Are my men that deep into their cups before the moon even rises? This is what my generosity brings?* Scowling, he strode to his tent entrance, pushing aside the flap angrily.

The scene that greeted his eyes only inflamed him further.

His men were either propped up underneath a cask with free-flowing ale pouring into their mouths...or they were fighting one another for mugs. Some were emptying their canteens to fill them with ale. Several soldiers had been stabbed; Captain Finkus was one of them.

"What are you doing?" Xaro bellowed.

All eyes looked up at him. Nobody said a word, but many moved to stopper the casks.

Xaro pointed to a man lying on his back directly underneath a cask. "You there, what is your name?"

"Bwodey, Sir. Bwodey Tomlinson from Misksh, Mastew Zawwow," he slurred.

"Brodey." Xaro narrowed his eyes with a mirthless smile, walking toward the young man. "Brodey from Misk. Would you mind telling me what possessed you to drown yourself in ale the night before we march? Was my order to limit yourself to a mild refreshment unclear?"

Brodey stuck his hands in the muddy dirt/ale mixture that had pooled around his head to try and at least sit up. His torso swayed while he gathered his thoughts for Xaro. "Cap'n Finkus said jus' one." He hung his head. "The ale is *soooo* good, though, Master. It's *special.*"

Something clicked in the back of Xaro's mind. He fetched a glass and smelled it. Smelled like ale—nothing particularly special. Just good ale. He wouldn't taste it; he would study it further in his pavilion. *If it was cursed ale...*

"Did you hear that thunderous explosion from our south? And why is Captain Finkus dead? What happened?"

Brodey tried to prop his back against the wheel of the cart carrying all the casks, but he started to slide off into the mud. He caught himself just in time, but swayed constantly. His eyes were glossed over like smooth stones look under a rippling puddle. "Mastuh Zarrow…the Cap'n woont let ush get our fill…but you don' understand. We *have* ta keep drinkin'. May I pleash have that cup, Mastuh?"

Xaro was incensed. "You *killed* Captain Finkus?"

Brodey jerked forward, toward Xaro's glass. "Pleash, jus' one more sip?"

"You weak, pathetic excuse for a man. We stand on the precipice of a siege, and you would squander your ale all in one night?" Xaro reached down and grabbed the man by his neck, hauling him out of the mud. "You gorge yourself on my generosity under an entire cask?" Drawing his sword, he ran Brodey through, slicing him open from stomach to sternum. Brodey cried drunkenly before pitching forward, his outstretched hand still longing for the ale.

"Who else is thirsty?" screamed Xaro, projecting his voice over the entire camp. All his men were paying attention now. *"Sober up now! Prepare yourselves for attack. You all have drunk poison, and I will rid us of this wretched brew."*

Jets of flame shot from Xaro's hands at the remaining casks, exploding them all. He was convinced that what was "special" about this ale was that it made one keep drinking, even to the point of murdering a superior officer who stood in the way, or just slowed consumption down.

As groans poured from his thirsty troops, he cast his attention to the south. He could see a large dust cloud over the mountains of Rookwood, and feared the worst. He swatted open the tent flap to his pavilion again, intent on prayer and re-planning his siege options. It may be time to summon his council one more time. *Hopefully Belara will bring back good news.*

Belara did not surprise with an update, however. "Enjoying the fruits of war, Xaro?" asked Malenec, seated on the chest in which Xaro stored the scroll, shield, and staff.

~Victor~

In war, rarely do plans unfold unmodified. Victor was waiting for Edward to return with news of his force to the south, when the entire country shook. The explosion came from the east—from Rookwood, he was certain—and it left him with an empty feeling.

The dust cloud hovering in the twilight over the mountain wasn't from spring cleaning, that's for sure.

And yet...*a better distraction I may never find.* Victor was *itching* to charge into battle. For good or for ill, the time to draw steel was now. *Where the hell is that golden-haired spell spinner?* He reached into his empty tobacco pouch and cursed.

"Commander," came a familiar voice behind him.

Victor spun around. The young man looked like a crumpled waterskin baking in the sun. *Spent.* "Edward. What is happening?"

The young mage took his leave to sit down without asking for permission. He leaned his back against the same large boulder that served as their lookout point. "Apologies, Commander, but this has been an exhausting scouting excursion."

"Sit, stand—whatever. What do you know, mage?" Victor pointed his empty pipe impatiently.

Nugget took a deep breath. "Magi is near death. He is in the hands of the Elfs, but his wound is grievous. I doubt he will live through the night."

Victor scowled. "The ogre's army?"

"Apparently, Magi put them all asleep. Our flank is secure, Commander. He is truly the most gifted mage I have ever seen." Nugget shook his head and wiped his eyes before looking up. "There is more."

"Go on."

"It pains me greatly to say this, but Rookwood has fallen, Commander."

"Fallen? To whom? Your traitorous roommate, the other one at sea?"

"I mean it has *fallen.* After racing to get Magi into the care of the Elfen Druids at Thalanthalas and, I *Teleported* to Rookwood when I heard the explosion. The castle has literally slid off the mountain, and destroyed the surrounding city. None could survive such a cataclysm. There is no Crown to go back to, Commander."

Victor stared at Nugget. *There is no Crown to go back to.*

He walked over to where the True Mage had plopped himself down. He tugged one of his mustaches. "You are certain of this?"

Nugget nodded wearily. "Seen by my own two eyes, just moments ago."

A dozen thoughts crashed into one another inside Victor's head:
What are we fighting for now?
Who will unite us?

Power abhors a vacuum; surely the winning general shall assume command.

The sleeping ogre is the spellweaver's final gift. Our flank is protected; let the elfs slaughter them while we crush these drunken fools outside Paragatha.

When I drive Xaro and his followers to the gates of hell, the people will need a new King. A victorious King. A King who fights. *That's what I do. That's who I am. Fate smiles on the bold. While others chase jewelry and ancient armor around the world, it is the* True Warriors *who protect the people. So it has always been.*

He smiled grimly, and reached out a hand to help the tired mage stand up. "Thank you, Nugget. I wish you had time to rest, but you don't. We are moving up our timeline to attack Xaro; we lose light by the minute. We don't have time to wait…we strike now, while there is confusion. Send word to our captains."

Nugget grasped his hand and hauled himself up. "Yes sir." He was gone.

Victor looked up at the mountains to the east. Night had fallen, and though he could no longer see dust hovering in the sky, he knew it was still there. The stars were obscured. He scowled again.

The True Warriors protect the people. So it has always been. So it will be again.

~Strongiron~

Deep in the folds of his subconscious, he heard a gentle prayer. He couldn't hold onto the words, but the voice was sweet and familiar. He wasn't in pain…not really. He thought he should be, but he wasn't.

Slowly the fog that was his memory began to clear. The shortest, closest memories began to crystallize first, because they were aided by his senses. He remembered the prayer because he just heard it. *What was being prayed about?*

He remembered the cool touch of water against his face. *Where did the water come from?*

He remembered soft breath tickling his whiskers. *Who was breathing on him?*

He remembered darkness. Lots of darkness all around him. *Where am I?*

"Strongiron?" whispered that same, sweet voice.

He opened his eyes. More memories flooded over him. At least, that's what it felt like. He slowly became aware of an enormous amount of weight on top of him.

"Strongiron?" came the voice again.

He licked his cracked lips. Another sensation—the taste of blood.

"Hrmmph," he grunted softly.

"Strongiron!" The voice was more insistent, and from right underneath him. The soft breath he felt on his face was coming from someone pinned underneath his body.

"Kari . . ?" he whispered, pulling a name through the fog.

"Thank Dymetra! You're alive." He felt dry lips press against his cheek, and more memories filled his head. He was coming around.

"Yes, apparently I am. And thankfully so are you." He pressed himself up, aware that he had to be crushing her. A bunch of stones shifted and he felt pebbles and dust begin to cascade atop them.

"Careful, my love! We are buried in stone. The cavern must have collapsed on us."

My love. That's right, I love this woman. "How long have we been trapped here?"

"I don't know. You threw yourself over me when the ceiling collapsed, and I prayed for help as the rubble fell atop us. Your armor seemed to protect you, and you created a little air pocket for me. I remember a stone hitting my head and I fell unconscious. When I awoke, my head hurt, and I could move my arms close enough to feel dried blood. I felt water from the underground lake, too. I've been awake for only a few minutes, but I can't move underneath you. I've been calling your name, and praying for healing for you, whatever might be broken. You saved me, Strongiron. I'd be dead if you hadn't thrown yourself over me as a shield.

"But now, I'd really like to move again. I just don't want to bring more rocks down on top of us…who knows how much is above us?"

Strongiron blinked. *As a shield...* He recalled shoving Kari underneath him, covering her as best he could. He remembered something hitting his head, but that phrase triggered another thought dancing on the edge of recollection.

"The Shield!" he exclaimed. "We came for the Shield." He thought about all those shields lining the walls of the mammoth underground cavern. "They're all buried now, too."

"First things first. If I *Levitate* some of these rocks, can you stand?"

Strongiron wiggled his fingers and toes. "I think so."

Kari called forth her magic, gently lifting rocks and pushing them off to the side. After about ten minutes of shifting rocks, they could both finally stand. They looked around. The blue *Everflames* still flickered along the cave walls, but shields were everywhere. Some still hung askew on the walls; others were buried. The statue of the kneeling man was shattered, its face cracked and lying in the debris, staring upward. The fountain was no longer running, and the water streams that had been arcing gracefully through the air were no more. Now, the underground lake was filled with stones, rocks, dirt, and shields.

They looked back at the entrance to the cavern. Of course, it was blocked with more rubble.

"What a mess." Strongiron said.

Kari canvassed the massive grotto as well. "At least the statue of Dymetra was unharmed by the cave-in," she pointed out.

Strongiron looked. The white marble statue across what used to be a small underground lake appeared unblemished, save for perhaps a fine covering of dust. *Not even chipped...*

He narrowed his eyes. "Yes. *Completely* unharmed. I think that's worth a closer look, don't you my love?" He turned to look at Kari, and fell in love with her even more when he saw her return his look of curiosity with one of her own—a single eyebrow raised, a half smile on her lips.

~Xaro~

"Malenec. What news of your attack?" Xaro's eyes flashed.

"The Elfs certainly had a fondness for fire. I would never have guessed that they'd burn down half of their beloved forest, but they did. And that miserable Queen...I would never have guessed that she would unhinge her own castle from the mountain, but she did." He smiled, but his angular face was drawn tight and lined with exhaustion. He spread his arms wide. He was still dressed in black, from his gloved hands to his soft boots. "Apparently they do not hold life in very high regard." His smile broadened. "Not that I blame them, of course."

"You *fool*! Rookwood was the seat of power in Elvidor. How could you let the Queen destroy it?"

Malenec tented his gloved fingers together. "Xaro, Xaro, Xaro," he said, shaking his head. "So close to our God, and yet so ignorant. I almost pity you."

Xaro took a step toward Malenec. "How *dare* you patronize me, worm. You think you are closer—"

Malenec stood. "I *am* closer, fool. *Far* closer to Kuth-Cergor. Whatever fantasies you have filled your head with, I can assure you they do not come from our God. There was *never* a scenario where you get to play King. *Never*, Xaro."

Xaro tilted his head. "You fancy yourself a *ruler*, Malenec?" He laughed. "Even the dead only follow you grudgingly!"

Malenec just smiled. "Exactly."

"You're mad, Malenec. Our God wants to be worshipped. The dead do not worship. He wants to return—to re-enter our land."

"The dead *do* worship, Xaro. They do whatever *I* tell them to do."

Xaro paused, his eyes flickering to the chest behind his necromancer. *If ever there was a time I could stand to know the absolute truth of a man's words*...he pushed the thought away. *None* of Her artifacts would work for him.

"I do not believe you, Malenec. Kuth-Cergor does not wish to preside over a dead world." *He can't wish that. I'm his chosen. Me! He asks me to conquer, to subjugate, to rule.*

"Tell yourself that. Better yet, ask him. I presume he still answers *your* prayers?" The condescension in his voice was thicker than butter.

"Your tone needs adjusting, worm. If you address me as such again, I will nail your tongue to a tree and silence your prayers forever."

"My silent prayers are still more powerful than any skill you may wield. You are nothing, Xaro. You are just another man who will die when the time is right."

Xaro had had enough. He would miss Malenec's talent to transform the dead into an army, but he could no longer trust the army to do his bidding. If he wanted a fight for supremacy, then let it be now.

He formed a javelin of lighting in his hand and sent a bolt directly into Malenec. The lightning seemed to strike a wall around the True Cleric and harmlessly diffused around him.

"What is this?" Xaro asked. And then he knew.

He looked at the small bulge on one of Malenec's gloved fingers, and he knew for sure. *Of course.* Darkness, Tarsh's account, Magi attacking his quarters...

"My ring... You filthy maggot, you have *my ring*!" he hollered.

Someone screamed outside the pavilion tent. Xaro turned his head. A drunken man, covered with blood, with an arrow in his chest stumbled in. "Mastew! Heaw me, pleash. I beg you!" He pitched forward.

"Get out!" he bellowed at the soldier. He turned around again. Malenec stood patiently, his eyes looking at the dying man with ravenous eyes.

"You," he said drawing his sword. "You can be dealt with in more ways than magical ones."

Malenec held up his hand, whispering a prayer. The sword became red-hot, and Xaro dropped it, cursing and shaking his hand. "As much as I've enjoyed our discussion, the time has come for our little team to disband. I am on Kuth-Cergor's team, and his alone. All your talents, Xaro, amount to wood before the fire. Your fate is to die, and when we next meet, *you* shall bow to *me*, for I will raise you from death to be my Lich! When I am fresh, your bones will dance for me, your magic will cast for me, your sword will swing for me, and your soul will scream for me.

"Enjoy these last days leading your men, Xaro. It matters not a whit to me whether you win or lose. All men who die feed my army and will sing my God's glory. All I require is death; you can amuse yourself trying to plan who lives and dies to the best of your abilities."

Malenec smiled. "You are destined to be my greatest undead creation. Until we meet again, take pleasure in that fact."

Infuriated, Xaro summoned a fireball and hurled it at his former lieutenant. The ball of flame split around him and burned two gaping holes in his pavilion tent, setting it ablaze behind the black-robed cleric. Framed in fire, he stood there laughing. "I would kill you now, but I am too exhausted to raise you after the efforts of this day. Besides, something deeply satisfying rests in knowing what the anticipation of your impending death will do to you; like an aging fine wine, your undead life awaits! But enough banter—goodbye, Xaro. Until we meet again…" Malenec was gone.

"Commandah…please!"

Xaro didn't immediately turn around. He stared at the fire consuming the rear of his tent. He waived his hand and a cooling, icy wind put the flames out. He turned to the dying man lying on his side, clutching the arrow in his chest. Blood trickled from his mouth.

Xaro curled his lip and picked up his sword in his blistered hand. He stabbed the drunken soldier in the neck as he walked out into the night air. A moment later, he saw fires flare up on the far side of camp. Around his tent, there were several drunken soldiers lying dead or wounded. He saw another man staring at him, badly burned on one side, leaning heavily on a sword. *What just happened in there? What is happening* out here?

For the first time in many, many years, Xaro had no idea what to do next.

~Victor~

His plan always centered on raids. Nothing was quite as terrifying to an army than death screams in the night springing up from tents and barracks everywhere at once. His men had broken up into small squads, each led by a Knight if possible, a True Warrior at minimum, and fanned out all over the countryside.

The directive was simple: *Kill until nothing moves—us or them.* Like a poisonous mist that drifts in and out, his attacks would randomly sweep one part of Xaro's camp before blowing over another, and another after that. His enemy had come for a siege; he was counting on them to never withdraw, and Victor would see these drunken butchers jumping at shadows and killing themselves in terror before the dawn broke. If they did...hopefully Peter's reinforcements could clean up the stragglers.

Random, uncoordinated attacks are hard to handle for trained men, and nearly impossible for drunken men to defend.

Victor himself led an entire squadron. He glanced over his shoulder in the direction of Rookwood. Even an hour or so later, after his men had taken their positions, some clouds of dust made the moon hazy as it shone from behind the once proud mountain.

He led the first raid himself. His mages spent their energy creating a cone of silence around the perimeter. The spell could be more simply maintained and for many more hours without unduly taxing his spellcasters. Victor didn't have many True Mages, but was grateful for the additional Sea Mages that had joined him. The key to his plans demanded absolute silence from scouts and sentinels. *Let the soldiers in camp scream their heads off...as long as they have no advance warning.*

Once the spell was cast, his best Ranger took out a guard with an arrow through the throat. Another guard posted next to him tried to shout a warning...but the sound was carried away like gnats in a hurricane. Not a soul heard, and Victor's men were on him. A few blades in the hazy moonlight put an end to sentinel number two.

Now comes the fun part. Victor crouched low, surrounded by the dozen men in his group. "These men we kill tonight have taken everything we cherish," he hissed. "You have all earned your Mark—tonight we show the world the resolve of a True Warrior. Any mercy in your heart needs to be saved for your brethren in Rookwood. Tonight we kill. Put thoughts of your family away—none of us know what we are going home to. Rookwood has collapsed, but I for one will go to hell before I let these maggots pick through the bones of our loved ones. We fight to the last man. No one lives. Are you with me, Warriors?"

It was a short speech, more whispered than shouted, and he imagined his captains were all making similar speeches to their raiding parties. A dozen shouts of agreement filled the night, their sound spurred away from Xaro's camp on the winds of magic.

Victor could feel the warmth of his bloodlust reddening his face. He loved every minute of it, licking his mustachioed lips. The first raid began with a nod to his men. Victor Charles Ethan Remington III turned and bolted toward the camp.

He followed a rocky path that was fairly flat, but it curved around a small hill. As he rounded the hill, the first tents could be seen dotting a valley with some thin forestry around the camp. Cooking fires were still lit, torches blazed, and inside the cone of silence, they could easily hear laughter and general merriment. *That will soon change.*

The first enemy soldier was lying on his back, clutching his canteen. He was away from the rest, twitching but unmoving otherwise. Victor broke off to see to him. As he approached, the man's glazed eyes looked at Victor, and his hands were shaking. "C-c-can you bring m-me some m-more—"

Victor dragged his still dirty blade across the man's throat. *I'm not your Steward.*

He turned and rejoined his regiment, and they quickly fanned out to engage in the slaughter amongst the tents.

Slurred shouts rang out. Tent poles collapsed. In the distance, near the middle of the camp, an enormous fire filled the night sky, and there were screams of dismay everywhere.

Victor's curiosity was piqued by the distant explosion and flames that lit up the night sky. However, there was a veritable smorgasbord of slaughter to be had in the fifty-foot kill zone all around him. Everywhere he turned he saw foes, some drunker than others, all with the same unsuspecting, stupefied look on their face that was easily twisted into anguish with accomplished swordplay.

I've been on hunts more challenging than this. Victor thought his plan was good—audacious perhaps—but he had not expected to carve up Xaro's men so easily. *Where is the black smoke, the mage-craft, the demon-god?*

A couple of his men had been killed, mainly from a sober, lucky archer or two, but he couldn't quibble with the first raid. They pressed inward, toward the wagons of flaming ale that Victor could now see. His men poured into another section of Xaro's camp, slicing down men where they sat. Remarkably, he had killed several men who chose to clutch their waterskins in one hand while fumbling for their blades with the other. *Pitiful.*

Victor turned his head to an enormous pavilion nearby—far larger than the others. Without warning, two enormous fireballs pierced the skin of the tent. The balls of flame flew to either side of him, singeing his mustaches and blowing him off his feet. His eyes were seared from the heat.

"Arghhh!" He cried. "Men, help me! I cannot see!"

He rolled around on the ground instinctively, and could smell the hair on his face smoldering. He rolled around until he came to an object on the ground. He felt around, and could feel wet, sticky leather.

Ignoring the pain in his eyes, he carefully opened them. One was completely blind. The other felt like pins were being shoved into it whenever air hit it. He could make out a body on the ground next to him, however.

His head pounding, he staggered to his feet and allowed his one good eye to crack open a sliver. *If ever there was a time for a damn cleric on the battlefield...*

One hand groping in front of him, the other using his long sword as a cane, he stumbled toward the other side of the pavilion tent. Everything was dark and blurry.

He did, however, see a large man standing in front of the tent, surveying the chaos, brandishing a sword.

And he did not look drunk in the least.

Chapter Twenty-Seven: The First Dawn

~Strongiron~

Kari and Strongiron slowly headed toward the statue of Dymetra, saving their prayers (or magic, in Kari's case) for whatever they may find. Climbing, stretching—and in some cases jumping—felt good after lying stiff for so long.

As they reached the statue, the blue *Everflame* cast a chilling light on the dusty white marble. Strongiron turned to Kari. "What do you think?"

She looked at the twenty-foot high chiseled sculpture, which was at least five foot wide at its base. "We should look for switches, levers. Perhaps it opens."

After fifteen minutes of searching—even *Levitating* up to the head—produced nothing, Strongiron pushed on the statue as well; it wouldn't budge.

Kari took a closer look at the base. "Let me try," offered Kari. Strongiron harrumphed. Weaving her *Levitation* spell, she lifted the entire statue and set it down ten feet away. "I thought I saw some indentations in the ground. This has been moved before."

Strongiron looked at the rock wall behind it. "I don't see anything."

Kari grabbed his forearm and pulled him toward the cave wall behind the statue. "That's why I'm here. Follow me." She plunged her arm straight through the *Illusion*, and flashed him a grin.

Strongiron shook his head but said nothing as he plunged through the wall with her.

"Ah, you two love-birds finally made it. I'd say I had my doubts, but you'd know I was lying," said Fate, who was leisurely sitting in a completely out-of-place chair in the corner of a large tomb.

"You again!" shouted Strongiron. "Much help you were when the roof collapsed on us! I thought you *wanted* us to find this Shield."

Fate hopped out of his chair, brushing his rich purple silk tunic smooth. "Want you to find the Shield? Why, whatever gave you that idea? I want order, but beyond that I don't care who wins your petty squabbles. The *patience* Dymetra extends to your race is, frankly, well beyond my comprehension. You sprang a trap set for you by someone who shows more urgency than a starving lion. You two seem more than content with your healing prayers. Far be it for me to choose sides."

Kari held up her hand before Strongiron could say a word. "Please, we are sorry, Fatum. Will you help us now?"

Fate smiled. "Yes, of course, Kari Quinlan. But not because you asked. Because *She* did. I will give you the same clue all who have sought Windomere's Shield are or have been given:

> *I am lighter than a feather, yet heavier than a stone. I am as plain as the noonday sun, yet as hidden as the noonday moon. I am the Shield of Life.*

He sat back down, draping a leg over the arm of his chair.

Strongiron looked at Kari. "What does that mean? 'Lighter than a feather, heavier than a stone?'"

Kari shook her head. "I'm not sure, but it must be in here. He would have met us out there in the cavern if the Shield was one of those that hung on the wall."

"You think so?" Fate asked innocently.

"Absolutely," agreed Strongiron.

He canvassed the tiny room, walking toward the coffin lying on a black marble dais. Empty shelves were mostly covered with cobwebs and empty flasks, with a scrollcase here and there. A plaque on one of the shelves looked recently disturbed; he picked it up and read the inscription: *Let death cover me like ice, and let ice cover my death.*

Strongiron handed it to Kari. "What do you make of this?"

She read it aloud and shrugged, handing it back. "Is this a clue as well, Fate?"

"This is not a game of 'hot and cold,' Miss Quinlan, and I am not some Oracle."

"Funny, I thought you liked games," snapped Kari.

"I do, and you have your one clue," Fate snapped back.

Strongiron moved toward the sarcophagus with a sigh. "Kari, let us have a peek inside. Perhaps he was buried with his Shield."

Kari nodded, and cast yet another *Levitation* spell, moving the top off the stone coffin. Strongiron bent over for a look.

Inside, perfectly preserved, was the body of an old man, arms folded across his chest. He wore a white robe that covered his body right up to his neck.

Strongiron let his shoulders sag. "No Shield, Kari."

She approached, tilting her head slightly. "Light as a feather, yet heavier than a stone…" she whispered. "Plain as the noon-day…"

"Strongiron," she said. "What if one of those shields out there *is* the right one? What if it is *light*, but we have to place it in his hands, removing the stone lid, which is *heavy*? What if it is out there, plain to see, but we have to *hide* it inside his coffin—"

Strongiron shook his head. God love Kari, but she was reaching and they both knew it. He turned to her and grabbed her hands, bowing his head. "We should have done this first, Kari. 'Dymetra, please forgive our delays. We are here now. If you truly wish Your Clerics to find this Artifact, guide our thoughts, Dymetra. Help us, for we are lost.'"

They finished their prayer and turned to Fate. "Don't look at me. Answering prayer is a bit above my pay grade," he said with a smug little smile.

They waited. No answers.

Strongiron looked at the plaque again. "Let death cover me like ice, and let ice cover my death," he said to himself. He looked at Fate. "How did Windomere die? I mean, in the end—I know he died when he and Quix…Quixay…"

"Quixatalor," helped Kari.

"Him, yes. Thank you. When they used that Scroll, but was that the killing stroke, Fate?"

"Ah. That is a story for another day, but I can tell you with certainty that he was murdered."

Strongiron looked at Kari, then over at the body lying in the stone coffin. He walked back to the corpse, lifting it into a sitting position. "My apologies, Windomere." He ripped the robes open, looking for a sign of a wound.

He found a deep hole through the heart, clear through the torso. But that wasn't what drew his attention. The tattoos did… Windomere's body was *covered* with them. They looked like runes.

"Will you look at that," whistled Strongiron. "What do you make of these, Kari?"

She reached out and touched them. Some were puffy and bumpy, others smooth. They stopped just below the neckline, but covered his arms, chest, and back. If they lifted him out of the coffin fully, Strongiron would bet the tattoos ran down his legs as well.

"They are ancient. I've never seen this language."

Strongiron showed her the wound, clearly a mortal stab of some sort that went through his entire body. *Light as a feather…*

"*Kari!* The tattoo runes! *That* was his Shield! Light as a feather, yet the burden of the gift must be heavy. The Shield was/is hidden behind his clothes, but clear as day when undressed. It fits, Kari. It fits better than any other idea we've had."

"It does." She turned to Fate. "Well?"

He stood up, straightening his bright purple trousers. "Well done, Clerics. You have found Windomere's Shield. I gave it to him myself, and so shall I give it to both of you, as neither would have found it on your own. Behold Dymetra's Quill." With a wave of his hand, Fate produced a quill pen, and Strongiron found his armor removed and his chest laid bare. "Come forward, Strongiron."

As he did, Fate began to draw those same runes on Strongiron's chest and back, the ink blending in with the contours of his muscles. The tattoos glowed briefly, before fading into dark ink.

"Step forward, Kari."

Nervously, she clutched her arms around her chest out of modesty, should her clothing tear away as Strongiron's. She was relieved that her leather armor did not, in fact, disappear from her torso.

Instead her legs were laid bare to Fate, Strongiron, and Windomere's corpse.

"Oh!" she exclaimed.

"Do not be shy, Kari. Come here I said. You will not be harmed."

She did, although her small clothes were all that covered her bottom half. Carefully, as with Strongiron, Fate began a series of intricate runes. Down her thigh, around her calf, up the other leg, and around her hips. They, too, glowed briefly before fading to colored ink.

"You two are now closer than most married couples, for you both share in Dymetra's ultimate blessing. From this point forward, *as long as your faith in Her remains strong*, no Dark Prayers may harm you. You are both sealed, two equal parts of a whole."

Fate regarded them both for a moment, a grave expression on his face. "Tenebrae crumbles all around. This Dark World—is one that needs your light. I don't know if you can save all of it, but perhaps you can save some. Dark powers have gathered to drive a dark agenda. Undead creatures are being created; their souls denied rest— an abomination. You can release those held in such bondage.

"Now, a final word. Your delays have cost your friends dearly. May have cost the Kingdom. Return to Elvidor quickly. You will find there much needs to be put right." Without even a goodbye, Fate disappeared in a flash of purple, leaving Strongiron and Kari half-naked inside the old crypt.

"Wait!" Kari shouted, but he was already gone. She turned to Strongiron.

"We should, uh, probably put our armor back on before we *Teleport*," he said with an awkward grin.

~Xaro~

In the fog of battle, a dozen tactical questions pressed against his mind, but Xaro fixed his thoughts on one overarching query that cast a long shadow over every other consideration:

What am I really fighting for?

If Malenec's goal was to cast doubt on his faith, he had succeeded brilliantly. *What is the point of winning a battle if my dead enemies rise to join Malenec?*

Xaro needed *time*. He needed to pray, he needed to meditate. He needed Kuth-Cergor to answer his Cleric, True or not. The middle of a battlefield was no place for such supplication.

As a burned man approached, Xaro called to mind Sands End, half a world away. His Art could not *Teleport* him across the sea, but his God certainly could. Back in his fortress, away from Elvidor, Xaro could pray quietly and contemplate his next move. It was his first impulse.

Nothing happened.

The burned man raised his sword and drove it into Xaro's upper arm. Lost in his prayer, he reacted too slowly, and the blade bit deep, below the armor and above his gauntlet.

"Argh!" he exclaimed, coming out of his failed prayer to focus on his enemy. "How dare you strike me, maggot!"

"Why, are you someone special?" asked the burned man, reversing his stroke to strike again.

Xaro easily switched sword arms and parried the blow. He cast the first spell that came to his mind—a *Force* spell—striking this annoying gnat full in the chest. The man collapsed backward into the ale-drenched mud around the pavilion.

"Am I someone special," mocked Xaro under his breath, but he paused. *Am I?*

Kuth-Cergor wouldn't answer his prayer, surely for a lack of faith, that much he knew. What he didn't know was whether he lacked faith in his God, or his God lacked faith in him...

Disgusted, Xaro called again on his Art, and *Teleported* away from the battle, away from his drunken men, to a quiet place in Elvidor. A place yet untouched by the winds of war, which he himself unleashed. A place where, if he was honest with himself, many of his initial plans were hatched, and where his troubles had also germinated.

Silent as a smoke-ring, Xaro *Teleport*ed across the Crystal Mountains, to the village of Brigg.

~Victor~

As Victor stirred, mud gathered beneath his arms like a child's snow angel. Turning his head full around to compensate for his bad eye, he spotted his sword half-buried in the nearby muck. Groggily he crawled over and grabbed it, pushing himself to his feet. Looking around, it appeared his plan had worked: lots of men lay dead with cups, goblets, canteens, and waterskins close at hand.

Victor turned his attention to the large pavilion tent. That man had cast a spell on him, and he only knew of one man that large, dressed as a warrior, who also cast spells. He cursed his misfortune of not finishing the man before Xaro *Teleported* away. *I could have ended this right here. I could have been legendary!*

Instead, he limped into the main tent, where he saw maps, books, scrolls, and a half-filled wine glass. Victor sighed. The man was gone.

He walked to the back and plopped himself down on a long chest to gather his thoughts. Exhausted and injured, Victor let his mind wander, tracing his finger absently over the runes carved into the chest. *I wonder what's in here…*

~King Herodius~

Grey light in the eastern sky signaled the breaking of the second-longest day in Herodius's life, dwarfed only by the ogre's invasion of his beloved isles.

Buoyed by a post-exhaustion burst of energy that only comes to those on the cusp of accomplishing something significant after much struggle, Herodius ignored Veronica's suggestions of rest. The ogre's camp was now in sight.

"Come, Veronica! For good or ill, we shall now see whether there is any Islander left who remembers from whence they came."

They came to a small bluff, overlooking the camp from a stone's throw away. Fires burned low, as if untended throughout the night. It looked, frankly, deserted. "Where is everyone?" he asked Veronica. "Are we too late?"

Veronica joined Herodius on the edge of the bluff, ignoring her instincts that an archer could probably *throw* an arrow at them, they were so close. She shrugged. "I don't know…wait! Look."

A couple of men stumbled from one of the tents. Soon others joined them. None of them were looking up at the bluffs; most went straight to their campfires to get them roaring. From the shade of their skin, he knew many were islanders.

Veronica turned to Herodius. "What are you waiting for, my King?" she whispered. "We should back away from these bluffs if you are not going to call out to them."

Before he could answer, the flap of one of the larger tents flew open, and the ogre Tar-Tan, Xaro's chosen General—Tar-Tan the Enslaver, as Herodius thought of him—emerged with a grunt. The King narrowed his eyes and rubbed the *1X5Z9* on his arm, turning to Veronica. "I was waiting for him," he hissed back.

Herodius took a deep breath and silently prayed a simple prayer to the One True God that had healed more than his arm. *Give me the words.* He stepped forward.

"Behold, Islanders! For whom do you fight? It is I, Herodius Cromwell, King of Elvidor. I have made Elvidor my home, and all of you are welcome here. Would you raise your swords against one of your own? Whatever promises the ogre has made, what profit lies in striking down your family, for that is what I am—one of your own. You know me—I tried to help us all escape, and I cried for those that could not. But see my mark!" He held up his arm. "Whatever wounds you bear, whatever loss you have suffered, I assure you that life goes on, and it can be good once again. But you cannot give up, trading your souls for the spoils of war. Fight for me! I beseech you! This is not who you are…*we are men of the Isles!*"

A short silence followed. Tar-Tan grabbed a spear. Then, he saw one of the islanders stifle a yawn and shake his head vigorously. The man shouted up at him, "Herodius?"

The ogre snarled something. "These men know better than to listen to ramblings of a token King! They have seen a God, and soon you will, too." He hurled the spear at him.

Veronica started running the moment the General drew back his arm. She tackled Herodius on the bluff just as the spear whizzed right overhead, and they both rolled away from the cliff in a cloud of dust. "I'd prefer you not be a martyr," she said, climbing off him.

Herodius stood up and walked over to grab the spear that had clanged off some rocks behind him, and used it as a walking stick to carefully approach the edge once again.

"My friends," he shouted. "Your General seeks to kill me. I came here to show you a different life. You have a choice: a soldier's life, or a farmer's. Slay this monster for me and join my Kingdom. We are not warriors! Follow me, and I will grant you land, and you can build a home here once again. Turn from this false God and this wicked General and live with hope in your hearts—hope for a better day. I had to learn how to hope once again, and I have. No matter what happens, I now have hope." He raised the spear and broke it in half over his knee.

"And you can too!"

Another Islander shouted "Herodius!" and raised his sword. Several more did as well. Soon they began chanting, *"Her-oh-dee-us! Her-oh-dee-us!"*

Tar-Tan's head swiveled. The Islanders began throwing their own spears at him. He parried the first one with his massive sword, but a second spear caught him in his calf. He growled and sank to one knee. Another spear caught him in the hand. Others grabbed their bows and began firing arrows. Even his thick hide couldn't rebuff arrows fired from that close. As the mob began forming around him, his kneeling body began to resemble a pincushion.

"I curse you, Islander! I curse you forever, you worm!" he bellowed.

One of the men dared get close enough and drove his sword straight through the ogre's throat. "That is better than you deserve!" he shouted. All that remained at that point was angry butchery.

A faint blur just outside the periphery of Herodius's vision stirred the air upon the bluffs. "You did it, my love!" came a familiar voice.

Herodius tore his eyes away from the grisly scene below to look at his Queen, running toward him.

"Najalas? But how..?" he asked as she ran into his open arms.

Veronica looked at the couple incredulously. "My Queen?" she said under her breath, barely audible. Then she shouted, "Wait, Herodius!"

The Queen had a small dagger in her hand, and had already sank it deep between his shoulder blades with a bitter laugh.

"NO!" Veronica shouted, catching Herodius as he slumped to the ground. She looked up and saw not the Queen, but a woman wearing a skin-tight, pure white dress, cloaked in white, with a cowl that capped her head in white as well. *Belara.*

"Don't bother, Assassin. The blade was coated with *flos venini.* I'll give you his last thirty seconds to say goodbye..." Belara disappeared in a wink.

"Herodius!" she cried. "I failed you."

The King turned his head toward Veronica, and coughed. "You...did nothing of the sort. If anyone failed, it was I—the Queen and I. We did our best to protect the people. We tried. Keep trying, Veronica. Tenebrae is worth fighting for..."

"Herodius? *Herodius!*"

His eyes shut, and his head lolled...

When he opened his eyes, he was no longer on the bluffs. The intoxicating scent of wildflowers drove the cloying memory of roses, vanilla, and other exotic spice fragrances clear from his mind. Something hard pressed against his cheek. *Stone.* He looked around and saw that he was on a beautiful path made of intricate stonework, the likes of which he could only imagine how long it must have taken to build. No two stones were the same shape, yet they fit together like a puzzle. He stood up immediately when he saw a lion yawning thirty feet from him in short grass, but the beast seemed barely interested in him.

He turned to look down the stone path and saw a beautiful woman with blue eyes and honey-colored hair walking toward him. *Could it be? Is this real?*

"Maria?" he yelled as he half-walked, half ran toward her.

She smiled with a nod, and embraced him. "Welcome home, my love. Welcome home. I cannot wait to show you how our kids have grown..."

~Strongiron~

The grey veil of pre-dawn light broke into an orange ball rising over the Sea of Joy, illuminating the vast devastation. Strongiron and Kari had *Teleport*ed from Windomere's crypt straight to Rookwood, and now the cold morning light shone behind them, revealing a city crushed under the weight of a mountain. To the citizens of Rookwood, Strongiron could only imagine their horror, watching stones larger than their own homes tumble down the great peaks, destroying everything in their path.

"An avalanche of rock," muttered Kari. "I never thought the Queen would use that…what did she call it?"

"The *Terraemotus*."

Kari nodded, and turned around in a slow circle, scanning the horizon. She saw a fleet still in the harbor, and a few dwellings near the outskirts of Rookwood still intact. "So many have died, Strongiron. Where do we begin?"

Strongiron blinked the dust from his ice-blue eyes and pointed toward a group of buildings in the distance. "There. We need to find out what is happening before we can do much of anything. Take my hand; we'll *Teleport* together."

A blink later, they were standing in front of a small two-story inn. The name of the place was hard to read; the long-faded sign hung by one rusty chain, jingling noisily in the breeze. Strongiron squinted.

"*The Last Call*," he said. "Looks indeed like a place one might call on last."

The door swung open, and an immense woman filled the doorway. The greasy apron she wore was cut low and strapped tight around her, making her look more like a holiday goose than an innkeeper.

"Thought I heard someone chatterin'. Bit early for a nip, but Lady Velvet's no judge. You best show me the color of your coin before I let you in, armor or no. This Dark World's turned darker by the day, and I know full well there ain't no other place to get away from *that* disaster." She narrowed her eyes and crossed her arms over her massive bodice, jerking her thumb in the direction of the fallen castle.

Kari stepped forward. "Lady Velvet, is that your name? We're not looking for a room. Just information."

"Ain't everyone?"

Strongiron smiled. "My Lady," he offered smoothly. "We have travelled far, and only wish to know what has happened since we left. We can see that Rookwood—both fortress and city—have been destroyed." He reached into his coin pouch and produced two gold crowns. "Can you tell us what happened? Surely you hear things, here on the edge of the city…" He placed the two coins into her hands gently.

She curled her sausage-sized fingers over them. "Mayhap I know some things."

"When did Rookwood fall?" asked Kari

"Yesterday. First the city flooded and half the boats in the damn harbor fell to the bottom of the sea. Queerest bit o' magic I've seen, and I've seen my share. People were *beggin'* to get inside that castle."

"But not you?" asked Strongiron.

"Me? Last time I set foot in there, some fancy-pants mage started gossipin' about me. Lady Velvet is fine right here…the waters never got to this part of town anyhow. But I knew they'd be lettin' in them creatures."

"Creatures?" said Kari.

"Dead folk, brought back to life. Evil stuff, if you ask me. Rookwood was crawlin' with 'em. More than one guardsman deserted his post, heading north, stoppin' here for a little liquid courage first. Lady Velvet don't judge."

"Are any men from the castle here now?" asked Strongiron eagerly.

Lady Velvet smirked. "Nah. They rode hard to get away from the fighting, or maybe to get into a fair fight further north. The buzz in the common room was that all the fighting was in Paragatha. The invaders were camped out there."

Strongiron looked at Kari and nodded. He turned to Lady Velvet and grabbed her hand, pressing two more pieces of gold into her meaty paw. "Thank you. May Dymetra bless you for your information."

And they were gone before she could say another word.

Strongiron and Kari materialized onto a muddy battlefield that smelled of blood, ale, and fire. Exhausted-looking men shoveled bodies into an enormous pile, performing their grisly task in grim silence. The only sound they heard was the wet clop of boots in mud until someone shouted, "Its Strongiron! Look, Strongiron is here!"

The men stopped hauling bodies and began to circle Strongiron, some clasping him, some saluting, all peppering him with questions. None could be heard over the laughter and raised voices. Strongiron looked at Kari. She returned his look with a nervous smile.

Suddenly a quiet began to spread over the mob, and cheers were replaced with hushed tones. The sea of weary warriors parted, and Victor limped toward the two of them. He was badly burned.

"Nice of you to join us, Cleric." Victor stood toe-to-toe with his former General, who dwarfed him in size, if not in gumption. "Swoop in for a visit?"

"Victor—" Strongiron began.

"Tell me," Victor interrupted. "Where is this Shield? Did you find it? Is it pretty? While you and your lady-friend toured distant lands, my men and I drove Xaro away. Not without cost, as you can plainly see."

Strongiron could see Kari starting to seethe from the corner of his eye. He reached out and grabbed Victor's shoulder before the General could flinch away. Victor winced audibly.

"Dymetra, if it be thy will, heal this man before he says another word." Power flowed through Strongiron, and the burned flesh fell away like ashes scraped from a grate. Moments later Victor stood before him with unblemished skin, keen sight, and flowing mustaches.

"Felt guilty for leaving me, didn't you?" he said smugly, scratching his face. "I told you we needed a Cleric on the battlefield. Might have saved the King, not to mention your friend, had you been here."

Kari felt her stomach tighten. "What friend?"

Strongiron quickly followed. "Where is Herodius?"

Victor looked over his shoulder. "Tell them, Edward."

Nugget stepped forward from the back of the crowd. "Hi Kari. It's Nugget. I made the climb."

"Nugget!" She ran over to him and hugged him, but then pulled away. "What friend?"

"Magi, Kari—it's Magi. He's…he's dead. A terrible sword wound. His body rests in Thalanthalas." He turned to Strongiron. "Herodius was killed by an Assassin an hour ago just south of here."

"By Belara, Strongiron. We were betrayed by that witch," Victor said bitterly.

Kari let Nugget go and walked over to Strongiron, clasping his hand. "I don't believe it. No. Surely *not!*" The crowd of warriors began to murmur angrily.

Vengeance and justice is on everyone's mind, thought Strongiron. *This will be a mob soon.*

Strongiron hugged Kari, but only for a moment. "My love…come. We must go visit both."

Nugget stepped forward trepidatiously. "I will *Teleport* to Magi as well. You should visit his body first."

Kari looked up at Strongiron. Her beautiful green eyes shone with the same look of hatred that enflamed everyone around them. "Let's go."

The three of them *Teleported* and reappeared before the gates of Thalanthalas faster than smoke before the wind. Strongiron saw the barren ground encircling the great Elfen city, but said nothing. *Clearly a tale for another day.*

Nugget led them past the sentries and into the inner fortress—the one part of the landscape that still supported plant life. Flowers, and especially trees, were still woven throughout the city.

Eventually they came to a healing room. Chief Chocktaw was present, along with his daughter, Lady Elyn. She looked up when they entered. Seeing Nugget, she said to him "He is nearly done."

Kari looked at the beautiful young elf askance. "What do you mean, 'nearly done'?" She looked at Nugget. "You said he was dead!"

Nugget shrugged. "If he isn't, he will be soon, Kari. I'm glad you could at least be here at the end. The Elfs have made him as comfortable as possible, given his wound. It's a death stroke, Kari. Whatever healing spell you used on Victor was impressive, but his wounds are not superficial."

Kari pushed Nugget aside and pulled Magi's sheets off his body. He was pale, barely breathing.

"Kari…" Nugget began.

Strongiron put his hand on the young True Mage's shoulder, smiling gently. "I assume you have never met a True Cleric, Edward?"

"Call me Nugget. And no, though I've met plenty of *false* Clerics. Don't get me wrong, that was a fine spell on our General. But Magi's wounds are…" his voice faded away as Magi sat up, following Kari's prayer. "What in all of Tenebrae…"

Strongiron patted the young man's shoulder and walked over to hug Magi whenever Kari let him go. "You look better now."

"Took you long enough." He laid eyes on the familiar face of a young man with golden curls. "Nugget? Is that you?"

After a few moments of stunned laughter, a round of hugs, and numerous 'thank-yous,' Nugget stopped all the conversation cold. "If you two are *really* True Clerics, we need to go see Herodius. Perhaps your God will heal him!"

The way was not far, but the four of them—even Magi, who claimed he never felt better—decided to all *Teleport* to where the 'islander rebellion' occurred that morning. History would later tell the tale of the place where Tar-Tan was betrayed by his slaves, and the King was betrayed by his own councilor.

Reappearing, they saw a huge pyre already built. The shock of seeing an oiled pyre on the verge of being lit sent Strongiron into action as soon as he got his bearings. He raced up to the Islanders, who were tossing body parts atop it. *Ogre* parts. Strongiron exhaled, then looked all around. "Where is our King? Where is Herodius?"

The nearest islander-turned-soldier looked at Strongiron. "You were his friend?"

"I crowned him King."

The islander nodded. "Follow me."

He led them to a tent that Magi immediately recognized. "Last time I walked into this tent I had a sword run through me. Maybe I ought to—" He stopped.

Veronica was kneeling next to Herodius, gently cleaning a wound on the back of his head when they all entered. She turned around.

"Magi? Magi!" She got up and ran over to him, hugging him tightly, kissing his cheek.

Strongiron looked at Kari, who cocked a single eyebrow. Nugget shrugged.

"I thought you were dead!" Veronica said. "I was told you had been killed."

He kissed her back. "Now you of all people should know how hard I am to kill."

Strongiron grabbed Kari's hands and walked back over to Herodius. By now several islanders had filed into the tent to view this homecoming. A small crowd was gathering inside the pavilion.

The True Clerics looked down at Herodius. Kari bent down to listen for even the faintest breath. Unlike Magi, who clung to life by a thread, Herodius had passed on. She looked to Strongiron.

"We can raise him. Like Dimitri."

Strongiron closed his eyes. He opened them after a moment and nodded. "Together this time. Let us pray."

Strongiron walked to the other side of Herodius's body and grabbed Kari's hands. A hush fell over the tent when it became obvious to everyone gathered what they were doing.

"Dymetra, if Your will allows it, return Herodius to his body. Restore his life to us." Strongiron said. Kari added, "Dymetra, You and You alone can do this. Use us to show all who have gathered that You are the One True God."

Though they were shielded from the outside, a wind blew through the pavilion. The tent shook, and the flap leading outside snapped noisily in the stiff breeze.

"Herodius is home now. His time on Tenebrae has passed. Let the man rest—his work is done, and he is filled with peace and

joy." The voice filled the tent, and everyone fell to their knees in awe.

The breeze stopped as quickly as it had risen. Strongiron looked at Kari, whose eyes were wide. He looked down at Herodius's face. The King was smiling. *Was he smiling when we walked in?*

Strongiron stood up and looked at the small crowd that filled the tent. "Dymctra has spoken. Herodius is not coming back."

The islander that led them into the pavilion stepped forward. "Herodius was a good man. He would have been a great King. Who will lead us now? Who will give us Justice for the evil of this day?"

As with Victor's army up north, Strongiron saw the thirst for blood in everyone's eyes. He looked at Kari, and saw the same steely determination in the depths of those green pools.

He reached out and clasped her hand, stepping forward and raising his voice over the din, proclaimed:

"We will."

THE DARK WORLD SAGA CAST, VOLUMES I AND II
(ALPHABETICAL)

Aaron: A food tester
Abel Steele: Opponent of Strongiron
Absynthe the Weak: Son of Torbeth, Ancient King of Elvidor
Ajax: Ancient True Warrior
Arkin Steele: Disfigured Warrior, opponent of Strongiron
Arrington, Lionel: Ranger from Brigg
Arrington, Lord: Overseer of Shoal
Axel Steele: Opponent of Strongiron
Barnabus: A smitty in Briz. Half-brother of Thimble
Belara Kassar: Niku's Number Two Mage, a gifted Illusionist
Belinda: Shopkeeper of *The Finest Livery*, (Assassin's Guild)
Benjamin: Sir Victor's Attendant
Bertram: Master-at-Arms in the Fighting Pits of Kekero
Bingham, Lord: Overseer of Ilbindale
Black-John: Village blacksmith in Brigg
Bollinger, Lord: Overseer of Misk
Brandon Gains: Large-scale farmer in Brigg
Brandon Massilon: Peter's son
Brody Tomlinson: Knight from Misk under Xaro's Command
Bronson: A deckhand on *The Modest Mermaid*
Bruno Stoney: Innkeeper at *Stoney's Drink*
Captain Grull: A leader under Tar-Tan
Chelsea Massilon: Peter's daughter
Cherokum: Elfen Scout
Cheyenne: Seasoned Assassin
Chocktaw: Elfen Chieftain
Corovant, Lord: Overseer of Gaust
Crystal: A serving girl at The Royal Steed
Daphne: Xaro's Enchantress mother
Diana: Elfen maidservant
Dimitri: Elder Druid of central Adimand
Dymetra: One True God
Eben: Druid child
Elmon: A miller from a hamlet near Briz
Elsa, the Ol' Shakoor: Northern Prophet
Elyn, Lady: Elfen Princess
Ethan Bollinger: Lord Bollinger's son
Faralon: Elfen True Cleric in Dariez

Fate: Demi-God also known as Destiny, or Fortune's Song
Felicity Massilon: Peter's wife
Galihali: Elfen Mage Guard
Garin Massilon: Peter's brother, a leper
Genevieve: One of Malenec's favorite zombies
Goodwin, Lady Melanie: Farmer's Widow in Brigg
Gwen: Elfen Maidservant
Hamath, Lord: Lord of Whilure
Hazelton, Lady Fran: Lord Daniel's wife
Hazelton, Lord Daniel: Overseer of Paragatha
Hector: Old Knight guarding Rookwood's Ale room
Helmut Bowhistle: First mate aboard *The Modest Mermaid*
Hem-see Rah: Ancient Elfen King
Herodius Cromwell: Islander from Uncharted Isles
Horace Packard: Large-scale farmer in Brigg
Jacyntha Blacksmooth (Jaz): Magi's Mother
Jamison, Lord Ian: Overseer of Shith
Jasper: Elfen True Cleric in Dariez
Jonathon Venerek: The Queen's Steward
Justin: Wight created by Malenec
Kari Quinlan: Mage in Brigg, trained under Marik
Karwin the Short: Warlord who overthrew Absynthe
Kenoshee Rah: Ancient Elfen Queen
Kensington, Lord: Overseer of Kekero
Kilroy: Captain of *The Fury*
King Alomar: King of Elvidor
Krishnan: True Mage, pursuing Alchemy
Kuth-Cergor: The Anti-God
Kyle Quinlan: Mage in Brigg, trained under Marik
Leonard: Captain of *The Cornucopia*
Linar: Druid of the Fertile Plains
Luther: Victor's Battle Mage of the Northern Army
Magi Blacksmooth: Mage from Brigg, trained under Marik
Malenec: A Dark Cleric
Manny: Fish peddler in Gaust
Manoramoshi: Elfen guard
Maria Cromwell: Herodius's first wife
Marik Kinshaw: Master True Mage, teacher of young mages
Markus: Captain of *The Queen's Arrow*
Michael: Alias for Magi Blacksmooth
Mika Lalonde: A Captured Islander, Mikel's wife
Mikel Lalonde: A Captured Islander, friend of Herodius

Miranda: Shopkeeper of *The Finest Livery*, (Assassin's Guild)
Morsus: The Master of Pain, a wight in the employ of Fate,
Najalas: Queen of Elvidor
Nathaniel Mist: Head of the Thief's Guild
Nepalacerta: A scorpion-like creature, with a lizard's head
Nikron: Water Merchant of the Dusty Plains
Niku Whitestone: Head of Magic for the Queen
Norman: Lord Bollinger's Steward
Nowahirim: Elfen True Cleric in Dariez
Nugget: Mage in Brigg, trained under Marik
Oliver Creighton: Lieutenant General under Victor's command
Omar: Great Isle Druid
Orion Tuitio: Xaro's Warrior Father
Palinor: Malenec's brother
Paul the Wanderer: Famous and accomplished Ranger
Peace-Arm Tuitio: Strongiron's father, Knight, Order of Thunder
Pendleton, Lord: Oversser of Oxen-Pace
Peter Massilon: Admiral of the Queen's Fleet
Phillip Xavier Trenton: Village Elder in Brigg
Phineas: True Mage in the employ of the Queen
Pilanthas: Ancient Elfen Prophet
Prithi: Druid of the Fertile Plains
Proventus: God worshipped by the Druids of the Great Isle
Quentin: Mage dispatched to Urthrax by the Queen
Quinn: Warrior dispatched to Kekero
Quixatalor: Ancient Archmage
Ragor Stri: Mage in Brigg, trained under Marik
Rebecca: A Ranger from Brigg, known as "The Lady Ranger"
Reginald the Third: Ancient King of Elvidor
Renee: Lady friend of Trevor Blink
Rhee: Female True Warrior under Strongiron's command
Robin Edgewild: Veronica's father
Roc-San: Warlord who rose to power after Karwin
Ronbar: A miller from Rookwood
Saalal: Great Isle Druid
Samir: Recruited Veronica
Serenity Hopewell: True Mage, student of Marik Kinshaw's
Sheila: Northern gypsy
Silas: Innkeeper of *The Royal Steed*
Silverfist: Head of the Assassin's Guild
Silvia Edgewild: Veronica's mother
Simon Brisbane: Captain of the Queen's Guard

Sindar: Warrior from Brigg
Skylar: Mage in Brigg, training under Marik
Solomon: Captain of *The Water Ghost*
Strongiron Tuitio: Warrior son of Peace-Arm
Tarsh Minster: Mage in Brigg, trained under Marik
Tar-Tan: Warrior half-ogre
Thimble: A dwarf travelling with gypsies
Thomas: Scribe in the Great Library of Gaust
Thorax: Iron God
Tinkle: A gypsy from the black markets of Paragatha
Tomas Blacksmooth: Magi's Father
Tonthor: Elfen guard
Torbeth the First: Son of Reginald, Ancient King of Elvidor
Trevor Blink: Talented Thief
Trimba: Great Isle Druid
Uriah: Druid child
Vartan: A cook at The Royal Steed
Velvet, Lady: Innkeeper at *The Last Call*
Venatus Carrion: Ranger from Brigg
Venia: Goddess of Charity
Veronica Edgewild: Talented Assassin
Victor Charles Ethan Remington III: Lieutenant General
Vincent: Lord Kensington's Son
Walter Arrington: Lord Arrington's son, Lionel's brother.
Windomere: Ancient True Cleric
Wyzle: Keeper of the Books, Great Library of Gaust
Xaro: True Mage who conceals his status
Yar: Great Isle Druid
Yelena: Druid of Central Adimand
Zachary: Druid child
Zender: The Mystic Under the Mountain
Zephyr (Captain Z): Captain of the boat, *Sheila's Bane*

ABOUT THE AUTHOR

Technically speaking, Steve began his writing career more than two decades ago as a teenager with the outline, map, and first hundred pages or so of what would become *In Pursuit of Wisdom, Volume I of the Dark World Saga*. It was always a project he promised himself he'd "get to" when he retired. Well, who among us is guaranteed tomorrow, right? So after some ungentle prompting from his wife of 17 years (and counting) and his best friend (looking at you, Mark), he dusted off the old Trapper Keeper notebook from the 1980's that housed his manuscript to see what kind of shape it was in.

(As an aside....if you ever have the opportunity to peek back through time at what was important or creative to your fifteen-year-old-self, Steve highly recommends it. It's, eh, illuminating).

After reading the hundred loose-leaf, yellowed, hand-written pages in the most God-awful cursive you can imagine...Steve scrapped it. He chuckled first of course, but scrapped it nonetheless. Fifteen-year-old Steve apparently wanted to take the story in a bit of a different direction than modern-day Steve. So that's a long way of saying his writing "career" began in earnest in 2012.

Between scribbling the plot foundation in the 80's and now, Steve enjoys his day job as a Managing Partner, Father to two amazing children, and Husband to the love of his life.

Look for him in the mountains.

CONNECT WITH STEVE M SHOEMAKE

To contact me and other useful fan-oriented information, visit our website at www.darkworldsaga.com.

Follow me on twitter @DWSauthor

Like us on Facebook at Darkworldsaga

And…for all the fans of the Dark World Saga, here's the unedited first draft of the prologue to Volume III, *In Search of Justice*…

PROLOGUE

~Malenec…in the not-too-distant past…back in Dariez…~

Late into the wee hours of the morning, Malenec sipped a cup of bitter tea that had grown cold. Hazy light from a mist-shrouded moon slanted in through one of the windows in the tower where he, Xaro, and Nowahiram huddled for their secret studies of dark prayers and darker worship. Heavy candles burned low, with the wax congealing down the sides in grotesque fashion. Nowahiram had his white cowl over his head, hiding his face in shadow. Malenec and Xaro each sat facing him patiently, watching him carefully unravel an old, delicate scroll.

"*This*, my acolytes," he began. "*This* is why you were sent to me."

"What is it, Master?" asked Xaro.

"*Aditus ab Inferno*. The Scroll of Entrance, Xaro. The process by which our God will return."

Skilled fingers slowly smoothed the dry parchment onto a low table between them. With a whispered prayer, Nowahiram summoned a *glowball* to shed some light on the slanted ruins that filled the page. Malenec leaned closer.

"Who wrote this, Master? I don't recognize the words."

The hint of a smile could barely be seen within the folds of his cowl, but his tone was patient and encouraging. "I wrote it; the cypher is mine and mine alone. The words came to me while meditating long ago, young one, but the time is near when you will both face your Clerical challenges. I would have you know the purpose of your training now, as set in motion by Kuth-Cergor himself."

"Tell us, Master!" said Xaro, leaning forward as well.

"Yes, I, too, would know our God's purpose," added Malenec, more calmly than he actually felt.

Nowahiram nodded. "Do you know what separates us from God?" he asked pointedly.

"Death, of course." Xaro looked over at Malenec for confirmation, to which Malenec simply nodded once.

"Correct. But there is physical barrier…a veil—the Veil of Orcus—that separates Kuth-Cergor from our realm – one that even he himself cannot cross unaided. The dead may cross to see him, and he may send the dead back to us as undead servants, but he is

531

prohibited from fully crossing the Veil." Nowahirram reached into one of the pockets in his alabaster robe and pulled forth a sheer piece of cloth. He held it up to a shaft of moonlight falling in from the tower slit.

"The Veil of Orcus must be ripped," hissed Nowahiram, tearing the cloth in two.

Malenec started to take another sip of cold tea but thought better of it, placing his cup beside him on the floor. "Where is this Veil, Master? How can it be torn?"

"South of us is a city once known as Kirin-Fein, which lay in ruins. I have been given a vision of that city, within which is an old temple—a temple whose followers unabashedly worshipped our God. Below that temple, we shall find a portal, and through that portal, we shall find the Veil. *That* is where Kuth-Cergor will re-enter Tenebrae in the flesh. A more glorious homecoming we will never witness—his entrance shall be magnificent, my acolytes."

Malenec tented his fingers. "You speak as if that is where we are all heading. If you've been given this vision, why wait for us? Why haven't you gone to split this Veil yourself? *Master*," he added.

Nowahirram reached up and drew back his cowl, with the moon, candles, and *glowball* all illuminating his dark features in the queer mix of light. "Do I detect a hint of insolence, Malenec?"

Malenec met the Elf's steady gaze with his own before inclining his head respectfully. "Not at all, Master. I am curious why the delay, that is all."

Nowahiram shifted his eyes to Xaro, then back to Malenec. Finally he took his index finger and slowly lowered it to rest on the old scroll. "*Aditus ab Inferno.* The prayer to open the portal and the path beyond is all written here. In my vision, for Kuth-Cergor to return, three of his devoted followers must join together to release him. If one man had the power to summon him physically, believe me, I would have done so long ago, for he aches to return. The Veil of Orcus, however, is not some tattered cotton shift that tears like a tavern apron. Two powerful devotees must grasp the Veil on either side, while emptying their faith into the sole act of ripping the Veil asunder much like a child's game of tug-the-rope."

Xaro nodded, but Malenec narrowed his eyes. "And what of the third?"

The old elf smiled at Malenec, his white teeth a glaring contrast to his dark skin in the shifty light. "Why, to welcome him, of course."

www.ingramcontent.com/pod-product-compliance
Lightning Source LLC
Chambersburg PA
CBHW072009020726
47501CB00006B/1746